THE VERDICT IS IN

THE VERDICT IS IN

Debra DeCrow

To order additional copies of this book, contact:
Xlibris Corporation
1-888-795-4274
www.Xlibris.com
Orders@Xlibris.com
62817

CONTENTS

DEDICATION

For Jeff

Acknowledgments

Acknowledgments are to Joyce for reading my rough draft and Pam for accuracy in editing. They have my gratitude for their long hours and perceptive suggestions that substantially improved the entire manuscript.

In addition, I would like to acknowledge Margo for her enlightening history of her young life in Germany.

I am gratefulness for their encouragement, support, and enthusiasm.

PROLOGUE

The only source of light in the dim room is a stream of sunlight running from a small window and down across the gray tiled floor. The room was small and sparsely furnished with a simple wood table and two chairs.

Nineteen-year-old Mike Overton sat in one of the chairs with his head tilted down, staring at the floor. His bleakness echoed in every line of his body.

He redirected his gaze toward the sound of voices filtering though the only door in the room. As the door swung open, a guard wearing a blue uniform stepped in and held it open for a man Mike did not know. The man had sandy blond hair; pleasant looking, and appeared proficient, dressed in a dark gray business suit.

"Knock on the door when you are done talking to him," said the guard, as he rattled a set of keys in the door lock.

Without a response, the stranger walked past the guard and approached the table. The guard stepped back out of the room, locking the door behind him.

As the man placed his brief case on the table he asked, "Are you Mike Overton?"

Mike looked up at the stranger and lightly nodded. "Yes, I'm Mike."

"My name is Campbell Mallary. Your parents retained me to represent you."

The nineteen year old squeezed his eyes tight to hold back tears, but that proved futile as they trickled from his closed eyes. "I did not kill her! Please sir, tell them I didn't do it!"

With empathy in his voice, the attorney reassured Mike. "I'll do what I can, but I need to get some information from you first." He smiled weakly, pulled out the other chair, and sat facing Mike.

Mike wiped his tear stained face with the back of his shirtsleeve. "I swear to God, I had nothing to do with her death."

Feeling some of the boys anguish the attorney showed compassion in his words. "I'm going to ask you questions that I'm sure you have already answered, but I need to hear the answers from you."

To give Mike a moment before continuing, Campbell busied himself in opening his brief case and pulling out reports. "Mike, can you explain where you got the watch?"

Gaining back some of his composure, Mike sat straight in his chair. "I found it in front of a Circle K store when I stopped for gas."

The attorney thumbed though a handful of papers drew out one sheet and read from it. "Was it the Circle K over on Kipling Street?"

"Yes, that was the one!" Without any hesitation Mike continued. "I didn't steal the watch! I found it in the parking lot while walking from the gas pumps up to the store."

The Overton boy gave his answers with such conviction Campbell knew he was telling the truth. "You have anyone who can give evidence as to where you got the watch?" He leaned his elbows on the table while anticipating an answer. "Was there anyone with you at the time?"

The boy's shoulders slumped. "No, my girlfriend and I got in a fight. She wanted to go home, so I took her home a little after eight. After I dropped her off, I went back to the dance. By the time I got back to the school, I changed my mind about going back inside. I just sat in the parking lot for a few minutes and then drove around for a while. Just before I went home, I stopped at the Circle K to get something to drink and to gas up my car."

Campbell looked up from his note taking. "You recall what time it was when you were at the convenience store?"

"I stopped for gas just before going home, and it was a little after eleven when I got home." With excitement in his voice, he announced. "The cashier at the Circle K saw me!"

"The police talked to the cashier, and he said he didn't remember you. He told the officer the store was busy that evening, with a lot of customers in and out."

Campbell reasoned, that even if the cashier could place Mike at the Circle K around eleven it would be of little help. The coroner's report determined the woman, Susanne, died between nine and twelve. Mike would need an alibi for earlier in the evening.

Campbell also considered that if the convenience store was as busy as the casher claimed, it would have only been a short time before someone stepped on or ran over the watch. With that in mind, Campbell knew there was the possibility that whoever dropped the watch was at the store at the same time as Mike. The attorney laid his pen to the side, leaned back in his chair and asked, "Can you recall seeing anyone around who may have dropped the watch?"

"I don't know. It was pretty busy." Mike ran his hands through his hair and expelled a long breath. "I wish I had never found that watch or tried to pawn it."

Campbell explained to Mike, "A friend of the dead woman noticed the watch was missing and described it to the police. Most police department will keep pawnshops updated with a list of reported stolen items. In this case, the watch had the woman's name engraved on the back."

The attorney sighed. "The pawn shop received the description of the watch Monday morning, and you tried to pawn it that same evening. The shop owner called the police right after you left his store."

Campbell hesitated a moment and then continued. "By you trying to pawn the dead woman's watch, you made yourself an obvious suspect in her murder."

Looking down at his open hands, Mike asked in a low voice, "When am I going to get to go home?"

The attorney stood and closed his brief case. "You have been set for an advisement of your rights this afternoon. Since, you have not been in any trouble with the law before this, I'm sure the judge will set a bond so you can go home." Mike's expression went rigid as he nodded his head in understanding.

Campbell took hold of his case, stepped around the table, and placed his hand on Mike's shoulder. "I will see you this afternoon." He smiled and squeezed his shoulder. "Please try not to worry. That's my job."

CHAPTER 1

Hendricks Law Firm

Campbell Mallary is an exceptional no-nonsense attorney and practices law at Hendricks Law Firm. The firm is controlled and own equally by Harlan and his brother Dean Hendricks. Although Harlan has more influence than Dean, both brothers have an arrogant manner about them. Harlan is known by his use of fifty-dollar words and a desire for prestige. Dean is the sort who is big on appearance, wearing Raja suits and driving classic sports cars.

Also on the firm's payroll is Randall, Harlan's playboy son. Randall is shiftless and unmotivated when it comes to holding his end up at the firm. If he came into the office at all, he was late and was sure to leave early, and in between, two hours lunch breaks.

Although Randall is not worth the cost of a bullet, one of the countless women he led on, then jilted, did not agree and paid him a visit one day. She was a chestnut-brunette who casually strolled into his office and pulled a thirty-eight special from her Gucci handbag. She shot at Randall, missed, and continued to shoot-up his office while he cowered under his brushed steel desk. Each time the gun emptied, she punched out the empties and loaded it again. She never stopped until she ran out of bullets. When she was done, calmly dropping the gun back into her bag, she walked out without a word. Randall never pressed charges, but for a long time, he took a lot of harassment over the incident. "Randall, you look as if someone shot at you and missed," and "Randall, did you ever get that smell coming out from under your desk taken care of?"

Most of the clients who come to Hendricks Law Firm are those who brought on their tribulations through their own greed, and Campbell was growing tired of trying to pass off their deceitfulness as truths. However, the Overton case was different. He was certain Mike had nothing to do with the murder of the women they found in the park. With Mike, it was a matter of being in the wrong place at the wrong time, coupled with a bad choice, and it was up to Campbell to prove that to the judge.

"MR. MALLARY, FELICITY Ricer is here for her eleven o'clock."

Campbell paused in his task of reviewing one of his client's files and looked up at his secretary who stood in the doorway of his office. He glanced at his watch and noticed his star client Miss Ricer, was twenty minutes late.

"Thanks Paula. I'm almost finished with this. Can you give me another ten minutes before showing Felicity in?"

With a disapproving expression, Paula placed her hand on her hip. "Thank you! I see you're going to force me into tolerating her spiteful attitude."

Campbell laughed and grinned back at Paula. "I guess it comes with the job."

Finding humor in Campbell's teasing, Paula smiled as she walked back toward her office. "Just remember, you owe me."

Paula Benson had joined the firm three years earlier and had worked as Campbell's personal secretary ever since. Very efficient and organized with her work, Campbell feels fortunate to have her as his assistant. Her first day on the job was the same day they delivered Campbell's new desk. Her professionalism and the timing of the desk delivery, earned Paula the nickname from her colleagues, as the adept secretary who came with the mahogany desk.

—

At ten minutes and not a second later, the door to Campbell's office opened and admitted a five-foot petite woman in her early twenties. She wore a scarlet red dress with bold yellow buttons struggling to hold the bodice of her dress together. Her shoes were the same bold yellow, three-inch heels with a bag and hat to match. Her shoulder length dyed auburn hair only made the vivid yellow hat look more intense. Nevertheless, that was what Felicity Ricer was all about; wearing flamboyant dresses with high hemlines and low necklines.

Typically, Dean was the one who handled the legalities for Slone Ricer and his daughter Felicity. On days Dean is not in the office, Campbell carries out matters that are too pressing to wait. Since Dean would be in court for the next two days and Felicity seemed to think the simpler things in life were always a dilemma, this was one of those days.

Felicity never tried to hide her irritation as she sat in the chair facing Campbell. "I was hoping to speak to Dean!"

Campbell swallowed hard, leaned back in his chair, and crossed his arms. "Dean is out of his office and you said your situation was urgent."

Felicity glared at Campbell, crossed her legs, and jerked her purse to her lap.

He cleared his throat and sat up straighter. "So Miss Ricer, what is your misfortune this time?"

Felicity hardened her glare. "Last night our driver left the keys in the BMW and someone stole it." She then waved her hand languidly, sounding prepared to go on for a while insulting their driver. "He is such a worm! I told Daddy a long time ago, he should get rid of him. He is so creepy the way he stares at me!"

Trying to keep down the sarcasm, Campbell responded. "Most people report a stolen vehicle to the police. Is there any reason why you never did that?"

Felicity flipped her hair with her right hand and answered without looking at him. "Me!" With distain in her voice she continued. "Do you know what those police stations are like? They are full of dirty disgusting criminals. Can you really see me sitting in such a filthy place?"

She paused long enough to hold her hand out with extended fingers in admiration of her red acrylic fingernails. "Daddy said he pays you plenty, and before he left on his trip he told me if I had any problems I was to come here. So here I am. What are you going to do about my stolen BMW?"

Although Campbell was livid from Felicity's rude behavior and remarks, he quite elegantly said. "I will go to the police station this afternoon and fill out a police report for you." He pulled a form from one of the desk drawers and handed it to her. "I will need your signature on this."

Felicity showed her annoyance by dotting the "I's" and crossing the "T" of her name with sharp jabs. With a flip of her wrist, she slid the form back across the desk. She pushed herself out of the chair and walked to the door to leave.

Campbell forced a final smile and replied. "Thank you Miss Ricer, you are always a pleasure. Please enjoy the rest of your afternoon."

Felicity departed, but not before turning and looking at Campbell as if he were some hideous life form, that someone dredged from the deepest part of a swamp.

Without doubt, Felicity's opinion of Campbell was unwarranted. Rather he was indisputably striking enough that one could think he had broken more then one heart.

In his early thirties, he stood a little less than six foot, at the perfect weight, and looked very professional in his tailored suits. Even so, there was something about him that said he wasn't really a "suit" kind of guy. That told you of course, when not at work, a suit was the last thing he wore. It would be blue jeans in the winter and shorts when the Colorado summers allowed it.

CAMPBELL WAS OF German descent and it showed in his sandy blond hair and blue eyes. His great grandfather, Jakob migrated from Germany at the age of sixteen in the early nineteen hundreds. After six years of living in New York, he tired of the crowds. He made the decision to get on a train, one that took him West and only stopped where the mountains were at their highest.

West of the "Great Divide" is where Jakob chose to make his home and live the rest of his life. The place he selected was right outside Addison, a small farming town that looked to be in the midst of the "three-country corner" where Germany, France, and Switzerland touch. With the tall Rocky Mountains looming overhead, it reminded him of the Vosges and the Alps that were close by the home he had left in Germany.

Jakob established his homestead and then married his "Gibson Girl" Addie Delaney, who was very pretty, with nut-brown hair, blue eyes, very fair skin, and the kind of face that looked vaguely Irish.

Out of the marriage came five children, a son and four daughters. Their great sadness was the early death of their youngest daughter Laura Belle, who died from influenza at the age of three.

While the other three daughters married and moved away, their only son Tracy, Campbell's grandfather, stayed on the farm after his marriage to Carlyn. She was a steadfast, beautiful dark-haired, green-eyed woman with integrity. Soon after their marriage, Carlyn gave birth to a son named Joshua, and who would become Campbell's father.

When Joshua was only eleven months old the Great War called, and his father enlisted. Tracy was a pilot for the United States Air Corps and died on a mission during the war. After Tracy's death, Carlyn continued to live on the farm where Joshua lived most of his life.

At nineteen, Joshua left home for a short time, and on his returned, he brought with him his young bride Mara, soon to be Campbell's mother. Mara was a petite carefree woman with sandy blond hair and blue eyes. She had a love of gardening and decorating, so much so that her flower arrangements took "Best of The Show" each year at Addison's County Fair.

Campbell was the first great-grandson who was born on that same homestead. Although he did not know his grandfather Tracy, he treasures his memories of his great-grandfather Jakob, who told of the homeland and adventures of coming to America.

"Opa", the German endearment for grandfather talked of the Black Forest, the area were he lived as a child. The name derived from the dense pine and firs that grew there.

Opa would tell Campbell in his broken English, "Schwarzwald is the German name for "thick with evergreen". You always should remember that name. That is where my mother and her mother came from."

Opa also told of the thermal springs that dotted the region, prized for their healing value.

Toward the north were low mountains that Opa called "Soft Mountains". He then would add, "And to the South is Switzerland with her high mountains".

In the region of Mainz and Koblenz, medieval castles and towers stood watch over the Rhine River. Campbell loved the way Opa would laugh his hearty laugh, and then whisper whenever he spoke of the Rhine River. "Campbell, you know what the great river is famous for?" He would lean in close to Campbell and whisper a little lower. "It is famous for its vineyards and great wine making!"

Spaetzle was a dish his great-grandfather loved and customary made it for himself. Campbell wondered if his own love of pasta came from his great-grandfather.

With the invention of the car and its popularity, Jakob brought a car but was still sure to own a horse. He explained. "Back home only the wealthy owned a horse to pull their wagons." His eyes flashed with excitement as he relayed his story. "When I use to write home and tell my mother I owned a horse, she was very happy and thought I had done very well for myself." Still chuckling he would remind Campbell, "When you grow into a man you must be sure to always own a horse. Remember, a horse is the mark of a wealthy and successful man."

When Opa was feeling a little under the weather, he always spoke of the "Herb-lady". She gathered herbs from the Black Forest and always had something that would make him feel better.

Opa loved Colorado, but he missed Germany. Campbell could recall his great-grandfather telling him how he longed to see Germany again. He would say, "When I was young they said I will want to go back home someday. I think what they say is true. The older I get, the more and more I think of home."

After high school, Campbell left home to attend college and establish his career. While he was away, his great-grandfather died in his sleep at the age of ninety-seven. Campbell felt privileged and grateful to have known his Opa who taught him many valuable lessons in life.

Although Campbell does not own a horse, some would consider him to have a fine career practicing law as an attorney in Denver.

He likes eating at the different varieties of restaurants, going to the clubs, and the availability of the different places to shop. Nevertheless, he is more like his great-grandfather than he realizes. He longs for the open spaces, clean air and wants to move back home out of the city.

For a while, the trips home to visit his parents seemed to satisfy the desire to move back. After his father passed away and then his mother two years later, his trips home became fewer. In addition, his ex-wife Amanda who hated the country had always been a deterrent. The long absences from home have only exacerbated his homesickness.

CAMPBELL PREPARED FOR his trip downtown to the police station with a dread. The traffic during that time of the day was horrendous, but it was necessary in order to file a missing report on Felicity's car. Before that, he had a court appearance pertaining to an animal cruelty case. An employee of a local veterinarian clinic was arrested and convicted of stealing and diluting pharmaceutical supplies, some of which were given to his client's dog during a medical procedure. With that, Campbell's client was holding the clinic liable for the actions of their employee.

Campbell knew they would prevail, but the whole affair bothered him. Although, the dog did suffer and was fine later, Campbell hated the idea of holding the clinic libel for a bad choice of employees.

Just before leaving, Ian Chatman, his friend and colleague, walked into his office. Campbell became acquainted with Ian during their freshmen year in collage, and they have been friends since. On Campbell's recommendation, Ian joined up with Hendricks Law Firm nearly a year after he did. Ian is the kind of person who is self-sufficient and adaptable. He has a zest for life, clever with words and has a quick comeback to anything a person says.

As Ian strolled into Campbell's office he asked, "Hey Campbell! Did you hear the Fashion Robber hit again last night? This time it was the Parker Meadows Shopping Center." Ian showed his distain on his face. "I heard when the Fashion Robber was speeding away he hit a shopping cart that belonged to one of those homeless people. The police was at the scene of the hit and run right after it happened because they were already on their way to investigate an alarm that was set at the department store that was just robbed."

Over the last three months, several department stores had been broken into, and the items missing were all name brand clothing. At each robbery incident, piles of clothing where found in front of the large mirrors located though out the stores. It appeared the robber tried on the clothes, took what fit, and discarded the rest on the floor. Thus the robber was tagged "The Fashion Robber" by the media.

"No, I didn't hear that," Campbell replied, as he reached for a bottle of Frappuccino from the compact refrigerator he kept in his office for just that purpose. It seemed lately he never had the time for his usual breakfast of oatmeal with orange juice or a banana with shredded wheat. He held a second bottle up to Ian.

Ian waved it off as he sat down on the brown leather sofa to the left of Campbell's desk. "Barbara has me on a diet."

Barbara is Ian's wife whom he met while she was working at the bookstore on campus during their college days. She is an attractive tall slender French Canadian woman with black hair and striking brown eyes. Barbara is the sort of woman who likes everything in order and will protect and cherish the person she cares for. She has the ability to make others feel good about themselves and loved.

Ian first met Barbara, he was so persistent in asking her to dinner, that she finally relented if he promised to leave her alone after one dinner. Although Campbell warned her that Ian's promises were no good, Barbara went out with Ian anyway. Campbell knew his friend well, and his warning proved true when after the first date, Ian continued to ask her out. With very little resistance, Barbara dated Ian exclusively for another year before agreeing to marry him.

"We are having a cookout Saturday," Ian said. "Barbara wanted me to ask you if you'd like to come over."

While still married to Amanda, Campbell did most of the food preparation. Although he was a good cook himself, he grew tired of his own. He had always enjoyed Barbara's cooking; she always made it delightful and creative. He liked spending time at their house and was always quick to accept any invitations that came his way. "Sounds great," Campbell replied.

As Ian reclined his six foot one inch frame on the sofa, he propped his feet on its arm and laced his fingers behind his head. "I do have to warn you, Barbara is doing her match-making again and has invited someone she knows from one of those seminars she has been attending."

Although Campbell had lost interest in getting into any serious relationship since Amanda, he knew he needed to get past it, but just had not had the courage to move on.

Back before Campbell knew Amanda, she worked and served drinks in one of the clubs where he occasionally went with friends. Amanda was always one who interpreted what she saw into what she wanted. She persuaded Campbell by asking him for a ride home. Up until then, Campbell had never even noticed her, but being the gentleman he was he graciously took her home. After that first evening, Amanda would call him on the phone and ask him to go out with her. Within a short time, she coaxed Campbell into marring her. Unfortunately, when Amanda decided she was tired of the marriage she took the easy way out and walked out without a backwards glance.

The way Campbell's week had already gone he felt as though he had no strength or desire to make small talk with someone he didn't know. He tried to construct a way of backing out of the invitation. He knew there would be no way of doing it gracefully, so he rejected the idea. He decided his only recourse would be to show up late and find an excuse to leave early.

Changing the subject Ian asked, "So Campbell, how are you doing with the Overton case?"

Campbell's shoulders fell under the weight of the question. "I just don't know," he admitted. "I'm sure Mike had nothing to do with the death of the women. The one thing in his favor is that they have no murder weapon, and the only evidence they do have is circumstantial. I only wished he had a more substantial alibi than driving around town alone."

"You did say the police caught him with the dead women's watch?" Ian remarked. "What about that?"

The lines around Campbell's mouth hardened. "The watch is the only thing that connects him to the murder, and he claimed he found it in a parking lot of a convenience store located over in Wheat Ridge."

"Wheat Ridge is a quite a ways from the park where that jogger found the body. I wonder how her watch ended up way over there."

Campbell agreed, "No doubt, whoever dropped the watch is involved in the murder, and I have to wonder if that person actually lives in the same area were the watch was found".

Ian nodded his head with understanding. "That's a thought, and it may be a tough one to prove. For the sake of Mike Overton, I hope you can. It's worth following up. If you want help with the case, let me know."

Campbell massaged his temple. "Thanks. If you can work a miracle, that would be of some help."

"I hear Harlan subjected you to Felicity Ricer again." Ian hesitated and cleared his throat. "You know, next time Felicity comes in, Harlan needs to get Randall to do the babysitting."

Campbell coughed to keep from chocking on his laughter. "Put those two together in the same room, they would kill each other within ten minutes!"

Ian sheepishly grinned. "That's my point, being rid of those two would do the whole civilized world a favor and make it smile. Not to mention, that would give Harlan an opportunity to do one act of kindness in his lifetime."

Campbell laughed at Ian's solution and dug in his pocket for his car keys. "I'm sorry to disturb your relaxation, but I'm off to court, then to the police station to fill out a report on a stolen car."

"Hey, I thought you might want to go to lunch?" Ian objected.

"No," Campbell said. "I need to get this done. Besides, I thought you were on a diet."

Ian still reclining on the sofa, made no effort to get up as his colleague walked toward the door to leave. "Are you going to stay here?" Campbell asked.

"I'm going to lie here, take a little snooze, and catch up on some sleep." Ian rubbed his face. "Last night Barbara kept me up late." Campbell gave Ian a sideways look of disbelief and Ian laughed at his reaction. "Our neighbors are out of town and their barking dog kept both Barbara and I up all night." He paused to yawn. "I think I'll be safe here where Harlan can't find me."

As Campbell walked down the hall toward the elevator, he saw Harlan come out of Ian's office.

Harlan approached, and he arched his eyebrows over the rims of his glasses. An annoying habit he had. "You see Ian lately?"

Assuming Harlan would not believe him, Campbell said, "He's in my office taking a nap."

Campbell knew he was right when Harlan turned and walked back down the hall. "Right! I'll catch him later; he must have already left for lunch."

AFTER FILLING OUT the police report and leaving his business card, Campbell strolled out of the police station. He looked at his watch and it read four fifty. It was getting too late to drive back to his office, so he decided to make a day of it and head home.

On the way, he stopped at the grocery store to pick up milk and a few other things. He was irritated with himself for forgetting and leaving the grocery list he had made that morning on the kitchen table. Now he would have to go by memory, and the way his workweek had been going, the prospect of remembering what was on the list looked bleak.

As always, Campbell parked at the end of the parking lot to get the extra exercise. As he approached the front doors, a woman came out of the store carrying a small bouquet of flowers. He glanced up, and when he made eye contact with her, she smiled pleasantly. After they passed, Campbell thought she looked familiar and wondered if he knew her.

After he was inside the store, he looked back over his shoulder through the glass doors, but she had already gone. He grabbed a shopping cart while assessing the situation. If he knew her, she must think he was a moron for not speaking. Of course, it had not helped matters that the sun had been shining in his eyes. He knew she was not one of his past clients, because he made it a practice to recognize and remember each one. He finally decided that she must have been someone who worked at the courthouse, a clerk, or someone like that.

―

It was a little after five by the time Campbell got out of the store and headed north on interstate twenty-five toward Thornton where he lived.

Campbell's house was a three bedroom contemporary style, which he had purchased at a bargain price while in his last year of college. He found great pleasure in spending time outdoors and in landscaping his yard completely on his own. It was an undertaking he had accomplished on weekends and evenings. The results were an eye-pleasing, aesthetic design that added a personal touch to the home's exterior.

The backyard was small and private with a spacious and beautiful stone patio overlooking flowerbeds. Back then, it had served as a nice place to entertain his college friends. Now it is a personal place to unwind and relax from a hectic day. In the mornings, it's a pleasant retreat with morning coffee, while reading the newspaper. Satisfied with the outcome, Campbell felt he had created a practical area for that part of his yard.

Campbell entered his back door and shifted a brown paper bag from hand to hand, as he dropped his keys back in his pocket. When he sat the groceries on the counter, he noticed he had three massages on his voice mail. He punched the button and listened to them while putting groceries neatly away. The first two were telemarketers and he quickly deleted those messages. The third was his brother Matt.

"Campbell, I almost forgot to tell you, a few days ago a woman from some tax office called. She wants you to call her back and left her phone number."

As Campbell wrote down the number, Matt concluded his massage teasing with a casual, "Hope you are not in trouble with the IRS." Campbell could hear the laughter in his brother's voice and had to chuckle a little himself. "I was only kidding—give us a call when you get time."

Matt is three years younger then Campbell and still lives in Addison, Campbell's hometown. His brother is married to Jennifer whom he met while vacationing in Virginia Beach. They have two small daughters, Madison and Natalie.

Since his parents passed away, most everyone gathers at Matt's house. Campbell though, likes the old house he grew up in, and still stays there whenever he's in town. The house is the same one his great-grandfather designed and had hired workers to help him build. It is a two story Victorian, six bedrooms with a large kitchen and dinning room, and with plenty of room for family and friends to meet together.

Going home to visit with family was one of Campbell's greatest pleasures. At the beginning of their courtship and marriage, Amanda would go there with him. Later, towards the end, she stopped going. She would tell him to go ahead, but then would sulk for days after his return. Other than a caretaker, the house now remains empty. Although there have been offers, both brothers agreed never to sell the old homestead.

Campbell glanced up at the kitchen clock and knew it would be too late to call the number Matt gave him. He assumed it was another telemarketer as the other two had been and was not overly concerned about calling.

Before heading to the bedroom to change clothes he paused to look at the grocery list that was still on the kitchen table. After running his finger down the length of it, he saw that he had only forgotten one thing and that was shampoo. He still had a little left and decided it could wait for another couple days. It was not worth the trip back to the store and he would be sure to get more on his next trip.

After he changed clothes, he made coffee, and since he had eaten a late lunch, he ruled against dinner. As he sat at the kitchen table waiting for the coffee to brew, he decided to start the new book he had purchased at Barnes & Noble. Although he is an avid reader, after a few minutes of reading, he found his concentration level was low and his thoughts kept drifting back to his brother's call. Hearing Matt's voice made him feel wistful.

Matt had initially suggested that Campbell should move back home and live in the old house after their parents were gone. At the time, he just started with Hendricks Law Firm and enjoyed working there. Since then things had changed and he often found himself dreading going to the office. He felt that way mostly when he had to face clients like Felicity and her father.

As he laid his book down and leaned back in his chair, he caught sight of the small television he had setting on one end of the table. He had brought it in from the bedroom when the larger one in the living room quit during a ball game one night. After the repair shop called and told him the television was too far-gone and should be retired, he bought a new one from Costco for the living room. Since that purchase, he had not bothered to return the small television to the bedroom. He decided to do it right then, and as he stood up from his chair, the phone rang. Campbell grabbed the receiver before the second ring. It was Sergeant Platt from the police station.

"Mr. Mallary, we found your missing BMW."

Campbell was astonished to hear how quickly they had recovered Felicity's car. "That was quick work. Where did you find it?" he asked in surprise.

"It was abandoned in a private parking space behind a bar, and the irate owner of the bar called it in. Parking is limited around there and the business owners jealously guard their spots," the sergeant explained.

Considering that most joy riders would drive a car until it ran out of gas or wrecked it, Campbell asked, "Was there any damage done to the car?"

"According to the officer who responded to the call, there is a scratch along the driver's side. His guess was the car ran into something or someone sideswiped it. The gas tank was empty and he assumed that was why the car wasn't driven away from the lot. Any idea Mr. Mallary, why the car would have been at that particular place?" questioned the sergeant.

While cradling the phone to his ear with his shoulder, Campbell reached in the cupboard for a fresh cup. "I don't have any idea, officer," Campbell replied truthfully. "I'll stop by tomorrow morning to look at the car and then I'll contact my client to see what kind of arrangements she wants to make."

Campbell thanked Sergeant Platt, and then ended the phone call.

After Sergeant Platt's phone call, Campbell forgot about the television he intended to move, instead poured himself a cup of coffee, and carried it into the living room.

He disliked the call he had to make to Felicity tomorrow. The damage to the car meant he would have to deal with another of

—

her temper tantrums and more of her insulting attitude. He hadn't gone to law school to be a spoiled rich girl's personal assistant.

He laid his head back in his chair and thought of how clients such as Felicity Ricer made him want, more and more, to turn his dream of opening his own law office into reality. Maybe it was time to seriously consider Matt's request, and return to Addison and make the old house a full-time home again.

CHAPTER 2

Felicity's Judas Goat

Campbell pressed the accelerator to merge with the morning rush hour traffic traveling toward Denver. It was Friday morning and he had plans to stop at one of his favorite restaurants for breakfast. He had missed breakfast every other day that week, but not this morning. His trip to the police station to check on Felicity's car could wait.

The Cracker Barrel located right off interstate twenty-five, at the one hundred and twentieth street exit on the way though Northglenn was frequently crowded with both tourists and locals. He hoped the restaurant was not busy then, and he could get in right away.

As he pulled up, he saw there were hardly any cars in the parking lot and things appeared to be going his way. Then out of the corner of his eye, he noticed a charter bus parked off to the side. It was full of senior citizens who were just starting to unload.

Although, he noticed the number of walkers and the wheelchairs being unloaded from the bus, he perceived instantly he would have to hurry to beat this hungry crowd and made the decision to park in close. He took a parking space right up front, rather than further out as he usually did.

Trotting toward the front door, he saw an older robust women moving very quickly toward him and with a good size crowd closing in behind her. There was not one hint of a waver, as the throng passed the row of Cracker Barrel's renowned rocking chairs that narrowed the path.

Campbell barely made it far enough ahead of the women to keep from feeling obligated into holding the door open for her. Standing first in line, he reflected that if he had hesitated in that race, he would still be holding the door for the whole busload that was continuing to push through the front doors.

As he followed the host to a table, the thought struck him that he may have forgotten his keys in the ignition of his truck. He quickly patted his pockets, and to his intense relief, he had remembered to grab them before he made his mad dash to the front door.

While Campbell ate his preferred breakfast of ham and eggs, minus the grits, his thoughts turned to Felicity and the theft of her car. He considered Felicity. She no longer goes away to school, holds no job, and continues to live at home. It gave him the impression she had no goals in her life and he could only speculate as to what kind of example her father has set for her.

Slone, her father, is a condescending and prideful man who Campbell guessed to be in his early forties. He seems to come in a close second to Randal Hendricks in patronizing the women. Slone dresses younger than his age and has skin that looks like it is in a perpetual state of a fabulous tan.

Campbell knew the Ricers lived in a gated Country Club community with good security and thought it was odd a thief was able, first to get inside and then be able to steal a car. Not only, would they have to avoid patrolling security, but also slip past a guard coming in and going out at the gate.

He recalled how three years earlier Slone Ricer had his house built down around the Country Club and during its construction, he had come up against the HOA about some of the things he wanted to do with the house. Slone came to Hendricks Firm for their help and when Dean could not find any loopholes in his

---

contract with the HOA, Slone made it known he was angry at not getting his way. To Dean's embarrassment, Slone had stormed out of the office, loudly announcing that Dean was incompetent and he had other ways of changing things. Apparently, Ricer got his way, because he had built his house the way he wanted and was now the new president of the HOA.

Slone is controlling and seemed to wield a lot of power over those who worked for him. Having him as a father makes it understandable why his daughter is so self-center and overbearing.

"Would you like more coffee?"

Jolted back to reality, Campbell glanced up at the smiling woman who was standing in front of him with a coffee pot in hand.

He picked up his cup. "No thanks, I'll have the check when you get the time." He swallowed the last of his coffee and placed the cup on his empty plate.

The server sat the coffee pot down on the table, reached in her apron pocket and pulled out her ticket book. "Sure, I have your ticket right here."

As she tore the ticket away from the pad, she apologized. "Thanks for waiting. We got a rush of hungry people all at once and it had us running for a while. Every Friday morning we get a busload of residents from Elmwood Independence Living Center."

Campbell considered her words and was certain he would keep in mind what she said and try to stay shy of the restaurant on that particular day of the week. He left a tip on the table and paid the check on his way out.

When he turned from the casher to leave, he fell in behind the same robust woman who had come in the same time he did. She was pushing a walker that seemed to have mysteriously appeared, and unlike earlier, her movements were slow and labored. Because of the close proximity of the stores displays, he couldn't go around her, which subjected him to slow short steps all the way to the front door. As he followed her, he wondered if she was actually the same woman he had the foot race with earlier. However, he was sure it was, because he recognized the ghastly purple floral dress she was wearing.

After getting through the door and around the creeping women, he walked past the row of rocking chairs, which where all occupied by passengers from the bus. As he walked down the walkway, the passengers all stared at him except for one man who gestured a small wave by lifting his hand. Campbell tipped his head and gave him a greeting as he passed. Toward the end of the row sat a fragile woman who leaned forward and smiled kindly as she watched Campbell approach. He saw her watching and smiled back as he walked her direction. Just before he stepped out into the parking lot, she called out with a gentle voice wishing him a nice day. Campbell half turned and looked over his shoulder. "Thank you and I wish you a good day also."

Just before backing out of the parking space, he scrutinized the first women who wore the purple floral dress. She was an imperious looking woman with a commanding nose and a voice that overrode all the others. She was antagonizing one of the men who were sitting in a rocker, who Campbell deemed to be the woman's husband. Campbell backed out and as he drove out of the parking lot, he checked the rearview mirror to see the bent old man give up his rocking chair to the old woman.

The incident made him reflect back on his relationship with Amanda. How would their marriage be now, if they had stayed together? He wondered if the elderly man and woman's performance was a prelude of what he and Amanda would have been after forty or fifty years of marriage. "That might have been us," he mused, as he once more headed for the police station and the mystery of Felicity's car.

SERGEANT PLATT LED Campbell though an eight-foot high chain link fence that housed only five cars. On the far left hand side of the lot sat Felicity's metallic blue BMW.

Sergeant Platt enlightened Campbell as to the details of the car's recovery, as they walked across the dusty parking lot. "Yeah, the car was parked in a private parking space behind a gay bar. The owner of the bar called to have it towed. When the wrecker service filed a report with us, the make and year matched your car, so it was hauled down here."

Both men walk to the front of the car to survey the damage. Campbell bent down and examined the three scratches that extended along the length of the left fender.

Sergeant Platt continued to talk. "Other then the scrape marks on the fender the car appears to be fine. Oh, and the hole in the radiator looks to be small enough, that it wouldn't take much to have it repaired."

While dusting his hands off, Campbell walked back to the driver's door and opened it. Platt trailed behind while filling Campbell in on the recent history of the car. "The keys were hanging in the ignition when the car was found. Majority of the reports we get on stolen cars are from people who leave their keys in the car."

Campbell looked inside the BMW and then leaned down to look at the adjustments on the seat. "Did anyone drive the car after it was found?" he asked Platt.

The Sergeant pressed his lips together and slowly shook his head. "No, not since the wrecker brought it in last night. When they found the car it was out of gas, it would be safe to assume the last driver was the suspect. Why do you ask? Platt eyed Campbell. "What are you thinking?"

Campbell stood and directed Platt's attention to the driver's seat. "The adjustment of the seat gives the impression that the last person who drove the car was a very small man or a woman."

"Mr. Mallary, I think you might be right!" Platt exclaimed as he stooped to look inside the car. "I would have to assume it was teenagers. We have had a real problem with auto theft involving kids who take the vehicles for joy rides and abandoning them once they run out of gas."

Campbell redirected the conversation back to the present situation, "I'll inform my client that her car was found and she can make all the arrangements to have it picked up. How long will you hold the car?"

"Well Sir," Platt replied. "We'll have to process and have it searched for evidence. In most car thefts, the suspect will leave something behind. If nothing else, they'll leave fingerprints. There have been a few instances where the suspect had dropped a wallet or even a driver license down along the side of the seat. We try not to keep the impounded cars any longer then necessary. Our first goal is to get the car back to the rightful owner and the second is to find the suspect."

Leaving the BMW for Sergeant Platt to deal with, Campbell returned to his office and he made the dreaded call to Felicity. Surprisingly enough she was not as upset with the damage to the car as he had expected she would be. Rather, she seemed more concerned with finding the suspect and her mindset seemed to be that their driver was the one who had stolen the car.

For all intent and purpose, it appeared to Campbell that Felicity had some sort of a vendetta against the driver. If that was not the case, he knew something was working under the surface, but he just wasn't sure what. Felicity would tip her hand eventually and he could wait.

Felicity was insistent that Campbell should personally go to the driver's house and arrest him immediately. He had to inform her firmly that his authority did not include taking suspects into custody and advised her to take her suspicions to the police. His business like tones only made her more angry and insolent. The phone call ended with Felicity banging the phone down at her end.

Before lightly placing the receiver back in its cradle, Campbell held it out in front of him as if still speaking to Felicity. Laughter in his voice he said, "Don't you know, rudeness—is a weak man's strength?" He then leaned back in his chair and grinned callously.

A small man or a woman, he mused. He considered that an interesting thought. He wondered if the Ricer's driver was a small man and why Felicity was so insistent that he was the thief. Felicity, is she the driver's Judas goat and trying to bring him to the slaughter? If so, then why?

CHAPTER 3

Friday Affairs

"Stacy, have you and Paul made any plans for your anniversary?" Barbara asked her sister-in-law, as she poured ice tea from a blue pitcher into two matching glasses.

Stacy is Ian's sister and the oldest by eight years. In their family of four children, two girls and two boys, Ian was the youngest. Though their father was a hard worker, he had spent most of his money on drinking and gambling. This forced their mother to work outside the home, leaving the children in Stacy's care. At the time, Stacy was only twelve, and still a child herself. Stacy had cared for her younger siblings before and after school, and during summers. Even though the children were close to their mother and tight knit as a family, mostly under Stacy's care, Ian at a young age grew to depend on her and look to her for his support. Stacy could always lift Ian's spirits and provided encouragement when times were tough.

As adults, Stacy and Ian are still dependable and loyal to each other. In addition, Stacy and Barbara were friends, and it was not uncommon for Stacy to drop by for a visit with her as they lived in the same area.

As Barbara poured their drinks, Stacy pulled a chair out from a small table nestled in the corner of the kitchen. The table was a nice place to sit and look out over the backyard. Barbara enjoyed gardening, and her well-manicured yard and flowerbeds were proof of her love of plants.

Stacy slid into the chair, as she answered, "No, we have no plans. Paul isn't much in to family celebrations."

Paul and Stacy have been married nineteen years and next mouth it would be twenty.

Barbara carried the two glasses of tea over and sat them on the table. "Twenty years is a China Anniversary, and I'd call that a milestone worth celebrating!"

Stacy took a sip of her ice tea. "I agree—it is a long time."

Barbara noticed Stacy didn't agree their upcoming anniversary was worth celebrating and seemed indifferent about the event.

As though reading Barbara's thoughts Stacy changed the subject and she brought up Barbara's dinner plans. "I'm sorry we can't come to your dinner tomorrow. You give such wonderful parties. Are you having a lot of people?"

Barbara sat down across the table from Stacy. "Not really, since you and Paul can't make it, there will only be the four of us. Campbell will be here and I invited a woman I met at the seminar, too."

"Barbara, are you match-making again?" Stacy accused lightheartedly.

Barbara's eyes sparkled with excitement. "Her name is Cassandra, and you're not going to believe this! She lived in the same little town as Campbell and she even knew him! They went to the same high school; she was two grades behind him, but has not seen him since he graduated and left town."

"Is she still living there? I mean in the same little town," asked Stacy.

"She left right out of high school and returned after her husband and only child were killed in a car accident."

"Both were killed," Stacy exclaimed with wide eyes. "Did she say what happened?"

"No, not really," Barbara said. "Other then saying they were only married a short time before the accident, that's all she said on the subject. I didn't think I knew her well enough to ask, and of course, I didn't want to pry. She did tell me she is a CPA and now has her own accounting office. She is a pretty impressive person."

Stacy sat forward on her chair. "Does Campbell know she will be there?"

"No, and Cassandra doesn't know he'll be there either. Isn't this fun?" Barbara giggled.

"You are kidding! I'm not too sure about that. I hope you know what you are doing," Stacy said with a worried look on her face.

With eyes wide in amusement, Barbara continued to fill Stacy in on the details. "At first I didn't even know she knew Campbell. After I asked her if she had family or friends in town, she told me about an old friend who she thought lived here. She hoped to get in contact with him, but didn't know if he had moved since she last heard about him."

"Don't tell me that same guy was Campbell!"

"How many people do you think there are who have the name Campbell Mallary and lived in a small town called Addison?" Barbara sat straight in her chair. "You are just going to die when I tell you what else she said!"

"Okay, tell me and let me die!" Stacy said.

Barbara leaned forward in her chair with excitement. "Cassandra said while in high school she had some real feelings for Campbell!"

"You mean she had a schoolgirl crush on him," said Stacy. "But that was a long time ago, Barbara, and a lot has happened since then. Campbell has had a bad marriage and divorce. She has not only been widowed but also lost a child. Their not the same idealistic teenagers they were then. It sounds risky to me".

"Don't you think every first love is special and never really fades?" Preoccupied with her thoughts, Barbara reached and pulled a spent leaf from one of the small potted herbs setting on the window ledge. "I think it's always there and just tucked away in a little secret place in our hearts."

"I think you can say that," Stacy said as she nodded her head and smiled. "First loves are nice and can be thought back upon with a great nostalgia." She then narrowed her eyes and folded her arms. "What does Ian think about all of this? He has to know she will be here for dinner!"

"He met Cassandra Thursday afternoon and knows she is coming to dinner." Barbara gave Stacy a mischievous smile. "He doesn't know either."

Stacy laughed. "I know my brother; if you want something to be a surprise, don't tell Ian! He likes a good gossip better than most women."

Stacy took the last drink from her glass before returning it to the table. "So my dear little match-maker what does this friend of yours look like?"

"She is very pretty, with light brown hair, not real tall and a cute smile." With her former excitement returning Barbara asked, "So do you think this is fate?"

Stacy toyed with her glass by running her finger along its rim. "You know me I don't believe in fate, but I have to say this has to be a little more than a mere coincidence."

Stacy stood and walked over to the sink. "Campbell is such a nice guy and he is like a younger brother to me. While in collage, he and Ian were always over at the house together." Stacy turned back toward Barbara and smiled. "If they were not working on Ian's old car, they were baby-sitting for me. Mostly while I did errands or ran to the store, but they were good at it too, even when it came to changing diapers!" Stacy chuckled. "Campbell is a great guy who needs to have someone who can be kind to him and treat him the way he deserves. Amanda was never that person."

Barbara laughed. "I agree, and if fate is what brought Cassandra and him together now, maybe that means she is the right person and they'll always stay together."

Stacy rinsed her glass and placed it in the sink. "I just hate it that I'm not going to be here to watch this unfold. You'll have to call me Sunday, and remember, I want a full report! I hope for your sake and everyone involved, it works out the way you hope."

Barbara saw her sister-in-law to the door. "I'll be sure to call you. And try to make some fun plans for your anniversary. You deserve a celebration."

"Barbara, you are such a romantic, and that could be one of the reasons why my brother adores you the way he does." Barbara gave Stacy a quick hug. "Remember it is your anniversary too, your China Anniversary."

As Stacy pulled her car into gear and backed down the driveway, in a quiet undertone she repeated Barbara's words. "China Anniversary, and so it is." But truth of the matter, she was hoping the anniversary would come and go without anyone noticing, and pass like any other ordinary day. Stacy had not always felt that way and even at one time, had marked that day as one of the most important days of the year.

Barbara giving this one a name made Stacy think back to their first anniversary and a conversion she had with Paul. A few days before the date, Stacy had asked Paul. "Did you know the first anniversary is paper?" Paul responded with, "So does that mean I should get you a roll of scented pink toilet paper for the occasion?"

At the time, Stacy had thought Paul was only trying to be amusing. But when their first anniversary passed without any acknowledgment from him, except a perfunctory thank you for her gift to him, she wondered then and even now if there was an underlying message in the toilet paper remark.

During that time, she was very hurt and tried to rationalize Paul's lack of concern. That incident marked the beginning of years of excuses she made to herself for Paul's selfishness and thoughtlessness.

The excuses stopped the day their teenage daughter Kathy pointed out how self-absorbed Paul was. Kathy told Stacy she wished her father showed as much enthusiasm for family activities as he did for his own personal interests.

"Dad never did anything with you Mom; it was always us kids who went with you. I think it eased Dad's conscience by sending us to do things with you. We loved going with you, but it would have been nice to do it as a family. I wish Dad loved being with us as much as you do."

Stacy knew her daughter was right and it became more obvious after the children had grown and left home. Now she spent most evenings and weekends alone while Paul continued to pursue his own hobbies. She had tried to join him and focus on his interests

—

40

but quickly understood that he preferred his friends to the company of his wife. She had often speculated that he married because he was more in love with the idea of being married then the person he married.

For twenty years, Stacy had let Paul take her for granted and she now come to realize, if ever there came a time he learned to value her, it would no longer matter to her, she no longer cared. It was time to begin building her own life, one that did not include him.

While waiting for a red light to change to green, Stacy's mind returned to Campbell. Although he had suffered when Amanda left him, she wondered if there would come a day he would realize how fortunate he really had been at her leaving. Staying married to Amanda would have been painful and frustrating, as she handed her grief out on a regular basis. She seemed to have her little ways of taking the joy out of anything they ever did together. He would have lived an unhappy life with someone who only cared for herself.

Campbell needed to let go of his pain and get on with his life. He might be getting a second chance with Cassandra that most people never achieved. It would be unwise of him to allow it to pass by and be gone forever. And maybe it was time for her, Stacy, to stop waiting for something that will never come. Maybe it was time for her to strike out on her own, but was it too late for her?

Chapter 4

The Soirée

Although Campbell had plans of showing up late and being the last guest to arrive, after he got to Ian and Barbara's he found he was actually the first.

Ian greeted him at the front door. "Hey Campbell come on in, we're out back. Barbara has me slaving over a hot grill." He directed Campbell toward the kitchen. "Would you like a beer?"

"Sure," Campbell said. "A beer sounds good."

Ian reached into the refrigerator, pulled out two bottles, and handed one to Campbell. "It's a new kind and I know you'll like it. The name of it is "Summer Ale". Last month, while Barbara and I were on vacation, we went into a microbrewery down the street from where we stayed. This was one of the bar's specialties. I tried it and thought it was excellent. I bought a case of it and brought it home with us. So, how do you like it, you think it has a nice flavor?"

"It has a nice golden color and good aroma." Campbell took a drink as he followed his friend out the back door and toward a smoking Bar-B-Q grill. "Not bad. The flavor is mild."

Ian walked over to check the grill. "According to the maker, the flavor goes very will with pheasant stuffed with wild rice and mushrooms. I couldn't get Barbara to go out and shoot a pheasant, so we'll have to settle for steaks."

Campbell laughed at his friend's humor. The smell of the food coming from the grill made him realize how hungry he was. He noticed that Barbara had already set the table, so he walked over to it to see what she had prepared. "The beer has an excellent flavor. I'm sure it'll go with what Barbara has here."

"For what it cost, it should be excellent," Ian said.

Campbell reached his hand in his pocket. "So are you saying I need to make a donation for the beer?"

"Of course not," said Ian. He laughed, then as an after-thought, he said, "Only after you drink five. Then it'll cost you."

Just then, Barbara stepped out the back door carrying a bowl of salad and walked across the patio toward the two men. "Ian, are you charging our guests for the beer they drink?"

She placed the bowl on a table that she had draped with a bright colored checkered tablecloth. The table setting looked festive with plates painted with rich patterns of orange and fiery red. She walked over and gave Campbell a quick hug. "Hi Campbell, welcome to our little soirée. It's good to have you here. Stacy and Paul couldn't make it, but I just got off the phone with Cassandra and she is on her way. She made a wrong turn and will be a little late."

This was Barbara's second try in finding Campbell what she calls a "life long companion". Barbara was just that sort of person wanting to make everything right. It's not that Campbell hasn't dated since Amanda. He's taken some very nice women to dinner, but he found they just didn't share the same interests as he.

As Barbara arranged napkins on the table, she voiced her disappointment that Stacy was not going to be there. "Stacy wanted to come in the worst way, but she had to help Paul's sister move their mother into Berrywood Nursing Home."

Campbell liked Stacy and thought she was a great older sister to Ian. "Too bad," he said. "Stacy has always been fun to be around and I was hoping she would be here. It's been a long time—really too long, since I've seen her. She sure keeps herself busy and it seems from your comments, she's always on the run."

After Ian turned the steaks on the grill, he walked back over to the table and took a drink from his summer ale. "Stacy has always been one to lend a hand, but I think Paul's family takes advantage of her. When they need any kind of help they're sure to call Stacy, but when it's time for a little fun or a good time they fail to remember her and the kids."

Barbara placed a small vase of flowers in the center of the table and stepped back to see how it looked. "Stacy is dependable when things need to get done, and she'll work hard at it and not stop until it's finished. She is also, funny and easy to be around."

Ian agreed. "My sister is a forgiving person and will tolerate a great deal for a long while." Ian laughed softly. "They need to beware of the day when Stacy has finally had enough. They'll stand around and wonder what happened."

Barbara nodded. "I agree with you, Stacy is one who will never talk badly to me about her family. I know her well enough and think it would be safe to presume that day is on the horizon.

"That family is so self-centered and could never see their faults," Ian said. "The sad thing is when Stacy has had enough, Paul and his family will never see they brought it on themselves. Rather, they'll wonder what is wrong with Stacy. By then she'll be beyond caring what they think."

Barbara placed her hand on Ian's back. "I think your sister can take care of herself, and she knows she has us no matter what."

Campbell paused in his task of lifting a cover off one of the bowls and inspecting its contents. "Stacy can bring humor to any situation. Ian, do you remember her marble cake?"

Ian started to laugh. "Do I ever! She really had me going!"

"I know," said Campbell. "We were over at Stacy's and as always, we were working on Ian's heap of metal he called a car back then. Stacy offered us a piece of cake she had just baked. While we were eating it, she said it was a box cake she got from the store. Then she casually said, "According to the outside package it's supposed to be marble cake, but I sifted it twice and could not find any marbles." Campbell paused to laugh and shake his head. "The funniest part of it all was the look on Ian's face, the way his hand stopped in med air just as he was about to take another bit of cake! It was hilarious!"

"I know," Ian said. "The look Stacy held on her face was so sober, I honestly thought she was serious. I could not believe my sister was that stupid to think real marbles actually came in a marble cake!"

"I think Stacy had you until she started laughing," Campbell exclaimed. "I have to tell you, I was about on the verge of believing her myself. She could always pull one over on us back then."

"You think that's bad, you should have grown up with her," Ian said. "Being the eldest and with our mother working, Stacy did most of the house cleaning. One time after she cleaned the bathroom she wouldn't let any of us kids take a bath. Her reasoning on it was she didn't want it to get dirty again."

Amused, Campbell asked, "So how long did you have to go without a bath?"

"Not long. Mom intervened and told Stacy to let us take our baths. Stacy made us agree to clean up the bathroom and hang our towels up. I know now that was what she wanted all along. She just liked getting her point across with humor instead of anger. She really wasn't and still isn't the yelling type."

Ian was still smiling. "She was a good sister at that. You know she brought my high school class ring for me? The family could not afford it, and I resigned myself not to get one. At that time, Stacy had already left home, married and was working. She said she never got a class ring herself and wanted to be sure I had one." Ian was smiling and Campbell thought he could see a little mist in Ian's eye. "That one gesture meant more to me then I could tell."

"What a wonderful story, and that sounds just like Stacy," Barbara said. "When she was over yesterday we had a great visit and we laughed a lot."

Ian slipped his arm around her waist. "Were you laughing at me?"

"No," Barbara said, as she smiled up at him. "We hardly talked about you at all."

Ian tried to look serous. "Are you saying I'm not worthy to be the topic of your conversion?" He dropped a kiss on the top of her head.

Ian then held his empty bottle up to Campbell. "You want another beer?"

—

"Sure, if you can spare another." Campbell tipped his bottle and took the last drink from it.

Ian grabbed it along with his own empty bottle and headed toward the back door. "Barbara, do you want anything while I'm heading that way?"

"Sure, bring back that tall, dark, and handsome man I have hiding in the bedroom closet."

Ian turned and walked a few steps backwards with his arms held out. "You see Campbell, what I have to put up with? That's why I call before coming home; it gives her time to get her boyfriend out of the house." He then turned and disappeared into the house.

Campbell laughed and then asked Barbara, "You want me do anything—you don't have a lid on a jar that needs to be loosened or opened?"

Barbara smiled back at Campbell. "Oh no, I think I have everything under control. We are only waiting on the steaks."

Campbell walked over to the grill and checked the steaks. The smoke from the grill changed direction and blew away from him. He chuckled to himself, thinking of how earlier it kept blowing back over Ian each time he even came close to the grill. No doubt, in Ian's case, the theory of smoke following beauty proved to be wrong. The sound of Ian's voice brought Campbell out of his thoughts.

"Look who finally got here!" Ian announced as he came walking out the door, holding the hand of the late arriving guest.

Campbell turned and saw a woman with brilliant eyes, nutmeg-colored hair, olive skin touched with soft red at her high cheekbones. She wore a turquoise blouse, which matched her slacks and sandals.

Barbara delighted, leaped from her chair. "Cassandra you made it, I'm glad you're here! I hope you didn't have too much trouble of finding your way."

As the two women greeted each other, Campbell realized this was the same women he had seen coming from the store two nights earlier.

"Campbell, I want you to met Cassandra," Barbara said with excitement. She was obviously delighted at engineering their meeting.

It took him a moment to collect his thoughts sufficiently to answer. "You're the same women I saw at the store Thursday evening."

Cassandra smiled broadly and held her hand out. "I'm pleased to meet you." Her voice trialed off as her eyelids flashed up and she touched a fingertip to her throat. "Campbell?"

Cassandra could see this stranger had the same blue eyes and broad smile as the boy she had a crush on while in high school. Yes, it truly was him!

Campbell wondered if he looked as puzzled as he felt. He recognized her, but he knew it was not from seeing her two days earlier. She knew him—his name. She seemed to expect him to recognize her, too.

"Campbell Mallary!" she exclaimed. Then noticing the confused expression on his face, she gave him an uncertain look. "You don't know who I am, do you? I'm Cassandra-Cassy. We went to high school together in Addison!"

"Cassy?" Campbell managed a shaky smile while he struggled to comprehend the incredible. Cassy was vitally standing before him! She was here in Ian and Barbara's backyard.

He tightened the grip on her hand. "When I saw you the other evening I was positive I knew you from somewhere, but I just couldn't place you!"

Cassandra now recalled seeing him as she walked from the store. What she had seen then was a well-dressed sophisticated stranger walking toward her, and as he came closer, she saw he had his eyes fixed on her. To keep from staring she smiled and quickly averted her eyes. That stranger was Campbell Mallary whom she had been hoping to find, and whom she did not even recognize when she saw him on the street!

"I tried to find you, but assumed you no longer lived here," she said as tears threatened to spill. "Just when I gave up, here you are standing right in front of me!"

"It's wonderful to see you. You look different. I mean in a good way." Campbell extended a comforting arm and hugged her, as she pressed her face against his cheek. He then pulled away and held her hand tight. "I've thought about you so many times over the years."

Ian looked confused as his mouth hung open. "You two know each other?"

Barbara chimed in, "Campbell and Cassandra attended the same high school."

Ian asked in surprise, "They lived in Addison at the same time?"

Without taking his eyes off his newfound friend, Campbell answered, "Cassy was a sophomore, and I was a senior. She sat two desks ahead of me in journalism and didn't even know I was alive."

"Campbell," Cassandra exclaimed. That is not true! I knew you were very much alive."

Campbell's thoughts darted back to their senior prom and how it took him all evening to muster up the courage to ask her for that one dance. After graduating, he saw her working at her father's drug store and considered asking her on a date. He knew he would be leaving for college the following week and decided against it. Now here she stood—

"Campbell, you want to give the lady her hand back?" Ian said laughing.

Campbell's glance darted from Cassandra to Ian and then back down to his hand. He apologized and let go of her hand.

"Hey, are we going to eat? I'm starving." Ian announced after he took the steaks from the grill and carried them on a platter to the table.

Campbell escorted Cassandra to the table and directed her to a chair. He then pulled a chair for himself next to her.

"We have so much catching up to do," he said. "You'll have to tell me what you've been doing since high school."

Barbara watched Campbell's reaction to Cassandra and could tell her two years of E-Harmony.Com for Campbell, just paid off. In an undertone, she told herself. "I know I got it right this time."

Ian leaned toward her and in between bites of food, he asked, "You say something Babe?"

"Oh, I was just saying Cassandra goes to the same seminar as I do and that's where we met."

Campbell leaning forward bracing his elbows on the table and asked, "Do you live here in Denver?"

"No, I moved back home—to Addison, over a year ago. It'll be two years next month."

Campbell was feeling disappointed that she did not live closer. He quickly asked her how long she would be in town.

"The last day of the seminar is Friday—in the afternoon." Cassandra then quickly added, "The classes are only half days and we get out at noon."

Ian leaned toward Barbara and whispered. "Right now if you and I dropped off the earth, no one in this backyard would notice."

While keeping an eye on Campbell and Cassandra, Barbara smiled and nodded in agreement.

Ian took a drink of his renowned beer. "Better yet, my dear wife, rather than dropping off the earth, let's just go in the house and make passionate love."

Barbara laughed and gave him a playful push. "Ian, stop it!"

Campbell and Cassandra stopped talking and both looked across the table to see why Barbara was laughing.

Ian quickly changed the subject. "Hey Campbell, did you forget about the beer I brought out to you?" He then offered one to Cassandra.

"No, but thank you anyway." Cassandra gave Ian an easy smile. "I have a bad sense of direction and already had trouble finding my way here. If I drank anything I doubt that I'd be able to find my way back."

"Barbara's that way." Ian raised his eyes, which had a teasing glint in them. "Oh, don't get me wrong. Her sense of direction is fine. It's all the drinking she does."

Barbara shot her husband a sideway look and tried to keep from laughing. "Ian Chatman, you are such a liar! She looked back in Cassandra's direction. "Don't believe a word this man tells you!"

Ian reached over, placed his arm across Barbara's shoulders, and pulled her close. "Her sense of direction is good because she found me."

Ian smiled over at Cassandra. "You have no need to worry about finding your way back. While Campbell was in college, he worked part time as a messenger and knows his way around the city very well. You'll be safe with him, and I'm sure he wouldn't mind seeing that you get home safely."

Campbell quickly agreed and asked Cassandra the name of her hotel. He nodded in acknowledgement. "I know exactly where it is. You can see it from the Interstate and I drive past it everyday on the way to work. When you're ready to go, you can follow me over in your car. That is if you don't mind."

Campbell brought a smile to Cassandra's lips. "Oh no, I don't mind at all. Actually, I would be grateful. I do fine with my driving, but if I'm not familiar with the area I do a bad job of it."

Campbell's eyes met and held Cassandra's eyes for a long moment. "Don't concern yourself, I'll see that you get back safely."

Redirecting the conversion Ian asked Campbell, "You left the office early Friday and I didn't get a chance to ask if you saw the report on that hit and run case."

"You mean the one involving the alleged Fashion Robber?" Campbell asked. "Did they find more evidence?"

"It seems the victim did in fact, get a good look at the driver," Ian said.

Barbara with her glass in mid air asked, "Did they say if the driver was a man or a woman?"

Ian was absently toying with a spoon, pressing it firmly against the tabletop and craning it around. When Barbara posed the question of the possibility of a woman as the driver, he looked up and met her eyes squarely. "No, but that is a thought! Who likes fashion better than the ladies."

"You're right," said Cassandra. "Since I've been here, I've kept up on what they are saying about the affair. I don't recall reading anything in the newspapers, where it tells if the stolen clothing were men's or ladies." She turned to Campbell. "Did the authorities mention anything thing about that?"

"No," he replied. "But that would be one way of determining if the thief was a man or woman?"

Ian laughed and leaned back in his chair. "I'm sorry to be the bearer of bad news. Some men prefer to wear clothing of the feminine gender. If you have any doubt, a drive down our fair city's most popular street will be very convincing."

"Ian," Barbara said while elbowing him in the side. Ian laughed and feigned injury. Still laughing she added. "Another thing to take into consideration is the clothing size, if everything is one size that would be of some help in finding the thief."

"A lot of stores sell clothing for tall and short people. For example, women less than five feet three inches are considered petite." Cassandra paused and smiled. "I know that because I am five foot three inches and I always look for clothes labeled petite."

The sharp lines between Campbell's brows were chiseled deep as he leaned back in his chair and took note of everything that was said. He considered a moment, then asked, "Ian, did the victim say what kind of car it was?"

"No, I don't think he knew. That seems to be the problem. If the police have no crime record on the suspect, it would be hard to find him even if the victim knows what he or she looks like."

"Unless the victim's description of the driver can be recognized by someone who knows or is acquainted with the suspect," said Campbell. "Do you know if the man has been released from the hospital?"

Ian shook his head. "No, the last I heard, he is still over at the county hospital."

"I think it would be interesting to hear what he has to say," Campbell said. "I'd like to talk to him."

Ian held up his arm and looked at his watch "It's too late to speak to him tonight, but I would do it first thing in the morning. They can release him anytime, and since he's homeless, you may not be able to find him after he leaves the hospital."

BARBARA OPENED THE cupboard and took out four desert bowls. "Campbell, did you like my surprise?"

Campbell leaned against the counter next to her, as she scooped ice cream into the bowls. "Yes, I think I'm still in shock from it all. I'm grateful for your little surprise."

His eyes and smile were tender as he remembered the old times. "Cassandra has always brought me joy and is a delight to be with." He sighed and said, "I think it's been ten or more years since we saw each other last."

Without thought he toyed and twirled each bowl, before pushing it over to Barbara to fill. "You say you only met Cassandra this last week?"

"Yes, I sat next to her at the seminar. When I asked if she lived here, that's when she told me she was from Addison. It wasn't until later that I realized she was from the same town as you are. The next day we took lunch together and that's when she told me about her friend. She said he used to live here and assumed he had moved. When she told me the name of her friend, I about fell over! Her friend was you!"

"You didn't tell her you knew me?"

"At first I was going to, but then I came up with this great idea. Don't you think I'm a genius?" Barbara asked without looking up from her task of spooning ice cream in the bowls.

"What would you've done if I had not come to your little party?

"I would've had Ian hunt you down."

Campbell looked right at Barbara and narrowed his eyes. "Ian knew about this?"

"No, Ian can't be trusted and I knew he would have told you," she said.

"That just goes to show, Ian's loyalties lay with me," Campbell said as a bright smile stretched across his face.

"Campbell, before you go back out, I think there's something you should know." Barbara turned and faced Campbell. "Cassandra's husband and only child, a son, were killed in a car accident."

Campbell turned his pained eyes to search hers. His voice was throaty. "When—I mean, how long ago did that happen?"

"I think about three years ago."

Campbell went to stare out the window at Cassandra. He had a hurtful frown on his face as he tried to make sense of the affair.

Barbara walked over and stood next to Campbell. "I think the only reason she told me is because I asked her about family. Otherwise, she seemed not to want to talk about it, and that's why I thought you should know."

Still looking out the window he asked, "How old was her child?"

"I don't know."

Campbell did the math in his head. "He couldn't have been much older then five or six."

"Did you know her husband? Did he live in the same town as you and Cassandra?"

"No, no, Cassandra left to go to school, and I think she met him there."

Barbara walked away from the window and back to dipping ice cream into the bowls. "Since she knows you, she may feel comfortable enough to talk to you about it."

Campbell turned toward Barbara. "Thanks, I'm glad you told me."

Barbara smiled and lightly laughed. "I think right now, you need to go out and rescue her from Ian. I'll finish up in here and be along soon?"

AFTER CAMPBELL PARKED in the hotel's parking lot, he quickly walked over to where Cassandra was just getting out of her car.

"Thank you, I hope this wasn't out of your way," she said as she slipped her bag over one shoulder.

He reached around her and closed her car door. "You know, it really is early yet. Would you like to go have a drink or a cup of coffee?"

Cassandra looked hesitant, and for a moment, he thought she was going to turn his invitation down.

Then she answered him. "If you don't mind waiting for me to run up to my room to get a sweater? Otherwise, I would love to go."

Assuring her he did not mind waiting, Campbell lightly placed his hand on her back and escorted her across the parking lot to the front of the hotel. When they stepped inside, he noticed a lobby to the left of the doors. He told Cassandra he would wait for her there. She reiterated she would not take long and then hurried toward the elevators.

As he waited in the lobby, he wondered what the proper etiquette would have been on that. Although, she was coming right back, should he have walked her to her room? If he did, would he stand outside in the hall or step into the room? As he was speculating what Emily Post's viewpoint would have been, he heard the elevators doors reopen and the click of heels on the Spanish tiled floor leading to the lobby.

He turned to see Cassandra walking toward him, and at that moment, he wanted to run to her like an excited child. He was able to somewhat contain himself and instead hurried, rather than ran, over to her. Together they exited the front doors they had entered less than fifteen minutes before.

As they walked across the parking lot, he considered that maybe he should have driven his truck to the front door so Cassandra would not have had to walk the short distance through the busy parking lot.

Without Cassandra realizing it, she put his mind at ease. "The fresh air is nice, kind of like a tonic that can complete any cure," she said. "During the summer months this is my favorite part of the day to walk and just to be out."

Campbell secretly commended himself for the choice he had made. Okay, you did good walking her to the lobby was the right thing to do. He then wondered why he was even worried about such details. He had never been that concerned with other dates, or around other women.

"I know what you mean," he said. "I guess I'm strange, but when I go grocery shopping I try and park my truck at the farthest end of a row from the store so I can walk and get a little exercise." There I go again. That was a stupid thing to say. No doubt by now, she probably wishes she had made an excuse and gotten away and safely back in her hotel room when she had the chance. Instead of these insane comments, can't you make some interesting small talk?

Cassandra smiled back at him and giggled a little. "No I don't think that's strange at all. I read a magazine article recently that stated we should do that exact thing. It's one of the little things we can do to keep fit. It suggested just those kinds of things to get in an extra 2000 steps each day."

With the sound of laughter in her voice, Cassandra casually added. "But what I think is strange that you are driving a SUV but you keep calling it a truck?"

Campbell laughed with her and agreed. "Yes you're right. I've always driven a truck and after so recently getting the SUV, I continue to call it a truck."

"There is actually nothing wrong with that. I like your "truck". I also like the color."

He looked at her in surprise. "The color is white."

Cassandra didn't answer, just laughed more. Campbell liked her easy manner; it put him at ease and made him feel good.

After Campbell opened her door for her, he asked, "You have any preference, coffee, or a drink, or where you want to go?"

"No, but since I haven't seen you for years, I'd hoped you would take me to one of the places you usually go to."

"You must really want to get bored, don't you?"

"Campbell, shame on you. Going to a place you like would be an adventure in getting to know you again. Try me and see if I get bored."

CAMPBELL TOOK HER to a little Italian bistro that had an intimate lounge with an atmosphere of Mediterranean chic, and offered white linen tablecloths and walls painted the sandy color of a seaside villa. The lights were low, with a Nora Jones song softly playing in the background.

Cassandra noticed there were only two other couples sitting at tables and one man sitting alone at the bar. Campbell took her by the hand and led her to a small table for two, a comfortable distance from the other couples. In the center of the table was a single candle and its flickering flame gave off a soft romantic glow.

"Campbell this is very impressive," she said. "If you are still trying to convince me how boring you are, you are doing a very bad job of it."

Soon after they ordered their drinks and the waitress hurried away, the man who was sitting at the bar slid off his stool and moved a little drunkenly over to them. He was a small man, with shaggy brown hair and his clothes looked too big for him.

As he approached their table, he said boisterously. "Campbell is that you? I thought that was you when you came in!"

He grabbed a chair from the next table and sat down alongside Campbell. "How's it going buddy? It has been a while! You get caught up on work at the office and don't have to work the grave yard shift anymore?"

Campbell's heart seemed to drop to the pit of his stomach when he realized who the man was. He was Nester, the janitor, who cleaned the offices for the Hendricks Firm.

Back when Campbell put in a lot of late hours at the office, Nester would come around and always want to talk and talk and talk. He was exasperating, with his endless chatter, so much so, that his interruptions ultimately ended Campbell working late. Now Campbell came to the office early whenever he needed to put in more than normal office hours on a project. Seeing him unexpectedly, it took everything in Campbell's power to be even somewhat congenial. He didn't want anyone interrupting his reunion with Cassy, especially this obnoxious man.

Nester called back over his shoulder. "Hey bar-keep. Put these two drinks on my tab and bring me another over here."

Campbell fought for control and he did manage to voice a calm protested. "Oh no, there's no need to do that!"

"Well, if I can't buy a drink for my old buddy and his lady friend then something just isn't right here!"

With Nester's presence, Campbell felt a lump gathering in his throat and he had to swallow to gulp away the emotion. Right at that moment, he wished Nester would turn into "Soylent Green". He felt embarrassed by the man and hated the idea of putting Cassandra though Nester's endless stream of stupidity.

Nester leaned in and spoke low to Campbell. "You know, I have to be careful who I drink with. If I drink too much, the women always take advantage of me."

Campbell cleared his throat and when he looked over at Cassandra to see if she had heard Nester, she was leaning back in her chair with her arms casually crossed, finding great amusement in Campbell's dilemma.

Eventually, Cassandra excused herself to go to the ladies room. Campbell would not have blamed her if she were using that as a ploy to get away from Nester. He just hoped she would come back and not sneak out and leave him stuck with Nestor for the evening. Blast the man!

When Cassy thankfully returned, she leaned in close to Campbell and slipped him a written note under the table where Nester could not see. Nester was so engaged in dominating the conversion that he never noticed the exchange of amused glances between them or Campbell secretly reading the note he held under the table. It read:

Please don't worry about me.
I am not bored—bored—bored.

56

Only minutes ago, Campbell was agitated, but thanks to this wonderful woman sitting next him, he was now trying to conceal his laughter. Out of gratification, he took her hand from her lap and incased it in both his. In response, she leaned toward him and laid her other hand on his.

Nester tipped he head back, drained the last of his drink before standing. "Sorry folks I have to go to the little boy's room." With a roguish shake of his finger, he warned. "Don't go anywhere, when I get back I will buy us another round."

Before Campbell could decline, Nester was already making his way back toward the hallway that led to the restrooms.

After Nester was out of sight Campbell stood, quickly pulled some bills from his wallet, and laid them on the table. He grabbed Cassandra by one hand and her sweater from the back of her chair with the other.

"Come on. Let's get out of here before he comes back!"

They hurried to the front door, and when they got outside, they ran to Campbell's SUV, laughing all the way.

When they got back to the hotel, they were still finding amusement in Nestor's bumbling intrusion on their evening and their wild dash to get away from him.

"What we did to Nester was awful," said Cassandra as they walked across the lobby. She reached into her bag, took out her key card, and handed it to Campbell. "I hope we didn't upset him too much."

"I will just look at it as saving a damsel in distress," said Campbell as they approached the elevator. "Besides, he was pretty wasted and probably won't remember any of it tomorrow."

The doors slid open and out stepped an older man and woman. Campbell caught the door for them and the woman rushed past him without a word. The man tipped his head with a thank you and followed the woman toward the lobby.

Just before the elevator door closed, Cassandra and Campbell could hear the woman berating the older man. "I like going there, and I don't see why we should change. I just hate it when you do that. I will just wait here while you go get the car and don't forget to—"

Campbell slid the key card in the slot and the doors closed, shutting out the woman's screechy voice. Campbell laughed. "It sounded as if she had an "I" problem."

Cassandra giggled. "That poor man."

Campbell then touched Cassandra's arm. "I had a good time tonight, in spite of the disaster at the La Bistro."

"It was a lot of fun tonight for me too, and I am glad you asked me to go with you." She said as the doors reopened, and she led the way down the hall toward her room. "Not only did you rescue me from a boring hotel room, but you took me on quite a venture."

"We could continue the adventure. Tomorrow is Sunday, and if you don't have plans, would you like to meet me for breakfast?" he asked. "After, I can show you around."

"Breakfast would be nice." She smiled up at him. "What time do you want to go?"

"Can I meet you here at eight?" He explained, "I hope that isn't too late, but I would like to stop by the county hospital. I have a feeling about something and have a couple of questions to ask the victim of that hit and run."

"That sounds intriguing," she said. "Eight will be just fine."

"Do you have a phone number I can call just in case my inquiry goes longer than I anticipate?" He asked.

Cassandra rummaged around in her bag and after a moment, she brought out a business card. "Here is my card," she said as she handed it to Campbell. Campbell glanced at it and saw her name printed in a burgundy color and down below was printed the familiar word of Addison, his hometown. The card included her business phone number and a cell number.

She laughed and held up a receipt. "For a moment, I thought I would have to write my number on the back of this receipt. Glad I still had one business card floating around in my bag."

"I'll exchange numbers and give you the number to my cell phone." Campbell paused to chuckle. "I'm not as organized as you are, so I may have to borrow that receipt myself."

She giggled at his wittiness. "Wait, and I'll get you a pen to write it with." She pointed to her door. "Please come in, stay, and I'll make coffee or order something from room service. We can pick up where Nestor interrupted our evening."

Campbell considered accepting her invitation, but he envisioned her hotel room and felt it would be like stepping into her bedroom.

He knew he could not trust himself to leave her once he did that, and regretfully declined her invitation.

He unlocked the door and held it for Cassandra. As she walked into the room, the door swung open wide where Campbell got a visual tour of the room. He saw it was a suite with a sitting room completely separate from a bedroom. He berated himself for declining her invitation and for even thinking that Cassandra would invite him into that kind of situation. She was too nice a woman to compromise herself, or him, in that manner.

She crossed the room to a small writing desk, took a pen from one of its drawers, and brought it back to him. As he took the pen, he lightly brushed his hand with hers. The warmth and the touch of her hand excited him. While he wrote there were no words passed between them, and he glanced at her from the corner of his eye. She had her eyes lowered watching him write the numbers. He suddenly felt self-conscious, stopped writing, and looked intently down at the top of her lowered head.

When she noticed he stopped writing, she looked up at him. He took her hand, squeezed it in a grip that demonstrated surprising gentleness. For a moment, they both concentrated on their joined hands. Releasing her hand, he then put his arms around her waist and pulled her to him. He felt her press in close as she put one arm around his neck and lightly rested against his chest.

Her hair smelled nice and when he touched his check to hers, it felt soft and warm. He held her just a moment longer than he probably should have. He stepped away, but not before slightly touching his lips to her cheek.

"Thank you." He said with words that caught in his throat. "After all these years, I can't tell you how I feel about finding you again." Stepping back from the temptation to stay too long, Campbell whispered, "I should go. I'll meet you tomorrow morning at eight in the lobby. Good night, Cassy."

CHAPTER 5

Regrets

"Mr. Thorson, you have a visitor," the plump nurse announced as she walked into the room with Campbell close on her heels.

The hospital room was painted infirmary arctic white and furnished sparsely with two hospital beds, one of which was striped down to the mattress and the other with rumpled sheets turned back as if recently vacated. On one of the over-the-bed tables sat a breakfast tray full of dirty dishes waiting to be carried away. The only window in the room had the blinds open and offered a view of the parking lot.

Rex was sitting in a wheelchair fully dressed and appeared eager to leave the hospital. His right arm was in a cast and supported by a sling tied around his neck. Tattooed on each one of the knuckles of his right hand were letters that made up his name: Rex T. Campbell could only assume by the poor workmanship and irregularity of the letters that either Rex or some other unskilled person did the tattoos. Rex looked to be in his early forties and had a scruffy beard and brown hair that hung down the length of his shoulders. He wore a faded red button up shirt and a stained pair of jeans rolled up at the cuffs. His tennis shoes looked to be new and Campbell could only speculate that one of the charities in town provided Rex with the shoes.

The nurse grabbed a clipboard from off the footboard of the unmade bed, flipped though the two page medical record, and scribbled something on it with a pen she took from the pocket of her blue smock. "Mr. Thorson, your Doctor is making his rounds now, he'll be in to see you, and after that one of our nurses will be in to wheel you down to the lobby." The nurse hung the clipboard back on the end of the bed and gathered a pile of laundry from one of the chairs. She turned and left without another word to her soon to-be-former patient.

As the nurse left the room, Rex glared at her and mumbled something under his breath that Campbell couldn't make out. Campbell could only assume from their behavior that Rex and the nurse didn't strike up a great friendship during his stay.

Rex then looked up at Campbell with a grimace on his face. "If you're from the police, please throw the cuffs on me and haul me out of here away from that devil woman. I pity the poor fool who's married to her. He'd have to take her everywhere he goes because she's too ugly to kiss goodbye." Rex laughed at his own joke, and when he did, Campbell could see that a good portion of his teeth was missing. "If I'd have to lay eyes on her again in a hundred years it'd be too soon!"

Campbell smiled. "No, I'm not with the police department. My name is Campbell Mallary, and I am an attorney. If you don't mind, I would like to ask a couple questions about the driver of the car that hit you." Campbell walked around the bed to stand in front of Rex.

"Mr. Thorson, I'd like to say I'm sorry about your misfortune and hope to get your help in finding the person who did this to you."

Rex started shaking his head. "Ambulance chasing won't do you any good here. I can't afford any lawyers; it just isn't in my budget."

Campbell held one hand up. "Oh, I do understand, and that's why we lawyers like to give someone like you a break once in a while.

—

Today, all my questions are free, and any answers you want to give me I'll not charge you for them either."

"Well, I guess you guys aren't so bad after all," exclaimed Rex. "So what did you want to ask me?"

Campbell knew he had better start asking questions fast, before Rex figured out what had just transpired. "Did you see the driver of the car that hit you?"

"I sure did and think she was trying to kill me! If she wasn't then she was doing a darn good job of acting like it!"

"You are saying it was a female who was driving the car?" Campbell asked, giving Rex his full attention.

Rex sat straight in the wheelchair. "You're darn right it was one of them females! I know it was, because she stopped and yelled out her window at me. She told me to get off the street and out of her way. I proceeded to tell the little twit the street is my home and I've more right to it than she does. That must have made her mad, because she backed the car up and went after me! That's when she crashed into my shopping basket, which held all my worldly possessions. Knocked it right out of my hands and up over the sidewalk. Threw my stuff all over! Gonna have to start gathering all over again." He shook his head in disgust.

"She spoke to you?"

"No she didn't speak to me at all, she yelled at me!" Rex nodded his head and scowled. "Kids these days have no respect for elders."

With peaked interest, Campbell asked, "So how old do you think she was?"

Rex thought for a moment while scratching his head. "I'm not sure, nineteen or twenty, maybe younger."

"Can I assume you got a good look at her and can identify her?"

"The little snip had red hair and a big mouth!" Rex said with one quick nod of his head.

Campbell chuckled. "You say her hair was red?"

"That's right, and a big loud mouth!"

"Is there any truth to the matter that your saw her come from the department store she had just robbed?" Campbell asked.

"I sure did! I was back behind the store sleeping—I mean resting my eyes, you know. I heard an alarm go off and when I looked up,

I saw her as plain as day coming out the back door with a load of clothes and stuff. She saw me looking at her and I think that's why she tried to do me under. You know, get rid of any eye witnesses."

"So you are saying she intentionally hit you?"

"You mean on purpose? Darn right, it was on purpose. But I almost got clear of her before she swerved to sideswipe me and broke my arm!" Rex paused and laughed quietly. "She came close to getting this bag I keep on my belt loop but she missed. This bag holds all my most important things. She got the rest of it, though. All my good stuff."

Campbell looked down and saw a battered Wal-Mart plastic bag on his lap. "Can you recall the color or make of the car?"

"It was too dark to see the exact color but I think it was green, maybe blue." Rex slowly shook his head. "The cops asked me that, but I'm not sure what kind of car it was. Not good at knowing cars. It was one of those fancy ones, I know that!"

Campbell knew he had acquired as much information as he could from Rex. "Mr. Thorson is there anyway I can get in contact with you in the future just in case I have more questions?"

"Now is there going to be any charge for those questions? You did say they're only free today. Not going to have any lawyer money in the future neither."

"Oh no, any investigation or court procedures are always paid by the people in cases such as this one."

"I don't know what people you are talking about but they must be pretty generous with their money."

Campbell only smiled. "Is there anywhere I could get in contact with you if I need to?"

"Well there is my sister; I might be staying with her until this arm heals up." He held his arm up and then jerked from the pain.

"I just don't know if I'm going to be able to stand her screaming kids. She has five and it sounds like there are ten when they get to fighting." Rex gestured by pointing his left thump at his chest. "That's why I'm my own man and don't need no screaming brats! Anyway, I check in with her now and again. Just to make sure she is doing okay, you know."

Campbell wrote down the sister's phone number and address. He thanked Rex for his information and before he left Rex asked him for money. Campbell pulled a twenty from his wallet and handed it to him. He figured it to be cheap insurance that Rex would be willing to talk to him again.

Rex was still thanking Campbell for the money as he walked out of the hospital room. Campbell could only hope Rex didn't spend it at the first liquor store he saw after getting out. Campbell then reconsidered. If his sister's five kids were as bad as Rex claimed, then the drink would be on him.

CAMPBELL CHECKED HIS watch, as he walked back though the double doors of the county hospital. He had told Cassandra he would meet her at eight. According to his watch, he had just enough time to catch the Interstate and then drop back down to the hotel where Cassandra was staying.

He reflected on his visit with Rex and considered it enlightening. He knew he had to get in contact with the police station where they were holding Felicity's car before it was moved. With what he had learned from Rex, he wanted to take another look at the damage to Felicity's car. He also wondered what kind of information the Ricer's driver may be holding and thought it would be beneficial to have a talk with him.

Campbell's thoughts returned to the traffic on the interstate as he noticed it slowing down. He wondered what the problem was, since on Sundays it typically moved along at a fast pace. He glanced ahead to an overhead sign that read; "Thirty minute delays are expected one mile ahead". He noticed the southbound lanes were moving along and he could only speculate there was a wreck ahead. He had already passed the last off ramp and it was too late to change his route. He had no other choice, but to wait it out and hope they could get the problem cleared up before the thirty minutes.

He reached into his console to retrieve the business card Cassandra had given him with her phone number on it. Instead of the card, he found the pen with the receipt he had been going to write his own phone number on and leave with her. He could not believe that he was that mesmerized with Cassandra that he had taken her pen without leaving his number. She must think him to be a moron, or at most a thief of other people's pens.

Still looking for her card, he pulled his wallet out and found it safely tucked away right where he had put it. He commended himself for being enough in the right frame of mind to accomplish that much. With the card in hand, he would call Cassandra and let her know he would be late.

However, when he grabbed his phone from the console and flipped it open, the light on the phone did not come on! All he could do was stare at the blank screen, while his heart dropped to his stomach. He could not believe he forgot to charge his phone the evening before. He was so frustrated with himself and felt like a prisoner in his own car. His only recourse was to wait it out and hope Cassandra stayed and waited for him.

While trying to analyze his feelings for Cassandra, a panic of not seeing her again came up inside him. Campbell came to realize then, that Amanda's tight grip on his emotions had been loosened. Cassy was restoring his trust.

Campbell had known Amanda never loved him, but hoped that someday she would. He could not understand what kind of hold she had on his emotions and he hated himself for it. Even though there were times he detested her, she had a way of taking advantage of his forgiving nature.

Amanda had never been faithful to Campbell and made very little effort to hide it. He had looked the other way with her infidelity and at the time, it seemed far easier to live with lies than to face up to the painful truth about how bad a mistake he had made marrying her.

His thoughts roamed back to a camping trip he and Amanda had gone on with a group of their friends and Amanda's brother-in-law, Jack, a short time after they were married. Amanda's sister stayed home with their new baby. Every one brought their own tents or campers and after the BBQ, there were a few drinks passed around. Campbell had been up early that morning and with the long drive up, bowed out of the party to go to bed.

Early the next morning he woke and realized Amanda was not in their tent. He thought it was odd that she would have gotten up before him, since she never did that at home. As a rule, he was always the first up, showered, shaved, and went on a thirty-minute walk, before Amanda even woke.

—

After dressing he stepped out of their tent, it was dawn with the sun still hidden behind the mountains. Eldon, one of the other campers was sitting at the campfire holding a cup off coffee. He held it up toward Campbell. "You want a cup? I'm the first up and thought I'd get the coffee going."

Before Campbell could answer, Amanda's brother-in-law Jack stepped from his tent with sleep in his eyes and hair standing on end. Right behind Jack and still half-asleep, was Amanda. When Campbell realized what he was witnessing, he was overcome with nausea and shock. Unable to face an ugly confrontation in front of everyone, he turned quickly around, walked to their tent, gathered up his shaving gear, and headed down to the river. Over the course of the weekend, he never found a time or way to tell Amanda he had seen her leaving Jack's tent.

So many times, he had thought of that event and tried to make sense of the whole affair. He knew at the time he should have confronted Amanda, but the shock of it only made him want to get as far from it as he possibly could. On the trip home, he had waited for an explanation from Amanda but none came. He finally decided to ignore it and assume that it was just a case of too much to drink and passing out in the nearest tent. He had always wondered if she was not even aware that he saw her come from Jack's tent, or if she just didn't care.

Although Campbell hoped that would be the end of it, the events did not stop with that. There were the hidden letters that came from other men, coming home early from a trip to find all his personal things and evidence that she had a husband swept off the dresser and stashed in drawers. Should he believe the story of the drunken man who followed Amanda home without any encouragement from her, to once again, deny what he couldn't bear to have confirmed? The worst was yet to come when one of their friends approached him and accused Amanda of sleeping with her husband. How many more events there were that he was not aware of, he could only try not to speculate.

Living those two years with Amanda had been like making a bad investment. Even though the bottom had dropped out, he was so far into it that all he could do was to keep hoping for a good return.

—

When it became obvious Amanda, too, was avoiding the issues in their marriage, he distanced himself from her even more by shutting down all feelings he had ever had for her. Now he wondered if he had buried his feelings so deep, they would never be found again. After she left, he'd had no more strength or interest in starting a new relationship with anyone.

With Cassandra, something shattered within him allowing his lost feelings to resurface.

CASSANDRA LAY IN her bed waiting for her alarm clock to go off. Her thoughts were on the day before and how she didn't want her time with Campbell to end. She wanted to keep looking at his smile of dazzling brilliance as he told his stories. He gave her a sense of excitement and she already missed his nearness and his tender concern for her.

The ringing of the clock on her nightstand pulled her out of her thoughts. The little green glowing numbers read five thirty. Cassandra reached over, silenced the alarm, and lay for a moment more. She was anticipating her breakfast date with Campbell and it made her smile.

Cassandra did not realize that would be the first morning since the death of her son and husband she did not wake with a dread in her heart. After the funeral, she went into her room, lay on her bed, and wished she could go to sleep and not wake up. She did go to sleep; however, she did not die. Rather, she woke with a wave of sadness that washed over her that morning and each morning after.

As she swung her legs out of bed and pulled on her robe, she walked over to the window and lazily stretched her arms above her head. What a gorgeous day! She made coffee in the little coffeepot the hotel supplied and while it brewed, she brushed her teeth, showered, and then dried her hair. By the time she was done, the coffee was ready.

She wrapped herself in one of the hotel's big white complimentary robes, took her cup of coffee, and snuggled in a deep chair to watch the weather channel. The weather forecaster predicted a nice spring day with temperatures in the eighties.

After her thirty minutes of what Cassandra called vegetating, she decided to finish with her hair and dress. The warm temperatures told her white capris with a bright pink blouse and sandals would be all right.

By the time she was dressed it still was only seven, which meant she had a few minutes to spare to work on her homework from her CPA classes. She would get a start on it now and then finish it later that evening. She usually didn't put something like that off until the last minute, but in this case, it had just worked out that way.

After she moved back home to Addison and opened her own accounting office two years ago, she had fulfilled her continuing education obligations in Denver. Ever since she had been in that sort of work, each spring after the rush of beating the tax dead line, she always took a two weeks vacation. Since she was alone now and had no one to vacation with, she thought it would be practical to roll her usual vacation and the CPA seminar in together.

Unlike some people, she hated to travel by herself and disliked sitting in a hotel room alone. Rather, she preferred to move about, look at the sights, and share all of that with a companion. When in a new place or while traveling, she was anything but independent, and she liked having someone to show her around and so-to-speak, take care of her.

This trip was an undertaking for her since it was her first long trip she had ever taken alone or without anybody to meet her when she got there. It was relaxing to do just what she wanted, but at the same time lonely. Up until the previous week before she met Barbara, she was beginning to understand the meaning of feeling alone in a crowded world.

She thought it was more than odd the way she tried to get in contact with Campbell, and just when she had given up, she met up with Barbara who knew him.

She glanced at her watch again. Although it was too early for Campbell, she decided to go downstairs a head of time and wait for him in the lobby. She didn't care if she seemed eager to see him, she was!

IN THE LOBBY Cassandra found a comfortable looking sofa and chair grouping to sit in as she watched for Campbell's arrival. To be sure, she did not miss him, Cassandra situated herself to face the wall of windows looking out across the front entrance of the hotel.

While waiting, she discreetly sneaked glances though the glass doors of the dining area at a young couple who were enjoying breakfast. The man said something that made the girl laugh and glance shyly up at him. The adoration in her face made Cassandra's heart throb thinking of herself with Campbell. She remembered every detail, every word spoken, and her own feelings from the day before with Campbell.

Cassandra recalled back to the days when she helped her father in his drug store and how on those particular days, she always hoped Campbell would come into the store. Most times, he did come in to buy some little thing for his mother or to have an ice cream. Although she felt timid and shy around him, he always gave her a pleasant smile and was sure to speak. The summer he left to college was the last time she had seen him until yesterday. Even though she had hoped to meet up with him again, they never did. Soon after she had graduated from high school, she had left Addison herself. They went their separate ways and she could only wonder if that was the way it should have been.

Her thoughts drifted back to what Barbara had told her about Campbell's misfortunes in life. Could she have spared him some of the heartbreaks by telling him how she felt about him back then? Although she adored him then, she felt she could not compete with the girls closer to his age. He was the class president and just as handsome back then as he was now.

When Cassandra looked at her watch, it was after nine o'clock. She had waited in the lobby for little over an hour. Campbell told her if he could not make it by eight he would call. Although, she brought along her phone and knew there were no calls, she checked for missed calls anyway.

A disappointment started to take hold of her. She wondered if he had misgivings and changed his mind. The thought of him not giving her his phone number began dancing in her head. At first, she thought he forgot to give her the number, but now a nagging doubt was settling in that made her wonder if he didn't want her to have it. She stood to go back to her room and glanced once more across the lobby as her brow furrowed with the pain of the disappointment.

After returning to her room, she crossed over to the window, rested her forehead against the cool glass, and stared out over the city. She was trying to make up her mind if she should go with her original plans before Campbell asked her to breakfast, or stay and study for the next day's seminar.

She sighed, leaned against the window, and decided against the homework. She knew her concentration level would be low and the homework could wait until that evening. She would do as she first planned. She would drive to Estes Park to browse the shops, galleries and take in a tour of the Stanley Hotel.

She knew it would do her good to get out and get her mind off Campbell. She grabbed her bag and as she headed down the hall toward the elevator. She was already feeling better, or so she told herself.

CAMPBELL RUSHED INTO the hotel, hurried to the front desk, and asked the clerk to call Cassandra's room. As the clerk dialed her room, Campbell remained calm on the outside but inside his heart kept repeating, "Please Cassandra answer—answer!"

"Sorry, there is no answer" the clerk said still holding the receiver to his ear.

Out of desperation, Campbell asked, "Can you let it ring a little longer?"

After a moment longer, the clerk shook his head. "Sorry, no one is picking up."

Campbell reasoned even if Cassandra was not in her room she had to be close by. If he could just call her on her cell phone, he would catch her before she got very far from the hotel. He asked the clerk for the use of the desk phone.

"I'm sorry it is against our policy," the clerk said. "There's a pay phone past the elevators, down the hall and to the right. Do you need change?"

After getting the correct change, Campbell hurried down the hall toward the pay phones. As he disappeared around the corner, the elevator doors slid open and Cassandra stepped out. She walked

—

though the lobby and out the double doors, leaving her phone on the window ledge in her room.

AFTER A DAY of sightseeing, browsing gift shops and galleries, Cassandra returned to her hotel room with high sprits. Although, Campbell was constantly on her mind, she was feeling better than she did earlier about the whole morning affair. Even though, with her youth she could not make the claim of having all wisdom, from past experience she had learned there are events of life that have to be moved to the side in order to move on.

After Cassandra shed her clothes and slipped on a gown and robe, she took a small package from a paper bag. She carefully opened the package as she sat in one of the hotel's high back chairs. Inside was a delicate vanity bowl, small enough to cradle in her cupped hands. The bowl was in the shape of a water lily and painted in hues of blush peach, feathered with streaks of pearl white radiating out from a golden center.

Cassandra had found the bowl in an antique shop and could tell it was hand painted. When she picked it up to examine it more closely, she saw someone had drawn ~~drew~~ a small heart on the back and added an inscription that read, "To Mom, Jenny". She wondered how an item that must have held such a high sentimental value to someone could have ended up for sale in a shop. It was obvious it was a gift from a child to their mother, and for that reason Cassandra bought it.

After a moment contemplating its sentiment, she placed the bowl on the side table and collected her dreadful homework that she could no longer put off. She walked to the window to look out before pulling the drapes close. When she glanced down, she was surprised to see her cell phone on the window ledge and not in her bag as she thought.

She checked the phone for missed calls. The first call was from a pay phone, and the second was a number she did not recognize or have a name with it. For a horrified instant, she stood there as if turned to stone and somehow knew it was Campbell who called.

She drew in a long breath, braced herself on the window ledge, and then dialed the number. She counted the rings as she slowly walked to her desk and sat. On the third ring a man's voice answered

"Hello."

Cassandra slumped back in the chair and swallowed hard. "Campbell?"

"Cassandra, is that you? Where are you?"

Tears willed almost instant and with a sense of excitement, she replied. "I'm back at my room. I got here just a few minutes ago. My phone was on the window ledge and not in my purse. When I checked for missed calls I saw your number, but I wasn't sure if it was yours."

With some embarrassment, Campbell began desperately to explain. "I know. I didn't give it to you, did I? Can you ever forgive me—especially for being late?"

"You were here! You came?" The heat encased her with a pain of regret for not waiting longer.

"I got tied up in traffic and I never had a way to call you right away. Like an idiot I'd let my cell phone go dead."

There was a dreadful silence. "You don't think I stood you up, do you?"

"Campbell," she said under her breath. She stared at her lap and groped for something to say. "No, well I mean—I didn't know what to think. So, I went for a drive."

"Would you like to meet somewhere? I mean—I can come get you." Campbell felt anxious and hoped she would give him another opportunity to be with her.

For a moment, Cassandra sat motionless. She wanted nothing more then to spend time with Campbell, but with a sheer force of will, she had to turn him down. "I already have changed out of my clothes and I have to prepare for my morning class." Although, she managed to speak lightly, her heart ached.

He closed his eyes, pressed fingers against his temples, before he spoke again. "You think we can get together tomorrow?"

His heart that has been empty for a long time trembled with hope that she would accept.

"I'll be at the seminar in the morning, but will be free around noon. I'm not exactly sure what time we get out. If you like I'll call you when I find out."

"Yes, of course. I'll give you my office number and this time, my cell phone too."

Campbell gave her the number, then with a wealth of emotion in his voice he said, "Cassandra, I can't apologize enough for this morning."

"Please, don't worry, its fine" she said. "I'll call you." Before hanging up, she wished him a good evening.

CHAPTER 6

Reveries

As Ian took his usual station on the sofa in Campbell's office, he noticed the tired look on his face. "You look tired, have a late night?"

Campbell seemed to be staring at a point beyond Ian. He then sighted again and dropped his chin. "No, I went to bed early, but just didn't sleep much." He paused for a long moment, lost in thought. "Cassandra thinks I stood her up."

Ian leaned back and crossed his arms. "Did you?"

Campbell retorted. "Of course I didn't!" He looked down at a document on the top of his desk and then back at Ian. "I asked her out for breakfast and was late getting there. We talked on the phone afterwards and when I asked if we could meet for a drink, she turned me down. She told me she had to stay and do some kind of homework for her seminar." He adjusted his reading glasses, picked up the document as if to read it, and then laid it to the side. "Cassandra agreed to meet with me this afternoon. She said she'd call when she found out the time she gets out of her class."

Ian stretched his arms over his head then laced his fingers behind his head. "So, you think that was one of those "don't call me, I'll call you" rejections?"

"No—of course not, Cassandra isn't that way." Campbell took his glasses off, laid them down, and then leaned back in his chair in thought. "I feel terrible for making her wait for so long. I just don't know how I feel—I just feel bad. To make matters worse, I don't know how she feels."

Ian smiled. "If it's any consolation, ever since Barbara has been going to that seminar she has been putting in a lot of time on reports and spread sheets. This weekend—mostly Sunday, it took her the best part of the morning. They really loaded her down this time. Maybe Cassandra truly did have homework that had to be done."

Campbell's thoughts raced back to Saturday evening when he asked Cassandra to go have a drink with him. The homework now explained her hesitation at accepting his invitation. No doubt, she must have lost valuable time while sitting around waiting for him all Sunday morning. Then if she thought he stood her up, he could imagine the great frame of mind in which that had put her. Her focus wouldn't be on any work sheets, it would be on him and the way he made her feel for not showing up. With that on her mind, she must have had to kiss away the rest of Sunday as far any level of concentration. If he saw her again he could be sure it wouldn't be so she could throw herself at his feet to thank him for the "F" she got in class that day. Why did he keep making a mess of things with this woman and why did it matter so much to him.

Campbell massaged his temples. "That clarifies things and maybe explains why she wouldn't meet with me last night. It could still be a convenient truth to put me off." He wadded up a piece of paper and tossed it in his wastebasket. "I don't know if that makes me feel better or worse. I trust that she'll call since she said she would."

Ian was still smiling at his friend, delighted to see that Cassandra was making a definite impact. "As far as the time they get out, Barbara never knows for sure. She told me it depended on how quick they get though that day's module. The only sure thing is they will not keep them beyond twelve o'clock." Ian laughed shortly. "Trust me. I can confirm what Cassandra told you was right. So if she doesn't call you before twelve, then I would think you are in trouble.

—

75

Campbell tipped his head aside, peered up at Ian. "You knew the facts all along and let me sit here and stew? I would like to express my gratitude for your thoughtfulness of finally cluing me in!"

Ian crossed his legs and beamed at Campbell's remark. Before he could say anymore, Paula walked in the office.

"Here are the documents and all I need is your signature." She handed Campbell the first file off the top of the stack of documents she held in her arms.

Ian stood and turned to Paula "Now, on the other hand, we have Paula who has been married for a long time and surely has all of the answers. Tell us Paula, if Campbell stood you up would you want to go out with him after that?"

As Campbell scanned over the papers, he hesitated long enough to give Ian a quick look. "Thanks, Ian! That paints a bad picture of me and puts Paula in a bad spot." He then grabbed his pen and scribbled his signature on the last page. "Paula, ignore everything this guy tells you." As a response, Ian tossed his head back in laughter.

Paula smiled and answered. "You think because I've been married for so long, I have all of the answers? I don't, but I do know if the woman you speak of is willing to make sacrifices, she will look past all the flaws, even being stood up. With sacrifices comes commitment, and no matter how sweet the romantic feelings were when a couple first fell in love, without a commitment a relationship will sour. Think about it. Would you rather have a relationship with some one who is committed to the union and who is in love with you or someone who is only staying out of obligation?"

"I think I want commitment, and Barbara and I do fine in that way. I can honestly say I value Barbara and know the sacrifices she makes being a good wife. I do know at times Barbara has her share of anxieties and I try to acknowledge them," Ian said. "We have our own interests but we take into consideration as to how much time we set aside just to spend with each other. That way we keep the romance going as well. It is kind of the icing on the cake"

Paula said. "You are right. Rather than just thinking of ourselves. We would want to ask what we could do to take more of an interest in the things that are important to our mate. Most importantly, we need to keep reassuring our wife or husband we are still good friends and lovers."

"I can honestly say Barbara is my best friend as well as the most desirable woman I know." Ian glanced over toward Campbell. "Sorry, Campbell I guess that leaves you only as my second best friend."

Campbell laughed. "Barbara has my sympathy."

Ian and Campbell teasing each other made Paula smile. "I do commend those who have been married for forty or fifty years. Don't get me wrong, but when you hear that, do you ever wonder if both—were truly happy? If in fact, was it one selfish, hard to live with person who found someone who was willing to tolerate and put up with him or her for that length of time, or was there give and take on both sides?"

Ian rubbed his jaw in consideration. "So what you are saying, in reality was, it is only the selfish one who has been happy for all those years?"

Paula sat in one of the chairs facing Campbell's desk, laid the documents on her lap, and started to sort though them. Without looking up, she answered. "I'm sure not all those long term marriages are that way. It would be safe to say most of them have been great marriages. Nevertheless, I believe there are some who choose to suffer in silence, becoming in effect, "great pretenders", as if all is well in their marriage.

"Don't you think for the other to be willing to stay for that length of time they had to be somewhat happy?" Campbell asked. "I mean, it couldn't be all gloom and doom?"

Paula answered him, "Sure, but I think they stay mostly because they are afraid of change. In time, they can shut down, distancing themselves from the marriage, and no longer have an emotional attachment to their spouse."

Campbell considered what Paula just said about the fear. Although he didn't know it at the time, he came to realize that was the very reason he stayed with Amanda as long as he did. He was afraid of the turmoil and the changes.

Paula gave Campbell the last document to sign. "It goes without saying, in any relationship we have to hear and feel the words that are spoken. What is more important is we need to listen to the words that are not spoken."

Campbell smiled at Paula. "Words of wisdom and on that I would have to definitely agree. As attorneys, Ian and I have to do that everyday."

Paula stood to leave. "Sorry, that is the end of "Dear Abby". I need to catch up with Dean and get his signature before he leaves."

Campbell handed Paula the document he had just signed. "Paula, one more thing, is there any chance we have the phone number or address of the guy who drove for Slone Ricer? I believe his name is Rudy Snider."

Paula jotted Rudy's name on a yellow legal pad she had resting on the top of the documents she cradled in her arms. "I'll look in the Ricer's file. If we don't I'll find it for you." She then headed out the door and then turned as if she had forgotten something. "One more thing Mr. Mallary—the women you stood up, you should ask her again—she'll go out with you. If you are this interested in her, she is too savvy a woman to let you get away that easily."

Campbell glanced over at Ian and smiled. "Thank you Paula that means a lot, coming from a women such as yourself."

Paula smiled, turned, and walked out into the hall and toward the elevator. While she stood waiting, she thought how her advice was actually describing her twenty-seven years living with her husband, Larry.

Paula was Larry's third marriage and she was only eighteen when they were married. Up until then she lived at home with her parents. She thought marriage was for life and a divorce was a disgrace.

Although as a wife she worked hard to please Larry, it seemed regardless of what she did, he always found fault. To this day, he still brought up incidents that happened years ago to only use against her.

When they were first married and when any disagreement came up, Larry would make Paula set facing him while he yelled and pointed out everything he thought was wrong with her. She fought hard each time not to cry, but the things he said hurt her deeply. Through her tears, she tried to work things out in her mind, to figure out of how she could change and make things better. That served to be only a frustrating and a exercise resulting in disappointment in herself, not realizing it was her inexperience and youth that keep her from measuring up to Larry's expectations. As time passed she gradually saw with Larry it would never be better.

She knows now, it was all in vain to try to reason with him when he got that way. When she tried to explain or defend herself, he took it as an interruption to his lectures or arguing. Trying only brought on Larry holding her down while he hit her on the arms and legs with his fist or a slap across the side of the head.

The hitting stopped eight years ago after Paula threatened him with a knife. Since then, Larry had resorted to pacing the floor and literally jumping up and down with his fists clenched. During his rage, he would come over to her and yell in her face or throw things at her, but he hadn't hit her with his fists again.

Though the years Paula learned after the rage was over Larry always acted as if it never happened and he expected her to do the same. Although, she wanted to scream herself, she had to put on a smile, because she knew if she didn't, it would start all over again.

Living with Larry was like walking on eggshells and working so hard at keeping the peace that every day became an emotional chore. She felt depressed and had even wondered if she was crazy.

Paula was not sure when it happened, but the dear young girl she was had died, and the woman she became had buried her feelings by walking out emotionally.

Larry could no longer hurt her with his cutting remarks. It was as if she had mastered the art of closing off the sound of clashing cymbals. She no longer derived any pleasure in listening to him nor found joy in sharing the simpler things of her days with him. She no longer cared and Larry was no longer a part of her heart. Paula was still committed to her marriage, just not to Larry.

Campbell was such a good guy; she hoped this woman would bring him romance as well as commitment. She hoped for him a marriage that she had once hoped for herself.

After Paula left, Ian stood to leave himself. Then as a second thought, he turned back facing Campbell. "Did you ever get over to see that bum at the county hospital yesterday?"

Campbell got up from his desk, walked over to a file cabinet and pulled out one of its drawers. "Rex Thorson? I did, and he gave me some very enlightening information. Enough so, that I think I need to have a talk with Rudy, the man who drives for Slone Ricer."

"The driver Felicity said she fired?"

"That's the one." Campbell removed a file from the cabinet and returned to his desk. "Felicity is claiming he is responsible for the theft of her car."

With heightened interest, Ian walked back over and leaned on the window ledge with his hands in his pockets. "Do you think he took the car?"

Campbell took his glasses off, laid them on his desk, and looked back in Ian's direction. "Ricers lives in a gated neighborhood and it would stand to reason that whoever stole the car, would have had to have access to the entire area.

Ian agreed. "You would think a secured community as that would be a deterrent to any thief."

"Thorson said the car that hit him may have been blue. That's the color of Felicity's car, and I think that validates a reason to investigate a little more."

Ian pushed himself from the window ledge, walked over, and stood facing Campbell. "Are you suggesting Felicity's car was involved in the hit and run?"

"The police found the car in an alley with the keys still hanging in the ignition. When I checked the car out, I took note of the way the driver's seat was positioned, and it appeared whoever drove it last was not a very big person."

"You think it was teenagers who stole the car?"

"That's what Sergeant Platt said." Campbell spoke with a sober intensity. "According to Thorson, the driver of the car that hit him was a woman and she had red hair."

"A woman stole the car?" Ian's eyes widened and his mouth fell open. "Felicity, she was the driver!" Ian laughed. "What are you saying? Are you telling me you think the car was not stolen, it was Felicity who wrecked her own car and did a hit and run?"

"Don't you think it looks that way? That is why I really want to have a talk with Ricer's ex-employee." With a little hesitation, Campbell laughed and added. "I guess I want to see how big of a guy he is and what color of hair he has."

Ian walked toward the door laughing. "If nothing else, you'll find out if the driver is a man or a woman."

"How many women do you know called Rudy?" Campbell jokingly asked.

"Other than on the Bill Cosby Show, I know none. But that doesn't mean it's impossible. A good lawyer waits for the facts to prove his theories. It will be interesting to see how 'Rudy' fits in with your facts." Ian glanced at his watch, "Nine-fifty. I have a client who will be here in ten minutes. I'd better run." He motioned a wave. "I'll catch you later. Tell Cassandra hello for me when she calls." Ian laughed gleefully as he disappears out the door.

ALTHOUGH CASSANDRA'S EYES were on the instructor, her mind was on the phone call she planned to make to Campbell. She rested her left arm in front of her on the table, then after a minute she secretly took a quick glance at her watch. Ten more minutes before break and she could make the call. She would tell Campbell the class was running ahead of schedule and she expected to get out early.

Cassandra's heart dropped a little at the thought of the possibility of Campbell being away from his desk when she called. Maybe she should have told him what time her break was, so he would have known when to expect her call. Maybe he has a secretary who could take her call, but then again, he never said anything about having a secretary. So many details of his life she didn't know about. She was counting on the opportunity to learn more about it since the last time she saw him. For a long time she had harbored a dream that someday she would know Campbell Mallary very well indeed.

Her thoughts flashed back to the evening before, and she now wished she met with Campbell even if it meant she would have had to stay up late getting ready for class today. Although she got to bed at a decent hour, she still didn't sleep with all the strands of her dreams swirling in her head.

Without humor, she laughed at herself. A full nights rest was a luxury she had not experienced since the death of her husband and son. Most were nights she would lie awake for hours before falling asleep, and if she did fall asleep right away, she would waken later to what she thought was the sound of someone ringing her doorbell.

When the news of the accident came to Cassandra, she was awakened from a sound sleep by the ring of the doorbell. Half asleep, she had grabbed her robe and hurried to the door. It was barely daylight and through the little window in the door, she could see it was a man. Thinking it was her husband who forgot his key; Cassandra opened the door only to see someone she didn't recognize.

Although he told her his full name, Cassandra always wondered why she could vividly remember his first name and not his last. Was it because his last name was tangled up with the word coroner? "I'm Ted—the County Coroner."

At first, she could not grasp what he was saying—there had been a terrible accident and her husband and child did not survive. When she was somewhat able to pull her thoughts together, Cassandra denied and tried to refute what she was hearing.

She recalled asking the corner the color of the car. At the time to anyone else, it may have seemed to be a silly question. However, she knew if his description of their car was wrong, that would have been proof that their car was not the one involved in the accident. It would have been someone else's car and her beloved husband and dear son were somewhere safe.

When the coroner told her they could not find the man's identification; she became desperate and grabbed at that bit of information as a ray of hope. With no identification, that could only mean somehow or someway they gotten her husband and son mixed up with someone else! Another ray of hope came when the corner asked Cassandra for a picture so he could make a positive identification. That could only mean that he was not sure himself and that what he was saying was not true!

Cassandra, frantic with fear showed the coroner one of their family pictures with her son and husband in it. She stood watching his face, hoping, and desperately waiting for him to say he was wrong. To tell her, "The man and boy in the picture were not the same who were killed by a drunk, who was speeding and driving too fast to make the curve in the road," or "That was not your helpless son who was thrown from the car and lying broken in the middle of the road." He never told her that, nor did he say, "You are not the one who will learn later that the drunk had walked away with only cuts and bruises, and you will have to try and not hate him for living."

It never happened that way. Rather, he kept looking at the picture of her son and husband with a painful silence. When he finally looked up, she was gripped by a sick feeling of dread, a dread much stronger then any she had ever experienced. It was at that moment Cassandra knew that her husband Brad and Kevin her child would never be coming home. Never—

Even after that one morning, she continued to wake to the haunting sound of the doorbell. She would hurry from her bed, peek out the window, and each time no one was there. At first, she wondered if someone was playing a bad trick on her, but soon realized it was something she was dreaming and played out in her own mind. After that, rather then rushing to answer her door, she would lie quietly in her bed, listening, and waiting for a second ring. When the second ring did not come, she knew it wasn't Ted who had the last name she could not remember. Rather, it was something she made up in her head.

Cassandra came to realize she could no longer stay in that same house or same town that held so many memories; Brad's favorite restaurant, Kevin's preschool, and even the store where she and Brad had brought Kevin his first bike. Rather than feeling comfort from the memories, they only served as painful reminders of what she had lost. Knowing she would never get past the ache of it all while living there, she left and returned to Addison. Her aunt who was her closest living relative lived there and it was home.

AFTER IAN HAD gone, Campbell, still smiling at his friend's humor swiveled his chair to look out the window. He was glad that Ian and Barbara liked Cassandra. Although they were kind to Amanda, he knew there were things about her they didn't like. He thought of what had Paula said about the unspoken words. He then wondered if Paula herself was the great pretender she was speaking about. There had been weariness in her voice, he remembered, when she spoke about obligation without friendship and intimacy.

He had to agree with her about commitment. A committed person will always do a far better job than the one who only feels obligated.

The ring of his phone pulled him back out of his thoughts. He turned his chair back facing his desk and he stared at the phone for a moment. His heart went weightless, lifting with a fluttering

---

expectancy of Cassandra calling. With a sense of excitement, he reached for the phone.

Relief widened his grin as he heard Cassandra's light clear voice on the other end. When she told him they would get out of the seminar early, he was obviously delighted.

"How about I pick you up at your hotel and we can decide where to go from there?"

He quietly listened to Cassandra's response; he then sat straight in his chair and laughed. However, his reply was completely serious. "No, cross my heart I will not stand you up."

Still smiling he leaned back in his chair and turned to gaze out the window again. "Don't you dare go anywhere until I get there!"

His eyes were filled with tenderness and he could not keep from smiling at her reply. "I'll see you then".

As Campbell hung up the phone, he felt a peace settle on him like a comforting blanket.

AS CASSANDRA PARKED her car, she wondered if she had arrived at the hotel before Campbell. She hurried from her car and as she walked toward the front door of the hotel, her face glowed with enthusiasm. With the sun shining and a little breeze that rustled her skirt as it passed, it made for a perfect spring day.

As she rounded the corner of the building, she saw Campbell sitting on one of the hotel benches reading a book. She was delighted, almost ecstatic to see him waiting for her. As she walked his direction, he looked up and with out hesitation he closed his book and met her halfway. He placed his left hand on her back, bent forward, and lightly kissed the corner of her mouth. With a friendly grin, he asked, "You want to have lunch?"

She looked in his eyes and noticed they were the same hazy blue as the sky overhead. "I'd like that."

He placed the palm of his hand on her elbow, "Do you need to go up to your room for anything before we go?"

Cassandra thought for a moment. "No I don't think so." Without thinking, she took his hand in hers. She then realized what she had done. It was nice and made her feel safe.

—

Leading her away from the entrance, he asked. "You sure you don't have to go up and let the dog or cat out?"

Cassandra started to giggle as a schoolgirl, his silly teasing made her delight in being with him. "Campbell you can always make me laugh, I don't even own a dog or cat much less have one in my room."

With that small awkwardness behind them, he looked down at her with a warm grin and tightened the grip on her hand as they strolled down the sidewalk. "I know a place we can eat that is close by and the food is good."

AFTER THEY SETTLED at their table, Campbell quickly looked at his menu then laid it to the side. He always ate the same thing when he came here. They were known for their chicken and mushroom paella and other Spanish Mediterranean dishes. He picked up his water glass and sipped from it as he studied Cassandra covertly.

She picked up her napkin, unfolded it, placed it carefully on her lap, and smiled up at the waiter as he placed the menu in front of her. As she looked back down to read it, Campbell took the opportunity to continue studying her face.

Campbell considered the slight curve of her mouth at rest and the way her lustrous pink silk blouse accentuated her faintly flushed cheeks. It made him weak just knowing, that someone like her actually cared for him. More of Amanda's dark hold on him slipped away as he watched Cassy look over the menu.

After the waiter left with their order Cassandra told Campbell, "I was really surprised to see you sitting on that little bench in front of the hotel. How long did you wait there?"

"Not as long as I made you wait Sunday morning. I left early to be sure nothing got in the way of me making it on time." He didn't want to tell her he had waited outside the hotel a good forty-five minutes to make certain he didn't miss her again.

"I'm glad I wasn't late," Cassandra said. "I would have felt terrible if I had made you wait for very long."

"You didn't need to worry. Even if you had been late, I would have waited until you got there. It would only have been fair. Besides, I don't mind waiting for a beautiful woman."

He grinned and made a production of clearing his throat. "I can just see the Denver post, "Denver man found dead on bench in front of hotel. Authorities say the man appeared to have been on the bench for sixty-eight days without food or water. It seems he ate the pages of the book he had been reading, but that didn't save him. People going to and from the hotel did not realize he had been there so long. Most-capable" Denver police officers are working on this strange case."

Cassandra was giggling "Campbell you have such an active imagination. You always had crazy tales when we were in school. Always something going on around you."

He was still smiling, but his eyes turned to a look of serious consideration. "I was so glad to see you again Cassy, as I had hoped to see you for many years each time I went home to visit." At the endearment, he grasped her hand and held it for a moment before lowering it back to the tabletop.

She could feel the blush spread all the way down her body. This was a surprise to her that he even thought of her, much less hoped to see her again. She lightly touched the back of his hand. "Did you not get my message?"

Not knowing what message she was talking about Campbell sat straighter and gave her an inquiring eye.

Cassandra explained. "I knew you lived in Denver at one time. I was not sure if you still lived here. When I found out I was coming into the city I called your brother and he told me he would give you my number and you would call me."

Campbell stared at her for a long moment. Matt had a message for him from Cassy? Why hadn't he given it to him when they last talked? He then recalled the message that his brother had given him, the one Matt thought was the IRS. "That was you!" He groaned, closed his eyes, and then opened them again. "Matt said you were with the IRS. Why do I ever listen to that guy?"

Still laughing she agreed. "So next time I'll know not to send messages through Matt?"

Not laughing any more he asked her, "Cassandra—will there be a next time?"

When Campbell said that Cassandra laid her spoon in the saucer, looked across the table into his eyes, and asked, "Is that what you want?"

He reached over and took her hand. "I don't know what I want, but I'm sure of one thing. While you're here in town I would like to spend as much time with you as I can. That is, as long as you are not spending all of it in your seminars."

Her heart stopped shortly before skittering madly onward. "Campbell, I would very much like that."

Just then, the waiter brought steaming plates of paella, and the smell of saffron and garlic stirred up their appetites. Digging into the rich, spicy food turned their conversation to lighter subjects. For the rest of their lunch and even lingering over coffee, Campbell and Cassy caught up on the parts of their lives that didn't involve either of their previous marriages. They found common taste in books and music but widely different ideas about what made a good movie. Talk flowed freely and they began to feel at ease with each other.

AFTER LUNCH, CAMPBELL held one hand out to Cassandra. He smiled, "Are you ready?" She walked over, met him, took his hand, and let him lead her out of the dimness of the restaurant and into the sunlight.

"Campbell, I would like to thank you for this afternoon and finding time for me."

In that instant, he stopped, turned to her, and took her by the shoulders. "Finding time for you . . . ? I don't think you have the slightest idea of how you affect me." Immediately the tension of mutual attraction was between them again.

For a moment, his face was within kissing distance from hers. She felt light-headed knowing that if he wanted to kiss her right there on the sunny sidewalk with people going about their leisurely afternoon errands she would let him. He looked at her face then gathered her into his arms and squeezed her. It sent a scatter of goose bumps up her back.

Stepping back and looking down at her. "I'm the one who had the most amazing afternoon." He then slipped an arm around her shoulder and they began walking up the sidewalk. "Since you like classical and easy-listening music, I know a place where we can sit out on a terrace and listen to some very good live music. The guy who plays the music comes straight from New Orleans. I'm not sure what his name is but I heard them call him Boo. He is very good on the keyboard and at playing the saxophone. They serve coffee or any other thing you want to drink."

Cassandra not wanting her time to end with Campbell accepted his invitation. "As you like that same kind of music yourself, I would love to go with you."

Letting his hand drop from her shoulder to the small of her back, he directed her toward the parking lot. "I'm afraid for you, that this lunch could last for days."

Momentarily his endearment left her wordless and his soft words warmed her. It cheered her to know that she was able to make him happy and that he wanted to spend time with her. She very much wanted to continue spending time with him, as well.

They moved slowly through the gift of the afternoon, their time together, luxuriant yet metered by the length. They contented themselves for the moment with occasional touch of finger or a meeting of eyes.

WHEN CAMPBELL WALKED Cassandra back to her room, it was late and the room was dark as they entered. He walked across the room and turned the lamp on next to the sofa. Without thought, he then glanced into the other rooms before going in and clicking on the lamp on the nightstand next to Cassandra's bed. With that done, he walked over and adjusted the air in the room to Cassandra's liking.

She stood, secretly smiling at him, flattered at the thought of him unconsciously not only showing his concern for her safety, but her comfort.

After he was done, he turned facing her. "I want to thank you for coming out with me and making me smile all afternoon. Would you consider meeting with me tomorrow?"

Simply happy Cassandra answered, "Of course, I was hoping we could. Where would you like to meet?"

"I'll meet you here like this afternoon."

Campbell walked over to her, put both his arms around her, and pulled the length of her against him. An ecstasy of emotions flooded Cassandra as her eyelids drifted shut and she touched his face. He kissed her on the forehead then followed the contour

———

of face. Cassandra could feel the rhythm of her heartbeat in her temples, her throat, and felt close to fainting.

He leaned back and smiled. "Just remember, before you go to sleep tonight, someone is thinking about you." He then touched her check with fingers and brushing the crest of her lips with his own. He then walked to the door to leave.

Cassandra took his hand and squeezed it in both of hers. "Thank you for a lovely time; it's been a long time since I felt this happy."

With a wealth of emotions in his eyes, he smiled down at her. "It was nice for me too, and I'd better go."

As he stepped out the door, he announced softly. "I'll meet you downstairs tomorrow afternoon." He then began whistling as he walked away.

Cassandra's legs were weak and she had to lean against the door she closed behind her for support. After a moment she walked to the window and stood there removing her earrings and unclasping her bracelet from her arm.

Later in the darkness, behind her closed lids she surrendered to her dreams. She could see Campbell's face and replayed their afternoon together; minute by minute, second by second until she fell into a restful sleep.

CHAPTER 7

Against the Odds

Campbell found the address he was looking for. It was an old white two-story house in what most considered a crummy part of town.

In front was a painted sign that read "Zola's Boarding House". The paint was peeling from its clapboard siding and most of the window screens torn or missing. The front porch, overgrown with vine, ran the length of the house. The sparse grass consisted mostly of weeds.

Campbell walked up the cracked sidewalk and when he stepped up on the gray porch, he noticed a good-size older women sitting in an overstuffed faded orange chair. Her hair pulled back tight in a ponytail was black with streaks of gray. She had leathery-looking skin with thick eyebrows as dark as her hair. Campbell assumed she was Zola.

With tight lips, she growled, "I saw ye pull up. You're looking for someone?"

Campbell casually stuck his hands in his pockets. "I understand Rudy Snider lives here."

"That he does, but not for long. He's behind on his rent!"

"Do you know if he's in? I'd like to speak to him."

The women raised her hand and shooed a fly off her arm. "He's probably still in bed. He's a lazy one, and he never gets up before noon.

Placing one hand on each arm of the chair, she pushed herself to a standing position. "I'll go in and holler at him."

As she walked to the door, Campbell could hear the boards of the porch creak from her weight. On entering the house, she let the screen door slam behind her. "Rudy—Rudy you awake! You got someone down here to see ye!"

Campbell figured Rudy's wakeup call must have roused him when he heard the women reply, "I didn't ask him his name! What do you think I am, your secretary now?"

The woman did not return. While Campbell waited for Rudy, he surveyed the porch. Back behind the old orange chair stood a discarded refrigerator that had a mountain of dusty newspapers mounded on its top. Down on the floor adjacent to it was what looked to be an old transmission and stacked next to the transmission were two bald tires.

At the other end of the porch sat a lawn chair with a bent and twisted frame. To the right of the chair was an old fashioned, stepped end table. The table held an ashtray made from a thirty-two ounce flattened beer bottle, which overflowed with cigarette butts.

Just as Campbell was running out of things to look at, a voice from inside the house drew his attention to the screen door. "You want to see me?"

Campbell turned and saw a tall slender man, who appeared to be in his early thirties, peering out though the screen door at him. As the man stood in the doorway, Campbell took note of his towering height and could only assume he wasn't the last to have driven Felicity's car.

Campbell introduced himself and asked, "Are you Rudy Snider?"

The spring on the screen door squeaked as Rudy pushed it opened with his foot. He stepped out from around the door and let it slam just as Zola before him did. He was dressed in jeans and a sleeveless faded black tee shirt with the logo "Harley Davidson" printed across the front. Around his neck, he wore a small crucifix that hung from a tarnished chain. "Yeah, I'm Rudy."

"I understand you where employed by Slone Ricer?" Campbell asked.

Before he answered Rudy then ran his hand though his dark brown hair that he had cut in a mullet, short on the sides and long in the back. "I worked for him up to last week, until his snot-nose brat thinks she fired me." He walked over, sat in the bent lawn chair, and pulled out a pack of Pall Malls from his shirt pocket. The bent chair twisted and squeaked from Rudy's weight. Campbell cringed and hoped the chair held together and didn't collapse.

Rudy tapped the pack of cigarettes on the palm of his hand. "The old man will be back in town Thursday." After tearing the cellophane away, he dropped it and let it drift to the porch floor. He lit one of the cigarettes then wiped and blinked smoke from his eyes. "I plan to have a little talk with him when he gets back and I'm sure he'll put me back on." He paused to take another drag from the cigarette. "I look at this as a little paid vacation."

While trying to avoid the stream of smoke that drifted toward him, Campbell told Rudy about the theft of Felicity's car and his theory of the car's involvement in the hit and run.

"Hey not me! I was nowhere around no hit and run!" Rudy adamantly shook his head. "Last I drove that car was two Saturdays ago. I drove the old man and his partner Kip Nelson over to some fancy condos by the golf course. I didn't even know the car had been stolen."

The topic of the condominiums by the golf course peaked Campbell's interest. "Do you know who Slone visited that evening?"

"It was some women the old man was pretty thick with. Most times, she would show up at the big house. That night was different. The old man was upset and had me drive him over to her place. I waited in the car while he and Kip went in."

"Both Slone and Kip went in the women's condominium" Campbell asked. "Can you remember what time it was?"

"Yeah, it was almost ten o'clock, and they were gone about thirty minutes before Kip came back out. He was cussing the girlfriend and said something about how she should have kept her mouth shut."

"Slone didn't return with Kip?"

Rudy picked a piece of tobacco off the tip of his tongue and wiped it on his pant leg. "No, we left him there and drove back to the big house."

"Did Kip say anything to you or give you any idea why he was upset?"

"No, but after we got back, he went in the house for a few minutes before coming back out and taking off in the car again. I don't know where he went, but it wasn't for smokes because he already made me stop for those on the way back. He told me he didn't need me. He was taking the car himself and I could have the rest of the night off."

Rudy picked up his lighter to light a second cigarette. He flicked the lighter half a dozen times before tossing it on the end table then dug in his jean pocket. He drew out a book of matches, pulled one of the matches free, and struck it twice before it flared. After lighting the cigarette, he once again, wiped and blinked smoke from his eye. He then continued, "That was the last time I drove that car. I took the old man to the airport the next day but it was in one of his other cars. Like I told you, I didn't even know it had been stolen."

Campbell knew Slone was out of town because Felicity told him, but she didn't tell him where he went. "Did Slone say where he was flying?"

"Down around the Gulf Coast of Texas. He makes a trip down there about once a month."

Campbell decided to bring the conversation back to the car. "If that was the last time you drove the BMW, can you think of any reason why Felicity is saying you're the one who stole her car?"

Rudy snapped his head around. "What! She's crazy!" Rudy took a drag on his cigarettes. "She probably wants to pin this on me for the same reason she told me I was fired. Last week I walked in and caught her and Nelson—Kip in the hay, if you know what I mean? I know darned well, Kip wouldn't want to let that cat out of the bag. If Slone found out, it could cost Kip his partnership. For herself, Felicity on the other hand, just doesn't care one way or another. You can't embarrass a whore. She's just mad I caught her with her pants down, so to speak."

Rudy took another drag from his cigarette and then stabbed it out. "Hey! Kip drove himself off in her car that night. Maybe she is trying to cover up for him." Rudy's eyes squinted as if another idea struck him. "Or maybe she wants to make sure I don't go to her old man to get my job back. Well, I didn't take off anywhere on my own in her car and I wasn't in any accidents, either. So, Miss Felicity is out of luck trying to make trouble for me. I'm clean and so I'm telling Slone when he gets back from Texas."

Figuring he had found out all he could, Campbell then thanked Rudy for his information but just before leaving, he turned back and asked, "One more thing, what was Slone's girlfriend's name?"

"Susanna. I'm not sure about her last name. I think it is Priest or something or another."

THAT AFTERNOON WHEN Cassandra arrived back to her hotel, she found Campbell waiting for her there as he said he would. He was sitting on the same bench he'd been on Monday reading a book.

When he saw her approach he smiled his great smile, stood, and waved her to a sit with him. After she sat down next to him, he lightly placed his strong comfortable arm around her shoulders.

"Would you like to go to an art gallery? I know some people don't care for them, so I won't be offended if you'd rather not."

Pleased again that one of his interests was the same as her own, she quickly replied, "No, I love art and wish I could afford to buy all that I like. Right now I have to be content with seeing it in the galleries." Her eyes brightened and her face glowed to an even brighter hue. "Yes, please. I would love to go with someone who shares my interests. We'll have to see if we like any of the same artists."

He checked to see if she needed to get anything from her room. After she answered no, he showed her down the walk toward the parking lot and his own car. "I have been fortunate to buy a few paintings. Other than my great grandfather, I'm the only art lover in my family and they think I'm crazy for spending an obscene amount of money on my purchases."

"You have original paintings from artists you admire? How nice!" she said.

—
94

He then sighed. "I took a couple art classes hoping I could learn to paint, but I have so little talent and my only alternative is to enjoy the work of others."

"You know, I do a little drawing myself," Cassandra revealed.

"I'd like to see some of your drawings sometime."

Wondering if she would accept an invitation to his house, Campbell ventured out and asked. "Would you consider coming over to see my paintings? I'd like to know what you think of them."

"I'm no expert, but I'm sure what you have is great. I'd feel honored and think it fun to see the kind of art that interests you enough that you would invest."

"How about we go to the gallery first then back to my house afterwards?" he offered.

Campbell then did a quick mental survey of his house and was somewhat sure he'd left it reasonably clean that morning. Laughing he said. "Trust me, the house is clean."

Suppressing her laughter, she said. "You already had the maid come in?"

Campbell sighed. "Sorry to say, I'm the maid."

"Oh, that's not good," said Cassandra. "You know what they say about bachelors?"

Giving her a sidelong look, he picked up her lead. "What do they say about bachelors?"

"How do you attorneys say it? I stand on the fifth." Cassandra laughed softly. "Is that the way it goes?"

He unlocked the car door and opened it for her. He then answered, "Most people who take the fifth are trying to hide something"

Cassandra's cheeks pinked as she quickly glanced up at Campbell. "Really?"

He bent closer to her and whispered in her ear. "Cassy are you trying to hide something?"

His whisper ticked her ear. "Yes I am." Then she looked down and giggled. "I'm a woman of mystery, you know."

Campbell put his hands on her shoulders and gently turned her to him. "Inside you is something special no one knows about, something sweet, and I'll find it." Cassandra looked up at him solemnly. He leaned forward and kissed her smooth forehead.

She lightly hugged him, her eyes shut. "Has anyone told you lately, how terrific you are? How you make a girl feel special?"

He touched his lips to her forehead once again. "No, the ugly truth is that I have a shallow, mundane, boring life. I'm wondering how I'll ever hold your interest."

For a long moment, they looked quietly into each other's eyes. Then seating her, he then walked around to the other side of his car. After getting in, he looked over at her. She smiled and gave him back a curious glance. Campbell then inquired, "And what are you smiling about or do I dare ask?"

"Oh nothing," she said. "Just felt like smiling." She gave him another quick glance. "Mundane and boring?" she said with a question. "Rather dashing I would say."

Just before he was able to protest, she laid one finger lightly on his lips. "If I'm not mistaken, yesterday you told me you never argue?"

He put the car in gear and smiled at her. "You win—this time."

CAMPBELL AND CASSANDRA spent a pleasant afternoon together at the gallery and enjoyed sharing their different opinions of the different displays of art.

Campbell favored Monet's style of painting with his use of vivid tones and colors and the way he captured the intricacies of natural light. He admired Monet's versions of volatile play of light on shadows as shown in the painting, "Village Street in The Lowering Autumnal Sun." Still life that featured traditional subjects was his preference such as Monet's painting, "Corner of the Studio."

Cassandra leaned more to Renoir's paintings that are notable for their vibrant light and saturated color. She liked Renoir's impressionist style and the way he made his figures softly fuse with one another and their surroundings, as in the famous painting, "Dance at Le Moulin de la Galette."

They both had a tendency of being drawn more towards landscapes. Cassandra desired the flower gardens and sunsets because they gave off the feeling of romance. Campbell appreciated the open-air and chose mountain scenes with trees and water.

—

Although they both agreed Picasso was a great artist, they did not care enough for abstract to want to take it home. Unless as Campbell said, "If they gave it to me free then I would most definitely not turn them down. I would take it home and brag about it until I drove everyone mad."

After they left the gallery, as promised, Campbell took Cassandra to his house to show her his paintings. She felt elated at last to be able to see that part of his life where he had lived for the years since she had known him as a young man. She knew his own home would tell her so much about the grown man Campbell had become. The house was in a cul-de-sac and clustered among trees and flowering bushes. It was a single story, which was no surprise to her, since she recalled him telling her that he didn't care for two story houses. His reasoning on that was he didn't want to climb stairs when he got old. When he said that she laughed, and reflected on how he would never be old to her. He would always be the young man she held dear in her heart.

As he opened and held the front door for her, she walked into a foyer illuminated by sunlight shinning though the two long stained glass windows on each side of the door. On one side was a Grayson English hall bench. On the opposite wall was a lovely matching rectangle table that held a cut glass lamp and a quaint old clock.

Campbell then pointed her though a large entryway and into a charming well-arranged room. The paintings he told her about were the first things that drew her attention. It seemed every square inch of the walls was covered by framed paintings, but in a very tasteful way. Not only did Campbell have an eye for art, but also, he was a very accomplished decorator.

With a happy laugh tinged with excitement she said, "Campbell this is very impressive and every bit as nice as going to a gallery. This is marvelous!"

Campbell stood watching her as she slowly walked from one painting to another. He relished the idea that she was right here in his house and enjoying his paintings. He was fascinated with her reactions and watched her face to see her expressions as she admired each detail of his collection.

Her eyes filled with a brilliant light and took on the color of a vivid sea green. There was something about her smile. He admired how the corners of her mouth dimpled as she quietly complemented his art in a quiet undertone.

She caught him off guard when she suddenly gave a quick look over her shoulder. "Campbell, tell me about this one—you're smiling—why are you smiling?"

"Just enjoying watching you." Her quick blush made him think he should change to an impersonal topic. "Would you like something to drink?" He made a motion toward the doorway that led though a dinning room and into the kitchen. "I have ice tea or would you rather have coffee?"

"Tea would be fine, but please let me help."

She followed him into the kitchen and surveyed the room with approval. "What a pleasant room." The kitchen was very cheerful and reminded her of a French country kitchen with butter-cream yellow cabinetry and black marble countertops. Windows ran the length of the wall over the kitchen sink and along the wall where a small breakfast table set surrounded by four chairs.

Cassandra walked over and looked out at the garden that was lying silently in the gathering dusk. The backyard had a row of lilac bushes that were in bloom stretching across the back. There were trees and flowerbeds full of spring flowers.

Cassandra recalled Campbell jokingly telling her how he was the maid, but he did not tell her he was also an excellent gardener. As she admired the landscaping, she commented. "You must have a busy grounds keeper?"

Campbell smiled at her wittiness. "Yes he is, but he has been pretty lazy the last two weeks and I need to give him a talking to."

He walked over to her and he sat their drinks on the table. "Would you like to sit out doors?" He gestured toward the patio.

Cassandra was agreeable and he directed her to a double door that opened out to a covered patio. As she stepped out, an evening breeze touched her brow like a concerned hand. It was soft, cool, and fragrant with spring.

He motioned her to a glider as he carried her drink to a small side table adjacent to it. When he sat next to her, he brushed her hip with his side. The urge to put his arms around her suddenly struck him but then he had second thoughts. He didn't want her to think he only brought her to his house to ravage her.

—

He took a drink from his glass. "After we get done here would you like to go out for dinner?" Cassandra agreed, but Campbell noticed a little hesitation in her answer. For a moment, he wondered if she didn't want to go and then recalled what Ian told him the pervious morning. He then asked, "Cassy, do you have work you need to do for your classes?"

"Yes, but don't worry, I'll find time to get it done." She wanted to be with Campbell even if it meant staying up all night to get those spread sheets done.

"I'm sorry I forgot you have that with this seminar. Did you have enough time to complete your homework last evening?"

Cassandra told him how she did part before bed and got up early the next morning to finish.

He noticed earlier that afternoon she had a folder she had carried with her when they left to go to the art gallery. "The folder you brought with you is that something you need to do this evening?"

"Yes, but don't worry I'll do it later, but please help me not to forget it when we get back to the hotel."

"Cassy, let me go out and get it for you. You can do it here."

She smiled. "Please, I wouldn't want to impose."

"I can assure you that you would not be imposing at all. I'm an avid reader and enjoy reading a little each evening. I'll read while you're doing your work. Then we can talk about dinner." He paused and laughed shortly. "I like doing the two puzzles that come in the paper each evening and that can take me awhile. That will give you the time you need without feeling pressured."

He made her giggle again. "Campbell, you are very intelligent and I can't see you being defeated by a puzzle in the newspaper for very long." She smiled and glanced up at him. "Anyone ever tell you that you have a highly developed since of humor?"

"Sure, my next job will be on the Johnny Carson show—I know, don't quit my day job!" He smiled. "I really only enjoy reading and working."

She turned her head and looked right at him and with a stern voice said. "I do have to ask reading and working is all you enjoy? The Campbell I knew had something going on all the time. As I remember, you had a great variety of interests. You belonged to most of the clubs the school offered. I doubt that has changed that much."

His face turned to a look of serious consideration, as if he knew that they had embarked on some grave enterprise. "As a matter of fact, I do like doing other things, but I guess I've spent a lot of time waiting for something that didn't happen. I prefer doing other things but not alone."

She felt weak at heart to think that the wonderful gentle man she once knew had found so much unhappiness in his life and wished it had been in her power to have saved him from it all. "Our hearts won't let us choose who we fall in love with, will they?"

"True," he said. "We go on because we have to convince ourselves that we can't be beaten out of life."

"Yes, and that's why we need to stop trying to live on memories."

Campbell wondered if Cassandra was talking about herself. Did he just breach her protective wall? "Cassy, is that what you have been doing?"

She looked down at her hands for a long moment before she spoke again. "When it seems all hope is gone, memories are all that's left."

Then to change the mood she smiled and uttered another little laugh. "It is just the two of us against the odds!"

Campbell watched the sunlight play across her delicately arched eyebrows and light the tips of her eyelashes to gold. He bent his head and kissed her gently on her neck. Cassandra leaned close and laid her head on his shoulder. He briefly considered kissing her again, then simply took her hand and squeezed it for a moment.

"I can't tell you how happy these last few days with you have made me," he said. "Thank you."

In response, she cradled his hand in both hers. Smiling she looked up at him. "Yes, they have been good days! Thanks to Barbara and her help, I'm glad I found you."

CHAPTER 8

Discoveries

Detective Harris was a tall man who looked to be in his med forties with brown hair and sharp gray eyes. He was standing at a file cabinet and looked up when Campbell entered his office.

"Mr. Mallary, thanks for stopping by," he said as he closed the door of the cabinet and stepped around it to shake hands with Campbell. "Come on in. Give me a moment while I get the keys for downstairs."

Campbell did a visual survey of the office. It was an open office with a bank of windows looking out over a larger office space full of activity. The setup reminded Campbell of Perry White's office from the show "Superman". The outer room was furnished with a number of desks that were occupied with busy personnel who were less fortunate than to have an office of their own.

The Detective reached over to a side drawer of his desk and took out a set of keys. "We've got the car downstairs, locked up for evidence."

Both men walked back out of the office and headed toward a hallway that led to a short flight of stairs. As they moved down the staircase, the Detective explained to Campbell, "While Rex Thorson was in the hospital, we had one of our investigators go over and question him about the hit and run. Although Thorson gave a good description of the driver, none of it matched anyone in our database. That seems to be our biggest problem in catching the suspect. That was a disappointment, since Thorson said he saw the suspect coming from department store. We knew if we could put our finger on the driver, we would actually catch the one who has been responsible for the chain of department store robberies. Up until you called with your suspicions of the BMW's involvement in the hit and run, we had no direction to go on this."

After Campbell had talked with Rex Thorson, he knew he was holding information that would be vital to the police. From Rudy's description, Campbell had no doubt their suspect was Felicity Ricer. Since the firm Campbell worked for represented Felicity and her father, he felt it would be best not to voice his thoughts in the matter. Rather, he made the decision to give out only the information he had on the car. He would let Harris and the police discover Felicity's involvement on their own.

Campbell said, "I thought it was little more than a mere coincidence that the car was reported to have been stolen the same evening and then found in the same general area as the hit and run."

As they approached the bottom of the staircase, the detective stepped off the last step onto a landing, pushed open a large door and held it open for Campbell. "The car is registered to Slone Ricer. With a little digging into the records down at the DMV, we came up with a Felicity Ricer, Slone's daughter. She is a match to Thorson's description of the woman who tried to run him down."

Both men walked though the door and into a dimly lit underground garage. Campbell could see Felicity's metallic blue car parked along the back wall with four other cars. He said, "After talking to Rudy, I came to realize the damage on the car fit the incident."

"I agree, and that's why we took a closer look at the car." Harris furrowed his forehead. "As I told you over the phone, we did a workup on fingerprints left behind. When we did a luminal test,

---

that's when the blood showed up in the trunk. It proved to be human blood and a lot of it! A little more then if someone cut their finger or had a nose bleed. It appears we have something bigger than a robbery and a hit and run case."

Detective Harris led the way over to the BMW, inserted a key, and opened the trunk lid. When Campbell looked in, he could see the outline of a blood spot about the size of a basketball. "Are you saying there was a body in the trunk?"

"I can't say that for sure," Harris said. "With that kind of blood loss, whoever it was had to be dead or close to it." Detective Harris closed the trunk and both men walked back toward the stairs.

"Did you find a match to the blood type?" Campbell asked.

"The lab is running that now, and we expect to get the results this afternoon or tomorrow morning." The detective glanced back over his shoulder. "You want us to call when it comes in?"

"Sure. How about the fingerprints?" Campbell asked, as he followed the detective back though the door of his office. "You get anything on that?"

"Yeah, other than a few unknown prints, we got three clear prints." Harris picked up a sheet of paper off his desk and read from it. "We got a match on the owner Slone Ricer and another set that belongs to a Rex Snider. We ran a check on Snider. The only thing that came up on him was a minor theft charge. Other than that, nothing very big. Majority of the prints belonged to Felicity Ricer. With the fingerprints, and you pointing out the close-up setting on the car seat, it appears she was the last to drive the car."

Harris tossed the sheet of paper back on the top of his cluttered desk. We have Felicity Ricer in custody. They brought her in an hour ago." Harris leaned back in his chair and laced his fingers behind his head. "Are you representing her?"

Campbell walked over and sat in one of the chairs facing Harris. "I have no plans so far. However, her father is a client of the firm I work for, and one of our lawyers may be representing her."

"Well, she's asking for you. She said her father hired you to take care of things while he's out of town."

"I'm working on something, and if my suspicions are correct, representing her or any part of her family could prove to be a conflict of interest."

—

Sitting straight in his chair again, the Sergeant pursed his lips. "She sure is a spiteful little girl isn't she—whiny, that kind of thing."

Harris crossed his arms and sat back in his chair. "We caught up with Rex Thorson over at his sister's house and brought him in. He identified Felicity as the driver of the car. With that we'll get a search warrant to look for the evidence to prove our theory that Felicity is the media's legendary Fashion Robber." He let his breath go in a weary sigh. "She said she knew nothing about the blood in the trunk. She's putting the blame on a guy who worked for her father. His name is Rudy Snider. We just sent an investigator out to talk to him to see what he has to say about it."

Campbell punched himself out of the chair and went to stand at the window to stare out. He turned and dropped his hands into his pockets as he leaned on the window ledge. "I talked to Rudy a couple days ago and he told me how he used the BMW to drive Slone over to his girlfriend's. It just so happened, the girlfriend lived in one of those high scaled housing complexes over by the golf course." Campbell's jaw tightened, as he looked straight at Harris. "Isn't that where they found that woman's body that my client Mike Overton has been accused of killing?"

"Yeah, some jogger found her about five in the morning. It was only two or three blocks from those condos."

"Rudy said he waited in the car while Slone and one of his thugs, Kip, went inside the woman's condominium. When Kip retuned to the car alone he was agitated and had Rudy drive him back to Ricer's house. After they arrived back to the house, Kip went inside for a short time and then left again in the same car. Since the car they drove that evening was Felicity's and with the blood in the trunk it would warrant a closer look."

Detective Harris had his sharp eyes fixed on Campbell. "Did he say when that was?"

"It was two weeks ago, the same evening the woman was killed. According to Rudy, Slone Ricer left town the next day."

"Did he say where Ricer went or when he planned to get back in town? I'd like to talk to him about that."

Campbell stood straight and walked over facing Harris's desk. "He said Slone went down to the Gulf Coast of Texas and he is expected to return the end of the week."

The detective's eyebrows came together. "I wonder what he is doing there. Does he work down there?"

"I am not sure what he does. Rudy told me he goes down there once a month." Campbell turned to leave. "I have a young client who is hanging in the balance. If you come up with any evidence that will direct attention away from him, give me a call."

Harris stood and planted his open hands on his desktop. "If the blood in the truck of that BMW comes up as a match to the dead woman in the park, I'll personally give you a call!"

SHORTLY AFTER CAMPBELL returned to his office, Harlan Hendricks arrogantly walked in unannounced. "They have Felicity Ricer down at the police station. She got herself into some kind of trouble. I need you to go down and take care of things."

The muscles of Campbell's jaw tightened, his eyes smoldered. He hated the way Harlan always expected him to drop everything at his command only to do what he wanted.

It galled him that the man wasn't as competent a lawyer as he was but insisted on treating Campbell like a legal assistant. With great composure, he answered Harlan without looking up at him. "I know, I understand they brought her in because she is involved with a hit and run."

Harlan looking annoyed as he shoved his hands in his pockets. He turned aside from Campbell and examined the paintings that Campbell had hung on the wall above his bookcases. "Well, Slone Ricer has us on a retainer and I'm sure he expects us to take care of the matter while he is out of town."

Harlan continued to stare at the three small impressionist works while he jiggled the change in his pocket, another habit Campbell found annoying. Campbell felt like throwing something at the back of his head to make him quit.

"Yes, whatever", Harlan said with his back still partially turned to Campbell. "Dean took this afternoon off and I need you to fill in for him with this client today."

Campbell wondered if Harlan even bothered to look at the schedule to see that he had already planned to take that afternoon himself. While Cassandra was in town, he wanted to spend time with her so he had Paula block off his afternoons for the rest of his week.

—

He had not taken any vacation for over a year and figured the firm shouldn't have any problem with him taking the time.

Harlan had originally brought Slone and his difficult daughter into the firm. Why wasn't Harlan taking care of this himself? Jumping at the chance to turn Harlan down, Campbell calmly replied. "I think it would be better if you got someone else to represent Felicity. If I did, it could become a conflict with the Overton case."

Trying to suppress his satisfaction at dropping that particular bombshell, Campbell quickly stood, in turn put his back to Harlan, and pulled out a file cabinet drawer at random.

Harlan turned abruptly back to face Campbell's back and asked, "How is that?"

While rummaging though his files and looking for nothing in particular, Campbell kept his back to Harlan. When he was able to contain himself and look somewhat dismissive, he turned back to face Harlan. "Give me a little more time and I think I can show a clear connection."

At Campbell's decisive tone, Harlan's eyes flicked to his face. After a moment's study, he turned away with a scowl. "According to the police, Felicity is giving them a bad time. She has been insulting the other prisoners and for her own protection they had no choice but to put her in her own cell."

Surprising himself, Campbell was able to answer with a very calm voice. "Maybe you can get Randall to go down and take care of matters. That is, if he's not too busy."

Harlan appeared uneasy and with a quick glance at his watch, he started for the door. He said hastily, "He seems to be the only one who's not busy. I better see if I can catch up with him before he takes off."

Campbell waved Harlan out of the room. He sat back down and leaned back in his chair smiling to himself. After a long moment, he came to realize, Harlan's absence was his cue to get out of the office himself.

He knew Cassandra would be back at her hotel soon and he didn't want to be late. He grabbed his briefcase and headed toward the door. He then hesitated and turned back toward his desk. He remembered telling Cassandra that he mostly read and worked while waiting for something to happen. He just realized something did happen—Cassy happened. He put his brief case back down next to the desk and left to meet Cassandra.

THE EVENING BEFORE, Campbell told Cassandra about a place he knew she would enjoy. "It's only about thirty miles out of town. The lake is beautiful. It's still too cold to swim, but we could bring a picnic."

After leaving the office his mood was light and happy. He hurried home to change into shorts, grabbed two cold drinks, and tossed them in a small cooler. He got to the hotel just before Cassandra and hurried over to her car when he saw her pull into the parking lot.

As Cassandra turned her car engine off, she looked up and her heart skipped a beat when she saw Campbell's bright face smiling at her as he walk to her car. She found it hard to keep from smiling herself and came to realize she felt more for him than she thought she could ever feel for any man again. He had given her much joy and happiness in the short time they had spent together. It frightened her to think that at the end of the week she would be leaving.

Campbell met her as she got out of her car. With a wealth of emotions in his eyes, he brought her close with a slight pressure at her waist and squeezed her briefly. The warmth of his arm lingered and it seemed she was floating on a breeze.

"You need help carrying anything up to your room?" He then touched the folder she had in her hand. "If you need this later this evening, let me take it for you."

Cassandra gave him the folder. "Yes, that will be needed. It will only take a moment to change clothes, then we can go."

He then placed his proprietary hand on her back and guided her toward the front doors.

As Cassandra changed, they both continued their conversation though her bedroom door that she had left slightly opened for that purpose.

"In the forecast they say we should expect thirty percent chance of light showers," she said.

"I think we'll be fine. It never rains at thirty percent," Campbell said as he aimlessly walked around the room looking at the pictures on the wall, touching the edge of desk, and then finally coming to rest as he stood watching out the window.

"You live here and you should know the weather better than I would. At home during the spring and summer months it seemed as though it rains every afternoon."

"I do remember those nice little rain showers, just enough to freshen up everything." Campbell said. "That may be why everything was so green at home"

"You're wearing shorts, so I'll follow your lead and do the same," Cassandra said.

While still looking out the window, Campbell called back. "I guess you can say I'm still a country boy at heart. I suppose my shorts make people laugh or cringe when looking at my legs, but I'm comfortable."

"Campbell, I don't know why you say that. Your legs are just fine."

Rather then Cassandra's voice sounding distant, it was quiet suddenly clearer and in the same room as he was. "Though, you are probably right about the country boy part," she said with the sound of laughter in her voice.

He turned from the window to see that she came out of her room dressed in white shorts and an electric blue colored blouse. She was smiling and added, "I'm only kidding".

He walked to her with open arms, a simple gesture meant to underline and emphasize his helplessness, but it was all her heart needed. She stepped into the circle of his arms and when they closed around her, she pressed her face against his shoulder and closed her eyes. It was her hair he touched first, her brow and then he tipped her chin his way and began kissing her. It was at first less then a kiss, rather, a reunion after their long separation, a hello again as his mouth lightly met hers.

After a moment, he stopped kissing her and tightened his arms around her. He met her eyes. "That was my way of getting even."

She was speechless and her expression was radiance tempered by incredulity. She thought if that was his way of getting even, she was going to kid him much more often.

Campbell stepped beside her and took her hand. "Are you ready for our adventure?" Still in a daze, she shook her head, "yes" and obeyed him as he pulled her through the door.

Campbell laughed an exuberant laugh as they headed down the hall. "We'll buy our lunch from the delicatessen at the grocery store and I'll even let you choose. The plastic grocery bag they give us is what we'll use as our picnic basket." He smiled his broad smile and looked down at her. "Does that sound good to you?" Cassandra smiled brightly back at him and nodded her head. He then tugged her a little closer to him as they left the building.

AFTER CAMPBELL TURNED his SUV off the pavement onto a gravel road, he drove only a short way before the trees on each side of the road opened up to a clearing. Cassandra could see a lake that simmered in the sunlight down a long graceful slope. Campbell pulled his SUV off the road into a parking area marked by railroad ties strung together end to end.

"It's so beautiful here," Cassandra said as she stepped out. She embraced herself and closed her eyes as she took a deep breath. "This place reminds me of home. No wonder you love it here!"

Campbell gathered up the cooler and their lunch. "Come on. I want to show you the lake." He took her hand and led her down though tall yellow grass scattered with little blue flowers. The grass whispered gently against her bare legs and tickled her knees. After they got down to the lake, they walked along the shore until they came to a small shelter surrounded by pine trees. Beneath the cover was a wooden picnic table.

Campbell placed the small cooler and grocery sack on the table. He then gestured Cassandra to sit with a sweeping motion of an open hand. "Lunch is served Madame."

They ate while watching ripples of water lap at the edge of the lake and trees with their circular dancing leaves. An occasional breeze would skip around them before moving on. Cassandra took note of the tranquility and peacefulness of their surroundings.

"This is very nice and feels good to get away from the city for a while."

"I agree, and it has been awhile since I've been here. Rather then putting in all of those late hours at work, I should come out here more. It's just that it's not much fun coming here alone."

"I'm glad you took time from your busy schedule to bring me here," she asked. "Did you have a good day at work?"

"Not bad. It was very interesting. I don't want to get over confident, but think I'll be able to help one of my clients more

—

than I had originally hoped. I need to thank you and also Barbara for helping me redirect my thinking."

Not understanding what part she played in things she asked. "Thank me, for what? I mean, I'm glad we were able to help, but you are going to have to explain."

"Remember when Barbara suggested the possibility of a woman being behind the department store robberies?"

"Yes I do," Cassandra said. "I thought if it was a woman, maybe the police should consider the size of the clothing that went missing."

"Not only that, but you also said a women who is less than five foot and three inches is considered petite. That got me thinking about one of my clients who is very short and wears some very flashy clothing." Campbell paused to take a sip from his drink. "She came to me last week claiming someone stole her car. The police found it in the general area of the last department store break-in and it appeared the car had struck something or someone. The victim of hit and run described my young client's car with her as the driver. I informed the police of this, and they have enough to prosecute her on both the hit and run and the robberies."

At that point, Campbell stopped talking and looked over to see that he had engaged all of Cassandra's attention. He apologized. "I'm sorry for all my rambling. I'll have to practice some self control and spare you from hearing more sordid law work."

She was amazed at what he just told her. "There's more?" Cassandra asked with enthusiasm. "Please, I want to hear."

"They found human blood in the trunk of the car and forensics is running a test on it now. If it comes out the way I hope, this will be one time I can bring a little justice to someone who deserves it."

She placed her hand on his shoulder. "Campbell that's great, but you have me a little concerned. Please be careful."

He took her hand and kissed the back of it before lacing his fingers in hers. "No need to worry. What bothers me more then anything is the way Harlan Hendricks takes on clients who seem to work the system with all their money and then expects me to represent them when they get caught being less than honest."

"Mr. Hendricks doesn't know what kind of person you are," Cassandra said. "I know you are an original unique person who is honest and truthful."

"Well, enough about me. I'll be getting conceited. Tell me about your seminar," he said while giving her a pleasant smile.

"After hearing about your day I don't even want to tell you about mine. It could never measure up to yours."

"No, you're wrong, I want to know." While still holding her hand he gathered both in his and pressed them to his chest. "I want to know all about you. I guess you may think I am crazy to be telling you this. I can't get you off my mind. You're there all the time. Hope that's not too uncomfortable."

The color of her cheeks pinked, as the blood rushed from her heart to her head. "No, you're not crazy. I'm flattered to be on your mind."

She wondered if he was in someway reading her mind. Since there first day together, he had been in her thoughts every moment of the day. Each morning before she opened her eyes, he was there in her brain. She couldn't get him out of her head, and didn't want to get him out of her head.

Before Cassandra could say more, there came a dull sound of thunder rumbling across the sky. The velvet sky darkened with clouds that carried a downpour of rain.

They both started too laugh. Campbell remembered their earlier conversion at the hotel. "That must be that thirty percent chance of rain. You want to make a dash or wait it out?"

At first the raindrops tapped softly on the tin roof of the shelter, then within seconds there was a hurrying of them. Cassandra hearing the sound of more and more rain chose to wait.

Campbell agreed with her. "It sounds like we just got caught in a cloud burst. It'll slow down."

He then noticed she had goose bumps on her arms. "You left your sweater in the truck." He then put his arm around her and pulled her close. She still shivered and turned to him with her crossed arms between her and his chest. She could feel the warmth from his body and his arms as he ran his hands across her back warming her.

She laid her head on his shoulder. "Have you heard the expression, you are like a hiding place from the wind?"

"Yes, have you heard the expression, you are as refreshing as the pouring rain?" They both laughed as he kissed her smooth forehead.

As they waited for the rain to slow before they could make a dash to the SUV, Campbell shared his plan of action. "Since the driver's side is closest, we'll get in from that side. Will you be okay climbing over the console?"

Cassandra was agreeable to his scheme. She was finding great humor in his well-thought out plan and was trying hard to keep from laughing.

He continued: "We will start out together and as we get closer I will run out ahead of you and have the door open by the time you get there. How does that sound to you?"

"Okay, but let's not forget the cooler. That would be terrible to get all the way there and look back to see it still sitting here on the table." She laughed until she cried and before she was done, Campbell had joined in with her laughter.

The rain slowed down a little. Quickly he then grabbed the cooler in one hand and put his other around Cassandra's waist. He looked down at her and asked, "Are you ready?"

They both ran up the little slope with Cassandra giggling the whole way, while Campbell encouraged her with his, "Hurry, Hurry!"

By the time they got to the SUV and tumbled in, they were wet and cold. Campbell quickly started the engine, turned on the heater, and then looked over at Cassandra. Her face glistened with little droplets of rain, while she was combing her wind blown hair with her fingertips.

Campbell leaned toward her, his eyes with their fascinating blue under-tint fixed on hers. "Do you know you are beautiful?" he asked.

She continued to look in his eyes as if she was trying to read the meaning behind what he just told her. She glanced away and then back again. "I must look like a drowned rat. Are you making fun of me?"

His eyes had softened. "No, I'd never do that." He smiled and stretched out his hand to touch hers. "You are beautiful."

She lifted her hands again to continue smoothing her hair. He reached over and took her wrists. "I like your hair like that."

He then pulled her to him and kissed her. He let go of her wrists and slid his warm strong hands up to her shoulders. He felt her respond as she put her arm on his chest and then placed the fingertips of her left hand on his right cheek.

After a moment, he then whispered to her. "We'd better go before we run out of gas." He then pulled away from her and put the SUV into gear.

"I have to warn you that driving home may be dangerous, because I'm not sure if I'll be able to keep my eyes off you."

With a little giggle, Cassandra rested her head on his shoulder and thought how she could walk all the way back as long as he kept his arm around her.

As they drove back, a ray of sunshine had sliced its way through the dark, brooding clouds.

CHAPTER 9

Trust Me with One Tear

After talking to Detective Harris, Campbell hung up the phone. He then leaned back in his chair and thought deeply about the conversation he'd just had. After a moment, he picked up the phone receiver once again.

"Paula, will you call Mike Overton and schedule an appointment with him, preferably this week. In addition, I'll need to talk to the DA about a dismissal on the case." Campbell paused and smiled. "Yes, if you can schedule the DA appointment before I meet with Mike that will work out best. Thanks Paula, I know I can always depend on you." After a moment of consideration, he turned to his computer monitor.

"Something is up with Randall! I just past him in the hall and he is not happy," Ian declared as he entered Campbell's office.

Without turning Campbell asked, "Did Randall say what was disturbing him?"

"He said something about Felicity Ricer and how Harlan is expecting the impossible. When I heard the name Felicity, I didn't stay around to hear the details. Your office door was the closest escape."

With a broad smile stretched across his face, Campbell turned in his chair. Ian stopped at Campbell's expression and then gave him a sideways look. "You know something, don't you? You plan to clue me in on what the upset is down at the Hendricks Law Firm?"

With a big grin still on his face, Campbell said, "Yesterday the police arrested a suspect on the department store break-ins."

"You mean they got the Fashion Robber?" Ian sat down in one of the chairs facing Campbell's desk. "Don't tell me the renowned "Fashion Robber" is Felicity Ricer!"

"That's right." Campbell leaned back with his elbows supported on the arms of his chair and his fingers laced together. "Harlan wanted me to represent her. I took your suggestion and recommended Randall."

Ian's face brightened with laughter. "You're not serious! No wonder Randall is upset."

Campbell told Ian how Rex Thorson identified Felicity as the driver of the car that hit him. In addition, he relayed the results of a further investigation of the car and finding human blood in the trunk.

"I just got off the phone with Detective Harris and the blood in the truck of Felicity Ricer's car is a match to the dead woman who was found in the park."

"You mean the woman that the Overton kid is accused of killing?" Ian narrowed his eyes. "What does Mike Overton have to do with Felicity Ricer?"

"Nothing," Campbell said with a sober look on his face. "He also had nothing to do with the murder of the woman. It just so happens that that dead woman was Slone's girlfriend."

"What!" Ian said as his eyes widened in surprise. "Slone's girlfriend was the woman they found! If that was the case why didn't he come forth when the authorities found her?"

"I think filling you in on my conversation with Ricer's driver will answer that question. When I went over to talk to Rudy about Felicity's car, he told me all about Slone and his girlfriend. When he said she lived by the golf course that caught my attention."

———

"You're right! The golf course is next to the city park where the body was found!" Ian exclaimed.

"I didn't know what to think of that and was not sure if, in fact, it was a mere coincidence. When I asked Rudy the name of Slone's girlfriend, he told me it was Susanna Priest. The dead woman's name is Susanna Bishop."

"Susanna Bishop—and Rudy thought her last name was Priest," Ian said while trying to comprehend what Campbell just told him. "I can't believe that! It was there all along and it only took the right person to ask the right question."

"I know," Campbell replied. "While talking to Rudy I noticed he was wearing a crucifix. I assumed he was of the Catholic faith and knew they have both priests and bishops."

Ian shook his head in understanding. "To someone like Rudy, a priest and a bishop would be one and the same."

"When Harris told me about the blood they found in the trunk of the car, things started to add up. That's when I knew I was right about my suspicions of Slone's involvement in the death of the woman. After I told Harris what Rudy said, they brought Kip Nelson in for questioning. Kip is a character that has some kind of a partnership with Slone. According to Harris, Kip claimed he was with Slone the evening Susanna called for help because she thought she had an intruder. Supposedly, someone broke into her condominium and they shot her before Slone and Kip got there. Kip told Harris by the time he and Ricer arrived at Susanna's she was already dead."

"That doesn't explain how her blood got in Felicity's car. Was Felicity with them?" Ian asked.

"No, they had used Felicity's car to drive to Susanna's. Slone then used the car to move the body from her condominium to the park. Kip told the police that Slone and the girlfriend were at odds with each other." Campbell's jaw tensed. "It was Slone's unscrupulous attempt to take suspicion off of himself. He wanted to make it appear that someone had killed her while she was out jogging."

With a perplexed expression on his face, Ian sat up a little straighter in his chair. "So how did Mike Overton end up with the watch?"

"Kip admitted taking the woman's watch and losing it. He thought he lost it when he and Rudy stopped for cigarettes on the way back to Slone's house. They just so happened to stop at the same convenience store over in Wheat Ridge where Mike said he found the watch."

Ian sighed. "The Overton boy was telling the truth."

Campbell nodded. "After Kip dropped Rudy off he returned and help Slone dispose of the body in the park." Campbell pressed his brow. "Pretty cold of Slone, waiting around the condo with her dead body until Kip got back"

"You're saying this Rudy guy knew nothing about it?"

"I think if he did he wouldn't have been as open with me as he was.

"So what did Rudy do to Felicity to make her try and set him up?"

"Nothing, I don't think she was necessarily trying to set him up." Campbell gave a short laugh. "Evidently, Rudy caught Felicity and Kip in a compromising situation. Since she needed someone to blame for the damage and the so-called theft of her car, Rudy was her best choice.

"Felicity's downfall was reporting the car as stolen," Ian said. "If she had kept quiet about it, none of this would have come about. She could have just gotten the car fixed and no one would be the wiser. Not to mention, Slone would have gotten away with his deception."

"That's true. I can't keep from thinking back to when Felicity came into the office and wanted me to report the car missing. The reason she gave for not reporting it herself was that the police station was full of dirty disgusting criminals." Campbell tightened his jaw, looked down at his desk and then back to Ian. "Felicity asked me if I could see her sitting in such a place as that."

"She said that!" Ian exclaimed. "I wonder what her thoughts are now, since she's one of those criminals herself, who's sitting in jail."

"I don't know," Campbell said. "Although, Felicity was always hard to take, I still have to sympathize with her and the situation she's put herself in. I also think her father needs to take part of the blame for her actions in all of this. Of course, his own situation isn't looking too good either. At the very least, he'll be charged with interfering with a criminal investigation and removing evidence from a crime scene. They're looking at paying a high price for their high-handed and selfish behaviors."

"So, do they know who broke in and shot Susanna?" Ian asked, bringing the conversation back to the murder. "Did Harris give a reason for the break-in?"

"I'm not sure," Campbell said. "Harris never said anything about it. I feel fortunate that he's told me as much as he has already."

"If it weren't for you scouting out that bum and Rudy, the police wouldn't have what they have now," Ian said. "Other than finding out who shot Susanna, it sounds as if the great mystery has been solved."

With a solemn look on his face, Campbell sighed. "You can't blame the police. With my association with Slone and Felicity, and as Mike Overton's lawyer, I was in a unique position to put information together. As for the murder of Susanna, I have to wonder about that. The coroner's report determined that Susanna died of asphyxiation. It appears to me that Susanna was still alive when she was in the trunk of the car. I don't think Kip is being entirely truthful about what really went on."

"That whole story of the phone call for help doesn't sound right to me either," Ian said. "I would think that the Bishop women would call 911 before she would call Ricer, especially if they were not getting along. If by chance she did call Ricer, why didn't he make the call for Susanna and see that she got the help she needed?"

"I thought about that. Since Susanna herself called Slone, it was obvious she was still alive. Slone can't use the excuse he didn't call 911 because he had the fear of being accused of Susanna's death. I'm having trouble finding the ring of truth in any this." Campbell paused in thought for a moment. "I'm sure Harris is aware of all of that and is just not saying too much right now. It well only be a matter of time before the police should get it all figured out. Right now, what matters to me is Mike Overton had nothing to do with Susanna's death."

Ian stood to leave. "Well I'm off. I have a client, who I have to meet in court within the next hour. I'll see you later this afternoon?"

"No, I'll be leaving in a few minutes to meet up with Cassandra. I arranged my schedule so I could take the afternoons off while she is in town."

—

"You never take time off work! And may I ask what kind of unprecedented power does this fair lady have on you?" Campbell ignored the question and diverted his attention to his monitor. Ian laughed at Campbell's reaction. "Okay, teasing aside, Cassandra seems like a very pleasant person. Although Barbara has spent more time with her than I have, we both like her. You see your way clear, maybe the four of us can have dinner, or you can come over to the house one evening."

"This afternoon I plan to take her to that car show they have in town this week," Campbell said as he glanced up from his monitor.

Ian raised his eyebrows. "You love old cars, but are you sure she likes going to those shows?"

Campbell was direct with his answer. "I asked her and she was agreeable. If she didn't want to go, she would have said so. She's just that kind of person."

After Ian left, Campbell thought about what his friend said. He then decided when he met with Cassandra he would ask her about the car show again. He wanted to be sure that she was fine with it and not just being nice. Since he had muddled things on Sunday, he wanted to be sure not to do it twice in one week.

CASSANDRA GOT OUT of class early and she hurried to her room to change in order to be back downstairs before Campbell arrived.

She only had to wait a short time before she saw him walking toward the hotel. She admired his sun-bronzed face with warm golden undertones and considered him a strong as well as tender man.

Although he was dressed causally, wearing jeans with a white polo shirt, he carried himself with easy confidence. That assurance seemed to desert him only in matters of the heart. She ascertained that Amanda had left deep scars on his confidence in that arena. Even then, any client of his would feel secure being represented by him, and Ian attested to his ability to form deep friendships. Yes, Campbell Mallary was quite a man.

When he caught sight of her, his eyes smiled, a little breeze ruffled his hair and made it look like filaments of gold. The joy she felt made her smile and she knew she had never loved him more then she did right then. She dreaded the thought of leaving him, but she knew that this would be her last day with him before going home the next afternoon.

As he approached her, she had a strange and marvelous feeling, as if she had just awakened.

"You got here before I did!" he said as he sat next to her and put his arm around her. "What a delightful surprise."

She gave him a small smile. "We got out earlier than we expected. The instructor told us they were giving us that extra time so we could prepare for the exam in the morning."

He put his hand over hers and squeezed it gently. "Maybe we should cancel the car show. It sounds as if you should study for tomorrow. I wouldn't want to be the cause of any problems for you."

"Campbell, don't be silly! You can never do that. Besides, all of this is mostly a repeat of what we've already learned. I'll do a little review this evening and I think that should suffice. I'm a pretty smart girl, you know," she teased.

"You're sure you want to go with me to the car show? I had no intention of being selfish and assuming that just because I enjoy that sort of thing, that you would also."

She gave him a smile and stood. "Campbell!" She rested her warm hand on the back of his neck—half on his hair, half inside his collar—while she passed behind him. "Let's go to the car show and see if we can find your 1950 Mercury."

His head snapped around and blue eyes registered surprise. She had turned and was already making her way down the sidewalk toward the hotel parking lot. He quickly stood, strode to her side, and again caught her hand in his. He felt the warmth of her hand and soft flickers passed heat to his heart. The occasional brush of her hip against his made him want her even nearer. He let go of her hand, place his arm around her waist and pulled her closer. Laughing he told her "You don't know what you're in for."

She gave him a sideway glance and smiled. After a short moment, she asked. "Will it make me blush?"

While grinning, he stared straight ahead without looking at her. "I hope so." He then glanced at her to see her reaction. "If you go with me, it'll be like living on the edge."

—

Cassandra looked up at him and replied with a calm voice, "On the edge, I can see clearer. I like being on the edge."

Campbell threw his head back in laughter and then pulled her even closer as they continued down the sidewalk.

ALTHOUGH THEY DIDN'T find Campbell's 1950 Mercury, they still enjoyed a nostalgic afternoon of classic automobiles with their faithful testimony of the steadfast technology of by-gone lifestyles.

Afterwards Cassandra returned with Campbell to his house for dinner. Soon after they arrived, Campbell pulled her into the kitchen and sat her at the table where she could review and prepare for her next day's class-exam and where he could see her while he cooked.

He told her. "I'll cook, and after you're done we'll sit and have a nice leisurely dinner with a glass of wine."

She suppressed a smile and did as he commanded. It took everything in her to concentrate, to avoid thinking of Campbell, who was only a few feet away in the same room. Twice when she looked up from her notebook, she caught him watching her.

Focusing hard, she was able to review her complete notebook to her satisfaction, by the time Campbell had dinner cooked and ready to put on the table.

As they ate, Campbell playfully teased her. "Now remember, no F's. Although A's are best, I'll not accept anything less then a C." He paused to laugh. "My father use to tell Matt and me that. Although, he was lenient a father in many ways, he always wanted us to do well."

Cassandra thought back to her younger days while living in Addison. "I remember your father, He used to come into the drug store all of the time. I worked there during the summer months and he was always very kind to me." She smiled at her memories. "He called me Miss Cassy. He and Father were always teasing with each other about one thing or another. You have obviously inherited teasing from him." She looked down at the table with a wistful expression. "The last time I saw him was when he came to my father's funeral. After that, I learned of his death. It was heartbreaking to think of him passing away. Another connection with Father was gone. I thought of you also without your dear father. I wasn't living

———

in Addison at the time. It was only after when I heard, so I didn't get to attend his funeral."

"My father's death was very hard on my mother—all of us really—then to have Mom die only two years later"—his voiced trailed off. Campbell was toying with the spoon at his place then pushed it to the side. "Sorry for not knowing for sure, your mother, I heard she died when you were young?"

"Yes, I was only two. I never knew my mother," Cassandra said softly. Father spoke of her all of the time and kept all of her pictures. I know he did that mostly for my benefit, but he truly loved her." She smiled pleasantly. "It's understandable that no one in Addison knew my mother. We never moved there until after she died."

"What brought you to Addison," he asked. "Did you have family there?"

"My Aunt Pam, my father's sister, lived in Addison with her husband Jim at the time, so we moved to be close to her. She treated me as a daughter and I feel blessed to have had her close while growing up." Cassandra took a drink from her glass. "Do you remember Mrs. Moorland the grade school librarian?"

Campbell's eyes brightened as his smiled spread across his face. "Mrs. Moorland is your aunt? I had no idea!"

Cassandra shook her head and laughed. "Yes, she's my aunt!" She was having fun and wanted to tell him more. "While we lived in Montana my father was a pharmacist." Cassandra smiled and opened her eyes wide. "Of course, since Addison had no drug store, my father opened one!"

"I liked going in there and sitting at the old fashioned soda bar while drinking a coke or eating ice cream." Campbell gave Cassandra a quick grin. "Then if you were there, that made it even better."

Cassandra could feel her face warm. "Campbell, really—I didn't know!"

Campbell sighed. "Too bad you sold the store."

"Oh, no, I never sold it!" she said. "Bruce and Joyce Charpnose only manage the drug store. Really, Bruce is the one who oversees the business. Joyce, his wife, owns the fitness center around the corner from the drug store, and that keeps her busy enough. I may sell in time, but for now, I'm finding it hard to do. I guess it just represents too much of my father's life and the times we spent together there." Cassandra paused to take a drink. "I never sold the house either. When I returned to Addison I moved back in it and have lived there ever since."

Campbell sighed. "Both your parents were so very young when they died."

"Mother was only twenty-six," she said. "My father told me the cause was the complications of carrying another child. Father was fifty when he died from the cancer."

Campbell laid his fork down on his plate. "I don't know if you knew or not, my father grew up without a father. He was killed during the war when Dad was only a child. Grandmother, with the help of my great grandparents, raised him. Great grandfather even had a house built for them to live in, right on the old homestead." He wiped his hands on his napkin and leaned back in his chair. "I know how you feel about not wanting to sell. Matt and I agreed not to sell the old farm. We have a wonderful caretaker who watches over the house and gardens around it. The rest of the land we have leased out for pasturage. I wish you could see the old house. Knock on wood. Someday I'll get the honor to take you there."

Cassandra folded her arms and gave him a smile that was on the edge of a giggle. "I would feel flattered, but first, I have to ask, "Knock on wood?"

He looked her in the eye and smiled back. "Are you making fun of me?"

"No," she said with laughter in her voice. "But it's been a long time since I heard that expression."

"That was something my mother always said."

"You were close to your mother, weren't you?"

Campbell reflected back. "Yes, we were. She was a strong woman but at the same time, very compassionate. As a child, there was no problem too big or too small that I felt I could not take to her. She had a way of resolving any fears I had and always made me feel good about myself."

Suddenly, irrelevantly, Cassandra wished her son had lived long enough to speak of her with the same adoring tenderness when she was gone. "My mother and I" were the words she held in her heart. She then quickly attempted to divert her thinking back to Campbell.

—

The look on Cassandra's face had brought Campbell back to the present. "I'm sorry. I think I must be talking too much about myself."

"No, I enjoy hearing about your family. I think I've been the one who has been doing all of the talking." Cassandra thought of how she felt comfortable with Campbell and told him things she usually never spoke about to others. He had away of drawing her out and she liked telling him her stories. She took another bit of food. "The food tastes good. You're a very good cook."

"Thank you for being kind. I'm really a very basic cook, enough to meet my own needs. I made a promise to myself to take you to a very nice place with very fine food tomorrow evening. I only waited until the end of the week because I knew you had to get up early all week. I didn't want to be the cause of you staying out too late."

Cassandra gazed at Campbell, not moving a muscle. She panicked when she realized Campbell was not aware she was leaving the next afternoon. "Oh Campbell, I'll be leaving tomorrow afternoon!"

Campbell jerked his head up and showed his dismay. "You're leaving tomorrow!" With a dry mouth, he continued, "I assumed you were going to stay though the weekend."

Her thoughts flashed back to when she had told him about her length of stay. Did she not make it clear, or did he misunderstand. "Campbell, I'm so sorry. I should have made sure you understood my plans."

Disappointment dragged at his spirits. "No. you're not to blame. I shouldn't have been so presumptuous." He touched her hand. "Do you have to be home for the weekend?"

"I have no commitments until Monday, but I only reserved my room until Friday morning."

Watching his face, she knew what he was thinking and continued. "I checked to see if I could keep my reservations at the hotel. There is a concert and two big conventions in town this weekend and they've already booked all their rooms. I called a half a dozen other places. None of them had any vacancies either. I just resigned myself to going home as planned."

His shoulders sagged. "I'm sure that car show has also helped to fill up all the lodging too. No doubt, there are places, but it's a

—

matter of finding them. I would never think of allowing you to stay in just anyplace where you weren't safe."

Color stole back to his face. "I have another thought. Would you consider staying at Barbara and Ian's? I am sure they'd be glad to have you. Ian just told me today how they both like you. Let me call and ask for you."

She was touched by his reaction. "Barbara told me she was going out of town this weekend. Her sister is getting married and Barbara is helping her with it." She shifted uneasily and lowered her eyes. "I wouldn't want to impose on anyone."

Campbell caught her hand from across the table. "You wouldn't be imposing. I want you to know that the time I have spent with you has made me so much happier this week—I can't explain how much. I wish we'd get to have more times together."

When she looked back at Campbell, she saw his eyes still on her. "I just feel terrible for you not knowing and making all your wonderful plans for us." Cassandra felt a tear go sliding down her cheek and quickly wiped it away with her knuckle.

He stood, walked over, and pulled her to him. As his arm went around her, he said, "Cassy, you can trust me with your tears. You can cry on my shoulder any time." She put her face against his chest for a long moment as he stroked and caressed her back.

While Campbell held her, he rolled over an idea in his mind. He thought about asking her to stay with him, but he couldn't decide if he should or not. He knew her well enough from high school to know she held some high standards. Among other qualities, that was one that attracted him to her, and he didn't want to, in any way, suggest compromising those standards. He had a good idea she would refuse him anyway. He could only wonder what kind of message he would be sending her by asking her to stay with him. Would she think it was an invitation for more than a place to stay?

"I feel so ashamed," said Cassandra, wiping her tears and now softly laughing.

"You have nothing to be ashamed about. I feel ecstatic at the thought of you wanting so strongly to spend a few more days with me." Campbell smiled back down at her. "Now I really believe I haven't been boring you."

He led her into the next room, seated her on the sofa, and sat down next to her. "You'll have to get back early so you can pack, won't you?"

"I can do it in the morning. I want to spend the rest of the evening with you."

"I don't want you to have to do that—I mean, put things off until the last minute and then have to hurry. I'll tell you what. I'll take you back to the hotel and wait there while you put your things together. After you're done, we can go someplace close to have a drink or cup of coffee."

Cassandra agreed to his suggestion. His understanding and tenderness proved to be a source of comfort to her. During this time of their disappointment, he had put his feelings to the aside and unselfishly consoled her with his words and actions. She was glad to have such a friend. Her feelings for him were growing stronger even as he was earning her respect and trust. She was glad to have found him again.

ONCE THEY RETURNED to the hotel, Cassandra packed her things while Campbell assisted as much as he could. As he watched her move about emptying drawers and folding clothing, his mind kept returning to his earlier idea of asking Cassandra to stay as a guest at his house. He was not sure how she would receive such an invitation, so he dismissed the idea each time it entered his mind.

When the packing was complete, they returned to the same little bistro he took her the first evening they met. As they walked in, he whispered in her ear, "Should I go in first to be sure Nester isn't in there waiting for us? I'm concerned for you, and think you may be too tired from all your packing to run away this time."

This made Cassandra giggle and clap her hand over her mouth. "Campbell, you have too vivid an imagination!"

Seated at a small table, Campbell thought Cassy looked so young and sweet in the candlelight. Her face was colored a delicate shell pink, her lovely lips curved in a smile. The animation in her face made her look like a delighted girl instead of an experienced woman who had faced loss and had to forge a new life for herself afterwards. She had such courage and strength but wasn't toughened by what life had handed her. He couldn't bear the thought of her leaving tomorrow. Contemplating his invitation again, he came to a decision.

—

He would offer it and if it offended, he would plead for forgiveness. He just couldn't let her go without making every effort.

As he loved to do, Campbell took her hand and covered it with both of his. "Cassandra, I do not mean any disrespect. It's just—that I don't want you to go home. My intentions are not meant to offend you, but I think I might have a solution that will enable you to stay here a little while longer." He hesitated before going on. "Would you consider staying at my house?" He paused, giving her a frankly worried look. "I have a spare room—it is a guest room."

She opened her mouth and nothing came out. The whole thing caught her off guard, and at that moment, she felt like a deaf mute. He was the only thing she could see—his hair, his mouth, and mostly his eyes. The rest of the world was gone. The look in his eyes told her he was feeling apprehensive and uneasy but she wasn't sure what to say to calm his fears.

He held her gaze and for one heart-stopping moment, he wondered what thoughts were going around behind her eyes. While still hanging on her hand with his right, he touched her shoulder with his left hand. "If you say no, I'll understand." Really, at that point, he wouldn't blame her if she called the evening off and demanded to be taken back to her room.

Still sorting out her thoughts, Cassandra bit her lip, looked down, hesitated, and turned her face up to his again. She gave him that frank, honest look he so admired.

Still, he was feeling anxious and quickly he told her, "The door to the guest room has a lock."

At last, he saw a small smile crease the corners of her eyes. She couldn't hold back her light laughter. "Are you telling me I'll need a lock for protection from you?"

"I hope I'm not scaring you," he said.

"No, you're too nice to do that." She smiled ruefully. "If I stay, what would the neighbors say?"

"They don't pay any attention."

She took a drink as she slowly chose her words and then looked over the top of her glass. "And what will you think?"

He smoothed his hand across her arm. "You're afraid I would think a little less of you? No, I would or could never think that of you! That's why it took me so long to even ask you."

—

She put her head down. "Thank you for asking. It does mean a lot to me. Please, will you give me time to think about it?"

His heart leaped as he thought there was still hope, she didn't say no! He then said, "I understand." He then leaned over and whispered in her ear. "The lock is a very big lock."

Cassandra gave him a sideways look and smiled. "I'll sleep on it and let you know tomorrow."

When he saw her eyes brighten with laughter, he felt gratified that she had not taken offense. "Regardless, I'll come over in the morning and help you with your luggage." He reached up and brushed back a single strand of her hair that fell across her forehead. A serious look crossed his face and with a dry, calm voice, he continued. "I want to say one last thing on the subject before leaving it alone—your stay will be all respectable. Cassy, I will not take advantage of the situation."

IN HIS BED, Campbell closed his book and turned off the light. After a while, he turned the light back on and reached for another book. His eagerness for morning and Cassandra's decision kept him tossing fitfully. Sleep was impossible for him that night.

In the kitchen, he poured himself a glass of water and while sipping from the glass he stood looking out the window. The full moon cast a blue light over the back yard. It was like an invitation to step out and sit for a while, so he did.

He sank back in the deck chair and listened to the distant noise of an occasional dog bark. He wondered if it was the same dog he had heard howling the night before. The warm breeze danced around his face as if it was taunting him.

Leaning his head back and looking at the bright stars, his thoughts drifted back to Cassandra. He envisioned her distinctive eyes with their dim green under tint and the graceful way she moved about as she packed her things. He remembered how the skin at the back of her bare neck felt on his fingertips. It fascinated him. The texture was finer than a watery silk.

He stood and crossed over the back lawn. The warm soundless night surrounded him, memories of the evening washed over him, and earlier memories of Cassy as a young girl, crowded into his mind, too. Through the years, Cassandra had changed. She was different

—

in good ways. In certain ways, though, she was the same, the way she shyly looked down when he had extended his invitation to her earlier that evening. The childlike lowering of her head, reminded him of her response when he would tease her at the soda fountain years ago. He had been attracted to her then, but never let her know. He had been also kicking himself for being such a brainless fool for not realizing she had cared about him. He wondered if he was blind or just stupid. Was it because he just never knew for sure and had a young man's insecurities himself back then? Now, he had a second chance, and this time he wasn't going to let it escape him. He wasn't going to sit back and wait or hope for something to happen. Rather, he would make it happen.

Although he had known the seminar ended Friday, it had still caught him off guard when she told him her plans. He blamed himself for thinking that she would stay the weekend. He was certain Cassandra would decline staying over and he needed to accept the fact she would be leaving tomorrow.

After reprimanding himself for dwelling on past actions that couldn't be changed, he made his way back to his bed. This time the sleep came quickly with his thought of old dreams being good dreams with potential. Even if they did not work out, he was glad to have had them.

———

CHAPTER 10

To Prevail

Using the keycard Cassandra had given Campbell the evening before, he took the elevator to the fourteenth floor. He knocked softly and only waited a moment before Cassandra opened the door.

She greeted him with a song in her voice. "Campbell, great you're here!"

She stepped back allowing him entry into the room. He noticed she was dressed for her last session, wearing a modest skirt with a fitted white, silk blouse that emphasized her figure. She wore no shoes and he detected a pair of black pumps setting next to a small table at the entryway.

He walked in and closed the door behind him. "Hope it's not too early. As I told you on the phone, I was up early and decided to come on over and help with your luggage."

"No, I'm glad you did. The truth of the matter, I couldn't sleep either. I was already up when you called."

Campbell tried to be witty. "You think it was my brain waves soaring your way that kept you from sleeping?"

Although he was the actual cause of her losing sleep, she knew not he nor his brain waves were at fault. Rather, it was her dreams of him swirling around in her head that disturbed her sleep. Whenever she closed her eyes, she saw Campbell walking down a sidewalk away from her. She dreamed that when she hurried after him, the sidewalk opened up and became a large room. The room was crowded with people who were dressed in evening gowns and tuxedos. When Cassandra looked down at herself, she was wearing only a nightgown. Embarrassed, she turned to rush from the room. As she was leaving, all the people in the room turned and looked her way. Cassandra recognized two of them as Brad, her first husband, and her son Kevin. They were sitting together at one of the round tables that encircled the room. Just as she got to the door, she saw her father standing next to a woman who looked like the picture of her mother. Even Ted the county coroner was part of her dream and held the door for her as she passed though it. Printed across the front of his pleated white shirt were the words, "Ted No Last Name". Quite suddenly, her dream had her back outdoors. This time she looked down to see she held a key and was trying to fit it into the lock of her car door. She remembered feeling anxious and wanting to go home as she desperately tried to unlock the car door. After what seemed like forever of trying to fit the key into the lock, the keyhole melted away and ran like gray paint down the side of her car. In her dream, she quickly stepped back from the dripping paint and bumped into Campbell who had quietly walked up behind her. He wrapped a warm blanket around her and guided her into his living room where a fire was burning in the fireplace. He led her to a sofa, sat down next to her, and cradled her in his arms. The last thing she remembered was laying her head on Campbell's shoulder and felling asleep.

The harsh sound of the alarm clock had brought her out of her fitful sleep. After quickly reaching out and turning the alarm off, she lay for a moment in thought. As Cassandra reconstructed her dream, she realized it didn't take a psychic to tell her she had never gotten over the loss of her father, her husband, and young son. She also felt that after a night of running around and seeing dead people, she was glad for morning and left her bed without regrets. It also didn't take a psychic to interpret Campbell being her rescuer or to recognize her own feelings of security and comfort with him mirrored in her dream.

Under the shower streams, she had to work hard at keeping her thoughts off Campbell. She could not even remember if she had shampooed her hair, so she washed it again to be sure. Yes, she was ready for a new beginning.

Right after she showered and while drinking her morning coffee, Campbell called. It was nice to hear his voice and she liked starting her day out by talking to him.

Cassandra smiled back at Campbell and repeated, "Brain waves?" Her eyes then sparkled with mischief. "Yes, good idea, I think I'll put all the blame on you for my lack of sleep."

He put his arm around her then placed the fingers of his left hand on her right cheek and turned her face toward him. "I don't mind. I'll take all the blame." He kissed her. The touch of his lips on hers made her cheeks warm and her heart race.

He stepped back and smiled down at her. "You have everything packed and ready to go?"

His gentle, friendly kiss had dazed her and all she could do was nod.

"You want to load the luggage in your car first or should we go for the breakfast I promised you?"

She looked at her watch. "I don't have to be in class until nine. We only have to be there long enough to take the exam, so it was scheduled later than the usual class at eight." She checked her watch again. "I think we have time."

"I know a nice place that has good food and is close by." Campbell looked over her shoulder, past her at her luggage and smiled his brilliant smile. "I think it would be a good idea to eat first. By the look of that stack of suitcases, I may need to build up my strength before tackling it."

Cassandra looked back at her luggage and saw it for the first time from someone else's perspective. It did look like a lot. She started to laugh and leaned her forehead against his chest. He bent his head down and kissed the top of her head affectionately. Her hair held the scent of her shampoo, which smelled like an early spring rain.

She tried to explain. "I know, I'm so bad! When I come to these seminars, I have to try to dress a little professional, but after classes, I want out of those and into casual, comfortable things. So, after I pack all those clothes, I end up bringing twice as much as the average or normal person. Otherwise, if I have to, I can travel very lightly."

"That's true," Campbell said. "All that's needed on a tropical island is a swimsuit."

"I don't know if I can pack that light," Cassandra said with laughter in her voice. "I'd have to take something more than just a bathing suit."

Campbell shook his head in agreement. "I think you are right about that. It would be a good idea to throw in a bottle of sun tan oil."

Cassandra gave him an amazed look and then laughed. Campbell smiled broadly, led her to the door, and held her elbow while she stopped long enough to slip on the black pumps. He then lightly placed the palm of his hand on her back as they hurried down the hall toward the elevator.

Just as they stepped into the elevator and the doors closed, Cassandra turned to him. "I want to thank you again for the very nice invitation to be your house guest for the weekend."

At that moment, a rush of blood flooded his heart and it made him feel the way he did each time they made the call, "The Verdict Is In". Each time the finding of the court was delivered, part of him wanted to hear what the decision was and another part didn't want to know.

Up until then, Campbell had avoided the subject. He felt he had a good idea what Cassandra's decision would be and knew it wouldn't be what he wished and hoped for. From his days of practicing law, he learned that just before the judge delivered the verdict, most times he would placate the party who did not prevail. It was as if he was smoothing things over just before the verdict went against them. Cassandra was either being very gracious or about to turn him down. His heart pounding, he braced himself for her answer.

Seeing the troubled look on his face, Cassandra became concerned. "Campbell!" Emotion tempered her voice. "You still want me to—to stay?"

He thought he could manage to keep his composure until he opened his mouth and started to stumble over his words. "I still want you? Yes, of course I still want you! You mean I want you to stay? Both!"

Finally, stumbling to a halt, all he could do was grab her by the waist and pull her to him. He trembled at the thought of losing her and held her tighter.

Getting back some of his composure he managed to tell her, "You know I want you." He spoke his words with passion yet, so softly, she almost didn't hear them. "Please, I want you to stay."

She felt the touch of his hand on her waist, warm palm, strong fingers, and it made her weak in the soul. For an instant, she forgot about the rest of the world and rejoiced. Seeing his eyes dance with the same excitement her awakening heart felt, Cassandra was glad she had made the decision to stay the weekend.

Up until he walked into her room, she was not sure what she would tell him. Her heart said, "Stay," but her mind was holding her back. Seeing his amusement over her luggage and the way he made her laugh at herself is what made her reconsider. His kisses and holding her so close and warm caused her to surrender to her heart.

Just as the elevator came to a rest, Cassandra pulled away and straightened herself. Campbell looked down at her and took her hand. "You know, we could have pushed the elevator button again."

She glanced up at him and then looked back down a bit embarrassed. He could see a little smile start to form at the corner of her lips. "I guess you are too much of a lady for that ploy."

She giggled and stepped out of the elevator into the lobby. With a sassy look, she replied, "Don't temp me."

Delighted in his own cleverness, he tightened the grip on her hand and smiled down at her as they strolled across the lobby and out the double doors of the hotel.

CASSANDRA HAD TO pummel herself into keeping her mind on what the class instructor was saying. She was finding it hard to do

—

with her thoughts filled with pleasant memories of her morning with Campbell. The last week with him made her feel as if she were coming back alive. He was rarely absent from her thoughts. He was with her everywhere she went and with her everything she did. Their first kiss made her weak and her legs feel as if they turned to water.

Although some time had past since they where young teenagers, she had not forgotten he was the first to win her heart. So much so, he was like a little gleaming light hidden in the back of her mind, which would light up whenever her thoughts went back to her school days or when she heard that one special little song. She always held the remembrance of him in a secret place in her heart. Although it was always there, it was only that morning she came to realize he was "Her First Love!"

"Cassandra," Barbara whispered as she leaned her direction. "What's so funny?"

"Nothing," she whispered back. "Why?"

Without taking her eyes off the instructor, Barbara replied. "You're smiling as if the instructor said something funny."

Cassandra sat up and looked straight ahead. "Oh sorry I never realized I was smiling."

Without another word, Barbara gave Cassandra a look out the corner of her eye and a smile of understanding. She felt that way herself, about Ian.

Although, she was not aware Cassandra would be staying the weekend at Campbell's house, she had a good idea of the way she felt toward him. Cassandra herself could not believe he had her so mesmerized she agreed to stay with him, something she would have never considered doing before.

Cassandra's thoughts went back to the dream she had the evening before. She was never one to believe that the subject of a dream had any special massage. Rather, she recalled reading that sometimes when a person was trying to solve a problem the solution could come to them during sleep. That meant that not all her sleep consisted of dreaming. Rather a portion of it was thinking and trying to work things out in her head. All week she had been trying to sort out her feelings and wondering if it was her memories of Campbell or Campbell himself that she was truly falling in love with. She now

—

knew her dream was her way of telling herself that she could move on and allowed herself to fall in love again.

Just before falling to sleep, she was trying to make up her mind if she should go home the next day or stay over with Campbell. The dream seemed as if she was asking for a blessing from those who were the closest to her on her decision. Although "Ted No Last Name" was actually a stranger to her, he was the only one she had had to hang onto during the most tragic time of her life. With that bond, she placed him in her dream where he held the door for her to go to Campbell. Most everyone dear to her was gone from her life and any strength and comfort they could provide they took with them. She stood alone for a long time and Campbell was the one who opened his hand out to her. He offered what she had lost. She was now ready to accept it.

CHAPTER 11

A Complete Dismissal

"**I** have to tell you, Randall isn't my favorite individual but he has my sympathy today," Ian said as he entered the office.

Campbell was just finishing a report and without turning his eyes from the computer monitor he responded, "What kind of grief has he brought on himself this time?"

Ian took a seat on the sofa, leaned back, and laced his fingers behind his head. "This morning they had the hearing to advise Felicity of her rights and set a bond. I was at the courthouse on another case and had a little time to kill, so I decided I'd step in and see how Randall was doing with his star defendant. I have to say, it didn't go well at all."

Campbell's face expressed his amusement as he turned in his chair and gave Ian his full attention. "I'm glad it's him and not me."

"In a material sense, Felicity had nothing to offer for bail. The authorities haven't found Slone yet or his money. Her BMW is no use to her since our city's finest have it locked up as evidence."

Campbell closed his eyes and thought a moment. "I believe the car belongs to Slone anyway," was his considered reply.

"Since she has nothing of any value, Randall was working toward getting her released on her own recognizance."

"That could work," Campbell said, "if she was bound and gagged before presenting her to the judge. Who was the Judge anyway?"

"Judge Hargis," Ian answered.

"Hargis is one of the most even-tempered judges we have. If Felicity could keep quiet and let Randall talk, it would have a good chance of working. What happened?"

"Hargis informed Felicity, regardless of her father's financial status, the court recognized her as indigent. Randall, the skillful attorney he is—." Ian had to pause to laugh, "Wanted to be sure his client understood what Hargis meant. I was sitting right behind them and heard Randall whisper to Felicity. He said, "The judge is saying you are in a state of poverty. Apparently, Randall had not discussed his strategy with his client. Felicity started screaming profanity at Hargis and when Randall tried to calm her, she slapped him across the face. Before he could retaliate, the guards were on top of them both. It took five guards to get the situation under control. As we speak, both Felicity and Randall are sitting in jail."

Campbell shook his head. "I never realized it would come to this. I almost feel guilty about setting Randall up as her lawyer." He then asked, "So, they never heard anything more on Slone? I mean, you would think someone would've made contact with him about Felicity's arrest. Surely, he is in touch with someone up here, or with Felicity herself, when he is out of town for this long a period. Especially so since he knows Ms. Bishop is dead and the police have to be looking into that situation."

"Last anyone has heard he is still down in the Golf of Texas," Ian said. "He has to know the authorities want to talk to him. Maybe he's hiding out."

"Makes a person wonder what his involvement is down there too," Campbell said. "I do know they have a lot of offshore drilling going on there."

Ian shot a quick glance at Campbell. "You think he has something to do with that?"

—

"I'm not really sure what he's into. Although, it was about a year ago Harlan sent Slone to me to draw up an insurance policy for him. It involved a barratry for ship cargo. By all accounts, it was for shipping supplies for oil rigs."

"I do know they have a number of drilling operation down around there," Ian said.

While in thought, Campbell mechanically tapped his pencil on his desk by letting it slid though his fingers a couple of times before laying it to the side. "I only have my suspicions, but I wondered if it's some kind of front for something illegal."

"Knowing Slone Ricer," Ian said, "I'd sooner think that of him then anything honest."

Campbell shrugged his shoulder "Who knows and at this point, not my business."

Paula tapped on the door just before walking in. "Mike Overton and his parents are here for their eleven o'clock. Here are the files you asked for." She laid the folder she was carrying on Campbell's desk.

Ian stood and walked over and leaned on the edge of Campbell's desk facing Paula. "My secretary Linda is leaving on maternity leave and this is her last week. How about you leave this slave driver and come down and take her place?"

Paula laughed at his wittiness. "Mr. Chatman, I am flattered, but no thank you. I do just fine here."

Campbell took the folder and started to flip though it. Without looking up, he answered Ian. "If you have it in your mind to swipe Paula away, it won't work. I know where Paula's loyalties lie."

Paula was not only a dependable secretary but also a good friend. When Campbell's mother died and he got very little sympathy from Amanda, Paula proved true. As a mother herself, she understood his close relationship with his mother and always offered words of encouragement.

To Paula's credit, while helping Campbell get past his anguish she had already had her share of grief, beginning with the death of her eldest child. Her son Eric was only twenty-five when killed in a terrible car wreck. Her son-in-law was the driver and had been speeding while in a fit of rage and jealousy.

At the time, Campbell could not understand Paula's forgiving attitude toward her son-in-law, but as things progressed, she came to hate him for killing her son. She had told Campbell the reason for the change of heart was that she never saw any remorse on her son-in-law's part. Campbell still thought that it was because Paula was still in a state of shock and couldn't see his only concern was for himself. Her own fair and honest nature caused her to give him the benefit of the doubt, until all doubt was removed by his consequent behavior.

Amy, Paula's daughter, saw it clear enough to divorce, the son-in-law. Divorce is not easy for anyone, and that included Paula who watched her daughter suffer though the guilt of her husband killing her brother and a failed marriage.

Right after Eric's death, Paula's was devastated further when she learned her grandchildren, Eric's children, were leaving the country. Eric's windowed wife was moving to Europe to live with her parents. To Paula that meant her visits with her dead son's children would become limited or come to an end.

Soon after their move to Europe the children's mother died. With the death of the mother, the children were left without parents and returned to the states. As the paternal grandparents, Paula and her husband were awarded guardianship of the children. With the help of their daughter Amy, they are now raising the children.

When things seemed to improve for Paula, Campbell recalled her telling him that her life story was the kind of material writers used in creating soap operas. They shared a laugh over that and were glad to be the kind of friends who could cry and laugh together, friends with a history of support and long understanding, much like his friendship with Ian.

Paula turned to leave. "I put Mike and his parents to the conference room. If you need anything else let me know."

"Thanks Paula," Campbell said.

Ian motioned to the door. "Do you mind if I come along and observe?"

"Sure. I'll be glad to have you." Campbell handed him a note pad. "You can take notes. Are you trying to hide out from the Randall and Felicity situation?"

"You know me like a book," Ian replied, as they both left the room and walked down the hall toward the conference room. "Though that isn't all, I'd like to see this happy ending."

"When Harlan hears Randall's in jail for contempt of court, he'll want to send someone down to post bail. That is not part of my plans for the day. If I can stay out of harm's way for one more hour, I'm home free for the weekend," Ian continued as he glanced at his watch. "I plan to leave early and meet up with Barbara for lunch. She's going out of town to visit her younger sister for a couple of days."

"Cassandra did mention to me that Barbara was leaving for the weekend," Campbell said.

"It'll be a well-earned rest and she deserves the time. I would go with her but, her sister will be getting married in two mouths, and I wanted to give them their time." Ian reached up and adjusted his tie. "By the way, how long is Cassandra staying?"

"She'll not be leaving until Sunday." Campbell knew Cassandra was feeling a little apprehensive with staying at his house, so he made the decision not to say anything about it to Ian.

They came to the conference room door and Ian stopped and turned to Campbell before opening the door for him. "You do know you both are welcome to come over to the house this weekend?"

Campbell gave Ian a thoughtful look. "Yes, I do know that, and thanks."

JAY OVERTON, A tall man with dark brown hair that was turning silver at the temples, sat at one side of table. Mike sat to his father's right with a vacant look on his face. With a look of concern, Jay kept glancing toward Mike as if trying to discern his thoughts. Jay rested his right arm across the back of Mike's chair. Without thinking, he occasionally let his fingertips brush the back of his wife's shoulder, as she was sitting next to Mike. Patty was an attractive woman with a well-arranged appearance, wearing a hairstyle most of which she had pulled high onto the crown of her head in an intricate knot.

The door then opened and as the two attorneys entered the room, both Jay and Mike stood. Campbell waved them to sit back down and made the proper introductions. "This is my associate Ian Chatman, He'll be sitting in with us today." Ian nodded to Patty and shook hands with Jay and Mike before taking a chair to the left of Campbell.

Campbell continued, "I want to thank you for coming in on with such, a short notice." He paused to take out his pen and open the folder he brought with him. "This shouldn't take too long."

Jay was overwhelmed with anxious anticipation. "Over the phone your secretary said there's been a change. Please, tell us what is happening!"

Campbell spoke quickly to relieve their anxiety. "Well, there's not going to be a trial."

With a puzzled look, Jay looked at Patty, then back to Campbell. "What! We don't understand!"

Mike's eyes were wide and his face looked intense. Without words, he waited to hear an explanation from his attorney.

Campbell continued. "The police found a witness to the murder and Mike—you are no longer a suspect."

With that news, Mike tried to hide his tears but they still trickled from his eyes, shut tight in an effort to stop the flow. Jay laid his hand softly on Mike's shoulder and squeezed it. "That's incredible! I can't believe I'm hearing right!"

Patty wiped tears from the corner of her eyes with a tissue as she reached out and grabbed Mike in a fierce hug. "Oh, Mike!"

Campbell looked over at Ian and thought that for a moment he'd seen him blink back a tear or two himself. He then spoke directly to Mike. "Mike, the witness admits to taking the watch from the woman's body and he claimed to be at the same convenience store on the same night you were. That exonerates you, as the watch was the only evidence they could find linking you with Ms. Bishop. They now know you had nothing to do with Susanna Bishop's death and that you were telling the truth about finding the watch."

With a tear-stained face, Mike looked directly at Campbell and spoke with a slight huskiness in his voice. "You knew I was telling the truth all along. Thank you for believing in me."

Campbell looked back at him for a long moment. "Yes Mike—I knew you were telling the truth." After another long moment, he continued. "But, it was a matter of convincing those who make all of the decisions."

Mike nodded his head. "I know," he whispered. Campbell could barely hear Mike, but looked at him with understanding.

After a moment had passed, Campbell continued. "I met with the DA about an hour ago and he agreed to move for a complete dismissal of all charges. You'll still have to appear before the judge but you need not concern yourself about that appearance. It's a formality."

A look of apprehension came across Mike's face. "Will you be there?"

"Yes, I'll be there. If the judge asks you any questions you don't understand, I'll be there to help you with your answers."

Campbell tried to ease the situation. "That's why they keep guys like me and Mr. Chatman around." Ian looked up from his counterfeit note taking, and to maintain a look of professionalism, he suppressed his laughter into a smile.

"Also I'm not sure, but they may summons you as a witness. If they do, all they'll want from you is to tell how you found the watch." Campbell closed his folder and clipped his pen to it. "I think that is about it, unless you have any more questions."

Mike stood and walked around the table to shake Campbell's hand. "No, I think you answered all of them. I want to thank you for what you did. I feel as if you saved my life."

With that last statement, Campbell did not know how to reply, but instead placed one hand on Mike's shoulder. "Miss Benson will need your signature on a few forms. She'll get in contact with you later. If you think of anything else before that, feel free to call me or my secretary."

Jay stood and shook hands with both the attorneys. "What more can Patty and I say other than thanks for giving us our son back. I think tonight we'll be able to sleep."

Patty wrapped her arms around her son. "Mike is our youngest. He has so many hopes and dreams ahead of him in his life. Because of you Mr. Mallary, he has them all back."

"Will, I'm truly happy it came out the way it did." Campbell rubbed his chin as in thought. "Mike before you go, I've got one more question. The night you were at the convenience store, did you by chance see a blue BMW?"

Mike shot a quick glace back at Campbell. "I did! I remember! I saw it while I was pumping gas. I thought it was a sweet car and envied the guy driving it."

Ian smiled and then looked in Campbell's direction. "It's just like you, to turn a suspect into a prime witness."

Mike and his parents had a confused look on their faces. Jay then asked. "The BMW, does it have anything to do with the dead woman and her watch?"

Campbell smiled, shook his head, and replied, "I have to say, Mr. Chatman is right. In this case, Mike is going to be of great value to the prosecution."

He turned in Mike's direction. "I'm sure they'll be in contact with you very soon. My advice to you Mike is until this is over with, don't discuss what you saw that evening with anyone other than the authorities."

Mike again had an anxious look on his face. "Everything is all right isn't it?"

Campbell laughed, "Everything is all right!" He then turned and directed his words to Jay. "Mr. Overton, I can guarantee they'll want to talk to Mike and possibly use him as a witness. When they do, please give me a call. I'd like to observe and be sure they handle things right where Mike is concerned."

"Thanks," Jay said. "I'll most definitely keep you up on things. You'll hear from us as soon as they contact us." He then escorted his rejoicing family out the door.

AFTER MIKE LEFT with his parents, Campbell looked at his watch. "It looks as if it's about time we get out of here ourselves. By now, Harlan must have heard about Randall's incarceration. He's probably scouting out a volunteer to do his dirty work. Let him do it himself this time."

Ian stood looking at his friend with his eyebrows furrowed and arms crossed. His voice was sharp and direct. "Campbell, I cannot believe you!"

"Why? What are you talking about?'

"You made it sound as if the police did all the work. You didn't even tell them you are the reason they have Kip as a witness. If you didn't go to the police with your suspicions, they would've let

Felicity's car go and would've never found Susanna Bishop's blood in the trunk."

With out looking up Campbell gathered up his folder. "You know how it is around here. I get tired of helping all of the Felicitys Slones and Randalls skirt around the law. Then when all is said and done, they treat their crime as if it was some little inconvenience in their life. The Overton case was different. They are a good family caught up in an unpleasant situation with no fault of their own. Their gratitude was enough merit for me. I'm not looking to make myself out a hero."

Ian thoughts turned to Jay Overton and the fine father he appeared to be, unlike his own father who was harsh and selfish. Most of his money went toward gambling and alcohol, opposed to buying the necessities for the family. While living at home, Ian couldn't recall one time his father ever came straight home with a full paycheck.

Ian still ached for his mother who continued to have hope in their father. On the days he was paid, she had sat in the dark, watching out the window and waiting for him to come home. Ian with his sisters and brother would wait with her until they were too sleepy to hold their eyes open. When their father finally came home, it was not until the early hours of the morning, without enough money left to pay rent, utilities, and food for the family.

At the age of fourteen, Ian had gotten his first job, and unlike most kids his age, he didn't spend the money on himself. He, like his brother and sisters before him, gave most of the small amount of money he earned to their mother to help her make ends meet.

With that same hard work and good grades, Ian was able to put himself though law school. He had worked at Hendricks Law Firm long enough to know Campbell was right. Mike Overton and his parents were different than most of their clients.

Ian reached over, picked the note pad off the table, and stuck his pen in his pocket. "You're right about that. I know exactly what you're talking about. I'm getting sick of it myself and it's an only a matter of time."

Campbell held the door for him. "Come on. Lets get out of here. You don't want to keep Barbara waiting, do you?"

"No, I'd never do that on purpose," Ian replied thinking again of his mother, patiently waiting. "I love my wife too much to let that happen."

CHAPTER 12

Shortage of Angels

Although Cassandra had been to Campbell's house on more than one occasion in the last week, he drew a little map for her anyway. She had laughed at the time he was drawing it, but now found it to be helpful.

As she drove, her thoughts were on the last few days. The way her life had changed gave her a breathless feeling. For the past two years, her whole life rotated around her accounting business. She worked long hours to keep from rattling around in an empty house and thinking of her dead husband and child. Now without dread, she was able to think of them, when before it was only a passing thought she pushed quickly from her mind. It was like brushing a wasp from her arm before it could sting. Even after the wasp flew away, the thought of almost being stung still lingered in her mind.

With Campbell's directions, she drove right to his house with no detours. She saw both his SUV and car parked in the driveway and knew he kept the promise he had given her that morning at breakfast to meet her and not be late. She parked in the drive, turned off the engine, and just sat for moment in thought.

She had no luggage to unload, since that morning Campbell had insisted on loading it in his SUV and bringing it to his house himself. He was so thoughtful and caring of her. It felt a little peculiar, but nice. Yes, it felt very nice.

She collected her purse and walked toward the front door feeling excited and just a little nervous. Before she could reach the door, it opened and Campbell stepped out. He stood where he was just a moment longer looking—then he went forward. Taking her hand, he pulled her on the step with him and kissed her lightly on the forehead. Yes, Cassandra was a very modern woman but she has not let go of her modestly and that quality, he highly valued in her.

"You have any trouble getting here?" He asked.

"No, with your cute little map I did fine."

"Cute?' Campbell replied light heartily. "I didn't mean for it to be cute, just correct, and informative."

"It was cute, and I think you did a very nice job of drawing the MacDonald sign and Ford Dealership on the corners I was to turn on." She laughed and his laughter joined hers. "It was a great help and I was glad to have had it. Thank you."

"Come on in, I already put your luggage in your room." He showed her down the hall. "It's the first door on the right."

When she entered the room, she saw a queen size bed next to a wide dark cherry wood, three-drawer nightstand, on which sat a lovely tiffany lamp. Behind the bed were two big windows over which hung sheer wine colored drapes. The bed was on a matching oval area rug. On the right was a cherry wood desk and on the left, adjacent to the door, were the closets, dressers, a very comfortable looking spindle chair, and a side table. The walls were covered with light wallpaper that had what looked like tiny flowers stenciled around the borders.

Campbell turned on the lamp then opened the window. A playful breeze flicked the hem of the drape. "You can close the window if that's too much air."

"No, it's fine." She ran her hand over the coverlet on the bed and straightened the gather in the overlay. "Campbell, this is a beautiful room!"

He was pleased at her approval. "I hope you'll be comfortable in here." He motioned toward the hall. "You can use the bathroom right across the hall. Don't worry about me. I have my own off my bedroom."

He then walked over to her and placed his hand lightly on her back. "Would you like something to drink?"

"Yes that would be nice," she said as she turned his way. "Do you have something cold?"

"Yes, I'll fix us both something and give you time to settle in." He started down the hallway, then retuned. "You know that lock I told you about? It's not as big as I claimed but if you look there is one on the door knob." She laughed and before she could say another word, he turned again and hurried down the hall like a mischievous boy well satisfied with himself.

In a distance, she could hear ice cubes hitting the inside of glasses and a phone ring. As Cassandra took her brush from her cosmetic case, the phone stopped ringing and the sound of Campbell's muted hello floated down the hall. She pulled the brush through her hair with deep, confident strokes. When she had finished brushing her hair, she could hear Campbell's muffled voice and knew he was still on the phone. Not wanting to intrude, she would wait in the room until he ended his phone conversation.

While waiting, she walked over to one of the windows and with her fingertips, she lightly pulled back the drape to look out. The window was on the far side of the house and looked out over a part of the yard she had never seen before. In the center of the yard was a birdbath with a backdrop of white bridal-veil bushes in bloom. To the right of the birdbath, was an arbor covered in trumpet vines and sheltering a comfortable looking bench.

Cassandra wondered if that creation was also Campbell's and if so, how many skills and talents did this complex man have that she had not yet discovered. That thought sent a thrill of anticipation through her.

"And on what adventures have your thoughts taken you this time?" Cassandra was so deep in thought that the sound of Campbell's voice made her jump. She turned to see him smiling while leaning on the doorframe with his arms crossed.

"Oh, you startled me!" Cassandra exclaimed.

Although his face was solemn, the corners of his eyes smiled. "You're having second thoughts?"

Looking confused she asked, "Second thoughts? I don't understand."

He said evenly. "You were in such deep thought. I thought you were regretting your decision to stay at my home."

Smiling and shaking her head, she looked straight into his eyes and with complete candor replied, "No, the only regrets I have is I didn't stay in such and wonderful room as this during the whole time I've been here."

With immense relief, he smiled back. "Well, the room is yours for the rest of your stay." He respectfully refrained from grabbing her and spinning her around, instead stuck his hands in his pockets, and sat in the spindle chair across the room from where Cassandra stood. "My mother decorated this room. When I first purchased the house, I did nothing with the room for a long time. It was an extra room and was only used when my parents came for the weekend." Leaning back and clasped his hands behind his head. "Most of the time I went home so they didn't come here that often." He chuckled a little. "My mother thought it was a terrible way to treat my guests, so she offered to decorate it. She redecorated the old homestead and was very good at what she did. How could I lose? My mother was happy, and out of it all I got a very nice-looking guest room."

He glanced behind her at the window she had been looking out. "I see you found my secret hiding place." Standing, he walked over to Cassandra and put his arm around her waist.

Cassandra leaned into him. "Your secret hiding place?"

"Well, not really. It was just a place to go when Amanda, my ex would get difficult. She was a very unreasonable person and rather than argue with her, I'd go out there with a good book until she settled down."

"You don't talk about Amanda very much, do you?"

"There is really not very much to say about her. As I say, she was a difficult person. I gave her my best and it just wasn't good enough for her."

Changing the subject, he looked down at her. "Come on, I made us something to drink, let's drink it before the ice melts." He left his arm around her waist as they walked across to the door. "I want

—

to hear all about the last day of your seminar and how you did on your exam." At the door, he removed his arm and with a smile and a bow, ushered her into the hallway. With a regal nod of her head, she led the way to the kitchen.

THE SERVER RUSHED over to their table, with menus tucked under her arm and water glasses on a tray. After she left, Cassandra opened her menu to study it.

Without looking at his menu, Campbell laid it to the side and instead he studied Cassandra's face. The little lamp over the table illuminated her face and defined the contour of her checks. He thought she looked wonderful—beautiful. He never noticed before, but there were the tiniest freckles that dotted her forehead and down the sides of her temples.

She glanced up. "You're not looking at the menu?"

"I come here a lot and already know what I want. You like seafood?"

She brushed back a wisp of hair that fell across her forehead. "Yes I do, I like shrimp the most, but other seafood, too." Trying to be coy she added, "I like fish sticks too".

He gave her his most serious look for at least fifteen seconds, before he laughed. "I don't think they serve fish sticks at this restaurant," he said with laughter in his voice. "They do have two of my favorites, Grouper and Tilapia, as entrée's."

She closed her menu and laid it down on the table. "Sounds great, you choose for me."

Campbell raised his eyebrows. "You're sure?"

With a little chuckle she replied, "I trust you with my heart and my stomach!"

He reached across the table and squeezed her hand. "Don't trust or give your heart away too quickly. It's the most precious gift you can give to anyone."

Before Cassandra could reply, the server retuned to give them their drinks and to take their order. As Campbell told the server what they both wanted, Cassandra smoothed the napkin on her lap and wondered what made him say what he did. Was it truly a warning to her, or was it something that had happened to himself?

After the server left, Campbell looked at her for a moment before a smile stretched across his face. He found it humorous in the way that one loose curl of hers kept falling across her forehead. Unconsciously she brushed it back, and then took a sip of her drink.

"If you don't mind, I want to stop at my office on the way home. It will only take a moment," he said.

"I don't mind."

"My secretary, Paula called me earlier this afternoon and said she left some papers on my desk that requires my signature. She'll need them first thing Monday morning. I have to be in court early and won't be in the office until later."

"You told me about one of your clients—I believe his name was Mike Overton." Trying not to pry she asked, "Are you still working on his case?"

He raised his eyebrows in surprise. "You remembered! Yes, I'm more or less still working with him. Just this afternoon I was able to tell him and his family that he was no longer a suspect. He'll be exonerated of all charges." He toyed with the edge of the little napkin that lay under his drink. "The police think they found a better suspect who may really have killed Susanna Bishop. Regardless of that, his testimony eliminates my client as a suspect."

"Campbell, that's great!' Her curiosity was spiked. "Susanna Bishops, is her names?"

"Yes, it was." He leaned forward, supporting his elbow on the arm of his chair while resting his chin in the palm of his hand. "You seem to be good at remembering people's name."

"I guess that comes from working with the public," she said. "I think it is good PR to remember my clientele's names."

Campbell agreed with her. "I learned if that there is only one thing I can remember about a person, then I should make it their name." Trying to draw her out he asked, "Tell me how you do that, I mean, remember names. Do you have some kind of method?"

"How I do it?" Unconsciously she circled the rim of her glass with her fingertip as she thought about her answer. "I try to remember a name by associating something with it." Cassandra looked down in thought then back up to met his gaze. "When my son was in preschool he couldn't remember his teacher's name, Mrs. Green. To help him I told him to think of the color of grass."

Campbell smiled his broad smile. "That work?"

She chuckled. "No, he kept calling her Mrs. Grass."

Campbell laughed aloud with amusement. This was the first time he heard Cassandra speak of her son. Although he was curious about him, and her husband, to keep from spoiling the moment and to keep the evening light and happy for her, he did not ask.

"I think that's exactly what this guy who works for Slone Ricer did," he said. "When I asked him for the name of his employer's girlfriend, he said it was Susanna Priest. While questioning him I noticed he was wearing a cross on a chain around his neck. I assumed he was Catholic and if I were right, it would be reasonable for him to get the name Bishop mixed up with Priest."

She leaned forward, propped her chin in her hands and devoted her attention fully to him. "So, who do they think killed her?"

"Kip Nelson, who also works for Slone Ricer, claims an intruder broke in her condominium and shot her."

"You think he's telling the truth?"

"Not really. I don't think Kip is as innocent as he wants everyone to think, and I suspect the police don't think so either. Whether he killed her or not, I'm not sure what I think."

"Very good Campbell Mallary! I think you missed your calling. You should have been an investigator."

"No, I only did the extra leg work because I had a gut feeling about this whole thing and didn't want to sit and watch someone like Mike have his life ruined."

A somber look crossed his face. "You know the night he was accused he had just left a high school dance?"

Cassandra smiled brightly. "Well thanks to you, he has a lot more dances he can go to."

"I don't know if I did him such a big favor after all." Trying to look somber, he casually held his drink with a slack hand. "Now he has a lifetime of going to dances and staring at all the girls who turned him down."

"Campbell! That's not true in your case."

His eyes remained clear and playful. "It is true!"

—

She had to wipe her eyes with the corner of her napkin. "Campbell, you're making me laugh!"

"You should be happy I never subjected you to dancing with me more than that one time—I'm the world's antithesis to Fred Satire. I can't dance a lick and I'm worse at singing"

"Fred Satire! You don't mean Fred Astaire?" Her eyes met his. "Campbell you're not fooling me. I know you can dance and I'd dance with you anytime."

"I wish I had been sure about that when we were younger," Campbell said. "I would have asked more than once."

He laughed and then looked serious again when he felt Cassandra's gaze on him. Her eyes were like a deep ocean that was keeping all of her secrets. He reached over and laid his hand on hers. His eyes burned with such love that the silence between them began palpitate with sensuality.

He broke the silence, "What I miss about childhood, is that it's nice believing in everything and everyone. It makes us feel secure, but later on we learn to be strong and depend more on ourselves. It makes us ready for disappointments."

Cassandra nodded softly. "It seems we're always in a constant state of change and there may be more disappointments ahead. Life is like that, not always easy, not always fair." She hesitated, arranging her thoughts before going on. "I think nothing is permanent except real love, deep love, <u>love that transcends time and place.</u> It is kind of a rope we cast to each other to keep each other from drowning in a sea of turmoil, otherwise known as life."

"Are you casting a rope to me?" Campbell asked.

She eyed him inquisitively, "If I cast one to you, would you grab hold?"

He looked back at her and sighed. Then shook his head and smiled. "So you're one of those people who answers a question with a question."

Without replying Cassandra picked up her glass, looked over the rim and gave him a playful smile.

AS CAMPBELL DROVE his car into the underground parking, he noticed Dean's silver colored Jaguar parked in his private parking space. "It looks as if Dean is working late this evening."

Cassandra did not know who Dean was and asked, "Is he someone you work with?"

Campbell grinned back at her. "I guess you can say that. He is Harlan's brother and controls fifty percent of the Firm."

"I heard you speak of Harlan but never Dean".

"Although they have equal holdings in the firm," he said, "Dean stays mostly in the background, while Harlan thrives on all the prestige."

Without hurrying, Campbell tuned the engine off and pulled the keys from the ignition. "Their father, Jack was honest, and with hard work, built up the firm. After he retired, he divided the operation between Harlan and Dean. None of Jack's integrity wore off on either one of his sons and he was never happy with the way they did things. I met Jack while he was still alive. He was a very intelligent and likable person."

Cassandra with interest asked, "I take it, he had a wife?"

"She had been dead for a long time, maybe fifteen or twenty years".

"He never remarried?"

Campbell leaned his head back on the headrest, as he recalled the different conversations he had with Jack. "No, not that I was aware of. He always talked about his wife. I think her name was Sarah. Jack believed in what he called a resurrection and a time she would be brought back to life to live here on earth."

Cassandra turned toward Campbell. "Most believe that everyone goes to heaven when they die."

"Not him, he told me he read in the Bible that a few do go to heaven, but most will be resurrected back on earth." Campbell paused in thought for a moment. "It seems he said they were called the great crowd or something like that. The earth by then would be a paradise, the way it was supposed to be in the beginning." He smiled and looked directly at Cassandra. "I guess that would leave his corrupt sons out of either place."

"Interesting I think the thought of living here is more appealing to me then going to heaven."

"I may have to agree with you on that." Campbell laughed quietly. "I'm not what you would call good heaven material. Besides, I'm not too sure what I would do there anyway."

Cassandra thought about that for a moment. "I don't think anyone has ever explained to me what they did there, other than walk around on golden streets."

Campbell chuckled. "You did say you liked to walk!"

"Campbell!" she exclaimed. "You're not being serious."

Still laughing Campbell continued. "Jack did say those who do go to heaven will rule as kings and priests over the earth. I guess that would mean there would have to be somebody down here to rule over. Otherwise, it would be kind of like having all chiefs and no Indians."

Cassandra smiled and shook her head. "Good thing no one put you in charge!" Although Cassandra laughed at Campbell's humor, she considered what he said.

During the services for her husband and son, the minister said they went to heaven. Her husband was a good person, but knowing him the way she did, Cassandra could not see Brad in heaven. Brad loved the outdoors and nature too much. He would not be happy if he had to live with golden streets and jeweled gates instead of trees, flowers and grassy places.

As far as Kevin her son, why would God need him more then her, his mother? She hadn't accepted that. The minister said our children are gifts from God, so why would he take his gift back? God is perfect in all of his activities. If that is the case, when he made all his angels, how did he miscalculate? Did he not have enough angels that he had to take her only son!

Campbell sensed her pensiveness, reached over, and ran his fingertips up and down her arm.

"Campbell, did Jack say anymore or tell you where he got his information?"

"Not really. You have to understand. Jack wasn't the kind of person who took things on hearsay or believed what was popular. Rather, he was one who would investigate and look into things himself. I can only assume he read all of that in his Bible."

Without saying anymore, Cassandra thought about how confused she felt and how it seemed no one could give her the right answers. Rather, she was always told it was not meant for her to understand everything. That didn't make sense when her minister said we were to come to an accurate knowledge and God is not a God of confusing.

Campbell's thoughts were still on seeing Dean's car. "I think that's odd."

"What, you think what Jack said was odd?" Cassandra asked.

"No, Jack makes sense. I think it is odd that Dean's working late." He checked his watch and then opened his door. "Come on, I don't want to leave you here alone."

He grabbed her hand and led her across the parking garage. "I only wanted you to come along for protection from Nester the janitor." Laughing, he put his arm around her waist and pulled her to him.

She looked up and gave him a carefree smile as they entered though the garage door that lead to an elevator. "Campbell, you are a tease. Have you seen Nester since we actually ran out on him?"

"No, he's harmless, just talks too much and interrupts my dates with beautiful women."

They walked from the elevator and down the hall and as they passed Dean's office Campbell heard muffled voices coming from the closed door. He considered tapping on the door to let Dean know he was there, but decided to pay attention to the uneasy feeling he had about Dean being in the office so late and went by without knocking.

He guided Cassandra on down the hall toward his office. After unlocking the door he held it for Cassandra. He followed her in and just before closing the door behind him, he heard Dean coming out of his office. Campbell glanced over his shoulder and was surprised to see Dean's cohort was Slone Ricer. Both men had their backs to Campbell and did not see him as they walked toward the elevator.

Campbell did not like Slone and was glad he had not made his presence known. He wondered if the police knew Slone was back in town and had an opportunity to question him. Campbell knew if Slone didn't kill the Bishop women himself, he had a good idea he was in the thick of it somehow and was glad they had avoided him.

Campbell showed Cassandra though Paula's office and into his own office. "Let me look. Paula said she would leave the reports on my desk." He stepped around the desk and pulled the chain on his desk lamp. The light that was diffused by a green shade, illuminated the top of the desk, and cast shadows across the room. "Here they are."

With the palm of his hand held out, he offered Cassandra a chair. "Go ahead and sit down, it will only take me a minute to sign these."

Cassandra sat in one of the leather chairs facing Campbell's desk. "So this is where you spend most of your time. I think I would be nervous if I were here for any other reason."

Without looking up he asked, "I make you nervous?"

She shot a quick glance at him, her eyes full of embarrassment. "No, not you, your office I mean, I would only be here for legal advice or if I was in trouble."

He found humor in her discomfort. "You are here alone with me-are you sure you're not in trouble?"

Her face warmed. "Campbell, you know what I mean."

A boyish smile that charmed her heart crossed his face. "I'm all done here. You ready to head on back?"

Before standing, he took a key from his pocket and unlocked the bottom drawer in his desk. Without Cassandra noticing, he quickly took a small handgun from the drawer and slipped it in his left hand pocket. He pushed his chair away from the desk and stood. Resting his right arm across her shoulders, he walked her out his office and though Paula's.

After they stepped out of the elevator, Campbell pulled Cassandra close and hurried her across the parking garage. While helping Cassandra into his car, his eyes surveyed the garage. He noticed the parking space where Dean had parked his Jaguar earlier was now empty. He wondered what Slone was driving and wished he had paid more attention to the other cars that were in the garage when he first got there.

Although the garage was quiet and nearly vacant of cars, he still felt anxious and hoped Cassandra did not sense his apprehension. In a matter of minutes, he drove out from the darkness of the underground parking and into the bright illumination of the streetlights. As he headed down the street toward home, Campbell felt more at ease and let his uneasy feelings fall behind him.

CHAPTER 13

Stories of Grace

As soon as Cassandra stepped into the room, she saw Campbell was working on a small painting. It was a country scene with fall colors and in the distance, snow-capped mountains. He was hovering over his work with such intensity he didn't hear her come in. Feeling like a spy, she stood there very quietly watching him concentrate. His mouth was slightly open and his eyes fixed on the canvas. After a few more minutes, he sat back, sighed, and then realized she was there. He gave her a quick smile. "How long have you been here?"

"Just a few seconds. I'm sorry. I didn't want to interrupt",

"It's okay. Perfect timing, I just finished." He stood from his chair. "Come, take a look."

She stepped closer and looked intently at the beautiful oil.

"It's a gift for you," he said.

"Really, Oh Campbell, it's beautiful." She said softly, her breath catching in her throat. "You were too modest when you told me you couldn't paint."

"After it dries I'll give it to you."

"Thank you, Campbell." Seeing him beam with pride over his surprise quickened her pulse. "I'll always cherish it." With an after thought, she asked, "Will it be dry by the time I go home? I wouldn't want to take a chance of smudging it."

"I can bring it to you." He paused. "That is, if you don't mind?"

A small smile crossed her lips and a gleam came into her eyes. "If I don't mind! Don't be silly. I'd be grateful if you did."

Campbell looked directly in her eyes. "Then that's what I'll do."

As he cleaned his brushes he asked, "Did you sleep well?"

"Yes, I did. I think I went to sleep as soon as my head touched the pillow. I sleep better when I'm not alone in the house. I presume it was because I felt secure just knowing someone else was watching over things."

Campbell laid his brush down and gently took her in his arms. "I'm glad you feel safe around me and I didn't mind at all watching over you." He kissed her and then held her for a long moment caressing her back. He could feel her warmth as she hid her face in his neck. She was real indeed, he thought, as he tried to construct, in his mind, a world that would feature them as a couple. Her business up there, his practice here—there could be a way when the time was right. He would make it happen. After a moment breaking contact, he asked. "I made coffee, would you like a cup?"

She kissed him on his cheek. "Thank you for the hug, it was nice." She smiled up at him. "I'd love a cup, please."

He caught her by the hand and pulled her into the kitchen. He took two cups from the cupboard and poured coffee in each of them. "Come on. Let's take our coffee out on the patio." He opened the door for her and after stepping out he asked, "Would you like to sit in my little hideaway?"

Cassandra answered him with a puzzled look on her face.

"You know my retreat, the one you saw from the window yesterday?"

"Oh, you mean your cute little garden! Yes, I would."

As she followed him around the corner of the house, they passed flowerbeds full of spring flowers and violets that spilled over into the grass. He took a seat on the bench and patted the place next to him. "Please, join me."

She sat next to him. "I feel privileged and love the thought that you want to share something private like this with me."

"Oh, I don't know if I'd call it that. I guess before I was the only one who had any interest in coming out here."

"Well, I think this is nice and special!"

"Cassandra, I think you are the one who is special."

With out a word she tipped her head and blushing, smiled back at him. She still wasn't used to such compliments, though they were lovely. She drank from her cup of coffee. "So, what's on the agenda for the day?"

"I really haven't thought of anything yet. I still owe you a weekend breakfast or brunch."

"You owe me?" she asked.

"You don't remember? The one we missed when I was late last Sunday." Hesitantly, he then went on and asked her. "Do you still think I stood you up?"

"No," she said "of course not!"

"You don't now, but I mean at the time, did you think I stood you up?"

She looked at his smiling eyes. "At the time I wasn't sure, but now I know that was not the case."

He caught her hand, pulled it to his lips, and kissed it. "Good! I'm glad."

Cassandra directed the conversation back to their plans for the day. "We don't have to do anything. It's your weekend and you may want to stay close to home."

"We can do that after brunch. I don't want to subject you to my cooking, so later on this evening we'll go out for dinner. How does that sound to you?"

Cassandra's face brightened. "I'll cook! You decide what you would like to eat and I'll prepare it."

"Okay, we can do it together, but we'll have to go shopping."

"Done! I think it will be fun," she said.

They both sat for a while, just enjoying the breeze on their faces and watching a hummingbird hover within a few feet over there heads.

Cassandra considered Campbell's earlier offer to bring the painting to her. Before that, she had wondered and achingly hoped that she would see him again. Still looking out across the yard she said, "Barbara asked if I would be coming back to see you."

Taking a drink of his coffee and not looking at her either, he asked. "What did you tell her?"

She glanced over at him and replied "Nothing. I don't know the answer, yet."

He turned and faced her then took her hand and kissed it. "Well maybe you'll have an answer before you go home." He waited, wondering what words would pass between them. She glanced up at him and without saying anything, looked back out across the yard. He smiled and thought to himself. "Cassandra, what kind of secrets are you hiding behind those eyes?"

He glanced down and saw a praying mantis inching along the edge of the wicker ottoman that served as a coffee table. "Are you afraid of bugs?"

Cassandra hastily looked his way. "It all depends!"

"Praying mantis," he said as he pointed to the one on the ottoman.

The praying mantis reminded her of an incident with her son when he was only four. "One summer when Kevin and I were out in our back yard, he brought back a praying mantis clinging to a stick." She lightly laughed as she recited the story. "Together Kevin and I watched the mantis as it watched us. After a while Kevin asked, "Mama, do bugs ever get tired of standing?" Cassandra laughed and Campbell joined her.

"That goes to show," he said, "kids see how it truly is. They say what's on their minds."

Campbell noticed her eyes glistened with tears. He took his napkin and gave it to her. As Cassandra wiped her tears, she hid her eyes. Campbell wondered if the tears were from laughter or sadness that she was trying to cover over.

He placed his arm around her shoulders and smoothed her cheek with his fingertips. Looking at her, he thought of how he saw a sweet-faced girl who thought she was on her own and was trying to protect her stories of grace behind a smile. A smile that hid a fragile and still grieving heart of a young mother and wife left alone after a tragic accident.

—

After a moment he said, "We both have had cruel events in our lives that we can't really run away from. We can escape for a little while but we can't run away."

"How can we escape if we don't run away?" she asked softly.

He paused to think about his answer. "You find another place to go inside yourself."

She questioned, "As you have found with your work?"

Surprised by her quick perception, he glanced over at her then stared back out across the yard.

Her eyes searched his face and then she asked, "Do you have something you're trying to escape from?"

"Not any more." Then he turned and looked at her with his eyes finally focusing on her. "It's okay to hide for a little while, but we will have to come back sometime."

"So it won't destroy us?" Cassandra asked her voice barely above a whisper that was not sure she had even spoken. Perhaps it had just been a thought.

With his eyes still looking into hers, Campbell repeated. "So it won't destroy us." He slid closer, leaned forward, and kissed her. With his arms still around her, he rested his lips against her hair. Cassandra found comfort in his embrace as she laid her head against his shoulder and looked out across the yard with it bright flowers and trees with leaves that rustled in the cool morning breeze.

CASSANDRA MADE THE table she set for dinner look festive by spreading it with a bright colored linen tablecloth. For a centerpiece, she arranged flowers from the garden in a small vase. Two lighted candles provided the final touch.

As Cassandra stood back to look at her handiwork, Campbell stepped up behind her and placed his hands on her shoulders. "You did a beautiful job," he said, kissing her affectionately.

"Thank you," said Cassandra. She held onto his hand and led him back to the kitchen. She lifted the lid from a pot on the stove and peeked in on the sauce that was cooking. "Did you know I started out in culinary arts before switching to accounting?"

Campbell planted his palm on the kitchen counter. "No, I didn't know that, and why didn't you pursue it?"

With a spoon, Cassandra dipped a bit of sauce from the pot and while cupping her hand under the spoon she offered Campbell a taste. "I'm not sure. I guess accounting was more feasible at the time."

Campbell accepted the sample and nodded. "Delicious. It's just right. Did you leave Addison right out of high school or stay for a while?"

"I stayed the summer and left the following fall."

"College, is that where you met your husband?" Campbell asked as he took two plates from the cupboard. "You said his name was Brad?"

Cassandra busied herself chopping vegetable for a salad. "I met Brad the last year of school but we didn't get married until after graduation. Then right away we had Kevin and I stayed home with him until he went to preschool." For a moment, she stopped in the act of dishing salad onto the two plates before continuing. "Kevin was nearly five—really only four." She said softly. "It seems we are like a mist and only here for a short time."

A pained expression grew on Campbell's face as he quickly glanced at Cassandra. "I'm sorry. I didn't intend to ask questions that forced you into talking on a subject that would make you feel distressed."

She stared at Campbell. "No, don't feel that way." She looked back down at the counter, "Although, at first you ache in places you did not even knew existed, or wonder how do you breathe again, but in time the pieces come back together." She glanced back up to Campbell. "I try to avoid the subject only because I worry about making others feel uncomfortable or putting them on the spot."

"I would hope you would never think that of me." Campbell laid his hand on hers. "Please, any time you need someone to listen, I can be trusted."

Cassandra smiled up at him. "Thank you, that means a lot." She laughed softly. "You don't know what you're in for."

Campbell gave her a great smile, picked up the two plates she had filled with salad and carried them to the dining room.

Cassandra asked, "If it's not too private an issue, why didn't you have any children?"

He returned and leaned with his back to the kitchen counter. "I wanted a child but Amanda didn't want any."

"Brad loved children and took Kevin everywhere." Cassandra looked distracted as she gazed out the window. "It was an overnight trip to see Brad's parents—when it happened. I didn't go because I couldn't take the time off. I stayed home—I had to work." She glanced toward Campbell and caught him staring her direction with kind eyes. She hesitated then busied herself wiping the counter.

He crossed the room and then turned her to face him. She drew herself up to her full height. He kissed her on one cheek then the other before kissing her on the lips. He then held her close in silence, their unspoken thoughts became the requiem for all the years they had not shared together.

CASSANDRA CLOSED HER eyes and drifted toward sleep, as she slipped deeper she found herself remembering—she sat upright and opened her eyes to an unfamiliar darkness. She held her breath, listening, the only sound she heard was a faint ticking of a clock. As her eyes adjusted to the darkness, she knew where she was.

She wondered what woke her or how long she had slept. She laid her head back on her pillow and turned to look at the clock. It told her, she had only slept for a little over an hour. She pulled the sheet up near her neck, rolled over, closed her eyes, and waited for sleep.

After a while she got back up, and without turning on a light she walked over, and peeked out her bedroom door. There was only a small light on in the hallway. To keep from waking Campbell, she tiptoed silently across the hall to the bathroom. Using the light from the hallway, she rummaged in her case and found a PM. She returned to the hall and walked softly toward the kitchen.

In the living room, Campbell sat reading by a single lamp beside his chair. When he heard the click of Cassandra's bedroom door, he stopped reading and listened.

Remembering where Campbell kept his drinking glasses, Cassandra took one down and tuned the faucet on ever so slowly to keep it from making any noise.

Campbell concluded Cassandra thought he was asleep and found humor at the thought of her not realizing he was sitting in the next room. He silently smiled and remained perfectly still to keep her from hearing him.

While sipping water from the glass, Cassandra walked over to the window and looked out. The sky was clear and stars were bright. She could see little flickers of light in and around the trees and bushes. As she studied the darkness, she came to realize the flickers were fireflies. She had heard of them but had never seen one before. They mesmerized her as they drew random lines and outlines in the dark.

Campbell didn't hear any more movement. He quietly laid his book next to him in the chair and softly walked through the dining room toward the kitchen. He paused at the doorway and saw Cassandra standing, looking out the window, holding a glass of water in her hand. Where any word or movement might have disturbed her, he silently crossed his arms and leaned against the doorframe. The moon cast its light on her pretty silhouette and made her even more alluring.

She wore a silk gown, the color mauve, embroidered with a fine feminine design, and snippets of delicate lace. The gown reached all the way to the floor, leaving her toes sticking out from under it. She had what appeared to be a matching robe draped over her arm leaving her shoulders uncovered. As he watched her peer into the darkness, he became curious as to what she was looking at. He glanced out another kitchen window that was closest to him and saw the fireflies doing their little dance while putting on a show for Cassandra. Secretly he continued to watch the fireflies with her.

Watching her, he mused that he had originally deemed her confident, self-assured, with great poise. As she watched the fireflies, now he also saw the woman who struggled with sorrow, loneliness and longing. He realized he was just beginning to know this complicated person. She needed someone to trust, someone who loved her deeply. He would have to be someone special he thought, because she was so special.

He glanced back out the window and saw movement out of the corner of his eye. He was not sure, but he thought he saw the side gate close. The night air was calm and he always kept the gate latched. Had someone been hiding in the darkness of the yard and had just now slipped out the gate? Since the gate was only in view of the window closest to him, he knew Cassandra would not have seen them.

He silently retreated into the dining room and quickly pulled back a corner of the drape covering the dining room window. He hoped to catch a glimpse of anyone running away. His eyes scanned the side yard, but he saw no one.

Before returning to the kitchen, he stood for a moment in thought. All the time he had lived in his house he had never heard of any problems with prowlers in the neighborhood. If there were a prowler, there was the possibility that they had not seen Campbell standing back in the shadows of the kitchen. Campbell had no doubt Cassandra's presences had alerted the prowler and made him run.

When he returned to the kitchen, Cassandra had not moved. This time he made his presence known. "So, who is creeping around my back door?"

Cassandra spun around. "Campbell, I thought you were sleeping!" She quickly pulled her robe over her shoulders. "I'm sorry. I couldn't sleep. I only came in to get a drink—and you have fireflies in your backyard!" Her eyes were bright with excitement. "I have never seen fireflies before!" Turning back to the window, she exclaimed, "Come, see!"

Campbell went and stood next to her and watched with her for a moment. "I was reading in the living room and thought I heard you."

She folded her arms around herself. "I slept for a while and something woke me. It seems whenever that happens, for the life of me, I can't get back to sleep." She turned to him. "The fireflies were a lovely diversion."

Campbell didn't want to tell her his suspicions of a prowler, but didn't feel comfortable leaving her there alone. "Would you like to come and sit with me for a while?"

"I took something that should make me sleep." She turned and walked with him back down the hall and into the living room. "I'll sit with you until it takes effect."

"You took a sleeping pill?"

"Oh no, it was only a PM."

He continued to stare at her and as his gleaming eyes met hers, his pulse quickened. He stepped closer and as he leaned toward her, she lifted her mouth in anticipation of his kiss. They kissed and then they kissed again only harder and deeper. He took her hand and gently brought her to the sofa. When he sat, he pulled her close and brought his lips to hers once again. He then pressed his lips to her hair. He fought to keep his voice even. "Oh, Cassandra," he said as he pulled away and took her hand. "I've gotten so I don't think of anything but you."

With laughter in her voice, she said. "You pretty much fill up all my thoughts too." She continued, her voice warm with sincerity. "Campbell, how am I ever going to leave you?" She could feel her defenses weakening. She wanted to trust this man with her feelings, with her heart. "I want to share more time—moments like this with you." She lowered her eyes and whispered, "Cherished moments."

He leaned over and lightly kissed her on her forehead, recognizing, even as his passion flared, that she was allowing herself to be vulnerable with him and that he needed to meet that trust with tenderness and respect. "We'll have more. Yes, a thousand times I tell you, we will have more."

She sucked in her breath, closed her eyes, and prayed for the right words to help her understand the things she didn't understand herself. "I feel so much for you, comfortable yet aware in every part of me, calm and giddy at the same time, silly and serious. Everything bright and happy in life will be gone if I can't see you."

He sat there fighting down a lump in his throat and swallowing back his surging emotions. He thought he had never heard anything so wonderful. "Cassandra, those are the words my heart has been longing to hear since that first evening together. Your trusting me with your feelings touches me deeply. I want you to know that I intend to guard and respect your feelings and return them with all my heart." Then he pulled her closer and kissed her, proving in every possible way that he loved her.

Cassandra had been right, knowing he was someone she could trust. She had genuinely loved him back in high school, and she genuinely loved him now. Her lips were at his ear. "Campbell," she whispered, as if the name were a prayer.

Still holding her close, he intertwined his fingers with hers. "I think that PM is starting to kick in."

She looked up at him and smiled. "I think you're right."

He stood and extended his hand to her. "Come on, it's time for you to go to bed." Cassandra obediently stood.

As he walked her back to her room, he asked, "You have the key to that big lock to your bedroom door?"

She laughed. "Campbell! Are you making fun of me?"

He laughed a rich joyous sound that seemed to come from deep inside him. "No, Cassandra, I'm not making fun of you. Rather, that's why I adore you, so much so that you have no need of a lock to keep you safe."

After Cassandra lay on her bed, she pulled the sheet to her waist. Campbell bent and lightly kissed her. He softly touched her shoulder, trailed his hand down her arm and holding her fingertips. "Pleasant dreams and I'll see you in the morning."

She felt like a child being put to bed. Half asleep, she smiled back. "Good night. All my dreams will be about you." She fell asleep as soon as she closed her eyes.

When Campbell got to the bedroom door, he tuned and looked back to see Cassandra was already asleep. With the possibility of a prowler still in his mind, he decided he would leave her door open and close it early in the morning before she woke up.

Before going to bed himself, he hid the gun he brought from his office in the drawer of his nightstand.

CHAPTER 14

The Intruder

S unny skies and a warm breeze greeted Campbell the next morning when he stepped out the front door of his house. As he loaded the last suitcase in Cassandra's car, he wished he could spend the rest of this beautiful day with her. He then reassessed his thinking. If the weather conditions were blizzards with five-foot snowdrifts, he would still want to spend the day with her.

He closed the trunk, walked around to the driver's side, and slid behind the steering wheel being careful not to disturb the adjustment Cassandra had on her seat. With knees bent to his chest, he turned the ignition to check the gauges.

The setting on the seat caused him to think again of Felicity. He was sure the police had found enough evidence to convince any judge or jury that she did the robberies at the department stores. He just didn't understand what her motive was or how she would have profited, since her father appeared to give her all the spending money she could want.

Campbell still had the same uneasy feeling he had had when he saw Slone Friday night with Dean. No doubt, Slone had to know who shot Susanna Bishop and would protect whoever it was for purely selfish reasons. On the other hand, if Slone felt in anyway threatened and thought he would be blamed for Susanna's death, he would sell out whoever had killed her. He would tell on his own grandmother if it got him off the hook. Slone was a man who would not stand by idle if he thought his lifestyle or livelihood was in danger. If murder was the only way of protecting it, Slone would either do it himself or have it arranged.

Before struggling out from behind the steering wheel, Campbell pulled the lever for the hood. He checked the oil, dropped the hood of the car shut, and walked back toward the front door of his house.

As he slowly ambled back up the steps, he recalled his earlier thoughts of how great the weather was and how he would like to spend the whole day with Cassandra. What mattered was just being with her, and that was far more important than where they were or how the weather was. Spending the last few days with Cassandra made him feel like he was breathing again. He didn't know if he could stand to see her leave. What she did to him scared him, but he liked it.

He strolled back down the hall toward the guest room and stood in the doorway. "I loaded the last suitcase and checked the oil. I think the car is ready to go."

Cassandra was putting on a pair of earrings while peering into the mirror that hung on the wall over the dresser. She turned to face Campbell. "You checked the oil? Thank you! You have always been so thoughtful and I see you have not changed." She grinned then looked back toward the mirror. "I wish you would have let me help with the luggage."

Campbell never replied, but only watched her while she put on the second earring. Dread squeezed his heart knowing that it would be agonizing to see her leave.

When she finished with the earring, she took one last look in the mirror and pulled back that same strand of hair that kept falling over her forehead. She snapped her bag shut and glanced back up and her eyes met Campbell's in the mirror. After a long moment, she turned his direction.

"I already miss you," he said, smiling tenderly.

Cassandra stood for a moment, then found herself steering like a sleepwalker into the opening of his arms.

He whispered with a catch in his voice. "In the last few days I've felt things that I didn't realize I could feel again." He wrapped his arms around her and she leaned into his embrace. "Something is happening and I don't want to let you go".

"I don't want to go either," she said, trying to hold back tears.

He kissed her cool wet cheeks, first under her right eye and then under her left. His kisses were as soft as a fluttering eyelash. He cradled the back of her head and kissed her softly on her lips. She then put her face against his shoulder and her eyes shut tight, still trickled tears. He squeezed her tighter and held her close in the safety of his broad chest.

While still holding her close, he reached over, pulled out a hand full of tissues from a box setting on the side table next to where they were standing. He bent down enough to look into her eyes and give her an understanding smile as he dabbed at her tears.

Cassandra then took the tissues and self-consciously wiped tears from her eyes. "Look at me. I planned not to cry. I'm too weak and it's your fault."

"My fault," he said. Campbell laughed and pulled her back into his embrace. "We'll see each other again."

Still wiping tears, "Will you come see me" she asked.

"Yes, and it will be soon. I just have a couple of cases I need to close and then plan to take a little time for rest." He beamed down at her. "Besides, I have to bring you that painting I promised you." He was trying to put her mind at ease, but in reality, it was himself he was trying comfort.

"Come on, I'll walk you to your car. I don't want you driving in the dark." He then turned, and with his arm pressing against her back, guided her down the hall toward the front door. "Are you doing okay now?"

Giggling, she replied, "I'm fine."

They walked down the steps and along the walkway before he replied. "Well, I'm not."

She raised her eyes to meet his gaze. Her reply was so soft that he barely heard. "Campbell, please—I'm sorry" After a long silence, she continued. "Before this week I planned to meet up with an old friend, reminisce, have dinner, and then each go on our separate ways." She struggled visibly with her emotions and managed to control them. "It seems I was wrong." She looked down trying to gather the right words. "This last week—I mean seeing you again, has changed everything."

He smoothed her hair away from her brow and studied her face. "Is that so bad?" He then drew her into an embrace and kissed her once again. "Please know I'll be thinking of you."

Still reeling from his touch and kisses, she smiled, nodded slightly, and stepped to her car. He opened her door and closed it after she got in. He leaned on the open window and looked down the driveway, then back into her eyes. "Will you please call me when you get home?"

"I will." She smiled back up at him. "I want to say thank you so very much for everything. It was kind of you to give up your afternoons to take me to the art gallery and that wonderful lake. The car show was fun also!"

"IT was my pleasure, and I'm delighted you had a good time."

"I did have a nice time." Cassandra gazed into his eyes and smiled. "I'm glad I stayed over so I could go to dinner with you. The room was beautiful—Campbell, thank you for making my stay so pleasant."

Campbell knew Cassandra had struggled with the decision to stay at his house over the weekend. He hoped she had no regrets and felt relieved to hear her say she was pleased with her stay. He smiled broadly. "I don't know about the neighbors, but I can assure you that I still think you're an outstanding lady."

Cassandra flushed, shyly looked down, then back at Campbell. "I hope I never made you think I didn't trust you."

"No I never felt that way. I have a very high opinion of you and glad you gave me a chance to prove that to you." He then leaned in and planted a little kiss on the tip of her nose. His eyes met hers then he gave her another little quick kiss but this time on her lips. "Call me when you get home. Please drive safely, and if you have any troubles on the road call me."

As Campbell stood watching her go, his stomach tightened, and he had to force himself not to rush after her. He wanted her to stay so he could take care of her but, simultaneously he needed and wanted her.

After she had gone, he slowly walked back up the sidewalk toward the front door. Once inside, the quiet of the house seemed to close in on him. He wondered how he was ever going to get past the idea of not having Cassandra near or the anticipation of seeing her each day.

He walked back and stood at the doorway of the guest room where she had stayed. Deep in thought, he leaned on the doorframe for a long moment. He needed a cure and he knew the best treatment would be to begin plans to see Cassandra again. He would occupy his mind with putting everything in order at work and then take a well-deserved vacation back home to Addison. With his strategy for seeing Cassandra again in place, he turned and pulled the door closed behind him.

THE HOUSE SOUNDED ominously quiet as the dark shadow of a woman entered. After softly closing the door she removed the single key from the lock and replaced it caringly back into her jacket pocket. The living room to the left of the entryway was dark. To the right a small light filtered from the kitchen beyond and faintly illuminated the dining room.

Although the woman called from a payphone in advance, she took a small flashlight from her pocket and tiptoed from room to room to be certain no one was at home. When it appeared she was alone, she hurried back to the living room. She strolled over to a row of built-in-cabinets that extended the length of the wall on the far end of the room. As she swung open double doors, a concealed safe was revealed. With ease she spun the combination knob to the right then quickly to the left and slowly back to the right. With a flip of her wrist, she pulled the handle and the door of the safe swung smoothly open.

The woman pulled out a handful of documents and quickly rummaged though them. Annoyed, she vented her irritation by shoving everything back and slamming the safe door closed. She turned and scanned the room before she walked though the dining room toward the kitchen.

Just as she entered the kitchen, the shrill ring of the phone broke the silence. Startled, she gasped, jumped back, and clasped her open hand to her breast. She stood for a moment to catch her breath before moving about the kitchen pulling out drawers and looking though cabinets.

The phone continued to ring and was a reminder to her to erase her own earlier call from the caller ID. After a moment, the voice mail took over and the ringing stopped. "Hello Campbell, this is Cassandra. You told me to call when I got home. I'm sorry I missed you. Call me when you get this massage. Goodbye."

The woman walked over and jabbed at the buttons on the machine. "Sorry Cassandra! Campbell will not be returning your call!" She gave the machine one last jab, "because he will not get your message!"

Abruptly she stopped when car lights flashed across the dining room windows as it pulled into the driveway. She rushed across the kitchen and quickly slipped though the door that opened out into the backyard. With ease, she latched the lock behind her then silently dissolved into the darkness.

THE EVENING HAD stretched before Campbell, long and empty. As an alternative to sitting at home and feeling miserable after Cassandra left, he drove to the grocery store to pick up a couple of items he needed. The diversion helped somewhat, but his thoughts kept returning to her, and how in a matter of days his life seemed to have become a new world of happiness and trust. She was more than he ever imagined possible for himself.

After he returned home, instead of going inside immediately, he leaned his head back on the headrest of his seat and a great emptiness came over him. He missed Cassandra even more than he dared to admit. He wanted to hold her in his arms, feel her warmth against his body, and smell the scent of her hair. Pulling his feelings together, he grabbed his bag of groceries, slid from his car, and headed to the back door of the house. It was dark and he wished he had left a light on before he had gone to the store.

As he rounded the corner of the house, a dark figure jumped out at him. Campbell jumped back nearly dropping the bag of groceries! With his heart in his throat he realized it was only Mrs. Devitte's cat.

"Scar!" He exclaimed. "What are you doing here?"

Mrs. Devitte was the elderly woman who lived next door. Three years earlier, her grandson had given her the cat, and Scarlet O'Hara was the name she had chosen for it. Campbell thought it was an odd name for a cat, and when out of hearing range of Mrs. Devitte, he condensed the name to "Scar."

The cat wound around Campbell's legs as he fitted his key into the lock. "Scar, would you get out of the way!"

As Campbell opened the kitchen door, Scarlet O'Hara rushed past him and into the house. "Okay Scar, have a quick look around because you are not staying long!"

Campbell flipped a switch and the overhead light lit up the whole kitchen. He sat the bag on the counter then walked over and grabbed the cat before it could jump up on the kitchen table. He carried it over and sat it on the back step. "Go home to someone who loves you more then I do!" He then quickly closed the door before the cat could rush back in.

Before putting the groceries away, Campbell checked his messages in hopes that Cassandra had called. He was disappointed to see there were no messages and wondered if she had forgotten. He picked up the receiver and dialed her number, but just before he pushed the last number he hung up. She would have not forgotten and may not even be home yet. It was early still and he made the decision to wait and call her later.

After making a pot of coffee, he poured a cup and carried it to the living room. At the entrance to the living room he abruptly stopped, stunned to see the doors of the cabinet standing open revealing the safe inside. Setting his coffee down, he hurried over and examined the safe for pry marks.

At one time he'd kept cash in the safe but now it held nothing of any great value to anyone but himself. He now mostly used the safe to store such thing as insurance papers and other documents to protect them in case of fire.

After seeing no pry marks on the safe and without opening it, he closed the cabinet and quickly moved to the front door to check for any sign of forced entry. Finding the door in good order, he took his gun from the drawer of his nightstand and walked throughout the house checking all the rooms. Once he secured all the windows and was satisfied no one was in the house, he returned to the living room.

As Campbell sat down heavily in his chair, he began drinking his coffee while working things out in his mind. No doubt, who ever had been in his house had a key or was very good at picking locks. The intruder didn't steal anything as far he knew, and was certainly not very bright, trying to open a locked safe, while there were other valuables in plain sight and more accessible. It was obvious the uninvited visitor was after something, but Campbell was not certain just what it could be. He was now positive that someone had indeed been hiding in his back yard the previous evening, and that it had not been his imagination when he had seen them slipping out the back gate, into the darkness.

CHAPTER 15

Monday Mania

"Mr. Mallary, thank you for stopping by Friday evening and signing those documents," Campbell's secretary said as she came into his office. "Again, I want to apologize for not getting them to you before you left the office."

Without looking up from his work, Campbell replied, "No need to apologize I was in the area anyway." He then glanced up and smiled at her. "It only took a moment."

Paula turned to leave, then stopped and pivoted back around. "Mr. Mallary, when I called you Friday afternoon, did I forget to tell you I would leave the documents on your desk?"

"No, you told me" Campbell said while continuing to be preoccupied with what he was working on. "They were right where you said they would be."

Paula inquired further, "Would you like anything else from the files?"

"No." Campbell leaned back in his chair now giving Paula his full attention, "Why do you ask?"

"I could tell someone was looking though our records over the weekend. I assumed it was you."

He stared at her for a moment and then asked, "You think someone was going though the files?"

Paula was quick with her reply, "No, no I wouldn't say that! What I meant was that if you need some kind of record or document, tell me which one you want and I'll find it for you." Looking perplexed Paula paused. "You're not the one who was looking in the file cabinet were you?"

Campbell pushed his chair back, stood and walked around his desk facing Paula. "Do you know which file was pulled?'

"No," Paula said as she directed Campbell back into her office. She pointed to a hydrangea setting on a small table that was nestled between two tall file cabinets. "When I came in this morning, a leaf on this plant was caught in one of the drawers of the cabinet."

Campbell cradled the leaf in his hand and examined it. He saw an impression stamped across the leaf that nearly cut it in half. "It wasn't that way when you left Friday?"

"The plant has always sat in the center of the table," she said. "Someone must have scooted it over and didn't notice they caught the leaf in the drawer as they closed it."

Campbell moved the plant back over to the left. "M-m-m, it appears someone moved the plant to the side so they could make room to set something on the table or to lay open a folder."

Paula nodded her head in understanding. "Then when they returned the folder to the drawer they forgot to move the plant back."

"It appears so," Campbell said as he stepped to the file cabinet. "What drawer was it caught in?"

Paula gestured toward the cabinet. "It was the third one down, the one that contains the files P-R."

Campbell reflected back to Friday evening when he saw Dean leaving his office with Slone Ricer and wondered if Dean was the one who was looking through the files. He slid the drawer out and pulled out the folder with Ricer's name on it. He flipped though it and saw nothing out of order then replaced it.

He turned back to Paula. "Didn't you just get done clearing out all the older records and moving them down to the archives?"

"Yes, I did it early this year," she said. "Did you need me to bring something back up for you?"

"No, that's fine." Campbell wondered if Dean had been looking for something related to Felicity's arrest. He tried to sort out in his mind what it would be, since Dean did most of Ricer's legal work and anything of importance would surely be in his own files.

That same uneasy feeling he had experienced Friday evening was still with him. "Paula, I think for a while, it would be best if you didn't work late. Please try to leave when everyone else does."

With a surprised look on her face, Paula anxiously asked, "Why, is there something wrong?"

"I'm not sure, but I think it would be safer for you not be here alone."

He took a few steps back to his office before turning back. "Paula, for right now, don't mention this to anyone even that you already transferred the old records down to the basement."

"Why, did I create a problem by doing that?"

Campbell considered how the transfer of files may have in fact, created a problem for Slone Ricer. Campbell laughed to himself and turned again to walk back toward his office. Over his shoulder, he said, "It may be a problem for some people but nothing for us to worry about."

With her hands on her hips, Paula gave him an inquisitive look for a long moment, then reached over and moved the hydrangea back to the center of the table.

"DETECTIVE HARRIS IS here to see you." Campbell looked up from his desk to see Paula walk into his office, followed by the Detective.

"Detective, please come in." Campbell quickly stood and walked from behind his desk with his hand extended. "What brings you to this side of town?"

The detective shook hands. "We're just doing a little investigating."

Campbell directed Harris to a chair. "What can I do for you?"

With a firm voice Detective Harris announced, "Last night, Dean Hendricks was found dead in his home."

Campbell part way back to his chair, pivoted sharply back to the detective, "Dean dead—how?"

Paula who was about to step out of the room, stopped, and turned with a gasp. Campbell moved to her side, rested his arm across her shoulders, and supported her to the nearest chair.

"My apologies, Miss Benson," said the Detective as he bowed his head. He then continued, "Someone shot Dean and it was his wife who found him. She was out of town over the weekend and discovered his body Sunday evening when she returned."

With compassion, Paula exclaimed, "His poor wife! What must she be going through!"

Campbell asked, "Do you have any idea who shot him?"

Harris crossed his arms. "We're just beginning our investigation. We have an ident officer over at the house taking pictures and dusting for fingerprints now. We haven't questioned any of the neighbors yet. Later this afternoon, we'll send an officer around. Hopefully someone saw something out of the ordinary, but since no one had called in an incident prior to Mrs. Hendricks' return home, we may not get much from the neighbors. We're pursuing all the usual avenues."

Campbell knew the detective's reasoning for the delay in questioning Dean Hendricks' neighbors. In neighborhoods such as the one Dean lived in, no one is ever home during the day. Through the weekdays, both husbands and wives are working, and their children are either in school or at childcare. A neighborhood such as his own usually had an elderly neighbor, such as Mrs. Devitte who is retired and stays home most of the time. In the poorer neighborhoods, both husband and wife are often home because nobody has either a job or the money to go anywhere.

Campbell walked over and sat back down at his desk. "They have any idea of the time of death?"

"The investigator from the medical examiner's office said it was either late Friday or early Saturday." Harris promptly said. "We've been checking around for the last person who may have seen Dean alive."

Paula quickly volunteered. "Friday evening after work was the last time I saw him. I passed Dean in the hall a little after five o'clock.

—

He wished me a good weekend." Her voice dropped to a strained whisper. "I can't believe he's dead."

While thinking intently, Campbell was toying with a pencil held long-ways in his hand. <u>Other then Slone Ricer, he had no doubt he was the last to see Dean Hendricks alive</u>.

He spoke in an even voice. "I returned back to work late Friday evening to sign some papers and saw Dean leaving his office." He laid the pencil to the side and sat straight in his chair. "He wasn't alone Slone Ricer was with him."

Detective Harris stared at Campbell for a long moment. "You know what time that was?"

"When I pulled into the underground garage I saw Dean's car and thought it was odd he was working late. I looked at my watch and it was exactly a quarter after nine.

"You talk to Dean?" asked Harris.

"No, I don't think Dean or Slone even knew I was in the building." Campbell paused and looked directly at Harris. "Maybe I should be grateful?"

The Detective's dark eyes focused on Campbell slowly and then he nodded. "Yeah, he said. "Yes, you could have been at risk yourself."

Paula looked apprehensive as her face turned pale. Campbell, you knew! Is that why you told me not to work late?"

He eyed her steadily, "No Paula, I knew nothing." Dropping his voice he added, "I only had a bad feeling."

A crushing weight came down on Campbell when he realized the danger he had put Cassandra in. He now had a good idea that the prowler and the break-in of his house had a connection to Dean's murder. With that in mind, he knew he had not only put Cassandra in danger by bringing her to his office but by inviting her to stay at his house.

Campbell continued. "Slone and Dean walked out together, but I'm not sure if they left in separate cars or not. Dean was driving his silver Jaguar and it was gone by the time I returned to the garage."

"The Jaguar was parked in Dean's driveway when our officers arrived," said Harris. "His wife said Dean never parked it in the driveway but always kept it in their garage. I have to wonder if someone else was driving the car."

"I assumed Slone's visit had something to do with his daughter Felicity's arrest." Campbell glanced over at his secretary. "Paula noticed that over the weekend someone had riffled though the files in her office."

Paula sat on the edge of her seat. "The hydrangea in my office was moved and who ever moved it shut one of its leaves in the drawer of the file cabinet."

A huge smile stretched across Detective Harris faces. "Really!" He chuckled a little. "So, do you know whose file they were looking at?"

Campbell interjected "I think they were looking at the file that belongs to Slone Ricer. Since Dean does most everything for Slone, I can't imagine what they were looking for in my files. There have been occasions I have done minor things for him, but nothing of great importance."

Campbell stood, walked around his desk, and then leaned against it with his arms crossed. "I might add, Saturday night I had a prowler stalking around my house and Sunday it was broken into and someone made a mess looking for something. I can't keep from thinking there is a connection between those two incidences and the files here at the office."

Paula looked stricken. "Your house was broken into!" Thoughtfully, she asked. "Since that was Sunday, that means they didn't find what they were looking for here on Friday."

"So where is the file?" Harris asked. "I'd like to look at it."

Smiling, Campbell replied, "You'll have to ask my secretary about that."

Paula looked embarrassed and felt put on the spot. "Once a year, we clear out the older records and store them downstairs in the archives. It was slow last month so I moved everything early."

"Interesting," Harris said thoughtfully. "If Dean didn't know you moved the files, the suspect must have thought Dean was holding out on him."

"If Slone is involved with Dean's death, I would think that will only tighten the noose around his neck with his involvement in the death of Susanna Bishop." Campbell said.

—

Harris shook his head. "If the possible connection between Dean and the Bishop case gets out, the press will be down on us like flies demanding to know more."

Campbell was curious. "Have the police questioned Slone in regards to Susanna's death?"

Harris looked straight at Campbell. "I didn't even know Ricer was back in town until you just told me. Without a doubt, he had more to do with her death than what Kip Nelson is saying. Not only that, the ident officer says all evidence is pointing to a third person who shot her."

"Although Ms. Bishop was shot, the coroner's report said she died of asphyxiation," said Campbell.

"That's another unanswered question. Someone must have wanted to make sure she was dead. If she was left alone, eventually she would have died of loss of blood." Harris looked down at the floor and shook his head. He glanced back up at Campbell. "One way or another, Ricer needs to be questioned. We will have to get an investigator on that as quick as we can."

Paula asked, "You think Felicity Ricer is the third person."

"No, they ruled her out," said the detective. "She finally confessed and definitely is the one who burglarized all the department stores."

"If you don't mind me asking," said Campbell "did Felicity give a reason why she broke into the department stores?"

"Yeah, she did," said Harris. He then smiled, "there was a time I thought I had heard it all, but this was a first. Apparently, the first store she allegedly robbed wouldn't let her take more than three garments at one time into the fitting room while she was shopping there. I gather Felicity caused some problems and made a big enough scene that the manager threatened to have her escorted from the store. Felicity took exception to it and out of spite she returned and robbed the store." He leaned back in his chair and crossed his arms over his chest. "She sure is a piece of work."

"Although they don't always enforce it, I think that is a standard policy for most stores," Campbell said. "So, did she say how she broke in?" I mean, that is a difficult feat for even a professional to get in without setting off the alarms."

"You're not going to believe this either," said Harris. "She never broke in. Instead, she stayed until they locked up and everyone went home. Then she helped herself to the whole store and took what she wanted."

Campbell said in surprise. "What did she do, hide in the restrooms or behind a rack of clothing?"

"No, she didn't hide at all. You know how the bigger department stores have their display of models—mannequins. In each of the stores Felicity robbed, she went in just before closing time. She took a garment off the rack, dressed up like a mannequin, and posed along side them. With her small stature, she blended in enough that none of the clerks even noticed her. After everyone left the store for the day, she was able to try on clothes at will."

"By the end of the day the clerks were probably eager to leave work and never paid any attention," Campbell said.

"I've seen that before," Paula said, "Some stores will hire models that are able to stand still for long periods of time. They are very good, enough so, that they hardly even blink their eyes. They can fool almost anyone into believing they are mannequins, until they change positions at one time!"

Harris chuckled. "Well, Miss Ricer must have that same knack. Too bad she didn't use it in a responsible and legal way."

"That, or maybe she should have gotten herself a nice hobby that would have kept her busy," Paula said.

"You mean a hobby like sharpening knives, watching people, and digging holes in her back yard?" Campbell chuckled.

Harris gave Campbell a sideways look and laughed while shaking his head. "We already have a few of that kind locked up in the state institution and don't need more."

Campbell smiled then turned the talk back to Slone Ricer's file. "Detective Harris, I know you want to do everything legal. If you have the right paperwork, we can go downstairs and look at that file."

Harris tossed his head back with an amused expression in his eyes, "You lawyers always want to keep things official." He reached into his suit jacket and pulled out a search warrant. "Yes counselor, I stopped and picked this up before heading over here."

Campbell pulled out the top drawer of his desk and reached for a key. "I'm only trying to make things easier for you when it comes time to face the judge with your evidence."

Harris stood from his chair to go. "I only hope the file will contain a motive."

"You don't need a motive for conviction," Campbell said. He then smiled. "Of course by figuring out why the victim was killed, it certainly helps figuring out who killed them."

"True" the detective said as he slipped his hands in his pockets and walked toward the door.

"Paula, we're heading down stairs. You'll be okay until I get back?" Paula stood and gave him a tired smile and Campbell smiled back. "If someone from the locksmith calls, tell them I'll call him right back."

As both men headed toward the lower level of the building, Harris asked, "I take it, you are changing the locks on your house?"

"I'm having the locks changed and getting back in the habit of setting the alarm."

Harris laughed harshly. "Most calls we get on house break-ins are from those who have alarms which have been turned off. The crooks are never off duty and never announce their plans of becoming a house guest either."

After they reached the lower level, Campbell unlocked a door and flipped the light switch, which lit up two rows of overhead lights. He went to the reference section that told him the general area to look in for the firm's records.

"We only keep the records for a short time. After that we contact the client to see if they want them before they are destroyed." He walked over to a cabinet and pulled out a folder. "Here it is, safe and sound!" Campbell handed it over to Detective Harris. "I'd appreciate you telling me if you find anything useful."

Harris nodded. "I'll get back to you within the week and you'll get this back when we're done with it."

IT WAS LATE afternoon when Campbell returned to his office. As he leaned back over his desk to punch up his computer monitor checking his messages, his desk phone rang. He picked up the receiver to hear his brother's voice on the other end.

—

185

"Hey Campbell, this is Matt. I haven't heard from you in a while and was wondering if you're still with us"

Campbell gave him a short laugh. "Oh no, I'm fine, I've just been busy".

"This Friday, Jennifer and I are having a little gathering with a few friends and we really would like for you to join us."

With all of the turmoil at the office, Campbell thought it would be a nice opportunity to get away for a day or two. Not to mention, he would get to see Cassandra. He could ask her to go to Jennifer and Matt's gathering. And, he would give her the canvas he had painted for her.

He was disappointed he hadn't heard from her the evening before and kicked himself for not calling her. At the time, he was so overwhelmed and unnerved at the thought of someone breaking into his house that he totally forgot to call until it was too late. He was anticipating calling Cassandra that evening after work.

"It sounds great! I'll take off work Friday and leave then." Campbell said.

"You staying in the old homestead like you usually do?" Matt asked.

"I think so."

"I know you like staying there, but remember you're always welcome to stay here with Jennifer and me. The girls will be looking forward to seeing their Uncle Campbell."

"Thanks for the invitation, but I do like staying at the old place. It makes me feel like I'm coming home each time I go there."

"I understand I feel the same way," said Matt. "Oh, by the way, did you get my message?"

"I did! You'll not believe who was trying to get in contact with me! You remember Cassandra Evens?"

"Oh, you're talking about the first message, the one I left last week? You mean to say it was Cassandra and not the IRS who was trying to get a hold of you!" Campbell could hear the laughter in Matt's voice. "I just saw her this afternoon and she was having lunch with Tom Larson."

Campbell remembered Tom from school. He was a grade ahead of him and a bully. Last time he was home, he had run into Tom and found he still didn't like him. He had a head full-slightly too full-of wavy black hair, a slightly too sincere smile and a slightly too firm handshake, reminding Campbell of a salesmen or politician.

Matt continued by offering Tom an unfavorable character reference. "He has been after Cassandra Evens ever since she moved back into town. Around town, Tom is not well-liked, and I think everyone just tolerates him. He's still living at home and sponging off his old man."

Campbell cleared his throat and asked awkwardly, "You think their lunch was a date?"

If Matt heard the strain in his brother's voice, he didn't let on. "Lunch, oh you mean with Tom and Cassandra. I'm not sure I never stopped to talk."

Campbell needed a chance to wrestle with his feelings and ended the call. "I'll see you Friday and give you a call when I get in."

He hung up and held the receiver in his hand. Was that why Cassandra didn't call him last night? Had he lost any chance he ever had with her by letting her go back without asking for a commitment? He replaced the receiver, slumped in his chair, and closed his eyes with the pain that squeezed up from inside him.

He then reconsidered his thoughts. Just because they were having lunch together didn't mean anything significant. Matt had said Tom had pursued her ever since she had returned to Addison. She was too fine a lady not to have told him if she already had a significant relationship going with someone else. The ugly doubts kept resurfacing to the top of his brain. Is that why she didn't call? Tom Larson, why him? Regardless, Campbell knew Cassandra had a hold on him he could not express or understand. Apart from Tom, he needed to see Cassandra again.

AS CAMPBELL PUT a dinner of leftovers in the oven and set the timer for thirty minutes, his mind turned once again to his day at work. First, to find out someone was going though the files, which could only be connected to the break-in of his house. Then the matter of Dean's death, and other than the murderer, he may have been the last to have seen him alive. The last event was Matt's phone call that left him at a complete loss.

He thought of his brother's phone call as he wiped down the kitchen counter. He didn't know what to make of Cassandra not calling him as she said she would, or her having a lunch date with Tom Larson. He was upset with himself for allowing his mind to become so preoccupied with the break-in of his house that he didn't think to call until it was too late. Even if he thought she may have been tired from her trip and had already gone to bed, he should have called her anyway. He could have explained and she would have understood. For no other reason than to let her know he was concerned that she got home okay. He should have called.

Campbell felt sure she was home from work by now and made the decision to call her. He grabbed his phone receiver and dialed her number. As he waited, he could hear her phone ring on the other end. His heart skipped with each ring. Then after about five rings, his heart dropped a little. Anticipating an answer from her voice mail, he continued to let it ring. He would leave her a message. She would know he did call and not think he was a complete cad and had forgotten about her already. When the voice mail answered, the recording said, "The voice mail is full and can't record your message". He could not believe what he was hearing. He decided he would wait and give her another call later. He would be in Addison in another four days and would be sure to go see her then.

While waiting for dinner to cool, he decided to read for a while to take his mind off the day's events. Just as he sat down and opened his book, the doorbell rang. He wasn't expecting anyone and it gave him a start. After laying his book down and walking to the foyer, he looked out the peephole. He was surprised to see Amanda, his ex-wife. Just seeing her made his emotions quickly change from confusion to annoyance. With reluctance, he unlocked the door, opened it and the scent of her perfume wafted in, permeating the room. He always thought Amanda was too generous when applying it and could tell she had not changed.

She just stood there smiling. "Hello, Campbell."

"Amanda." He nodded, keeping his voice level and cool.

"Can we talk for a few minutes?" She asked when he didn't immediately open the screen door.

Without smiling, he unlatched the door and she came inside. Campbell knew letting her back into his life would only bring more pain. His lack of welcome and warmth went against the grain but

—

he was protecting himself. He had no polite choices, not with this woman.

Amanda stalked into the foyer and followed Campbell as he walked back into the living room. She sat on the edge of the cushion of the overstuffed chair that she knew was Campbell's favorite and the one in which he always sat. Campbell took the chair across from her. She didn't speak for a long moment. "You're looking well," she finally said.

Campbell's demeanor was business-like. "What can I do for you Amanda?"

She gave him a confident smile. "I was thinking, actually I was hoping, that you might be free for dinner tonight."

Campbell's posture stiffened and he sat up straight. "Amanda, what is it you want from me?"

She sighed and tried to sound wounded. "I miss you and my life feels very empty without you."

Campbell remembered a time he would have weakened but now her display of misery had no meaning for him. If he were not a gentleman, he would have laughed. "I'm sorry you feel your life is empty."

She appeared not to notice the sarcasm in his voice. "I'd like for us to try again."

His eyes darkened as his face lost its controlled aloofness. "Amanda, why would you want to put yourself though all that grief again? I don't want or need it myself."

Not bothering to hide her disdain, "Fair enough", she replied. She stared at him and carefully considered her next statement. "I'll tell you what. Don't make your decision right now. Think about it." She dug in her bag, produced a card, and held it out to him. "Once you've made your decision, you let me know."

To Campbell the card had no merit but he graciously took it and laid it on a side table without looking at it. He wondered if she was deliberately being obtuse. He then said evenly. "I already made my decision."

She shooed his words away with a flip of her wrist and then walked toward the front door. "No need to show me out. I know the way."

Nevertheless, he got up and accompanied her. Just before she stepped out the door, she turned and put her arms around him.

Without a response, Campbell only let his arms dangle. His face was rigid, set, looking right past the screen door into the night. Her performance sickened him. As she continue to cling to him, he reached up and calmly removed her arms from around his neck.

She winced and her eyes stormed. "Oh Campbell, you know your life is no good without me. You just won't admit it yet. I'll not trouble you again. When you're ready you'll have to come to me. C'est la-vie." She then hurried out the door and down the steps.

Outraged as he felt, he still had to fight down a hysterical impulse to laugh. He could not believe he was ever so young and romantic, that he had allowed himself to be deceived by Amanda's wiles. As he closed the door, he hoped she would stand by her word and not contact him again.

After she had gone, he recalled that not one time had she said she was sorry or apologized. She never even said—she loved him. Although, he had cried back then he would not now allow her back into his mind or heart to bring chaos again.

Campbell opened his book to read and then closed it. Leaning his head back in his chair, he remembered something Cassandra told him. "We shouldn't allow our disappointments in life to destroy us." Amanda was, in fact, his greatest disappointment and he would not allow her to destroy his life.

He reopened the book and began to read. In an undertone, he whispered. "Thank you Cassandra, for giving me the strength."

CHAPTER 16

C'est la-vie

As Campbell got off the elevator and headed toward his office, Ian stepped out of his door just as Campbell passed by.

"You're just getting back? Paula told me you were filing a continuance on one of Dean's cases."

Campbell gave his friend a smile and kept walking. "I've two more of his cases I have to postpone before the end of the week and a preliminary hearing to prepare for this afternoon."

Ian fell in step with him. "Harlan also spread some out my way. The best thing to do is to file continuances where we can and take care of everything that can't wait."

"One positive thing is that the clients have been somewhat understanding," said Campbell.

Ian checked his watch. "I had a cancellation on one of my own cases this afternoon. Let me help you on that preliminary."

"Sure, I can use all the help I can get. We get this day behind us the rest of the week should be fairly painless."

Ian, his usual light-hearted self, laughed and joked, "When they find who killed Dean, we'll file a suit against them for putting us under duress."

Without speaking, Campbell looked at Ian with a half-kidding, half-exasperated, expression.

Paula looked up as both men entered her office. "You have a visitor," she informed Campbell.

"Thanks Paula." Campbell tossed his head with a wicked grin. "Ian told me he would do that preliminary hearing for me. Will you bring the file into my office so I can help him with it?"

Ian gave him a sardonic look. "Paula, don't believe a word of it."

Amused, Paula smiled. "I'll bring the file."

Campbell strolled on into his office. "Detective Harris, I didn't expect you back this soon!"

The detective was sitting in a chair, looking through the folder he held in his lap. When Campbell entered the room, he stood and smiled.

Campbell half sat and half leaned on the edge of his desk. As he folded his arms across his chest, he asked, "You find anything of help in that file I loaned you?"

Before Harris could answer, Ian stepped into the office followed by Paula. Ian reached out and shook Harris's hand. "Detective, it's good to see you again."

Harries nodded his head. "Mr. Chatman, Mrs. Benson."

"The Detective was just about to tell me what he found in the file we have on Slone Ricer." Campbell then turned to Detective Harris and asked, "You mind if Ian and Paula sit in?"

"No. Not at all," The detective continued, "Mr. Mallary, do you recall procuring cargo insurance for Slone Ricer?"

Campbell remembered when Slone had asked for the insurance and recalled how he and Ian had speculated on his reasons. He shot a glance Ian's direction and saw an unmistakable slight grin. Keeping his composure Campbell answered, "Yes, I drew that up for Slone a little over a year ago."

Harris sighed. "Cargo insurance sounds innocent enough. At least, that's what I thought until the US Drug Enforcement Administration contacted me. It seems they, along with Customs, have been tracing Slone Ricer's actions for quite some time."

Detective Harris grimaced and sat back down in his chair. "Slone has been involved in using offshore oil drilling rigs as a cover for smuggling drugs. The drugs were off-loaded from ships onto the oil drilling platforms and then flown by helicopter up to the Gulf of Texas coastline. Slone arranged for them to be picked up there and brought on into the United States."

Ian glanced over at Campbell. "That explains all the trips to Texas."

Campbell took a seat at his desk. "The information given me by Slone was that the cargo consisted of equipment used on drilling rigs."

"Most of the cargo actually was legitimate and very expensive. That's why Slone secured insurance on it. When customs found the illegal drugs, Slone knew it would be a matter of time before they found out that the equipment was insured, and then they would go looking for the name on the insurance policy. The signed policy you held in your files was the only thing that tied Slone to the illegal cargo, and he was desperate to get his hands on it." The detective fixed his eyes on Paula. "We suspect Dean is the one who was going though your files."

Campbell looked Ian's direction and explained. "Dean couldn't find Slone's policy because he wasn't aware Paula had already taken it downstairs along with all our other old records."

Detective Harris continued with more details. "Slone was heading out of the country when the Feds picked him up yesterday morning. According to Slone, Dean was blackmailing him by withholding the policy. He threatened Dean until he gave in and told him the policy was here in your office. When Dean couldn't find it, Slone thought he was lying and still holding out on him. Although Slone admitted to having Kip Nelson follow Dean to his house to search it, he denies having anything to do with Dean's death. The investigators confirmed that Kip was the one who actually shot Dean, but they can prove Slone was also there when it happened. Kip and Slone both are being charged with murder one, abduction, transporting and conspiring to sell illegal drugs, and the list goes on and on. It's too long to say."

The sound of the phone ringing in Paula's office drew everyone's attention. Paula turned toward the door. "That's my phone. I'd better get back to work. Mr. Mallary, call me if you need anything else."

Campbell only responded with a nod of his head. His thoughts were caught up with the evening he had brought Cassandra to the office and the danger in which he had inadvertently placed her. Was Kip hiding inside the building or secretly watching them while they were in the garage? Seeing Dean shortly before his death was disturbing, but the threat of Kip lurking around in the dark, watching him and Cassandra was unnerving.

Harris turned toward Campbell. "Since they couldn't find the policy at Dean's house that may explain the break-in at your house."

Campbell spoke huskily. "They didn't waste any time. They were skulking around my house Saturday evening and broke-in the next night."

Campbell had a look of weariness about him as his thoughts raced back to Saturday evening when he had seen the prowler in his back yard. He recalled Cassandra telling him something had awakened her but wasn't sure what it was. The room she had stayed in was toward the back of the house where she would've heard any unusual sound. Although awake, he had been in the front part of the house and wouldn't have heard anything. He had no doubt that seeing Cassandra standing at the window had caused them to run, but only to return the next evening.

"I'm sure whoever was in your house was after the policy," said Harris. "That would explain why nothing else of value was stolen."

Ian still leaning against the doorframe suddenly stood up straight. He looked over at Campbell, "It was a good thing you were gone when they broke in, my friend. The same thing that happened to Dean could've happened to you."

Campbell replied, "I went to the store and was gone for only a short time. They had to have been watching my house waiting for me to leave." To Campbell, the whole thing was unsettling and he could only be glad Cassandra had already left for home and was safe from any threats.

Harris nodded. "We got a little more information on the Susanna Bishop case, too. As we could have guessed, Kip was not completely

---

194

truthful in what he told the police. I mentioned the other day the ident officer thought there was a third person involved." The detective looked directly at Campbell, and with an edge of apology in his voice he said, "After questioning Slone and looking at the evidence that was collected, we now know the third person was a woman named Amanda. I'm told—she's your ex-wife?"

Harris's words rocked Campbell back and his arms dropped loosely to his sides as he stared in disbelief at Detective Harris "Amanda! You're not serious—you're saying she—you mean murder?" he stammered.

Detective Harris quickly replied. "We believe Amanda shot Susanna Bishop, but she didn't kill her."

Hearing about Amanda's involvement in Susanna's death caused a great swell of sadness to sweep up from inside Campbell, but at the same time, it didn't come as any surprise. He thought of Amanda as a shallow woman who may have finally come to realize what far-reaching consequences could come with her selfish lifestyle. He felt sadness at the waste of her life.

Campbell exchanged a rueful glance with Ian. By the pained expression that flitted across Campbell's eyes, he obviously had mixed feelings about this latest report on Amanda. Campbell smiled fleetingly and broke contact. Ian folded his arms over his chest, leaned against the open door, and waited.

The detective watched the dark gravity of Campbell's face for a long moment before he gave out more details. "Apparently Slone was playing both ends, with Susanna here and Amanda in Texas. Amanda found out about Slone's relationship with Susanna and to make a long story short, she shot Susanna to keep her away from Slone. Right afterwards, she called Slone and told him Susanna threatened to tell the police about the illegal drug deal and so she shot her to protect him. Slone believed her and with Kip's help, he disposed of the body. He chose the park to make it appear someone killed her while she was out walking. Slone hoped that would take attention off him or anyone who knew her well enough to tell the police about their relationship. After taking her from the trunk of the car, they discovered she was still alive. Since they thought she was a threat to them, Kip took the plastic they had her wrapped in and put it over her face until she stopped breathing."

—

"That's callous," Ian said. "They need to lock him up and throw away the key. In fact, both of them."

Detective Harris shook his head. "Sorry about it being your ex-wife, Mr. Mallary. We do have her safely in custody so she isn't a danger to you."

Campbell considered that, then sighed and murmured. "Things don't always turn out the way you hope, do they?"

Detective Harris stood to leave. "I'll return that file as soon as the Feds return it to me. I'm sure it won't be until after their trials."

Campbell stood. "Thank you for coming over. Though it was a shock, I prefer having heard it from you rather than hearing it on the radio or reading it in the papers."

Harris walked to the door to leave, stopped, and turned as if he forgot something. "Oh, one more thing. One of the oil Companies that operate those particular offshore oil drilling rigs is partly owned by our former President." He then turned and held his hand up in a wave as he went out the door.

Ian tightly smiled at Detective Harris as he left the office. He then walked over and sat in the chair facing Campbell. "Sorry about Amanda. Do you want to go home early? Why don't you let me do that preliminary for you?"

Campbell swiveled his chair to look out the window. After a long moment, he turned back to his desk facing Ian once more. "Thanks, I'll do it, but you can help." He smiled weakly and bent his head to his work. Without looking up, he spoke, "I think hearing about Amanda's involvement with Slone came as much of a shock as finding out she shot Susanna Bishop."

Disheartened, Ian looked at his friend without saying anything. Campbell continued, "You know, she came by Monday evening. I can't help but think since Slone was not available for her to use as her pawn she was after me as her next choice." He laughed shortly and murmured, "C'est la-vie".

Trying to lighten things Ian joked, "You're learning French now?"

Campbell shook his head. "That was the last thing Amanda said to me as she was leaving the other evening." He reiterated, "That's life"

Both long time friends were quiet for a few minutes, each busy with his own thoughts. Eventually Campbell lifted his head and looking at Ian, he spoke again, "While Cassandra was here, she told me I should let go of what was too painful to hang onto." With a sigh of regret, he said. "I reasoned that I had already done that but I believe her advice is still good for me. Maybe learning to let go of pain is just an ongoing part of living."

Ian tapped his pencil calmly and deliberately on the desk. "I agree with the advice, but I believe what's good for you is Cassandra herself."

Without saying what was on his mind, Campbell looked at Ian for a moment and then averted his eyes before Ian had a chance to read anything into his expression. He agreed with Ian and knew how he felt about Cassandra. He just didn't know how strong her feelings were for him.

CHAPTER 17

Mrs. Devitte's Cat

The warm breeze that rustled in the leaves of the trees at Campbell's back didn't ease his mind, nor did the warmth of the sun ease his tension. The news of Amanda's involvement in murder kept haunting him.

He wondered how long she had had a relationship with Ricer. Campbell knew Slone was a womanizer but also knew Amanda made herself an easy target with the kind of lifestyle she led. Since he and Amanda had separated three years earlier, he had only seen her one other time. That was when she had dropped by his office to have him sign off on a car he bought her while they where still married. At the time, she told him she wanted to sell the car and move to Texas where she had a job waiting for her. She hadn't told him what her job would be and he hadn't cared or bothered to ask. Since he'd found out that Ricer was making monthly trips to Texas, he could only speculate that Amanda's job down there also had something to do with Slone.

Detective Harris said she had asked for him but he didn't even want to see her, let alone advise her. He firmly dismissed the guilt he was feeling. He didn't believe in her and would not be a good defense lawyer for her. She would just have to find other counsel that didn't involve him.

As he walked down the sidewalk to collect his morning newspaper, he heard Mrs. Devitte's gentle voice call to him from her yard. She was a fragile woman who stood up where she had been plucking flowers from her garden. She lifted a slender hand to the brim of her straw hat and called, "Campbell is that you?"

Campbell waved and walked toward her at the far edge of his yard. "Mrs. Devitte, you're out early this morning."

"I'm in charge of arranging centerpieces for the senior citizen dinner tonight." Bending into the flowers again and snipping stems she said, "I saw Amanda the other evening."

Campbell's mind raced back to Monday evening when Amanda had come by and asked him to reconcile. Although he had heard she was back in town, he had been surprised to see her at his front door. When she first left town, it felt as though someone had lifted a huge weight off his shoulders. Life had been so much easier, less stressful when he didn't have the risk of running into Amanda around town. Although he had wished it would stay that way, since her return that hope had melted away as quickly as a block of ice left out on a sidewalk on a summer day. Thoughts of Amanda only distressed Campbell. "Yes, she stopped by only for a moment," Campbell replied with a strained smile on his face.

The elderly woman discerned Campbell's painful expression. "I'm not one to pry into my neighbors affairs. I only saw Amanda because I was out looking for Scarlet O'Hara."

"No, of course not," Campbell said while collecting himself, as he didn't want to upset his dear little neighbor. "I didn't think that of you at all."

"I wouldn't want anything to happen to my cat and I always keep her in at nights." Mrs. Devitte smiled with amusement. "I'd just gotten home from the Senior Citizen Sunday Night Social and when I opened the door that cat slipped right out!" She cut more flowers and laid them in a basket. "I didn't want to worry about her all night so I went out looking for her."

Campbell considered her words for a long moment. "That must have been the night Scarlet O'Hara came over to visit me."

"That pesky cat!" said Mrs. Devitte. "Next time she does that, just shoo her home!"

"I've never been very successful at herding cats, but I'll do my best." Campbell smiled, then excused himself, "I'm running late this morning and need to be on my way." Before leaving he added, "Your flowers in the basket are going to make some very striking centerpieces."

Mrs. Devitte smiled up at him. "Thank you. You're a very kind neighbor."

Campbell dug in his pocket for his car keys as he walked back across his yard. It was only after he was sitting in his car that he started to sort out his thoughts. <u>Amanda was at his house Monday but Mrs. Devitte said she saw her Sunday.</u>

At first, he thought the elderly woman had gotten her days mixed up. He then realized that couldn't be the case since Mrs. Devitte had spoken of just returning from a Sunday social. Sunday evening was also when her lost cat had found its way to his back door.

All the evidence pointed to Amanda as the person who was in his house Sunday evening. Since there was no forced entry, he was certain <u>she still had her house key</u> and had used it to get in. He should have changed his locks as he had meant to and just never had gotten around to it.

Campbell climbed out of his car and headed back to the house. When inside, he went straight to the cabinet and opened the safe that was inside it. He stared at the disarray of the contents and fought down the emotions that threatened to overwhelm him. Amanda knew the combination and he was now convinced that she definitely was the one in his house Sunday. His eyes grew fiery, and his mouth hardened. Without a doubt, <u>he knew she was looking for the insurance policy for Slone.</u>

The list was a long one, lying, adultery, illegal entry, theft, attempted murder and he didn't know what else she had been involved in with Slone. As Campbell sat back in a chair, his shoulders slumped, weighed down by the memory of a woman whom he once thought he had loved. How could he have been so blind to her true character?

A thought struck him then, one so terrible that it froze him where he sat. When Matt had asked him if he had gotten his message, Campbell had thought he was inquiring about the one he had left the previous week. Matt had said something about a first message—was there a second one? If there was another message—what had happened to it? More importantly, were there other messages, possibly one from Cassandra that he hadn't gotten?

Campbell pushed himself from the chair and hurried to the kitchen to check his voice mail—nothing! Picking up the receiver, he brought up the menu and then pressed the button for the call log. As he scrolled down the missed calls, he came across Matt's name and number. He did call! The date showed his brother had placed the call that same Sunday evening his house had been broken into.

Campbell scrolled to the next phone number—it was Cassandra's number! He felt an uncontrollable emotion boil up from inside himself while he stood staring at the little blue glowing letters with Sunday's date below it. Cassandra had called and someone had erased her message! Amanda was the only one who could have done it! She had erased all the messages, and why? Campbell continued to scroll though the list of phone calls on the call log. He then saw the call Amanda had made from the pay phone and the time indicating that she had called while he was at the store. It was clear to him that she had called ahead of time to be sure he was not at home. In the process of hiding her deceitfulness, she had erased all of his messages and given herself away. Amanda walked in, went though everything like a common thief, and then returned the next evening to try to seduce him. Was he that blind to think he could ever have found something of any value in Amanda?

All along, he thought Cassandra was the one who had distanced herself from him. A terrible sense of foreboding had begun to fill his mind. What must Cassandra be thinking of him for not returning her call?

All week long, his thoughts were about her no matter how busy he kept himself and the memory of her popped into his mind constantly. <u>He missed her</u>, but now he wondered if he had let her slip away!

He felt an ache in his chest when he realized that perhaps he couldn't love her back, not the way she ought to be loved. Regardless, he knew what he felt for her, that it was real love and that he needed to see her again. He grabbed for the receiver to call her and then placed it back on its cradle. After a moment of thought, he picked it up again and dialed his office.

"Paula, I won't be coming into the office today. I'm heading out of town a day earlier than planned. Can you handle everything?"

Paula assured him everything would be fine, "I think all of Dean's cases have been taken care of. Ian was already here this morning and told me that if Harlan brings you anymore of Dean's work to let him know, so he can help you cover it. I don't think you have to concern yourself about it anyway. Penny, Harlan's secretary, said he called and said he wouldn't be in for the rest of the week and all of next week. So we'll see you Monday?"

"Yes, Monday. Wait, I don't know for sure. If I won't be back Monday, then I'll call and let you know."

He went to his room and pulled out a bag. As he packed, he thought how he felt about Cassandra, but he didn't want to tell her over the phone. This had to be said in person, where he could see her face, her eyes, and know if he had a chance.

He picked up the canvas he had painted for her, and before wrapping it, he took a long hard look at it. He whispered. "Give me time, Cassandra." He laid the canvas down and pulled the brown wrapping paper over it. "<u>Give me time to find a way to tell you what I want you to know</u>."

CHAPTER 18

Turning of Shadows

It was exactly twelve thirty as Campbell arrived at the city limits of his hometown. It still had its small town atmosphere. He drove past the park with its tall pine trees and well-maintained flowerbeds. Two story buildings lined the business section with the usual array of grocery stores, drugstore, boutiques, post office, and restaurants.

He glanced at the business card Cassandra had given him the first night they were together. According to the card, he was only a couple of blocks from her office. Campbell's heart began to beat faster wondering how receptive Cassandra would be to his showing up unannounced. He drove a little further down the street towards the bank, notable for its prominent clock tower. To the far side of the bank he saw her office, and neatly painted in white letters across the front window read, "Cassandra Evans-Certified Public Accountant". Parking in a convenient space available just across the street from her door, Campbell prepared himself for their meeting.

Campbell stepped into an office with thickly carpeted floors and sound deadening ceiling tiles. He saw to his right a waiting area with a contemporary casual sofa and chair grouping. To his left, sitting behind a desk was a young receptionist with short blond hair and blue eyes. To Campbell she had appeared to be in her early twenties or maybe even fresh out of high school.

As he moved her direction, she smiled and asked. "May I help you?" When he told her he was there to see Cassandra, she inquired if he had an appointment. After hearing his answer she apologetically said, "She went home for lunch."

Campbell was familiar with the street Cassandra lived on and would have no problem locating it. He did feel by having her exact address it would make it easier to find though. He lightly thrummed his fingers on the desk. "I take it you won't tell me where home is?"

The young receptionist's face turned red from embarrassment. "I'm so sorry, but she'll be back at one o'clock. You can wait or come back later."

After he left the office, Campbell drove directly to the street he had remembered as the one where Cassandra lived. Fortunately, right after he had turned the corner onto the street, he recognized Cassandra's car parked in the driveway of a white frame house. Two stories high, it boasted a wrap-around porch and green-shuttered windows. He thought there was a Victorian grace to the old house as he parked in the drive next to her car. Climbing the steps, he noticed colorful pots of geraniums grouped near the door and at the far end of the porch, white wicker chairs with bright, colorful pillows. Very inviting he thought, and hoped Cassandra would be as inviting. Nervously he knocked and then waited, shifting from foot to foot.

Within a few moments Cassandra opened the door, startled, her hand flew to the row of buttons on her blouse. At last, her hand fluttered outward and she stammered in her gentle voice, "Campbell?" Then as if to assure herself that she was awake, and was really seeing him standing at her door, she repeated, "Campbell!"

Campbell tried to read the expression on her face and wasn't sure. He knew she was unprepared for his presence but couldn't discern if it was a happy shock or just a shock.

—

She was so adorable, so desirable in her surprise at his appearance that he had to fight the temptation to catch her in his arms, to tell her nothing in the world mattered now that he was there. Instead, afraid that would completely overwhelm her, he only spoke, "I know you weren't expecting me."

She regarded him mutely and then to his surprise, she smiled brilliantly. When Campbell saw her smile, the anxious look slowly faded from his face as he softly let out the tense breath he had been holding. He tried to dig in his brain to find the right words but ended up blurting out, "Cassandra I'm so sorry for not returning your call."

Her face flushed at once. Well, so much for finesse. He was already knee deep in it so he might as well bumble on, "I have to explain. I didn't know you called until this morning. When I found your call on my call log, I threw clothes in a bag and drove here as quickly as I could."

With quick understanding, she responded to him. "You think I'd get angry because you didn't return my call?" She brushed at her forehead as if a stray hair were getting in her way. "I'm not going to say I wasn't disappointed, but I wasn't angry with you." She stared at him, still obviously struggling to pull herself together. "I shouldn't have assumed—just that I thought—." He waited for her to collect her thoughts. Rather, she pulled on his arm. "Please, come in, here you come to see me and I let you stand outside."

He stepped in and paused in the open door peering in, taking a minute to absorb the sights, sounds, and scents. She drew him on into a neat front hallway and passed a long mahogany table that held a single lamp and a group of small pictures. She said not a word more, but guided him down the hallway and into the kitchen.

Cassandra moved efficiently around the kitchen, while Campbell intently watched her face as she made small talk. Although the light in her eyes, her quick smile, and the animation in her expression were charming, he got the sense she was concealing her true feelings.

She poured two cups of tea from a yellow teapot and carried them from the kitchen into a gaily-decorated sun porch at the back of the house. There she pressed him into a cushioned love seat and position herself on the matching footstool. She avoided his eyes and busied herself by brushing at her lap to smooth a winkle from her skirt.

He sat and simply looked at her for a moment. "Can I ask you a question?" He used his fingers, firm and reassuring, to turn her face toward his. He gathered his brows tightly over curious eye. "You really think I forgot about you? You were my first thought in the morning and last thought before I went to sleep at night. Cassandra, all that matters to me is you and me, our relationship."

Although Cassandra didn't reply, he could tell she was considering his words. She looked troubled and he smoothed his hand gently up her arms to quell her agitation. "I need to say something to you." He paused and looked a little embarrassed. "When I thought you had not called my first impulse was to call you immediately but I wanted to give you time. I wanted to talk to you but it's just that—I wasn't sure about how you felt about things—about me."

Cassandra interrupted him, "Campbell, what you need to know is that on the day I left your house I stopped at a convenience store before leaving town. A woman I didn't know followed me into the restrooms and told me she was your wife."

Campbell's pulse raced as an icy finger of dread hurried down the ridge of his spine. "Amanda?"

Cassandra looked at him with pleading eyes. "I can only assume she was Amanda. She told me you and she were trying to restore your marriage. She threatened me and told me I should stay away from you."

Campbell was aghast at the thought of Cassandra being put in such jeopardy and could only wonder if there was finally to be an end to Amanda's menace. He took Cassandra by the shoulders and looked into her eyes. "What Amanda said is not true! Rather, it's one more of her fantasies that has led her to her own demise."

Campbell told her how Amanda broke into his house, her involvement with Slone Ricer, and her intent to kill Susanna Bishop. Cassandra looked at him with alarm, speechless.

She tentatively stretched her arm out to touch the side of his face. "Campbell, I'm so sorry you had to go through all of this. When you didn't call, I wanted to call but—." She paused and looked down at her hands. "I need to ask. Where is Amanda now? I mean is she in jail?" Her eyes now focused on his as she spoke emphatically "My feelings for you have not changed."

With her words, Campbell's heart turned over. It was an incredible feeling, a quick pang in his chest that left him spinning. He put his arm around her waist and with a gentle tug, he pulled her from the footstool until she fell next to him into the shelter of his arms. He then kissed her with every ounce of pent-up energy inside himself.

For Cassandra, dreadful thoughts fell behind her. His kisses made everything all right. The intimacy of the gesture warmed her face. She was blushing like a teenager, a becoming pink that heightened the brilliance of her eyes, eyes no longer filled with tears.

The hand he had been pressing against her back now stroked her hair. "When I discovered you called and I didn't return the call, I was heartsick. I drove here as soon as I could and hoped you would forgive me." He laughed shortly. "I feel fortunate you even let me in your house."

She sat back and studied his face. Then with amusement written on her face she said, "You thought I'd kick you out of my house?"

"No, you're too nice, but I would have deserved it. This makes twice. Not only did I not return your call, I stood you up on our first date." Her smile faded as she continued to look in his eyes.

Answering the question he knew was still on her mind, "Yes," he said. "Amanda was arrested earlier this week and will be detained until a bond is set. I'm not even sure if they will let her out on bail or not. It all remains to be seen and will be up to the judge." Campbell pressed his brow and signed. "They have some serious charges against her with a lot of evidence both corroborating and direct. To be honest, I think she would be considered a flight risk."

"How do you feel about her situation, about her?" Cassandra asked.

Campbell looked at her for a long moment, considering his answer. "Amanda has made some unwise decisions that have caused her problems. I only wonder if I could have helped her and done something differently a long time ago to prevent this. However, I have no desire to go to her rescue now and won't even consider being her lawyer or in any way involving myself in her case. She is no longer my responsibility and I know that now."

Cassandra covered his hand with hers. "Campbell, you have to consider, some of us unexpectedly get caught in things that are out of our control. An example would be a rainstorm. Whether we get just a little wet or completely drenched may depend on where we happen to be standing when the rain begins to fall. To what extent we are personally affected is often a matter of timing and circumstances over which we may have little or no control."

Before continuing, she studied him, indecisive about being critical of his ex-wife, but after a long moment continued, "Amanda's situation was different. She had control." While still holding his hand Cassandra cupped it in both of hers. "Imagine, a man who by choice, neither eats properly nor gets sufficient rest. Eventually it leads to serious health problems. Should he blame others? No, the man has merely reaped the bitter consequences of his own poor judgment. We should not be quick to blame those around us for every adversity we experience." Campbell nodded his head in agreement. She could see his eyes light from within as his understanding of her words freed him from the last vestiges of guilt concerning Amanda.

He then pulled her into an embrace with a ferocity that almost alarmed her. "It sickens me to think of the risk all of this has put you in! I'm so sorry for putting you through this."

"I admit once I got home I was reluctant about calling you, but I called anyway. Before I left, you had asked me to call and so I did. When you never returned my call, I was apprehensive about making a second call." Campbell could hear a quaver in her voice. "Not because I doubted you. I didn't know Amanda or know what she was capable of or not capable of doing. I was not only concerned for my own safety but also for yours."

Campbell pressed his brow while trying to work things out in his brain. He didn't know how long Amanda had been stalking his house, but he was sure she was watching the evening Cassandra stayed there. "Amanda must have seen you at the house and followed you when you left." He held her hands and squeezed them tight. "You trusted me! I can't apologize enough."

"Campbell, you have nothing to apologize for. You had no control over Amanda's actions. Please, don't think this will keep me from putting my whole trust in you."

"Amanda is like a toxin and poisons everything she comes in contact with. The vexation she caused me was like carrying around a wet bag of sand."

Cassandra smiled at him whimsically and repeated, "A wet bag of sand?" Her hand covered her smile. "For a suave lawyer you sometimes have a funny way of expressing yourself."

With satisfaction at having lightened their conversation, he looked her up and down carefully. His eyes lingering for an extra moment or two on her face before he changed the conversation, "Your secretary said you came home for lunch. You have your lunch yet?"

"I just ate something simple." A smile stretched across her face. "So, you met Jelynn. She graduated from high school this spring and plans to attend collage this fall. She'll only be working for me through the summer. Was she nice?"

"Yes, she was very nice, and spoke in that precise, high-pitched voice secretaries tend to use when they are talking to people who are slightly retarded, inebriated, or otherwise incapacitated."

Cassandra eyed Campbell curiously. "She did?"

He threw his head back and laughed. "No, I only wanted to get a reaction from you." Absurdly pleased that he still could razz her, he suppressed his laughter. "She was nice and very professional."

Cassandra smiled and watched him in his delight. His eyes were so full of delight and desire that he made her heart pound. "Campbell, I'm glad you came and it feels so nice to have you here. I've missed you."

He took her in his arms and closed his eyes. He breathed in her familiar scent, moving his lips down her cheek to her neck. He tipped her head at an angle that made his next kiss, a kiss on her lips, intense. While still embracing her, he laid his head against the back of the sofa as Cassandra silently rested her head in the curve of his arm. She found comfort in his embrace. His voice was deep and lazy as he asked, "You have to go back to work soon?"

Without moving, and still in the protection of his arm she answered, "I've one appointment I can't put off, and after that, the rest of my day is free." She didn't want to return to work and then wondered how much more time she would have with him. "How long are you planning on staying?"

Still with his arm around her and without looking at her, he answered nonchalantly, "Forever."

"Campbell, you're a tease!"

"Actually, I came to invite you to dinner at my brother's house this Friday so I'll be staying through the weekend."

Cassandra's heart leaped. "You'll be here all weekend?"

"All weekend. I'll be staying at my parents' house. Matt always wants me to stay with him, but I like spending time at the old place."

"Were you serious about your brother having a dinner party or were you still being a tease?"

"No, I wasn't teasing. He and his wife, Jennifer, invited me to dinner. I wanted to ask you to go with me as my date. I'll pick you up." He hesitated. "That is, if you don't already have plans."

She giggled. "I'll have to check my calendar." After she let a moment pass she added, "If I did have plans, I'd be sure to cancel them. You would have to come first."

The thought of Cassandra considering him that important made him feel absurdly happy. Smiling, he smoothed her hair and toyed with a curl for a long while before he spoke again.

"While you're back at your office, I'll go over to the old house and get settled in. My brother doesn't expect me in until tomorrow, so I'll stop by his place and let him know I'm here." He turned and looked at her face. "Can we meet after that? I'd like to take you to dinner."

"Yes, that would be nice and I will look forward to it, but why don't you let me cook dinner for us here?"

"No, I want to take you out, but I'll take a rain check for tomorrow? I like eating home cooked food as long it's not my own."

"Since I have Jelynn to schedule appointments, I'll take tomorrow off. I'm hoping to keep this afternoon appointment short." Cassandra massaged her temples. "Do you remember Tom Larson, from high school?"

Campbell grew tense with the sound of Tom's name and hoped Cassandra didn't notice. "I do, he was a grade ahead of me."

—

"He's the one I'm meeting with." She drank the last of her tea, returned the cup to its saucer, and leaned back in the curve of Campbell's arm. "He's in trouble with the IRS and he expects me to work miracles. He'll be upset when he hears how much money he'll have to come up with for them."

Campbell reflected on Matt's version of why Cassandra was with Tom. It made perfectly good sense! She was having a business luncheon with him. Ah, the joys of an older brother. I'm going to kill Matt. I'm not going to kill him dead. Rather I want him to know why he is dying!

Keeping his expression bland, Campbell nodded. "While in high school, Tom ran with an unfavorable crowd. His trouble with the IRS is no surprise."

"I remember how he and his friends stood around the drug store and made cat calls to any girl who walked past," she said. "He intimidated me then and still makes me uncomfortable today."

Campbell squeezed her and pulled her in a little closer. "During one of the school's baseball games, Tom was pushing his weight around with Steve Pace. After the game, Steve and I along with Mitch Denison locked Tom in the outhouse."

Cassandra clapped a hand over her mouth. "Was that you? That story went around the whole school for a long time. Nobody ever knew who did it."

"Do you remember the way they always put those portable potties out by the parking lot?" Campbell chuckled. "We were one of the last to leave the game. As we were rounding the bleachers, we saw Tom pull his car right up to one of them and hurry into it. Mitch came up with the idea, and without a thought, I jumped in Tom's car, pulled it into gear, and steered while Mitch and Steve pushed. Without Tom knowing, we backed it within an inch of the outhouse door. We took off running and never stopped until we reached Kelso's Five and Dime on Main Street!' We sure took a chance, if Tom had caught us, the three of us would have died that very night!" Campbell paused to laugh and to wipe at one corner of his eye with his forefinger. "I'm not sure how long he was detained, but rumor has it, he was stuck there until the night watchmen found him."

—

211

Cassandra turned his direction and fell against him laughing. "I heard he was there for two or three hours!" she finally managed to gasp.

Campbell liked the way she looked at him, approving, and admiring. He found himself feeling energized around her. Amanda had always made him feel deflated, his ego bruised and sore. He began to expand on his deeds with the despised Tom Larson.

"Another time Mitch got to him was the summer Tom's father made him get a job. Tom pumped gas at Maxwell's gas station where Mitch knew the mechanic. The mechanic told Mitch about a Morgan Roadster sports car he had done some repairs on. They were waiting for the owner, who was British and from out of town, to pick it up. They didn't know when he would be back in town but they were expecting him in the next day or so."

"Just about closing time that same day Mitch saw Tom working alone so he called the station from a pay phone right cross the street. With his best British accent, he told Tom he was the owner of the car. He really wanted to pick it up that evening but he was a couple of hours away. If Tom would keep the station open until he got in town, he would make it worth his time. He made the promise of a hundred dollar tip." Campbell leaned his head back with laughter. "A hundred dollars back then was a lot of money for a teenager. Tom was so greedy he played right into Mitch's hands."

Cassandra adored Campbell's rich laugh and could not remember seeing him as relaxed and cheerful as he was then. Watching him with his delight in his tales, she admired his broad forehead and strong jaw line. Her heart was full of love for him.

With amusement still in his eyes, Campbell shook his head. "That Mitch was crazy but sure gave us a laugh. He kept driving past the station just to see how long Tom would wait for the phantom Englishman. By midnight, we got tired of watching and headed home. On our last trip pass the station, we saw Tom walking aimlessly around the pumps and watching down the street. Mitch waved as we drove by and Tom waved back. Tom's wave wasn't what you would call a friendly wave."

"Oh no!" Cassandra exclaimed. "Do you think Tom knew it was Mitch who made the call?"

"No, Tom always waved to Mitch that way." Campbell took Cassandra's hand and spread his finger out to match hers. "I could almost feel bad for what we did, but Tom was such a spiteful person back then."

"Campbell, how am I ever going to look at Tom without thinking of what you guys did to him and keep from laughing?"

Campbell gave her one more squeeze then stood with his cup and took hers to carry back to the kitchen. "I guess that comes with the job." He smiled back at her. "If it's any help, I'll be thinking of you all the time."

Cassandra stood and followed him. "Did you know Mitch is a funeral director now? His sister who was in my grade told me he's married with one child and lives back east."

Campbell placed the cups in the sink and leaned against the counter with his hands in his pocket. "No, I didn't know that, but I'm not surprised. Although Mitch was a prankster, he was a kind person with a lot of good qualities. If he was tough enough to keep Tom from getting to him, he'd be strong enough to offer a little comfort to those who have lost loved ones in death. I think his compassion for people is what made him go after Tom. He hated the way he treated Steve Pace and others like him and was compelled to do something about it."

Campbell looked down at the floor. "You know Steve Pace was killed while in the Marines?"

Cassandra leaned on the counter next to him. "No, I didn't know that. I'm glad he had a friend like Mitch."

Campbell put his arm across her shoulders. "I'm glad too."

After a long moment passed, Cassandra spoke again. "I hate the fact that I have to go back to work and leave you. Especially with you only being here until Sunday."

"I'll be back." He turned and embraced her. "One of the hardest things I've done in my life was to let you go the day you left to come home. I didn't want you to go. I wanted you to stay—just to be with me." His eyes found hers and he seemed to drink her in with great pleasure.

Her lips trembled and then broke into a tremulous smile. "Campbell," she whispered as if his name were a prayer. She spoke so softly he barely heard, "I think I would have stayed."

WHEN CAMPBELL ARRIVED at his brother's house after parting from Cassandra, he called out as he entered the front door. He heard Matt's voice come from the direction of the kitchen. "I'm back here making coffee. We weren't expecting you until tomorrow."

As Campbell entered that room, he saw his brother standing at the kitchen counter with his back toward him. Unlike his regular T-shirt and jeans, he was wearing khaki trousers with a real button-down-the-front shirt.

After a lot of time and self-discipline, Matt had earned his engineering degree and now worked for Addison as their City Engineer. Matt was easy going, craved stability, and enjoyed comfort. All of which made him a great husband and father. He was also an incredible provider for Jennifer and the girls. His older brother was very proud of Matt.

Matt partly turned as he measured coffee from a small blue canister. "I just got off work. I'll have us a cup of coffee in a minute."

Campbell walked over and slapped his brother on the back. "How's work? They treating you good down at City Hall?'

"They keep us busy, but not as busy as you've been." He gestured Campbell to a chair. "I read a couple of articles in the City Tribune that mentioned Hendricks, the firm you work for."

"I know. It's a long story and I'll have to tell you all about it later." Campbell pulled out the chair. "Where are Jennifer and the kids?"

Jennifer is picking the girls up from daycare. They should be here anytime. Are you just getting into town?"

"I've been here since noon. I came over early to see Cassandra Evans."

"Cassandra Evans—really," Matt said, as he lowered his brows ominously. "She's not hooked up with Larson?"

A soft scrape sounded in the doorway of the kitchen and both men turned to see Jennifer.

"No, Matt, she's not with Larson!" Jennifer said. "Give Cassandra more credit than that! I hardly know her but I do know her enough to know she wouldn't want anything to do with the likes of Tom Larson."

Jennifer walked over to where Campbell sat. "It's so good to see you and you're looking well." He stood and greeted her with a quick hug.

"Campbell, do not pay any attention to anything your brother tells you!" She stood next to Matt and pressed a hello kiss on him, then punched him in the shoulder. "He's worse than a gossipy old lady who never gets the facts right!"

Campbell thought about his earlier plans of severely punishing his brother, but after he saw Jennifer doing it for him, he dropped the idea all together.

Matt with his right arm around Jennifer's waist pulled her tight against him. "Yeah, but you love me that way."

Jennifer held Matt's hand reaching across and catching his hand as he had rested it on her hip. "Tom Larson would like for Cassandra to go out with him, but she knows he's a jerk!"

Matt nodded. "I think he's been after her since she came back to town. He's already been married a half a dozen times."

Jennifer placed three clean cups from the dishwasher next to the coffee pot, before putting away the rest of the dishes. "He can't keep a wife because he's not a nice person. Cassandra is only doing some accounting work for him. You can bet that's no picnic for her."

Matt grabbed the basket full of utensils from the dishwasher and started sorting silverware into a drawer. "So Campbell, are you "dating" Cassandra?"

Campbell's face warmed and he could feel it radiate from him like heat from a stove. "I don't know if you can call it that, but we spent some time together when she was in the city for a conference. Ian's wife, Barbara, was at the same conference and invited her for dinner one evening, along with me." He laughed quietly. "It was a very pleasant surprise for me and—well, she hasn't thrown me out of her life yet."

Matt held a fork to examine it before tossing it back into the basket. "I know my brother he has always been one who would never kiss and tell."

Jennifer closed the dishwasher door and sat at the table across from Campbell. She propped her fist against her chin. "Although there are a few available suitors in town, Cassandra hasn't shown any interest in any of them. Like I say, I really don't know her, but

I think she's been using the time to deal with the death of her husband and child. It has had to be terrible for her."

Jennifer leaned back in her chair, crossed her arms, and fixed her sharp eyes on him. "Campbell, if you have caught Cassandra Evans' attention, she must think you're something special. She strikes me as a real lady."

Matt poured coffee and brought the cups to the table. "Any woman who can't see how special my older brother is has to be crazy or blind."

Campbell's heart nearly burst from Jennifer's words and he derived encouragement from them. He knew he was in love with Cassandra, but was not sure of the way she felt for him. He looked down to keep Jennifer from reading his eyes and was glad for Matt's distraction.

Matt still standing, sipped at his coffee. "Tom Larson won't be happy when he finds out he has some competition. Watch your back. I think he's unstable and I don't trust him even a little bit."

"Uncle Campbell!"

Campbell turned to see his three and five year old nieces running toward him. Madison, the five year old climbed on his lap with little effort, while Natalie struggled. Campbell pulled her up on his lap next to Madison. "Hey, do I know you? What did you do with my two favorite nieces, Madison and Natalie?"

Madison's eyes opened wide. "Uncle Campbell, it's us!"

Campbell feigned surprise. "Well, I guess it is! You both have grown so big I hardly recognized you!"

Madison was jumping on his lap. "Uncle Campbell, you're funny!"

Campbell laughed and pulled them close. "I need a big hug!"

With her face only inches from Campbell's, Natalie asked. "Did you bring us a prize?"

"Yes I did, but you'll have to wait until tomorrow." Campbell looked at Matt. "I forgot their surprise back at the old house."

Matt bent down, tweaked Natalie's cheek, and patted Madison fondly on the top of her head. "Campbell, you don't have to bring them something each time you visit."

Natalie held her arms out for Matt to take her. He swung her in the air before standing her on the floor. She hurried to Jennifer to sit in her lap. "How does the old place look?" Matt asked. "I haven't driven out there in awhile."

Campbell took Madison's toy car and ran it across her arms and neck until she shrugged and giggled. "Things look good. Bob and Nell are doing a nice job of keeping the old place up."

Matt nodded. "They do well, but I sure would like to see it occupied. I know how much you always liked it there and still hope someday you'll consider moving back."

"It would be good to have you around," Jennifer said. "Ever since Carl Bonnell retired, Addison has been without a really good attorney.

"What about Howard Gregory," Campbell asked. "And Terrance Miller—didn't he just open his practice?"

"Gregory should have retired a long time ago," Matt said. "It takes him too long to get anything done. Terrance—he just plain does a poor job."

Madison bounded from Campbell's lap and rushed out the back door. Matt grabbed Natalie before she escaped past him. "Where are your shoes? You're not going anywhere until you get them on!" He tucked her under his arm like a football. "Sorry Campbell, I'll be right back. I have some shoes to locate."

Campbell turned to Jennifer. "I can't believe Carl retired. He and Dad were good friends for years. Did you know his father served in the Air Corps with Granddad?"

"Yes, Matt told me your families go back a long ways." After a moment, she asked, "Are you staying for dinner tonight?"

"No, thanks anyway—I'm taking Cassandra out to dinner."

"You do know you can bring her here Friday night for dinner?"

He smiled. "I do know, and already asked her, and she accepted."

"I'm glad to know you are friends with her. I think she has needed someone for a long time, it just took her awhile to find that out for herself."

Jennifer reached over and touched Campbell's hand. "You shouldn't let Matt make you feel badly about not moving home. Although, it would be nice to have you back here, Matt understands you have a satisfying practice and a house that has been your home for a long time. Your happiness is what matters most to us."

A great swell of sadness swept up from inside Campbell when he thought of how Amanda had dashed all his plans to pieces. Although it had taken Cassandra in his life before he could truly get over the way Amanda had tossed away their marriage like a piece of rubbish, her involvement in murder and threatening Cassandra still pained him. It seemed the whole affair had changed his view of his work, his home and even of himself. How could he have been such a fool? He knew he had to be honest with himself now and admit he needed to get out from under the weight of the negative things in his shattered world, in order to make room for what was positive. He wanted to make room for Cassandra, and it was only a matter of finding a way to accomplish the changes.

Jennifer studied him with narrowed eyes. "I think the years I have lived with Matt classify me as an expert in the study of the Mallary men's underlying feelings. Right now, I am looking at a certain man who is crazy about a woman. I can feel your love for her working below the surface and about ready to burst forth."

He glanced at her in surprise. "Jennifer you amaze me." He laughed lightly. "I wish you could look in your crystal ball and tell me how Cassandra feels about me."

She looked at him over the rim of her coffee cup. "Could a woman be in love with a man and not know it? I have seen it before. You may be the one that has to make it happen and the one who is going to make the dreams come true." She returned her cup to the table. "It is up to you, Campbell. If love is in your grasp, reach out and grab on to it."

Campbell regarded her thoughtfully. "I think you're right. I need to reach out with all the strength I have."

CHAPTER 19

Crossing Oceans

Matt greeted Cassandra graciously and led her and Campbell along a rosewood paneled hall to the back of the house. Soon they were out on a patio, built of stone that glowed in the flickering light of tea lights in terra cotta jars. Here Matt introduced Cassandra to Jennifer. With flattering warmth, Jennifer advanced and extended her hand. "Cassandra, I'm very glad to meet you at last."

Campbell's heart skipped at the thought of Cassandra's presence with his closest family members. He could only wonder if that was the way his father had felt, the first time he had brought his mother home to meet the family.

"Campbell, they told me you would be here!" Campbell turned to see an older man with commanding eyes, firm jaw, and a shock of black hair beginning to show streaks of iron gray.

"Carl Bonnell!" He gripped the older man's hand warmly. "Good to see you. They tell me you have officially retired."

The older man answered in the affirmative, "Yes, I finally did." He put his arm out to a fragile woman who came and stood next to him. "Ruby has been after me to retire for a long while."

Ruby responded, "Campbell, how nice to see you again."

"I don't know if you know Cassandra Evens." Campbell lightly placed his hand on Cassandra's back. "This is Carl Bonnell and his wife Ruby."

Carl smiled at Cassandra. "Oh yes, I knew this dear lady as a child and she just recently did some financial planning for us."

Ruby took Cassandra's hand. "My dear, it's always a pleasure to see you. I just saw your aunt Pam the other day at the post office. She is looking very well."

Cassandra smiled pleasantly. "Yes, that must have been the same day we met for lunch. Aunt Pam told me she had seen you just that morning and that you both had a very nice visit."

Carl's level eyes sought Cassandra with warm friendliness, and he gestured toward Campbell. "Don't let this amiable fellow's pleasant face and polite words camouflage his steel-trap legal mind."

Campbell laughed with boyish jubilance. "Thank you. A compliment coming from someone like you means a lot."

Between narrowed lids, Carl's brilliant eyes met Campbell's eyes. "That was no compliment. It's the truth!"

Matt carried over a tray of cheese tapas and sat it on a table, festively covered with a bright yellow tablecloth. In the center sat a white basket filled with assorted pink and yellow daisies mixed with tulips, carnations, and little white monte casinos.

Carl reached for one of the tapas. "Carl, you've already had two of those", Ruby lightly scolded. "I don't want you to end up like that poor George Larson."

Carl laughed and kissed the top of Ruby's hand. "I guess that's what I love about this woman. She takes good care of me."

"That's all right Carl, the good stuff is coming later," Campbell said as he took an hors d'oeuvre for Cassandra and one for himself. "I think my sister-in-law is a very fine chef, and we have my brother to thank for not keeping Jennifer's cooking all to himself."

Matt leaned against the railing that ran the length of the patio. "George Larson is a pretty decent, likable man. He's been on that ventilator at home, with a private nurse watching over him for some time. Has his doctor determined if he'll ever get off of it?"

"You haven't heard?" Carl asked. "George's nurse found him dead early this morning. They think someone unplugged his ventilator."

Matt stood up with a jerk. "Unplugged, how could that have happened?"

Campbell glanced over at Cassandra. She sat motionless, and by the stressed look on her face, he knew her thoughts were on Tom Larson, George's son and the time she had spent consulting with him. Campbell moved closer to her, stood behind her, and placed his hands on her shoulders. He felt her draw in a shaky breath as if shivering at the memory. As she reached up and laid her hand on his, he felt her relax again.

"How did it happen?" Matt repeated.

Carl pursed his lips. "They don't think it was an accident. Someone had tampered with the alarm on the ventilator and George's gold watch was missing, along with some of his dead wife's jewelry." He paused and rubbed his chin thoughtfully. "Both Tom, George's son, and the nurse said they were asleep and didn't hear anything."

Matt settled back comfortably on the railing and folded his arms. "They have any suspicions as to who may have done it?"

"I'm not sure," Carl said. "If they do, they are not saying anything or I believe I would have heard about it."

Campbell asked. "Did anyone else have anything missing, or was it only George and his wife's things that were stolen? Any household valuables missing?"

Carl's eyes slowly focused on Campbell and then he nodded. "Yes," he said. "Yes, the only things missing belonged to George and his wife."

Campbell's thoughts swung to the previous evening when he had seen Tom Larson what must have been just hours before his father's death. He and Cassandra had stopped for a drink at Bella's Wine Bar. Right after they arrived, he had noticed Tom sitting alone at the bar. When Tom glanced up, Campbell gave him a silent nod. Tom looked annoyed as he quickly turned his back to Campbell and swilled the last of his drink. Campbell had just reasoned that the guy had always had a chip on his shoulder and still lacked manners. No doubt, nothing had softened Tom's disposition since the last time Campbell had seen him.

After the server had seated Cassandra and him at a corner table, Tom had stood with his hands on his hips and looked Campbell's way with a sullen scowl on his face. He gritted his teeth, whirled and hurried out of the room, barely avoiding a collision with a passing server.

Cassandra had never seen Tom nor had even been aware he was at the club. After hearing the circumstances surrounding George's death, Campbell was glad of it.

Just then Jennifer announced dinner was about to be served, and the guests drifted toward the dining area. Campbell took Cassandra by the arm. "You doing okay?" he asked.

"I wasn't until after you came and sat with me. Everything's all right now."

"I hope this whole Larson situation didn't scare you."

"You were there before I had time to be too afraid, and then I wasn't afraid at all. Thank you for that. I feel infinitely grateful for your presence." Cassandra smiled up at him.

AFTER DINNER, Jennifer came over and sat down beside Campbell. She smiled and gestured toward Carl Bonnell who was occupying all of Cassandra's attention. "Campbell, I see Carl has taken your date away from you."

Folding his arms, Campbell nodded and smiled. "Carl is a good person. I'm glad to see the way everyone here has welcomed Cassandra."

"Why wouldn't they? I liked her at once! She has a nice voice, beautiful eyes, and she sparkles."

Earlier in the evening, Jennifer had noticed Campbell standing behind Cassandra's chair, putting his wide hands on her shoulders and stroking the sides of her neck while teasing her. Cassandra had craned her head around to grin up at him. The affection between them was so obvious, the way they enjoyed each other and teased while using words with double meanings for things only the two of them understood.

Jennifer leaned back in her chair and glanced Cassandra's way. "I have to tell you at present, I'm seeing a woman absolutely in love with you."

Campbell grinned sheepishly. "I don't know. All I'm sure about is whenever I'm around her, I'm happier than I've been in long time." He laughed shortly. "I can stand in a courtroom and deliberate in front of a judge and jury all day, but when I'm around Cassy, I stumble over my words like a tongue-tied teenager."

"Campbell Mallary stumbling over his words, image that!" Jennifer leaned toward him, her arms folded on the table. "Your first day here, Matt and I could see how happy you were."

"I can't understand what happened, but I do know my life is in need of a change"

Her eyes were tender with sympathy. "Through no fault of your own, you've had a rough go of it. You did the best you could. It's time for a change, a time for you to find some happiness. I hope Cassandra is the one who can do that for you."

He drew in a breath of desperation. "I don't deserve her, but I need her."

Jennifer's mouth widened in a grin and then she said. "Don't you think that decision is up to Cassandra? Have you asked her?"

"Jennifer, you have always been a remarkable sister-in-law. I can't recall you ever handing out bad advice."

AFTER THE DINNER party, Campbell walked with Carl and Ruby to their car.

"Campbell, I didn't want to say anything in front of the others. When you asked for clarification of items taken from the Larson house, I knew what you were thinking. I believe we had the same thoughts, correct me if I'm wrong." Carl had a preoccupied frown on his face as he looked across the yard. "I'm referring to a common mistake thieves make. If someone were trying to make it appear a thief broke into their own house, usually it's not their own personal property that's missing. Rather, what's missing are items that belong to other members in the household."

Campbell nodded. "It seems Tom is the only other person who lives there and he didn't have anything of value stolen."

"The investigators always look at the family first, so I'm sure they'll check Tom out thoroughly." Carl paused in thought. "I'm not sure about a motive though. While he was alive, George gave Tom everything he ever needed or wanted."

"Unless Tom owed a lot of money," Campbell added hastily. "I knew George, and he always helped Tom in any way he could. However, when Tom got himself, in trouble that's where George drew the line. He'd make Tom work it out."

Carl laughed shortly. "That George was quite a character." He then narrowed his eyes. "You think Tom got himself in some sort of difficulty?"

"Cassandra told me Tom owed money to the IRS. Of course, she didn't and wouldn't say how much, but it sounded like a good amount."

Carl's steel, gray eyes widened. "Now, I know where you are coming from, that information could be corroborating evidence. If anything comes of this, Cassandra may be holding information needed to strengthen or supplement other evidence against Tom."

Campbell nodded in agreement. "Although you're retired, I think you're still in a position to hear it first. If it appears that the authorities need the evidence Cassandra holds, will you call me?"

"Yes, you know I will!" Carl said. "I'm still friends with the District Attorney and we have morning coffee together like always. I'll keep you up on the case and anything that transpires."

"Thanks Carl," Campbell replied with an anxious expression.

Carl laid his hand on Campbell's shoulder. "Don't worry. I can understand how you are feeling. If that happens, I'll advise Cassandra and give her counsel until you can get here."

"I don't want to impose on you, but you're someone I know I can depend on."

"No, don't ever think you're imposing. You're like family and I'm glad to help." Carl smiled and got into his car. "It would be good for our fair city to have someone with your skills practicing law here. When I started out, I was with a big firm as you are now. I have no regrets about moving back to Addison. Although it's a small town, I kept busy—too busy really." He reached over and took his wife's hand. "Ruby and I've been happy here and I think we have done okay."

—

Campbell nodded. "Addison has always been home to me too." He paused in thought. "I think I know how Grandfather felt. He always spoke of Germany. He said the older he got, the more he longed for the old country. I can only be grateful that unlike my grandfather, I don't have an ocean to cross to get back home. The only thing that separates me from home is making the right decision."

"Sometimes making the right decisions can be like crossing an ocean." Carl eyed Campbell for a long moment as if he was trying to discern his thoughts. "I thought a lot of your grandfather. It was a sad day when he passed away. He left many fond memories in Germany but he knew this was where his friends and family were."

Campbell smiled and waved to Carl and Ruby as they drove down the driveway. While walking back across the yard toward the front door, his thoughts raced back to his childhood. He knew all about fond memories. He also knew he didn't want something as vast as an ocean to separate him from them or his family.

Just as he stepped up on the front steps, the door opened and out stepped his brother Matt. "Hey, I was wondering where you went!"

"I just stepped out to say goodbye to Carl and Ruby."

Matt smiled and leaned on the railing of the porch. "I'm glad they came tonight. They are an amazing couple to be around. Both of them have a wealth of wisdom to share with us young folks. Each of them is highly respected in Addison."

"Where is Cassandra?" Campbell asked. "I hope she didn't think I deserted her?"

"Don't worry, Jennifer has her occupied. She is showing her baby pictures of the girls." Matt chuckled. "Although, you better get in there fast. When I left I think the next picture album in the stack is the one that has our baby pictures in it."

Campbell started across the porch for the front door. "If Cassandra takes one look at those old pictures of us, she'll never want children."

"You know how women are, they think all baby pictures are cute. Jennifer thinks they are and so will Cassandra." Matt walked over and sat down in a glider that was to the right of the doorway. "Tell me what is going on with the firm you are working for. I read in the paper that one of the owners was found murdered in his home last weekend."

Campbell stepped back and walked over to his brother. "Yes, he was shot at his house and it was his wife who found him. In my opinion, one of his clients, Slone Ricer, instigated it. That is, if he didn't pull the trigger himself." Campbell took a chair across from Matt. "The night it happened I had returned to the office and saw them leave together. Neither one of them saw me or even knew I was there."

"You can't be serious," exclaimed Matt. "You could have been involved if they had seen you!"

"That, or maybe I could have prevented it. If Slone knew he had had a witness, Dean might still be alive."

"All I know, is those people are crazy. I'd like to see you get out from under all of that, Matt said.

"I'm thinking pretty strongly that way myself," Campbell said as he stood again. "But I have to remind you, we may have something similar happening right here in Addison.'

Matt stood. "You mean with George Larson?"

Campbell walked over to the door and opened it. "I'm not sure. All I know, is things don't seem right with that either. And it sounds like the authorities agree."

"I guess only time will tell," Matt said, as he followed his brother inside.

—

CHAPTER 20

Only One Dance

The maitre d' escorted Campbell and Cassandra into an elegant room with a warm cherry wood interior, frescoed ceilings and white linen tablecloths. He sat them at a small table adjacent to double glass doors that opened up to a terrace. Tiny lights illuminated the terrace with its boarder of bright flowers and greenery.

After the maitre d' took their order for drinks and left, Cassandra caught Campbell's hand. "This is wonderful, what an excellent setting—don't you think the atmosphere is just magic?"

Campbell thought Cassandra had never looked lovelier or more desirable than she did then. Sparks of laughter flitted in her eyes and made them, light up. Her fair skin was flushed with candlelight. She wore an ivory dress with tiny pearls sewn onto the collar and forming a lacy pattern on the bodice. On her wrist was an elegant gold bracelet, inset with a small watch with tiny gold hands and numbers.

He squeezed her hand gently and leaned across the table keeping his eyes steadily on hers. "Yes, I think it's like magic, and I'm glad you like it." Interrupted by the waiter approaching the table with two glasses of white wine and a basket of bread, Campbell sat back.

After taking the white linen napkins by his fingertips and draping one each across Cassandra and Campbell's laps, the waiter inquired in a heavy French accent, "Have you decided what you would like for dinner?" He recommended the Bouillabaisse as a first course. "The assorted shellfish and seafood is fresh and in a saffron tomato broth. Our chef has hand-selected the finest ingredients available for this dish. I'm very sure this would be very pleasing to your and the madam's palate. Bon Appétit!"

After Campbell and Cassandra agreed on the bouillabaisse, the waiter departed. Cassandra gave Campbell a bright smile. "This is very charming. Thank you for bringing me here."

In the background, music began to hum softly. Cassandra looked across the room in that direction. On a small balcony, surrounded by an elegant spiraled railing, stood a woman singing, accompanied by a three-man band. Just below the balcony were couples dancing on a small dance floor.

"The band is very good," Cassandra said. "And the singer has such a lovely voice. The song she's singing is beautiful and I have always loved it. Although it seems to be a little sad, it's about a man who's asking the love of his life to come away with him. He tells her if she would, nothing else will matter, and he would never stop loving her." Cassandra laughed softly. "I'm such a romantic, and hope that she takes him up on his offer."

With laughter in his voice, Campbell replied, "Will you take me up on my offer to dance with me?"

"Campbell Mallary, you told me you couldn't dance!"

With a hint of amusement he said, "I can't dance, but I hope you'll dance with me anyway.

Her thoughts raced wildly, eyes on him. She couldn't focus on anything but the heavenly sense of being close to him when she was in his arms. "Campbell, although I've only ever danced one dance with you, I can testify that you did okay then."

"Okay!" His eyes sparked with mock indignation. "Is that what you're telling people now—I'm only okay?"

The amusement in his voice sent the warm color of pink to her cheeks. "No, I'd never tell anyone you're okay! I mean—Campbell you're embarrassing me. You know what I mean. You know how I feel about you."

Their eyes met and he gave her a long probing look. He thought to himself, "No, Cassy, I don't. Please, tell me how you really do feel about me." He broke the silence, "Come on. I don't want you to be the girl I've only danced with once."

As he took her arm, he noticed her skin was smooth and her hands were graceful. He caught her close in his arms. He could smell the sweet fragrance of her perfumed hair and feel the warmth of her body close to his.

Cassandra felt that electric shock again when he touched her and the place where he held her arm tingled. Campbell was even a better dancer then he had told her, and she thought he left nothing to be desired as a dance partner.

Campbell touched his lips to Cassandra's ear so she could hear him over the music. "You're the love of my life. I'm glad you agreed to dance with me." He then gave her a kiss on the forehead.

Cassandra steadied herself against the whirling of her brain. Love of his life! Did he just say he loved her? Did she not realize she loved him and always had? Was she taking his decency, tenderness, and generosity for granted? Was she going to let him get away—she might never see him again—without telling him, how she felt toward him. Why was she standing there like a stone statue? She must tell him she loved him. "Campbell!" she said under her breath. Her lips parted—then shut tight—she was speechless.

Campbell felt Cassandra lean into him as if for support. He hugged her with a comforting arm as she pressed her face against his shoulder. He heard her whisper his name so softly he wasn't sure if she had actually said it. He wondered what she was thinking. He then whispered to her, "Cassy, I don't want this to end—just the two of us." She pressed closer to him and he tightened his hold on her. He knew he was caught and desperately in love with this amazing woman.

CHAPTER 21

The Legacy

Campbell watched as Cassandra tore the brown paper from the painting. She gazed intently at the canvas a long time before she spoke. "It's such a lovely painting, Campbell. I love the way you made the sunlight appear to shine down between the trees."

"While I was painting that, I thought of a quote I read once," Campbell told her. "It said that love stands at the center of our lives, just as the sun is the center of our universe." He laughed softly. "I don't want to come across as some kind of poet or rhymester. I just liked the saying."

She glanced toward Campbell. "I never heard that before, but I think it's nice, and so very true."

"You think it's true?"

"Yes, I do, and I also think your painting is very good. Art is an expression of emotion as well as perception, and I can tell you had strong feeling when you painted this."

His thoughts drifted back to when he had painted the canvas. She was right. He did paint it with deep feelings, and they were feelings about her, a great lady, sweet and lovely. In Cassandra, he could see strength of character and courage, which had taken her through some tragic times. She was a lady who could love deeply, whose warmth shone brightly, and he wanted her to love him in such a way.

"I did have strong feelings while I worked on it," he said, "I think you're saying that you like it and think it is good?"

Without taking her eyes off the painting, she shook her head. "I'd never tell you something was good if it wasn't." She caught his gaze and smiled back at him. "Ever since the day you told me it was mine, I've been anticipating where to hang it. I thought about hanging it in my bedroom so it would be the first thing I saw when I woke each morning."

He liked the thought of her putting that much importance on his work. Feeling light-hearted he teased, "Why would you want to make that the first thing you saw each morning? I'd think it would put you in a bad mood for the rest of the day."

She turned her head his direction, and smiled at him. "Campbell, you can always make me laugh."

She knew she could beat him at his own game. Although Cassandra thought better of saying what she said next, she said it anyway. With her back to him, she answered nonchalantly. "I suppose since I don't have you to look at each morning I'll have to take the next best thing and that would be this painting." Fighting to keep from laughing she continued, "Since I spend most of my time at my computer, I decided this would be the best place." She stood and carried the painted over and hung it on the wall over her computer desk. She stood back to examine her handiwork. "I think it looks perfect there, what do you think?"

When he didn't answer, she stole a glance his direction. She saw his handsome face was pale and his whole manner changed. He appeared to have gone deaf, dumb, and blind.

"Campbell, do you think this is a good place to hang it?"

Campbell felt every nerve tingle as he stared at Cassandra. Her expression seemed to suggest some secret and amusing knowledge. He responded with an obviously false, sinister expression, amusement glinting in the depth of his eyes. "If you keep looking at me that way I'm going to have to kiss you."

—

Her cheeks dimpled with laughter and her eyes sparkled. "So do you think if you stole a kiss I wouldn't love you any more?"

Campbell's heart went wild, performed a somersault, and began to pound. "I would hope not!" He advanced with outstretched arms. "Come here, I can't talk when you are so far away." He then caught Cassandra in his arms, kissed her throat, her eyes, and her lips. Cassandra lost her breath for a minute. He continued to hold her in his arms for a long moment after the kiss, before he spoke. "You still love me?"

Continuing the levity Cassandra crossed her heart in the childhood gesture. "Hope to die!" She stood her full height and pressed another kiss on his lips. He could hear the laughter in her voice as she murmured in his ear. "You are the center of my universe, and who of us can live without the sun or love?"

"You would make a very good poet!" He laughed and held her tight for a long while, then he looked back up at the canvas and recalled her asking if he liked where she hung it. "Yes, I think I like it there. You made a good choice," he said, kissing the top of her head affectionately.

Cassandra looked back at him, studied his face, smiled, and slowly nodded. "Yes, I think you're right, I did make a good choice."

He looked back down at her with feigned innocence. "Are you talking about my painting?"

Her face was confident as she softly smiled back at him and answered, "No, I'm not talking about your painting."

Campbell threw his head back in laughter. "I'm glad you like the choice you made." He then pulled her a little more closely. "This afternoon will you come with me to the old homestead? I would like to show you the old place. I have something in mind. I want to share it with you."

"Can we?" Cassandra exclaimed with excitement in her eyes. "I'd love to go!"

CASSANDRA GLANCED DOWN at the panorama spread out before her. As they drove she thought of how the scene would make a perfect post card.

"You like the scenic view?' Campbell asked as he glanced over at her. "It's a lot different from what we see while living in the city. The countryside has a calming effect on me and I miss it."

—

"I know," she said. "I think that's partly why I moved back home. I prefer calm, unhurried to frenetic."

Campbell turned into a lane marked by two stone columns and drove up the hillside under the canopy of century-old trees.

"Whenever I come up here I always have good memories of my parents and grandparents. I remember all the barbecues and gatherings we had, and I still miss having them."

As they rounded the corner, Cassandra could see Campbell's beloved house. It had two stories, with three steeply pitched gabled roofs and a tower toward the front of the house. The lovely front porch ran the width of the house with a long set of stone steps. The first story was finished with a light brown wood siding. The second story, the trim, and shutters on the windows were bone white.

"Campbell what a wonderful house! When you spoke of it as the old house, I had never envisioned it looking as grand as this!"

"It is an old house!" Campbell replied. "I never thought of it being grand. To me it is just always home."

The driveway pitched to the right and the parking area was just adjacent to the house. Cassandra could see that behind the large house there was an elaborate garden with a gazebo. There were some maple trees, green ash, and pine, and trimmed bushes lining the pathways.

"Bob and Nell Bergner have been taking care of the place. They live in the little cottage on down the road." Campbell pointed in the direction of a grove of trees. "If you look closely, you can see it though the trees.

After grandfather died while in the Air Corps, great grandfather had the cottage built to give my grandmother her own little place to live. That's where our father grew up, and after he married our mother, they lived here in the big house. This is also, where Matt and I were born. We lived here all though our childhood. That's why we could never bring ourselves to sell it. Bob and Nell do a good job of caring for the place and that makes it possible for us to keep it. Later on I'll take you down to meet them."

As Cassandra stepped out of the car, she felt a cool breeze and inhaled the crisp scent of pine. "It's so very nice here—what a treasure!"

"Come on in. I'll show you around the inside."

Cassandra thought the entryway was bright and homey with light blue curtains and a cushioned chair and settee done in a light blue pattern.

Campbell led her into a room that had a stone fireplace with a richly carved mantle above it. The floors in the room were polished light oak with big thick area rugs in floral designs. The walls had large paintings depicting rustic country scenes and ocean scenes in rainbow colors.

Campbell followed Cassandra's eyes as they looked intently at the paintings. "My grandfather loved art too, as you can see."

Charming was the word, Cassandra thought as she ran her hand along an overstuffed copper colored sofa.

"The house has six bedrooms, four upstairs, and two downstairs. As you can tell from that number, grandfather liked to entertain and always had overnight guests." Campbell gently placed his hand on the small of her back. "Come on and I'll show you the kitchen."

He showed her through an arched doorway that led into the dining room and past an antique dining table set with six chairs and a matching china cabinet. They then entered the spacious modern kitchen. He smiled with his arms extended out. "You see, to entertain we have to cook, for them and this is a kitchen big enough to do it in." The open eat-in kitchen had adequate room for a family to move around the kitchen freely. It was designed around a red brick hearth, and featured modern appliances. Walls painted with natural tones of brown and matte gold wrapped around the cabinetry, and large windows let the warm sunlight stream in. The elements of open cupboards and shelves displaying baskets, rich red and intense yellow ceramics, and copper cooking utensils made Cassandra immediately conjure up an image of a Tuscan kitchen in the south of Italy. The floor was laid with terra cotta tiles, and in the center, stood a sturdy kitchen island with a granite countertop finished off with wrought iron drawers pulls.

Campbell then gestured toward a good-sized table that sat in front of a large bay window. Lace curtains billowed out, dancing in a lively late afternoon breeze. "This is where we ate all our meals except for dinner. We always ate as a family in the dining room for that meal."

"I'm thirsty. Would you like something to drink too?" Campbell asked as he headed toward the large refrigerator.

Cassandra smiled and nodded. "Yes, that sounds great."

He poured tea into two tinted glasses and handed Cassandra her drink, tilted his own glass up and drank thirstily.

Sipping her drink, Cassandra wandered back toward French doors that opened out to the back of the house.

Campbell walked over and lightly touched her on the arm. He loved touching her, making sure she really was there and not just a lovely dream. He took her drink and sat it on the counter. "Come on, I'll show you the outside." He opened the doors and they stepped out onto a sunny stone patio bordered with flowers that glowed like many-colored jewels. Below the terraced yard lay a lovely stretch of green hills, and at the base sat a small lake, clear as a blue mirror reflecting a snow-capped mountain peak in the distance.

Campbell then stepped up behind her and wrapped his arms around her waist. She could feel his strong hands gently pulling her close to him. She leaned into him, laid her head back against his shoulder, and turned her face toward the sky. As she enjoyed the comfort of his arms, she watched a lone hawk overhead glide effortlessly below wispy clouds like gossamer scarves of white flung carelessly across the sky.

She sighed. "Campbell, how can you stand not to live here?"

He affectionately kissed her on the side of her neck. "I wonder that myself."

She trailed her fingers along his arm. "You think someday you'll move back here?"

"Yes, I think so. It seems lately I've thought about it more than usual." He squeezed her a little tighter. "Now that you've told me you're passionately in love with me, I plan to go home, pack all my worldly belongings, and be moved back before the end of the week."

Cassandra expressed her amusement and turned to face him. She could see his joy. His eyes were as blue as the skies behind him and sparkled with a child's delight. "Campbell, I do love you, and I have loved you long before we met again at Barbara and Ian's. When you left that last summer and I thought I would never see you again, I took all my wonderful memories of you and hid them away in my heart to keep them safe. I still love those memories, but I love you more."

"Cassy, I wish, I had known that back then." He gazed down at her, took her by the shoulders, and pulled her into his embrace. She tipped her head up and he kissed her softly on the lips. After his kiss, he held her still as he stroked her hair. "Being with you has convinced me that certain things are missing in my life. I wish it were as easy as moving within a few days. After I left your house last night, I stayed up trying to figure things out and thinking of us together." He stepped back and still holding her, he smiled down at her. "All that is dear to me is right here in Addison and I have to wonder why I'm not living here." Cassandra lifted her hand and touched his face. He kissed her tenderly then caught her hand and pulled her down next to him as he sat on a garden chaise. Still holding her hand he said, "Although I've made some good friends in Denver like Ian and Paula, I know with the recent events at Hendricks Law Firm, it's only a matter of time before they move on themselves."

Cassandra placed her hand on his arm to comfort him. "I understand and think of Barbara as a friend, as you do Ian."

He turned to face her. "For a long time, I've thought about leaving Hendricks and opening my own law office. The time never seemed right, or I just never had the courage." He held the hand she had resting on his arm. "With you, I know now I can do it. Since Carl Bonnell retired, it seems Addison is in need of a good attorney. As soon as I get back to my office, I'm going to begin making plans to transfer my practice here. Carl has practiced law here in Addison for years. He's found it to be satisfying. He said he and Ruby have been happy here."

Cassandra was ecstatic as she brought her hands to her mouth and then let them flutter down to grasp Campbell's arms. "Campbell, that is wonderful!" She wrapped her arms around him and hugged him. Her eyes were bright with tears. "Yes, I think you'll be very successful here!"

Campbell laughed at her reaction to his announcement and returned her embrace. "I have to agree with Matt," he said. 'This house has been empty far too long. Although it will take time, I'm starting right away to get things going. I want to move back so I can be close to you too."

"Campbell, that's the best news I have heard since—forever!" With excitement in her eyes, she asked, "Your brother—Matt, does he know? Have you told him yet?"

—

"No, I wanted to tell you first." He stood and took her by the hand. "Come back inside. I want to show you the best part." He led her back into the kitchen and down a small hall that opened up into a stately room. Two walls of the room were covered with shelves full of books from floor to ceiling. Across one end of the room was a wall of windows that looked out over the same little lake they were admiring earlier. The room also had a stone fireplace similar to the one that stood in the living room. In front of it was a grouping of sofa and chairs, complete with end tables. A heavy iron and stone coffee table complemented the room, as it sat in the center of the grouping and pulled it all together.

"This is my grandfather's library. He loved books and spent a lot of time in here."

Cassandra walked over to admire the books and then turned to where Campbell was standing. "What a cozy room. One could feel safe from the world here."

"I spent a lot of time here with my grandfather, mostly during the winters. There was always a fire burning in the fireplace, and it was great to relax while watching the snow drift down and cover the lake."

Campbell leaned on the edge of a large heavy desk that divided the side of the room with the shelves of books from the rest of the room. He crossed his arms and smiled brilliantly, "This is my new law office! What do you think?"

Cassandra looked at him with surprise. After a moment, she wrapped her arms around herself as she slowly turned looking at the room once again. She turned back to face him and gave him a smile of approval, "Perfect!" She laughed softly, "Campbell, what a great idea!"

"Come here." He showed her though a side door that opened up into another large room. "You are now looking at my secretary's office and waiting room. With a little remodeling it will work very nicely." He pointed to a large carved wooden door. "That door opens outside to a driveway at the side of the house. Any clients I have can park there. The main driveway will be left for private parking." Campbell held his hands up. "This setup was grandfather's private retreat and it's perfect as an office, completely separate from the rest of the house. Having my practice out of town shouldn't be any problem. It is only a four mile drive and I've had clients who drove further than that just in Denver."

"Just think of the beautiful view they'll have while driving here," Cassandra exclaimed. "No traffic jams either." Her eyes met his and the corners of them creased into a smile. "All of this has been here all along and just waiting for you just to see it."

Campbell agreed and thought of how certain things in life could be viewed as simple and taken for granted. Sometimes they can be recaptured and other times lost forever. He pulled Cassandra back into the library. He stepped over and drew a brown leather covered book from one of the shelves. "This is one of the books grandfather carried all the way from Germany."

Cassandra gently took the book from his hand. "This is a lovely old book. What a treasure!" Gold lettering was embossed on the cover and the pages were thin and delicate. As she opened the book, she saw at the beginning of the first chapter an illustration of a fragile looking woman sketched in black ink. Her lose curls flowed about her head, across the page and curved into the letters of the words. "Cassandra eyes brightened. "Campbell, look at the way the artist made the locks of her hair turn into the words!" He smiled and watched as she turned the pages. She then looked back up at him with an astonished look on her face. "It's all written in German!"

"I know and I can't read a word of it!" He was amused at her reaction and leaned his head back in laughter. "But don't you think it's a great book?"

Cassandra laughed. "Campbell, you are crazy! Yes, I do think it's a beautiful book. Did your grandfather read to you from it?"

"He did. It's a book of poems his mother gave him before he left Germany."

"You remember any of the poems or what they were about?"

Campbell smiled again. "No, I have no idea what the book says. When grandfather read it aloud it was in German and he didn't translate it."

Cassandra stood with her hand on her hip. "Campbell, are you teasing again?"

"No, I'm telling the truth. Even though I didn't understand a word of it, I still liked the sound of grandfather's voice as he read and spoke his language."

She turned back to the front page. "I'll bet the poems are about a lovely lady like the one on the first page."

"You think the poems are telling about her bad hair day?"

Cassandra gave him a sideways look. He laughed shortly and then looked serious. "I do cherish the book, not for what it says, but rather the value grandfather put on it and his mother before him."

"Campbell, I think it is such a great heritage to have and to hold."

He took the book and admired it while in thought. He looked back at her. "I can't help but think of the book as a true friend whom I took for granted. Years later I learned to cherish it and came to an understanding of its value."

Campbell's eyes met Cassandra's and her cheeks turned a pink as she looked intently at him. He reached over and cradled her in his arms. In a husky voice he said, "Cassy I cherish you and will never again take you for granted. You do understand that, don't you? Yes, the house, Matt and his family, disillusionment with Hendricks, all of those things are factors. But the most important, the driving motivation for me to be in Addison is my need to be near you." He kissed her right cheek and then her left before he cupped her head so he could tip it at an angle that made his next kiss a kiss on her lips. In between kisses, he told her how he loved her and how he could never be complete without her. He let his kisses trail down her neck.

Cassandra's heart began to race and the room seemed to be spinning. "Campbell, I do love you. My heart won't give me a choice. It's telling my brain I'm madly in love with you."

He held her close, and laughing said, "Please Cassy, for my sake, pay attention to your heart!"

The distant ring of the phone interrupted their laughter. "I wish I could just let that ring and not answer it, but I think it's Matt. He said he would call, so I'd better answer it." Campbell pulled Cassandra closer. "Don't go anywhere. I'll be right back." He dropped his arms and stepped back. "I'll get rid of him as quick as I can." He chuckled, "I hope it's not Nester who's calling!"

"Campbell!" She exclaimed, "I doubt if he even has your phone number!"

"Blast that man!" Campbell said. You don't know Nester. He'd find a way." He walked toward the door. "I'll get us more to drink while I'm gone."

"Let me get our drinks," Cassandra said.

"No, you're my guest," he called over his shoulder as he walked toward the door. "Please sit and relax and I'll be right back."

Cassandra sank into an armchair and gazed out the window as she thought of Campbell's plan to return to Addison. She had hoped for this for so long and now that it was about to happen, it scared her a little. Even then, she was not going to let her fear stop her from trusting Campbell. She knew that with Campbell she could endure anything that would come her way. He had renewed her hope and taught her how to believe all things.

The house was quiet, except for the far-off chimes of the grandfather clock she had seen earlier standing at the foot of the staircase. Cassandra laid her head back and closed her eyes for only a moment.

When Campbell returned with two drinks in hand, he found that Cassandra had drifted asleep. She had told him earlier that morning that she had not slept well the previous evening, so it came as no surprise that she had fallen asleep. Not wanting to wake her, he quietly sat both drinks down on an end table and lowered himself down in one of the large cushioned chairs.

He picked up a book he had started to read the day before, but found he could not concentrate. After reading the same paragraph twice, he knew it was hopeless and closed the book. He leaned his head back and watched Cassandra sleep. It gave him a good feeling to see her right there with him in the house that represented so many good things.

He studied Cassandra's face and saw her as a unique woman. Her beauty had never seemed more radiant than at that moment. Her warm golden skin glowed, tinted with pink around her smooth forehead and cheeks. He took note of how her dark eyelashes appeared even longer with her eyes closed. As his eyes followed the line of her delicate cheekbone down to her full lips, he tried to grasp the idea that she really did love him. He felt that with Cassandra he could make something out of his dreams and have the kind of success that truly mattered. He could survive any disappointments and failures. She would be worth any sacrifices and struggles they would endure together.

He stood and took a coverlet from the back of the sofa and unfolded it as he walked over to where Cassandra slept. He softly laid it across her and at that moment, her eyes opened in surprise.

"Oh, I'm so sorry! I only wanted to close my eyes for a moment!" She sat up straight. "I didn't mean to fall asleep!"

"No, there's nothing to be sorry about," he said softly. He then held his hand out to her. When she pushed the coverlet to the side and took his hand, he pulled her from the chair and led her to the sofa. "I want you to come over here where it'll be a little more comfortable."

"Oh, no, I can't do that!"

"I know you didn't sleep last night, and I think you'll feel better after a little rest. Beside, it is all selfishness on my part. I don't want you falling asleep later when I tell you my boring little stories."

Campbell sat on one end of the sofa, laid a sofa pillow in his lap, and motioned her to lie down. "Here, I'll be your pillow."

Cassandra grinned and obediently lay down on her back with her head on the pillow. "You know Campbell, your stories are not boring I find them very interesting and most entertaining."

"Really? You're going to pay now, because I've tons of them to tell." He bent down, kissed her on the forehead, and stroked her hair.

"Sleep a little and later I'll take you to one of my favorite places to eat. Of course if you'd rather, we can stay in and just eat here."

Cassandra smiled softly. "You take such good care of me. Campbell, for a long time I have felt as if I had been cast overboard and have just been drifting along. You have made me stronger, given me courage, and filled my heart with hope. I'll always love you for that." She giggled and then quoted, "As sure as the sun will shine." Then while still smiling, she closed her eyes and floated silently into sleep.

Campbell laid his head back and thought of how quite suddenly his life seemed complete again. He softly laid his arm across Cassandra's waist. She placed her fingertips in the curve of his hand. Between them, no words needed to be spoken. To Campbell, all was good, and then he too closed his eyes.

9 781441 534897

Urban growth: an approach

Urban growth: an approach

BRIAN T. ROBSON

Lecturer in Geography, University of Cambridge
Fellow of Fitzwilliam College, Cambridge

METHUEN & CO LTD

First published 1973 by Methuen & Co Ltd, 11 New Fetter Lane,
London EC4P 4EE
© 1973 Brian T. Robson
Printed in Great Britain by William Clowes & Sons Limited,
London, Colchester and Beccles

ISBN 0 416 66950 6 Hardback
0 416 78710 X Paperback

To Glenna,
Mark and Peter

Contents

Tables

Figures

Preamble

My centre is giving way, my right is in retreat; situation excellent. I shall
attack.   MARÉCHAL FOCH

Students of the city seem always to be one jump behind reality. The roundabout
designed in the '40s is built in the '60s; multiple-storey car parks arise in the
centre as multiple shopping centres begin to expand in the outskirts of towns;
the form and the functioning of the city change so rapidly and are so little
understood that our gropings to tackle problems often produce solutions to the
reality of the past rather than the present. For more conceptual problems, the
time lag is even greater. The writings of sociologists and anthropologists in the
early twentieth century focused on a rural-urban dichotomy at a time when such
a distinction had become largely artificial; the human ecologists derived a
theory of the city in the 1920s which was outdated almost at the time of its
writing; geographers continue to elaborate concepts based on distance constraints when increasing mobility has begun to erode the effects of spatial
friction. Much of the theory of urban geography is predicated on a view of cities
which no longer exist. They are not unitary, self-contained, definable entities,
since the strands of control, influence and effect pass casually beyond the
bounds of administrative areas or densely built-up zones. Such conceptual lags
are inevitable. Time is needed to refine, to verify and to explore the conceptual
frameworks in which theory is couched and it is only on the foundation of some
securely-based notions about the recent past that more intelligent guesses about
the present and future can be made. One need feel no necessary embarrassment
in talking of the 'industrial city' when we are already far advanced in the
post-industrial age, since the tasks and the interests of the academic are different
from those of the planner, the politician or the futurologist.

Many urban theories make the necessary assumption that the city can be
defined as a unit and the fact that such an assumption was more clearly met in
the past than the present suggests the value of looking at earlier rather than
contemporary data as material to test the concepts of present-day notions. Here,
the cities of nineteenth-century England and Wales are studied to examine the
assumption that urban population growth obeys a law of proportionate effect —
a law which states that, in a set of cities, there is a common rate of growth
irrespective of city size, and that individual cities depart from this general rate
by random rather than systematic amounts. The approach is an aggregate one;
concentrating on the characteristics of the whole set of places rather than upon

individual towns. It differs in consequence from much of the writing of urban history which has tended to study the events, the stimuli and the checks experienced, in some unique combination, by only one or a very small number of towns. The two approaches complement each other rather than vie as alternatives; the results of the present study demonstrate the general tendencies inherent in the demographic history of towns while at the same time suggesting the wide bounds within which individual places may grow more or less rapidly than other places of comparable size. The unique events of history add the detail which helps to explain this individual variance, but the overall aggregate curve of growth sets limits to this variation; for the small towns there is considerable scope for individual variation, while for the large town there is considerably less.

At the outset, it was hoped to develop a formal system-based approach to urban growth: regularities in city sizes and in the nature of the overall growth process being seen as symptoms of the inter-relatedness of the individual towns in an urban system; the aim being to isolate the negative and positive feedback loops by which the system achieves stability or progressively alters over time. That this aim was gradually abandoned in favour of a less ambitious and more pragmatic approach, is salutory. It suggests both the limitations imposed by the nature of much of the available data and also the dubiousness of many of the wider claims that the concepts of systems can be applied as working tools in the analysis of social phenomena. The approach is, however, more theoretical than empirical. Even though it draws on the experience and the material of the nineteenth century, its basic concerns are more with the underpinnings of urban theory than with the nineteenth century *per se*. As such it is hoped that it might provide a perspective against which the detailed histories of individual cities might be placed, as well as throwing some new light on the more general questions of urban growth and the diffusion of innovations.

In addition to the specific acknowledgements made in the body of the text, I must thank those people who contributed so much to the preparation of this book. In particular, I owe a considerable debt to Miss Helen Gibson for her valiant and intelligent typing of the manuscript and to Mr Michael Young and Mr William Kirkland for the skill with which they prepared the illustrations.

PART 1

Introduction

CHAPTER 1

Defining the city

I have therefore looked at the subject without reference to the rivalries of particular towns, and must be understood to admit that in the absence of scientific boundaries comparisons of one place with another can seldom be altogether just.

T. A. WELTON

Ever since the town has been studied there has been agonized debate about its definition.[1] Much of this debate has been contributed by those concerned with the origins of urbanization who, in trying to establish the points in time at which towns first emerged, have needed to clarify with some precision the ways in which 'towns' can be distinguished from objects which are not 'towns' and have therefore needed to develop unambiguous criteria to define their objects of study. It is from this type of concern that the various definitions based on legal (Maine 1861; Maitland 1898), economic (Pirenne 1925) and sociological (Childe 1936; M. Weber 1958) elements have been added to the emphasis on the purely physical aspect of the town as a densely built-up area. In studying more recent periods, the problems of definition have, if anything, become less easy to resolve. Once the legal forms of urban government were codified, once the division of labour and the development of specialized occupations had become fairly widespread, once, concomitantly, the long-distance traffic in men, messages and materials had grown to considerable proportions, and once the built-up area itself had grown to a relatively large size, the distinction between town and country may have looked reasonably precise, but it was not long to remain so. Today, in the developed world, one still thinks and talks of 'towns' as distinct from 'the country', but if it is city air that makes men free who is not a free man in the western world?

By way of introduction, this chapter will attempt to go a little way in clearing the ground for a study of towns by looking at the problems of their definition both in a theoretical and in a more purely operational fashion. It will, however, be more than mere introduction since how we define towns, and how in consequence we measure them, will have great effect upon the studies upon which we might embark and the conclusions which might be reached.

---

[1] The terms 'town' and 'city' will be used interchangeably without any difference being implied.

THE TOWN AS AN OBJECT

In the literature of philosophy and, to a growing extent, in that of geography there is a concern about what is infelicitously called 'entitation'. Any attempt to establish or explore relationships needs first to specify the objects which are to be related in some appropriate manner; and the test of whether the definition is appropriate is that it should be meaningful in terms of the function and the performance of the objects. If a study is concerned simply with description, the stringency of this need is relaxed, but where the concern is with function then it becomes of some moment. Since we shall be concerned with the functions of towns and the relationships between them, the requirements of definition become somewhat taxing and a discussion of the difficulty of thinking of towns as functional objects is not amiss.

Philosophers have suggested a number of types of object: structurally integrated objects, which have volume and whose parts are physically connected; areal aggregates, which are collections of elements physically close to one another but not necessarily structurally bound together; and non-areal aggregates, which are collections defined by some sort of similarity which warrants their being thought of as a 'class'. A beech tree would illustrate the first of these objects, a wood the second and the concept of 'tree' the third. G. P. Chapman (1971) follows Fiebleman (1954) in suggesting that the most meaningful object, and the only one which can be used where functional performance is of interest, is what he calls the 'first-order object of study'. This is an object which can be specified in terms of its morphology, taxonomy, composition, physiology, ecology, chorology and chronology; an object, in other words, which has shape, which is composed of a set of identifiable elements determining its internal functioning, which can be related to other objects defined at a similar scale and having relationships with it at the next-higher scale level, and which varies both over space and time. Such a first-order object of study, meeting these strict requirements of definition, is something which can 'perform' and which can be thought of as a unit at one scale level and part of some more inclusive unit at a higher level of scale. The difficulty, of course, is that such objects can only be defined with any confidence at the extreme ends of the continuum of scale. It is relatively easy to define the successively higher-scale objects of atom, molecule, cell, organ and organism; conceptually it is relatively easy to define the world or the solar system; but it is in the middle ranges of scales where definition becomes difficult and where the blurring of first-order objects and areal aggregates occurs. Geographers have dealt with a multitude of objects at a variety of scales, but the majority of objects with which they are concerned falls right in the middle of the disputed ground between what can and cannot readily be regarded as first-order objects of study. The suggestion that they are concerned with objects above the scale of the atom and below the scale of the universe (Chorley and Kennedy 1971, p. 4) must be regarded as a light-hearted intrusion upon geographers' notorious academic licence, but certainly much of their concern is with objects which are defined in terms of spatial proximity rather than any necessary structural bonding between the component parts — the 'region' being the classic instance. The same, of course, is true of the town. The classic definition of urbanization is provided by Tisdale (1942) who suggests that urbanization is the process whereby increasing proportions of a nation's population are drawn into areas which, being relatively densely settled and relatively large, can be thought of as cities. Here there are two objects involved — the nation and the city — both of which are areal aggregates, but neither of which could be claimed with confidence to meet Fiebleman's strict definition of a first-order object of study. The town, conceived of as an area of densely populated land, may or may not function as a unit, but it would be a brave man who would suggest what exactly it is that functions and what is its sphere of operations. Seen in terms of economic activity, many of the inhabitants of such a built-up area may not work within it and many of the people who work within it would certainly live at considerable distances from it. Likewise, other activities (or performances) of the town as an areal aggregate may affect and involve people from outside its spatially-defined boundary. Such activities would include shopping, recreation, entertainment, the making and execution of a whole variety of political and economic decisions and a host of formal and informal contacts between people and activities.

This is simply to emphasize that, while one can recognize discrete areas which are relatively compact and densely populated, such areas do not necessarily operate in functional terms as units or solely within their own confines. It would seem difficult, if not impossible, to define an unambiguous first-order object to describe 'the town'. Of course this is not an uncommon difficulty; it afflicts all disciplines dealing with objects of middle-order scale. The botanist, for example, is faced with the same problem in trying to define a plant community in terms which would meet the rigour of Fiebleman's definition of an object and many of the suggestions derived from botany bear close resemblance to the functional regions defined by the geographer. For the town, such functional regions have been demarcated in terms of spheres of influence (Dickinson 1947; Smailes 1947; Carter 1955), but the conclusion which arises is not surprising; that no one town has a single sphere of influence, but rather has a set of indistinct spheres each of which differs in varying degrees from the other depending on the particular activity which is used as an indicator of the town's influence on its surrounding area. The tributary area from which a baker draws his custom is very different in extent from that from which a specialist jeweller draws his custom. In terms of the ascending scales of objects, it might be possible to define a baker's shop at a low spatial scale for the hours while the shop is functioning and, at a higher spatial scale, it may again be possible to define a functional object comprising the shop and the households served by it. But when one aggregates together all of the bakers' shops and the jewellers' shops and the multitude of other activities which take place within the town, one has so jumbled a set of low-scale objects comprising the town that any definition of a single functional area which describes the operational extent of the town is faced with so complex a collage that only heroic Occam's-razor decisions could hope to provide any resolution.

One is therefore faced with the problem at the outset that any definition of the city is of necessity bound to be far from satisfactory as a description of the varied types of effect and contact that towns have. Probably in no case could one hope to define a town in terms which would satisfy the requirements of a first-order object of study. But for what objects could one draw such definitions except those of organisms and scales below this?

OPERATIONAL DEFINITIONS

It is against this seemingly intractible conceptual background that the various attempts to resolve operational definitions have been made. The most monumental and conscientious of such attempts have come from America where the Census Bureau distinguishes between such varied definitions as the *Standard Metropolitan Statistical Area* and the *urbanized area* (U.S. Bureau of the Budget 1967), and where Kingsley Davis and his associates at Berkeley have applied common definitions to towns throughout the world (International Urban Research 1959; see also Gibbs 1961). These attempts have tried largely to demarcate towns as built-up areas and they draw attention to the evident unsatisfactoriness of using administrative areas based on political or governmental boundaries. The two main criteria which most often are used in place of political boundaries are, first, some critical population size and, second, some critical level of settlement density, by means of a combination of which villages or non-urban settlements might be distinguished from 'towns'. Such discussion is of great value in making comparisons between sets of national statistics on urbanization, but it obviously cannot resolve the more fundamental problem of the inappropriateness of purely physical definitions of urban areas.

The difficulty has become increasingly severe as the process of urbanization-industrialization has progressed and, with it, the increasing mobility of populations both urban and rural. Increasing physical mobility, allied with the spread of the means of non-physical communication, have tended to pull apart the tightly-bounded town as it has conventionally been thought of. The telephone now enables people to make long-distance contact fairly effortlessly; radio and television disseminate the culture of cities almost universally and instantaneously; and the projection of three-dimensional images by holography (Berry 1970, p. 49) holds out the awesome prospect of the 'embodied' contact of people taking place without their physical movement. Such developments, with the more immediately evident effects of the greater ease and speed of physical movement, have meant that distance has increasingly become less of what Warntz (1967) called a constraining tyranny and, as its power has lessened, so have the tight compaction of cities and the relatively narrow compass of the areas which they affect and which are affected by them, broken down.

A useful distinction which clarifies this effect is that between urbanization on the one hand and the urban process on the other (Popenhoe 1965; Friedmann and Miller 1965; Friedmann 1966b). Reference has already been made to Tisdale's definition of the former as a process by which increasing proportions of people are drawn into cities. One can define the urban process, on the other hand, as that by which increasing proportions of people, irrespective of whether they actually live in cities, are *involved* in ways of life, modes of thought and types of activity which are somehow 'urban' rather than 'rural'. At a time when the tyranny of distance was considerably greater than now, the city's effect was largely restricted to areas within its own spatial extent. Only those who lived within its walls were markedly subject to urban life-styles and were caught up in social and economic activities and types of behaviour which were urban. To this extent urbanization and the urban process could be thought of as roughly synonymous or largely overlapping. Today however, in the most urbanized and economically developed areas, the two are certainly not synonymous. People are sucked into the urban ambit whether or not they live within what we would conventionally define as a town in terms of its built-up area. Indeed, with the general tendency for the populations of large towns to decline where one uses relatively narrow boundaries to define those towns, it might even be said that urbanization is diminishing whereas the urban process gallops on apace.

It is this substitution of an 'urban field' in place of the more familiar 'urban area' that underlies Berry's attempts to define broad swathes of territory and population which are tributary to central cities in the United States (Berry 1968). His definition is based on flows of journeys-to-work and he shows that the streams of commuting produce city areas which overlap and interpenetrate each other in a complex jigsaw within the more densely settled areas of the manufacturing belt, but which elswhere rather accurately dovetail into one another so as to parcel out much of the whole national territory between the various central cities. Such an exercise is of course subject to the same criticisms that might be levelled at any study based on one of a variety of types of spheres of influence, but it is not without interest that Berry finds that no less than 96 per cent of the total American population lies within the set of urban regions which he produces as against only 67 per cent within the census-defined Standard Metropolitan Statistical Areas. Almost the entire United States population thus lives within areas in which at least some portion of the residents have their work in large urban centres and it is significant that it is within those interstitial areas which fall outside these functional economic urban areas that the highest indices of social and economic ill-health are to be found: higher unemployment, lower levels of formal education and other such indices being found in the few areas which lie outside the enlarged compass of the modern city.

THE EVOLVING MEGALOPOLIS

These progressive changes in the role, scope and form of the town have given rise to a number of well-known urban typologies which are based on their changing salient features. The typologies range from the hypnotic writings of Mumford (1938 and 1961) to the prognostications of H. G. Wells (1902 and nicely reassessed by Berry, 1970) and the work of self-styled 'futurologists' such as M. M. Webber (1963, 1964 and 1968). Whatever their tone or stance — gloomy in the case of Mumford, excited in the case of Wells and bland in the case of Webber — the various writers tend to be in remarkable agreement both in regard to the structure of their typologies as well as to the analysis of the principal agents underlying the changes, which are seen as consequences of technological development and particularly improvements in communication (Boal 1968). Mumford's catalogue of eras — eotechnic, paleotechnic, neotechnic and bio-technic; terms originally coined by Patrick Geddes — are basically tied in to the predominant technologies of successive periods and especially to the prevailing fuel technologies. Webber provides a more sociological stress by emphasizing changes in the types of social relationships between individuals, but such changes are themselves the result of alterations in the means of communication. The substitution of face-to-face contact and the primacy of the local community as a basic social group by the emergence of what he calls 'non-place communities' composed of interest groups, is an indication of the greater range of contacts which have been made possible by the greater ease of both physical and non-physical communication. Again, as far as the physical form of the various types of cities is concerned, the compilers of urban typologies draw heavily on changes in the types of internal and external urban transport as the explanations of change.

The urban typologies suggest that the predominant categories of city would comprise the pre-industrial, the industrial and the post-industrial city, each of which would be characterized by differences both in their physical form as well as in their preponderent types of social and economic activities. The pre-industrial city, which has been categorized most extensively by Sjoberg (1960 and 1965; see also the dissenting views of Vance 1971), is characterized by a tightly compact physical form and by social and economic roles which are not highly specialized. Even where one finds, in the exceptional case, pre-industrial cities of some considerable population size, the constraint of distance still produces a 'walking city' since there is a suggestion that the larger pre-industrial cities tend to be composed of a number of relatively distinct component parts each of which conforms roughly to a standard spatial module set by the possible radius of walking and each of which might be physically separated from the other by internal town walls or distinct quarters.[1] The essence of the physical form of the pre-industrial city is therefore its compactness, so dramatically portrayed by such engravers of late medieval European towns as Hogengerg.

The industrial town, by comparison, reflects the loosening of these spatial bonds by the advent of more efficient inter-urban transport and of the simultaneous and gradual transformation of economic and social roles with the development of large-scale factories. The industrial city therefore shows both a much greater specialization of roles amongst its inhabitants and also a much greater physical spread which breaks down the circular compaction of the pre-industrial city. It may be that the industrial city was still compact since intra- as distinct from inter-urban transport was late in improving, but it sends out major tentacles of growth along the main arteries of movement and also, with improvements in both transport and in the techniques of organization, the upper limit of population size which can function as a single whole becomes greater and enables the appearance of cities of considerable size.

The post-industrial city is, superficially, a very different animal. The process of social and economic specialization has progressed even further in terms of fragmenting the roles which individuals play. And, in terms of its physical form, the bounds of the post-industrial city become quite unrecognizable. Not only do improvements in internal transport make it possible for the interstices of the tentacles of earlier growth to be filled in (this perhaps being a feature of the late-industrial rather than the post-industrial city), but increasing numbers of the inhabitants and activities of the city are no longer found within it. The relaxation of the distance constraint has the effect of emphasizing and encouraging the development of groupings of people and sets of economic and social contacts which no longer depend upon physical proximity, but rather upon like interests or complementarity in terms of the contact activity itself. People, in other words, do not merely or even necessarily form social contacts with neighbours, but develop ties with others in terms of shared interests rather than residential proximity. For the city as a whole, with its much greater potential range of control and influence, the once separate and distinct agglomerations of buildings can no longer be taken as delimiting a single functional city entity. Instead there has emerged a polycentric form or a loose amalgamation of centres into a larger and more complex megalopolis (Gottman 1961; Hall 1966). This physical form – or rather the emergence of this formless form[2] – is best seen in the development of vast 'concentrations' of urban areas

---

[1] It is interesting to note that Marshall (1968) suggests a similar pattern for nineteenth-century industrial towns such as Blackburn and Bury, each of which contained discrete cells centred around a major workplace.

[2] The grammar used to describe post-industrial cities tends often to resort to such antithetical terms as 'community without propinquity' and is indicative of the fact that the quasi-technical language has not yet caught up with the physical reality of the ways in which towns have developed. Notions of continuous space and Euclidean geometry still permeate the terms and have to be countered by the negatives which suggest their inappropriateness.

in the United States. Planners in that country have coined conglomerate names to describe these emergent 'megalopolitan' areas which are as grotesque to the ear as are the phenomena to our conventional urban notions: 'Boswash' for the area between Boston and Washington; 'Chipitts' for the area between Chicago and Pittsburgh; and 'Sansan' for the San Francisco to San Diego area.

While these typologies seem to point to very similar conclusions, they do not suggest that the periods during which one urban 'type' was superseded by another can be pinpointed with any precision. Instead, they have emphasized the role of particular mechanisms whose operation is considered crucial in the long run in the emergence of a distinctively different urban form. These mechanisms emerged and became dominant only over relatively long spans of time. Moses and Williamson (1967) stress, for example, the importance of the motor lorry in improving the internal movement of manufactured goods and raw materials within the city and thus in freeing factories from central locations and in breaking the grip which the centre of the city for so long had on its constituent parts. This was a gradual rather than a sudden development. Since implicit in many of the typologies is the importance of electrical forms of communication replacing mechanical ones, it might be imagined that one could date the emergence of the spatially-unconstrained post-industrial city to the early part of the twentieth century. Certainly it is not merely a product of the last few decades since the megalopolis has emerged very gradually out of the large metropolitan complexes which existed in the nineteenth century and the distinctiveness of the metropolis was recognized by contemporary writers long before the Second World War. For example, the last stage in the urban typology of Gras (1922) was the development of the metropolitan region defined in terms very similar to the later descriptions of post-industrial cities. The Chicago ecologists too, despite their preoccupation with the internal structure and especially the more central parts of a single 'industrial' city, recognized the larger-scale emergence of a distinctive metropolitan complex (McKenzie 1933). Even earlier than this, Mackinder had talked of the influence of London extending widely throughout southern England in terms which are strongly suggestive of precisely the same sort of phenomenon:

In a manner all south-eastern England is a single urban community; for steam and electricity are changing our geographical conceptions. A city is no longer an area covered continuously with streets and houses. The wives and children of the merchants, even of the more prosperous of the artisans, live without — beyond green fields — where the men only sleep and pass the Sabbath. The metropolis in its largest meaning includes all the counties for whose inhabitants London is 'Town', whose men do habitual business there, whose women buy and spend there, whose morning paper is printed there, whose standard of thought is determined there. East Anglia and the West of England possess a certain independence by virtue of their comparatively remote position, but, for various reasons, even they belong effectively to Metropolitan England. Birmingham, in Industrial England, is the nearest independent community, with its own heart-beat, with subject boroughs which call it 'Town', with its own daily newspapers guiding opinion not wholly dictated from London. (Mackinder 1902, p. 258)

The gradual recognition of what are considered to be radically different phenomena poses the question of the extent to which these urban types really are different in kind or merely in degree. Is it the confidence of hindsight and the happy blurring of detail through lack of data which enable writers to categorize the pre-industrial city as being so simple and so unitary? Is the dispersed post-industrial city so very different from the industrial city out of which it emerged? Any resolution of such questions would require both more data than are readily available and a separate monograph. It is however worth briefly posing the question of the extent to which the apparent differences are as much matters of the scale at which data can be collected in urban studies as of more fundamental differences of kind.

It may be that, while cities have grown in physical size, our own conceptual scales have not kept pace and our measuring instruments have remained of constant size. This might be illustrated with the familiar example of the shape of population density curves within cities since the literature on the topic suggests that, conforming to the notion that today's cities are different animals, the density curves have progressively changed over time. The regular downward slope of density gradients as one moves outwards from the city centre has been one of the happy lynch-pins in the geographers' quest for spatial regularities and one which has been widely exploited. Following Colin Clark's (1951) first demonstration of a regular negative-exponential decline, the same regularity was shown for countless other cities and the factors universally advanced as explanation invoked the importance of the central city in terms of the bid-rent functions of residential and other land users for all of whom the central city had positive utility. Subsequently, however, this monolithic certainty began to be frayed as writers began to take greater account of the central density crater caused by non-residential land uses and varieties of higher-order surfaces were used to fit the density data (Tanner 1961; Newling 1966 and 1969). More recent still is the suggestion from Berry (1970) that the idea of a density decline is being turned inside-out since population densities now show signs of increase rather than decrease as one moves away from the central business district. This suggestion would appear to tie in neatly with the notion of a post-industrial city which is different in kind from the industrial city which first gave rise to the classic pattern of density decline. It would also find a parallel in the similar erosion of confidence in the existence of a regular distance decline in land values away from the city centre (see, for example, Yeates 1965). Might it not, however, be the case that such apparent differences in the modern city are the result of the scale at which such patterns are measured? Non-residential land has always existed within cities and, if, as seems not unreasonable, it has tended to be found in more central areas, there must long have been a central crater of population density. The fact that the extent of central non-residential land has increased as the area of the city has increased seems undeniable, but the consequence for making comparable measurements of density in cities of different size is that one ought to adopt a unit of observation which differs depending on the extent of the city. That density appears to increase with distance may therefore be a consequence simply of the greater absolute extent of the central city even though relatively the same pattern of centre and periphery may still hold. Once again, the problem may resolve itself into one of trying to define an appropriate extent of what is meant by 'city' and an appropriate module for the constituent parts of which it is composed. The explanation for density curves suggested by Casetti (1967), which relies on the balance of the diametrically opposed forces of desire for centrality and desire for greater space, could as well account for the regular gradients suggested by Clark as for the 'distance accretion' suggested by Berry. Gulliver in Brobdingnag was shocked at the coarseness of the women's skin. Had he been a Brobdingnagian, and not, as he was to them, a dwarf, the women would have appeared as smooth, and no doubt as titillating, as the regular density curves of small cities do to the geographer.

This long digression might perhaps suggest that, while it has indisputably grown larger, while its inhabitants have more widely specialized roles and while its contacts may be more widespread more complex and less contiguous, the modern city may still be the old writ large and that certain of the apparently radical differences are as much a product of scale as of kind.

ESCAPING THE DILEMMA

Nevertheless, we are still faced with a dilemma in that, however the city is defined, all of the operational definitions still leave unanswered the conceptual problem that a city cannot be isolated as a functional operating unit in spatial terms. If it is narrowly defined, many of the people intimately involved in its activities will be excluded; if it is generously defined, many of the people included will be involved only marginally if at all. This suggests that, if we wish to isolate a set of cities with a reasonable amount of confidence in our spatial definitions, a useful compromise might be to turn to earlier rather than more recent periods of time. The extent of flows of commuting into central cities can provide some useful guidelines of the degree of relative self-containment of cities at different periods, and there is a variety of evidence which suggests the changing extent of the journey-to-work over the last century, which demonstrates the gradual widening of the catchment areas of towns. For the nineteenth century it is true that there is little substantive material since census data on place of work and place of residence have only been provided very recently and there are no substantial surveys of such movements comparable to those of the twentieth century. What evidence there is, however, does paint a picture of very short distances separating the worker from his work. Charles Booth's discussion of the casual labour market in London (Booth 1902-3; see also G. S. Jones 1971) gives some idea of the forces making for uncertain employment of large proportions of the working population of the nineteenth century and of their consequent need for access to centres of employment at a time when regular contracts of work were not the normal means of labour supply. The nature of the hiring process, at least as far as many of the unskilled workers were concerned, was conducive to a strong centralizing of the homes of the poor so that they were accessible to the central places where labour was hired. Warnes (1970) gives some suggestive evidence for the town of Chorley by plotting the places of residence of people in particular occupations and the places where such occupations were carried out. While such information is only suggestive in cases where there is more than a single place in which people of a given occupation could be employed, the patterns for mid-nineteenth-century Chorley do show very strong residential concentrations of certain occupations such as miners and quayside workers around the few places where such work was available. From other scattered sources the picture emerges that journeys-to-work were certainly short on average, but that a minority of workers could travel considerable distances even in the nineteenth century. In North America, for example, Goheen's work on Toronto shows that workers in the legal city could be drawn from wide quarters throughout the area for particular occupations (Goheen 1970). Likewise, Pred's maps of the journey-to-work for New York engravers and for miscellaneous industrial occupations in the first half of the nineteenth century (Pred 1966, pp. 196-215) show a generally tight bunching of homes around places of work, but with a certain small fraction of journeys of over two miles. For Britain, the evidence of the mid-1880s submitted to the Royal Commission on the Housing of the Working Classes suggests that it was only the more skilled and better-paid of the artisans who were able to travel distances of more than a few miles. The effects of improving internal transport were limited to a very small sector of the population until well into the 1890s (Dyos 1953 and 1955; Pollins 1964; Kellett 1969, chapter 11; see also Vance 1967) so that, in the words of Hobsbawm (1964, p. 8), for the unskilled artisan, 'all that lay beyond a tiny circle of personal acquaintances or walking distance was darkness'. In a large metropolis such as London, the nineteenth century was almost entirely a period when the great majority of workers lived close to their place of work and when many of the work-places themselves were highly segregated into distinct occupational districts as Hall's (1962) maps of certain of the trades in furniture and clothing suggest. Even though a minority of people travelled long journeys to work in central cities, the predominant pattern of the century was for urban areas to be relatively self-contained employment areas.

For the contrasting picture of the more recent period, there are much more comprehensive and reliable data. Lawton (1968a) has compared the patterns of journey-to-work in 1921 and 1951 for England and Wales and his maps show clearly the increasing pull of the cities, or conversely the increasing spread away from cities of the homes of those who work there. They also suggest that, even in 1921, considerable numbers of workers lived well outside the city limits of the places in which they worked. The massive surveys of Liepmann (1944) for Britain and of Loewenstein (1965) for America provide further corroboration. Liepmann implies in much of what she writes that the lengthening of the journey to work was, in 1944, still a relatively recent phenomenon in Britain and many of her examples certainly demonstrate that relatively large proportions of workers still lived close to their place of work. A survey of Longbridge car workers in Birmingham in 1937, for example, showed that almost one-half lived less than five miles from the factory. Two surveys within London in 1936 found not dissimilar proportions: workers at Standard Telephones and Cables Ltd, with predominantly male employees, had 60 per cent living within five miles; and the tobacco firm of Carreras, with largely female workers, had almost 90 per cent living within the London postal area (Liepmann 1944, pp. 133-45).

While today the blowing apart of the once discrete and relatively self-contained city, which is suggested by the concept of the post-industrial city, is well reflected in the complex overlapping of work-spheres which cover almost the whole of the national territory of developed economies, the process by which the association between place of work and place of residence has become distended is by no means a new phenomenon. It has been developing for as long as means of communication have made it possible for people to move other than on foot with relative ease and increasing speed. The fact that this has been a gradual process means that, giving emphasis to the built-up area of towns and the labour force drawn into that area, it would be difficult to suggest any period for which one could confidently draw bounds to a spatial definition of a city. The further back in time that one goes, however, the greater can be one's confidence in the boundaries that are used.

NINETEENTH-CENTURY TOWNS AS TESTING GROUNDS OF THEORY

The discussion may appear to have moved some way from the problem of urban definition. Certainly the concern has been more with the operational than with the conceptual problems, but if urban population is defined as that collection of people which is affected by work and economic transactions which are characteristically urban — the secondary and tertiary occupations within the context of a sophisticated market economy — then the economic areas traced out by the flows of journey-to-work go some way towards providing a viable measure. Drawing such areas at the present day would raise a host of problems of non-contiguous space since people 'belonging' to city x might live in city y and people living in villages close to the city might not 'belong' to it whereas others in more distant villages might. Such geometrical problems set interesting challenges to the conventional spatial notions of geographers and, while far from being resolved, reactions to them have begun to sketch out the non-Euclidian geometries which would be necessary to tackle them (Tobler 1963; Harvey 1969). But in the absence of ways in which one can readily identify a city and its population as a discrete object, it would seem that the further back in time one goes, the greater the confidence that can be placed in the meaning of the urban populations which can be derived. Since our concern is with population change in towns, this suggests the nineteenth century as a fruitful period in which to test ideas and examine data. Nineteenth-century towns may not have been self-contained, but they were discrete entities to a far greater extent than the complex and sprawling blotches on the map of the twentieth century. Obviously the larger places, such as London or provincial towns of the standing of Manchester, Liverpool or Birmingham, drew upon and affected large tracts of land and large numbers of people from outside their built-up areas and did so to a greater extent as the century wore on. Writing in 1848, and drawing comparisons with the seventeenth century, Macaulay wrote of London, 'The town did not, as now, fade by imperceptible degrees into the country. No long avenues of villas, embowered in lilacs and laburnums, extended from the great centres of wealth and civilization almost to the boundaries of Middlesex and far into the heart of Kent and Surrey' (quoted in Briggs 1968, p. 730). Even though London was later to become, as Mackinder so presciently noted or as Wells so truly prophesied, a metropolis extending its influence over virtually the whole of the country, it was still the case that the divorce between urbanization on the one hand and the urban process on the other had progressed significantly less far in the nineteenth than it has in the twentieth century.

The nineteenth century may, then, offer something of a useful compromise between the unmanageable complexity of defining urban populations at the present day and the utopian state alleged for the self-contained pre-industrial city of early medieval times. It is also, more obviously, a practicable period with which to deal since the demographic data of the censuses and the great wealth of other less general sources of information fully justify Sir Richard Giffen's contemporary epithet of the period as 'the statistical century'. Cairncross (1949, p. 67) considered that changes in the scale and structure of nineteenth-century society meant that there 'are few better quarries for the theory of economic development than Victorian England'. Certainly, for testing theories there is a vast mine of information provided by the censuses, even though, in the words of the well-known quotation, the stones in that quarry are of little use until they are dug out, shaped and built up in an intelligent fashion. Since our concern will be with testing ideas rather than with problems of policy, we would be better served by turning to an earlier period and looking at the nineteenth century as a context in which to develop hypotheses about the nature of the objects we call towns.

CHAPTER 2

City systems and size distributions

If a model can be developed which, when suitable parameters are fed in, fits everything from the rise and fall of New England stone masons to hospital management and the decay of the city, we may question whether the general system has not become so general as to become operationally meaningless or philosophically otiose.

TIMES LITERARY SUPPLEMENT, 1971

Concerned as they are with so wide a variety of data and with *collages* of those data, it is not surprising that geographers have turned to the concept of systems in their efforts to tease out the relationships in which they are interested. For American geography the notion of the subject as a study of systems has even had a semi-official stamp of approval in the publication, under the auspices of the Association of American Geographers, of *The science of geography* (National Academy of Sciences 1965; see also Association of American Geographers 1968) which argued, following Ackerman's Presidential Lecture of 1963, that the subject was concerned with the study of physical, political and economic systems with locational analysis as an overall set of tools through which such systems might be understood in their spatial context. Reactions to this suggestion in particular and to the application of systems' notions in general have not been lacking. Thoman (1965) protested at the emphasis given to location and the lack of attention paid to historical geography in the agenda formulated in *The science of geography* and Chisholm flailed at general systems theory with an oddly constructed two-tailed whip; it was at once nothing but 'plain common sense' yet an 'irrelevant distraction' (M. Chisholm 1967, p. 51).

Despite such reactions it is apparent that the notion of 'system' is an attractive one to geography. That great prop of geography, the natural region — as conceived by de la Blache in particular — is a system *par excellence* since the concept underlying the recognition of the region is that the various elements which comprise it are given a unity and a distinctive coherence by the interconnection and interdependence which characterize them. This, at its simplest, is what 'system' is all about. As Chorley and Kennedy (1971, p. 2) suggest, it is essentially a *gestalt* concept in which the relationships between the elements make it greater in sum than the mere addition of the constituents of which it is comprised. As Angyal (1941) notes, the difference between an aggregate and a system is that in the former the parts are added while in the latter they are arranged.

A commonly quoted definition of a system is that by Hall and Fagen (1956) who state that a system is 'a set of objects together with the relationships between the objects and between their attributes'. To define and isolate such systems a number of aspects need to be considered. First is the set of objects themselves and here the appositeness of the discussion of first-order objects of study in the previous chapter is apparent. For middle-order objects like the city the geographer is faced with insurmountable difficulties in trying to define an object called 'the city' in functional terms and these problems become of some importance in considering the effectiveness of the application of systems' ideas to urban studies. However one goes about defining the objects of study, they form the elements of any system. The second essential component is the set of attributes of those elements. The cities, or whatever may be the object of study, must have some definable attributes which can be measured and which will provide some indication of the performance of the object. Third, the relationships between the elements need to be specified. These are the connections between the objects which make the system more than a collection of independent parts. Fourth, it must be possible to adduce the state of the system; that particular conglomeration of values of the attributes of the elements which obtains at some given time. Finally, as an over-riding consideration, one needs to specify the relationship of the system to the environment in which it operates. This raises the twin problems of defining the appropriate environment for the system as well as of determining the degree of open-ness or closure of the system itself. This latter point has raised innumerable bogeys in the various studies which have used a systems' framework. Many have used the assumptions which pertain to closed systems in which the state of the system may be expected, by the second law of thermodynamics, to tend towards some form of maximum entropy.[1] In practice of course, virtually all of the systems which are considered in geography are only in varying degrees of closure so that some form of steady state replaces maximum entropy as the 'goal' towards which the system tends. Drainage basins export water to other basins or to the ocean and in turn import water from the atmosphere and from other basins. A nation's economy is likewise supported by imports and exports of goods, people and ideas from and to areas outside its boundaries. How such lack of complete closure affects the performance of the system in question and of the goals towards which it might be hypothesized to develop, are questions calling for some refined discussion. Certainly the common analogy with the tendency for differences in temperature

---

[1] For the physical sciences, the concept of entropy derives from the tendency of a system to assume the most random molecular state. Systems, in other words, are likely to become disordered. The reason for the tendency is that random molecular motion more probably produces a disordered than an ordered state. Entropy is the property by which the disorder is described quantitatively so that a more disordered state has a higher entropy than an ordered state. In transferring such concepts to urban studies two problems stand out; how can one measure order and disorder and how can one translate the notion of molecular activity into the context of the 'performance' of the city.

of a gas in an enclosed cylinder to equalize over time, cannot be accepted at face value in the application of systems' concepts to social and economic observations.

The use of such systems' ideas within geography has certainly only begun to face the difficulties of transmuting these concepts into ones appropriate to the data used by geographers. Two of the main stumbling blocks have been the confusion between different approaches to systems and the imprecision of the terminology of systems. On the first, Harvey (1969, pp. 471-80) recognizes three sorts of systems' approach. First is systems' analysis in which the concepts of systems developed in biology, the electrical sciences, cybernetics and other physical sciences have been applied to the social sciences simply as tools of analysis for unearthing the relationships of complex bodies of material. Second is the theory of general systems which is an attempt, developed in the writings of Mesarovic (1964), to explore the syntax of systems. Third, and perhaps most controversial, is general systems' theory which, in the hands of von Bertalanffy (1950) and of Boulding (1956), has attempted to demonstrate the universality of explanatory structures by tracing out the isomorphism between systems comprised of very different types of phenomena and thus to establish the lineaments of a grand general theory cutting across the conventional disciplines. The distinction between the writings of Mesarovic and von Bertalanffy is by no means clear-cut, but the contrast between attempts to develop systems' theory as an interdisciplinary philosophy on the one hand and the use of systems' concepts as working tools of analysis on the other is certainly marked. That many criticisms of 'systems' theory' fail to recognize such differences is an example of the confusion which occurs in the literature. At a more detailed level, it is also abundantly clear that there is great confusion in the use of terminology, even in the literature of the physical sciences. So fundamental a concept as entropy is given widely varying interpretations and in this, as in the interpretation of 'systems' analysis' in general, semantic fashion has outstripped semantic clarity (Wilbanks and Symanski 1968). As Langton (1972) has concluded, the euphoria which has sometimes accompanied the discussion of systems' theory in the geographical literature has often been misplaced or at least not supported by sufficiently clear elaborations of its applicability.

SYSTEMS IN THE STUDY OF TOWNS

Most of the attempts to use the concepts of systems within human geography have, either explicitly or implicitly, turned to the more limited use of systems' analysis rather than to the more wide-reaching theories of general systems. Their success has proved rather variable. There have been two main types of application: either the somewhat vague recourse to the terminology of systems and the use of its concepts to provide frameworks within which data are organized or parallelism between phenomena suggested; or the more precise use of certain measures taken from the literature of systems and applied to a more limited body of data. As instances of the former, Berry (1964) has linked together a number of the recurring generalities in urban geography in an attempt to argue that all can be seen under a single neat umbrella. He argues that, in looking at cities, the regularity of density gradients, the tessellations of spacings and sizes and the overall size distribution of cities, provide systems within systems which can be represented by various sets of accounting equations which embody the relationships between the attributes of the city objects. In similar vein, Olsson (1967) draws together the same sets of regularities in tracing the connections between central-place theory, regularities in distance interaction and the stochastic processes which can be taken as underlying them. The more rigorous applications of systems' ideas however have evolved from extensions of 'social physics' and the gravity concepts applied to human populations by Stewart (Stewart 1947; Stewart and Warntz 1958; Neft 1966). The now considerable body of work which has developed such gravity concepts in the context of entropy-maximization has followed the lead of Wilson (1970) whose work on deriving the most-probable states of certain probability distributions has given birth to a wholly new approach to the analysis of the internal structure of cities. Wilson's work has explored various trip-distributions and particularly the journey-to-work and it has translated the gravity models, which have long underlain much of the geographical interest in movement, into but one of a whole family of models of interaction which have subsequently been used as the building blocks for models both at an urban (for example: Crowther and Echenique 1972; Anthony and Baxter 1971) and a regional (for example: Cripps and Foot 1969) scale.

In these latter applications, the use of systems' concepts has been of a more limited sort, as distinct from the much more all-embracing arguments of Berry and Olsson. As Wilson says, the difference is that entropy is used as a measure of a probability distribution and the object of trying to maximize entropy for any particular distribution has been to assess the most probable state of a system whose elements can be defined with some precision and for which distinct constraints can be specified. In his own work, taking a set of origin and destination flows, he produces a matrix of trips which are constrained such that the sum of the elements (the T_{ij} terms which measure trips from origin to destination) equals both the total origins and the total destinations, and the summed total of expenditure on travel in the system equals the overall amount of capital spent on travel. His measure of maximum entropy then represents the most likely state of the system and can be used, in aggregate terms, to distribute trips within the matrix of origins and destinations.

This brings us back once again to the nub of all attempts to use systems' concepts. If the nature of the system cannot be defined with sufficient precision, the application of measures of system becomes inappropriate and unrevealing or, at the very least, difficult to interpret. If there is difficulty in defining towns in the first instance and even greater difficulty in specifying the nature of the linkages between those 'towns', then the use of systems' concepts in justification for empirical regularities takes on more than a slight air of mysticism. For a limited and clearly defined set of objects and their relationships, measures of entropy may have meaning, but for the 'city' as a whole it is difficult to know what they may be. Such doubt surrounds not only those studies which make more nebulous recourse to the language of systems, but also many of the more formal applications of systems' ideas as well. Both G. P. Chapman (1970) and Curry (1964), for example, use cities as their objects of study in using information theory and systems' analysis in the study of the sizes and spacings of settlements. It is interesting to note the difficulty which Chapman finds in interpreting the quantitative measures which he derives to analyse the patterns of settlement distribution and size and equally to note the difficulty of translating Curry's abstract system-based arguments into an urban context without the invocation of some vague and unspecified teleological forces.[1]

CITY-SIZE DISTRIBUTIONS

One of the most frequently advanced justifications for regarding sets of cities as systems has been the appearance of regularity in the distribution of the population sizes of the component places. The regularity of size distributions has been a source both of interest and of frustration within urban geography for a considerable time. While some have argued that it is an indicator of the system-like nature of cities, others have poured scorn on what has been seen as a mindless exercise in curve fitting. Geographical interest in size distributions owes much to Zipf's *National unity and disunity* (1941; see also Zipf 1949), although, as Rosing (1966) has pointed out, Zipf was by no means the first person to point to the regularity of city sizes; Auerbach in 1913, Lotka in 1924 and Singer in 1936 had each previously drawn attention to it and it had not escaped the notice of the Chicago ecologists of the 1920s (Goodrich 1926). Lotka, a statistician, reached a gloomy conclusion after further study of the application of rank-size curves to other data: 'Frequency distributions such as these have a wide range of applicability to a variety of phenomena, and the mere form of such a distribution throws little or no light on the underlying physical relations' (Lotka 1926, quoted in Rosing 1966). Despite this, Zipf's work gave rise to a great deal of subsequent speculation both about the form of the curves which best described city sizes as well as about the mechanisms which might give rise to them.

The first focus of such enquiry was on the contrast between the size distribution suggested by Zipf and that implicit in the earlier suggestion by

[1] See below, p. 29.

Jefferson (1939) of the existence of 'primate' cities. Zipf's 'rule' states that, if cities are ranked from the largest to the smallest and if P_r is the population of the rth-ranked city and P_1 that of the largest city, then city sizes can be described by the simple expression $P_r = P_1 \cdot r^{-1}$. In other words, the second largest city will have a population one-half that of the largest, the third will have a population one-third that of the largest and the nth-ranked city will be one-nth the size of the largest. The 'rule' is referred to as the rank-size rule since rank multiplied by size will be a constant value (equal, of course, to the size of the largest place). Such a distribution of sizes will obviously plot as a straight line on logarithmic paper and the slope of the curve, given by the exponent of $1 \cdot 0$ to which the denominator is raised, will be $45°$. The simple Zipf formula can be made more general (Stewart 1947; Berry 1961) by introducing a variable exponent, q, which will steepen or flatten the slope, but still preserve the linearity of the size distribution. Various ways of expressing this straight-line plot using different values for q are shown in fig. 2.1.

A contrasting plot, which would not be a straight line, would arise from Jefferson's suggestion of urban primacy; 'All over the world it is the Law of the Capitals that the largest city shall be supereminent, and not merely in size, but in national influence' (Jefferson 1939, p. 227). Again, to generalize this, the 'primate' pattern would therefore lead to the expectation that a set of cities would contain one or a small number of very large places with a distinct gap between it and an array of very much smaller places.

It is this suggested dichotomy which has given rise to much empirical classification of the size distributions of national sets of cities and to attempts to relate the different curves to aspects of the social and economic characteristics of the countries concerned. Both Colin Clark (1967) and Berry (1961) have drawn up typologies based on size distributions. Clark plots the cumulative frequency of cities against population on logarithmic paper and distinguishes the following types: a pattern of 'primacy' in which the largest cities are disproportionately large so that the right tail of the distribution flattens out; an 'oligarchic' pattern in which, while the number of primate cities is kept in check, there is an over-representation of cities of middle orders of size; and a 'counter-primate' pattern in which the largest cities are under-represented so that the right tail of the distribution steepens. Examples of these different patterns, recognized in such graphical ways, are shown to apply to a variety of countries and Clark discusses, somewhat cursorily, the reasons why different curves might fit different countries. Berry's distinctions are drawn between 'primate' size distributions on one hand and 'lognormal' on the other, with a variety of transitional types between these two extremes. He in fact sees the various curves as parts of an evolutionary scheme in which 'lognormal' distributions might be expected to evolve from 'primate' ones. Like Clark, Berry suggests reasons for the fit of particular curves to particular countries and we shall return to his explanations later in the discussion.

Figure 2.1   The rank–size array: alternative graphical plots. In each diagram the same three size distributions are used

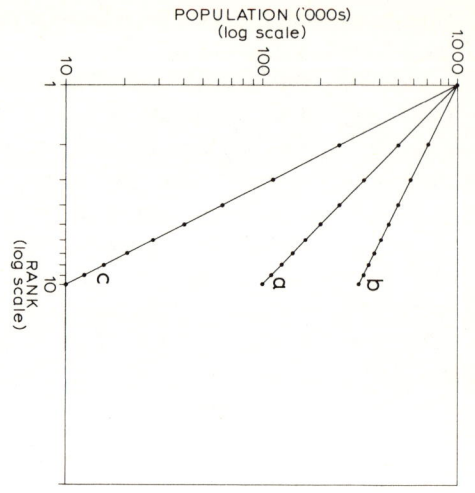

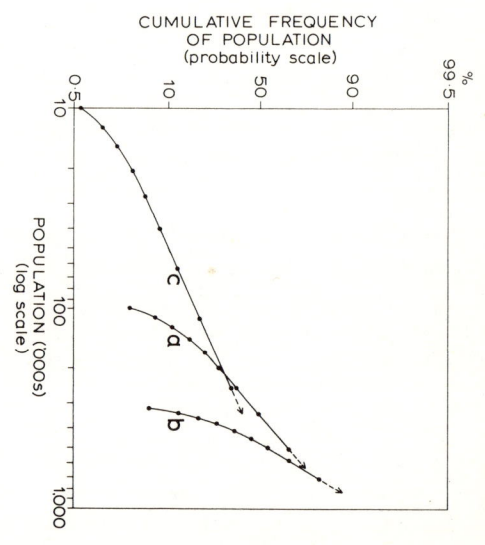

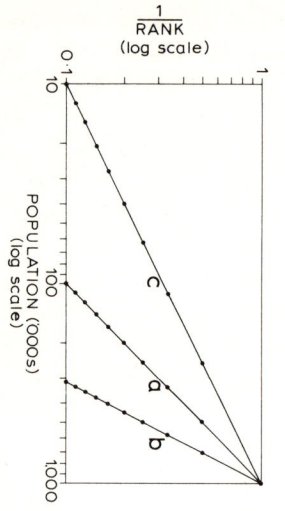

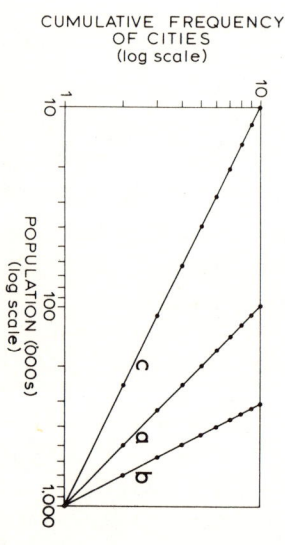

a $P_r = P_1 r^{-1}$ b $P_r = P_1 r^{-0.5}$ c $P_r = P_1 r^{-2}$

THE VARIETY OF FREQUENCY CURVES

Zipf's rank-size curve is, of course, only one of a number which could be used to describe frequency distributions which are highly skewed and city-size distributions are only one of a variety of types of social and economic phenomena which assume this sort of shape. Many other curves have been suggested and subsequently explored both by statisticians and geographers as predictors of a multitude of phenomena. Zipf himself looked at other data such as the frequency of words used both in speech and in writing and many of the alternative frequency distributions have been fitted to such phenomena as income distribution,[1] population sizes of countries, sizes of firms, the number of publications of scientists and winnings at gambling (for examples of a wide variety of such phenomena, see Kendall 1961). The lognormal distribution has been a popular candidate to describe many such frequencies. Simon (1955) has suggested forms of the Yule distribution and the various forms of Pareto distribution have equally been widely suggested.

The variety of frequency distributions and cumulative frequency distributions which have variously been espoused presents a number of difficulties, chiefly that the distributions are not greatly dissimilar from each other and so are difficult to distinguish. Zipf's law is a higher-the-fewer rule, of which Pareto's equation is a particular case; Zipf's generalized equation is, in turn, an approximation of the much more general Yule distribution. With skewed distributions of the sort used to describe city-size distributions, it is only the right-hand tail which is used to provide a fit to the data and, even though the distributions as a whole may be differently derived, their tails may virtually be indistinguishable given the relatively crude measures of fit which can be called upon. This can clearly be seen in the common assumption that the lognormal and the rank-size distributions are identical, an assumption which Berry makes throughout his work on size distributions. The falsity of this assumption can be seen graphically by comparing identical arrays of city sizes. Figure 2.2 illustrates, for a rank-size array, both a plot of rank against size on logarithmic paper and of cumulative frequency against size on logarithmic probability paper. Where only large cities are used the discrepancy may not be severe, but where smaller city sizes are used, the array of sizes must obviously curve downwards away from the straight-line plot expected on the basis of the assumption of lognormality.[2] Ferguson (1969, Part 2) has provided a formal demonstration of the mathematical lack of equivalence between the rank-size and lognormal distributions. Even though their right tails may be similar (that is, where larger sizes of places are used), the two distributions are not identical. The use of lognormal

[1] Champernowne's (1937) study of income distribution is of particular interest as an early use of transition probabilities before the development of Markov methods.

[2] See also fig. 2.1.

A

B

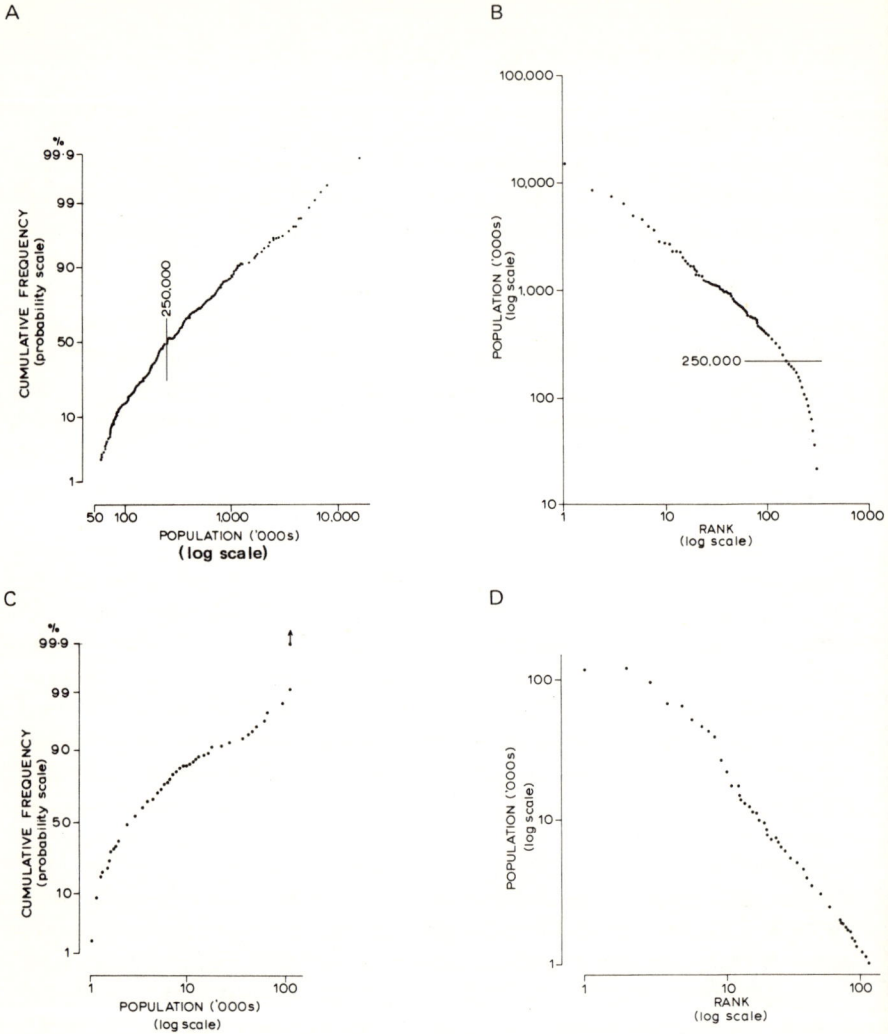

C

D

Figure 2.2   The rank-size array: plotting data on logarithmic and log-normal graphs. Data are identical in A and B (Berry 1969) and in C and D (Ferguson 1969)

assumptions to test the rank-size rule is thus fraught with difficulties, amongst which is the choice of a lower population threshold at which places are included since the various graphical portraits of size arrays plotted on logarithmic probability paper produce different slopes, and in certain cases different forms of curve, depending on the threshold size at which cities are selected as qualifying for entry to the city 'system'. In addition, even if the arrays do conform to a lognormal plot, they are not necessarily rank-size curves.

FITTING THE CURVES

Both in fitting and in testing the fit of size distributions there are further difficulties. Tests of the rank-size rule have used a variety of approaches. Stewart (1958), for example, looks at the five largest cities of countries throughout the world and concludes, on the basis of the fact that the ratios of sizes do not conform exactly to the expected progression — 1·0, 0·5, 0·33, 0·25, 0·2 — that the rank-size pattern does not hold. Rosing (1966) also uses only the largest five cities, but fits a curve with a slope of 45° and tests the significance of the chi-square values which indicate the fit between observed and expected sizes. Again he draws a negative conclusion both from this test and also on the basis of the lack of relationship between the residuals from these curves and various measures of the economic development of the countries. Whereas Stewart's method of fitting a curve to the largest place makes the unreasonable assumption that all places other than the largest may be out of kilter, Rosing appears to use the more precise method of least-squares fitting. Browning and Gibbs (1961) provide a rough approximation to this least-squares procedure which involves calculating the expected population of the largest place by summing the reciprocals of all of the city ranks, and then deriving the expected populations of other places as fractions of this in the progression 0·5, 0·33 etc. Such methods all assume that the fit is to be against the simple rank-size plot using an exponent of 1·0, but the most usual method is least-squares regression which produces both a variable intercept and a variable slope to the curve (see Duncan and Reiss 1956, pp. 25-8 for an early example). The goodness of fit can then be tested by using chi-square, although the further difficulty arises here that the density of point observations varies along both axes so that differential weight is given to the large and the small places in the fitting of the curve.

The most extensive test of the various alternative curves is that by Quandt (1964) who examines no fewer than eight types of distribution which are tested against city sizes amongst other types of data. Since the Pareto type-I was fitted by two different methods — using least squares (Pareto type-1a) and the method of maximum likelihood (Pareto type-Ib) — a total of nine tests was used in all. The city-size data were treated in a variety of ways: by using a basic set of cities of over 50,000 population; by using the same set, but with 50,000 subtracted from each observation; and by looking only at the upper half of the distribution. The goodness of fit was tested with the Kolmogorov-Smirnov statistic which, as Quandt admits, is not a wholly satisfactory test since it measures only the overall displacement of the expected and observed curves and cannot compare the two curves along their entire range. Of the distribution functions most commonly invoked in the case of city sizes — the lognormal and the Pareto — it is of considerable interest to see that Quandt found that each proved to provide a best fit to one or other of the various data sets. For example, with the full set of cities of over 50,000 population, all four distributions met the critical value so that it was not possible to reject the null hypothesis that each could have generated the sample set of city sizes; but, of the total of nine tests, the distribution function which performed best was the Pareto type-Ia, second was the Pareto type-Ib, third was the Pareto type-II and fifth was the lognormal. A second approach involved comparisons of the lognormal and the two Pareto functions with the coefficients of the Lorenz curves of the city sizes and, here, it was the Pareto type-II and the lognormal which proved to be the best predictors. Finally, using in place of the Kolmogorov-Smirnov a new statistic which incorporates observations at each point along the whole array of observations, Quandt suggests that the lognormal is a much better description of the modified set of city sizes (with 50,000 subtracted from each population) than for the unmodified set, thus to some extent reinforcing the suggestion made above that the lower population threshold of size which is selected in testing such distributions is critical both in fitting and testing the fit of distribution functions.

Quandt's survey is of interest in a number of ways. First it suggests the difficulty of establishing the goodness of fit of such frequency distributions. Second, and only partly consequent upon the first point, it suggests the even greater difficulty of distinguishing between the fit of various of the alternative distributions. Each is closely similar to the other and, while no single one could explain all the sets of data at which Quandt looks, for any one set of data more than a single distribution will give a reasonable estimate of the actual observations. It is this latter point which provides the most telling statistical weakness of the voluminous literature which argues for one rather than another frequency distribution as an explanation of such socio-economic data as city sizes. Quandt concludes that 'the distributions under consideration are all fairly similar; they probably exhibit smaller deviations from each other than a perfectly error free sample would exhibit from the actual one' (Quandt 1964, p. 22).

There is a close parallel between such curve-fitting exercises applied to city-size distributions and the attempts to fit probability distributions to the frequencies of observations in spatial quadrats which are found in the geographical literature on point-pattern analysis (Harvey 1966 and 1968). In this latter literature, such distributions as the negative binomial and the Neyman type-A have been compared with empirical data on the frequencies of point observations such as settlements. The conclusions which emerge suggest the difficulty, similar to that of city-size distributions, of identifying unambiguously which of several distributions best fit the appropriate data. Furthermore, as Dacey (1968, p. 61) notes, no fewer than six different generating processes might give rise to a distribution such as the negative binomial. Harvey, reflecting on this, has suggested that the point-pattern analyses are examples of what he calls 'over-identified' models since, without further information, it is not possible to infer which of a number of theories might be most appropriate

(Harvey 1969, p. 166). This parallel suggests that one might profitably turn to the process explanations which have been suggested for the various city-size distributions to see to what extent they too might be thought of as over-identified, since, as has been suggested, the critical right-hand tails of these distributions are similar and yet the distributions themselves are severally produced by different types of generating process.

EXPLANATIONS OF CITY-SIZE REGULARITIES

Three general types of explanation of city-size distributions might be recognized: concepts derived from central-place theory; ideas based on principles of maximization or optimization; and notions based on the assumption of the random growth of city populations. The three are by no means clearly distinct. The second and third in particular overlap considerably since random growth is usually seen as a product of the same types of varied and multiple stimuli which lead to the overall entropy-maximizing steady states which underlie many of the second types of explanation. It is useful, however, to discuss the three separately.

The first is the only one which does not allow for any operating dynamic process of growth since central-place theory has never been couched in dynamic terms. A central-place approach is therefore hard to reconcile with a system which grows by small increments as do city populations. There has, however, been a number of attempts to demonstrate the compatability of the carefully balanced geometry of central-place theory, with its expectation of distinct breaks in a hierarchy of centres of different levels, on the one hand, and the regular and continuous size gradation of the rank-size rule on the other. If such a relationship could be demonstrated formally, it could be argued that the spatial rationale of central-place theory − optimal space-filling and distance minimization on the part of consumers − would apply equally to the rank-size rule. The suggestion which has been most fully explored is that, while distinct hierarchical levels do exist, as central-place theory would suggest, the multiplier by which the population size of cities at one hierarchical level is 'blown up' to that of the next level is a random multiplier so that the steps of the size distribution are blurred into a continuous rather than a stepped curve. This attempted resolution has been widely invoked, but its only formal demonstration (Beckmann 1958) is undermined by a number of statistical and operational mistakes which have been pointed out by Dacey (1966) and, more especially, by Parr (1969; see also Beckmann and McPherson 1970). Parr (1970) has provided a review of these attempts to resolve the two size distributions and, while unable to demonstrate the compatability of the two, does show that the rank-size distribution can produce parameters consistent with central-place hierarchies so that, to this extent, the conceptual bases of the two are not substantially dissimilar. There is still however no formal proof of the idea, conceptually appealing though it may be.

Berry (1967, chapter 2) has suggested a slightly different mechanism by which the theory of central places and the empirical observations of rank-size distributions might be reconciled. He suggests that at different regional population densities the threshold sizes of the identical hierarchical levels in a central-place system will differ since, at a lower population density, even though the trade area of a given mth-level town will increase, the increase will not be sufficient to keep the supporting tributary population at the same size as that for an area of higher density. Thus, while in a small and relatively equally densely populated area, city sizes might be expected to show distinct hierarchical breaks, when a number of such small areas, each with its own regional population density, are aggregated together the differently-sized hierarchical steps would blur the overall distribution of city sizes into a more truly continuous curve. Again, attractive as the idea may be and despite the demonstration that threshold sizes do vary with regional population densities, there is nowhere a formal demonstration that the blurring would produce a lognormal, a rank-size or any other form of distribution. The distribution would presumably be dependent upon the particular *collage* of areas and densities which were pooled to form the aggregate 'system'. Even if the suggested isomorphism between central-place theory and the rank-size rule could be demonstrated, this first set of explanations would in any case be subject to the same damaging criticisms which have been widely levelled at central-place theory.

The second set of explanations calls rather loosely upon a number of somewhat ill-defined 'principles'. Zipf's own explanation invoked the joint effect of what he saw as two opposing forces: one being a force of 'diversification' by which a large number of small places develop, benefiting from locations close to widely distributed raw materials and thus minimizing their transport costs; the other being a force of 'unification' whereby a small number of large places develop to minimize the transportation costs to the consumer. The emergence of a rank-size distribution reflects the achievement of 'balance' between these opposing tendencies, although it is by no means clear how such balance emerges or why it should lead to so striking a regularity as Zipf was trying to explain. A similar sort of mildly mystical force appears to underlie many of the explanations which have been couched in terms of entropy. When Berry and Garrison, for example, talk of the rank-size distribution being the outcome of a random state and 'as such it is a condition of entropy' (Berry and Garrison 1958, p. 90), it is far from clear what they mean by 'entropy'.

There are, however, more satisfactory explanations invoking maximization or optimization which call upon more formal statements of entropy-maximization. The most precise has been applied not to city sizes, but to word frequencies. Mandelbrot (1953), drawing on information theory, derives a word-frequency distribution in terms of a principle of maximizing information content and, in similar vein, derives a frequency of word lengths in terms of maximizing efficiency or, alternatively, of minimizing cost. The closest parallel to this in the city-size case would seem to be Curry's (1964) rather less precise attempt to derive a city-size distribution. He suggests the following approach, which draws on the notion of random behaviour and the concepts of information theory. If N people are divided between Z settlements, with i being the number of people in each settlement and n being the average number of people per settlement, the cumulative distribution when entropy is maximized will be $P_1(1 - e^{-i/n})$. This, Curry suggests, produces a situation in which the ratio of the population of the $m + 1$st city to the mth city will be constant. This would obviously give a rank-size pattern, but it is not clear from his exposition how this ratio is derived. Nor, indeed, is it clear how one might translate this notion into processes of city growth although in a later paper Curry (1967, p. 231) appears to suggest that the rank-size pattern results in minimizing the length of the journey to shop in a central-place system.

Another, and very novel, derivation of a theory of city sizes which involves minimization is that of Evans (1972) who views cities as being composed of 'coalitions' of manufacturing firms. Each city's size is a linear function of the number of firms contained within it and, for each firm, economic returns are a function of city size. Each firm will tend to join the coalition of that size which minimizes its production costs and a general equilibrium will be achieved as an n-person game in which each firm, acting independently, joins coalitions of other firms. As an example, assuming that proportional deviations from the optimal coalition size result in equal proportional changes in production costs, Evans derives a model of city sizes in which each city is three times the size of the next largest place. Despite the attractiveness of the general approach of the paper, however, the detailed size distributions which are produced are highly dependent upon the initial assumptions which are made about the numbers of firms for which particular size coalitions are optimal.

A further approach, involving optimization rather than maximization, is represented by explanations which call on the principle of allometric growth in city systems. Stemming from the fascinating work of biologists such as D'Arcy Thompson (1917), allometric growth suggests that there is a constant ratio between the growth rate of an organ and of the organism of which it is a part. The farmer who measures a pig's weight from its girth rather than by heaving it onto a weighing machine, is a practical advocate of a principle of allometry linking width and weight in living organisms. Translating the biological notion into the city case, the proponents of allometric growth argue that, if one plots two curves of city sizes at successive times, the horizontal shifts represent the growth of the organism as a whole (the addition of new cities into the urban system) while the vertical shifts represent growth of the component organs (the changes in the individual city populations). Where the two curves are parallel, as

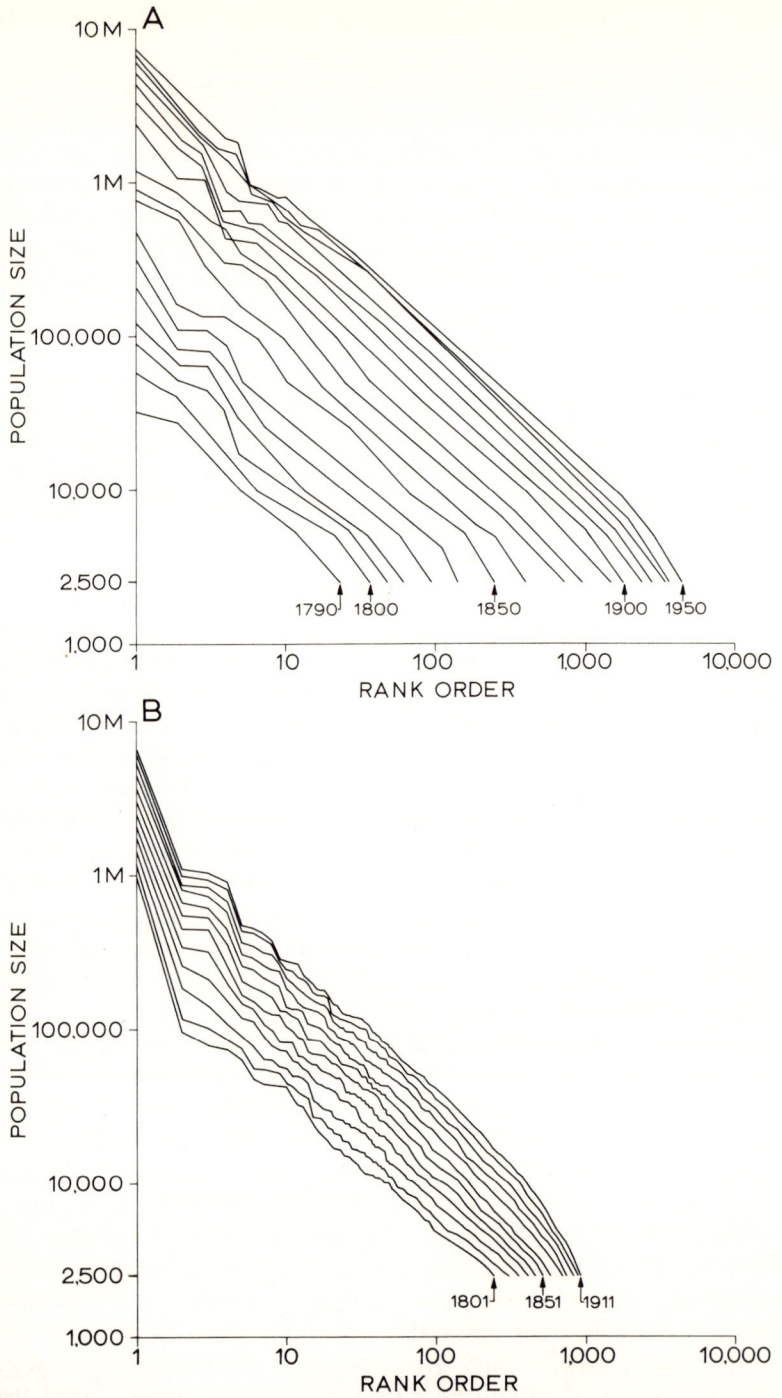

Figure 2.3 The size arrays of cities over time: (A) United States, 1790–1950 (B) England and Wales, 1801–1911

indeed is often the case in empirical data (fig. 2.3), then the ratio between the two is constant, as the law of allometric growth would suggest. Nordbeck (1965 and 1971) first introduced the idea to geography in looking at the constant ratio between city population and area, seeing allometric principles on the basis of a number of logarithmic relationships which he demonstrated both for this and for a number of other relationships applying to social and physical phenomena. Woldenberg (1967) has translated this allometric approach to the arguments surrounding city-size distributions by suggesting that rank-size plots are the consequence of an allometrically-growing central-place system.

The difficulty underlying acceptance of these various arguments which invoke principles of optimization or maximization is how the 'principles' might be translated into real-world conditions. The problem of trying to define an object called a 'city' has already been discussed briefly in relation to the application of systems' notions in general. This basic difficulty makes it extremely problematic as to what it is that the various explanations which call on optimization or maximization are trying to optimize or maximize, since, if one has difficulty in isolating the object itself, it is even more difficult to conceive of that object having some goal towards which it 'operates'. And, given the complexity of the relationships between the component parts of the total city whose population size is being used, it is unrealistic to attempt to single out one component and claim that it is shopping or space or whatever which is the sole element being optimized or maximized. Perhaps it might only be claimed that, by using the expectation of a maximally-probable state in a situation of such complexity that it can be thought of as 'behaving' randomly and thus subject to the laws of probability, measures of maximization can provide operational definitions of unconstrained situations against which departures will appear significant as clues to the types of constraint which operate within the system. This idea that the rank-size or the Pareto or the lognormal forms of city-size distributions may represent ideal unconstrained states and that it is the variations from these ideals which should be of interest as indications of the existence of constraints, is a suggestion which has certainly received much support in the literature on rank-size distributions (for example: Olsson 1967, p. 35; Berry 1964, pp. 149-50; Rosing 1966).

The third set of explanations of the city-size regularities looks explicitly or implicitly at the growth processes which are implied by different types of frequency distribution or which produce such distributions. They suggest that a rationale for the appearance of a given distribution may therefore lie in the reasonableness of the growth assumptions which are used. Two slightly different growth processes have been assumed: the first that, within any particular size group of cities, the towns will grow by a random proportion of their previous population; the second that any individual city will grow by a random proportion of its existing population. The former assumption underlies part of Simon's stochastic model of size distribution. He suggests (Simon 1955) that a

Yule distribution describes a variety of data including the city-size case. His argument for the Yule as a generating process is developed by using a word-frequency illustration. Given S words in a text, the probability that the S + 1st word has already appeared i times is assumed to be proportional to the number of words that have already appeared i times. A second assumption is that new words will appear with a constant probability. The right tail of his cumulative distribution — $f(i) = a \cdot i^{-c} \cdot b^i$ — reduces to the frequency equivalent of the rank size when b equals 1·0 and so the second assumption, which can be translated into the city case as being that new cities will be added to the system at a constant rate, becomes important in terms of the closeness of the b parameter to this figure of 1·0. It is Simon's first assumption, however, which deals more directly with the growth of existing cities since it argues that city growth would be random within a given size range of cities; in other words that fresh population would be added to existing cities as a constant, but random, proportion of their existing size. This assumption of random growth within groups of city sizes is a relatively weak one since it allows *individual* city growth to be influenced by the growth rate of previous periods (Steindl 1965; Simon and Bonini 1958; and, especially, Ijiri and Simon 1964). A given individual city which grew rapidly in one time period might, therefore, still be expected to grow rapidly in a subsequent period and, so long as its temporally-autocorrelated high growth rate was compensated for by some other city which grew commensurately slowly, the overall distribution of growth rates within that size class of cities might nevertheless be randomly normal. The assumption could, therefore, readily embrace the case of individual cities which were favourably placed with respect to growth so that an individual city's growth might be 'determined' yet the distribution of the size class as a whole still be random. E. N. Thomas' (1967) growth assumption is more restrictive. In deriving a rationale for a lognormal size-distribution, he assumes that growth will be random for any individual city and will therefore not be influenced by its previous growth rate. Thomas argues that, given this assumption and starting from a set of cities whose population at the outset is normally distributed, after a sufficient number of periods of small incremental growth, the distribution will converge on the lognormal. Looking at empirical data from Iowa, he finds that this lognormal model provides a less good fit than a log-lognormal model which he suggests as an alternative, but the importance of his paper lies in the rationale which it suggests for the lognormal curve which has been so widely used in describing city sizes. It is, of course, the case that most of the writers who have tested for lognormal distributions have equated it and the rank-size distribution so that one rapidly gets into deep water in trying to match the sets of growth processes which they have assumed to the particular frequency distributions which they have tested.

These two mildly different growth assumptions have provided the background to a number of the studies of city-size distributions which have called somewhat vaguely upon the complexity and hence the essential randomness of urban growth rates. Once their article is stripped of its systems' language, this is the argument underlying Berry and Garrison's (1958) explanation of city sizes. Most explicitly, Berry himself has advanced this argument in relation to his work on the relationship of 'lognormal' patterns of city sizes in various countries and their degree of economic development. He argues (Berry 1961 and 1969) that a 'lognormal' pattern can be expected to characterize those countries in which — because of their size, their complexity, their long history of urbanization and their well-developed linkages which bind all of the cities into a single economic nexus — there are many and varied growth stimuli operating on their cities. This is in distinction to countries which are small, or have only begun the process of urbanization, or which have a dual economy with only one set of places being tied in to commercial activity, and in which the growth stimuli might be few and might be restricted to a subset of places so as to produce differential growth between one set of places and another. Essentially, the underlying rationale is that of providing reasons to expect a common growth rate to apply to the whole array of cities, a growth rate which would only be disturbed by random fluctuations about that mean. It is not clear whether it is the Simon or the more restrictive Thomas assumptions which are invoked, but the general argument is for some form of random growth.

More recently, Berry (1969 and 1972) has added to these notions a connection with the growth stimuli which arise from the diffusion of technical innovations throughout a national economy and argues that, where a country is integrated into a single economic system, the spread of such innovations would filter through the whole array of cities in a manner which would lend support to his assumption of random growth. This argument has also been pursued by Ward (1963) in a paper whose argument is worth repeating in some little detail. He argues that many of the models of size distribution require random urban growth and that, while this may be reasonable so far as the purely biological mechanisms of birth and death rates are concerned, much urban growth is the result not of natural population change, but of migration. Indeed, it might be argued that all growth within a city is the product of migration since those people who are born and remain within a particular city can be considered to have made a decision to migrate a zero distance. If one therefore considers all growth to be a product of migration and if that migration is considered to be the product of differential economic opportunities within the cities, then it is the factors affecting the number of economic opportunities within cities towards which attention should be directed. Ward argues that the differential distribution of such opportunities can be considered to be the result both of technological change within a given city and of the expansion of its market opportunities. Both of these can be subsumed under the effects of market expansion in a general way since technological change can only find commercial expression through the willingness of consumers in a market to buy the products of a new technology. He then argues as follows:

> The size of the population of a city is a measure of its market size so that market-expansion opportunities depend for their occurrence on the number of inhabitants a city possesses. The opportunities characterized in this way then occur with a relative frequency (probability) which is proportionate to the size of the market. There is some minimum city size below which the probability of occurrence of opportunities is much smaller partly because there is less effective search by both prospective entrepreneurs and prospective migrants, and partly because the basic natural and technological material for opportunity creation does not exist in any quantity. These assumptions are sufficient to generate the Paretian city size distribution. (Ward 1963, pp. 215-16)

Thus, in terms of a rather more extended argument which ties in the effects of migration and the spread of technological change, Ward suggests — although not in formal terms — a reason why city growth above a certain size of city might be a constant fraction of previous size with some disturbance term added in the form of a distribution of probabilities around this common rate.

SYSTEMS AND CITY SIZES

The discussion has so far looked at the various types of frequency and cumulative frequency distributions which have been suggested as generators of city sizes and at some of the explanations offered in support of the regularities which appear. Behind most of this concern with size distributions has been the belief that regularity betokens the existence of a system of cities. In the light of our earlier criticisms of the application of systems' concepts to such vaguely-defined objects as cities, what conclusions can be reached in respect of the validity of such claims?

A study which has tried to carry the idea of systems of cities to a logical geographical conclusion is Harris' (1970) work on Russian cities and, despite its novelty, it demonstrates that the use of size distributions as an indicator of city systems is a very blunt-edged tool. Harris suggests that, for any given territory, the emergence of a regular rank-size array might suggest the existence of a functional system. Within a national area, it might happen that a number of sub-systems would be found, reflecting the lack of overall connectedness of the national economy. These system and sub-system characteristics might, he suggests, be isolated by studying the size distributions of the component cities. Supposing, for example, that a rank-size plot betokened the existence of a functional system and that, in a given area, one had three such plots which reflected the existence of sub-systems within the whole area, then the superimposition of their respective size distributions would lead to a curve of the sort traced out in fig. 2.4 by the line J1, J2, J3, K4, K5, K6, L7, L8, L9 . . . S28, S29, S30. If ten such sub-systems were included, the curve would be traced by the line, J1 . . . J10, K11 . . . K20 . . . S91 . . . S100. In each case, while the lower end of the curve would increasingly approximate the rank-size curve, the upper end would be marked by noticeable breaks above which the slope would

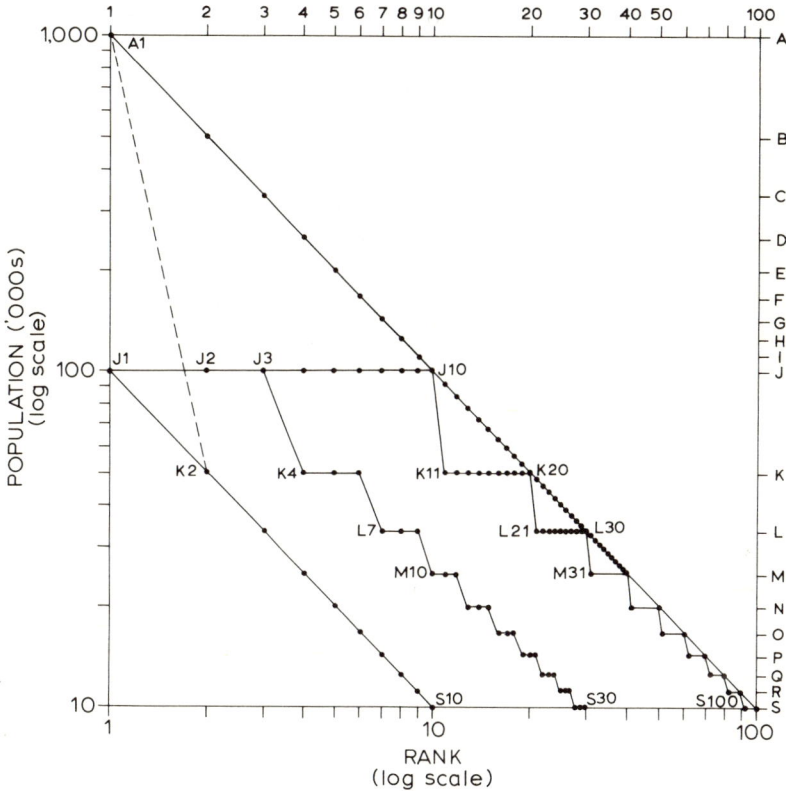

Figure 2.4   An idealized scheme of aggregates of city-systems. *Source:* Harris (1970)

approximately be zero. Only if the ten regions were to be 'fully integrated into a single functionally co-ordinated and interacting urban system' would one expect to find the 100 cities distributed in the rank-size curve of A1, B2 . . . J10 . . . S100. He suggests that a distribution 'with a flat top . . . and several "steps" down the line warns that the cities plotted may represent several relatively independent regions with little functional integration' (Harris 1970, p. 132). Conversely, a distribution in which the curve steepens at the upper end – as in A1, K2, L3 . . . S10 – would suggest that the largest city is disproportionately large because it may 'serve' a much larger area than is encompassed by the cities included within the plot. He uses these ideas to study the size distributions of the Soviet Union and to derive a regionalization of the country based on the shape of the curves of subsets of cities. His partitioning of the country produces twenty-four regions of which no fewer than fourteen have principal cities and boundaries which are identical to those of the major planning regions of the USSR.

Such an exercise is a most interesting attempt to take to its logical conclusion the idea, so widely advocated, that 'lognormality' or rank-size distributions are indicative of complex interacting functional systems. The technique is, however, of little analytical value since it can hardly be hoped to provide a sensitive or diagnostic measure of whether a particular city or set of cities does or does not 'belong' to some hypothesized 'system' or 'sub-system'.[1] Nor, indeed, would it necessarily be the case that the sub-systems would form distinct spatially-discrete areas.

Indeed, in the whole of the work on city sizes, there is much confusion, great difficulty in distinguishing the different distributions, many problems in drawing inferences about processes which might give rise to them and even doubt about the goals of the exercise itself because of the notorious difficulty of arguing about the processes underlying static cross-sectional forms when so often, according to the principle of equifinality, many different processes give rise to identical end-product forms. At no point can one turn to any of the studies of size distributions and claim with confidence that they demonstrate the effectiveness of a systems' approach. As a means of analyzing an array of city sizes, the notion that the set of places comprises a system is an attractive one, but until the objects themselves can be defined *in toto* and until the linkages which determine the relationships between them can be specified, one must accept the conclusion that the existence of regularities in such data suggests relatively little about the substantive phenomena themselves.[2] Kendall (1961, p. 15) puts it rather elegantly:

> It may well be that such things as wars, strikes, epidemics and accidents can all be represented by a common model — a Statistical Theory of Disaster would make an attractive study. It is hard to resist the conclusion . . . that in unifying our observed patterns in this way we are approaching something akin to fundamental laws and moving towards that synthesis which is one of the main goals of scientific endeavour.

But, he adds:

> Nobody would claim we have got that far.

[1] It is interesting that the size distribution of the 100 largest cities in the world as a whole produces exactly the same 'steps' (although not the same slope) as in Harris' idealized diagram. Doubtless only the more heroic would draw conclusions from such an observation.
[2] A conclusion which echoes that of Lotka in 1926. See above, p. 20.

We are forced to a rather pessimistic conclusion about the value of the numerous exercises which have tried to argue that city-size regularities can be taken as evidence of the system-like character of sets of cities. If our concern is with substantive aspects of cities, rather than with probability theory *per se*, the study of size distributions appears to be an elaborate maze which ends only in a cul-de-sac.

CHANGE OVER TIME AND THE PROCESS OF URBAN GROWTH

A brutal, but effective, path out of a maze is to cut through the hedges. Instead of following yet more curves of size distributions, a more profitable avenue, and one which has been surprisingly little explored, is the study of the dynamics of the urban growth which underlies city sizes. Despite the many assumptions about growth rates which have been used, studies of urban growth itself are remarkably few and yet it is the way in which the component cities grow or decline which determines the shape of the size-distribution curves. For empirical data, there is still little detail known about a number of fundamental questions. Do cities in fact grow by a constant but random proportion of their existing sizes? If this 'law of proportionate effect' holds (Gibrat 1931), what are the mechanisms by which it is sustained and what are its implications for our views of urban systems?

The approaches to such questions have mostly adopted rather tangential routes. There has, first, been an attempt to study changes over time in the shape of size-distribution curves. Some of these have suggested that the curves tend to approach towards some form of straight-line logarithmic plot. Bell (1962), for example, suggests this for Israel and Berry (1969) supports the suggestion in his comprehensive review of data from countries in the developing world.[1] Berry concludes that this tendency might support the argument that increasing numbers of a nation's cities are progressively drawn into the ambit of modern urban-orientated market economies and that the suggestion might have planning implications for isolating the constraints within a national economy which obstruct the development of a maximally-probable size distribution and one which betokens the rapid spread of assumedly beneficial growth stimuli throughout the whole hierarchy of places. The study of such changes in the shape of size distributions also gives some rather aggregate indications of the way in which the set of places is growing over time.

A second dynamic approach to urban growth and change has been the study of shifts in the ranks of cities over time. Carter (1969), for example, looks at correlations between the ranks of cities in Wales at successive decades in the nineteenth century. His argument hinges again on a vaguely-specified systems'

---

[1] Although this tendency for city sizes to approach a straight-line distribution is certainly by no means general. Friedmann (1966a, pp. 146-50), for example, notes the persistence of a 'primate' pattern in Venezuela. This is but one of many counter examples.

approach to the growth of cities since he sees an urban system as evolving through cyclical phases of genesis, transition, sorting and climax in which major technical and organizational changes and exogenous stimuli produce new patterns of regional demand and so lead to further cycling of the genesis sequences. He takes the populations of Welsh towns at each decade from 1801 to 1901, ranks each place from largest to smallest and calculates an overall rank correlation coefficient for each of the intercensal decades. The results demonstrate that the coefficients are markedly lower in the period 1861-81, suggesting that the injection of coal-mining towns into the system in this period corresponds to a new phase of urban genesis which leads eventually to the emergence of a new city system. Such a study of changes in the rank ordering of towns can reveal, albeit tangentially, something of the nature of urban growth and can certainly, as Carter suggests, point in a rather aggregate fashion to periods of marked change in the distribution of individual city growth rates. Other studies which have looked at individual city rank-orders, have pointed to the tendency for shifts in rank to be small at the upper end of the size array, but to be very considerable as one moves to progressively smaller cities. Luckermann (1966) shows that the shifts in rank of the largest cities in the United States conform to this pattern. The same is true of data for British cities. Figure 2.5, for example, plots the ranks of certain cities in England and Wales over the period 1801-1911. The cities which are included are the twenty-five largest places in 1801 and their ranks and populations are shown at each of the twelve successive dates. London, the largest town in 1801, retained its rank throughout the whole period. Manchester and Salford, starting in the second rank, had fallen to third place by the end of the period at the expense of Liverpool which had moved from third to second. Birmingham retained its rank of fourth throughout the whole period. All of these larger places, indeed, show relatively little change in their rank orders over the whole period. On the other hand, with the smaller places there is a tendency for increasingly large fluctuations to occur at smaller city sizes. Some places move rapidly up the rank hierarchy: Leicester, for example, was 21st in 1801, had moved to 13th by 1891 and retained this rank up to 1911. Other places moved very rapidly down the hierarchy: Exeter, for example, began at 20th position, and had fallen to 65th by 1911, even though its fall was halted briefly in the period 1821-41. Other places show more fluctuating fortunes: Coventry, which began in 19th position, had fallen to 48th by 1881, but climbed back to 33rd by 1911.

Analyses of such changes in rank order can reveal much in detail about the demographic fortunes of individual towns and they appear to suggest the ways in which growth occurs in a set of places. The literature of urban growth includes more than a few such instances of the study of changes in rank order (Madden 1956a; Luckermann 1966; Borchert 1967; Lopes 1972; and, a precociously early example, G. G. Chisholm 1897, p. 525). The aggregate patterns which have appeared and which are illustrated by the example of England and Wales, suggest

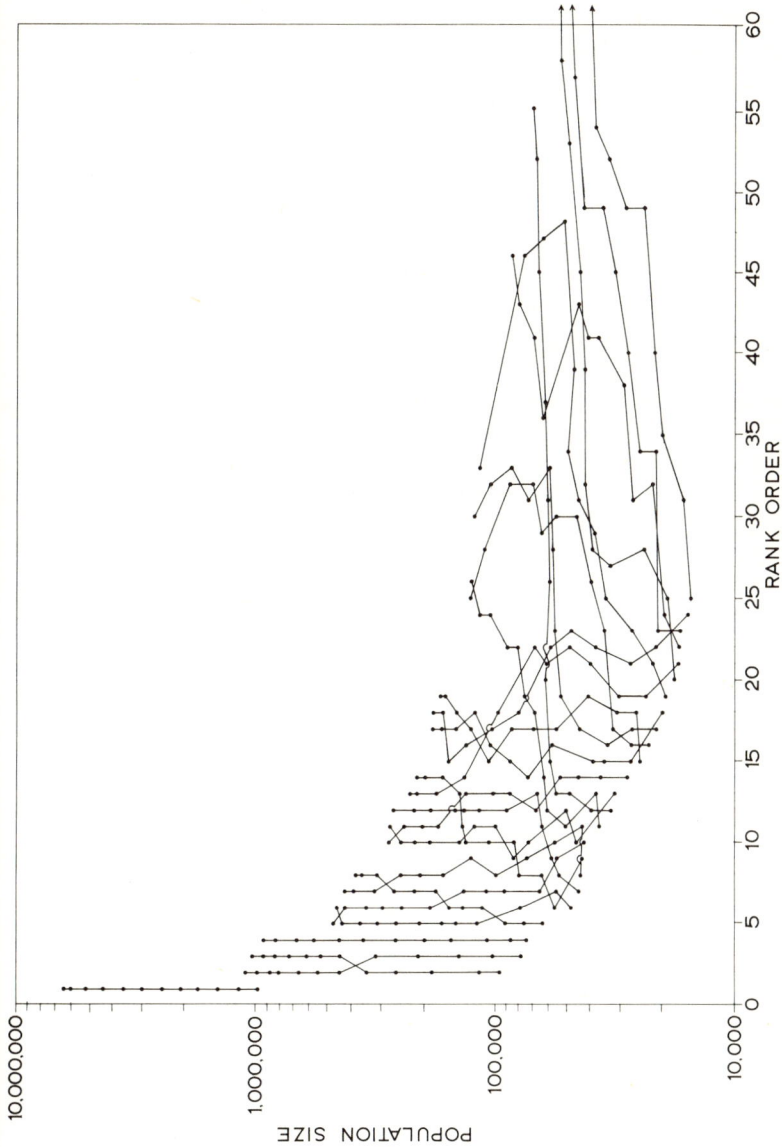

Figure 2.5 Changes in rank order, 1801–1911. Successive ranks of the twenty-five largest towns in England and Wales in 1801. Each line represents one town; the lowest dot shows its rank and size in 1801 and successive dots show its rank and size at each decade up to 1911. The towns (ranked in their 1801 order) are as follows: London; Manchester/Salford; Liverpool; Birmingham; Gloucester; Leeds; Portsmouth; Newcastle/Gateshead; Plymouth; Sheffield; Norwich; Bath; Nottingham; Hull; Sunderland; Medway Towns; Stockport; Bolton; Coventry; Exeter; Leicester; York; Norwich; Oldham; Chester

the stability of the upper end of the size array of places and the great fluctuation of sizes at the lower end. Had fig. 2.5 included more than a mere handful of ranks and had it included places which started at lower ranks and subsequently moved into these higher ranks, this impression would have been reinforced.

This might suggest that a more formal statistical analysis of rank changes over time would be one way in which to study the growth and the fluctuations of growth in a set of cities. The difficulty in such an approach, however, is twofold. First, the degrees of freedom of places to change rank within the hierarchy differ from one rank to another. The largest place of all cannot increase its rank; it can only either retain its first position or fall to a lower rank. If we take a constant set of places, the very smallest place can conversely only retain its rank or increase it; it cannot fall in rank. That place in the very centre of the array would appear to be the only place which has an evenly-balanced probability of plus and minus changes, since there is an equal number of ranks above and below it. Secondly, however, since the size distribution of places will be highly skewed, the absolute difference in population between adjacent ranks at the upper and lower ends of the distribution will be very different. The probability is that there will be a much greater absolute difference in the population sizes of the first- and second-ranked places than between the 100th- and 101st-ranked places; and that the absolute difference in population between the nth-ranked place and the $n - 1$st place will be greater than between the nth and $n + 1$st place. This means that only slight differences in the growth rates of small places might lead to marked changes of rank whereas even marked differences in the growth rates of large places may produce no changes in their ranks. The effect of these two characteristics is that the probable distribution of shifts in the ranks of places will not be normally distributed,[1] and that the probabilities will differ from different initial rank positions. Thus, the probabilities for the largest, smallest and middle places will be highly right-skewed, highly left-skewed and somewhat right-skewed respectively and, while the first two distributions would be highly peaked, the third would be flat topped. This is simply to say that a change of one rank position has very different connotations for a city of 1,000,000 than for a city of 10,000 population.

If an analysis of rank changes were to be attempted, it would therefore be necessary to calculate the different *expectations* of shifts in rank for each different initial rank and these would then form norms against which the *actual* changes in rank could be compared. The task would be complex and probably impossible, but in its absence it would not be possible to interpret the significance of any changes in rank ordering; nor could any pattern of rank shifts, such as the suggestion of stability in the upper end and fluctuation at the lower end of the array of places, be translated with any confidence into suggestions about the variation in growth rates of the set of places.

[1] Thus the centrally-ranked place will *not* in fact have a uniformly distributed probability of moving up or down as was suggested above.

To develop and test ideas about the growth rates of towns, shifts in rank ordering would therefore not appear to be a workable surrogate for a study of the actual population changes of urban areas. We must therefore turn to the actual populations rather than the rank orders of cities to see to what extent Gibrat's law of proportionate effect may hold and what implications this or some other pattern of urban growth may have upon both the theoretical notions of cities and the empirical data of urban sizes. If our interest was primarily in the distribution of city sizes, any findings which were made about the processes of urban growth could then be fed back into the development of appropriate mechanisms by which such distributions were generated and either maintained or altered over time. Enough has been said already to suggest that this is not a topic worth pursuit. Instead, we shall turn to a study of urban growth rates *per se*, ignoring the sterile debate on size distributions — which may form a useful context, but not a profitable goal — and avoiding the wilder claims of the proponents of systems' approaches.

PART 2

Analysis

CHAPTER 3

The growth of cities in England and Wales in the nineteenth century

Facts alone are wanted in life.   CHARLES DICKENS

It seems clear that, whatever interest the size distributions of cities may have in themselves, greater interest attaches not to the static curve of sizes, but to the growth processes of towns which first generate and subsequently maintain or alter the curves. The various attempts to derive theoretical distributions have worked from sets of assumptions about these growth processes, but have not explored the extent to which their assumptions may be reasonable or may be met with in the real world. Such an examination seems long overdue, less for the light which it might throw on notions about rank-size curve, than in its own right as telling us something about the nature of urbanization. In this chapter we shall therefore look at data on the growth of towns in England and Wales in the nineteenth century to see to what extent empirical questions about the process of urbanization can be answered as well as to develop some more general ideas about urban growth.

Two preliminary points might be made before turning to an examination of the data. First, if our interest lay in the consequences of urban growth processes on size distributions, by looking at empirical data we would not be able to derive a model of the effect of urban growth on *generating* city sizes; data on the growth of cities will suggest only what some given size distribution may become at a future date.[1] The data could therefore help in understanding the way in which a size distribution might be maintained or might alter over time, but not how it would initially be generated. Second, a word might be said both about the time and the area to be studied. As to the period, it has already been argued that the nineteenth century — Giffen's 'statistical century' — can be regarded as a most useful compromise period in Britain between the pre- and post-industrial periods. Not only does this mean that, so far as our individual units of observation are concerned (call them 'objects' if one will), one can place greater confidence in the necessary assumption that each town is relatively more self-contained, and hence relatively more of a unit or object, than would be the

---

[1] Unless, of course, one were to demonstrate formally that the model of the growth process would *inevitably* lead to a given size distribution after a sufficiently long time period irrespective of the initial starting distribution — an argument which has been applied to a number of the stochastic growth processes (for example, E. N. Thomas 1967).

case for twentieth-century cities, but it is also the earliest period for which one can have recourse to the demographic data of the censuses. Although the census data are very far from being entirely reliable, they are much more so than any other comparable source and have the inestimable virtue of providing an almost complete coverage of urban places for a long period of time.[1] So far as the area of study is concerned, there are obvious limitations in using only England and Wales as an overall unit. It must be recognized, however, that whatever unit were to be selected, there would always be the problem of the lack of closure of the boundaries of the 'system'. England and Wales were much affected, in terms of their economic growth and the growth of their towns, by concurrent developments in Scotland and in Ireland — more obviously so in the case of the recurrent waves of immigration from the latter unfortunate country. Equally, developments in areas outside the British Isles would have their effects. Nevertheless, in what follows, the two countries will be regarded as forming a closed system, immune from developments from outside. In so doing, considerably less than full justice is done to the complex interlinkages between national economies, but the study of international economic development cannot easily be subsumed in a single parameter within a model of national urban growth. Even within the general framework of economic history there is considerable doubt about the totality of the effect of international linkages. The voluminous literature on 'long waves' in the development of a variety of countries suggests that the shocks to one national economy were echoed elsewhere and the late nineteenth-century indicators of the economies of Britain and North America have led Brinley Thomas (1954) to suggest their linkage within what he calls an 'Atlantic economy' in which the crests and troughs of the two moved in inverse harmony.[2] Saul (1962a), Habakkuk (1962b) and others, however, have doubted the functional connection of the two areas, arguing instead that fluctuations in indices such as house-building are essentially of domestic origin. The case is by no means yet proven and, while there is obviously much room for further study of the effects of international trade upon nineteenth-century England and Wales, it must fall outside the province of this study.

URBAN POPULATIONS

To measure the growth rates of individual towns, one needs to assemble population data for successive times for a number of defined urban areas. This

[1] The various local eighteenth-century surveys, from which much detailed demographic data can be derived, suffer both from the patchiness of their coverage as well as their lack of coincidence in time.

[2] The argument has been extended beyond Britain and America. Schumpeter's (1939) classic work on business cycles drew Germany into the circle and a number of countries of white settlement have also been seen as linked to the fluctuations of Britain from whence their principal funds of capital were derived (see, for example, the discussion in B. Thomas 1972; and, on Australia, the dissenting views of Butlin 1964).

mmediately raises a number of the problems of definition which were earlier discussed in connection with what is meant by a 'city'. At what point does a collection of people and buildings become a town; how can one define the areal extent of a given individual town? Such problems have long bedevilled any work which looks at changes in urban populations over time and they account for the uncertainty which must hang over any estimate of the relative sizes of urban and rural populations within any country, no matter how reliable its census information. A tentative definition of a city has already been made which suggested it as an area which contains a relatively large number of people, which is relatively densely settled and in which the majority of the population is involved in activities which are not agricultural. This provides at least guidelines to help resolve the difficulty of classifying urban and non-urban areas. The population data which are used have been taken from the mammoth recalculations of nineteenth-century census returns undertaken by Mr C. M. Law and kindly made available by him. Law (1967) recalculated urban populations for urban areas which were more realistically defined than the administrative areas given in the census returns and, in defining towns for this purpose, he used three criteria which a place needed to meet to qualify as a 'town': a minimum size of population; a minimum density; and a criterion of spatial clustering.

The minimum size is taken at 2,500; a threshold which is large enough to exclude many of the purely mining communities which sprang up in counties such as Durham during the later part of the century and also large enough to exclude most of the small market towns which never attracted industry to them, which relied almost wholly on supporting their tributary agricultural areas and which often suffered radical population decline in the later part of the century. It might be argued that, rather than taking a fixed population size as a criterion of qualifying as a town, a better yardstick might be a variable or sliding size-threshold, so that, as the century progressed, a successively larger figure would be used as a minimum size. This would certainly accord with the realistic argument that the scale of efficient size increases with time as technical and organizational expertise improves and raises the level of scale economies and the lower threshold of efficient operation of units.[1] The use of such a sliding minimum would, however, have two main disadvantages. Not only would it be as difficult to justify the selection of any particular threshold at a given time as to select a constant threshold, but it would also introduce difficulties in handling towns whose population, even though remaining static or growing only slowly, would yet 'die' out of the urban 'system' as the threshold became progressively higher. As Friedlander comments with reference to just this problem of varying minimum size thresholds, 'It seems that there are no simple or unique answers to these questions and there could probably be good arguments in favour of different approaches to such problems' (Friedlander 1970, p. 423).

A theme which forms the underpinnings of much of the argument of Social Area Analysis which has looked at changes in the internal structure of both cities and national economies (see, for example, Shevky and Bell 1955; Udry 1964; McElrath 1968).

Law's density criterion was fixed at a figure of one person per acre which, as he says, would be a very low figure for urban areas, but a very high figure for rural areas. It is thus a useful yardstick for deciding which of the parishes or areas surrounding an administrative urban area should be included in the total urban population or, indeed which administratively-defined non-urban areas should be regarded as towns. Since the censuses for England and Wales give population data for administrative units which are often seriously underbounded as descriptions of urban areas, it was this criterion which was used to define the basic areal extent of urban areas.[1]

Finally, the nucleation criterion takes account of the attempt to define towns as spatially continuous built-up areas. In a number of the parishes of England and Wales, even though the criteria of minimum population size and minimum density are met, the population is dispersed in a series of small communities over a relatively wide area and the several communities are not physically contiguous. In the nineteenth century, this was particularly the case of many settlements in South Wales and parts of northern England, where, most usually, mining communities were found scattered discretely throughout large parishes. In such cases these populations would not be regarded as a single urban area even though meeting the first two minima.

THE DATA

These three criteria therefore underlie the redefinition of urban places used throughout this study, and the population figures on which the subsequent analyses are based depend critically upon the validity of the criteria. They depend as well upon the varying accuracy of the census returns. Undoubtedly, the census improved over time. It is generally agreed that the first two censuses, in 1801 and 1811, failed to include a significant proportion of the population although estimates of that proportion differ (Taylor 1951; Krause 1958). Thereafter, the census figures are much more reliable, but by no means perfect. A marked improvement came after 1841 when a new approach to the collection of the data was instituted. In the first three censuses, information was provided by Overseers of the Poor in the several parishes — a somewhat casual exercise which suffered from a number of potential dangers, not the least of which was

---

[1] In the United States, the Bureau of the Census — for long much more alive to the inadequacy of purely administrative definitions of urban areas than the British Census Office — began to experiment with more extensive definitions of urban aggregates as early as 1910 when statistics were given for 'Metropolitan Districts'. In 1950, data were reported both for 'Urbanized Areas' and 'Standard Metropolitan Areas'. Subsequently, the 'Standard Metropolitan Statistical Area' was added (for definitions, see U.S. Bureau of the Budget 1967 and, for the 'Urbanized Area', Carter 1972, p. 24). The nearest British equivalent — the 'conurbation' — falls between these two American definitions and suffers from the fact that it is still composed of administrative units.

that the whole operation might be spread over a number of days thus increasing the risk of double counting. The *Report* on the 1841 census (*Parlimentary Papers*, 1843, XXII, 5), in evaluating the role of the Overseers, considered them to have been 'a body of men, in many parts of the country, fully competent to the task thus imposed upon them, and anxious to discharge it to the best of their ability; but in some districts, from want of education, or habits of business, and from ignorance of the importance and real object of the inquiry they were conducting, essentially unfitted for it.' For the 1841 census the country was divided by local Registrars into as many as 35,000 small Enumeration Districts, each of which was assigned to one enumerator who was required to undertake the enumeration 'in one day'. The 1841 census also postdated the reform of urban areas effected by the Municipal Corporations Act which meant that many new urban areas were recognized as administrative units for the first time and the boundaries of all the boroughs and municipalities were faithfully demarcated in maps signed in the spidery hand of R. K. Dawson (*Parliamentary Papers*, 1837, XXV-XXVIII). From 1851 onwards, the census authorities also began to produce tabulated statistics of urban and rural populations helping at least to sharpen the awareness of the distinction between what were then considered as urban and non-urban areas.[1]

The two most troublesome of the urban definitions are, of course, those of the very largest and the smallest towns. As the nineteenth century progressed, the largest towns grew to incorporate once-separate peripheral communities. Given the definitions adopted, had the peripheral boroughs or communities been regarded as discrete places before being submerged into the sprawl of their neighbouring giants, once they *had* been submerged they would have 'died' as towns and the larger places correspondingly would have appeared to increase rather suddenly during the decade in which the amalgamation was assumed to have occurred. The largest urban areas have therefore often been amalgamated with certain of their neighbouring communities to produce a generous definition and the population totals of the adjacent areas have been included in the overall total once the density criterion outlined above had been met. Thus, the definition of London traces out an area which, at its most considerable extent, includes, in addition to the Administrative County, a number of peripheral areas which can be considered to have become part of the metropolis by 1911 − the end of the period of study. In the north for example, Southgate, Edmonton, Tottenham, Wood Green, Hornsey, Finchley and Hendon came to be included; in the east, Woodford, Walthamstow, Wanstead, Leyton, Ilford, Dagenham, Barking, and East and West Ham; in the south, Bromley, Penge, Beckenham, Croydon, Mitcham, Merton and Wimbledon; and in the west, Richmond, Barnes,

---

[1] Accounts of the successive census changes are given in Interdepartmental Committee on Social and Economic Research 1951, and, especially, in Drake 1972.

Mortlake, Chiswick, Brentford and Ealing, Acton, Hanwell and Willesden.[1] Certain of the large provincial northern towns also include peripheral boroughs or communities. For example; Manchester eventually grew to include not only Salford, but also Stretford, Droylesdon, Prestwich and Failsworth; Liverpool includes Birkenhead; Sheffield includes Handsworth; Birmingham includes Smethwick; and Newcastle includes Gateshead.

For the smaller places, the main difficulty lies in estimating the early populations of certain places which grew very suddenly. With the very rapid urban growth of the nineteenth century − a growth for which the experience and the administrative machinery of early Victorian England were largely unequipped to deal − a number of difficulties occur in the calculation of the populations of towns which are 'born' into the system when they reach a figure of 2,500 or over. The great majority of places which were not already 'towns' by 1801, were 'born' with populations of less than 5,000 and the progress of their subsequent rises and falls in population can be taken with some confidence. A number of places, however, first appear with populations considerably larger than this and it is clear that for some of these the inadequacies of the census data mean that it is impossible to trace the early history of their demographic expansion. This means that there will be some undercounting of the real number of smaller 'towns' and that the early growth rates of such places cannot be included in the subsequent calculations. Table 3.1 lists all those places which were 'born' with populations of 10,000 and over and also a regional distribution of the total numbers of places 'born' at 5,000 or over. It is clear that the great majority of these places is comprised of two types of town. First are the mining towns of Durham, Northumberland and South Wales and the manufacturing towns of Lancashire, the West Riding and the Black Country. Many of these places grew very rapidly from very small origins and some tended to be designated as separate administrative areas only at a relatively late stage in their growth so that it is impossible to attach population figures to them until a sufficiently fine administrative net was created. Second are the towns which became dormitory suburban areas very late in the nineteenth century or in the first decades of the twentieth. This accounts for the relatively large numbers of places 'born' at suspiciously high figures in the counties surrounding London.

Not all of these places are reflections of the inadequacies of the census information, however. A number of Victorian towns were genuinely 'born' with

[1] In the light of this broad definition of London, it is interesting to note Hobsbawm's discussion of London as a labour market. Unlike other conurbations, London developed a single wage rate which applied theoretically to the whole urbanized area throughout the nineteenth century. Its extent, understandably, widened throughout the period: for example, in 1834, the tailors' union claimed jurisdiction over an area with a four-mile radius from Charing Cross; in 1865, the compositors claimed an area with a radius of fifteen miles. This was markedly different from provincial conurbations. South-east Lancashire, for example, was still a mosaic of trade-union districts with different wage rates as late as 1906. Tyneside, in 1806, was divided into three districts of the Amalgamated Society of Engineers and five of the relevant semi-skilled union (Hobsbawm 1964, pp. 4-5).

Table 3.1 *Towns entering the urban 'system' with large initial populations*

A. Towns 'born' with populations of 10,000 or over

Town	Reference	Date 'born'
Staleybridge	CHE 29	1851
Glossop	DER 17	1851
Jarrow	DUR 24	1871
Shotton	DUR 36	1911
Aldershot	HAM 1	1861
Bournemouth	HAM 5	1871
Bacup	LAN 8	1861
Eccles	LAN 27	1871
Heywood	LAN 35	1831
Mossley	LAN 54	1871
Coalville	LEC 3	1891
Enfield	MDX 2	1861
Oakengates	SAL 7	1891
Burslem	STA 6	1831
Coseley	STA 9	1871
Sedgley	STA 21	1871
Chertsey	SRY 6	1891
Saddleworth	YWR 88	1871
Stanley	YWR 103	1891
Abercarn	MON 1	1891
Abersychan	MON 3	1871
Ebbw Vale	MON 8	1871
Aberdare	SWA 9	1851
Barry	SWA 10	1891
Caerphilly	SWA 14	1901
Gelligear	SWA 15	1901
Ogmore	SWA 20	1901
Pontypridd	SWA 22	1871
Rhondda	SWA 25	1871

B. Distribution of all towns 'born' with populations of 5,000 or over

(i) Distribution by date (ii) Distribution by county

Date	No. 'born'	Area	No. 'born'	Area	No. 'born'
1801	0	Buckingham	1	Northumberland	3
1811	0	Cambridge	1	Salop	1
1821	0	Cheshire	4	Stafford	6
1831	5	Derby	5	Surrey	7
1841	8	Durham	14	Sussex	2
1851	10	Essex	1	Warwick	2
1861	9	Hampshire	3	Worcester	2
1871	36	Hertford	2	Yorks (NR)	4
1881	6	Kent	2	Yorks (WR)	9
1891	18	Lancashire	10	Monmouth	10
1901	6	Leicester	1	N. Wales	2
1911	8	Lincoln	1	S. Wales	10
		Middlesex	3		
Total	106			Total	106

very high populations. Middlesbrough is perhaps the classic example of a newly-created Victorian town. It enters the list of 'towns' — and hence of the calculations of this study — in 1841 at a population of almost 6,000 and by 1861 had reached nearly 20,000. Three further examples can be quoted as illustrations of the mining, industrial and residential categories which comprise the great bulk of the genuinely mushrooming towns which form part of table 3.1. Ashington, in Northumberland, shared in the late nineteenth-century growth of parts of the concealed coalfield of the North East and its population figures read as follows: 1871 — 1,002; 1881 — 2,091; 1891 — 5,307; 1901 — 13,972; and by 1911 it had almost reached 25,000. It was therefore 'born' in 1891 at the very high figure of over 5,000. Scunthorpe grew on the basis of its iron workings in the last quarter of the nineteenth century and its population figures read: 1871 — 1,852; 1881 — 5,173; 1891 — 7,255; and by 1911 it had reached almost 20,000. Royal Leamington Spa developed as a resort and dormitory area much earlier in the century and its figures read: 1821 — 2,183; 1831 — 6,209; 1841 — 12,864; and by 1911, after a period of stability and even slight decline, it stood at over 26,000. In each of these three cases the particular town — illustrating a different and typical type of mushrooming growth — entered the system at figures well above the critical threshold of 2,500, but the first population figure can be used with some confidence as the earliest datum for that place as a 'town'. In other cases where towns enter at a high population figure, the first population datum must be treated with less confidence and the early figures are simply impossible to derive because of the inappropriateness and inflexibility of the administrative boundaries for which data are reported in the census. This would be the case, for example, with Bournemouth which is treated as a single aggregate together with Poole. The joint population figures can only be derived from 1881 onwards. Before that date, even though separate figures for Bournemouth alone could have been used, the subsequent addition of Poole would have created a quite artificial boosting of population at 1881, so that the aggregate 'town' is considered as having been 'born' at a figure of just over 30,000 in 1881.

Problems of definition of this sort are an inevitable conjunct of any work on urban growth. Despite such difficulties, and despite the variable quality of the census sources from which the populations have been recalculated, Law's figures provide as sensitive and accurate a set of estimates of urban populations as one could hope to derive.[1] Certainly in that they apply to areas which approximate as closely as possible to the actual and changing extent of the built-up area of nineteenth-century towns, they provide better estimates of urban populations than do the raw census data on which so many previous studies have had to be

---

[1] Only an impossibly laborious calculation based on the information contained in enumerators' books could provide a more sensitive set of populations and this source is, of course, available only for census dates between 1841 and 1871.

Table 3.2 Numbers of towns in different size groups

| | Size Group ('000s) | | | | | | | | | | | | | | | | | | |
| Date | 2·5–4·9 | | 5–9·9 | | 10–19·9 | | 20–39·9 | | 40–79·9 | | 80–159·9 | | 160–319·9 | | 320–639·9 | | ≥ 640 | | Total |
	No.	%	No.	%	No.	%	No.	%	No.	%	No.	%	No.	%	No.	%	No.	%	No.
1801	160	62·50	47	18·36	32	12·50	7	2·73	8	3·13	1	0·39	0	—	0	—	1	0·39	256
1811	190	61·69	64	20·78	31	10·06	12	3·90	7	2·27	3	0·97	0	—	0	—	1	0·32	308
1821	200	55·40	89	24·65	38	10·53	20	5·54	9	2·49	3	0·83	1	0·28	0	—	1	0·28	361
1831	207	50·24	115	27·91	44	10·68	26	6·31	13	3·16	4	0·97	2	0·49	0	—	1	0·24	412
1841	226	48·60	121	26·02	62	13·33	32	6·88	13	2·80	7	1·51	2	0·43	1	0·22	1	0·22	465
1851	234	44·91	135	25·91	85	16·31	31	5·95	23	4·41	8	1·54	2	0·38	2	0·38	1	0·19	521
1861	255	43·97	153	26·38	91	15·69	40	6·90	24	4·14	9	1·55	4	0·69	3	0·52	1	0·17	580
1871	274	39·65	201	29·09	111	16·06	55	7·96	28	4·05	13	1·88	5	0·72	2	0·29	2	0·29	691
1881	270	36·00	215	28·67	135	18·00	65	8·67	37	4·93	17	2·27	7	0·93	1	0·13	3	0·40	750
1891	293	35·13	230	27·58	159	19·06	77	9·23	41	4·92	20	2·40	8	0·96	2	0·24	4	0·48	834
1901	290	32·77	225	25·42	190	21·47	89	10·06	49	5·54	23	2·60	11	1·24	4	0·45	4	0·45	885
1911	274	29·69	243	26·33	193	20·91	109	11·81	56	6·06	29	3·14	11	1·19	4	0·43	4	0·43	923

Note: Percentage figures are percentages of the total number of towns at each date.

based — as, for example, in the figures given by Mitchell (1962, pp. 24-7) which have been widely quoted elsewhere (for example, Banks 1968).[1]

THE NUMBERS OF URBAN PLACES

If we look by way of introduction at the set of places which these definitions produce during the period 1801-1911, the easiest way to familiarize ourselves with the material is simply to look at the changing numbers of towns in each

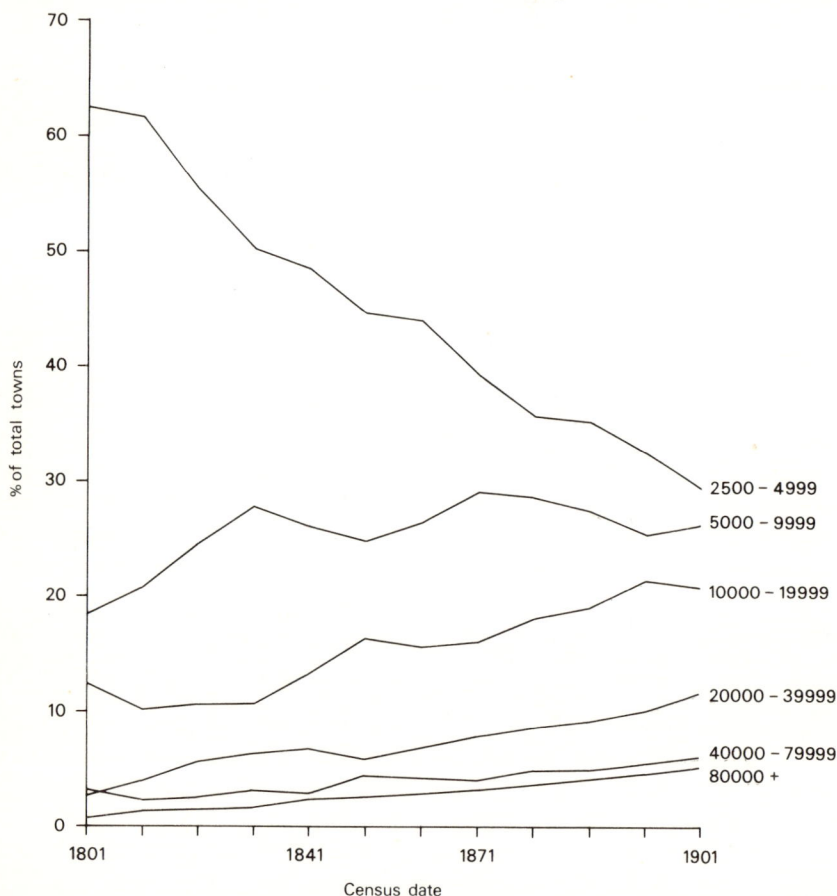

Figure 3.1   Percentages of towns in different size groups in England and Wales, 1801-1911. Details are given in table 3.2

[1] The same would be true of the heroic calculations of nineteenth-century commentators such as A. F. Weber (1899) and Welton (1900). In calculating percentages of the urban population for England and Wales as a whole, Law (1967) compares the results based on his urban definition with the figures suggested by the census itself and by Price-Williams (1880), Welton (1900), A. F. Weber (1899), and Vince (1955).

population size class over the whole span of the twelve dates. Table 3.2 shows the number of towns in each of nine size classes which have been selected so that each size class is a constant factor of twice that of the previous class. It can be seen first of all that the number of towns increases rapidly from a mere 256 in 1801 to as many as 923 in 1911. Secondly, within this increasing number of places, the proportional representation of each size class changes in a fairly systematic fashion. The percentage of towns in the size range 2,500-4,999 falls progressively from over 60 to under 30; that in the size range 5,000-9,999 rises from less than 20 to almost 30 and then falls to level off at about 25; percentages in the size ranges above 10,000 tend almost universally to increase throughout the whole span of the period. Figure 3.1 traces these changes, showing the relatively greater rise in the numbers of large places at the expense of the smaller.

CHANGES IN SIZE

These are simple descriptive statistics which give some preliminary idea about the numbers of places which are to be studied and also suggest that there may be regularities in the changing sizes of those places which could lead to the development of hypotheses about urban growth. It is not, of course, the number of towns in which our interest lies, but the population changes of individual size groups of towns at successive decadal intervals. The first, and simplest, way in which this might be studied is to plot the movements of individual towns between the eight size classes during each pair of census dates. These are shown in table 3.3 which gives transition matrices for each of the eleven successive periods. Each matrix shows the number of places which start the decade with populations in one size class and end the decade with populations either in the same or some different size class. The row entries show, for each size class, the classes in which towns ended the decade; the column entries show, for each size class at the end of the decade, in which size class the places had started the decade. In the first decade, for example, 160 places had populations in the size class 2,500-4,999 in 1801; by 1811, of these 160 places only 135 were still in that size group, twenty-four had increased their populations into the size group 5,000-9,999, one place had lost population so as no longer to qualify as a 'town', and so forth. The totals of the rows and columns can be interpreted in the same way: the totals of the rows show the number of places in each size group in 1801; the totals of the columns show the numbers in each size group in 1811.

Attention might be drawn to four points in these matrices. First, the range of movement between categories is relatively small. This is very much a function of the large ranges of population which are included in each size category. For a place to move from the mid-point of one size group to the mid-point of the next higher group, it would need to double its population during the course of the decade. It is therefore not surprising that there is only a minority of cases in

Table 3.3   *Transition matrices: numbers of towns in population size groups at successive dates*

Size group		0	1	2	3	4	5	6	7	8	Total
					No. in 1811						
	0	625	53	0	0	0	0	0	0	0	
No.	1	1	135	24	0	0	0	0	0	0	160
in	2	0	2	40	5	0	0	0	0	0	47
1801	3	0	0	0	26	6	0	0	0	0	32
	4	0	0	0	0	6	1	0	0	0	7
	5	0	0	0	0	0	6	2	0	0	8
	6	0	0	0	0	0	0	1	0	0	1
	7	0	0	0	0	0	0	0	0	0	0
	8	0	0	0	0	0	0	0	0	1	1
Total			190	64	31	12	7	3	0	1	308/256

Size group		0	1	2	3	4	5	6	7	8	Total
					No. in 1821						
	0	573	53	0	0	0	0	0	0	0	
No.	1	0	147	42	1	0	0	0	0	0	190
in	2	0	0	47	17	0	0	0	0	0	64
1811	3	0	0	0	20	11	0	0	0	0	31
	4	0	0	0	0	9	3	0	0	0	12
	5	0	0	0	0	0	6	1	0	0	7
	6	0	0	0	0	0	0	2	1	0	3
	7	0	0	0	0	0	0	0	0	0	0
	8	0	0	0	0	0	0	0	0	1	1
Total			200	89	38	20	9	3	1	1	361/308

Size group		0	1	2	3	4	5	6	7	8	Total
					No. in 1831						
	0	522	46	3	2	0	0	0	0	0	
No.	1	0	161	39	0	0	0	0	0	0	200
in	2	0	0	72	17	0	0	0	0	0	89
1821	3	0	0	1	25	12	0	0	0	0	38
	4	0	0	0	0	14	6	0	0	0	20
	5	0	0	0	0	0	7	2	0	0	9
	6	0	0	0	0	0	0	2	1	0	3
	7	0	0	0	0	0	0	0	1	0	1
	8	0	0	0	0	0	0	0	0	1	1
Total			207	115	44	26	13	4	2	1	412/361

Table 3.3—*Continued*

					No. in 1841					
Size group	*0*	*1*	*2*	*3*	*4*	*5*	*6*	*7*	*8*	*Total*
0	468	46	8	0	0	0	0	0	0	
No. 1	1	175	31	0	0	0	0	0	0	207
in 2	0	5	82	27	1	0	0	0	0	115
1831 3	0	0	0	34	10	0	0	0	0	44
4	0	0	0	1	21	4	0	0	0	26
5	0	0	0	0	0	9	4	0	0	13
6	0	0	0	0	0	0	3	1	0	4
7	0	0	0	0	0	0	0	1	1	2
8	0	0	0	0	0	0	0	0	1	1
Total		226	121	62	32	13	7	2	2	465/412

					No. in 1851					
Size group	*0*	*1*	*2*	*3*	*4*	*5*	*6*	*7*	*8*	*Total*
0	413	46	7	2	1	0	0	0	0	
No. 1	0	187	39	0	0	0	0	0	0	226
in 2	0	1	89	31	0	0	0	0	0	121
1841 3	0	0	0	52	10	0	0	0	0	62
4	0	0	0	0	20	12	0	0	0	32
5	0	0	0	0	0	11	2	0	0	13
6	0	0	0	0	0	0	6	1	0	7
7	0	0	0	0	0	0	0	1	1	2
8	0	0	0	0	0	0	0	0	2	2
Total		234	135	85	31	23	8	2	3	521/465

					No. in 1861					
Size group	*0*	*1*	*2*	*3*	*4*	*5*	*6*	*7*	*8*	*Total*
0	350	54	6	3	0	0	0	0	0	
No. 1	4	196	34	0	0	0	0	0	0	234
in 2	0	5	110	20	0	0	0	0	0	135
1851 3	0	0	3	68	14	0	0	0	0	85
4	0	0	0	0	26	5	0	0	0	31
5	0	0	0	0	0	19	4	0	0	23
6	0	0	0	0	0	0	5	3	0	8
7	0	0	0	0	0	0	0	1	1	2
8	0	0	0	0	0	0	0	0	3	3
Total		255	153	91	40	24	9	4	4	580/521

Table 3.3—*Continued*

		No. in 1871									
Size group		*0*	*1*	*2*	*3*	*4*	*5*	*6*	*7*	*8*	*Total*
	0	241	77	25	9	2	0	0	0	0	
No.	*1*	2	197	52	4	0	0	0	0	0	255
in	*2*	0	0	124	28	1	0	0	0	0	153
1861	*3*	0	0	0	70	20	1	0	0	0	91
	4	0	0	0	0	32	8	0	0	0	40
	5	0	0	0	0	0	19	5	0	0	24
	6	0	0	0	0	0	0	8	1	0	9
	7	0	0	0	0	0	0	0	4	0	4
	8	0	0	0	0	0	0	0	0	4	4
Total			274	201	111	55	28	13	5	4	691/580

		No. in 1881									
Size group		*0*	*1*	*2*	*3*	*4*	*5*	*6*	*7*	*8*	*Total*
	0	184	53	6	0	0	0	0	0	0	
No.	*1*	0	214	58	2	0	0	0	0	0	274
in	*2*	0	3	149	49	0	0	0	0	0	201
1871	*3*	0	0	2	84	24	1	0	0	0	111
	4	0	0	0	0	41	14	0	0	0	55
	5	0	0	0	0	0	22	6	0	0	28
	6	0	0	0	0	0	0	11	2	0	13
	7	0	0	0	0	0	0	0	5	0	5
	8	0	0	0	0	0	0	0	0	4	4
Total			270	215	135	65	37	17	7	4	750/691

		No. in 1891									
Size group		*0*	*1*	*2*	*3*	*4*	*5*	*6*	*7*	*8*	*Total*
	0	98	68	12	6	0	0	0	0	0	
No.	*1*	2	221	46	1	0	0	0	0	0	270
in	*2*	0	4	168	43	0	0	0	0	0	215
1881	*3*	0	0	4	108	23	0	0	0	0	135
	4	0	0	0	1	54	10	0	0	0	65
	5	0	0	0	0	0	31	6	0	0	37
	6	0	0	0	0	0	0	14	3	0	17
	7	0	0	0	0	0	0	0	5	2	7
	8	0	0	0	0	0	0	0	0	4	4
Total			293	230	159	77	41	20	8	6	834/750

Table 3.3—*Continued*

	Size group	0	1	2	3	4	5	6	7	8	Total
					No. in 1901						
	0	41	53	3	3	0	0	0	0	0	
No.	1	8	231	53	1	0	0	0	0	0	293
in	2	0	6	168	56	0	0	0	0	0	230
1891	3	0	0	1	129	29	0	0	0	0	159
	4	0	0	0	1	60	16	0	0	0	77
	5	0	0	0	0	0	33	8	0	0	41
	6	0	0	0	0	0	0	15	5	0	20
	7	0	0	0	0	0	0	0	6	2	8
	8	0	0	0	0	0	0	0	0	6	6
Total			290	225	190	89	49	23	11	8	885/834

	Size group	0	1	2	3	4	5	6	7	8	Total
					No. in 1911						
	0	7	34	7	1	0	0	0	0	0	
No.	1	4	238	43	5	0	0	0	0	0	290
in	2	0	2	191	31	1	0	0	0	0	225
1901	3	0	0	2	156	32	0	0	0	0	190
	4	0	0	0	0	76	13	0	0	0	89
	5	0	0	0	0	0	43	6	0	0	49
	6	0	0	0	0	0	0	23	0	0	23
	7	0	0	0	0	0	0	0	11	0	11
	8	0	0	0	0	0	0	0	0	8	8
Total			274	243	193	109	56	29	11	8	923/885

Note: Size groups are as follows:

0	< 2,500	5	40,000–79,999
1	2,500–4,999	6	80,000–159,999
2	5,000–9,999	7	160,000–319,999
3	10,000–19,999	8	⩾ 320,000
4	20,000–39,999		

which towns appear in cells more than one away from the diagonal. On the whole, such large movements tend to be restricted to the smallest range of town sizes which suggests that it is only in these towns that one might expect to find very high percentage growth rates. Second, it can be seen that the matrices are all 'absorbing' matrices, that is to say that it is not possible for a town to move from one size class to every other of the size classes within the matrix — a requirement which would have to be met for the matrices to be 'regular Markov matrices' (Kemeney and Snell 1960). For this to be possible, the rows would need to have entries in the cells both above and below the diagonal. Instead — and particularly in the higher population sizes — the pattern is for towns either to continue in the same size class or to move up into the next higher size class.

Thus, if a given initial distribution of town sizes were to be powered up by successive multiplications by the transition probabilities,[1] all of the towns would eventually end up in the highest size class since, once above a certain population size, the probability of moving *down* into a lower size group becomes remote or non-existent. Third, the pattern of town 'births' is of interest. These 'births' are shown in the entries given in the 'zero' row and which fall in columns other than the 'zero' column – in other words, places which start a decade at populations below 2,500, but which end with populations greater than that figure. The rapid growth in the number of such new towns has already been noted, but here the pattern is shown much more clearly. The great majority is 'born' in the lowest size category with populations between 2,500 and 4,999, but many are 'born' in the later decades at figures well above this and it is some of these places whose early population figures are impossible to derive (see above, pp. 50–2). Fourth, and conversely, the entries in the 'zero' columns which do not fall in the 'zero' rows show the pattern of 'deaths' of towns – those places which fall below the threshold of 2,500. In most cases these represent places whose population hovered uncertainly around the threshold figure and declined below it for some of the twelve dates. Lyme Regis, in Dorset, for example, grew to over 2,500 by 1831 and reached a peak of 2,852 in 1851, but then declined so as to fall below the threshold in 1881 and only reappeared above it in 1911. Similarly, Dursley in Gloucestershire had a population above 2,500 from 1811 to 1851, but then fell below and again reappeared in 1911. Market Rasen and Alford, in Lincolnshire, both grew above the threshold only by 1861 and then fell below it in 1881 and 1891 respectively and had not reappeared again by 1911. The overall number of such places which 'died' – or fell out of the list of 'towns' – is relatively small. They present far fewer operational problems in deriving population totals than do some of the places which were 'born', not only because of the smaller number involved, but also because, when an administrative core had once been defined for such places, appropriate figures tend subsequently to be given in the census returns.

These are the main features of the transition matrices. In general they show that the great bulk of towns cluster along the diagonals of the tables, confirming in a very approximate way an expectation that urban growth would tend to occur at a rate common to the whole set of towns. A sharper focus is needed, however, before anything more precise or of greater interest than this general description might emerge. There are two possible avenues which could be explored: first the formal use of Markov methods in analyzing the structure of these matrices; and second the adoption of a regression format in looking at the relationship of opening and closing sizes at successive dates.

---

[1] The transition probabilities would be given simply as a weighting of the raw observations of the matrices. Thus, for each row, the probabilities would be the cell entries divided by the row total. These would give the probability of staying in the same size class or moving to another by the end of the decade.

MARKOV METHODS

The use of Markov methods was not pursued, even though there are some interesting examples of their use in closely similar fields. Markov methods involve the use of transition matrices of change as probabilities by which an initial distribution of observations is successively transformed over a number of iterations until the distribution converges on a terminal distribution vector which represents an equilibrium position to which the probabilities tend irrespective of the values of the initial vector. Alternatively, the number of iterations which are needed to reach the final absorbing state — when all the observations will have fallen into a group from which they do not again emerge — can be calculated for an absorbing matrix. Fuguitt (1965) has used such approaches in looking at population changes in small towns in the United States. For decades in which the pattern of size changes produces regular stochastic matrices, the equilibrium vectors produced by successive applications of the transition probabilities are derived and comparisons between them suggest that markedly different transition probabilities apply from one decade to another. The same differences are also seen by comparing the length of time taken to reach absorption: of the eight decades studied, the decade 1890-1900 shows the most rapid change, reaching absorption in the equivalent of 350 years and with 130 years being the average time which it would take for a place to move from a population of less than 500 to over 5,000; by contrast, the decade 1920-30 showed the slowest change with figures of 4,510 and 3,820 years respectively. In Britain, Lever (1972) has also used Markov methods to examine urban growth for the period 1951-71. He tries to isolate 'most favoured' town sizes by calculating the final vectors of town sizes which result by successive applications of the transition probabilities of 1951-61 and 1961-71. Again, like Fuguitt, he discovers that the transition probabilities differ between the two decades[1] and, in any case, his derivation of a terminal vector of sizes is made less convincing by the fact that his initial matrices contain very few observations and that the matrices themselves consist of a number of absorbing sub-matrices rather than single regular matrices.

Markov methods have been widely used in studies comparable to these of the changes of town size. In the literature of the social sciences, the phenomenon of social mobility has been studied in this way (Prais 1955; Beshers and Laumann 1967), but the closest parallel is in the study of business-firm sizes, the most comprehensive work being that of Adelman (1958). Its particular interest here lies in the way in which Adelman deals with the troublesome categories of observations which are 'born' and which 'die'. Most of the applications of

[1] The fact that marked differences occur between the probabilities of successive decades means, of course, that the successive application of one set of probabilities over a long period of time must be seen in terms of its analytic rather than its predictive value.

Markov methods have ignored these categories and deal instead with an un-changing number of observations — be they towns, firms or whatever. Adelman, however, incorporates them by including in the transition matrices a very large 'reservoir' from which new firms can be created and into which existing firms can disappear. This would be the equivalent, in our transition matrices, of the 'zero-zero' cell in which appear all the places which are less than 2,500, but which are larger than that at some date in the period 1801-1911. Adelman demonstrates that the size of the entry in this cell makes no difference to the eventual equilibrium vector which is produced by the transition probabilities.[1]

Despite the interest of such approaches, Markov methods were ignored here partly because of the unreasonableness of using a simple assumption that the transition probabilities would remain constant over a long period of time, but more particularly because, as has already been noted, all of the matrices were absorbing and thus it would have been possible to calculate only the expected time to absorption for the probabilities of each decade. This, by itself, would have produced somewhat of a sledgehammer statistic which would tell one little about the structure of population changes besides the speed of the overall rate of change.

REGRESSION OF OPENING AND CLOSING SIZES FOR EACH DECADE

Instead, a regression approach would seem of much greater value as a first exercise in looking at the details of the nineteenth-century growth processes which are hinted at in the transition matrices. It was suggested in the last chapter that one might hypothesize that towns grow by some common overall rate, but that the common rate is subject to fluctuations from one town to another. This hypothesis suggests a regression formulation of the following sort:

$$X_t = a + bX_{t-1} + \epsilon;   [3.1]$$

where X_t is the population of a town at time t; a and b are constants; and ϵ is a normally-distributed error or disturbance term. If the growth of the set of places were to conform to the law of proportionate growth, the value of b would be expected to be $1 \cdot 0$ and the overall change produced by this growth within the total population of towns would be represented by the constant a which would measure the vertical displacement of the curve. The variances in the growth rates of individual towns would be contained in the error term. The interest in this formulation is twofold: first in the extent to which real-world data do produce a value of b which is not significantly different from $1 \cdot 0$; and second in the increasing concentration produced in the distribution of urban populations by the value of both the b term and the disturbance term.

[1] The difficulty of dealing with a variable rate of 'births' and 'deaths' is discussed below, pp. 69–70.

CONCENTRATION OF URBAN POPULATION

Before turning to the statistical regression, we might digress a little to expand on this latter point about the growing concentration of population. If it were to be found that empirical data on urban growth fitted a regression model in which the value of b was greater than $1 \cdot 0$, this would mean that larger places tended to grow more rapidly than smaller places and the consequence on the size distribution of those places would be that the slope of the frequency curve would grow steeper as increasing proportions of the total population were contained within the larger cities at the expense of the smaller. There is, indeed, some evidence that the slopes of more developed countries tend in general to be somewhat steeper than those of less developed countries. Lopes (1972), for example, in criticizing the distinction between 'lognormal' and 'primate' size distributions, suggests that attention should instead be focused on the relation-ship between the degree of economic development of countries and the *slope* of their size-distribution curves.[1] He finds that the correlations between the slope coefficients and indices of economic development for a number of countries are positive and quite high and, while the calculation of slopes is very much dependent upon the lower threshold of size at which cities are selected, the results would tend to support the notion of increasing urban concentration over time. In practice, however, the great majority of studies of rank-size distribution curves has found that the curves at successive dates tend to be parallel with each other and tend to settle down at a slope of approximately $45°$.[2] In the regression format of the closing size on the opening size of cities, if we find a b value of $1 \cdot 0$, will this then explain the parallelism of size curves?

In fact, so long as there is a disturbance term around the common growth rate, even a value of b equal to $1 \cdot 0$ will still produce increasing population concentration over time. The connection of concentration and the nature of urban growth is best seen with a simple example. Suppose one takes a set of 128 cities each of which has an identical population at some given time t_1 — a situation perhaps representing an early stage of unspecialized development in which each place is relatively independent and serves only a small and relatively self-contained tributary area (a statistical parody, in fact, of the pre-industrial city). Let us assume that each city has a population of 10,000; then a measure of concentration which might be used is the percentage of the total population contained in the ten largest places and this, at time t_1, would be $7 \cdot 8$. Obviously if each individual city were subsequently to grow by an identical rate, the percentage of population contained in the ten largest places would remain unchanged no matter how many time periods were involved. However, if we

[1] A suggestion which was advanced much earlier by Singer (1936) and Allen (1954).
[2] The successive curves of city sizes in the United States (fig. 2.3) demonstrate the point, see above, p. 30.

assume that there is even a very slight random fluctuation of individual city growth around this common rate, the effect is very different. Let us assume that this fluctuation conforms to Simon's (1955) growth model, so that the disturbance term is identical within any band of city sizes. This fluctuation can be of the following order: within each size band, half of the cities will stay the same size, one-quarter will increase by 10 per cent, and one-quarter will decline by 10 per cent.[1] The progression of sizes will then be as follows:

	Size of city							Total number of cities	% of total population in top 10 cities
Time	*7,110*	*7,900*	*9,000*	*10,000*	*11,000*	*12,100*	*13,310*		
t_1				128				128	7·81
t_2			32	64	32			128	8·59
t_3		8	32	48	32	8		128	9·28
t_4	2	12	30	40	30	12	2	128	11·53

The percentage of the total population which is found in the ten largest places increases progressively over time from 7·8 at time t_1, to 8·6 in t_2, 9·3 in t_3 and 11·5 in t_4. Despite the fact that there is a common overall rate of growth and that the fluctuation around that rate is the same for groups of larger and smaller places, the degree of concentration will increase. Only if there is *no* fluctuation whatsoever and a common rate of growth, will concentration not occur. The greater the degree of fluctuation the more rapidly will concentration take place. Interest in the regression formulae should therefore be focused upon the size of the disturbance term as well as upon the closeness of the *b* term to 1·0. Only some form of countervailing tendency in the growth of cities will prevent increasing urban concentration from occurring.

This phenomenon of concentration was discussed very early by Galton who recognized the need for some form of 'regression towards the mean'[2] if the growth of units was not to lead to growing concentration. In the study of business-firm growth, this requirement has been discussed by Kalecki (1945) and by Prais and Hart (1956) and a similar regression towards the mean has been recognized in the study of IQs of parents and children.[3] A somewhat parallel

[1] By using size bands, this growth process conforms to the weaker assumption discussed above, pp. 31–2. It means that it is perfectly possible for any given city to increase consistently over successive decades. The percentage growth rates used in this instance should be regarded as departures from the overall average growth rate which is taken as being zero.

[2] So as not to cause confusion between the statistical technique of linear regression and Galton's term 'regression', the latter will be referred to as 'regression to the mean'.

[3] On average, the children of parents with high IQ tend to have slightly lower IQs than their parents and children of parents will low IQ tend to have slightly higher IQs than their parents. The regression towards the mean level of IQ operates to prevent the distribution of IQs from becoming progressively distended.

phenomenon can be seen in the discussion of positive and negative feedback effects in regional economic development.[1]

The need for some retarding element in order to maintain concentration at a constant level has briefly been noted in the case of urban growth (E. N. Thomas 1967) and the suggestion of retardation in the growth rates of individual cities has been discussed most fully by Madden (1956b and 1958) and Williamson (1965b; Williamson and Swanson 1966). It is by no means clear, however, that one can as yet reconcile the apparent stability of size-distribution curves with the inevitable tendency towards increasing concentration which is a concomitant of the urban growth process of proportionate effect which has so often been assumed in studies of urbanization.

REGRESSION   ANALYSIS   OF   NINETEENTH-CENTURY   URBAN GROWTH

Bearing in mind the discussion about urban concentration, our regression formulation can now be re-expressed in the following terms:

$$X_t = a + (1 + c)X_{t-1} + \epsilon; \qquad\qquad [3.2]$$

where c is Galton's constant — the negative weighting which is necessary to retard the growth of large places relative to small places by an amount which will maintain the level of concentration in the distribution under consideration. Obviously, this is directly the equivalent of equation [3.1] since the c term equals the slope coefficient, b, minus $1 \cdot 0$. Equation [3.2] simply argues that, to produce a distribution whose component units grow while maintaining the overall stability of the distribution, the larger units have to grow more slowly than the smaller. The size of the negative weight, c, which is required for stability will depend on the size of the disturbance term, ϵ, since, as was shown above, concentration will tend to increase more quickly the larger the variance around the common growth.

Table 3.4 shows the regression coefficients of towns' opening and closing sizes for each of the eleven decadal periods between 1801-11 and 1901-11. Throughout, the natural logarithm of population sizes has been used in the calculations. There are two points of particular interest. First, it is apparent that the values of b, the slope coefficient, are in every case very close to $1 \cdot 0$ which suggests that the growth of these nineteenth-century cities is governed by an

---

[1] Hirschman (1958), Myrdal (1957) and others argue that economic inequality is the product of cumulative growth which is aided by 'backwash' effects within a national economy and that, only at a later stage, is the level of inequality dampened by 'spread' effects operating from growth centres as negative feedback replaces positive. In a study of a number of national economies over time, Williamson (1965a) supports this temporal progression. Some of the checks to cumulative growth which have been suggested for national growth centres could obviously be applied directly to the growth of large cities.

Table 3.4 Regression of urban populations: closing size on opening size of towns at successive dates

Decade	No. of towns in calculation	Intercept (a)	Slope (b)	b − 1 (c)	Coeff. of determination (R^2)	Standard error of estimate ($s_{X_t \cdot X_{t-1}}$)
1801–11	256	0·009	1·017	0·017	0·977	0·128
1811–21	308	−0·047	1·028	0·028	0·980	0·127
1821–31	361	−0·147	1·037	0·037	0·978	0·128
1831–41	412	−0·159	1·035	0·035	0·970	0·160
1841–51	465	−0·186	1·037	0·037	0·978	0·131
1851–61	521	−0·086	1·024	0·024	0·968	0·166
1861–71	580	0·112	1·006	0·006	0·959	0·200
1871–81	691	0·049	1·013	0·013	0·967	0·183
1881–91	750	−0·012	1·015	0·015	0·975	0·166
1891–1901	834	0·065	1·008	0·008	0·974	0·166
1901–1911	885	0·148	0·998	−0·002	0·978	0·159

Notes

1. All calculations are for $X_t = a + b X_{t-1} + \epsilon$, where X_t is population at date t.
2. Values are for natural logarithms of town populations.

approximately constant proportion irrespective of city size. Second, however, it is not without significance that, with only one exception, all of the values are slightly higher than 1·0. If we subtract 1·0 from each of the values of *b* (thus giving the value of *c*), it can be seen that it is only in the final decade that Galton's constant gives a negative weighting. Indeed, there would appear to be a pattern of some regularity in the changes of the value of *c*. In the early decades it tends to increase in size, but in 1861-71 it falls markedly and stays at a low level until it actually falls to a negative value in the very last decade. If anything, therefore, the regression model of closing size on opening size suggests a weak positive relationship with the size of city for the early decades of the century, but that in the final quarter of the century and the first decade of the twentieth

Table 3.5   *Concentration of the urban population: percentage in the largest towns*

Date	A *Total no. of towns* *used in calculation*	B *% of total urban population* *in largest 10% of towns*	C *Rate of change*
1801	250	61·63	1·006
1811	300	62·02	1·013
1821	360	62·81	1·024
1831	410	64·31	1·020
1841	460	65·57	1·020
1851	520	66·88	1·017
1861	580	68·02	0·994
1871	690	67·58	1·015
1881	740	68·37	1·012
1891	830	69·18	1·000
1901	880	69·18	0·987
1911	920	68·28	

Note: Column C gives the ratio of the percentages (column B) at time *t* to those at time *t* + 1.

century this positive relationship was weaker and turned to a negative relationship in the decade immediately before the First World War. In all cases however, the relationship between size and growth rate is never strong.

The results of the regression approach might therefore suggest two conclusions. First that, at this aggregate level, the assumption that urban growth is a random proportion of existing population size does not appear to be unreasonable. Second that, since there is a marked disturbance term throughout and the variance of individual cities' growth rates is not compensated for by a negative *c* term which would produce 'regression to the mean', one would expect that the level of population concentration would have increased for all except possibly the final decade. The extent to which such growing concentration occurred during the nineteenth century is suggested in tables 3.5 and 3.6 which show, for

Table 3.6 Concentration of the urban population: dispersion of sizes

Set of towns	No.	Starting year			Closing year		
		Mean ($\bar{X}$)	Standard deviation (s)	Coefficient of variation (V)	Coefficient of variation (V)	Standard deviation (s)	Mean ($\bar{X}$)
1801–11	256	8·608	0·801	9·308	9·408	0·824	8·763
1811–21	308	8·623	0·813	9·434	9·583	0·845	8·819
1821–31	361	8·694	0·840	9·665	9·935	0·881	8·872
1831–41	412	8·768	0·878	10·012	10·345	0·922	8·915
1841–51	465	8·816	0·915	10·373	10·708	0·959	8·957
1851–61	521	8·886	0·947	10·661	10·939	0·986	9·011
1861–71	580	8·923	0·976	10·939	11·030	1·002	9·086
1871–81	691	8·977	0·979	10·903	11·027	1·008	9·141
1881–91	750	9·061	1·014	11·187	11·342	1·042	9·188
1891–1901	834	9·096	1·037	11·398	11·468	1·059	9·236
1901–1911	885	9·170	1·065	11·610	11·553	1·074	9·299

Notes
1. Each set of towns is comprised of those which had populations ≥ 2,500 at both the start and close of the decade shown.
2. Values are for natural logarithms of town populations.

the whole period of 110 years, both the percentage of the total urban population which was contained in the top 10 per cent of the cities as well as the standard deviations of the whole array of cities. It is evident that both measures suggest similar conclusions; that the rate of concentration increased in the period up to 1861, but thereafter slowed down somewhat and that concentration decreased in the final part of the whole period.

We might try to draw together some of these apparently disparate forays on the body of data by developing the ideas inherent in the regression model. The results suggest that equation [3.2] provides a useful model by which to represent the growth of cities over successive dates. It argues that the population of a city at one date is some common proportion of its size at an earlier time irrespective of that size, but that there is a (log)normally-distributed fluctuation in the growth rates of individual cities which can be seen as a disturbance term common to the whole set of places. The empirical data which fit this model therefore provide, for nineteenth-century England and Wales, some support for the idea of a form of stochastic growth process which has been the underpinning of many of the theoretical models of city-size distributions. However, this is to ignore the generally positive value of the c term which suggests that there is a deviation away from constant growth to one with a slightly positive relationship with the previous size of a city. This, and the variation in individual growth rates which is given by the ϵ term, suggest that the particular growth process operating in the nineteenth century would not lead to a stationary size distribution of cities, but rather one characterized by increasing concentration of population. Ideally, it would be of some interest to calculate the value of the c term which, for a given value of ϵ, would produce a distribution which would become neither more nor less concentrated over time. We know that a positive c term will lead to greater concentration, but how large a negative term would be needed to halt the progress of concentration? The calculation of such a value would be very easy were one dealing with a constant set of cities, but the fact that the set of places is increasing in number complicates its calculation unduly. Here is one of the further difficulties encountered in dealing both with the 'birth' of new places and the 'death' of declining places. It will be recalled that the second of Simon's assumptions about growth was that new places (or, in his case, new words) were added at a constant rate and that it was this rate which determined the closeness of the convergence parameter of b to a value of 1·0 in the growth formula noted earlier.[1] The rate of addition of new places in nineteenth-century England and Wales, however, was far from constant. Table 3.7 shows the 'births' of towns as a percentage of the total number of cities at the start of each decade and shows that this percentage declined from a 'high' of over 20 down to almost 12 in 1851-61, then rose markedly almost to 20 once again in 1861-71, but thereafter fell drastically to figures of less than 10 in all but one of the following decades

[1] See above, p. 32.

and ended with a 'low' of under 5 in 1901-11. Such varying rates of addition to the set of places complicates our assessment of Galton's constant — the value of *c* which would be required to maintain a stable distribution. For decades when the rate of entry of new places is high (assuming, as is the case, that the majority of 'births' was in the small size groups), the effect will be to increase the rate of concentration of population, whether measured in terms of the percentage of population found in the largest 10 per cent of the cities or in terms of dispersion. The opposite will apply when 'births' are low so that the markedly lower ratio of 'births' in the last quarter of the period would have the effect of increasing the concentration to a lesser extent so that the declining rates of

Table 3.7   *The rate of addition of new towns*

Decade	A Total no. of towns at start of decade	B No. of new towns at end of decade	C B as % of A
1801–11	256	53	20·70
1811–21	308	53	17·21
1821–31	361	51	14·13
1831–41	412	54	13·11
1841–51	465	57	12·26
1851–61	521	63	12·09
1861–71	580	113	19·48
1871–81	691	59	8·54
1881–91	750	86	11·47
1891–1901	834	59	7·07
1901–1911	885	42	4·75

concentration in that period must be seen as the product both of the falling value of *c* and of the falling ratio of 'births'.[1]

There are therefore three types of function which influence the extent to which a size curve will be stable or will show increasing concentration over time. Where the variance of the growth rates, ϵ, is high, concentration will proceed more rapidly; this concentration will be countered or exacerbated depending on the value of *c* — only where *c* is of a 'sufficiently' large negative value will concentration tend to be reversed; but in addition the rate of entry of new small towns has to be considered since it will tend to distend the tail of the lower end of the size distribution and it will do this to a greater extent when the rate is high than when it is low, with the consequent effect of increasing the speed of concentration.

[1] Fuguitt (1965) draws a parallel conclusion in suggesting that much of the apparent decline of very small communities in the United States is more a product of the declining rate of incorporation of new small places than of the actual decline of existing small places.

A DISAGGREGATED APPROACH

So far the data on urban size and growth rates have been studied in aggregate terms. It would be profitable to look in more detail at the growth rates of towns by analyzing not the whole set of places, but sub-sets of the whole population. This might throw more detailed light on the nature of urban growth in nineteenth-century England and Wales.

So that the individual growth rates of towns can be more readily comprehended, the actual populations, rather than the natural logarithms of populations, will be used. Further, in estimating the actual growth rates of individual towns, a slightly more complex measure of growth has been used than is normally the case. In the overwhelming majority of the work which has studied growth rates, a simple rate of population increase has been calculated for each decade, given by the formula:

$$G_{t-1.t} = (P_t - P_{t-1}) . P_{t-1}^{-1};$$ [3.3]

where $G_{t-1.t}$ is the growth rate between the times $t - 1$ and t; and P is population. A more realistic estimate of the rate of growth and one which, as Gibbs (1961, p. 108) suggests, is a close approximation to a compound growth rate, is given by expressing the denominator of the equation not as the initial population of a place at $t - 1$, but as the mid-point population between the opening and closing dates. The calculation of growth is then given by the following:

$$G_{t-1.t} = (P_t - P_{t-1}) . \left(\frac{P_t + P_{t-1}}{2} \right)^{-1}$$ [3.4]

The use of this estimate of growth rates would seem to have two advantages. First, it is a more accurate assessment of growth since population change is a continuous not a discrete phenomenon and the estimated mid-point population is a closer approximation to the changing base from which increments to or decrements from the population occur during the course of a decade. Second, its use has the effect of altering the distribution of growth rates in such a way as to help counter the tendency of simple growth rates to be positively skewed.[1] This tendency has been widely noted (Madden 1956a; Lampard 1968, p. 128), but the fact that studies have produced sets of growth rates which have a long tail of very high values is partly the result of using simple rather than compound measures of growth. By comparison with a simple rate, equation [3.4] tends to compress the high positive growth rates and expand the negative rates. For

[1] It was partly to correct the different and much more extreme skew of town sizes that natural logarithms of population size were used in the regression analysis above, pp. 65 *et seq.*

example, a town which increased in population from 10,000 to 15,000 over the space of a decade would be considered, by using the simple growth rate of equation [3.3], to have a growth rate of 50 per cent; if it were to decrease in population to a figure of 5,000, it would be given a growth rate of −50 per cent. However, by using equation [3.4] which would involve denominators of 12,500 and 7,500 for the case of growth and decline respectively, its growth rates would be considered as 40 per cent in the case of expansion and −111 per cent in the case of decline. The tendency for positive skew in the distribution of growth rates is therefore counteracted to some extent by the use of this second estimate of growth and the assumption of normality which underlies parametric statistical tests will be more likely to hold true. The growth rates used in the following analysis are therefore all based on the somewhat modified form of equation [3.4] which approximates the compound rather than the simple growth-rate formula.

Growth rates for each town were calculated during each pair of successive census dates in which the town had a known population of over 2,500. The numbers of observations at each intercensal period are therefore comparable with the numbers used in the regression study: for the first decade there are 256 observations; for the final decade there are 885. The scatters of observations for each of the eleven decades are shown in fig. 3.2 which plots the growth rate against the population size of places on semi-logarithmic scales.

On casual inspection of these diagrams, the first clear impression is of the increasing number of observations during the whole period; the galaxies of dots become much denser in the later decades as more and more towns are 'born' into the population. Second, if one squints sufficiently hard, discernible patterns can be seen. It is clearly true, as the earlier regression analysis suggested, that growth and size are virtually unrelated. If one visualizes lines representing the average growth rates across the whole span of city sizes during each decade, then the lines would be roughly horizontal, suggesting that the whole set of places can be characterized as having a common growth rate around which disturbance occurs. If these lines are horizontal, then their vertical shifts upwards and downwards from one decade to another represent differences in the overall growth rate during the different decades.[1] For example, the average growth-rate lines for the earlier and middle decades appear to be characterized by average growth lines somewhat higher than those of the later decades and thus the whole set of places must have grown on average by a greater amount during the earlier part of the period. A third comment on the diagrams, however, must be that it is quite apparent that the scatter of observations around the imaginary average growth

---

[1] The relationship between these scatters of growth rates on the one hand and the earlier regression analysis of equation [3.2] on the other is quite apparent. A horizontal line of average growth rates corresponds to a slope coefficient of $b = 1\cdot0$ in the regression of closing on opening population sizes. The scatter around the line of growth rates equals the disturbance term, ϵ.

lines is not constant with increasing size of town. The disturbance appears to grow distinctly less as one moves from smaller to larger towns.

These latter two points are obviously of some importance in relation to our ideas about the overall growth rates of sets of cities and deserve a more detailed examination than the simple inspection of scatter diagrams. They are of importance because of their bearing on the stochastic growth models which have been widely assumed to apply to urban growth. Gibrat's law — or the law of proportionate effect — would state, as has been seen, that growth would be a common proportion of existing size and, as a strict and necessary version of the law, that the error term around this proportionate growth would be normally distributed. We therefore need to test whether or not these two properties are met in the empirical data of nineteenth-century growth in England and Wales.

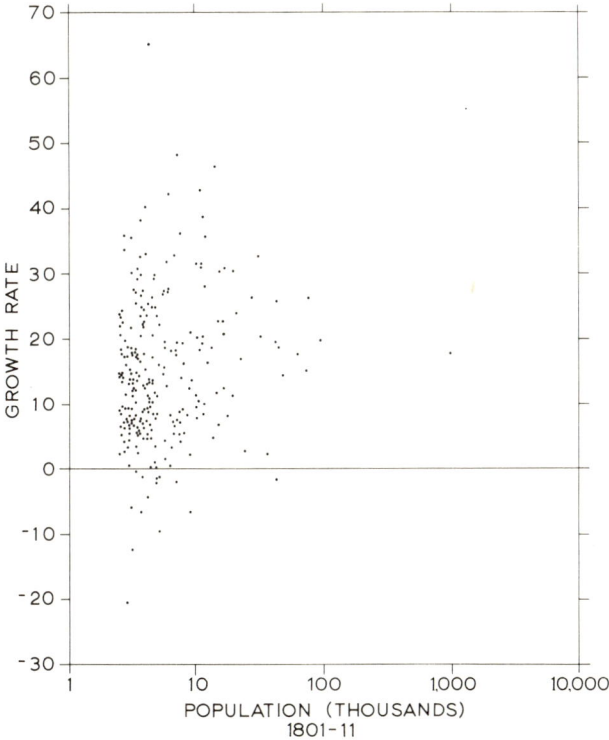

Figure 3.2 Growth rates and town size in England and Wales, 1801–1911. Note: A small number of places in the lower size ranges have growth rates greater than 70 per cent and are not shown in the scatter diagrams. The numbers involved, for each decade, are as follows: 1801–11, 1; 1811–21, 3; 1821–31, 3; 1831–41, 3; 1841–51, 3; 1851–61, 9; 1861–71, 13; 1871–81, 10; 1881–91, 6; 1891–1901, 11; 1901–11, 9.

continued

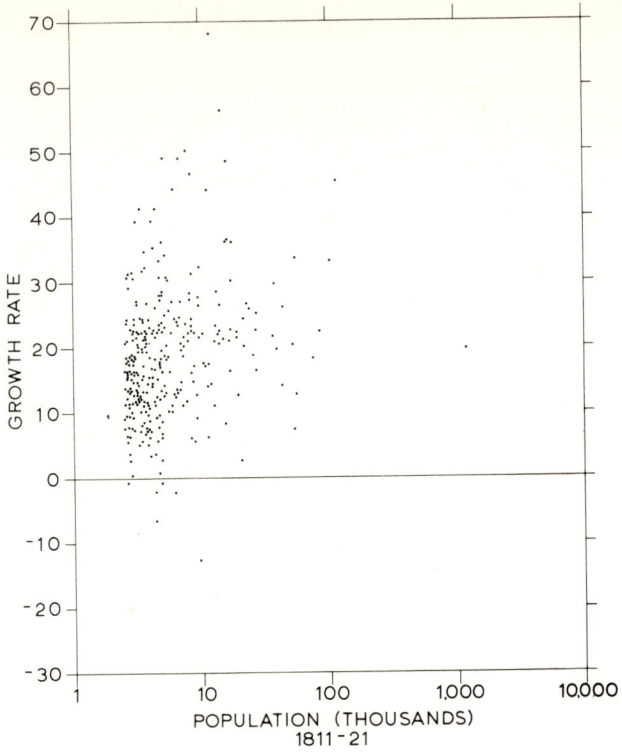

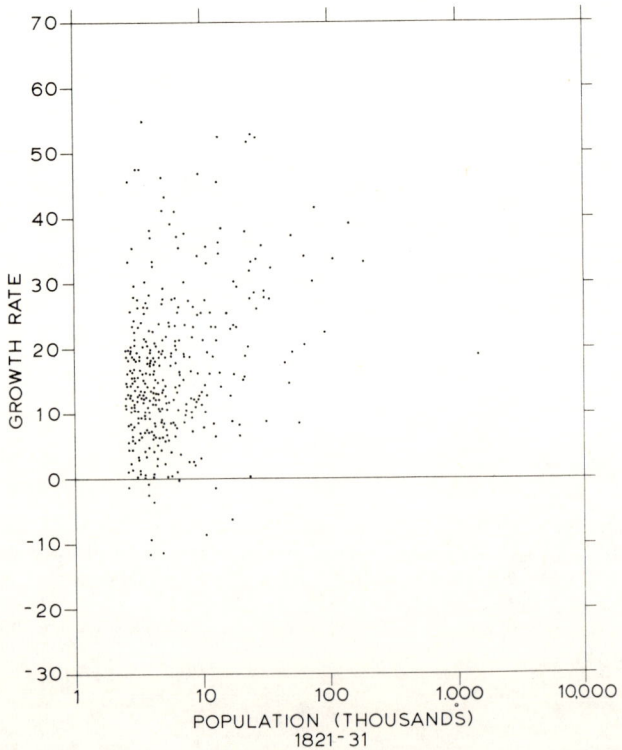

Figure 3.2 (*continued*)

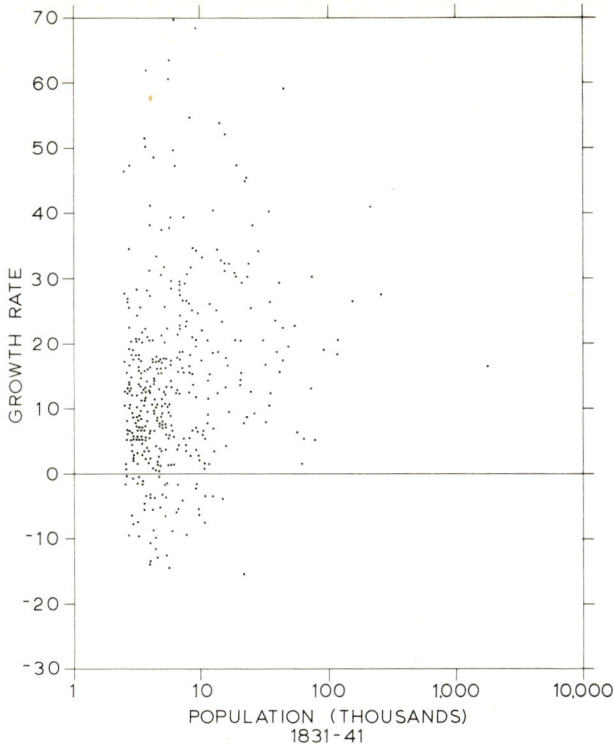

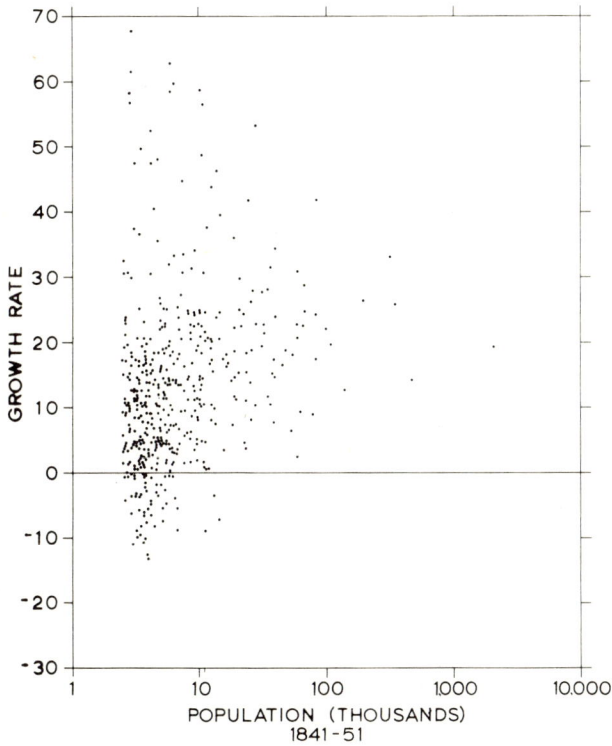

Figure 3.2 (*continued*)

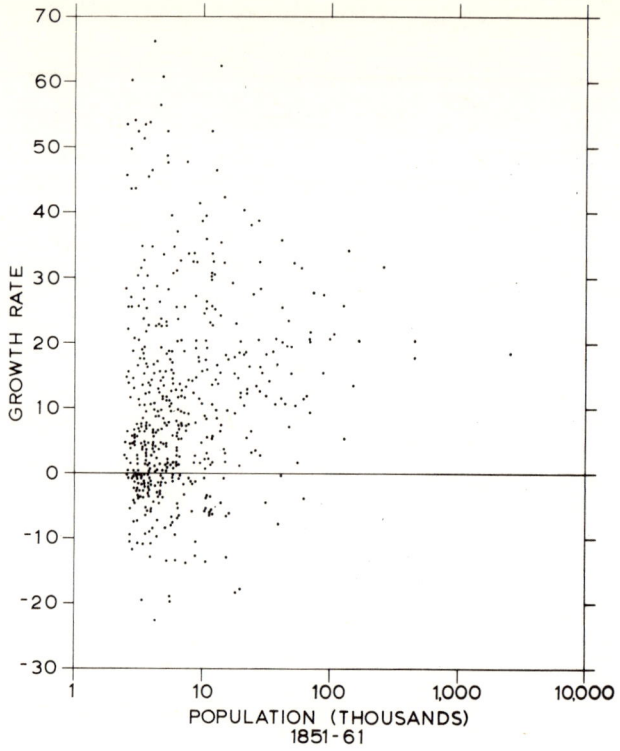

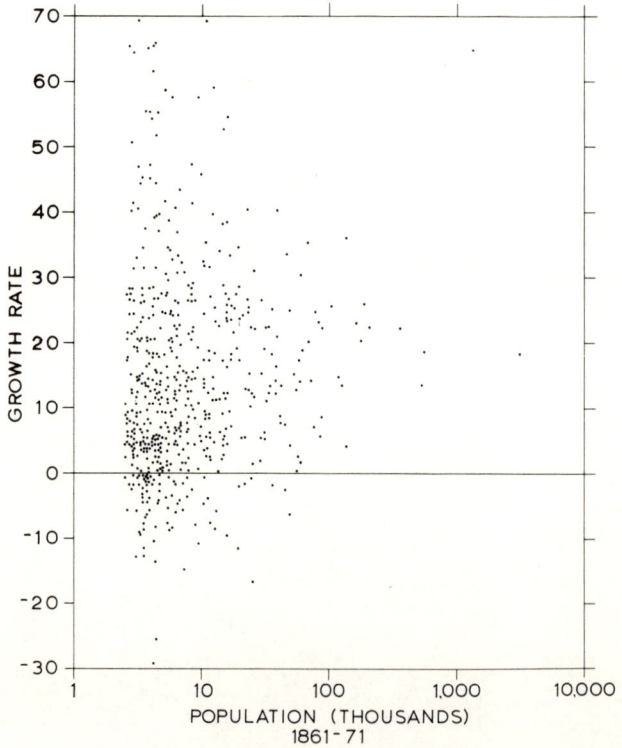

Figure 3.2 (*continued*)

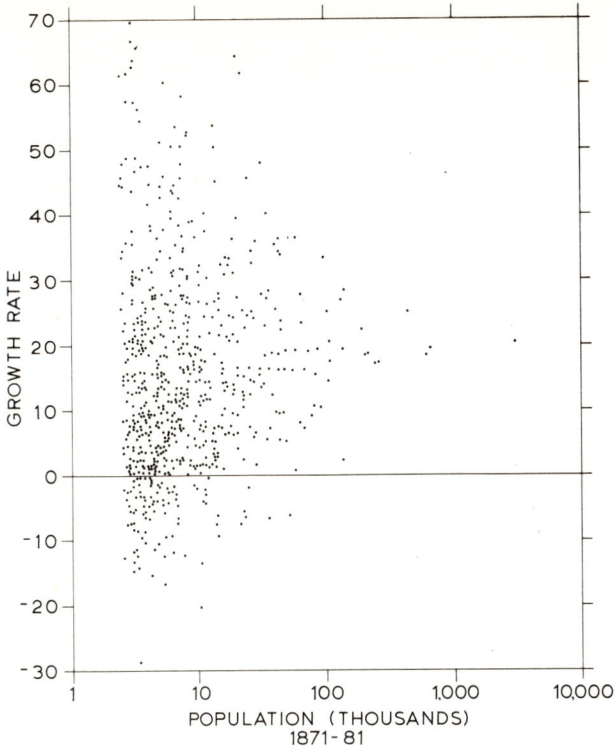

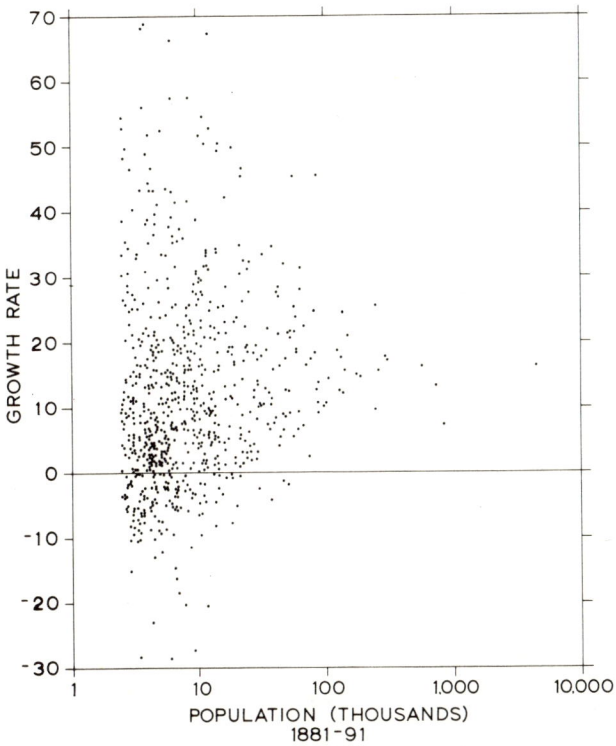

Figure 3.2 (*continued*)

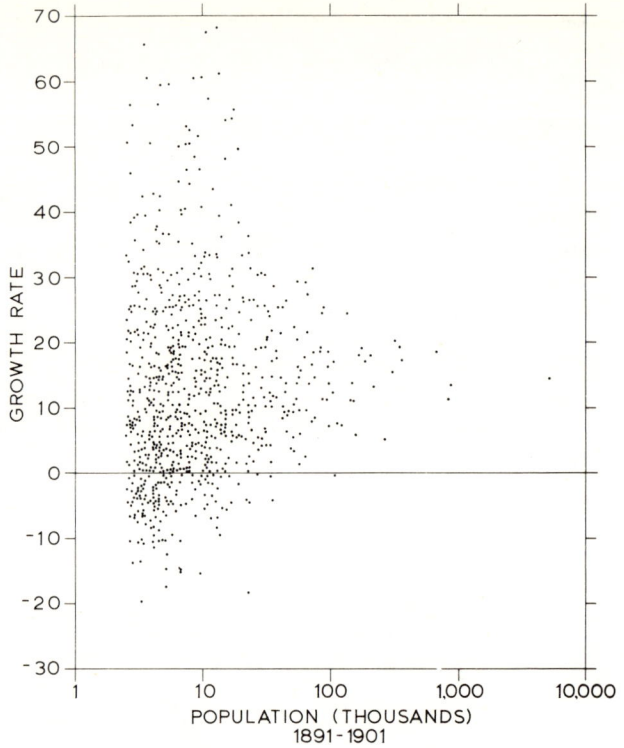

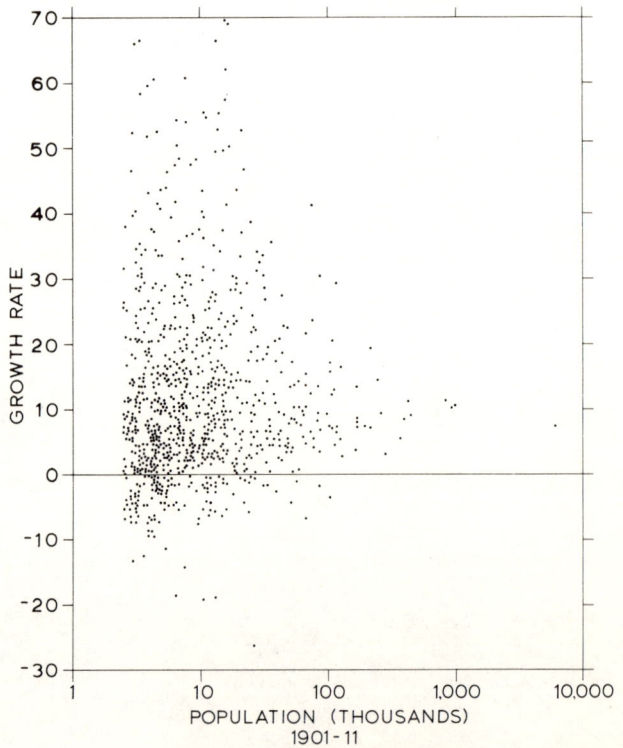

Figure 3.2 (*continued*)

One way in which this might be approached is, again, to use a regression model and table 3.8 gives the results of simple regressions of the following form:

$$G_{i.d} = a + b \log P_{i.t} + \epsilon; \qquad\qquad [3.5]$$

where G and P are respectively the growth rate and population of town i during the decade d which starts at time t.[1] The standard errors of these regressions formulations are, of course, very large, reflecting the expectedly low amount of explanation provided by the regression since the regression lines are virtually horizontal. Apart from the somewhat unreliable fact that the slopes of the

Table 3.8   *Regression of growth rates on town size*

Decade	Intercept (a)	Slope (b)	Standard error of estimate ($s_{G.P}$)
1801–11	0·71	3·94	12·11
1811–21	−4·63	6·43	11·67
1821–31	−14·63	8·53	12·59
1831–41	−15·80	7·97	15·49
1841–51	−18·59	8·49	13·81
1851–61	−8·31	5·35	17·09
1861–71	10·26	1·47	18·98
1871–81	4·28	3·06	17·58
1881–91	−1·83	3·67	15·91
1891–1901	7·25	1·72	16·45
1901–1911	14·95	−0·54	15·52

Notes: Values are for the equation $G_{i.d} = a + b \log P_{i.t} + \epsilon$, where $G_{i.d}$ is the growth rate of town i during decade d; and $P_{i.t}$ is the population of town i at the start of the decade.

relationship between size and growth rate are positive for all but the final decade, the regression approach is of little analytic value.

A more profitable approach is to test the means and variances of growth rates for sub-groups of town sizes. Again, the size categories of 2,500-4,999, 5,000-9,999, and so forth, in which each group is twice that of the lower group, have been used. The values of the means and standard deviations for each of these size groups in each decade are given in table 3.9. The results are plotted in fig. 3.3 in which the means of each size group are joined by thick lines and thinner lines are drawn above and below them at one standard deviation from the means. These diagrams, and the data of table 3.9 on which they are based, are simplified descriptions of the galaxies of points showing the growth rates of each individual town.

Equation [3.5] differs from the earlier regression equations of [3.1] and [3.2] in that it uses growth rate rather than closing population size as dependent variable. See above, p. 62 and 65.

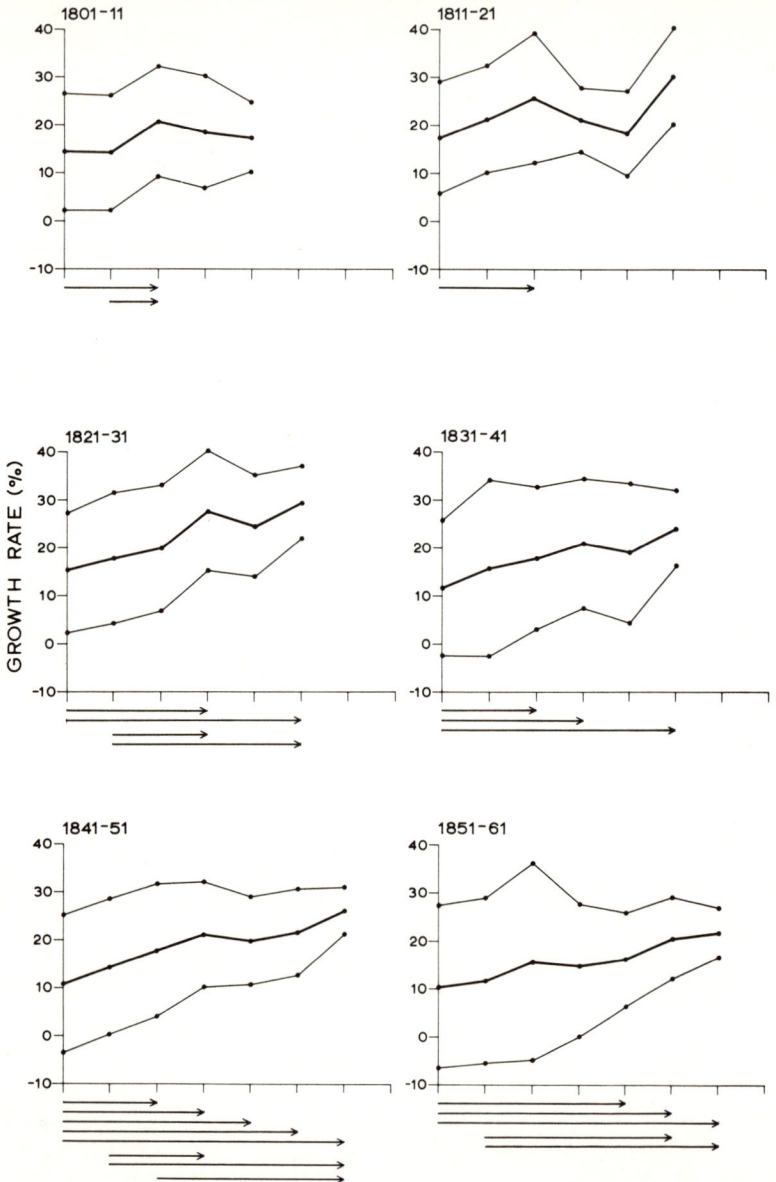

Figure 3.3　Growth rates and town size: means and dispersions. The diagrams summarize the data shown in fig. 3.2. Arrows below each plot show those size groups with mean growth rates significantly different at the 1·0 per cent confidence level, the arrow head points to that size group with the *higher* mean (see details given in table 3.10)

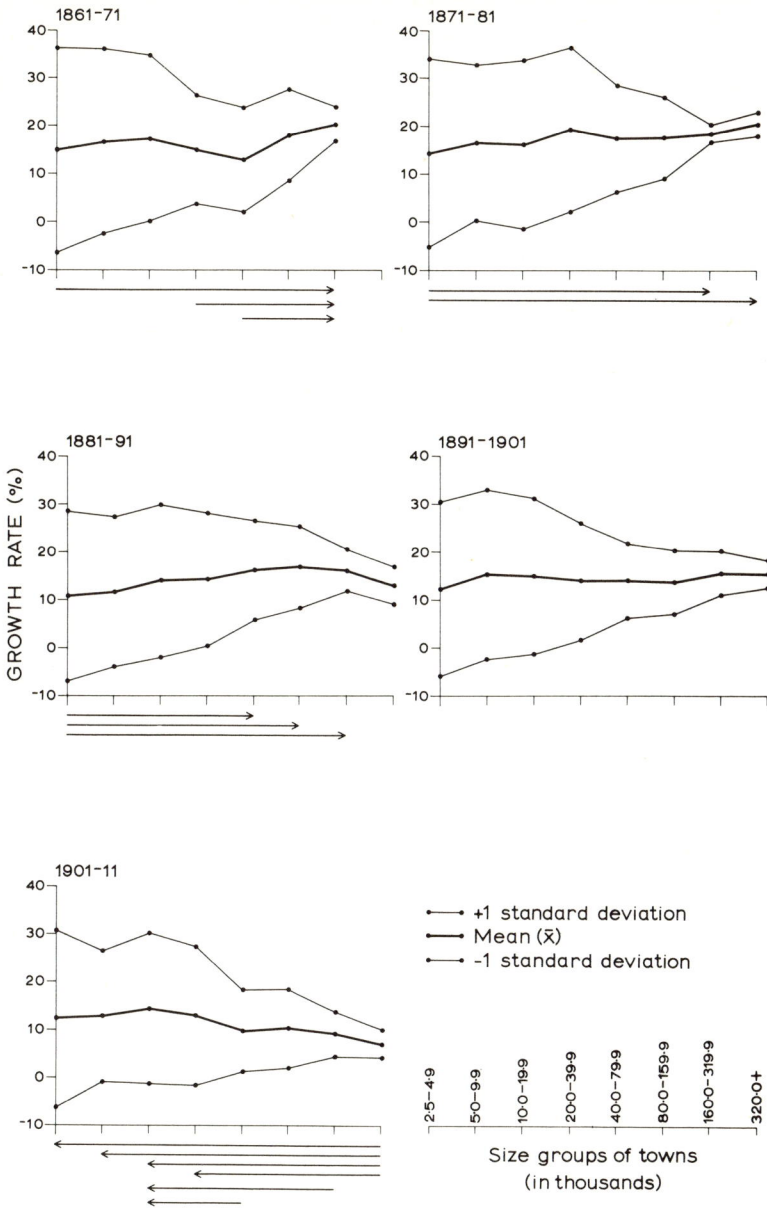

Figure 3.3 (*continued*)

Table 3.9 *Means and dispersions of growth rates of towns in different size groups*

Period		2,500-	5,000-	10,000-	20,000-	40,000-	80,000-	160,000-	320,000-
					Size group ('000s)				
1801–11	N	160	47	32	7	10			
	$\bar{X}$	14·5	14·3	20·7	18·6	17·5			
	s	12·3	12·1	11·6	11·6	7·4			
	V%	85·0	84·9	55·8	62·5	42·2			
1811–21	N	191	64	31	12	7	4		
	$\bar{X}$	17·5	21·3	25·8	21·3	18·4	30·3		
	s	11·7	11·2	13·5	6·7	8·7	10·1		
	V%	66·5	52·5	52·1	31·3	47·3	33·4		
1821–31	N	200	89	38	20	9	5		
	$\bar{X}$	15·3	17·9	20·0	27·8	24·6	29·6		
	s	12·0	13·6	13·1	12·4	10·5	7·5		
	V%	78·6	75·9	65·5	44·5	42·7	25·5		
1831–41	N	207	115	44	26	13	7		
	$\bar{X}$	11·7	15·8	18·0	21·0	19·1	24·3		
	s	14·2	18·4	14·9	13·4	14·5	7·9		
	V%	121·0	116·6	83·0	63·9	76·1	32·4		
1841–51	N	227	121	62	32	13	7	4	
	$\bar{X}$	10·8	14·3	17·9	21·1	19·9	21·8	26·2	
	s	14·3	14·2	13·8	10·9	9·1	9·0	4·9	
	V%	132·0	99·1	77·3	51·7	45·6	41·4	18·7	
1851–61	N	231	135	85	31	23	8	5	
	$\bar{X}$	10·3	11·6	15·6	14·8	16·2	20·6	21·8	
	s	16·9	17·3	20·5	12·8	9·8	8·5	5·1	
	V%	163·6	148·9	131·5	86·4	60·6	41·1	23·5	
1861–71	N	255	153	91	40	24	9	8	
	$\bar{X}$	15·0	16·9	17·5	15·1	13·0	18·4	20·6	
	s	21·3	19·2	17·4	11·3	11·0	9·5	3·5	
	V%	141·7	113·7	99·3	74·4	84·1	51·5	17·0	
1871–81	N	274	201	111	55	28	13	5	4
	$\bar{X}$	14·6	16·8	16·5	19·8	17·8	18·1	18·9	21·0
	s	19·6	16·3	17·6	17·2	11·1	8·5	1·8	2·6
	V%	133·8	97·0	106·8	86·8	62·2	47·0	9·6	12·2
1881–91	N	268	215	135	65	37	17	7	4
	$\bar{X}$	11·0	11·9	14·2	14·6	16·5	17·3	16·6	13·3
	s	17·8	15·6	15·9	13·8	10·4	8·5	4·4	3·7
	V%	161·3	131·3	112·0	94·8	62·9	49·0	26·2	28·1
1891–1901	N	285	230	159	77	41	20	8	6
	$\bar{X}$	12·3	15·4	15·0	14·1	14·2	13·9	15·8	15·7
	s	18·2	17·7	16·2	12·2	7·7	6·6	4·5	2·9
	V%	147·6	114·6	107·9	86·4	54·1	47·9	28·6	18·4
1901–1911	N	287	225	190	89	49	23	11	8
	$\bar{X}$	12·4	12·9	14·5	13·1	10·0	10·5	9·4	8·6
	s	18·5	13·6	15·8	14·5	8·5	8·2	4·6	2·6
	V%	149·1	105·4	108·8	111·1	85·2	77·8	49·3	29·9

Notes: For each size group, observations are as follows: N = number of towns, $\bar{X}$ = mean growth rate, s = standard deviation of growth rates, V% = coefficient of variation (%) of growth rates.

In testing the two properties of Gibrat's law, the evidence on the relationship of variance and population size is unambiguous. In virtually every case, the standard deviations and the coefficients of variation grow progressively smaller for the larger size groups. While the progression is not necessarily smooth, there is a tendency throughout for there to be a gradual fall in the size of the variance with successively larger city-size groups. The assumption of uniformly-distributed error around the line of proportionate growth is clearly not met.

On the second Gibrat property — the invariance of the means of different size groups — the conclusion is less immediately apparent. The regression analyses have both suggested slight positive relationships between growth and size. Here, with more disaggregated material, we can use more discriminating tests of whether this is or is not significant. In making comparisons between the mean growth rates of the different size groups allowance has to be made for the fact that the size groups have different variances as well as different numbers of observations, and that the standard tests comparing means are consequently ruled out. However, an appropriate test which does take account of the different variances and numbers of the observations is that suggested by Aspin and Welch (1949; for its application to business firms, see Singh and Whittington 1968, pp. 75-80). The results of using the Aspin-Welch test in comparing the significance of the mean growth rates for each of the size categories are shown in table 3.10 which plots significant differences at the 5·0, 2·5, 1·0 and 0·5 per cent confidence levels. Taking the 2·5 per cent level, for example, it can be seen that, in the decade 1801-11, out of a possible total of ten comparisons between the means of size groups, only two are significantly different. In all of the eleven decades there is a total of 230 such comparisons in which no fewer than 58 show that one mean is significantly higher than another at the 2·5 per cent confidence level.[1] There is a marked pattern in the distribution of these significant differences from one decade to another. The earlier decades show a much larger number of significant differences than do the later decades and in all cases the pattern of differences is one of higher mean growth rates being found in the larger city sizes. In the later decades, there are relatively few such significant differences and in the very final decade a completely different pattern emerges with larger cities tending to have significantly *lower* average growth rates than smaller cities. This changing pattern is clearly seen in fig. 3.3 in which differences between means which are significant at the 1·0 per cent level are shown by sets of arrows for each of the decades.

This is a most interesting finding and one whose implications need to be spelled out both in terms of the theoretical notions of urban growth and in terms of the nature of the facts of the growth of towns in England and Wales in the nineteenth century.

[1] The exact pattern of significant differences would, of course, depend upon the particular size groupings whose means are chosen for comparison, but the overall tendency in these sets of sizes over the eleven decades is relatively clear.

Table 3.10 *Significant differences between mean growth rates in different size groups*

1801–11

	2	3	4	5
1		+++	0	0
2		+++	0	0
3			0	0
4				0

1811–21

	2	3	4	5	6	7
1	++	++++	+	++	++	++
2		0	0	0	++	++
3			0	−	0	+
4				0	0	++
5					+	+
6						0

1821–31

	2	3	4	5	6
1		++	++++	++	++
2		0	+++	0	++
3			++	0	++
4				0	0
5					0

1831–41

	2	3	4	5	6
1	++	+++	++++	+	++
2		0	+	0	++
3			0	0	0
4				0	0
5					0

1841–51

	2	3	4	5	6	7
1	++	+++	+++	++++	++	++++
2		+	+++	0	+	+++
3			0	0	0	++
4				0	0	0
5					0	+
6						0

1851–61

	2	3	4	5	6	7
1	0	++	+	++	++	++
2		0	0	+	++	++
3			0	0	0	+
4				0	0	++
5					0	+
6						0

1861–71

	2	3	4	5	6	7
1	0	0	0	0	0	+++
2		0	0	0	0	+
3			0	0	0	0
4				0	0	+++
5					0	++
6						0

1871–81

	2	3	4	5	6	7	8
1	0	0	++	0	0	++	++
2		0	0	0	0	0	++
3			0	0	0	0	++
4				0	0	0	0
5					0	0	0
6						0	0
7							0

1891–1901

	2	3	4	5	6	7	8
1	0	+	+	+++	+++	+++	0
2		0	0	++	++	++	0
3			0	0	0	0	0
4				0	0	0	0
5					0	0	0
6						0	0
7							0

1901–1911

	2	3	4	5	6	7	8
1	0	0	0	0	0	–	0
2		0	0	–	0	–	–
3			0	–	–	–	–
4				0	0	–	0
5					0	0	0
6						0	0
7							0

1871–1881

	2	3	4	5	6	7	8
1	++	0	0	0	0	+	+
2		0	0	0	0	0	0
3			0	0	0	0	0
4				0	0	0	0
5					0	0	0
6						0	0
7							0

Notes

1. Entries in matrices are as follows:

   + } Mean of column size group is higher or lower than
   – } mean of row group

   ++++ significant at 0·5%
   +++ significant at 1·0%
   ++ significant at 2·5%
   + significant at 5·0%
   0 not significant at 5·0%

2. Significance of differences is assessed by using values of

$$v = \frac{(y - \eta)}{\sqrt{(\lambda_1 s_1^2 + \lambda_2 s_2^2)}}$$

   where $y = (\bar{X}_i - \bar{X}_{i+1})$ = difference between means of size groups; $\lambda_i = 1/N_i$, where N_i is number of towns in size group i; s_i^2 = variance of size group. See Aspin and Welch (1949) and supplementary tables in Pearson and Hartley (1966, table 11).

3. Size groups are as follows:

1	2,500– 4,999
2	5,000– 9,999
3	10,000– 19,999
4	20,000– 39,999
5	40,000– 79,999
6	80,000–159,999
7	160,000–319,999
8	320,000–

   In the earlier decades, larger size groups have been merged to keep the number of towns in each cell $\geqslant 4$.

4. Details of N_i, $\bar{X}_i$ and s_i are given in table 3.9.

First, in terms of Gibrat's law of proportionate effect, both the decreasing variance of growth rates with size and this relationship between average growth rate and population size suggest that neither property of Gibrat's law are met.[1] During all the decades, variance decreases with city size and in only some of the later decades are the mean rates of growth of larger size groups not significantly higher than smaller sizes. This finding adds considerable weight to our earlier observation that the regression of growth on size tended to be positive. Now that the suggestion of the regression analysis is complemented by the more rigorous finding of significantly higher growth in larger city-size groups, it can be said that a uniform urban growth rate cannot be proven for most of the decades of nineteenth-century England and Wales. Were our tests of stability in the distribution of city sizes sufficiently powerful, the effects of this unequal growth could be demonstrated. The effect of higher average growth rates in larger towns would be to steepen the slope of plots of size against rank at successive decades as urban concentration progressed. If the average rate of growth grew progressively greater for larger towns, this would not necessarily have the effect of destroying an existing logarithmic-linear plot between rank and size, but it would certainly alter the overall shape of the distribution. In terms of an expectation that city sizes are distributed as the right-hand tail of a lognormal distribution, it would mean that the tail would become increasingly elongated as the degree of concentration of the population progressed. However, our second finding — that the variance of growth declines with city size — would tend to have a retarding effect upon this rate of concentration. To expand this point, one need only think back to the earlier discussion about the effect of the disturbance term in the regression formulae of equations [3.1] and [3.2]. The greater this term — the greater, that is, the variance in growth rates — the quicker

---

[1] No comparable formal tests of the applicability of both of the Gibrat properties to urban growth have been discovered. Thompson (1965b) has looked at the relationship of size and variance in his study of the growth rates of Standard Metropolitan Statistical Areas in the United States in the decade 1950-60 and finds the same pattern of declining variance amongst larger cities. His suggestion (Thompson 1965a, p. 22) on the relationship of growth and size is that, above a certain size of city, no cities decline in size and that there is a common growth rate. This he likens to an 'urban ratchett': 'at a certain range of urban scale, set by the degree of isolation of the urban place, the nature of its hinterland, the level of industrial development in the country, and various cultural factors, some growth mechanism, similar to a ratchett, comes into being, locking in past growth and preventing contraction'. The reasons adduced for this ratchett-effect are the diversification of industry, the existence of political power, the huge fixed investments, the rich local market and the steady supply of industrial leadership and innovativeness which characterize large urban economies. Thompson's later discussion of the relationship of cyclical instability and the size of a local economy (Thompson 1965a, p. 160) are also of some relevance here. Because of their industrial structure he hypothesizes that large places will approximate more closely to national cyclical patterns, but that smaller places will show greater variability since some have predominantly stable and others predominantly unstable industries. Studies of business-firm growth have tested Gibrat's assumptions much more extensively. Conclusions on firms' sizes, mean growth and variance of growth have differed somewhat both between and within studies in Britain and America (for a summary, see Singh and Whittington 1968, chapter 4).

will be the increase in concentration, assuming that the slope of the regression is held constant. In the regression model it was assumed that the disturbance term was both (log)normally distributed and was homoscedastic — in other words, that the variance was equal irrespective of size group. Since the disaggregated empirical data show that the variance is distinctly heteroscedastic and that it is the larger places which have smaller variance in their growth rates, the size of the disturbance term is lower for larger size groups and they will therefore tend to spread out in size less rapidly than will smaller places so that the overall rate of concentration of population will be less than would be suggested by the overall variance of the total set of places.[1] If this finding were to be fed back into the regression formulae to produce a model which might characterize the level of population concentration and the future sizes of sets of towns, the regression formulation would need to have added to it a vector of correcting factors given by the declining variances of larger groups of towns or it would need to be further partitioned into sets of equations of the following sort:

$$X_{t.s} = a + (1 + c) \cdot X_{t-1.s} + \epsilon_s; \qquad\qquad [3.6]$$

where the subscript s is a size group of cities and the ϵ_s term would become smaller for increasing values of s. Obviously this is a far less attractive form of growth model since it is less general than equation [3.2] and because, without calibrating it for particular sets of data, it is impossible to use it to generate expected plots of future city-size distributions.

A more general suggestion from our findings, however, would be that there is great value in the more empirical historical study of sets of towns as against the more general theoretical growth models which draw on micro-economics and the behaviour of the firm. Lampard (1968, p. 95) suggests that there is a need 'for a distinctive *developmental* perspective on the evolution of city-regions, a perspective that allows for greater disaggregation and, at the same time, yields generalizations of a somewhat lower order than those of formal theory'; and even the economist Thompson (1965a, p. 60) says, 'It may be that a rigorous synthesis of many . . . case studies is needed to unlock the secrets of the urban growth process: the economic historian may have fully as much to contribute to urban growth theory as either the economic theorist or the econometrician'. It is this view which has buttressed the present concern with a more historical and a less formal systems' approach to the study of urban growth.

TWO QUESTIONS

Two interesting puzzles are posed by our findings on the empirical data of nineteenth-century urban growth. The pattern of urban growth which is outlined by the analysis of the scatter of means and variances calls first for the

---

[1] This would mean that any attempt at calculating the value of Galton's c at which concentration would not occur would be even more complex than suggested above, pp. 69–70.

development of ideas about how urban growth in a set of cities produces a pattern of declining variance with increasing city size and what factors might determine the varying slope of the relationship between growth rate and size. Second, since the relationship between growth rate and size appears to have changed during the course of the nineteenth century, how can this change be explained? Looking at the diagrams of average growth rates (fig. 3.3) and the results of the Aspin-Welch tests in table 3.10, the nature and timing of this change can be more precisely specified. There appear to be two types of pattern: on the one hand there is a scatter of urban growth in which average growth is positively related to city size; and on the other, a pattern in which growth and size are virtually unrelated so that the curve of average growth is not significantly different from horizontal.[1] In both cases the variance declines

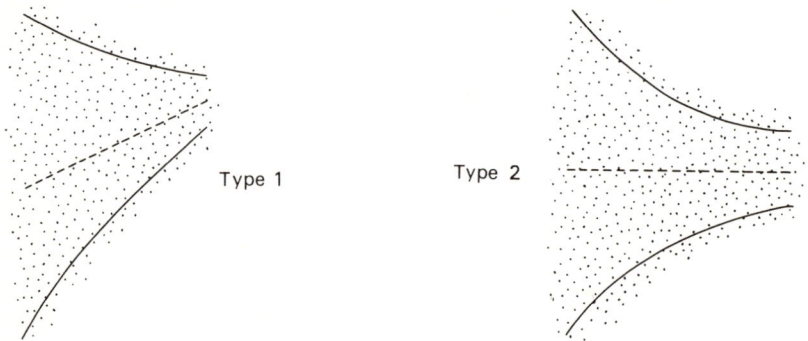

Figure 3.4   Two ideal types of growth in a set of towns

regularly about the average at larger city sizes. These two patterns are crudely represented in fig. 3.4. Can one specify the decade at which the change from the first to the second of these patterns occurred? Table 3.11 shows the percentages of the total number of observations in each decade in which the average growth rate was significantly different. It is clear, both from this and from the actual values of the means in table 3.9, that the proportion of significantly higher average growth rates is considerably lower in the decades after 1861 than in those before. The pattern of the first two decades is somewhat ambiguous, reflecting perhaps the greater imperfections in the census material, but they would both nevertheless appear to be closer to the first than the second of our ideal types. The third, fifth and sixth decades however conform very closely to our first ideal pattern in which growth is positively related to size; the fourth decade is less clear. The decades from the seventh onwards – that is, from 1861-71 – tend to grow increasingly close to the second pattern in which size

[1] These are, of course, idealized types. They ignore the pattern of the final decade in which the relationship is negative. Clearly, during the final quarter of the nineteenth century the once strongly positive relationship grew progressively less so until, by the final decade it had become negative.

and growth are virtually unrelated and this is especially clear in the decade 1891-1901. By 1901-11, the pattern has become the reverse of our first type with growth being lower for larger city sizes.

Table 3.11 *Percentage of comparisons between size groups in which larger towns have mean growth rates significantly higher than smaller towns*

Decade	level of significance	
	1·0%	*5·0%*
1801–11	20·0	20·0
1811–21	6·7	46·7
1821–31	26·7	53·3
1831–41	20·0	46·7
1841–51	38·1	61·9
1851–61	23·8	52·4
1861–71	14·3	19·0
1871–81	7·1	17·9
1881–91	10·7	28·6
1891–1901	0·0	10·7
1901–1911	21·4	39·3

Notes
1. Calculated from Aspin-Welch tests given in table 3.10.
2. For the final decade, 1901–11, the values show the percentage of comparisons in which large towns have significantly *lower* mean growth rates.

It is to discussion of these two questions that the bulk of the subsequent chapters is devoted. Chapters 5 and 6 develop a model of urban growth which attempts to simulate the declining scatter of variance around an average growth rate which can either be constant for the whole set of towns or can slope upwards to give a positive relationship between growth and size. Chapter 7 looks at certain aspects of late nineteenth-century Britain to throw light on the changing relationship of growth and size in England and Wales after 1861. But before turning to these, we must look at the spatial pattern of the growth rates which have been discussed in this chapter to see the extent to which general spatial patterns can be discerned which might throw light on the notion of sets of towns as formal systems with feedback loops and control mechanisms being reflected in the spatial pattern of their growth.

CHAPTER 4

Spatial patterns of urban growth

The eternal silence of these infinite spaces terrifies me.   B. PASCAL

It is obvious from what has so far been said that the average rate of growth of a whole set of towns explains much of the expected growth of an individual town from within that set. Even when our model is disaggregated to produce average growth rates for differently sized sub-groups of that set, however, the model still suggests that there will be considerable deviation around the mean for individual cities. The growth model is a relatively weak one since, even though within a size group the fluctuation around the mean is random, for any individual town within that size group, growth from one decade to another can be consistently high or consistently low. The model, in other words, can accommodate the preferential growth of particular places during successive periods. The question then arises of how one explains the fluctuations of individual towns around the average growth rate of their size group.

In attempting to explain this scatter of individual growth, the most obvious approach for the geographer is to study its spatial pattern to see to what extent interpretable general features emerge which might throw light on the dispersion of growth rates. Does the existing literature on the spatial structure of economies suggest hypotheses which might be tested for the empirical data on nineteenth-century urban growth?

TWO SPATIAL HYPOTHESES

Two hypotheses may be proffered: first that, at a macroscopic scale, growth rates may fall into one of two patterns — either a single national pattern with one major core area of higher growth and a penumbral outer area with lower growth, or a regional pattern in which distinct regions show markedly different growth rates from each other and act as 'sub-systems' within the whole national area; second that, at a smaller scale, growth rates may decline with distance from regional metropolitan areas.

The literature from which such hypotheses are derived covers a wide span. Implicit in much of the geographical work on cities is the notion that, at successively higher levels of scale, functional urban regions 'nest' in to one another to form elements of an urban system at a higher scale. This of course is the skeletal argument of central-place theory which, while derived for areas much smaller than the whole national territory, has provided a major springboard for national studies. One of the earliest and most thorough of the national studies is Bogue's (1950) work on metropolitan dominance in the United States.[1] In it he demonstrated the way in which, at a macroscopic scale, a large variety of social and economic indices declined in value as one moved progressively away from the sixty-seven major metropolitan centres of the country. He argued that one could see the metropolitan centres as poles around which regional population distribution and types of economic activity were articulated and that, like the ecological community from which he drew his analogies, the constituent elements of the metropolitan community could be seen at a variety of territorial scales comprising 'dominant', 'subdominant', 'influent', and 'subinfluent' communities each of whose sphere of influence nested in to the next higher level. There have been many subsequent studies in the spirit of Bogue's, more especially within the United States, but, after the development of the concept of economic growth poles, such spatial analyses of national patterns of economic development have been extended to a wide variety of other countries both in the developed and developing worlds (for a geographical review see Keeble 1967).

Since the work on the United States has been the most fully developed, it is worth looking at it in some greater detail in order to exemplify the argument. The national economic structure which is suggested is one composed of an economic core region embracing the manufacturing belt which stretches from New York to Chicago and which 'performs' the role of national focus for the whole economy. Both within and beyond this core area, however, there is a large number of regional cores – or growth centres – which act as organizing poles, but at a regional rather than a national scale. Perloff's analysis is one of the most impressive (Perloff *et al.* 1960). It argues that the pattern of economic growth is more clearly seen if subdivided into two components which together make up the total shifts in regional employment: differential shift which is an intra-industry difference in the growth of regional employment by which, within any industry, certain regions grow more rapidly than others; and proportionality shift which is an inter-industry difference in which certain regions grow more rapidly because of their larger proportion of rapidly-growing industries. While the overall spatial pattern of total employment growth between 1939 and 1954 shows a wide scatter throughout the United States, when broken down into these two components the underlying spatial structure of growth becomes more

[1] The similarity between Bogue's ideas and central-place theory is striking. Bogue worked from the very different tradition of the human ecologists and, at the time, was unaware of Christaller's (1933) work which diffused to the English-speaking world very slowly, being first introduced to the United States in 1941 in a rather unexpected source, the *American Journal of Sociology* (Ullman 1941).

apparent. Differential shift is high within an essentially peripheral area with high growth being found in the fringe areas of the west, south-west and Florida, while within the manufacturing belt only the western edge shows high growth. Proportionality shift, however, shows a very different pattern with a distinct concentration of high growth within the manufacturing belt and only very small outliers in the fringe areas of Florida, southern California and Washington State. Perloff interprets these patterns in the following terms. The national core area of the long-established manufacturing belt is picked out by the measure of proportionality shift since its developed advantages of established infrastructure and access to the whole national economy foster within it the leading sectors of industry. The innovations associated with these new growth industries only filter out at a later date to the more peripheral parts of the country. The peripheral areas, on the other hand, grow predominantly on the basis of more localized access to raw material resources and also grow, again at a more local scale, on the basis of a process of infilling produced by the regional economy meeting successive demand thresholds which provide market opportunities for regional economic growth. The 'macro-geography' of the United States today suggests a much less clear emphasis on the national predominance of the manufacturing belt, but Perloff's analysis of the post-war period certainly accords with the idea of a single dominant national core area with regional sub-systems being subordinate to this core at a higher spatial scale. Exactly the same spatial pattern can be seen in the study *Metropolis and region* (Duncan *et al.* 1960) which looks at the structure of metropolitan centres of over 300,000 population in the United States. Here, it is the classification of metropolitan centres which reflects the same dichotomy that Perloff isolates. On the one hand there is a set of widely-spaced metropolitan centres which act, very much in the spirit of central-place notions, as centres which provide services for the localized regions which surround them. On the other hand, there is a set of much less regularly-spaced centres which are predominantly industrial and manufacturing complexes and which, largely concentrated within the manufacturing belt, rely on access to the market of the whole national territory.

For the United States one therefore has a body of well developed studies which points to the existence of an overall national economic system articulated around the twin principles of localized access to an immediate tributary area and generalized access to a national market. In very general terms, the economy can be conceived as a 'system' comprised at lower scales of 'sub-systems' which nest in to one another. The literature on the spatial patterning of urban growth has been able to call on certain of these ideas (Madden 1956b), but has also been able to isolate consistent spatial regularity in the growth of cities because of the particular sequence by which the country's urbanization proceeded. With the frontier of development being pushed progressively further west, the historical process of urban growth in the United States can be seen as a consistent sequence of western expansion followed by subsequent infilling and it has been this rather marked spatial pattern which has been most strongly emphasized by the geographical studies of urban growth (Luckermann 1966; Borchert 1967).

For Britain, there is not the same body of massive studies of the whole national urban system. However, the general outline of the spatial pattern of economic development is familiar. Looking at a longer span of time than just the nineteenth century, the changing importance of the national core area around London appears quite clearly. Before the industrial revolution, London's dominance of the national economy was unchallenged. Not only was population overwhelmingly concentrated in the South East — as Mantoux's (1928, pp. 350-3) rather charming maps reveal[1] — but the influence of the Metropolis extended over a very broad swathe of the country. Fisher (1935), for example, has shown the increasing extent of the area upon which London drew for food in the period from 1540-1640 and Wrigley (1967) has suggested the importance, in the following century, of the market represented by London on the production of foodstuffs and raw materials elsewhere in the economy and also, through the effects of migration, on changing the attitudes and horizons of a large proportion of the total population.[2] 'Town' to the man of the eighteenth century meant simply London — all the rest was 'Country' — and this contemporary evaluation was an accurate reflection of the marked difference not only between the population, but also the importance of the Metropolis by comparison with its nearest rivals. Even by 1801, there was an enormous differential between London — with its population of almost one million — and the largest provincial towns, none of which had reached 100,000. With the industrial developments of the nineteenth century this spatial pattern of dominant Metropolis and subservient provinces was radically altered. While previously growth and activity had flourished in the South East — in what Sir Cyril Fox called 'Lowland Britain' which, certainly since Roman times, had enjoyed an almost uninterrupted monopoly of political power and economic wealth — the growth of industrial production was focused on the mineral-bearing and carboniferous areas of 'Highland Britain'. The pattern of demographic changes illustrates this radical alteration to good effect. The counties which showed a continuous rise in their proportion of the total population between

---

[1] There are surprisingly few maps of population distribution in eighteenth- and nineteenth-century Britain. Petermann's splendidly detailed maps which accompanied the 1851 census are an outstanding exception. For periods before 1801, however, virtually no attempts to map regional distributions can be found. Those in Usher (1921, pp. 95-9) give a somewhat different impression of density than do Mantoux's.

[2] Later developments in the sources of London's food supplies are suggested by Wetham (1964) who suggests that the radius from which milk was supplied widened rapidly at the end of the nineteenth century. Whereas in the 1860s milk 'warm from the cow' was supplied from stalls within London itself or from out-of-town farms at places such as Hendon, Dulwich and Highgate, by 1900 central London drew either directly on sources within thirty to fifty miles away or, through railway depots, on distant sources in Dorset, Wiltshire and Derbyshire.

1801, 1861 and 1921 were overwhelmingly those of 'Highland Britain':
Northumberland and Durham, Yorkshire, Lancashire and Cheshire, Staffordshire, Worcestershire and Warwickshire and Monmouth and Glamorgan. In
'Lowland Britain', by contrast, only the metropolitan area itself and the area of
the south-east coast and Hampshire basin continuously expanded their percentage of the total population throughout this period. The twentieth century,
however, has seen a reversal back towards the older pattern of population
concentration in the South East. Between 1921 and 1961, those areas which
increased their proportional representation of population were all south of the
Tees-Exe line; indeed, within that area, only Lincolnshire, East Anglia and the
metropolis itself did not increase their percentage and in the case of the latter
this was a reflection simply of the localized spill-over of population beyond the
boundaries of London itself.[1]

Nineteenth-century developments can be seen therefore as something of an
interlude in the longer-established pattern of metropolitan dominance. The
expansion of the northern industrial areas, however, occurred in different
regions of the country at somewhat different periods as the wave of growth
industries progressed through the sequence of textiles, iron and the development
of the railways, coal and, by the early years of the twentieth century, the motor
car.[2] Largely on the basis of different factor endowments these various growth
impulses had their greatest effect in rather specific areas of the country: cotton
textiles in south-east Lancashire; woollen manufacture in West Yorkshire and
Lancashire; iron in the West Midlands, Teesside and south Yorkshire; coal in
South Wales and the North East. It is perhaps these industrial provincial nodes
which might be seen as forming the cores of regional sub-systems in the
development of the nineteenth-century economy. Briggs (1963), for example,
suggests that one can characterize the developments in terms of the leading
regional centres each of which developed sequentially as the 'leading cities' of
their period: Manchester he calls the 'shock town' of the 1840s; its role was later
assumed by the Yorkshire towns of Leeds and Bradford, each vying with the
other in building bigger and more substantial municipal monuments to their
provincial grandeur; subsequently Birmingham assumed the mantle of leading
city, reaching its apogee under the civic gospel of Chamberlain in the 1870s;
only by the 1880s or 1890s had London again begun to reassert its domination,
a domination which differed from that of the provincial cities in that it was
national in scope. Read (1964) makes a similar point, although suggesting
different dating, in tracing the rising strength of provincial influence in the

1 This description of regional percentages is based on Osborne (1964). Of the many studies
of regional population distribution, an excellent cartographic portrait of the late nineteenth-
century population changes is given by Lawton (1968b) who uses detail at the level of
registration districts. For the early twentieth century, a useful study of the 1921-51 period is
that by Willatts and Newson (1953).
2 A simple cartographic sequence of the spread of urbanization, 1851-1951, is given by
Friedlander (1970).

nineteenth century. He suggests that it was Manchester and Birmingham which were the two dominant cities, the lead having changed from the former to the latter in 1857. Briggs suggests that the successive rise of provincial centres might be traced out by the opening of local institutions such as Literary and Philosophical Societies[1] or by the development of provincial newspapers, whose subsequent decline in the twentieth century again reflected the re-establishment of London's national dominance. Kitson Clark (1962, p. 103) has suggested yet a further rough index of progress in suggesting that the medical enlightenment of various towns might be measured by the date of establishment of medical officers of health; Leeds having appointed one in 1866, Manchester in 1868, Birmingham in 1872 and Newcastle — 'normally in these matters a laggard' — in 1873. Indices such as this are, as Kitson Clark himself recognizes, only a crude and imperfect measure even of medical progress, let alone of the general importance of provincial centres. Nevertheless, it seems indisputable that a discernible sequence of regional development did occur during the nineteenth century with first one then another area feeling the full effects of the technical and industrial progress of the period.

POPULATION AND ECONOMIC GROWTH

It is in the light both of such empirical studies and of the more theoretical writings that one might hypothesize that the spatial pattern of urban growth rates might reflect the existence of sub-systems of regional cities by showing patterns of distinctly regional growth in the earlier part of the nineteenth century to be followed later by growth focused predominantly in the London area as inter-regional differences became subordinate to the dominance of the Metropolis. In the language of systems, one might say that the once distinctive regional sub-systems would eventually become less clearly evident as the whole national system developed around a single core area. In making such a suggestion one is of course using urban growth as a surrogate for the expansion of rates of general economic activity and one is assuming that higher rates of population growth are valid reflections of more general economic expansion. This may not be as unreasonable an assumption as may at first appear. Demographic growth is the product both of natural and migrational change and, even though it would appear that differences in fertility were more marked in nineteenth- than in twentieth-century Britain,[2] a number of grounds can be suggested as to why one

---

[1] Most of which pre-date Victoria's accession. The sequence of foundation dates however is suggestive: Manchester 1781; Liverpool 1812; Leeds 1820; Sheffield 1822 (Briggs 1963, p. 44).

[2] For the regional differences in fertility, valuable estimates of the disparities in the early part of the century are provided by Deane and Cole (1962, pp. 106-22). For the most recent period, the fall in regional differentials is well illustrated by a comparison of the patterns of fertility rates in 1911 and 1931, which shows not only the lower average, but more particularly the markedly smaller regional dispersion by the latter date.

can argue that, in the nineteenth century, migration acted to bring the distribution of population and economic growth into close harmony to a greater extent than it has in the twentieth century. First it can be argued that the characteristics of nineteenth-century industry made it less likely that population by itself would attract industry to it because of the greater proportion of heavy and capital-goods industries which were more tied to raw materials than to access to markets.[1] Second, it might be argued that at least one of the possible reasons for higher fertility in certain areas was the very proximity of employment opportunities represented by local industries.[2] Third, and most significant, one can argue that the impediments to migration were significantly fewer in the nineteenth than in the twentieth century. It is impossible to make accurate comparisons between the amounts of mobility in the two centuries since even the best estimate of nineteenth-century migration are far from perfect, applying as they do to such large areal units as counties and being measures of net rather than gross movements.[3] The imperfect evidence does suggest, however, that the rate of movement was significantly higher for the nineteenth century. Friedlander and Roshier's (1966) figures for movement between counties suggest an overall fall in the longer-distance net movements within the country from the last quarter of the century and, while much of this represents the substitution of emigration for internal migration, the differences between the nineteenth and twentieth centuries within Britain is marked. At a local level, Pritchard's (1972) study of movement within Leicester notes that the most striking difference between the pre- and post-First World War periods was the sheer fall in the rate of gross residential turnover produced both by movement within the town as well as movement to and from it.

Certainly a number of convincing explanations can be proffered in support of higher mobility in the nineteenth century. First the prevailing economic and demographic conditions of the period would favour high rates of movement.

---

[1] Although it would be a gross exaggeration to say that industry was not attracted by the existence of a large potential labour force in an area. Obviously the relationship of industry and population is two-way. London itself – in absolute terms the largest industrial complex in nineteenth-century Britain – had few raw materials other than those imported from outside, although it could be argued that linkages with existing industries acted as 'raw materials' which attracted new industrial activity to the Metropolis. It would be true to say, however, that population by itself would attract economic growth *relatively* less in the nineteenth than the twentieth century (Wrigley 1965).

[2] Deane and Cole (1962, pp. 114-16) suggest that seven of the ten counties with the highest rates of natural increase in the period 1701-1830 were Cumberland, Westmorland, the North and West Ridings of Yorkshire, Derbyshire, Staffordshire and Shropshire – a belt of counties all but enclosing the textile area of Lancashire and Cheshire. They comment, 'An obvious inference is that the rise of Lancashire stimulated the growth of population in the surrounding areas, and that part of the population increase was then syphoned off into Lancashire itself'.

[3] Newton and Jeffery (1951) suggest that, for the period 1948-9, of the population changes in most of the areas studied, net migration was less than 5 per cent of the total gross migration of population.

Higher fertility and larger family size[1] increased the potential pressure for movement and the greater regional differentials in wage rates in a population much of which lived close to or below subsistence level meant that the economic incentives to mobility were high. But second, and of especial importance, are the differences in the housing structure of nineteenth- and twentieth-century England and Wales. The greater ease of moving house in the nineteenth century acted as enabling agent in translating the desire to move into high rates of mobility. The important difference lay in the structure of tenures. The nineteenth-century housing market was predominantly one of privately-rented accommodation and the proportion of owner-occupied housing was very small; thus reducing the legal and financial restraints upon moving. By contrast, the expansion of local authority housing after 1919 with the residence requirements which are needed to qualify families for tenure,[2] the relatively rapid expansion of the owner-occupied category, and the various decontrol-on-vacancy acts passed in relation to privately-rented furnished accommodation have all introduced dampers on twentieth-century mobility.

If this difference in the gross rates of mobility in the nineteenth and twentieth century existed, it lends considerable additional weight to the argument that migration effected a much more rapid and sensitive adjustment between population and employment opportunities in the nineteenth century[3] and so bolsters the assumption that population growth reflects economic growth and can be considered to be 'caused' by it. Even though most of the growth of towns was the direct product of natural increase rather than directly the consequence of migration,[4] it can be argued that people who are born in an area and opt to stay there are making a zero-distance migration decision which will not be entirely independent of the employment and economic opportunities of that area.[5] We can therefore draw on the wider body of theory about the spatial

[1] Statistics of these differences are provided by Mitchell (1962) and are discussed in, for example, Carr-Saunders and Jones (1927) and Marsh (1958).

[2] The lower rate of mobility amongst council tenants is discussed, for example, by Brooks (1967). Donnison (1967, p. 210) suggests, however, that they move as often as other tenure groups.

[3] Saville (1963, p. 2) emphasizes the importance of the New Poor Law of 1834 as a major element in first freeing labour from the restrictions of the seventeenth- and eighteenth-century settlement laws. With the introduction of the poor law, he says, 'the labour market was now as efficiently adapted to the requirements of expanding industrialism as political legislation could achieve'.

[4] Even in London – the recipient of so large a proportion of the total migrants within the country (C. T. Smith 1951) – total population grew by approximately equal contributions of natural increase and migration in the period 1851-91 (Shannon 1935). The importance of natural increase in the growth of provincial towns is shown by A. F. Weber (1899, p. 244). In the final part of the century, the contribution of migration was even lower. The increase in population in the Bristol area after 1871, for example, was almost wholly the consequence of natural change (Shannon and Grebenik 1943, p. 12). And Welton (1911, pp. 15-16) shows that for the decades 1881-91 and 1891-1901, even of the towns with the largest gains by migration, the proportions were above 20 per cent only in very few cases.

[5] An argument of Ward's (1963) which has already been noted above, p. 33.

pattern of economic growth to derive spatial hypotheses to test against the patterns of population growth in Victorian towns.

THE MEASURE OF URBAN GROWTH

First, however, we need to derive an appropriate measure by which we can compare the growth rates of towns. From what has been seen already of the scatter of urban growth rates, it is apparent that direct estimates of growth are inappropriate because of the relationship between the size of a town and the expected variance of its growth rate. The scatter of growth rates is very wide for small places and relatively narrow for large places. Plotting the spatial incidence of growth rates would thus tend to emphasize small places at the expense of large; the probability of London having an abnormally high or low growth rate in any decade would be rather low, whereas the probability for, say, Penzance, would be very much greater. Some form of standardization is therefore needed which will take account of these differences. The most suitable is the use of z, or standard, scores. These express each town's growth rate as a deviation from the average growth rate of the size group to which it belongs in any decade. For example, table 3.9[1] shows that for the decade 1901-11 the means and standard deviations of growth rates in the largest size group of towns were 8·57 and 2·56 respectively and in the smallest size group they were 12·40 and 18·48. Thus, for the largest towns, places whose growth rates lay between the two limits of 11·13 and 6·01 would be within plus or minus one standard deviation of their size group average; whereas, for the smallest towns these upper and lower limits would be 30·89 and −6·09 respectively. To qualify as being 'unusually' rapidly or slowly growing, a town would therefore require different growth rates depending on the size of the town being considered.

The translation of individual town growth rates into standard scores accords with the urban growth model which has been discussed earlier since it takes account both of the varying means and varying disturbance terms which apply to groups of town sizes. The calculation follows the standard formula:

$$z_i = \frac{G_{i.n} - \bar{G}_n}{\sigma_n};$$

where $G_{i.n}$ is the growth rate of the ith town whose population places it within the nth size group of towns: G_n and σ_n are the mean and standard deviation of the nth size group. To take an example: Birmingham had a population which put it in the largest size group in 1901 and had a growth rate of 11·28 per cent in the decade 1901-11; Newquay, in Cornwall, lay in the lowest size group of towns and had a very much higher growth rate of 34·53 per cent. Despite these different absolute growth rates, however, it can be seen that, in relation to other

---

[1] See above, p. 82.

towns of similar size to themselves, both places stood in approximately the same relationship to each other. The standard scores of the two places are as follows:

$$z_{\text{Birmingham, 1901-11}} = \frac{11 \cdot 28 - 8 \cdot 57}{2 \cdot 56} = 1 \cdot 06$$

$$z_{\text{Newquay, 1901-11}} = \frac{34 \cdot 53 - 12 \cdot 40}{18 \cdot 48} = 1 \cdot 20$$

The growth rates of both places thus lie just over one standard deviation above the mean of their appropriate size group.

The derivation of these scores has been gone into in some little detail because it is important that, in studying the patterns of standardized growth rates, the nature of the statistics is clearly understood. Measured in this way, the fact that a town has a 'high' growth rate means, not that its absolute percentage rate of growth was high by comparison with the national average in the particular decade, but that it was high in relation to the scatter of growth rates of towns of comparable size. Thus each decade will have approximately the same proportion of places with 'high' and 'low' standard growth rates irrespective of the national average; likewise, even in decades in which the average growth of large places is higher than that of smaller places, not all of the larger places could appear as having 'high' standard growth rates since it is the deviations from the average of the size group rather than the whole set of places which are measured. There is a variety of base lines against which to measure 'high' growth rates. The one selected here has the great virtue of taking into account the varying scatter of growth within different size groups of cities and of conforming to our model of urban growth.

THE SPATIAL PATTERN OF STANDARD GROWTH RATES

The pattern of growth during the eleven decades from 1801 to 1911 is shown in figs. 4.1-4.11. For each decade, places with growth rates of above or below one standard deviation from the mean of their appropriate size group are distinguished from towns which grew or declined by less than this.[1] The maps produce a striking sequence which provides a fascinating commentary on the progress of urbanization during the nineteenth century. The patterns of relative growth rates, both for individual towns and for regional clusters of towns, tend strongly to confirm the well-known pattern of nineteenth-century economic

---

[1] In discussing the patterns of above- and below-average growth rates, places whose growth was over one standard deviation below the mean will be referred to as 'declining' places. The term is used in a *relative* sense. In certain cases — more especially with small places — the populations of such towns did show an absolute decline in numbers, but more usually they expanded absolutely even though at an 'abnormally' low rate. The numbers of places which showed absolute decline in any decade can be seen in the sequence of diagrams in fig. 3.2 (pp. 73-8).

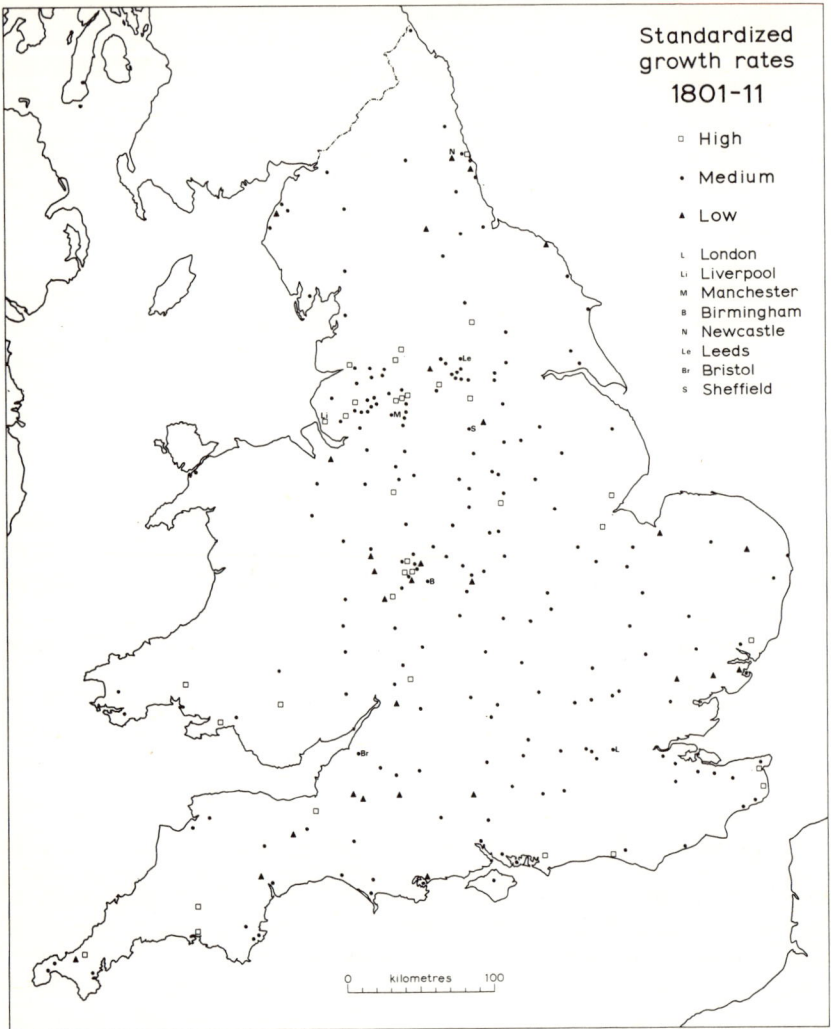

Figure 4.1 The spatial pattern of urban growth in England and Wales, 1801–11. Standardized growth rates are as follows: high = ≥ 1 standard deviation above the mean for the appropriate size group; low = ≤ 1 standard deviation below the mean for the appropriate size group; medium = between ±1 standard deviation from the mean of the appropriate size group. Details of means and standard deviations for each size group are given in table 3.9

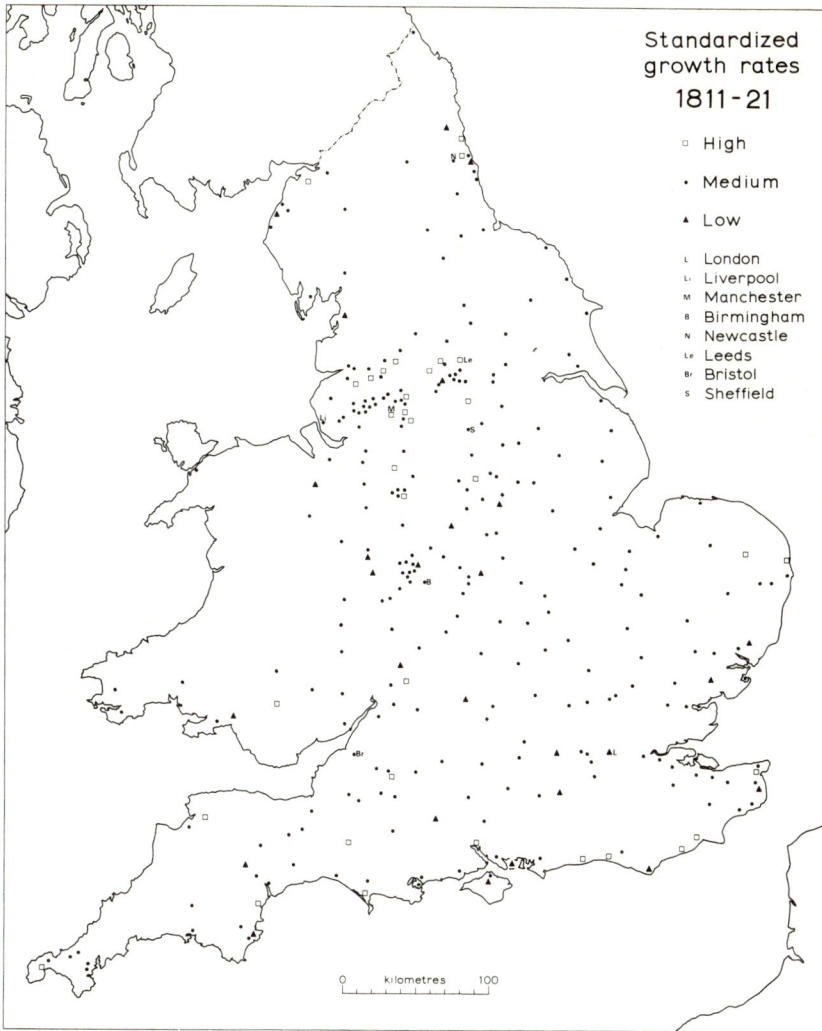

Figure 4.2   The spatial pattern of urban growth in England and Wales, 1811–21. For explanation, see fig. 4.1

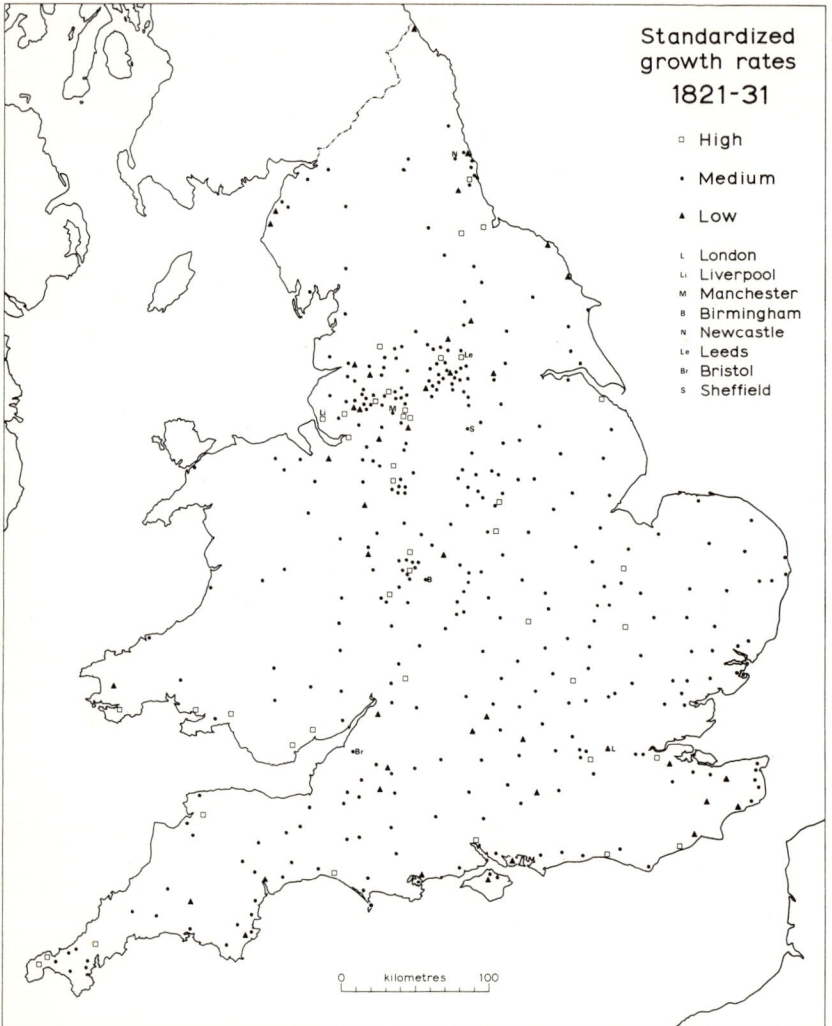

Figure 4.3 The spatial pattern of urban growth in England and Wales, 1821–31. For explanation, see fig. 4.1

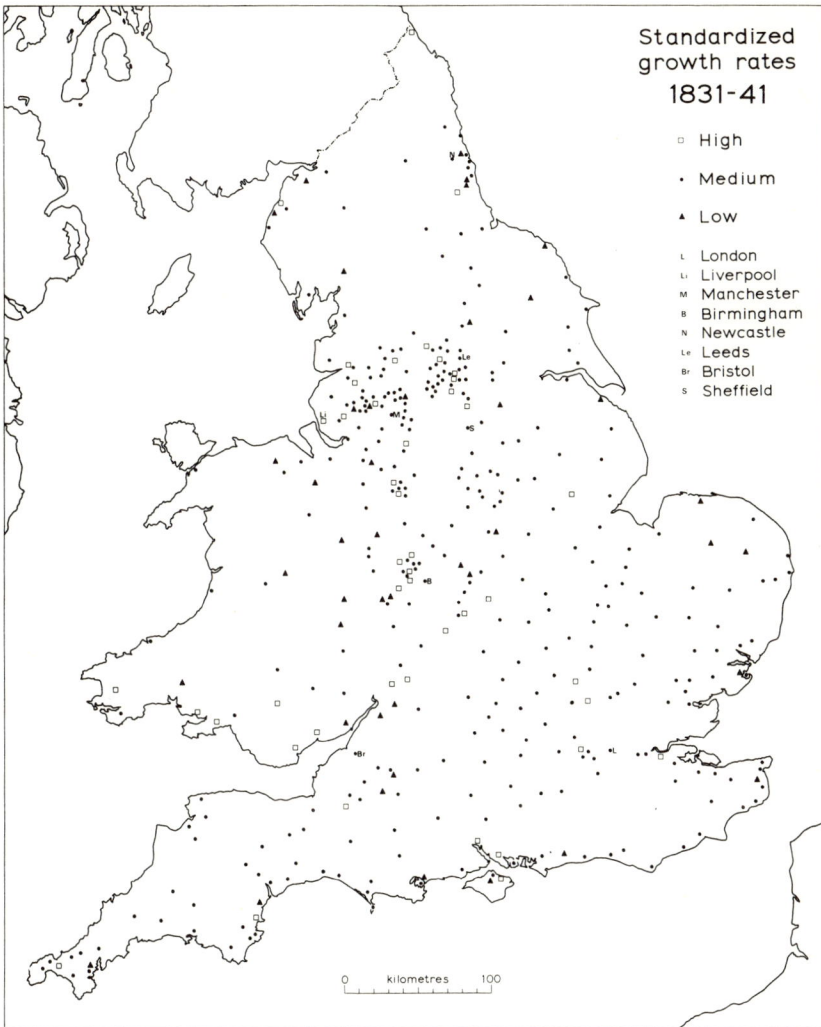

Figure 4.4 The spatial pattern of urban growth in England and Wales, 1831–41. For explanation, see fig. 4.1

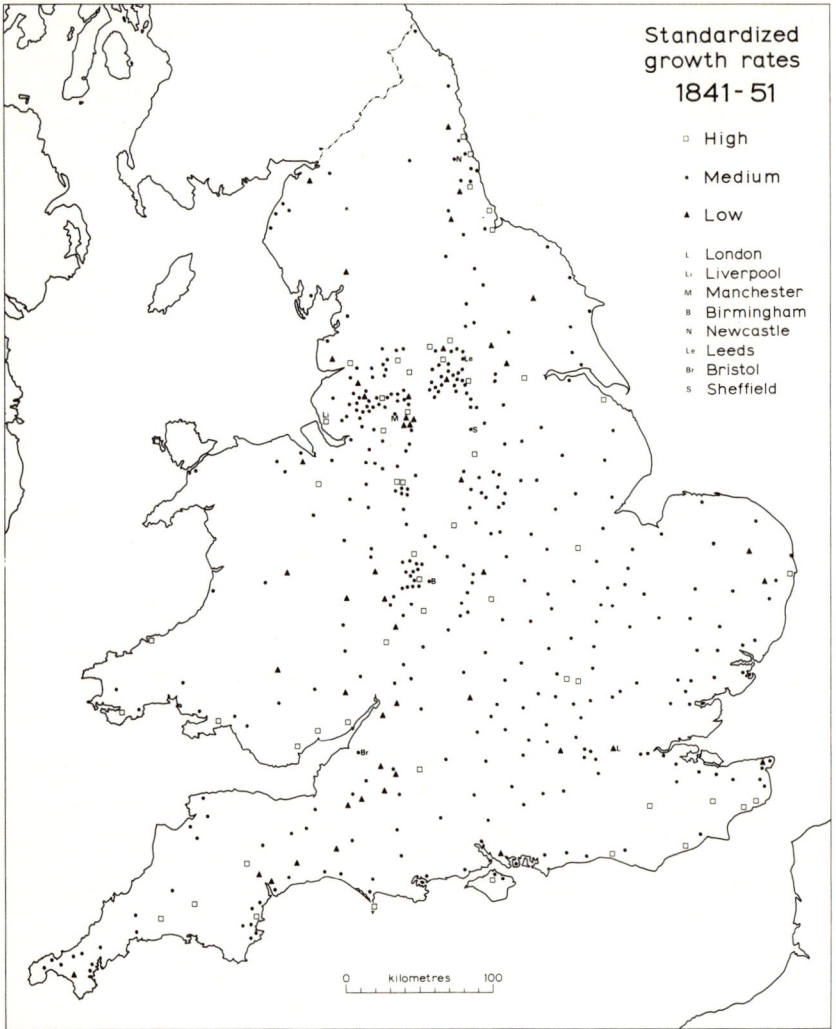

Figure 4.5 The spatial pattern of urban growth in England and Wales, 1841-51. For explanation, see fig. 4.1

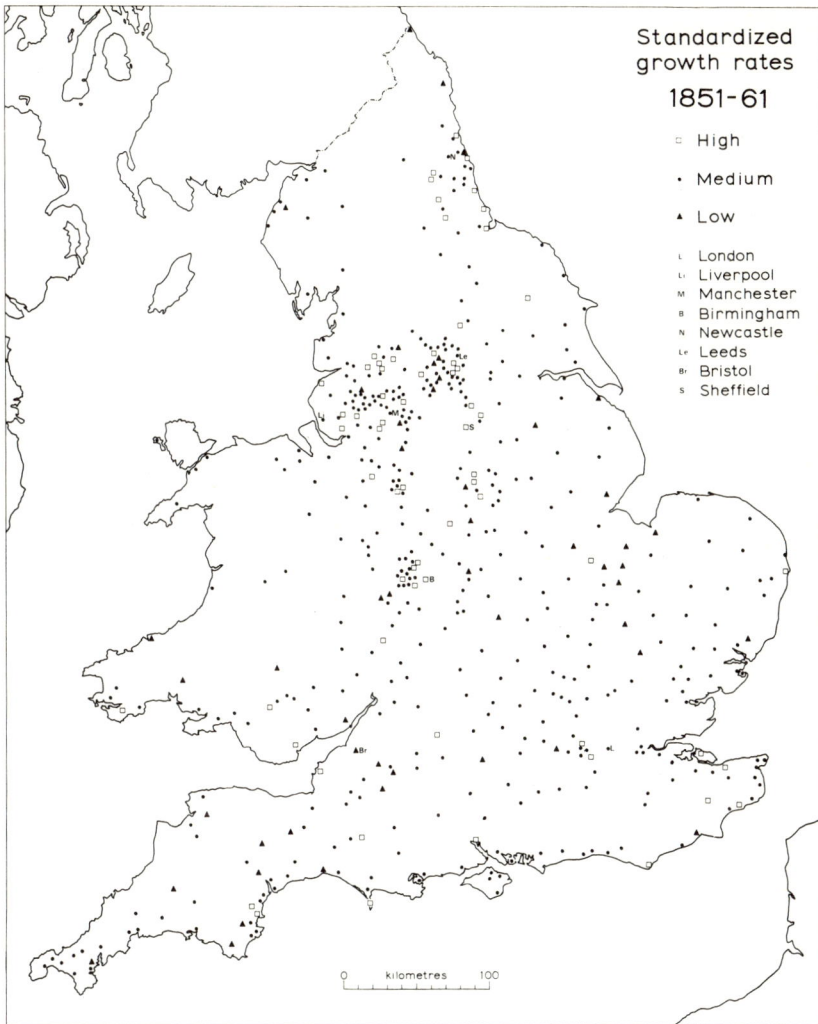

Figure 4.6 The spatial pattern of urban growth in England and Wales, 1851–61. For explanation, see fig. 4.1

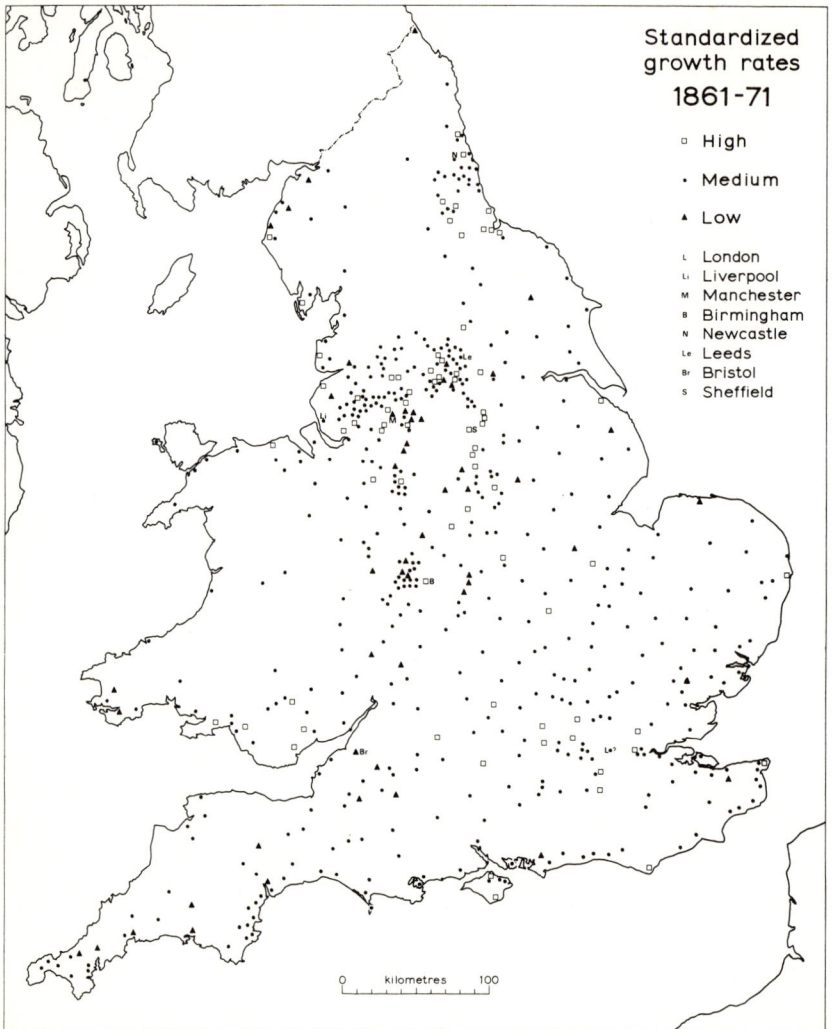

Figure 4.7 The spatial pattern of urban growth in England and Wales, 1861–71. For explanation, see fig. 4.1

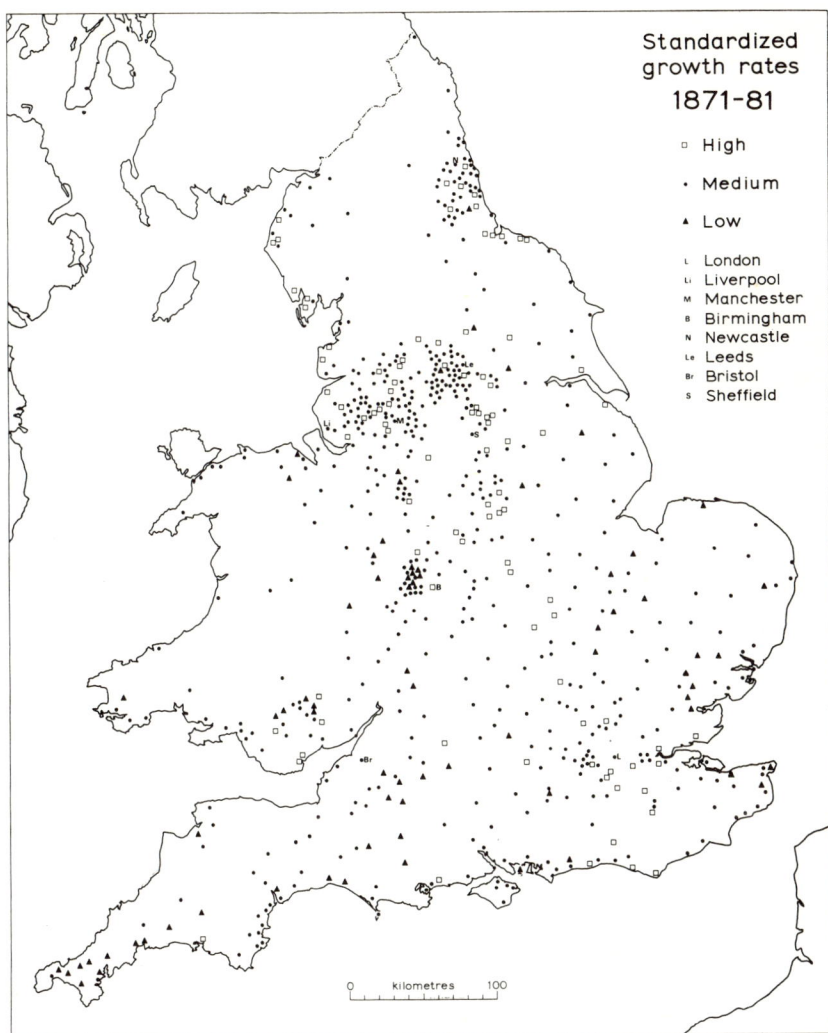

Figure 4.8 The spatial pattern of urban growth in England and Wales, 1871–81. For explanation, see fig. 4.1

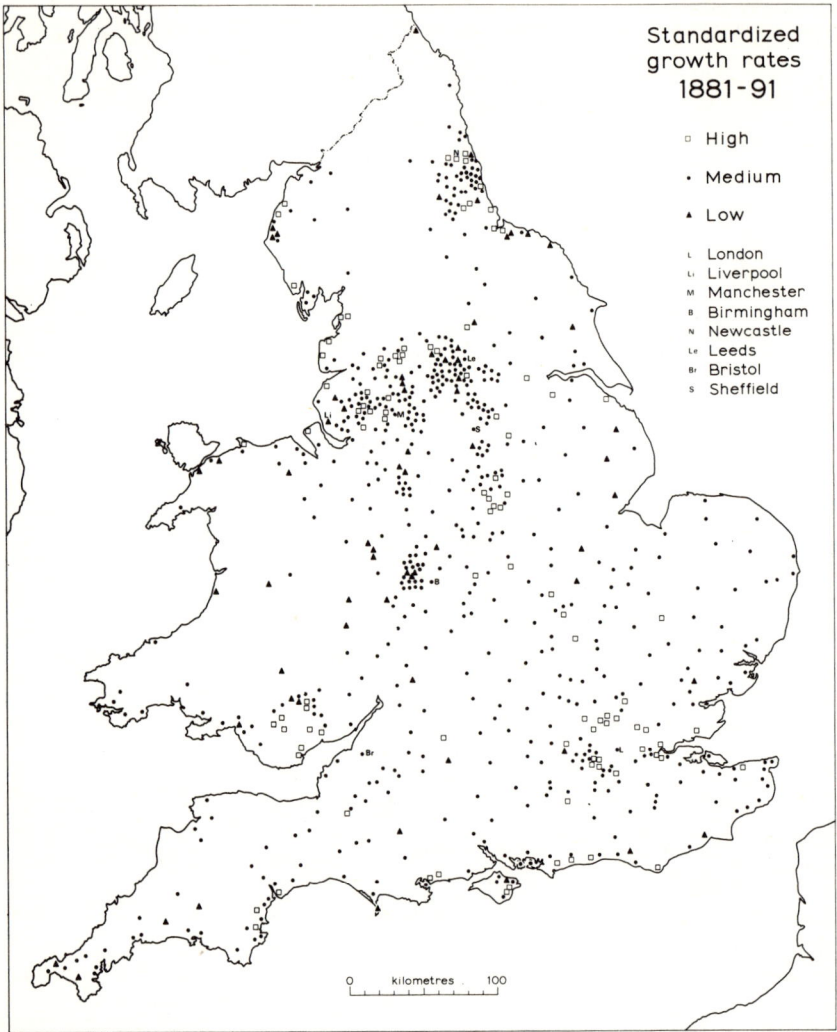

Figure 4.9 The spatial pattern of urban growth in England and Wales, 1881-91. For explanation, see fig. 4.1

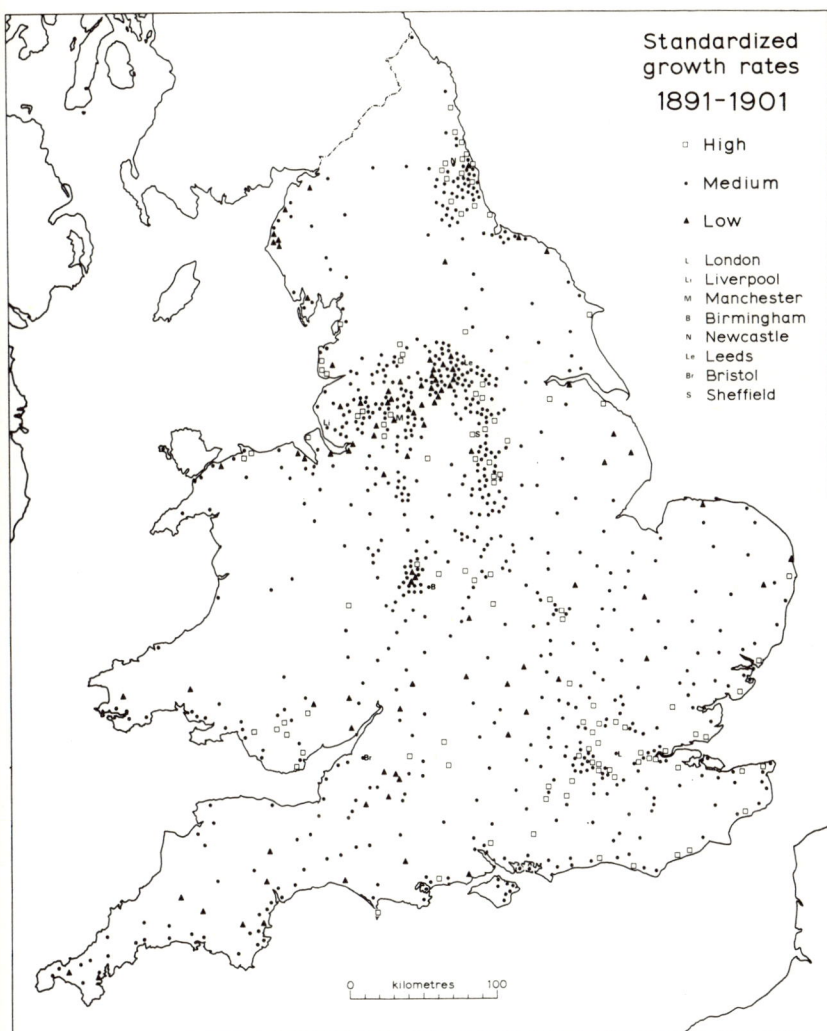

Figure 4.10   The spatial pattern of urban growth in England and Wales, 1891–1901. For explanation, see fig. 4.1

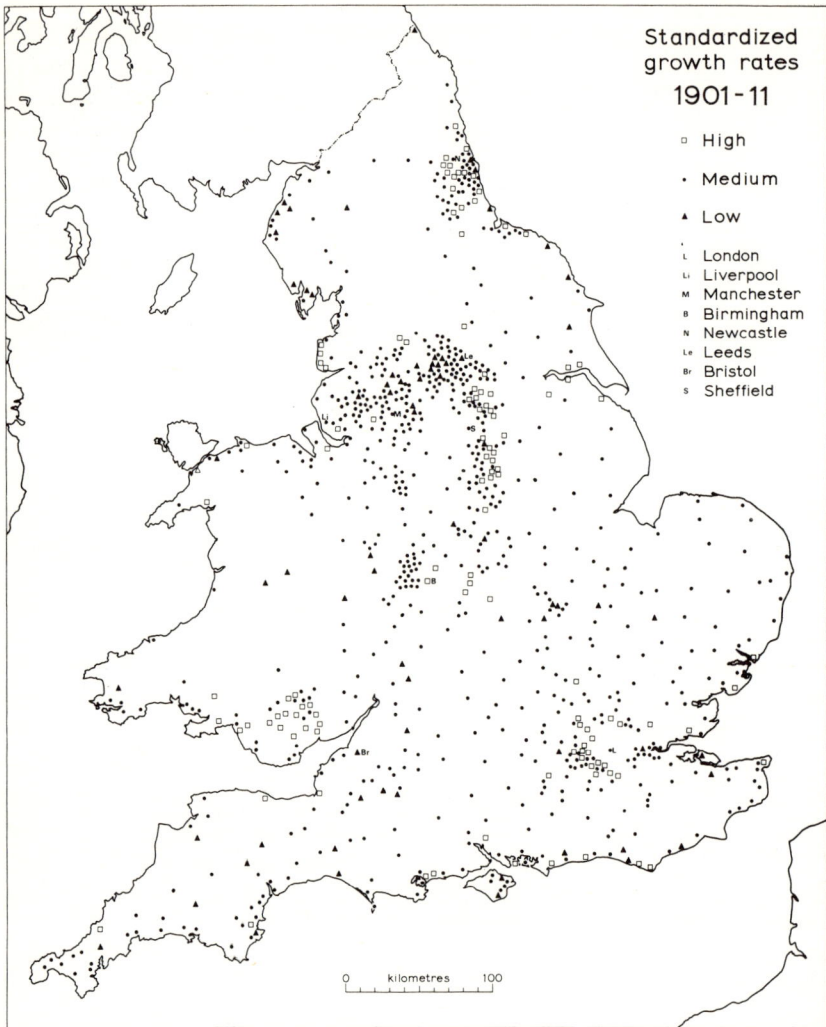

Figure 4.11   The spatial pattern of urban growth in England and Wales, 1901–11. For explanation, see fig. 4.1

development. The earlier decades are dominated by the rapid growth of towns in the textile areas of Lancashire and, at a slightly later date, the woollen area of the West Riding of Yorkshire as well as of the towns of industrial Staffordshire. In the 1820s and 1830s the older textile towns of the West Country and East Anglia decline. After the middle of the century, decline becomes very marked in the more remote agriculturally-based areas, but at the same time newer industrial areas such as Teesside, south Yorkshire and Nottingham-Derby appear. By the final quarter of the century, the metropolitan area begins to show rapid growth while the coalfield areas of South Wales and the North East — for long having had a small scatter of growth towns — both develop strongly as areas of more uniformly high growth. Throughout the whole period, in addition to the differences between the rural and industrial areas and between the metropolitan and non-metropolitan areas, there is a strong undercurrent of growth in resort towns, particularly in coastal resorts. In the early decades, it is the coastal resorts of Sussex which show rapid growth; later, it is the resorts of Devon; and, in the early twentieth century, such striking developments as the growth in the resort towns of north Lancashire are a feature of the two decades following 1891.

It can therefore be said with some confidence that these population changes appear to be useful surrogates of economic growth in general in that the pattern of growth seems to make sense in terms of our knowledge of the industrial and economic history of the period. These qualitative descriptions, however, are very much more the field of the economic or urban historian than the geographer and they would better be amplified by detailed histories of particular industries or particular areas. Can one go beyond this by analyzing the spatial pattern of urban growth? The two hypotheses which have threaded their way as background to this discussion seem to be promising avenues to explore at the somewhat macroscopic scale of our interests. The first is that, particularly in the earlier decades of the century, there should be regions of distinctly high urban growth found in those areas which were undergoing rapid development as the temporal sequence of growth industries caused expansion in distinct regional sub-systems of cities. Second, within any sub-system of cities, one might expect to find a distinctive pattern of spatial growth in which the impetus of growth first occurs in one or a few centres and only subsequently filters out to more distant towns.

REGIONAL GROWTH PATTERNS

The first hypothesis was studied in two ways. First by the use of trend-surface analysis and second by a simpler comparison of the variance of urban growth rates within regions of England and Wales.

Trend-surface analysis is a method of fitting progressively higher-order polynomial equations to a set of x, y, z observations in which the x and y values are co-ordinate data and the z values are observations of some variable, in this case the standardized growth rates.[1] In fitting the surfaces a least-squares solution is used to fit, in two dimensions, first a linear, then a quadratic surface, and so forth. The results, as might be imagined from the complex patterns of the maps of growth rates, were not encouraging. In none of the cases did even the sixth-order surface produce any significant reduction in the sums of squares of the initial observations. This can be seen by looking at some of the results for selected decades. Table 4.1 shows the percentage reduction in the sums of squares for three decades which were chosen as being ones which suggested a relatively simpler pattern than others. Even by the sixth surface, the reduction of the original scatter is only 16, 18 and 10 per cent for the three decades. If one had a

Table 4.1   Trend-surface analysis of standardized urban growth rates

	Percentage reduction in the sum of squares					
	1801–11		*1811–21*		*1831–41*	
Trend-surface	*%*	*Cumulative %*	*%*	*Cumulative %*	*%*	*Cumulative %*
First-order	0·3	0·3	4·6	4·6	0·5	0·5
Second-order	2·4	2·7	0·1	4·7	1·4	1·9
Third-order	6·6	9·3	3·7	8·4	1·1	3·0
Fourth-order	2·1	11·4	2·0	10·4	2·7	5·7
Fifth-order	2·0	13·4	3·0	13·4	1·5	7·2
Sixth-order	2·3	15·7	5·0	18·4	2·3	9·5

Note: Numbers of observations in each decade are as follows: 1801–11 – 255; 1811–21 – 308; 1831–41 – 409.

relatively small number of distinct growth areas in which growth rates of individual towns was high and fairly uniform, one would expect levels of explanation somewhat higher than these figures. It would seem to be the case that, even though certain areas were growing rapidly, the rates of growth of the individual cities which comprise these areas were by no means uniform. Lancashire in the early decades, for example, may have been growing rapidly, but this did not mean that all the towns within, say, the south-east of the county were growing at uniformly high rates, but rather that the area had a higher-than-average proportion of towns which were growing even though at the same time a number of places was growing at well below-average rates. This is exactly the pattern found by Madden (1956b) for nineteenth- and twentieth-century growth rates in American cities of over 10,000 population. He too found that certain areas of rapid growth could be recognized, on the average, but that within each

[1] Trend-surface analysis has been widely used in geomorphology (for example: Chorley and Haggett 1965; Rodda 1970), but has also been applied to the study of the distribution of social phenomena, as for example in the study of urban social structure (Williams 1969).

such region the distribution of growth rates of individual places was scattered throughout every quintile of the overall distribution of growth rates.

The patterns of the trend-surface analysis do, however, appear to confirm our earlier descriptive account of the pattern of growth (fig. 4.12). The macroscopic

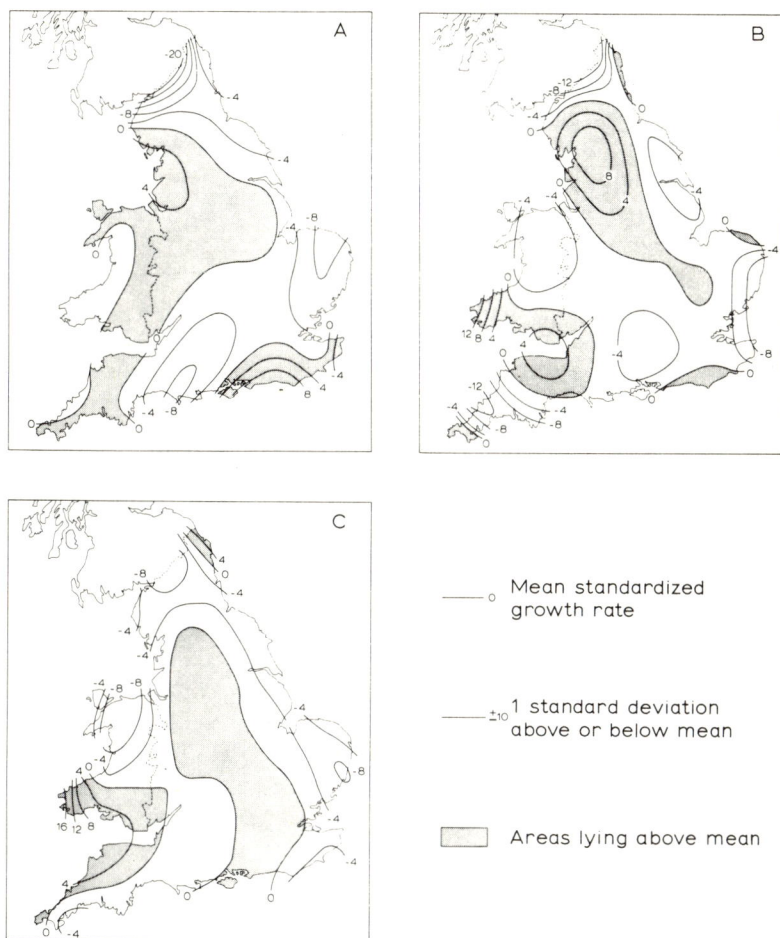

Figure 4.12   Trend surfaces of urban growth rates. Sixth-order surfaces for three selected decades: (A) 1801–11; (B) 1811–21, (C) 1831–41

patterns of the polynomial surfaces show that, in the first decade, the focus of high growth was in the North West with some suggestion of high rates along the south coast; in the second decade the North West again has high rates with markedly lower rates of growth in East Anglia and the South West; and the

decade 1831-41 shows a pattern of higher rates roughly in the area of
Staffordshire, again accompanied by a belt of high rates along the south coast
and with lower rates in the peripheral areas. Interpretation of these surfaces
should obviously not be taken very seriously since they evidently 'explain' so
small a fraction of the total variance of the original growth rate data. While of
some little interest as generalized descriptions of the complex pattern of growth,
the trend-surface analysis cannot take us very far in understanding the spatial
pattern.

A clearer understanding of the regional complexity of individual urban
growth rates can be seen in the second approach to the problem in which
averages and standard deviations of growth rates for sets of towns grouped by
regions are studied. The thirteen regions which have been selected are simply
aggregates of counties made on the basis of their general industrial similarity;
they are an attempt to aggregate the whole set of places into a small and
relatively homogeneous set of areas. Counties are used as the basic units which
are joined purely for the convenience of calculation. It would have been possible
to ignore the county groupings and derive more truly homogeneous sets of cities
on the basis of a formal regionalization procedure, but, anticipating the findings,
this was considered unnecessarily elaborate.

Table 4.2 gives the results of this exercise and, since the growth rates of all
places have been included rather than simply isolating those which exceeded plus
or minus one standard deviation from the mean, the calculations supplement
the spatial distributions portrayed earlier.[1] The full picture of the spatial
scatter of growth rates can be seen to be extraordinarily complex. Most of the
thirteen regions show a wide scatter of towns in every category of growth rate
class. The particular divisions between each class in the table were selected so
that each class would include 20 per cent of observations if the growth rates
were normally distributed.[2] In fact, in most of the regions and for most of the
periods, the percentage distribution of places is little short of an even spread of
20 per cent in each of the five classes of growth rates, suggesting that no area is
one with uniformly and significantly high or low growth rates. There are,
nevertheless, certain tendencies apparent within each area which give a useful
picture of the pattern of urban growth during the nineteenth century. This
spatial pattern is clarified if the growth rate data are re-expressed as ratios of the

---

[1] See above, figs. 4.1 to 4.11.

[2] Thus: the central class runs from minus to plus 0·253, a range which includes 20 per cent
of observations under the normal curve; the second and fourth classes run from these limits
to figures of minus and plus 0·842; the first and fifth classes are greater than minus and plus
0·842. These figures apply since the standardized growth rate data have been calculated with
a mean of 0·0 and a standard deviation of 1·0. It can be seen that the total growth rates of
all places at the various decades are not normally distributed, but have a slight positive skew.
Had the initial growth rate data been calculated on the basis of simple rather than
compound growth, this skew would have been considerably more pronounced. See above,
pp. 71-2.

Table 4.2 *Frequency distribution of growth rates by region*

	$\bar{X}$	*s*	% in growth class 1	2	3	4	5	Total no. of towns
NORTH EAST								
1	−0·65	0·92	31·3	50·0	6·3	0	12·5	16
2	−0·16	0·75	27·8	11·1	38·9	5·5	16·7	18
3	−0·35	1·02	28·6	28·6	23·8	4·8	14·3	21
4	−0·39	0·95	31·8	22·7	18·2	18·2	9·1	22
5	0·14	1·38	20·7	20·7	13·8	24·1	20·7	29
6	0·52	1·40	9·1	30·3	6·1	21·2	33·3	33
7	0·41	1·17	9·3	23·3	23·3	16·3	27·9	43
8	0·34	0·96	3·3	27·9	21·3	21·3	26·2	61
9	−0·04	1·05	18·8	31·9	20·3	10·1	18·8	69
10	0·31	1·16	12·8	23·1	21·8	17·9	24·3	78
11	0·43	1·06	9·9	19·8	17·3	21·0	32·1	81
CUMBRIA								
1	−0·42	0·43++	28·6	28·6	42·9	0	0	7
2	−0·06	0·65	12·5	50·0	0	25·0	12·5	8
3	−0·51	0·79	25·0	37·5	12·5	25·0	0	8
4	−0·52	0·78	50·0	25·0	12·5	0	12·5	8
5	−0·50	0·50+	25·0	37·5	25·0	12·5	0	8
6	−0·51	0·41++++	22·2	55·5	11·1	11·1	0	9
7	−0·32	0·91	36·4	36·4	0	18·2	9·1	11
8	0·41	1·23	0	46·2	15·4	7·7	30·8	13
9	−0·16	1·21	28·6	35·7	0	14·3	21·4	14
10	−0·68	0·64+	53·3	26·7	13·3	0	6·7	15
11	−0·89	0·70+	41·2	47·1	11·8	0	0	17
WEST YORKSHIRE								
1	0·14	0·84	9·5	19·0	28·6	23·8	19·0	21
2	0·40	0·86	4·2	8·3	45·8	16·7	25·0	24
3	−0·02	0·85	17·2	27·6	10·3	27·6	17·2	29
4	0·43	1·22	7·0	11·6	27·9	34·9	18·6	43
5	−0·01	0·95	14·6	31·2	27·1	12·5	14·5	48
6	0·17	1·07	7·4	35·2	20·4	14·8	22·2	54
7	0·26	1·03	12·9	22·6	17·7	24·2	22·6	62
8	0·16	0·92	8·9	30·4	17·7	22·8	20·3	79
9	−0·02	0·79++++	13·5	25·8	24·7	24·7	11·2	89
10	−0·15	0·99	22·2	29·3	22·2	16·2	10·1	99
11	−0·01	1·09	13·3	35·2	22·9	11·4	17·1	105
NORTH WEST								
1	0·01	1·22	7·7	5·1	15·4	43·6	28·2	39
2	0·59	1·33	4·4	15·5	24·4	33·3	22·2	45
3	0·22	1·16	17·3	21·2	21·2	21·2	19·2	52
4	0·14	0·97	13·6	22·0	25·4	20·3	18·6	59
5	−0·03	0·89	14·7	26·5	25·0	22·1	11·8	68
6	0·31	1·03	10·6	14·6	32·0	20·0	22·7	75
7	0·33	1·39	12·9	22·3	25·9	14·1	24·7	85
8	0·44	1·06	4·9	20·6	23·5	29·4	21·6	102
9	0·20	1·10	14·0	20·6	27·1	15·9	22·4	107
10	−0·17	1·07	25·6	26·5	24·8	11·1	12·0	117
11	−0·22	0·73++++	13·3	41·7	25·8	13·3	5·8	120

Table 4.2 (continued) *Frequency distribution of growth rates by region*

	$\bar{X}$	s	1	2	3	4	5	Total no. of towns
					% in growth class			

WEST MIDLANDS

	$\bar{X}$	s	1	2	3	4	5	Total no. of towns
1	0·11	0·60++	18·5	33·3	14·8	7·4	25·9	27
2	−0·04	0·65++++	9·4	25·0	37·5	18·8	9·4	32
3	0·18	0·72+++	8·1	10·8	40·5	24·3	16·2	37
4	0·46	1·21	10·0	22·5	10·0	22·5	35·0	40
5	0·31	0·84	4·2	18·8	27·1	29·2	20·8	48
6	0·28	1·07	9·6	25·0	23·1	21·2	21·2	52
7	−0·21	0·77+++	16·6	33·3	22·2	20·4	7·4	54
8	−0·13	0·90	16·6	28·3	28·3	20·0	6·6	60
9	−0·32	0·67++++	16·6	38·3	31·6	11·7	1·6	60
10	−0·10	0·79++	14·8	39·3	23·0	9·8	13·1	61
11	−0·20	0·82++	11·5	50·8	18·0	8·2	11·5	61

NORTH MIDLANDS

1	−0·09	0·80	0	20·0	53·3	6·7	20·0	15
2	−0·19	0·74	15·8	31·6	26·3	15·8	10·5	19
3	0·03	0·62+++	0	38·1	23·8	28·5	9·5	21
4	−0·23	0·56++++	8·7	43·5	26·1	17·4	4·3	23
5	−0·18	0·81	18·5	37·0	29·6	11·1	3·7	27
6	−0·26	0·80	20·7	51·7	6·9	10·3	10·3	29
7	−0·14	0·91	16·6	38·9	22·2	5·6	16·7	36
8	0·39	0·98	6·8	25·0	20·4	15·9	31·8	44
9	0·24	0·80++	1·9	25·0	32·7	17·3	23·1	52
10	0·25	0·79++	3·3	23·0	32·8	21·3	19·7	61
11	0·24	1·04	5·4	36·5	20·2	21·6	16·2	74

EAST

1	−0·09	0·80	13·0	26·1	30·4	17·4	13·0	23
2	−0·34	0·75++	16·1	32·3	35·5	12·9	3·2	31
3	−0·04	0·62++++	9·1	39·4	21·2	18·2	12·1	33
4	−0·26	0·48++++	10·5	42·1	36·8	7·9	2·6	38
5	0·08	1·05	7·7	28·2	41·0	15·4	7·7	39
6	−0·64	0·65++++	30·2	46·5	16·3	2·3	4·7	43
7	−0·35	0·65++++	15·6	48·9	24·4	6·7	4·4	45
8	−0·38	0·78++	24·4	40·0	13·3	15·5	6·7	45
9	−0·45	0·64++++	29·2	47·9	12·5	4·2	6·2	48
10	−0·28	0·84	24·5	40·8	12·2	8·2	14·3	49
11	−0·15	0·79++	12·0	46·0	26·0	0	16·0	50

SOUTH WEST

1	−0·05	1·52	24·1	31·0	20·7	6·9	17·2	29
2	0·10	1·24	17·6	29·4	14·7	20·6	17·6	34
3	0·13	1·39	22·0	17·1	24·3	24·3	12·2	41
4	−0·16	0·85	21·2	27·6	25·5	14·9	10·6	47
5	−0·32	0·94	34·6	23·1	23·1	11·5	7·7	52
6	−0·37	0·83+	20·4	46·3	24·1	1·9	7·4	54
7	−0·55	0·60++++	25·4	54·5	9·1	10·9	0	55
8	−0·72	0·63++++	42·9	37·5	12·5	7·1	0	56
9	−0·32	0·68++++	20·7	37·9	29·3	5·2	6·9	58
10	−0·62	0·47++++	35·5	41·9	16·1	6·5	0	62
11	−0·44	0·61++++	27·9	47·1	10·3	7·4	7·4	68

Table 4.2 (continued) *Frequency distribution of growth rates by region*

	$\bar{X}$	s	1	2	3	4	5	Total no. of towns
			% in growth class					

	$\bar{X}$	s	1	2	3	4	5	Total no. of towns
SOUTH								
1	−0·47	0·61++	26·7	46·7	13·3	6·7	6·7	15
2	−0·11	0·88	20·0	35·0	15·0	10·0	20·0	20
3	−0·33	0·85	19·0	42·9	19·0	4·8	14·3	21
4	−0·03	1·14	20·0	32·0	24·0	12·0	12·0	25
5	0·15	1·27	20·0	24·0	24·0	16·0	16·0	25
6	−0·06	0·92	14·3	42·9	14·3	14·3	14·3	28
7	−0·17	0·77+	12·9	48·4	22·6	6·4	9·6	31
8	−0·53	0·84	37·8	29·7	24·3	2·7	5·4	37
9	−0·02	1·13	23·1	41·0	7·6	10·3	17·9	39
10	−0·03	0·98	20·0	37·8	8·9	13·3	20·0	45
11	−0·08	0·87	17·0	31·9	23·4	17·0	10·6	47
SOUTH MIDLANDS								
1	−0·29	0·42++++	6·2	50·0	25·0	18·8	0	16
2	−0·28	0·57+++	17·6	29·4	23·5	29·4	0	17
3	−0·21	0·64++++	18·5	33·3	25·9	14·8	7·4	27
4	0·01	0·58++++	3·4	44·8	17·2	27·6	6·9	29
5	−0·16	0·84	9·1	51·5	18·2	12·1	9·1	33
6	−0·27	0·67++++	18·2	36·4	24·2	15·2	6·1	33
7	0·04	0·78+	8·6	37·1	17·1	20·0	17·1	35
8	−0·18	0·84	21·6	40·5	10·8	10·8	16·2	37
9	0·02	0·96	12·2	41·4	19·5	14·6	12·2	41
10	−0·09	0·84	27·6	19·1	14·9	23·4	14·9	47
11	−0·33	0·55++++	18·0	46·0	22·0	12·0	2·0	50
SOUTH EAST								
1	0·12	1·01	9·7	16·1	38·7	19·4	16·1	31
2	−0·22	1·04	27·5	37·5	10·0	12·5	12·5	40
3	−0·12	1·06	20·4	36·4	18·2	13·6	11·4	44
4	−0·11	0·83	10·9	37·0	26·1	19·6	6·5	46
5	0·05	0·88	6·0	40·0	22·0	18·0	14·0	50
6	0·16	0·91	4·9	29·5	29·5	19·6	16·4	61
7	0·20	0·82++	5·6	23·9	23·9	32·3	14·1	71
8	0·08	0·98	15·4	29·6	22·0	13·2	19·8	91
9	0·42	1·05	5·8	25·2	13·6	27·2	28·2	103
10	0·53	1·02	4·1	19·7	21·3	24·6	30·3	122
11	0·31	1·12	10·7	20·8	27·7	16·9	23·8	130
WEST								
1	−0·28	0·74	15·3	53·8	0	23·1	7·7	13
2	−0·37	0·68+	25·0	31·3	25·0	18·8	0	16
3	−0·13	0·82	21·1	10·5	42·1	15·8	10·5	19
4	−0·63	0·94	41·7	20·8	25·0	8·3	4·2	24
5	−0·13	1·02	23·3	40·0	10·0	10·0	16·7	30
6	−0·29	0·55++++	8·8	47·1	32·4	5·9	5·9	34
7	−0·42	0·58++++	25·0	38·9	22·2	11·1	2·8	36
8	−0·51	0·58++++	22·5	55·0	10·0	12·5	0	40
9	−0·77	0·67++++	50·0	32·5	15·0	0	2·5	40
10	−0·29	0·79++++	24·4	35·5	17·8	15·5	6·6	45
11	−0·53	0·67++++	31·9	44·7	14·9	4·2	4·2	47

Table 4.2 (continued) *Frequency distribution of growth rates by region*

	$\bar{X}$	s	% in growth class 1	2	3	4	5	Total no. of towns
SOUTH WALES								
1	0·88	0·82	0	25·0	0	0	75·0	4
2	0·13	0·86	20·0	0	40·0	20·0	20·0	5
3	1·17	1·23	0	12·5	12·5	25·0	50·0	8
4	1·37	1·25	12·5	0	0	25·0	62·5	8
5	0·99	1·20	0	11·1	11·1	44·4	33·3	9
6	0·46	1·16	15·4	7·6	30·7	23·1	23·1	13
7	0·49	1·13	0	35·3	23·5	11·7	29·4	17
8	0·09	1·32	29·6	22·2	7·4	11·1	29·6	27
9	0·64	1·41	13·8	6·9	34·5	10·3	34·5	29
10	0·40	1·14	6·5	25·8	22·6	19·4	25·8	31
11	1·16	1·18	0	10·8	8·1	27·0	54·1	37
DATA FOR ALL REGIONS								
1	0·00	1·00	14·5	27·7	23·0	17·2	17·6	256
2	0·00	1·00	15·9	26·2	25·5	18·8	13·5	309
3	0·00	1·00	16·3	26·9	23·5	19·1	14·1	361
4	0·00	1·00	15·5	28·2	23·5	18·9	13·8	412
5	0·00	1·00	15·2	30·0	24·0	17·6	13·1	466
6	0·00	1·00	13·5	34·2	22·6	14·1	15·6	518
7	0·00	1·00	14·2	33·7	20·8	16·5	14·6	581
8	0·00	1·00	16·6	31·2	18·9	16·9	16·3	692
9	0·00	1·00	16·7	30·3	22·0	14·6	16·3	749
10	0·00	1·00	18·6	28·8	20·7	15·6	16·2	832
11	0·00	1·00	14·3	35·4	20·9	13·4	16·0	887

Notes

1. Standardized (z) growth rates are used throughout; the five growth classes of columns 4–8, being as follows:

    1 $< -0·842$ 4 $0·253$ to $0·842$
    2 $-0·842$ to $-0·253$ 5 $> 0·842$
    3 $-0·253$ to $+0·253$

2. $\bar{X}$ and s are, respectively, the means and standard deviations of the standardized rates. Areas whose growth rates are 'bunched' more tightly than those for all regions (i.e. areas showing some homogeneity of urban growth) have standard deviations significantly *lower* than 1·0. These are distinguished (in column 3) for the following confidence levels:

    ++++   5·0%
    +++   2·5%
    ++   1·0%
    +   0·5%

3. For each region the rows refer to decades running from Period 1 (1801–11) to Period 11 (1901–11).

4. Regions are composed of towns from the following groups of counties (abbreviated as in Appendix B):

    North East (DUR, NLD, YNR); Cumbria (CUM, WLD); West Yorkshire (YWR); North West (CHE, LAN); West Midlands (STF, WAR, WOR); North Midlands (DER, LEC, NOT, RUT); East: (CAM, LIN, NFK, SFK, YER); South West (COR, DEV, GLO, SOM); South (DOR, HAM, WIL); South Midlands (BED, BER, BUK, HUN, NTS, OXO); South East (ESS, HRT, KEN, LONDON, MDX, SRY, SSX); West (HFD, SAL, WALES except GLAM, MON); South Wales (GLAM, MON).

appropriate rate for all of the towns within England and Wales as a whole and these figures are shown in table 4.3. A figure greater than 1·0 in any period means that the particular region had a larger percentage of towns falling within the particular class of growth rates than did the whole set of towns for England and Wales during the same period; a figure below 1·0 means that the region had a smaller percentage in that class than did the whole set of towns.

The towns of the North East started off the period with a predominantly low set of growth rates; they had higher growth in the decades from 1841; and by the end of the century the area was clearly one with a predominantly rapid set of growth rates. Cumbria includes very few towns throughout the whole period and its figures are therefore less reliable, but it would appear to have been an area whose towns grew at lower rather than higher rates with the exception of the period 1871-91. West Yorkshire had a rather variable pattern of urban growth, but with a tendency for there to be an over-representation of rapidly growing places throughout most of the period. The North West had a larger-than-expected number of places with rapid growth in all of the decades up to 1891, but thereafter it had more places in the classes of less rapid growth. The West Midlands shows most consistently rapid growth in its cities in the middle decades from 1831-61. The North Midlands appears to have grown most consistently in the latter part of the period, with large proportions of places in the high growth rate classes in the decades from 1871. The East and the South West both show a consistent pattern of predominantly low urban growth; the South West showing this pattern somewhat earlier than the East. The South and the South Midlands show no particularly clear pattern over time. The South East, by contrast, shows a very marked pattern with decline in the period 1811-31, followed by average growth rates in the following decade and increasing proportions of places in the classes of more rapid growth from 1841 onwards. Wales and the Border shows predominant decline during most of the period; while South Wales shows a very distinctive pattern having had high proportions of its towns in the highest growth class for every decade of the period.

These patterns of urban growth in the thirteen regions accord very closely with the fluctuating economic fortunes of their respective regions, but it is quite evident at the same time that there is little suggestion of there being sets of urban regions with homogeneously high or low growth rates. Even in South Wales — the smallest area geographically and the one in which one might expect greatest homogeneity — while there are high proportions of places in the class of the very highest growth rates, these proportions exist alongside significant numbers of places which were found in the classes of lower, or indeed lowest, growth rates.[1] Given this wide scatter of growth rates of towns within regions of England and Wales, it is impossible to talk of regional sets of cities with uniformly high growth rates reflecting the expansion of successive growth industries. The spatial pattern of urban growth is too complex to be teased out by simple spatial or geometric analysis at this aggregate scale.

[1] A scatter which is confirmed by the standard deviations shown in table 4.2.

Urban growth

Table 4.3 *Relative growth frequencies by region*

Period	Ratio of regional % to overall % in each growth class				
	1	2	3	4	5
NORTH EAST					
1	2·16	1·81	0·27	0·00	0·71
2	1·75	0·42	1:53	0·29	1·24
3	1·76	1·06	1·01	0·25	1·01
4	2·05	0·81	0·77	0·96	0·66
5	1·36	0·69	0·58	1·37	1·58
6	0·67	0·89	0·27	1·50	2·14
7	0·66	0·69	1·12	0·99	1·91
8	0·20	0·89	1·13	1·26	1·61
9	1·13	1·05	0·92	0·69	1·15
10	0·69	0·80	1·05	1·15	1·50
11	0·69	0·56	0·83	1·57	2·01
CUMBRIA					
1	1·97	1·03	1·87	0·00	0·00
2	0·79	1·91	0·00	1·33	0·93
3	1·53	1·25	0·53	1·31	0·00
4	3·23	0·89	0·53	0·00	0·91
5	1·65	1·25	1·04	0·71	0·00
6	1·64	1·62	0·49	0·79	0·00
7	2·56	1·08	0·00	1·10	0·62
8	0·00	1·48	0·82	0·46	1·89
9	1·71	1·18	0·00	0·98	1·31
10	2·87	0·93	0·64	0·00	0·41
11	2·88	1·33	0·57	0·00	0·00
WEST YORKSHIRE					
1	0·66	0·69	1·24	1·38	1·08
2	0·26	0·32	1·80	0·89	1·85
3	1·06	1·03	0·44	1·45	1·22
4	0·45	0·41	1·19	1·85	1·35
5	0·96	1·04	1·13	0·71	1·11
6	0·55	1·03	0·90	1·05	1·42
7	0·91	0·67	0·85	1·47	1·55
8	0·54	0·97	0·94	1·35	1·25
9	0·81	0·85	1·12	1·69	0·69
10	1·19	1·02	1·07	1·04	0·62
11	0·93	0·99	1·10	0·85	1·07
NORTH WEST					
1	0·53	0·18	0·67	2·54	1·60
2	0·28	0·59	0·96	1·77	1·64
3	1·06	0·79	0·90	1·11	1·36
4	0·88	0·78	1·08	1·07	1·35
5	0·97	0·88	1·04	1·26	0·90
6	0·79	0·43	1·42	1·42	1·46
7	0·91	0·66	1·25	0·86	1·69
8	0·30	0·66	1·24	1·74	1·33

Table 4.3 (*continued*)   *Relative growth frequencies by region*

	Ratio of regional % to overall % in each growth class				
Period	1	2	3	4	5
9	0·84	0·68	1·23	1·09	1·37
10	1·38	0·92	1·20	0·71	0·74
11	0·93	1·18	1·23	0·99	0·36
WEST MIDLANDS					
1	1·28	1·20	0·64	0·43	1·47
2	0·59	0·95	1·47	1·00	0·70
3	0·50	0·40	1·72	1·27	1·15
4	0·65	0·80	0·43	1·19	2·54
5	0·28	0·63	1·13	1·66	1·59
6	0·71	0·73	1·02	1·50	1·36
7	1·17	0·99	1·07	1·24	0·51
8	1·00	0·91	1·50	1·18	0·41
9	0·99	1·26	1·44	0·80	0·10
10	0·80	1·37	1·11	0·63	0·81
11	0·80	1·44	0·86	0·61	0·72
NORTH MIDLANDS					
1	0·00	0·72	2·32	0·39	1·14
2	0·99	1·21	1·03	0·84	0·78
3	0·00	1·42	1·01	1·49	0·67
4	0·56	1·54	1·11	0·92	0·31
5	1·22	1·23	1·23	0·63	0·28
6	1·53	1·51	0·31	0·73	0·66
7	1·17	1·15	1·07	0·34	1·14
8	0·41	0·80	1·08	0·94	1·95
9	0·11	0·83	1·49	1·19	1·42
10	0·18	0·80	1·59	1·37	1·22
11	0·38	1·03	0·97	1·61	1·01
EAST					
1	0·90	0·94	1·32	1·01	0·74
2	1·01	1·23	1·39	0·69	0·24
3	0·56	1·47	0·90	0·95	0·86
4	0·68	1·49	1·57	0·42	0·19
5	0·51	0·94	1·71	0·88	0·59
6	2·24	1·36	0·72	0·16	0·30
7	1·10	1·45	1·17	0·41	0·30
8	1·47	1·28	0·70	0·92	0·41
9	1·75	1·58	0·57	0·29	0·38
10	1·32	1·42	0·59	0·53	0·88
11	0·84	1·30	1·24	0·00	1·00
SOUTH WEST					
1	1·66	1·12	0·90	0·40	0·98
2	1·11	1·12	0·58	1·10	1·30
3	1·35	0·64	1·03	1·27	0·87
4	1·37	0·98	1·09	0·79	0·77
5	2·28	0·77	0·96	0·65	0·59

Table 4.3 (*continued*)   *Relative growth frequencies by region*

Period	Ratio of regional % to overall % in each growth class				
	1	*2*	*3*	*4*	*5*
6	1·51	1·35	1·07	0·14	0·47
7	1·79	1·62	0·44	0·66	0·00
8	2·58	1·20	0·66	0·42	0·00
9	1·24	1·25	1·33	0·36	0·42
10	1·91	1·46	0·78	0·42	0·00
11	1·95	1·33	0·49	0·55	0·46
SOUTH					
1	1·84	1·69	0·58	0·39	0·38
2	1·26	1·34	0·59	0·53	1·48
3	1·17	1·60	0·81	0·25	1·01
4	1·29	1·14	1·02	0·64	0·87
5	1·32	0·80	1·00	0·91	1·22
6	1·06	1·25	0·63	1·01	0·92
7	0·91	1·44	1·09	0·39	0·66
8	2·28	0·95	1·29	0·16	0·33
9	1·38	1·35	0·35	0·71	1·10
10	1·08	1·31	0·43	0·85	1·24
11	1·19	0·90	1·12	1·27	0·66
SOUTH MIDLANDS					
1	0·43	1·81	1·09	1·09	0·00
2	1·11	1·12	0·92	1·56	0·00
3	1·14	1·24	1·10	0·78	0·53
4	0·22	1·59	0·73	1·46	0·50
5	0·60	1·72	0·76	0·69	0·70
6	1·35	1·06	1·07	1·08	0·39
7	0·61	1·10	0·82	1·21	1·17
8	1·30	1·30	0·57	0·64	0·99
9	0·73	1·37	0·89	1·00	0·75
10	1·48	0·66	0·72	1·50	0·92
11	1·26	1·30	1·05	0·90	0·13
SOUTH EAST					
1	0·67	0·58	1·68	1·13	0·92
2	1·73	1·43	0·39	0·67	0·93
3	1·25	1·35	0·77	0·71	0·81
4	0·70	1·31	1·11	1·04	0·47
5	0·40	1·33	0·92	1·02	1·07
6	0·36	0·86	1·31	1·39	1·05
7	0·39	0·71	1·15	1·96	0·97
8	0·93	0·95	1·16	0·78	1·22
9	0·35	0·83	0·62	1·86	1·73
10	0·22	0·68	1·03	1·58	1·87
11	0·75	0·59	1·33	1·26	1·49
WEST					
1	1·06	1·94	0·00	1·34	0·44
2	1·57	1·20	0·98	1·00	0·00
3	1·29	0·39	1·79	0·83	0·75

Table 4.3 (*continued*)   *Relative growth frequencies by region*

Period	Ratio of regional % to overall % in each growth class				
	1	*2*	*3*	*4*	*5*
4	2·69	0·74	1·06	0·44	0·30
5	1·53	1·33	0·42	0·57	1·28
6	0·65	1·38	1·43	0·42	0·38
7	1·76	1·15	1·07	0·67	0·19
8	1·36	1·76	0·53	0·74	0·00
9	2·99	1·07	0·68	0·00	0·15
10	1·31	1·23	0·86	0·99	0·41
11	2·23	1·26	0·71	0·31	0·26
SOUTH WALES					
1	0·00	0·90	0·00	0·00	4·26
2	1·26	0·00	1·57	1·06	1·48
3	0·00	0·47	0·53	1·31	3·55
4	0·81	0·00	0·00	1·32	4·53
5	0·00	0·37	0·46	2·52	2·54
6	1·14	0·22	1·36	1·64	1·48
7	0·00	1·05	1·13	0·71	2·01
8	1·78	0·71	0·39	0·66	1·82
9	0·83	0·23	1·57	0·71	2·12
10	0·35	0·90	1·09	1·24	1·59
11	0·00	0·31	0·39	2·02	3·38

Note: The growth classes, the periods and the composition of regions are as given in table 4.2

SPATIAL PATTERNS: GROWTH RATES AND DISTANCE

The second hypothesis suggests that growth impulses in a set of cities will be filtered out from certain cities to others so that a temporal lag will occur between their respective growths or that growth rates will decline at increasing distances from the growth centre.[1] Once again, such an hypothesis derives from the notion that the interconnections between towns form urban systems and sub-systems. The most impressive studies which have attempted to disentangle patterns of leads and lags in sets of cities have used rates of unemployment as indicators of economic health. King, Casetti, and Jeffrey (1969), for example, have postulated a model in which the activity levels in a given city are the effect, first, of levels of activity in other cities and, second, of the effects of national factors whose consequences are delayed by various time lags, the duration of which depends on the linkages of the given city. Looking at unemployment data

---

[1] These are, of course, different notions: the first suggesting a temporal and the second a spatial pattern. However, both are derived from the hypothesis that the influence of towns upon each other are channelled through a network of linkages which help define the system of cities. In the ensuing 'test' of the hypothesis it is assumed that these linkages are spatially determined. With better data, the more realistic assumption that the linkages follow the hierarchy of urban size could be studied in the way in which it has been examined for present-day Swedish towns by Wärneryd (1968).

for 1960-64 for midwestern cities of the United States, their analysis isolates three sub-systems of cities centred on Pittsburgh, Detroit and Indianapolis; the latter two lagging behind the first. Other cities within the area show less interaction since their linkages are less with the regional than with the national urban system.[1] At a finer scale, Bassett and Haggett (1971) have studied the pattern of leads and lags in towns in south-west England using lag correlation and cross-spectral methods to analyze the time series of monthly unemployment figures. Their results suggest a complex pattern of leads and lags amongst the set of places with the upturns and downswings of such places as Swindon, Stroud and Bath leading those of Bristol by periods of from six to one months and Gloucester, on the other hand, lagging by some two months. Analyses of this sort have suggested most interesting methods of unravelling the economic interlinkages between towns, but they are extremely demanding in terms of data requirements (Granger 1964). In studying the growth of cities of the nineteenth century, one set of data which would seem to provide observations of a sufficiently fine temporal mesh are the annual statistics on house building collected by Weber for a large number of individual towns in Britain. Parry Lewis (1965), in looking at these data, himself suggests the potential value of studying inter- and intra-regional lags in the movements of the individual house-building series. In the building boom of the 1890s, for example, the great majority of areas followed the national trend with a downswing occurring in the early part of the 1900s. South Wales, however, showed a markedly different regional pattern with house building continuing at high rates into the late 1900s.[2] Even such data on house building, however, provide observations only at annual intervals and, since the connections between rates of building and population increase are by no means in happy accord and since house building is in competition with other economic activities for many of the same factors of production so that many of its swings move inversely to indicators of more general economic activity, it would seem that a study of house-building activity rates would not reveal much about the demographic expansion of urban areas.[3]

---

[1] Chicago is one of these latter, nationally-orientated, cities. Such a distinction accords neatly with the national and regional dichotomies of the American urban system which are noted above, pp. 91–2.

[2] This difference might be seen as a consequence of the continuing high rates of migration into South Wales. Maps of net migration flows (Friedlander and Roshier 1966) show that the dramatic reversal of migration in South Wales occurred after the decade 1901-11; up to 1911 immigration into the area was very heavy, but after 1911 outmigration to the South East began in large numbers. See especially B. Thomas (1930).

[3] The relationship between house building and population pressure (as measured by the number of empty houses) has been studied by Saul (1962a, p. 129) who suggests that 'though building was normally influenced by the level of empties obtaining, at the height of a boom there may be a considerable lag before building was reduced in the face of the high empties and the effects could also be much delayed before the upswing got under way.' See also the similar conclusion reached by Cairncross (1953, pp. 27-33). The most generally agreed opinion is that building activity appears to be less a direct indicator of economic expansion than of migration. Cairncross (1953, p. 25) called the building cycle 'little more than a migration cycle in disguise'.

An approach to the analysis of leads and lags in rates of urban growth which provides a more spatial focus and is less taxing in its data requirements is provided in the study by Casetti and Semple (1968) of urban growth in small towns in southern Ontario. They found that growth rates tend to decline in magnitude with increasing distance from a limited number of growth centres in the area: three centres being found which formed an arc of growth around the head of Lake Erie from which, at increasing distances, the growth rates of other towns fell; two further centres were found to the north-west of this from which, at increasing distances, growth rates rose. Impressive amounts of explanation were provided by the isolation of spatial growth trends from these five points. Distance from the first growth point alone explained almost 70 per cent of the total variance in the growth rates during the decade 1950-60; and almost 95 per cent of the variance was explained by the joint 'effects' of all five points.

The technique suggested by Casetti and Semple was applied to one of the decades in the sequence of urban growth in England and Wales. The method used involves superimposing over the whole area a grid of x,y co-ordinates; from each intersection of the grid, linear equations are then fitted expressing the growth rates of all towns as some function of distance from the intersection; the intersection with the best fit is then taken as the point from which growth either declines or increases; the residuals from this regression equation are then used as observations for the fitting of subsequent equations, and thus the choice of a second, a third and nth points from which growth either decreases or increases. One therefore picks out points which successively explain the largest amount of the observed growth (or residuals) in terms of distance decay or distance accretion. For an area as large as England and Wales, it would be unreasonable to anticipate that growth might be related to distance from a single point, but some form of transformation of the distances would obviously enable one to steepen the fall-off in the distance effect and so isolate regional growth centres.

The results of applying this technique to the growth rate were not encouraging. Table 4.4 shows the results for the decade 1801-11 and it can be seen that the amounts of explanation which are afforded are extremely small. This might be expected from all that has so far been said of the complex spatial pattern of growth during the nineteenth century and the results are yet again confirmation of the absence of any simple geometrical pattern of growth rates at this macroscopic scale of analysis. The points which are selected are nevertheless of some small interest since, despite their low reliability, they do make some sense in terms of the details of the growth rates of the chosen decade. In all cases, the various permutations of the growth rates — either the raw growth rate data or the standardized rates — and the distance transformations — either using a reciprocal or a logarithmic transformation — make little difference to the patterns which emerge. The first growth point which is isolated falls in Lancashire with a tendency for growth to decrease at increasing distances away from it. The second point, isolated both by the first and second tests, falls within an area on the coast of Kent, again from which point growth rates tend to fall. The two other points which are isolated fall in the vicinity of Whitby in Yorkshire and within the west of Wales, from one of which growth rates tend to rise. It is interesting to note that the points in Lancashire and in Kent accord with what has already been seen of the spatial pattern of growth rates in this decade, but, given the amount of explanation provided by these four points, it is evident that one would need to isolate a very large number of points before being able to account for any large fraction of the total variance. The conclusion must be that, at this spatial scale, the pattern of urban growth is too complex for such techniques to have any great analytic value. Only at a much more detailed

Table 4.4   *Growth centres, 1801-11*

Location (national grid references)	*Correlation* (*r*)	*Cumulative* (*r²*)	*Distance effect*
(*a*) *Reciprocal of distances and raw growth rates*			
1st centre 371.416 (near Bury, Lancs.)	0·22	4·7	decrease
2nd centre 638.155 (near Dover, Kent)	0·17	7·6	decrease
3rd centre 260.251 (central Cardiganshire)	0·12	8·9	decrease
(*b*) *Reciprocal of distances and standardized growth rates*			
1st centre 371.413 (near Bury, Lancs.)	0·23	5·4	decrease
2nd centre 638.155 (near Dover, Kent)	0·16	8·0	decrease
(*c*) *Logarithm of distances and standardized growth rates*			
1st centre 391.407 (near Oldham, Lancs.)	−0·23	5·1	decrease
2nd centre 488.513 (near Whitby, Yorks.)	0·16	7·5	increase

Notes
1. For explanation of method, see text.
2. The final column shows whether urban growth rates tend to increase or decrease at increasing distances from the selected 'growth' centre.

level of study — looking at the distribution of growth rates both at a finer temporal scale and within much smaller areas of the country — might one unearth any tendency for spatial regularity.

CONCLUSION

The various analyses of the macroscopic spatial pattern of urban growth have produced uniformly negative results. Even though the generalized patterns do accord with knowledge of the regional economic growth of England and Wales, the details of the spatial patterns can only be interpreted in terms of the particular factor endowments and historical events which underlay the growth of certain towns and the decay of others. There is little in the spatial pattern, at the scale at which it has been studied, which could be interpreted better by a geographer than by the descriptive expertise of the historian. At the national scale, it appears not to be the case that there were regions (or spatial sub-systems) which underwent uniformly rapid growth or decline during the nineteenth century. Rather, particular areas showed rapid average rates of urban growth because they had a higher-than-average number of rapidly growing towns, but at the same time they also had significant numbers which grew at rates similar to or below the national average. Nor, again, at the scale at which we have looked, can it be said that there are key growth points at greater distances from which the growth rates of the majority of other towns decline. It may well be that such patterns could be found at a smaller scale of study or with population data for periods less widely spaced in time than a decade. The latter information cannot be derived for any large number of places and the former approach lies outside the national frame of reference adopted in the present study. All that can be said in general terms is that the spatial pattern of nineteenth-century urban growth shows most dramatically the very marked shift from the early boom of the northern textile and metal-working areas and the much later growth of the towns within the South East. Before one could argue that this general pattern is suggestive of the early development of distinct sub-systems and the later development of a more unitary system focused on London, one would need both more sensitive indicators of the existence of systems, as well as a good deal of non-Euclidian spatial ingenuity.

We must, therefore, return to the two unresolved problems of urban growth which were outlined in the last chapter in an attempt to explain the scatter of urban growth rates and the particular decline of the average growth rates of large places in the final third of our period.

PART 3

Approaches to explanation

CHAPTER 5

Technical innovations and the scatter of urban growth

He that will not apply new remedies must expect new evils.

FRANCIS BACON

The first aspect of urban growth to which we shall turn is the decreasing scatter of growth rates which are found at increasing city sizes. This is the more interesting because it is the more general of our two findings from the data of nineteenth-century cities. There are many possible lines of explanation which could be explored. First a purely statistical approach could be adopted and it could be argued that large units might be expected to have small variances simply on the basis of elementary statistical theory. If growth is the result of the addition of employment opportunities, a slight fluctuation in the number of factories added to a town of 1,000,000 will make less proportionate difference to its growth than it would in the case of a town of 10,000. The arrival of one new firm would barely ruffle the smooth growth curve of Birmingham, but could cause a marked upswing in the curve of Bewdley. Second, and as amplification of this first statistical explanation, it could be argued that towns are a collection of some more fundamental 'unit' at a lower level of scale[1] so that a very small town might be seen as consisting of the summation of, say, 100 such 'units', a medium sized town would be composed of 1,000 units and a large town of 100,000 units. Then, while the variance in the growth of each of these units would be the same, the greater the number of units the less would be the overall variance on the assumption that, the distribution of probabilities of growth of each unit being normal, the addition of increasing numbers of these units would produce an overall growth closer and closer to the average.[2] Such an approach, however, would suffer from the fact that it is difficult to identify the basic units so that the explanation is singularly unrevealing of the nature of urban growth. Whereas in the case of the growth of firms, one can distinguish the respective units of divisions and branches of an overall firm which could be considered to

[1] The problems of definition which would be involved here hark back to our earlier discussion of defining objects at successive levels of scale.
[2] An explanation which has been considered in the parallel case of business-firm growth rates (Singh and Whittington 1968, p. 93, footnote 2).

form the basic units, the constituent parts of an urban economy are both more numerous and less easily identifiable.

An alternative approach might be to argue that large cities are the organizing poles of a regional economy and that much of their economic vitality derives from the commercial activities involved in the servicing and marketing functions which they offer to the more specialized subservient industrial towns within their hinterland. Thus, while the upswings and downswings affecting particular industries would have marked effect on a town whose economy was closely tied to that particular industry, the large regional centre would continue to flourish on the basis of the many activities which it performed for other towns not dependent on the declining industry. While it is certainly the case that many of the large towns had a greater variety of industrial activities within them than did smaller places — Birmingham's welter of trades being the prime, although slightly unusual, instance — the absence of detailed occupational or industrial data for towns in the nineteenth century means that it would be impossible to estimate with any accuracy the proportions of industrial and commercial activities within individual towns.[1]

Instead, the line of argument which will be pursued here turns to the connection between urban growth and the spread of innovations which can be argued to underlie the economic vitality of towns. It will be argued that the characteristics of entrepreneurial diffusion can produce patterns of growth rates which conform to our empirical finding that the variance of growth decreases with the increasing size of towns.

In the aftermath of Schumpeterian writings, there has been a widely-accepted belief in the importance of technological innovations rather than capital inputs as a factor in urban growth. In the city of today, growth is as much a product of tertiary activities as of manufacturing and, with the growth in white-collar occupations, the largest cities are now characterized by very extensive office development and the growth of service rather than manufacturing industry. For the nineteenth century, this was much less the case. Although London had for long been the most important commercial centre in the country, it too was a very substantial centre of industry — the largest in the country in absolute terms — and industrial activity together with its associated activities, particularly transportation, provided work for very considerable numbers of the employed

---

[1] While occupational data are given in the earlier censuses, the early classifications are far from satisfactory (Booth 1886). Only in 1911 — and more fully in 1921 — was a separate distinction drawn between occupational and industrial classifications. For periods before this, see the heroic attempts of Welton (for example: 1868-9; 1869; and 1897-8) to work towards the current notion of primary, secondary and tertiary activities. For an attempt to derive occupational data for a single town during the second half of the nineteenth century, see Bellamy (1952). The problems and potentials of using such census data are well discussed by Armstrong (1972).

population.[1] For the majority of towns it was industry which provided the bulk
of employment opportunities of nineteenth-century towns. And the advent of
new types of industries and the growth of existing ones depended very much
upon the development and application of new industrial expertise, which either
improved existing practices and so increased production relative to inputs of
capital, labour and materials, or else introduced entirely new types of economic
activity. Both of these types of expansion in industrial activity within towns
would tend to be self-generating in that they would widen markets and set the
stage for further expansion in production and they would also encourage the
development of new activity in a host of related types of manufacturing and
servicing activity which were linked to the original industry by 'forward' or
'backward' linkages. The application of the ideas of Bessemer and Siemens, for
example, made possible the production of vast quantities of relatively cheap
steel in the 1860s and, more especially, the 1870s. But this in turn had
consequent effects on activities which handled the ores and fuels, on those
which used steel both in heavy construction, as in shipbuilding, and in the lighter
finishing trades, and all of these activities in turn had effects on the growth of
the multitude of services called into play to provide housing, urban facilities,
transportation, capital and the host of infrastructural and service requirements
called for by the additional labour so produced.

Ramifications such as these may have had effect either within a single town
or more generally, but the nature of the process is clear; there is a form of
positive feedback effect in which growth calls forth additional growth in a
cumulative and circular fashion. Models of this process seem themselves to have
been subject to the same positive feedback effects since there is an enormous
literature on cumulative causation both at regional and sub-regional scales. For
the growth of cities, a relevant suggestion is that proposed by Pred (1966) which
is illustrated in fig. 5.1. He envisages two feedback loops which are associated
with an initial growth impetus produced by new or enlarged industrial activity
within a city during a period of manufacturing predominance. The first of these
loops is traced through an initial multiplier effect which is the product of the
growth of the manufacturing function itself plus the growth of manufacturing
activities with which it is linked. Associated with this is a secondary multiplier
effect caused by the concomitant expansion in construction and tertiary
activities. This first loop leads to the expansion of the local or regional market
on which, Pred claims, the manufacturing industry is dependent; so that, with
expansion, new threshold levels are reached and growth in the industry and its
labour force continues to cumulate. The second loop is associated with the

[1] Hall (1962, pp. 21 and 183-5) calculates that, in 1861 the percentages employed in
primary, manufacturing and service activities were respectively, 24·0, 33·2 and 39·2 for
England and Wales and 3·0, 31·7 and 61·0 for London. One-quarter of the service activities,
however, is comprised of building and transport employment.

argument that growth in production increases the likelihood of further new inventions and innovations within the local economy and so leads to yet further growth which will be produced by them. Such a notion of positive and cumulative causation in the growth of local manufacturing economies seems widely to be accepted and there is certainly evidence that technological innovations generate fresh industrial activity and in turn are more likely in the context of a vibrant than a stagnant economy.[1]

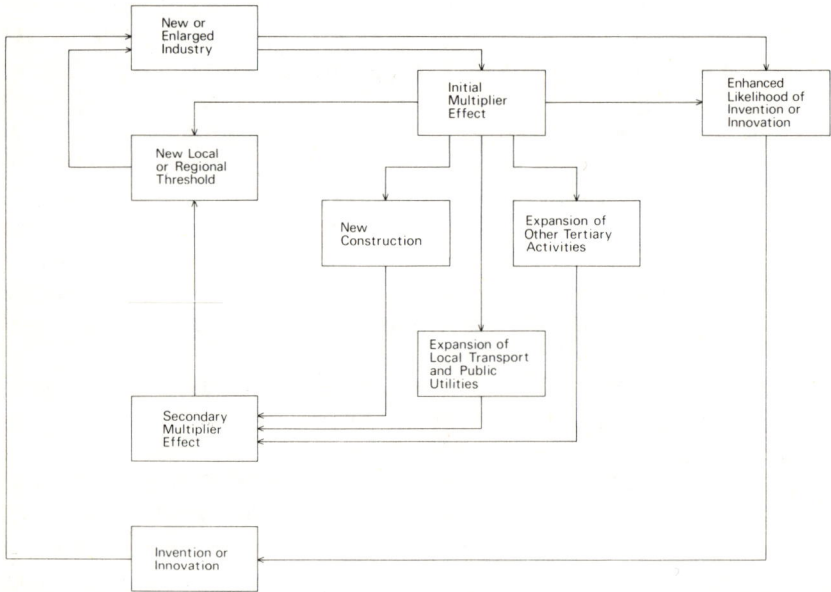

Figure 5.1   The process of urban growth: circular and cumulative causation. *Source:* Pred (1966)

It is this concept which must partly be held responsible for the considerable interest which has been engendered in the manner by which innovations diffuse throughout an area or an economy. The most voluminous of this literature deals with the temporal and structural aspects of innovation diffusion rather than its spatial characteristics. Rogers' (1962; see also Rogers and Shoemaker 1971) early summary of literature draws most strongly on work within agriculture and the social sciences and is still an invaluable compilation of evidence of the

[1] Schumpeter (1939) argued that innovations appear in 'clusters' over time as bottlenecks in related industries spurred the development and application of new techniques within industries which were linked in their productive processes. There is some disagreement amongst economists as to whether innovations are developed more in periods of slack or of full activity (see for example, Mansfield 1969, pp. 106-7).

existence of a logistic curve of acceptances of an innovation over time and also of the relationship between the characteristics of the adopters and the date at which they adopt — whether they are 'leaders', 'early-' or 'late-majority', or 'laggards' in the temporal process. There is in addition a flourishing literature in epidemiology (for example, Bailey 1957) and in the spread of technology (see, for example, the summary in Mansfield 1969). It is, however, the spatial aspects of diffusion with which our main concern will lie and, although late in developing, there is now an accumulating body of empirical and theoretical literature on which to draw (Brown 1968). Hägerstrand was the first to contribute a distinctly spatial approach to the formal analysis of the diffusion of innovations and his *Spatial diffusion of innovations* has already become one of the few 'classics' of modern geography because of its careful unfolding of a spatial argument and its incorporation of more general spatial theory.[1] The focus in this and much subsequent geographical study of diffusion has been on the process of contagious diffusions. The acceptance of TB controls amongst farmers, the spread of pastoral subsidies, of foot and mouth epidemics, or of tractors are all processes which can be seen in terms of a progressively advancing frontier of diffusion. In such studies the logistic curve of the temporal process of adoption can be directly applied to the spatial case. The logistic expression is given by the following:

$$P = \frac{U}{1 + e^{a-bT}};$$ [5.1]

where P is the percentage of adopters; U is some upper saturation limit; T is time; and a and b are parameters. With spatially-continuous diffusion, this equation can readily be made to apply to the spatial rather than the temporal case by expressing the a and b parameters as some function of distance from the place of first adoption — as in Casetti and Semple's (1969) study of the spread of tractors in a rural area. Alternatively, as in Hägerstrand's case, the spatial spread can be simulated in a Monte-Carlo fashion by which the probability of adoption is made a function of distance from individuals who have already adopted.

The logic of such spatially-continuous diffusion models is that, first, there is a relatively uniform distribution of population 'at risk' and, second, that the likelihood of adoption is a function of distance because it is determined by face-to-face contacts through the network of private communications which link individuals together. Such assumptions may meet the case of many agricultural innovations where the variance in the size of farms may not be large, where their distribution is relatively uniform and where, even after the widespread development of the mass media of communications, the decision to

[1] Although see the criticism of Hägerstrand's interpretation of patterns of 'neighbourhood' spread in Cliff (1968) and Cliff and Ord (1970, pp. 285-9).

adopt (as distinct from the fact of *knowing* about the innovation)[1] may still depend on face-to-face contacts. The case of adoption of innovations by towns, however, seems not to meet such requirements. As adopting 'units', towns are both discretely located in space and there are much more marked differences in their sizes than is the case for either farms or private households. Furthermore, many of the relevant innovations are of a different sort from those which have been studied in the contiguous diffusion of agricultural innovations. It is useful, here, to differentiate between what Pederson (1970) calls entrepreneurial and household innovations: the first being those which are adopted by organizations or by composite decision-making bodies; and the second those adopted by individual households. The difference is illustrated, for example, by the spread of television stations on the one hand and the spread of individual television sets on the other. The latter is obviously contingent upon the prior spread of the former, but there are more fundamental differences than this. The entrepreneurial innovation is one which will usually involve a larger capital outlay and a greater element of risk and is more likely to be based on a somewhat more 'rational' economic assessment of the appropriate market potential of the innovation. They also differ in that the entrepreneurial innovation is essentially competitive; whereas the fact that a household adopts a television set in no way precludes the adoption of sets by other households — indeed the essence of the diffusion argument is that it is likely to encourage rather than discourage such further adoption — once a firm or company establishes a television station in a city the probability of further companies setting up stations is more likely to be reduced than enhanced. Only when the market potential for a particular innovation is sufficiently great to support more than a single entrepreneurial innovation is one likely to find more than a single adoption in a given town. For commercial entrepreneurial innovations, the size of the potential market is therefore a consideration of the first importance and the size of the adopting unit — the town — is therefore critical. This adds a new element to the emphasis on space and distance. In looking at the diffusion of innovations in sets of towns it would appear that both size and distance need to be taken into consideration.

The importance of size of town in the spread of urban innovations has long been noted (Bowers 1937; McVoy 1940; Crain 1966), and indeed, Hägerstrand himself recognized the need to incorporate the influence of the size hierarchy into any study of diffusion within a set of towns. He distinguishes between a 'neighbourhood' effect on the one hand and an 'hierarchical' effect on the other: the former being the process of contiguous spread which geographers have studied in some detail; the latter being a diffusion from larger to smaller places.

---

[1] A distinction well illustrated by Ryan and Gross (1943). The stages at which mass media are of great importance are the very early ones of 'awareness' and 'interest'. In the later stages of 'evaluation', 'trial' and eventual 'adoption' the role of personal contact through friends and neighbours becomes paramount. See, for example, Mansfield (1969, p. 129).

He argues (Hägerstrand 1966, p. 40) that the 'frontier of urban diffusion' will be found in the successive ranks of the hierarchy of towns:

The point of introduction in a new country is its primate city; sometimes some other metropolis. Then centres next in rank follow. Soon, however, this order is broken up and replaced by one where the neighbourhood effect dominates over the pure size succession.

The need to consider the importance of size of towns has therefore been recognized, but the unresolved problem is how best to combine the joint effects of both size and distance in studying the diffusion of urban innovations, since the two have largely been treated apart from each other. On the one hand there is a wealth of literature on spatial diffusion which argues that, through various forms of communication networks whose structures are influenced by distance, innovations are likely to spread outwards from one or more originating centre in a spatially-orderly fashion. On the other hand there is a somewhat less voluminous literature which argues that, for entrepreneurial rather than household innovations, diffusion will filter downwards through the size hierarchy of cities because of the importance of minimizing risk and the economic importance of the size of market area. Representative of this latter approach is Boon's (1967) development of a diffusion model which traces the spread of information through a rank-size distribution of towns, but which does not consider the spatial distribution of those places. Similar to this is Berry's (1972) study of the diffusion of television stations in the United States over the period 1940-68. Berry uses a regression framework which equally ignores spatial aspects and concentrates on city size.[1] Having shown that the date of adoption is strongly linked to the size of the adopting city, his regression models have, as independent variables, a number of estimates of the size of the urban areas and in addition a number of measures of certain individual city characteristics which appear to be important causes of disturbance in the relationship between date of adoption and size.

The pattern of innovation diffusion through an urban system might best be thought of, however, as a combination of both the distance and the size effects. Given a particular urban innovation, its spread within a system of towns might be expected to follow both the size hierarchy and a distance spread simultaneously. Boutiques might first blossom in London and soon after spread to Birmingham, Manchester, Liverpool and Leeds, but at the same time there is a greater likelihood of their spreading to Andover, Bishop's Stortford and Chelmsford than to Aberdeen, Blyth and Carlisle. The logic for the hierarchical spread would be in terms of lessening the economic risks in a larger potential

---

[1] Of the independent variables, the only one which acts as a form of surrogate for distance effects is the population potential of each city. Population potential — being calculated as a spatially continuous variable — does incorporate an element of location into Berry's regression formulation, but only in the most indirect fashion.

market; and, for the 'neighbourhood' spread, the logic would be in terms of imitation of the innovation by proximate places which would have a higher probability of exposure to it. Two studies have attempted to follow this approach by combining both size and distance elements into models of diffusion in sets of urban places. Hudson's (1969) attempt takes as its starting point the formal geometry of Christaller's central-place pattern; he postulates a set of m levels of centres in which centres at the jth level are spaced apart at distances of $q^{i/2}$ where j equals $(i + 1)$ and i runs from 0 to $(m - 1)$. A town P_1 is then said to L-dominate a place P_2 through a chain of L information links. When L equals 1·0 (in other words when a message travels directly from P_1 to P_2 in only one step) P_1 is said to directly dominate P_2. The likelihood of a message passing from P_1 to P_2 is given by the expression for the demographic force of P_1 on P_2 and, since this involves both the distance between the two places and their respective population sizes, this expression subsumes the two aspects which we need to resolve together. It argues that, with respect to some originating centre which is a potential source of messages about an innovation, a place with a large population which is distant from the originating centre can be thought of as being equivalent to a smaller place which is closer to the origin. Thus the hierarchical and neighbourhood processes need not be thought of as separate and in such a central-place system one cannot think of a single type of jth-level place, since the length of the chain which links it to a potential source of messages has also to be taken into account. Hudson then assumes that each place which has heard the message about an innovation then tells every other place which it directly dominates. The process can be represented by a matrix which records the first-hearing times of places in which the columns are the order of the centre and the rows represent time. The result of the process outlined above is to produce column vectors which are binomially distributed and which therefore cumulatively produce a logistic curve of 'knowers' in the total population of places and also that the means and standard deviations of these column vectors[1] are functions solely of the parameters of the initial geometry of the central-place system – the spacing constant, q, and the number of levels in the hierarchy, m.

Pederson's (1970) model draws upon only slightly different sources since it is developed in terms of gravity ideas and the rank-size rule which give him a distance and hierarchical effect respectively. He assumes that once a place has adopted an innovation it will begin to send out messages about it to other places which have not adopted, at a rate which is determined by the gravity equation:

$$I_{i,j} = k(P_i P_j) . d_{i,j}^{-b}; \qquad [5.2]$$

where $I_{i,j}$ is the amount of information sent from place i to place j; and where P and d are population and distance respectively. The total amount of information

[1] These values gauge the respective strengths of the size effects and the distance effects: the wider the scatter and the closer the means of the columns, the less important will be the effect of town size.

received by a place which has not adopted is then simply the summation of all such flows from towns which have adopted since the time of their adoption. Thus, at time t_n, the total information at place P_i will be:

$$\sum_{j=1}^{i-1} [(k . P_i P_{j.m} . d_{i.j}^{-b}) . (t_n - t_m)] ; \qquad [5.3]$$

where $P_{j.m}$ is the population of place j which adopted at date m. Towns will adopt once the fund of information has reached some critical level and will then subsequently emit messages themselves to places which have not adopted. Pederson's model thus combines the size and distance effects in a single form similar to that of Hudson. In Pederson's case, it can be seen that both the size and distance processes are limiting cases of the model which are approached as the exponent b tends to zero and infinity respectively. This is seen very clearly if the city-size distribution is approximated by the rank-size expression $P_i = P_1 . r_i^{-a}$, in which r_i is the rank of the ith town. If this expression is substituted in equation [5.2] we get the following:

$$I_{i.j} = k P_1^2 . r_i^{-a} . r_j^{-a} . d_{i.j}^{-b} \qquad [5.4]$$

Here one can conceive of the ranks r_i and r_j as hierarchical distances between places, exactly equivalent to the physical distances between them (fig. 5.2); and it can be seen that as the b term is made infinitely large physical distance becomes all-important in determining the nature of the diffusion process, whereas, as it approaches zero, it is the hierarchical distance which will dominate in determining the rate at which places receive messages. The applications of this model which are pursued by Pederson suggest conclusions about the determinants of the speed of innovation diffusions and about the shape of size distributions of cities, but do not consider the consequences of this link between innovations and urban growth upon the nature of urban growth processes.[1]

We have here some most pertinent ideas about the spread of urban innovations which consistently suggest that diffusion in a set of towns might follow a path both down the levels of the urban hierarchy and spreading outwards in space from places which have already adopted. While fitting such embryonic models to empirical data has still a very long way to go, it does seem that there is some agreement about the expected general form which urban

---

[1] On the latter he argues that once a town has adopted it will grow in size by a given percentage during each subsequent period of time. Starting from a central-place hierarchy of sizes he shows that the stepped size distribution will then be converted into a smoothed curve over time and that the shape of the curve is strongly influenced by the value of the distance term, b: with $b = 1.0$ a straight-line plot results; when $b > 1.0$ a concave curve (typical of a 'primate' size distribution) emerges.

diffusion might follow. It would be characterized as a process whereby simultaneously an innovation would spread along three levels: down the urban hierarchy of sizes; out from areas of high population potential to lower population potential; and, at a more local level, outwards in space from one centre to smaller centres adjacent or close to it (Berry and Horton 1970, p. 87). This process neatly accords with Hägerstrand's (1967b, pp. 7-8) picture of the network of contacts of individuals which can be seen at national, regional and local levels, but the rationale for the hierarchical spread derives both from the flow of information and, depending on the characteristics of the innovation concerned, the degree of risk associated with different market areas. The

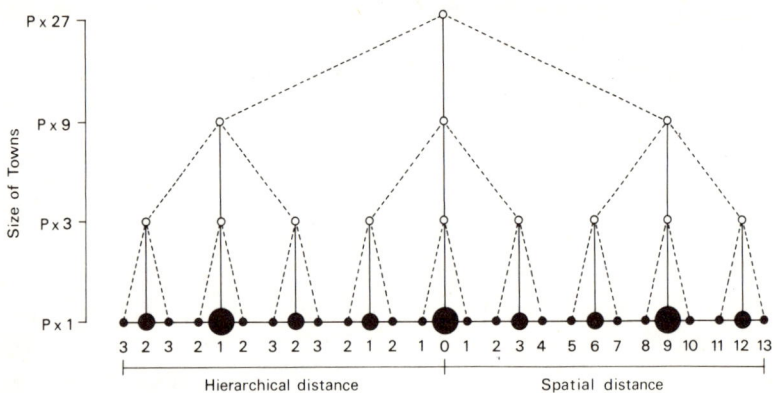

Figure 5.2   Diffusion in an urban system: hierarchical and spatial distance. *Source:* Pederson (1970)

respective importance of the hierarchical and the neighbourhood effects would therefore differ depending on the characteristics of the innovation. Those involving large economic risk or those in which technological constraints or scale economies favoured their adoption in large market areas would be determined more by hierarchical than by neighbourhood considerations.

If these ideas, albeit very roughly sketched, provide the material for an attractive model of innovation diffusion in a set of towns, to what extent do empirical data conform to the expected patterns? The difficulty in trying to answer this is, first, that tests of the fit of essentially probabilistic notions of this sort are notoriously difficult and also that, since we are trying to argue about urban growth in a nineteenth-century context, sufficiently detailed data are hard to come by. On the first point of testing the fit, this has long been a problem in all of the more well-established spatial diffusion work from Hägerstrand onwards. We have seen that Berry used a regression format to test the fit of the hierarchical spread of television stations and he found percentage explanations generally of the order of 60 per cent. This test, however, takes no account of the spatial patterning of the spread. Hudson simply tests his model in an aggregate and temporal fashion rather than at the level of individual places by looking at the curve of total hearings over time. Perhaps, in view of the problem of providing sensitive measures of fit for probabilistic models in space, one might simply look at patterns in a more purely qualitative fashion to see to what extent particular innovations appear both to show a general relationship to the size of towns and, at the same time, seem to spread out from larger centres to proximate smaller centres.[1]

On the question of data, there is a number of studies of the diffusion of technical innovations for the period of the industrial revolution. Among the more notable, with examples both from America and Britain, are studies of the diffusion of tinplate manufacture (Minchinton 1956), of Cornish pumping engines (Von Tunzelmann 1970), of iron technology (Walsh 1966), of the draper loom (Feller 1966) and of steam power (Temin 1966). But all of these studies consider the spatial dimension only incidentally. Pred (1966, pp. 106-10) provides another example in his study of the numbers of patents taken out in the United States for the three dates 1860, 1880 and 1900 in eleven cities which were to become the country's leading metropolitan centres and another five large, but declining, cities. He shows the general relationship between the numbers of patents and the size of the manufacturing population of each of the cities.[2] Perhaps the most directly relevant example, however, and one which looks explicitly at the spatial and hierarchical aspects of spread is Krim's (1967) study of the spread of urban tramways in the United States which shows very effectively the simultaneous operation of the three factors of hierarchical size,

---

[1] If one were to test this process in a more formal manner, a regression format would appear to be most appropriate. This would involve a series of regressions for successive time periods of the form $X = a + bY + cZ + e$; where X is date of adoption, Y is population size and Z is distance from the nearest town which had already adopted by the given date. This would, however, be far from satisfactory. Once the spatial element is added, the pattern of one period becomes partly dependent on that of the previous period and any deviation — even though in itself explicable in the probabilistic framework — will tend to be amplified. The empirical data discussed later in this chapter show the way in which innovations often spread densely throughout a particular region following adoption by the major regional centre. While the whole process can be described in terms of hierarchical and spatial diffusion, a formal test of 'goodness of fit' of this probabilistic expectation would require the incorporation of so much real-world data (for example, which of the various regional centres happened to adopt early in the sequence) that the test would rapidly become circular — a problem not uncommon in attempts to test probabilistic notions in situations involving spatial 'autocorrelation' (see Pred's comments, in his postscript in Hagerstrand 1967a, where he discusses this problem in relation to Morrill's work on the evolution of settlement patterns in Sweden).

[2] The fact that patents — which measure *inventiveness* rather than innovation — are taken out predominantly in urban rather than non-urban areas is discussed in, for example, Feller (1971).

population potential and distance decay which have been outlined as providing the controls of urban diffusion.

Given the very sparse number of studies which look at both spatial and hierarchical spread in sets of towns, it would be useful, before developing a model of the connection between the spread of innovations and the growth patterns of cities, to look at some examples which might illustrate the operation or lack of operation of our expected spread mechanism within nineteenth-century England and Wales. Since our argument is that technical innovations act in a cumulative fashion to boost the population growth of towns, it might appear that the best examples to study would be those which were explicitly connected with the major technical advances and industrial development of the industrial revolution. These might include the spread of the Boulton and Watt steam engine (see, for example, Lord 1923) of the late eighteenth and early nineteenth century; the spread of the major textile innovations or of those in iron and steel such as the open hearth or Bessemer processes; or the spread of the railway. Undoubtedly such innovations include the most important of what Rostow would call the 'leading sectors' behind the growth of the British economy, but they all tend to have a number of deficiencies as indicators of the way in which innovations in general might have diffused through the set of British towns. The technological innovations, for example, are specific to those particular places which practised, or which came to practise, the specific activity for which the innovations were relevant, so that the population of places 'at risk' would be specific to the particular innovation being considered. Railways suffer from a different drawback as a general indicator. The spread of railways undoubtedly had profound effects upon the growth of those towns which were part of the network,[1] as well as having more direct effects upon those places, such as Swindon or Darlington, which became major construction and servicing points for the railways themselves. But as a general indicator of diffusion amongst a set of towns the fact that railways are a two-dimensional rather than a one-dimensional phenomenon makes it difficult to characterize their spread amongst a set of towns which are one-dimensional points. The fact that a railway is built from London to Manchester, for example, means that points along the line will also 'adopt' the innovation if stations are built there, but the fact of their adoption is more contingent upon the characteristics of the terminal towns than upon their own.

Instead of looking at the major technological innovations we shall therefore

[1] For the midwestern United States in the period 1870-1900, Higgs (1969) uses multiple regression to test ideas about the growth of cities. One of his variables is the number of railway connections which a town has and he finds an 'ambiguous' relationship. He comments (pp. 374-5): 'Undoubtedly cities without rail connections stood little chance of growing substantially. But once a few railway lines had been secured, it by no means followed that procuring additional lines would guarantee further growth.' Railway connections, it might be argued, are necessary, but not sufficient elements in fostering urban growth.

look briefly at some selected examples of organizational entrepreneurial innovations. Specifically we shall look at three innovations which may, at first sight,
seem to form a rather motley collection: gas works and urban street lighting;
building societies and, in particular, Starr-Bowkett building societies; and
telephone exchanges. While a rather odd assortment of 'innovations', all three
had evident effects upon the internal functioning and, in the case of the
telephone, eventually upon the external relations of nineteenth-century towns.
None is explicitly connected with a particular type of town and, while none
could be considered a major manufacturing stimulus in the sense of Pred's model
of cumulative and circular causation, each can be considered a significant
entrepreneurial innovation which would fall within the scope of his secondary
multiplier effects. Certainly in the opinion of contemporaries, gas works and the
telephone were considered of some considerable importance to the way in which
towns functioned and, in a minor way, each would have effects upon a town's
population both in terms of the direct employment which they offered and,
perhaps more importantly, in terms of their spin-off effects on other types of
activity — both in terms of related industrial activities and of the general
attraction to migrants of towns which, having the innovations, were considered
more 'progressive' or more efficient. The building societies, as will be discussed,
were never a really major force in terms of the overall building activities of
nineteenth-century towns. The justification for looking at the pattern of their
diffusion is that, like the first two, building societies are *general* indicators of
entrepreneurial innovations, but, unlike the first two, they are an innovation
with very different economic implications in terms of the element of economic
risk involved in their adoption.

BUILDING SOCIETIES

Building societies are not the most obvious innovation with which to examine
our ideas about spatial and hierarchical diffusion. The housing market of the
nineteenth century was relatively little affected in quantitative terms by houses
built through such societies although Cleary (1965, pp. 286-9) estimates that as
many as one in every seven or eight houses built in the 1860s were built under
the auspices of or with money loaned by building societies.[1] Nevertheless, they

[1] Studies of individual towns give little quantitative indication of the relative contribution
of building societies to the housing market. They do, however, suggest that they had a more
than trivial effect. Church (1966, p. 263) notes that one of the hosiery manufacturers of
Nottingham borrowed money from building societies to build housing for his employees
towards the end of the nineteenth century. A number of the contributors to S. D.
Chapman's *The history of working-class housing* (1971) also suggest the impact of the
societies in specific towns: in Leeds the earliest back-to-back housing was built through
terminating building societies (p. 102); in Nottingham they appear not to have played a part
in early developments although 'money clubs' did (pp. 140-3); in Birmingham their effects
can be shown to be of some importance (pp. 235-9); and in Ebbw Vale they had the effect
of improving the standard of housing in the second half of the nineteenth century (p. 297).

did provide one source of capital for house building and their adoption may be taken as an index both of this and of the more general economic adventurousness of a town. They are also clearly entrepreneurial rather than household innovations in that the decision to start a society had in the nature of things to be undertaken communally and in the light of expectations about a sufficient number of individuals being interested to provide a relatively large and continuing flow of money into the funds from which loans were made. The way in which the knowledge of building society objectives and methods was spread also ties in with our ideas about the importance of communication networks, especially in the early years of the growth of the societies. Cleary (1965, pp. 9-10), for example, suggests that they developed out of the friendly societies which made provision for hardship and illness in a time of some general financial insecurity. The earliest of the building societies usually met in local inns and drew for their membership upon local patronage.[1] In such circumstances the spread of knowledge of the societies might be seen as being not only through the solicitors, accountants and other professional classes, who, in the early years, occasionally and, later, usually acted as the organizers, secretaries or initiators of the societies, but also through the face-to-face contacts of the members who participated in what were often relatively informal organizations. To this extent one has a nice interplay between the size-of-market aspects determining the potential number of members on the one hand and the private communication fields which provide the rationale of spatial diffusion models on the other.

Easing the provision of housing for the less affluent was the underlying, if not always the real, motive in the foundation of building societies. The elements of gambling and investment which were widespread in the later years of the century were not always absent in the early years, but were certainly far less frequent. And even though few of the societies drew upon the really poor for their membership, they did provide a means of saving and thrift and, for some, of access to housing amongst the relatively better-paid of the artisan classes and of what would now be called the lower ranks of the middle class. The ostensible aims of the societies always included the provision of housing or of capital for housing, but the means by which these objectives were furthered were very varied and underwent considerable changes as the century progressed. The early societies usually worked on some variant of a plan involving the payment of subscriptions (of the order of 10s per month — no mean sum in a population a

---

[1] The continuation of the connection with local inns is seen, even at late dates, by the names of many of the societies which were derived from the place where they met. Societies founded in the north in particular suggest the frequency with which inns were the meeting places especially of the terminating societies: in Bury there were the following building societies — the British Oak Inn, the Stanley Arms Inn; in Huddersfield, the Fleece Inn, the Queen's Head Inn, the Ramsden Arms, the Sir John Falstaff, the Temperance Hotel and the White Hart Inn; in Manchester, the Salford Arms, the Mitre, the Golden Oak amongst others; in Oldham, the Hart and Feathers, the Black Swan Inn.

large proportion of which earned less than 20s per week)[1] until the fund was large enough to have provided each shareholder a house, at which point the society would be broken up. They were thus all *terminating* societies which, even if successful, had relatively limited life-spans. Some of the societies themselves arranged the building of the houses. There were obviously many difficulties involved in such a scheme. First, the process could be a very long one since, as Cleary notes, with twenty members paying 10s a month it would be almost ten months before a first advance of £100 could be paid and almost as long before the second £100 advance would be possible even though later, with the interest on swelling funds, advances would come more rapidly. Second, the fact that fixed subscriptions had to be paid until the termination of the society made them very inflexible as regards membership. After the early years, the heavy backlog of subscriptions made it almost prohibitive for new members to join existing societies so that additional members could only readily be incorporated by the founding of successive societies so that the funds of a second society could be augmented from the reserve funds of the first (Cleary 1965, p. 56). Thus one finds long sequences of offspring societies formed in cascade from their parent: the first of a society called the Birmingham Building Society was formed in 1842, a second and third in 1845, a fourth in 1846 and a fifth in 1848; the first of a Manchester society, the Manchester and Salford Building Society, was formed in 1843, a second in 1845, a third in 1849, a fourth in 1851 and a fifth in 1853 (Brooks' *Directory* 1855). A third problem was connected with the provision of housing by societies where they built houses themselves. Problems inevitably arose in providing identical houses for members who had subscribed, or were to subscribe, equal amounts; the member getting a house early obviously had a great advantage over a member who got one much later. The first of these problems could, of course, be met by the society borrowing money, which helped to accelerate the process of providing returns for the subscriptions. The third problem was eased by the societies disengaging themselves from the provision of housing *per se*, but, even with the relative security afforded by the legal recognition of building societies under the 1836 Act, the terminating societies were still faced with considerable problems in ensuring regular payments of subscriptions and in equalizing the returns to their members. It was out of such problems that the idea of permanent societies grew, in the 1840s. The permanent society aimed to enable members to take out shares at any time during its existence and to give the borrower of money a fixed period over which to make repayments so that the total sum to be paid could readily be calculated. Thus advances for fixed terms of five, ten, fifteen years

[1] Estimates of weekly wages taken from Baxter's 1867 classification in *National Income* are given in Best (1971, pp. 94-9). The same source suggests that the average annual income-per-head in England and Wales was £32. Figures such as these must, of course, be treated with some circumspection.

and so forth could be offered in place of societies having to demand sub-scriptions for an indefinite period until it wound up. Cleary (1965, p. 48) and Price (1958, p. 129) differ in their attribution of the originator of the permanent principle, but the fact of the rapid growth in the popularity of permanent societies in the period from 1845 when the Metropolitan Equitable was formed is beyond dispute.[1]

If the introduction of the permanent principle and the growth of permanent societies was the first major change in the rapidly altering aims and principles of the building society movement, the second was the more conscious introduction of the element of gambling and pure finance which came in the 1870s and 1880s. Gambling had always played a part in the movement as can be seen from the early tontines. Cleary (1965, pp. 10-11) quotes the very early case of the St John's Street Tontine formed in Swansea in 1791. It had 100 members who subscribed for five years to build five houses which were then to be let. The income from these houses was to be shared amongst the surviving members until their number was reduced to ten. At that point the houses were to be sold and the proceeds divided between the ten remaining members, or they were to continue to be let until only five members remained and the houses would be allocated to them by casting lots. Ballot societies, which grew and flourished much later in the nineteenth century, and of which the Starr-Bowkett society was a representative type, made appeal to the same sort of gambling spirit as such early tontines and in certain instances were far removed both in spirit and in practice from direct involvement with housing in any way.

Briefly this sets the background to the early developments of the building society movement. In looking at the way in which it spread through time and over space, one is severely handicapped by the intractible nature of the data. By their very nature many of the societies were of very short duration. The average life of the terminating societies may have been of the order of ten years, but many were wound up very soon after their foundation. The records of societies were also very haphazard as the Royal Commission on Friendly and Building Societies (*Second Report* 1872) found when it tried to collect material on their growth and operation. There was no central register of societies and, even though the local clerks of the peace in England and Wales held copies of the rules of the societies once they had been certified, the information supplied by the clerks to the Royal Commission was very inadequate since it failed to distinguish between the dates of foundation of new societies and the alteration in the rules of existing societies. This is a recurring and serious problem in trying

---

[1] The spread of permanent societies indirectly helped open the way for the development of Freehold Land Societies which grew out of the agitation for reform of the suffrage in the 1840s and aimed to help people to buy sufficient property to qualify for parliamentary voting rights. The connection of influential figures such as Cobden and Bright with these aims in turn helped to give respectability to the principle of permanence upon which the land societies operated.

Table 5.1   *Early building societies*

(*a*) *Geographical distribution*

Region	Date of first society	Societies
West Midlands	1775	Birmingham (1775, 1781(3), 1785(3), 1791(3), 1794, pre-1795); Dudley (1779, 1786, pre-1795(2)); Rowley Regis (1792); Wednesbury (pre-1820); Netherton (1821); Kidderminster (1822)
West Yorkshire	1785	Leeds (1785, 1787, pre-1814); Horbury (1793); Bingley (1806); Mirfield (1806); Skipton (1806, 1807, 1823); Bradford (1823, 1824, 1825(6)); Slaithwaite (1825)
South-east Lancashire	1792	Droylesden (1792); Cheadle (1806); Manchester (1817, 1820(2), 1821(2), 1822, 1823, 1824)
North Lancashire	1793	Preston (1793(2), 1822); Longridge (1798, 1822); Burnley (1799, 1815, 1820)
Potteries	1807	Burslem (1807); Tunstall (1816); Leek (1824)
Scotland	1808	Glasgow (1808); Selkirk (1815); Kilmarnock (1824)
London	1809	Greenwich (1809)
West Lancashire	1818	Liverpool (1818, 1825)
Cumbria	1824	Carlisle (1824)
North East	1825	Gateshead (1825(2))
North Wales	1825	Caernarvon (1825(2)); Bangor (1826); Pentir (1827); Eryri (1827)

(*b*) *Dates of formation*

	Pre-1780	1785	1790	1795	1800	1805	1810	1815	1820	1825
Number of societies	2	6	2	12	2	0	8	3	8	27

Note: Numbers in brackets after dates in table (a) show cases where more than one society was formed in a single year.
Sources: Price (1958), Cleary (1965), Beresford (1971).

to assemble material on the date of foundation of societies. For example, after the introduction of permanent societies, many of the terminating societies transformed themselves into permanent ones. The Home Office list of societies collected in 1859 (*Parliamentary Papers* 1859, XXIII)[1] shows a number of

[1] Fewer than 200 societies are recorded since there was no compulsion upon societies to make returns.

societies which changed their status in this way in the period of the early 1850s. The Great Grimsby and North Lincs Permanent Building and Investment Society had originally been founded as a temporary society in 1847 and became permanent in 1851; the Deal Walmer and East Kent Society was founded as a terminating society in 1846 and became permanent in 1852; the Industrial and Mutual Society of London was formed as terminating in 1852 and became permanent in 1857. In using the date of foundation given in various sources, the foundation date given may sometimes be either the date of the original foundation or the date of a change in the composition, or perhaps simply the name, of a society.

We can, nevertheless, make some cursory study of the spread of societies by using data on the dates of foundation gathered from a number of sources. Those used here are primarily the various directories issued from the 1850s onwards by Brooks, Rouse, Kent and Braund and the *Building Societies' Gazette* and the returns issued in Parliamentary Papers by the Registrar of Friendly Societies with whom a majority of building societies was registered. By amalgamating the various listings and dates of foundation provided by these sources one can derive, for the middle period of the 1850s — a time at which the movement had spread widely throughout the country — what would appear to be a reasonable estimate of the distribution of the societies at a point in time.[1]

For the very early period after the foundation of the first society — Ketley's Building Society founded in Birmingham in 1775 — the picture is particularly hazy since, even though Price (1958, pp. 59-67) produces a list of sixty-three societies known to have been formed up to 1825 to which Cleary (1965, p. 283) adds a further six, there must have been many more than this founded in total, about which nothing can be said.[2] It can be seen from table 5.1 however, that the spread of those very early societies about which there are data suggests the very strong regionalization of the diffusion. Starting in the West Midlands, the growth of societies was restricted very largely to the industrial areas of the Black Country, the Potteries, the North West and the West Riding. Indeed, the first known society in London dates from 1809, over thirty years later than Ketley's.

---

[1] It would have been possible to use the dates of foundation to look at the spread of societies over time, but the data are not sufficiently reliable to allow one to place any great confidence in the patterns so produced.

[2] Details of an additional society formed before 1825 are given by Beresford (1971, p. 102). This was the Crackenthorpe Garden Building Club which built back-to-back houses in Leeds and whose articles of agreement were drawn up on 3 November 1787. That there were many other early societies for which details are unknown is suggested by references to societies from Lancashire and Newcastle being prominent in the agitation which eventually led to the 1836 Act (Price 1958, pp. 80-3). These two areas do not feature as prominently as might be expected in the list of those societies for which details are known. Similarly, in the framing of the 1836 Act, constant reference is made to societies being formed 'on the Liverpool plan' which suggests a greater early development of societies in that town than is suggested by the data of table 5.1.

While the data are incomplete one can make some tentative observations on the early pattern of spread which is revealed. First there is a distinct regional bunching which could be interpreted as a reflection of the operation of some form of 'neighbourhood' effect. This can be seen in the bunching of societies in the Preston-Longridge area in the north of Lancashire, but is perhaps most clearly seen in North Wales in the period after 1825. In October 1825 the Caernarvon Building Society was formed and in the two subsequent years four further societies sprang up all within the Caernarvon area: in July 1826, the Bangor Benefit Building Society; in February 1827, the Pentir Building Society; in October 1827, the Caernarvon Union Building Society; and, also in October 1827, the Eryri Building Society (Cleary 1965, p. 283). In the light of the very localized nature of the membership and the generally informal manner in which such societies operated, it would not seem unreasonable to suggest that word-of-mouth transmission of knowledge of their operation and of their objectives would lead to a strong distance-decay element in their spatial spread which would help to account for the pattern of very strong regional clustering amongst these very early societies. Second, it is of no little interest that, where societies 'penetrated' a region for the first time, it was usually to the major, or one of the largest, towns within the region. Not only did they start in Birmingham, but the first society in Yorkshire was in Leeds; in the Potteries the first was in Burslem; and in Lancashire, Manchester, Liverpool, Burnley and Preston each fell within the ranks of the larger cities of their respective regions and all had early societies. While not trying to read too great a significance into the data, it would appear that the twin ideas of spatial contiguity and of inter-regional space jumping to the larger regional centres would adequately explain much of the diffusion suggested by these early societies.

When we turn to later periods after the 1836 Act, the number of societies has grown considerably although the data problems are still severe. Estimating the total growth in the number of societies is made difficult by the problems of registration discussed above, and the various estimates of total numbers vary widely. Contemporary commentators give estimates which vary up to as many as 7,000 in 1867 (Scratchley 1867). Price (1958, p. 237) suggests that by the centenary of the movement, in 1875, between 6,500 and 7,000 societies had been founded. A more cautious and justified estimate, based on the figures of the 1871 Royal Commission, is that by Cleary (1965, pp. 44 and 286-9) who suggests that a total of 3,500 societies were founded between the passing of the 1836 Act and 1869 and that at any one time during this period the maximum number in existence was unlikely to have exceeded 1,500 by any substantial margin. These figures certainly accord with the contemporary directory data which, while far from complete, suggest that figures of this order of magnitude seem reasonable. The data in table 5.2(a) are based on compilations from various sources and show the dates of foundation of societies which were in existence in 1853. Given the uncertainty surrounding the material, it is better to consider

Table 5.2 *Terminating and permanent building societies in England and Wales, 1853*

A. DATES OF ESTABLISHMENT

Date	No. of provincial societies		No. of metropolitan societies		Tot
	Terminating	Permanent	Terminating	Permanent	
pre-1843	18		2		2(
1843	4		18		2?
1844	14		19		3?
1845	20	1	65	2	8?
1846	46	1	56	0	10?
1847	36	5	42	2	8?
1848	29	4	15	5	5?
1849	25	9	10	2	4?
1850	38	12	10	6	6?
1851	21	16	14	7	5?
1852	27	12	13	3	5?
1853	28	14	21	4	6?
pre-1850	59	2	1	0	6?
Date unknown	96	5	81	4	18(
Total	478	81	367	35	944

B. GEOGRAPHICAL DISTRIBUTION

Number of societies

Region	Terminating	Permanent
North East	30	2
Cumbria	8	0
North West	206	13
West Yorkshire	56	8
East	16	5
North Midlands	8	2
West Midlands	48	11
South Midlands	9	0
South East	39(406)	16(51)
South	14	8
South West	29	12
Wales and Border	5	3
South Wales	10	1
Total	478	81

Notes
1. For the composition of the regions see notes to table 4.2.
2. Under the South East, the figures in brackets include the totals for London and the South East.
Sources: Rouse (1853); Brooks (1854 and 1855); Kent and Braund (1884); *Parliamentary Papers* 1859, XXIII.

simply the snap-shot picture of the total numbers of societies at a given date rather than drawing inferences about the details of the temporal and spatial spread of societies from the dates of their foundation.[1] Table 5.2(b) suggests that, by the early 1850s London's late start had certainly not prevented an eventual blossoming of societies within the Metropolis and, indeed, the 1840s saw a very marked boom in the foundation of London societies. The terminal date which has been selected, 1853, postdates the period at which permanent societies had begun to develop and their expansion after 1845, especially in the South East, is noticeable. The great majority of permanent societies was found in southern England and, indeed, while terminating societies continued well into the last quarter of the nineteenth century in the north, and especially in Lancashire, the growth of permanent societies continued to become especially marked in the southern and eastern counties.[2]

The expansion of societies over time shows a discontinuous expansion in numbers. We have already seen the rather uneven expansion of the very early decades when the initial growth accelerated only very slowly, almost stopped during the Napoleonic Wars, and then accelerated markedly in the 1820s. Likewise in the later period there is some evidence of variations in the rate of expansion — with the 1840s, 1860s and 1880s being decades of more-than-usual expansion. When we look at the distribution in 1853 (fig. 5.3), it can be seen that societies had spread widely throughout the country. The particular interest in the diffusion however is the relationship with the rank size of towns. Table 5.3 plots the spread of societies against the set of towns ranked in order of their populations in 1851. The percentage of places with societies falls regularly as one moves to successively lower ranks of towns and the average number of societies in towns with societies also falls with decreasing town size. Of the top thirty towns only two places were without either a terminating or permanent society. One was Bath and this omission is in itself somewhat misleading since no fewer than four of the societies based in Bristol included both 'Bristol' and 'Bath' in their titles. The other place was Merthyr Tydfil — an anomaly which may arise as much because of the generous definition of the population of the 'town' as because of the inappropriateness of the process of hierarchical diffusion.[3] It would appear that all of the high-ranking towns in the middle of

[1] The coverage and accuracy of the data appear understandably to be best for the metropolitan area and worst for Wales and the North East. It is difficult to believe, for example, that some of the towns in which early building societies developed — such as in the Caernarvon area or Dudley in Worcestershire — did not have further societies founded in them in the period up to 1853.

[2] The geographical distribution of permanent and terminating societies for a later date, 1873, is given by Cleary (1965, p. 46) and shows the continuing preponderance of permanent societies in the metropolitan area.

[3] On the difficulty of defining Merthyr, see Davies (1926) who uses census figures and interpolates smooth waves of population growth on the basis of patterns of migration and economic development in the area. As was noted above (p. 48), the amorphous valley towns of South Wales present quite intractible problems of definition.

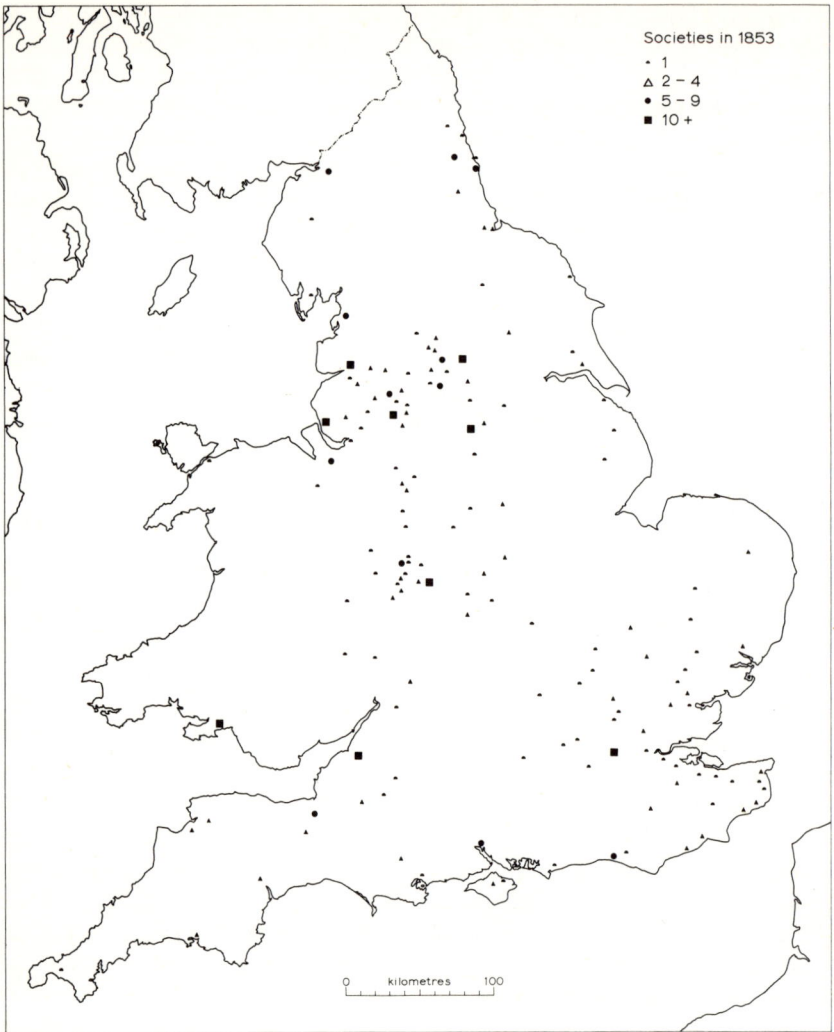

Figure 5.3   Terminating and permanent building societies in England and Wales, 1853

the century were very likely to have adopted building societies even though the total number of places with societies included also a large number of small places with only one or a few societies in addition to the large towns some of which, like Manchester with no fewer than ninety, had very large numbers. It is also interesting to note that in regions in which there is a low density of societies almost invariably one finds that the early societies in the area were in the major towns which would thus appear to lead the way in the pattern of spatial diffusion: this is true, for example, of East Anglia where Norwich had societies; of the Nottingham-Derby region where the only known societies were in the two county towns; of Leicestershire where again the county town had societies; of the Hampshire basin where Southampton and Portsmouth had societies; of the North East where Middlesbrough, Newcastle and Sunderland were represented; and in South Wales where Swansea, no doubt benefiting from its long

Table 5.3 *Hierarchical diffusion of terminating and permanent building societies, 1853*

Towns ranked by 1851 population	Total towns in each group	Towns with building society in 1853 No.	%	Total no. of societies	Average no. of societies per adopter
1 ⎫				402	(402·0)
2–10 ⎭	10	10	100·0	223	22·3
11–30	20	18	90·0	71	3·9
31–60	30	19	63·3	57	3·0
61–100	40	19	47·5	41	2·2
101–150	50	21	42·0	41	2·0
151–210	60	19	31·6	26	1·4
211–280	70	12	17·1	17	1·4
281–360	80	16	20·0	23	1·5
361–450	90	5	5·5	7	1·4
451–521	71	5	7·0	5	1·0
places < 2,500		27		31	1·1

connection with early forms of investment societies, had as many as eleven building societies. While such evidence is by no means as convincing as that which might be produced by a dynamic analysis which the poor data forbid, it is nevertheless suggestive of a process whereby the largest regional centres, those high in the rank order of towns, first adopt the innovation in question.

There is, too, some rather elusive evidence of the proximity effect, the second of our diffusion principles. It is this second process which provides the long tail of smaller towns which had societies. There is, for example, a particularly dense spread of societies in the South East spreading out of London. Almost all of the places in Kent[1] with populations of over 2,500 are represented by societies and the same is true of a large proportion of those towns in Essex lying close to London. Similarly, of the very small places which had societies — places so small that at no time during the period 1801-1911 did their populations rise above

[1] It was, of course, in the coastal towns of Kent that rapid urban growth rates were found during most of the decades of the nineteenth century.

2,500 to qualify them as 'towns' by our definition — an overwhelming proportion was found within the wider ambit of the Metropolis: such places included Amersham, Beaconsfield and Cheddington in Buckingham, Battle in Kent, Dunmow and Manningtree in Essex and Eaton Bray in Bedfordshire. Drawing inferences about the importance of spread effects from such cross-sectional evidence is obviously fraught with peril, but the inferences are certainly supported, frail as the ground may be. And a further independent strand of support is provided by the tendency — evident in the distribution of 1853, but much more apparent in the later spread of the 1860s — for the permanent societies, as distinct from the terminating ones, to be found much more densely developed in the areas both in and around the Metropolis than in the northern parts of England and Wales.

STARR-BOWKETT BUILDING SOCIETIES

The notion that the two principles of hierarchical diffusion and more localized spread go some considerable way in describing the diffusion of building societies can be looked at in more detail in the history of the Starr-Bowkett building societies. The history both of the originators and of the rise and fall of the Starr-Bowkett societies has the curious air of frenetic tragi-comedy which pervades so many Victorian enterprises. They boomed over a period of two decades to a growing accompaniment of dubious financial machinations and eventually were outlawed leaving a legacy which was neither undeniably bad nor demonstrably good. Bowkett certainly appears to have had the admirable intention of helping the lower-paid groups to have access to housing in his initial elaboration of his scheme and the later, and somewhat equivocal, involvement of R. B. Starr seems to have caused him some dismay. Bowkett's scheme was first advanced in 1843. It involved the formation of a society in which members paid subscriptions of $9\frac{1}{2}$d per week and at the end of a period were to draw lots for an interest-free advance to be secured by a mortgage on house property, the winner of the draw subsequently paying back both his subscription and a repayment on his advance so as to clear the loan over a period of about ten years (Bowkett 1850). The continuing flow of subscriptions together with repayments would enable subsequent ballots for further advances to be held with increasing frequency until all members would have had an advance and any surplus accruing from fines and defaulting would then be repaid to the members. A certain number of Bowkett's societies were formed in the 1840s (Tompkins 1845, p. 301), but his 'Ninepenny-halfpenny' societies had only a limited success partly owing no doubt to the familiar problems of the terminating societies: the long period involved before the successful termination of the societies and the consequent temptation for those unsuccessful in the early draws to withdraw their subscriptions; and the unequal advantage accruing to those who made the earlier successful draws. Their limited success must also have owed something to the hostile reception generally given to the principle of his societies. The great burgeoning of Bowkett's principle came very much later and in the hands not of Bowkett but of Richard B. Starr who made alterations to the rules which he then copyrighted (Starr 1878). Starr's own return from the enterprise came, with increasing profit, from the fees which he charged to the local secretary and the solicitor and surveyor of the societies. The particular attraction to potential members in Starr's scheme appears to have been the opportunity which it offered for purely financial gain in a gambling context. The goal of a loan on the security of property was a valuable asset which could be sold and, as Starr altered his rules in 1877 so as to force members who had been successful in the balloting but who wished to dispose of their appropriation, to sell it to the society itself, the society could then, if it so wished, become a simple lottery in which money for housing never changed hands (Cleary 1965, p. 107). Increasingly, gamblers rather than prospective home owners appear to have played a larger part in the balloting and the increasing publicity afforded by innumerable court actions against Starr and his obvious financial success in the scheme attracted imitators in the form of a rash of other balloting societies which grew rapidly in the 1880s until, with the Building Societies Act of 1894, balloting was made illegal in future societies and the further formation of new balloting societies was abruptly checked.

In tracing the spread of the Starr-Bowkett societies, details of which have been taken from directory sources and from Parliamentary Papers, one is helped enormously by the fact that, since they were centrally controlled under the copyright of Starr, as societies were formed their sequential number was incorporated into their title. It appears to be impossible to discover the exact nature of the founding of the societies since, although copies of Starr's rule books exist, no record has been discovered of the procedure by which he founded or attracted new societies.[1] It is reasonable to assume that he himself must have canvassed for the formation of new societies as well as being approached by potentially interested groups wishing to start societies. Whether this involved his travelling from place to place for custom is not clear although it appears to have been not unlikely. So successful was his business in the 1880s indeed that he claimed to have employed fifteen people to aid him in the promotion of societies (Cleary 1965, p. 107).

If we take it that the number allotted to each society is the sequential order of foundation of that society the difficulty of attributing a precise date to its formation is obviated. This has great advantages since there is some difficulty in fixing such dates since not all societies were registered with the Chief Registrar

---

[1] For example, a pass book of the 433rd Starr-Bowkett Society, registered in 1881 and founded in Southampton, is in the Southampton City Record Office (ref. D/PSR/66/1). Papers of either Starr or Bowkett have not been discovered.

of Friendly Societies and, of those which were, not all were registered immediately after their foundation. Starr claimed that the first society was formed in London in 1862 (Cleary 1965, p. 105) and the subsequent progress seems to have been very rapid: the first 150 societies seem to have been founded by 1874 and there was a spate of registrations after the 1874 Act so that at least 200 had been registered by 1876 and over 700 by 1885.[1] Starr claimed that the 999th was formed in 1891. We are, however, less interested in the impossible task of trying to trace a precise time-curve of formations than of plotting what one can of the spatial spread of the societies and for this purpose the numbers of the societies have been used. Taking the first 600 societies to be formed – a number which covers the period over which the majority of new places which

Table 5.4   *Data on Starr–Bowkett building societies*

Society numbers	Total with data	England and Wales		Scotland and Ireland
		London	Provincial	
1– 50	26	26	–	–
51–100	28	27	1	–
101–150	29	22	7	–
151–200	41	21	20	–
201–250	49	21	28	–
251–300	50	19	31	–
301–350	49	11	38	–
351–400	49	15	34	–
401–450	47	9	35	3
451–500	46	10	35	1
501–550	50	17	30	3
551–600	50	13	34	3

Sources: Kent and Braund (various dates); *Parliamentary Papers* (various dates); Building Societies Gazette (1874).

formed societies had founded their first society – details have been traced for all but eighty-five of the societies. Seventy-four of those which have not been traced were in the early period up to the first 160 societies at a time when, as table 5.4 shows, the majority of societies was still being formed in London. One can be reasonably confident that, since our interest is in the date of a town's first society, these omissions are less serious than might at first sight appear. The societies are plotted in figs 5.4 to 5.9 which show the locations of existing and newly-created societies in sequence from the first 200 up to the 600th society.

[1] These figures are based on entries in the directory sources and in *Parliamentary Papers*: the directory for 1874 notes the 144th society; the date of registration of the 212th is given as 1876; and Kent and Braund's 1885 directory notes the 734th society.

Table 5.5   *Hierarchical diffusion of Starr–Bowkett building societies*

Towns ranked by 1881 population	Total towns in each group	No. of places adopting up to the Nth society					% of places adopting up to the Nth society				
		200th	*300th*	*400th*	*500th*	*600th*	*200th*	*300th*	*400th*	*500th*	*600th*
1– 10	10	3	7	9	10	10	30·0	70·0	90·0	100·0	100·0
11– 30	20	3	7	14	18	18	15·0	23·3	70·0	90·0	90·0
31– 60	30	6	12	18	23	25	20·0	40·0	60·0	76·7	83·3
61–100	40	3	10	18	23	24	7·5	25·0	45·0	57·5	60·0
101–150	50	2	11	16	21	28	4·0	22·0	32·0	42·0	56·0
151–210	60	—	1	5	10	12	—	1·7	8·3	16·7	20·0
211–280	70	—	3	5	11	17	—	4·3	7·1	15·7	24·3
281–360	80	2	3	3	5	9	2·5	3·8	3·8	6·2	11·3
361–450	90	1	2	3	6	10	1·1	2·2	3·3	6·6	11·1
451–550	100	1	1	3	5	6	1·0	1·0	3·0	5·0	6·0
551–650	110	—	—	2	2	3	—	—	1·8	1·8	2·7
651–749	89	—	—	—	—	3	—	—	—	—	3·4
Places less than 2,500		—	1	2	4	7	—	—	—	—	—

The two processes of hierarchical filtering down the ranks of the size array of towns and of outward spatial spread to local towns are clearly apparent. Some idea of the strength of the hierarchical filtering can be got by considering the relationship with the size rank of towns in 1881. Table 5.5 shows that the pattern of diffusion follows the size hierarchy even though there is a wide scatter of early adoptions in small towns. The percentages of adoptions falls with some regularity as one progresses to groups of smaller towns. Equally, the average number of societies in adopting towns declines with smaller town sizes (table 5.6).

Table 5.6   *Average number of Starr–Bowkett societies for towns adopting by the 600th society*

Towns ranked by 1881 population	No. of towns with society	Total no. of societies	Average no. of societies
1	1	209	(209·0)
2– 10	9	52	5·8
11– 30	18	49	2·7
31– 60	25	45	1·8
61–100	24	35	1·5
101–150	28	37	1·3
151–210	12	15	1·3
211–280	17	20	1·2
281–360	9	10	1·1
361–450	10	10	1·0
451–550	6	6	1·0
551–650	3	4	1·3
651–749	3	3	1·0
Places < 2,500	7	7	1·0

The succession of maps suggests the spatial sequence of this diffusion. Up to the 100th society, the spread consisted of a multiplication within London and the one society found outside, the 94th, was formed in nearby Kingston-on-Thames. The spread out into the provinces began with the second hundred societies; with the 141st at Northampton, the 157th at Southampton, the 169th at Hanley in the Potteries, the 178th at Coventry, the 186th at Norwich, the 180th at Colchester, the 193rd at Great Yarmouth, and the 198th at Liverpool. All of these places were the largest or large towns within their regions. However, in addition to this spill-over down the ranks of the regional hierarchy, the density of societies within the metropolitan area as a whole shows a marked thickening. Not only did societies multiply within London, but many of the smaller proximate towns adopted the Starr-Bowkett innovation. The list includes not only the larger places such as Brighton, Maidstone, the Medway towns and

Existing Society

New Society

Appropriate figures
for London:
53
43

Figure 5.4   Starr-Bowkett societies in England and Wales: spatial spread of the
1st to the 200th society

Canterbury, but also a further two societies at Kingston and new ones at
Brentwood, Bishop's Stortford and Cheshunt.

In the sequence of societies from the 201st to the 250th, the same two
simultaneous processes can be seen. New regional centres make their appearance;
Birmingham, Sheffield and Manchester. At the same time outward spread within
already-colonized regions either continues, as in the south-east and eastern
regions, or, as is most clearly seen in the Potteries, new clusters of local towns

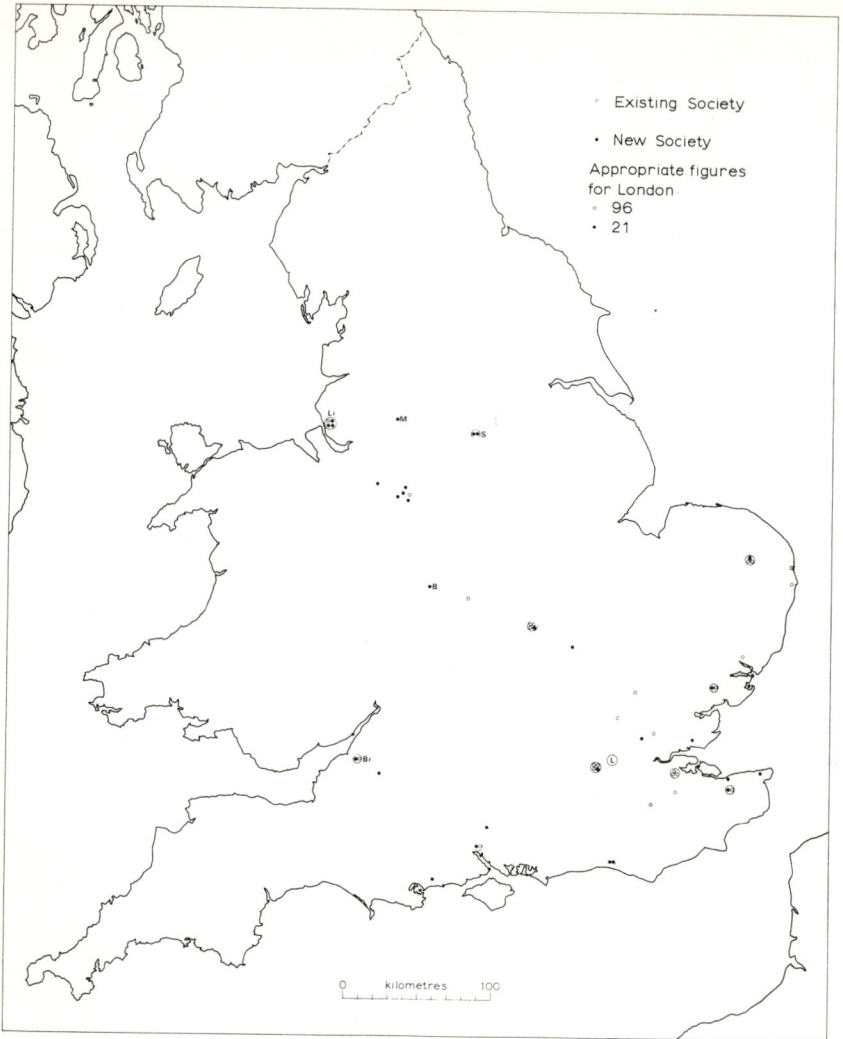

Figure 5.5   Starr-Bowkett societies in England and Wales: spatial spread of the 201st to the 250th society

adopt following the lead of a regional centre. In the period of the 251st to the 300th this process of local infilling is taken up in Lancashire and in the Black Country with new societies being formed in the smaller towns to join the established ones in the regional centres of Liverpool, Manchester and Birmingham. At the same time as this localized spread, hierarchical diffusion can be seen in the appearance of the first society in yet a further region – in the textile towns of the West Riding – with the founding of two societies in Bradford. In

Figure 5.6 Starr-Bowkett societies in England and Wales: spatial spread of the 251st to the 300th society

the next sequence, from the 301st to the 350th societies, the process of colonization within Lancashire continues and further new regions are freshly opened-up with societies being formed in the regional capitals. The North East first appears with Sunderland in the coalfield area and Stockton in the Teesside area; South Wales appears with Cardiff and Newport; and the south-west peninsula is first colonized, not through Plymouth or Exeter, but the third-largest of the Devonshire towns, Torquay, which lay in the midst of the belt of

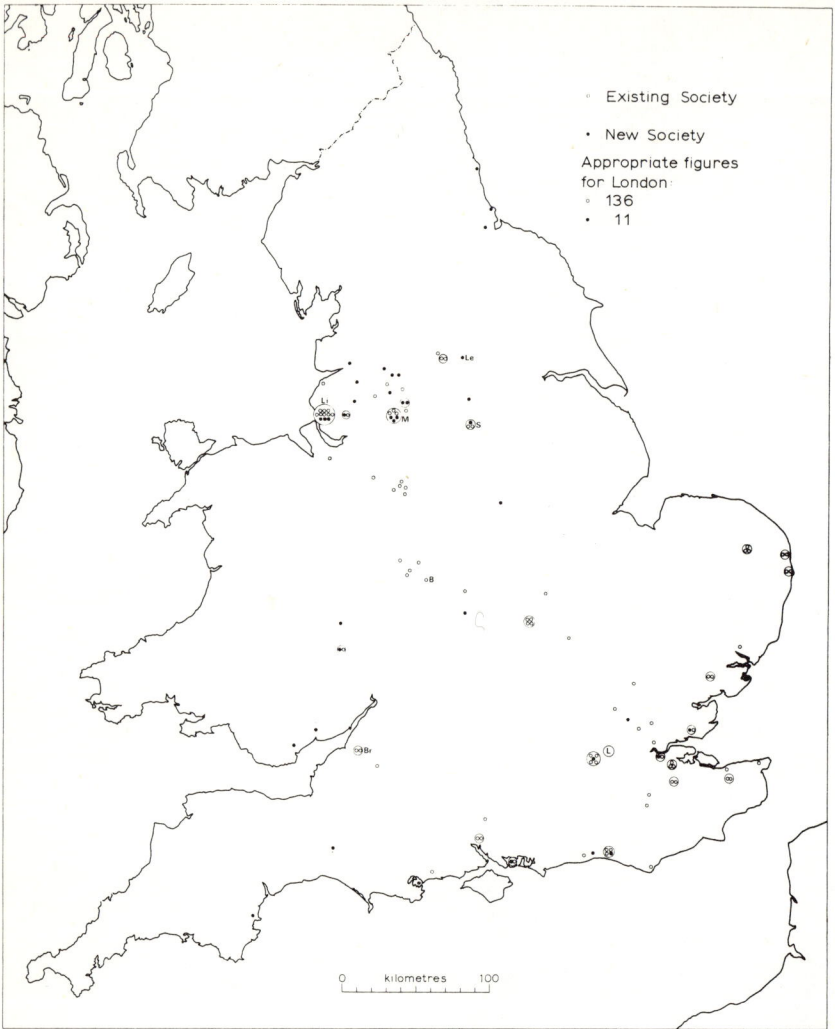

Figure 5.7   Starr-Bowkett societies in England and Wales: spatial spread of the 301st to the 350th society

seaside resorts which were the fastest growing towns of the otherwise demo-graphically-stagnant peninsula. The later developments up to the formation of the 600th society continue to illustrate the operation of these twin processes. In particular, the development of new societies in the South West during the 'period' from the 450th to the 500th society is very striking. First, in Somerset, societies were developed in rapid succession at Chard (the 456th society), Crewkerne and Yeovil (465th) and Wells (470th); then Devon was equally

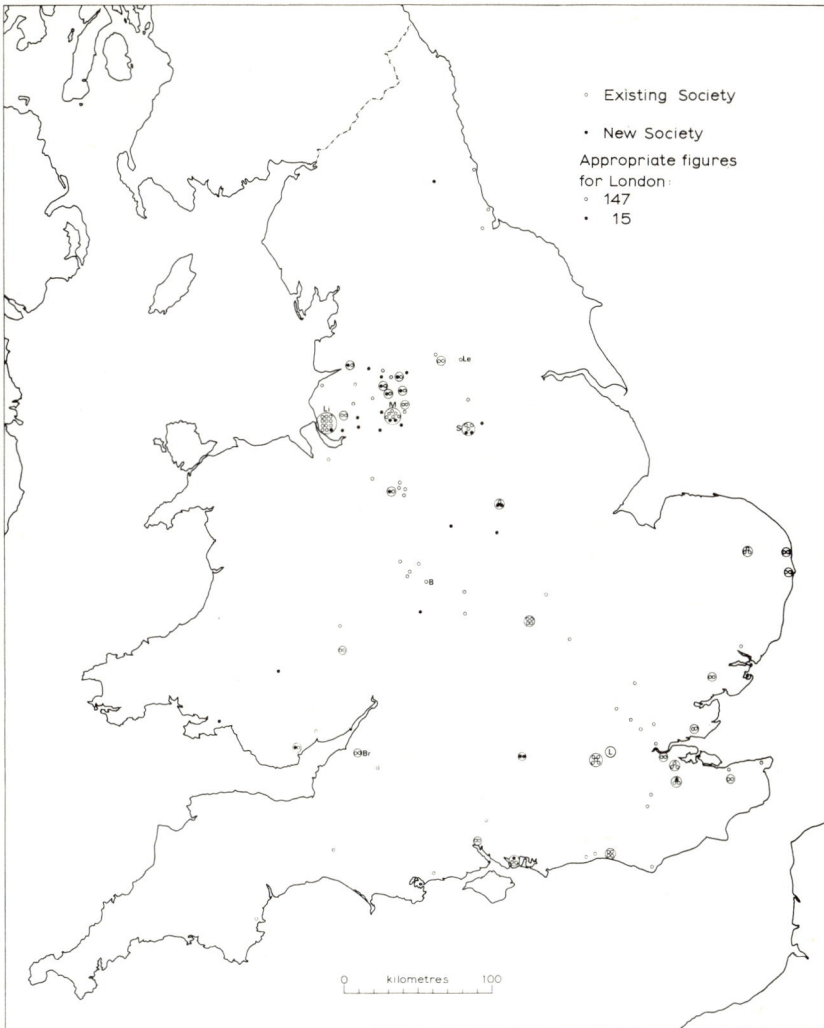

Figure 5.8   Starr-Bowkett societies in England and Wales: spatial spread of the 351st to the 400th society

rapidly colonized, with societies at Exeter (486th), Paignton (495th), Torquay 2nd (496th), Plymouth (498th) and Exmouth (499th). Developments in the North East in the 'period' between the 400th and 500th societies, likewise illustrate this same neighbourhood process. Following a lag after the foundation of societies in Sunderland (339th society), Stockton (340th), and Hartlepool (344th), others followed in fairly rapid succession: Jarrow (402nd), Sunderland 2nd (417th), Middlesbrough (421st), South Shields (436th), Middlesbrough and North

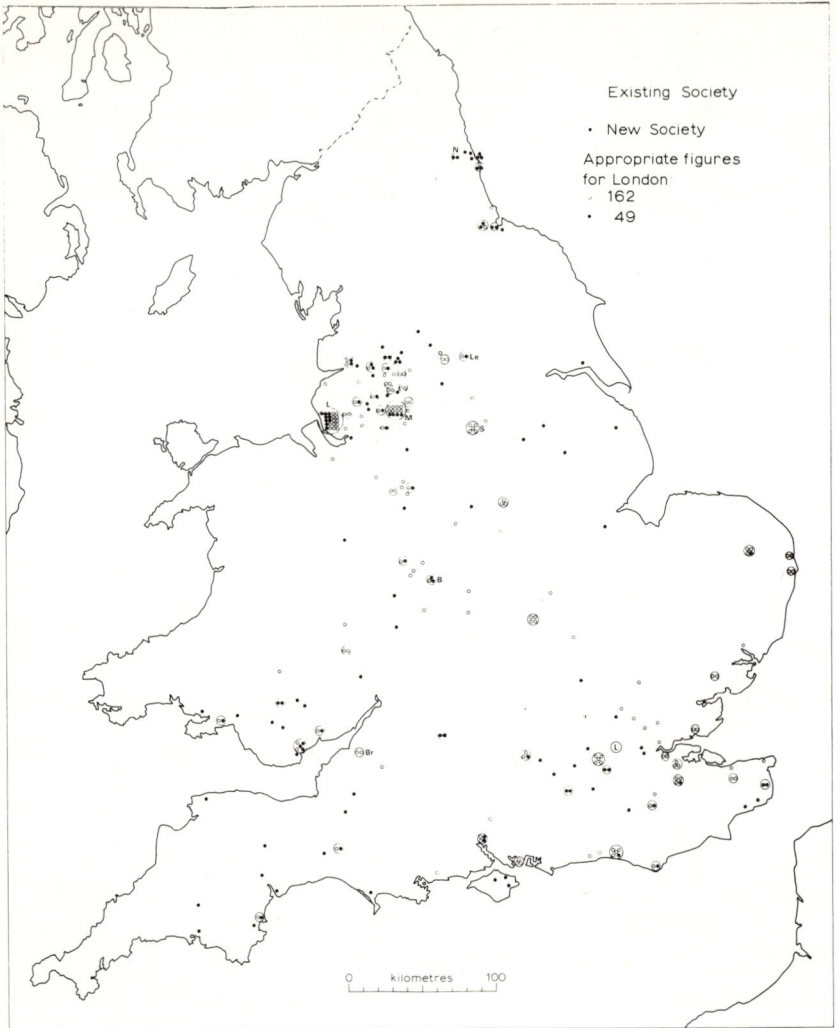

Figure 5.9   Starr-Bowkett societies in England and Wales: spatial spread of the 401st to the 600th society

Ormesby (438th), Tynemouth (452nd), South Stockton (454th), South Shields 2nd (462nd), Gateshead (477th), Stockton 2nd (481st), and Newcastle (489th). The development of Starr-Bowkett societies in the West Riding of Yorkshire was markedly lower than might be expected. This was a result of competition from the plethora of similar balloting societies – the Richmond, Model, Perfect Thrift, Mutual and others – founded in the 1880s after the success of the Starr-Bowketts and which were strongly developed in the area.

The spatial pattern of spread of the Starr-Bowkett societies is therefore a remarkably consistent one. Spread occurs first by the filtering down of societies to the regional centres or the largest towns within regions and subsequently societies spread out to other, and smaller, places within the region while at the same time consolidation occurs within regions which have already been colonized by this process. Looking at England and Wales as a whole, the two processes of hierarchical filtering and spatial spread occur simultaneously, but within any region the one precedes the other.[1] While it appears to be impossible to establish whether these societies were formed purely on the initiative of people within the various towns concerned or whether Starr or his assistants travelled from one region to another to drum up support for the scheme, the significance of these patterns remains unaffected. If the genesis of the societies was local it can be argued that the combination of hierarchical filtering and local spread would appear to be the way in which information about innovations would tend to travel in the commercial context of the nineteenth century. If people considered the Starr-Bowkett scheme attractive and feasible, the spread of formation of societies was therefore dependent upon knowledge of the idea or upon contact with its successful operation elsewhere and the probabilities of these events would seem to be explained well by our joint diffusion processes. If, on the other hand, societies were formed by Starr himself, on proselytizing missions to the provinces, we can then say that, taking him as representative of business or commercial entrepreneurs in general, such entrepreneurs must have evaluated the commercial prospects of general innovations such as this in terms consistent with our notion that innovations will diffuse simultaneously down the hierarchy and outwards from large regional centres to smaller local towns.

TELEPHONE EXCHANGES

The invention and spread of the telephone were events of considerable commercial significance to urban development. In looking at the adoption of this innovation it is clear that one is on much firmer ground in arguing that the adoption or failure to adopt could have had direct economic consequences for individual places. Of the commercial significance of the telephone there is little doubt. As Preece (1882) commented in the early 1880s, 'In 1877, it was a scientific toy; it has now grown to be a practical instrument.' It was, moreover, an instrument in which manufacturers and business men expressed great interest from the outset. Many of the early experiments in telephony were conducted on business premises. Experiments with the Edison carbon telephone in 1878, for example, used one of the longest private lines then in existence owned by the mustard firm of J. & J. Colman which linked their works in Norwich with their

[1] The same process is true of Scotland and Ireland to which societies spread rather late. Again the regional centres lead the way: in Scotland, Edinburgh formed the first societies (the 415th, 493rd and 548th) and was followed by Bo'ness (543rd); in Ireland it was Belfast (the 428th, 447th and 596th) to be followed by Ballymena (515th), Dublin (568th) and Derry (591st).

offices in Cannon Street in London (*Electrician* 1, 1878, 302).[1] The early plans
to establish exchanges were usually greeted with great enthusiasm by the
business communities of the towns concerned, as, for example, in the proposal
to establish exchanges in Cardiff and Newport which was 'being heartily taken
up by the merchants of both places' (*Electrician* 6, 1881, 149). In Glasgow – a
town in which the telephone was to become more comprehensively developed
than probably any other in Britain – the exchange opened by the company of
D. & G. Graham established separate medical, legal, commercial and
stock-brokers' exchanges and to them added a manufacturers' exchange in the
early 1880s (*Electrician* 6, 1881, 98-9). In the internal organization of urban
areas, the telephone was also considered of great value. Many of the various
offices of town councils were connected by telephone to plant under municipal
control at early dates, no doubt with the hope and the effect of improving the
working of the various activities of the internal government of the urban area.
Wolverhampton, for example, constructed a line of some eight miles between the
water works and the pumping station and subsequently connected this line to
the water engineer's office in the town hall (*Electrician* 8, 1882, 242).
Particularly in the early years of its development, it was to the business and
manufacturing communities that the telephone companies looked for potential
customers. In his report to the third ordinary meeting of the South of England
Telephone Company in 1887, the chairman made the following observations:

> The district in which we work is not a very promising one as regards business.
> We have few large towns, Brighton being our largest. I may say we have no
> manufacturing or commercial centre to compare with Bristol, Birmingham,
> Liverpool, Manchester, Newcastle and Glasgow. Reading, and its biscuit-
> baking industry and Norwich, with its mustard manufactory, are our best.
> Our district is composed mainly of residents and agriculturalists; the former
> do not require the telephone, and the latter, I much fear, cannot afford to
> pay for them. (*Electrician* 19, 1887, 173)

Claims and counter claims for having invented the telephone dragged through
American courts well into the late 1880s (*Electrician* 22, 1888, 35) since in the
1870s there was a variety of types of equipment used in telephony some, but
not all, of which used different principles for their receivers and transmitters.
Whatever the date and whoever the inventor, there seems little doubt that the
telephone was first introduced to Britain in a demonstration at the British
Association meeting in Plymouth in 1877 (Preece 1882) and that it was rapidly
promoted by the formation of London- and provincial-based companies founded
in the late 1870s. The two principal companies – The Telephone Company

[1] Sources of data on the development of the telephone are primarily the weekly journal *The
Electrician* and the papers collected in the archives of the General Post Office. The former is
referred to in the text as *Electrician,* followed by the volume, year and pages; the latter is
referred to as *GPO* followed by the reference number of the appropriate archive.

Limited (Bell's Patents) which was floated in 1878, and The Edison Telephone Company of London Ltd which was floated in the following year — were joined to form The United Telephone Company in an amalgamation in 1880. In the provinces a variety of companies was formed both as subsidiaries of the London company and as independent enterprises. The plethora of separate companies and the, at times, extremely bitter fighting between them, was no doubt encouraged by the fact, as Baldwin (1925, p. 91) comments, that Bell's receiver and Hughes' microphone were both instruments of simple design and so readily lent themselves to simple forms of construction and to experimentation. Out of the flurry of formations of fresh companies both in London and elsewhere, a much simpler pattern of control had evolved by the late nineteenth century. Through amalgamations and take-overs of smaller companies, the 1880s were dominated by the United Company in the metropolis and a series of regionally-based companies elsewhere: the South of England Company; the Lancashire and Cheshire Company; the Western Counties and South Wales Company; the Northern District Company covering the North East, Cumbria and part of Scotland; and the National Company covering Yorkshire, Nottinghamshire and much of Scotland. In the face of the increased potential competition with the expiry of patent rights, amalgamation of these main companies was begun in 1889 by the agreement of the United and the Lancashire and Cheshire companies to be subsumed into the National and this process continued with the take-over of the other companies until, by the early 1890s the National Company stood virtually in a monopoly with its only competitor being the Post Office itself. The state finally bought out the National Company, taking over its plant in its entirety in 1912 to create a state telephone service.[1]

There is some difficulty in establishing the date of adoption of the telephone in particular towns. Ideally, the spread of adoption could best be measured by the opening of exchanges in towns, but this is complicated in a number of ways. First, the opening of exchanges is nowhere recorded formally. The companies were licensees of the Post Office and had to apply to the PO for licences to operate exchanges.[2] However, the material on licences is far from complete and

[1] The only exception to total control by the Post Office was the town of Hull which was in the hands of the local authority — the sole vestige of an earlier flurry of interest in municipal telephony. For a very readable account of the early history of the telephone see Baldwin (1925). A more general account is provided by Webb (1910).

[2] This position arose out of a court decision in 1880 that the private telephone companies infringed the state monopoly in the telegraph (see below, chapter 7, p. 225). An instructive illustration of the operation of hierarchical filtering of information through the largest places in a set of towns — a process strongly underlying much of our earlier discussion of diffusion — is provided by the way in which the Post Office disseminated news of this court victory over the Edison Company. The result of the court decision was sent by telegraph in October 1880, to local postmasters who were instructed to inform the editors of the principal morning newspapers. At the same time, they were to place an advertisement in the newspapers which drew attention to the fact that 'in order to meet the convenience of the public, the Post Office is now prepared to establish in any town a system of intercommunication by means of the Telephone instrument . . .' The towns to which these

the date of obtaining the licence was very often different from the actual opening of the exchange. The opening of exchanges in the early years of the development of the telephone were not surrounded with publicity and glamour as were later openings (Baldwin 1925, p. 116) and notices of their opening only rarely appeared even in local newspapers. Secondly, the transition from private lines to full exchange services was a gradual one. Frequently an area would have one or a number of private lines linking private houses with offices, linking a residence with its lodge or its stables, or linking different branches of a single company. Out of such private lines, an exchange would often eventually be built and full exchange services then be offered to the general and business publics.[1] Thirdly, there are many cases in which meetings of local bodies established their interest in the opening of an exchange and in which the telephone companies then promised its immediate execution, yet the exchange may not have been opened for some considerable time after such interest was first expressed. For example, a meeting to discuss the opening of a Gloucester exchange was held as early as February 1880 (*Electrician* 4, 1880, 169), yet an exchange appears not to have been opened until June 1887. Likewise, even though the town council of Derby was experimenting with telephony in 1881 (*Electrician* 7, 1881, 209), an exchange was only opened in 1888.

It is for such reasons that the date of establishment of even the very first exchange in Britain is in some doubt. Different authorities suggest London, Glasgow, Manchester — 'all that documentary evidence has produced so far is that there is very little to choose between the claims of the three exchanges . . . to priority' (*National Telephone Journal* 6, 1910, quoted in Baldwin 1925, pp. 117-18). For our purposes, rather than rely on what data have been collected on the actual opening dates of exchanges in individual towns, three dates have been selected at which to illustrate a static cross-sectional approach to the diffusion. The first date is the end of 1881, at which time the early adopters had opened exchanges despite the opposition of the Post Office which itself had begun to open its own services by converting certain of its telegraphic services to telephone circuits. The second date is the end of 1886, at which time, with a

---

messages were sent were selected from 'a list of towns in which daily newspapers are published receiving regular supplies of news'. Those places selected, in addition to the principal London newspapers, were: Aberdeen, Belfast, Birmingham, Bradford, Bristol, Cardiff, Cork, Darlington, Dublin, Dundee, Edinburgh, Exeter, Glasgow, Huddersfield, Hull, Ipswich, Leeds, Leicester, Liverpool, Manchester, Middlesbrough, Newcastle, Newport, Norwich, Nottingham, Plymouth, Sheffield, Southport, Sunderland, Swansea and York. (*GPO*, E.13267/1889/Post 30.) Of the twenty-five largest towns in England and Wales in 1881, only eight are not included in this list.

[1] Accompanying the annual statements of many of the early regional companies are lists of exchange and private lines open at the appropriate dates. They show that a number of towns had often established long private lines well before the opening of full exchange services: for example Huyton in Lancashire, Windermere in Westmorland and Bishop Auckland in Durham for long had a number of private lines well before the opening of exchanges; and a private line connected Alnwick and Alnmouth in Northumberland long before exchanges were opened at either place.

relaxation of the adamant refusals by the Post Office to grant licences, the number of exchanges had covered large areas of the country and the system was poised to develop a full-scale network of services by the connection of regional systems through the development of trunk lines. The third date is the end of 1892 by which time an inter-regional trunk network had been established and the telephone was beginning to spread even to very small places. The data have been taken from a number of primary and secondary sources. Of the primary sources, the records of the GPO Archives are invaluable even though surprisingly not as complete as one would have expected for so recent a period. Notes and articles in *The Electrician* have been extensively relied upon to establish dates of openings, as have the reports of the various companies to their annual meetings. For the final date, Gunston (1907-8) provides a survey which is probably as accurate as could be wished since he was himself an employee of the National Telephone Company which, at the time that he wrote, enjoyed a virtual monopoly and which doubtless enabled him to draw extensively on documentary evidence which appears no longer to exist. In addition, the telephone directories are useful supplementary sources, particularly in the period from 1896 when the National Company issued an annual directory covering the whole country. Before this date, a number of directories listing the subscribers and activities of separate companies were intermittently issued and a few have adventitiously been preserved and are in the GPO Archives.[1]

The pattern of diffusion which emerges from the compilations based on these sources produces a striking picture. For the first date (fig. 5.10) the spread is restricted almost entirely to the very largest towns in England and Wales.[2] Of the exchanges shown as being open by 1881, all of the largest towns in the West Midlands, north-west Yorkshire and the North East had exchanges, as did Bristol in the South West. London by this date had as many as fifteen exchanges (Baldwin 1925, p. 75)[3] although, as applied throughout the early history of the

[1] Directories preserved in the GPO are as follows: Northern District Telephone Company, 31 January 1886 (*GPO*, 1/6); *idem.*, July 1889 (*GPO*, 1/10); Post Office Telephone List of Subscribers to the Newcastle-on-Tyne and District Telephone system, 21 March 1887 (*GPO*, 1/9); *idem.*, 31 August 1892; *idem.*, 31 December 1892; *idem.*, 30 June 1893; *idem.*, 30 April 1896 (*GPO*, 1/12); Lancashire and Cheshire Telephone Exchange Company, January 1886 (*GPO*, 1/7); National Telephone Company, Midland District, September 1886 (*GPO*, 1/8); *idem.*, Nottingham District, 1 January 1885 (*GPO*, 1/5); *idem.*, Thames Valley District, May 1894 (*GPO*, no ref.); *idem.*, (northern England and Midlands), 1891-2 (*GPO*, 1/11).

[2] Developments in Scotland have been excluded from this study even though, in proportionate terms, they were far more impressive than those in England and Wales. The exchange opened by the company of D. & G. Graham in Glasgow in March 1879 would appear to be the first ever opened in Britain (Baldwin, 1925, pp. 117-18) and the spread of further exchanges and the growth of a trunk-line system in central Scotland were far more dense than in virtually any area south of the border.

[3] By December 1881, these fifteen exchanges served a total of some 1338 subscribers. London in fact lagged behind many of the provincial cities both in terms of the quality and extent of the telephone service. Annual meetings of the United Company in the 1880s frequently dissolved into acrid attacks on the failings of the London company by comparison with its regional offshoots.

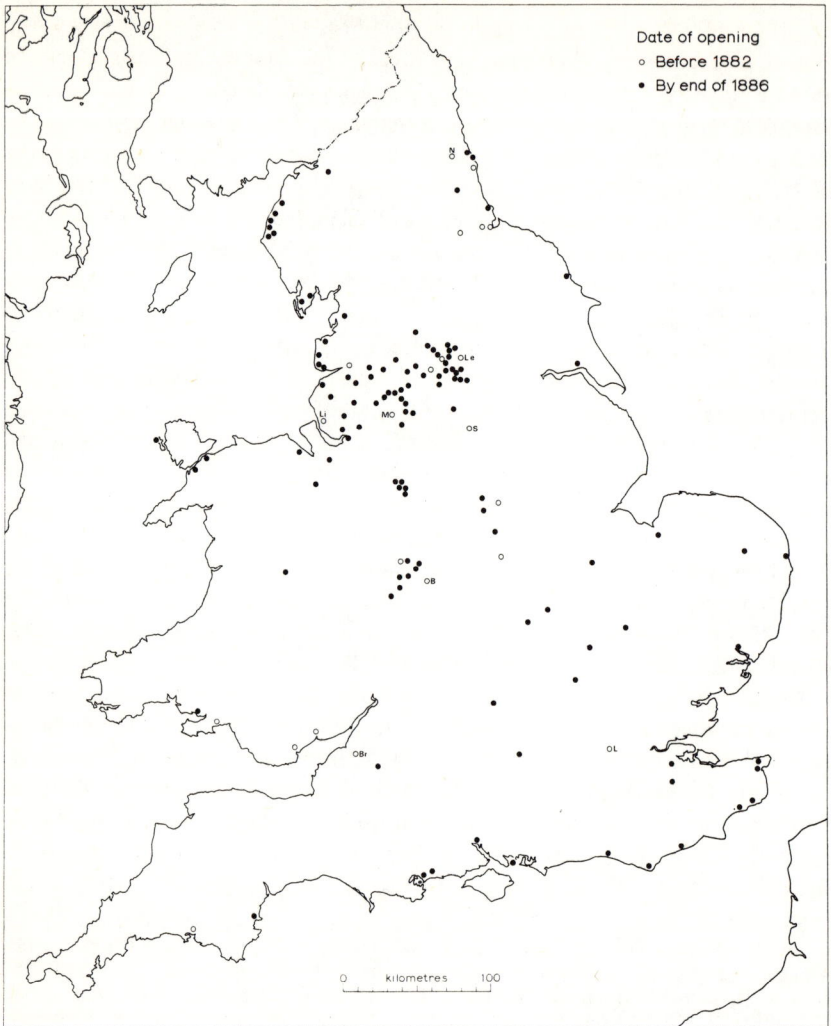

Figure 5.10   Telephone exchanges in England and Wales: spatial diffusion 1881-6

telephone in the Metropolis, exchange areas tended to be very small, and served relatively few subscribers.[1] The Newcastle and Plymouth exchanges had an interesting early development. The first Plymouth exchange had been opened in

[1] The size of area and of population served by exchanges could vary very widely; the largest being found in northern towns. In 1887, for example, within the area of the Northern District Company, Sunderland's single exchange served 215 subscribers, whereas that at North Shields served a mere 5 (*Electrician* 18, 1887, 194). Such differences add weight to the use of the date of opening of the first exchange and the exclusion of subsequent exchanges in towns where more than one were opened.

July 1881, but was then refused a licence by the Post Office and was forced to close in October of the same year and was not reopened by the company until 1885; the Post Office in the meantime having opened its own exchange in December of 1881 (Baldwin 1925, pp. 110-11). Likewise in Newcastle, a company exchange had been opened in 1881 and, being refused a licence, was forced to close in July 1882 and eventually reopened in May 1883. The Post Office started its own exchange in the town in October 1882 (Baldwin 1925, pp. 146-8). Indeed, the whole of the North East was an area of considerable Post Office activity. The first exchanges in Middlesbrough, Stockton and Darlington and, later, in Hull, were started by the Post Office and it was because the department had 'established exchanges worked both by ABCs [the telegraphic system used by the Post Office] and Telephones' (*GPO*, E.4806/1881/Post 30) that licences were refused to private companies to establish exchanges in these towns.

By 1886 the spread of exchanges had been considerable (fig. 5.10). With the establishment of the regional companies, there was a number of provincial exchanges scattered across the counties of southern England, and particularly those of the South of England's exchanges along the south-east coast, but the most striking developments had been in the industrial areas where both Lancashire and Yorkshire had a very large number of exchanges. The other industrial districts were almost as flourishing. The Potteries and the West Midlands each had exchanges in most of their larger towns, and the North East, both in the hands of the Northern District Company and, to a lesser extent, of the Post Office, had continued to expand its coverage. Only the Nottingham-Derby area and the towns around Sheffield appeared to be markedly deficient at this date.[1]

By 1892 the spread of coverage was very wide indeed, (fig. 5.11) with large numbers of new exchanges having opened in South Wales in particular as well as in the non-industrial areas of Kent and Devonshire and in the area of the Lancashire and Cheshire Company which extended to cover the towns of North Wales.

The essence of this pattern of diffusion can be seen most clearly if the dates of adoption of exchanges are again plotted against the population of the towns. This is done in table 5.7 where, for groups of towns ranked by their populations in either 1881 or, for the final date, in 1891, the numbers and proportions of places which had adopted by the three dates are shown. The fall in the percentage of adopters as one moves into lower population sizes is very regular.

[1] In Chesterfield, in Derbyshire, an exchange was eventually opened by the National Company in 1887. Just prior to its opening it was said that the town 'was probably at the moment the most important town in the country without [an exchange]' (*Electrician* 19, 1887, 469). The commercial significance of the establishment of exchanges is suggested by the importance attached at the time to the fact that Chesterfield would also be linked by trunk line to Nottingham and Sheffield, thus 'bringing not less than 10,000 firms within hail of the local exchange'.

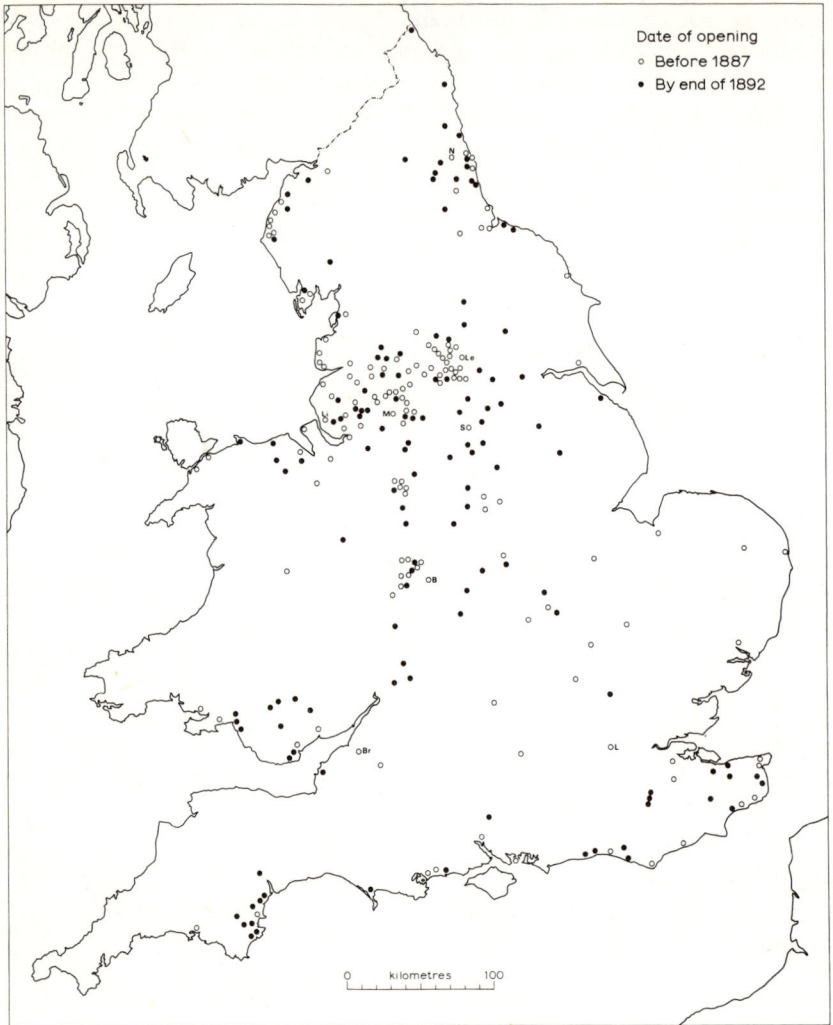

Figure 5.11   Telephone exchanges in England and Wales: spatial diffusion 1886-92

At the first date, the top ten towns had all adopted and, of the other adopters, almost all were found in the top thirty places. By 1886 all but two of the first fifty towns had adopted, but the scatter of other adopters had begun to creep very rapidly down the ranks of population size with no fewer than seven places of less than 5,000 population having had exchanges established. By 1892 this process had continued with infilling of the upper town ranks and large numbers of places in the very small population sizes having exchanges. By this final date, of the top 100 towns, only seven appear not to have had exchanges. Rhondda in South Wales was the largest of these exceptions and its anomalous position can be accounted for by the problems of defining the Rhondda as a town. Of the remaining six, all opened exchanges soon after 1892: Kingston-on-Thames and Swindon in 1893; Colchester and Crewe in 1894; Gravesend in 1895;[1] Enfield in 1899. At the other end of the size range, there was a number of places with populations of less than 2,500 (and thus not qualifying as 'towns' by our

Table 5.7   *Hierarchical diffusion of telephone exchanges, 1879–92*

Rank of towns[1]	No. of towns in each group	No. of places with exchange			% of places with exchange		
		1881[3]	1886[3]	1892[3]	1881[3]	1886[3]	1892[3]
1- 10	10	10	10	10	100·0	100·0	100·0
1- 30	20	9	19	19	45·0	95·0	95·0
1- 60	30	3	22	30	10·0	73·3	100·0
1-100	40	1	21	34	2·5	52·5	85·0
1-150	50		22	34		44·0	68·0
1-210	60		13	27		21·7	45·0
1-280	70		9	30		12·9	42·8
1-360	80		6	21		7·5	26·3
1-450	90		6	20		6·7	22·2
1-550	100		5	20		5·0	20·0
1-660	110		3	12		2·7	10·9
1+	—[2]		1	12		1·1	6·9

Notes
For 1881 and 1886, towns are ranked by their populations in 1881; for 1892, they are ranked by populations in 1891.
In the final group of ranks the 1881 distribution has 89 observations, the 1891 distribution has 174 observations.
Dates are for the end of each year.
Sources: Baldwin (1925); Kingsbury (1915); Gunston (1907-8); *Electrician* (1878 onwards); PO Archives.

criteria) which nevertheless had exchanges by 1892. Excluding exchanges in the suburban areas around major towns (such as Moseley and Selly Oak in Birmingham, Clifton in Bristol, Kemp Town, Hove and Preston in Brighton, Headingley in Leeds) there appear to be at least twenty-eight exchanges open at that date in places smaller than this population limit.[2]

[1] Some doubt surrounds the date of opening of the Gravesend exchange. A report of the South of England Company in 1886 claimed that a Gravesend exchange had already opened (*Electrician* 17, 1886, 270), but the report of the third ordinary meeting of the Company in the following year suggests that an exchange had not been opened by that date (*Electrician* 19, 1887, 152).

[2] These places therefore do not appear on the maps of diffusion – the suburban exchanges, as with all of the London ones, have been treated as part of the town in which they occur. See above, pp. 49–50, for definitions of certain of the largest towns.

The diffusion of the telephone exchange appears to have followed guidelines very similar to that of building societies. The same two principles of size and proximity are apparent in both. The differences lie in the relative importance of population size in providing the early and main determinant of the pattern of spread. In the case of the telephone, size was obviously of considerable importance. The potential returns from installing the various switching equipment, lines and personnel could only be realized if a sufficient number of subscribers could be found and consequently size of population offered one of the most important incentives for the establishment of an exchange. The state telegraph service had earlier provided some warning of this since, after its initial hopes of establishing telegraph offices in villages throughout the country after the state take-over in 1870, it had been forced later to demand guarantees of certain levels of usage before the Post Office undertook to open offices. Likewise with the telephone, it is apparent from the comments of company managers that it was the size, and more particularly the industrial and commercial sizes of a town which lay uppermost in their minds in determining whether or not to go ahead with the installation of an exchange. There was, however, more to the diffusion than mere size alone. From table 5.7 it is apparent that even quite small places were developed at relatively early dates. Almost invariably these unusually small early adopters were towns close to larger places which had previously adopted. Most are therefore to be found in the industrial areas of Lancashire, Yorkshire and Staffordshire. The principle of proximity operated no less clearly than did size, even though, in comparison with the spread of building societies in which the economic consequences of size were not as serious, the proximity effect is much more subdued. This localized spread effect was the consequence not so much of imitation (although the lobbying by town councils and local chambers of commerce from relatively small towns must no doubt have been prompted partly by knowledge of the successful working of the telephone in places which they knew), rather was it connected with the regional policies of the respective companies in whose hands the developments were undertaken. And the spread within a region such as the North West was very much affected by the rapid growth of a network of telephone trunk lines which connected up the emerging exchanges and which in turn affected the future establishments of exchanges. Gunston comments: 'It is not the rurality or size of a town which is most likely to make it a latecomer in the telephone network. It is rather its remoteness from and inaccessibility to the busier and more crowded areas' (Gunston 1910, p. 73). Whereas, with the development of a trunk network, very small places may have got exchanges because they lay with the line of trunk development, other places which lay off such lines often had to wait very much longer for telephones. Thus Wigton in Cumberland (with a population in 1891 of less than 4,000) had an exchange by 1892 no doubt because it lay on the line of the network of trunks connecting the towns of west Cumberland with Carlisle. On the other hand, places in the southern part of

England which lay off the main trunk lines from London to the industrial north and those northern towns remote from the main centres in the north had to wait until the very end of the century before they got exchanges even though their populations may have been quite large. The eastern part of the country suffered notably in this respect; Grantham, for example, with a population in 1901 of over 17,500, had its first exchange as late as 1900 and it was by no means an isolated example.

Earlier it was stressed that the innovations which would be studied were one-dimensional *point* activities which would illustrate the diffusion of innovations amongst a discontinuous set of towns. The development of a network of telephone trunk lines may appear to contradict this claim. However, the fact of the development of the trunk system did not make the diffusion of the telephone an inappropriate innovation for our purposes, mainly because the period which has been studied largely predated the establishment of a national system of trunks. The early telephone developments indeed were expressly denied the opportunity to develop inter-town communications since the Post Office, which licensed telephone developments, wished to protect its telegraph monopoly. The very early licences were issued for defined radii around the specific towns in question. Licences issued before 1881 included the following typical radii (*GPO*, E.4806/1881/Post 30): Birmingham and a radius of 4 miles from the central post office; Halifax and a radius of 3 miles; Wednesbury with a radius of 1·5 miles; Leeds with a radius of 5 miles. Such restrictions were universally applied wherever early licences were issued. In the early years of development, indeed, there was little real comprehension of the potential scope of long-distance telephony. No doubt some of the apparent disbelief in the long-distance potential of the telephone was not as disingenuous as might first appear since it was in the interests of the advocates of the telephone to underplay its potential competition with the state telegraph. A leading article in *The Electrician* of 1881 argued that 'the telephone is to the telegraph what the car or omnibus is to the railway . . . there is a limit to the extension and multiplication of the telephone', and concluded that the creation of a wider network through overhead wires or cables should not be attempted since it was only a local instrument (*Electrician* 7, 1881, 200). Not only, from our post-Beeching vantage point, does the comparison seem singularly ill-chosen, but, given the vacillating stance of the journal with respect to the telephone, it is also difficult to know whether such a judgement was being passed on purely technical or political grounds. Disbelief in the feasibility of long-distance telephony does, however, appear to have persisted for a considerable time. Commenting on reports of successful experiments of telephony over a distance of 200 miles in the United States, a correspondent to *The Electrician* in 1886 (16, 332-3) discussed claims that the practical working of the telephone between London and Birmingham – a distance of 113 miles – was not possible and debated whether or not this was so. Later still, in 1888 (21, 12-13) *The Electrician* commented upon the amalgamation of companies, suggesting that this was being hastened by the growth of the trunk system – 'The rise and progress of this branch of their business [the trunks] has been almost as much a surprise as the rise and progress of telephony itself ... it is now to all intents and purposes a telegraph worked by telephony.' The conclusion was that, had this development been foreseen by the Post Office, its attitude to licensing would have been even more restrictive, given its interests in protecting the state telegraph service.

While the awareness of the potential of long-distance telephony appears, for whatever reason, to have been slow, the actual development of a network of trunk lines evolved inexorably from the start. Early hopes of inter-town links were dampened by the undoubted problems of insulation, but in the provinces long-distance trunks appear at very early dates. Leeds was connected with Bradford as early as 1880 and by the middle of the 1880s there was a number of small regional networks each of which was separate but which were eventually to be linked in to a national network. Such limited trunk developments were best developed between the major towns around Manchester, Leeds, Birmingham and Sunderland. With a new system of licences after 1884, however, trunk line developments proceeded quite rapidly and a series of networks developed which eventually were linked one to another, particularly in the areas of the Lancashire and Cheshire Company,[1] the Yorkshire area in the hands of the National Company and the North East under the Northern District Company. London was remarkably isolated by comparison. Its first inter-town link was completed only by 1884, and this only connected it with Brighton. It was not until 1890 that a line was opened connecting London with the industrial centres of the north.

Figure 5.12 shows the network which had evolved by the end of the period of our immediate interest– in 1892/3. By this time, not only was London linked to the relatively dense networks of the industrial regions, but many of the originally separate networks in other parts of England and Wales (for instance in South Wales, and the South West) had been joined in to the evolving national system. What needs to be stressed in relation to our particular interest in the diffusion of the telephone, however, is the novelty of such a national network by 1892 and the fact that, throughout the greater part of the 1880s, the development of this net had been in disconnected regional sub-networks.[2] The effects of this trunk line development were to reinforce, or provide a stronger economic rationale for, the essentially local spread of the diffusion of the

[1] Which company had, by 1887, almost one-third of its total length of wire used for inter-town connections (*Electrician* 19, 1887, 217).

[2] The differences between the developments of the telephone and the railway networks illustrate the differing importance of long-distance connection in the two. The railway network very rapidly became a national one (see, for example, the maps of its extent in 1840 and 1850 in W. Smith, 1953, p. 161), whereas the telephone was essentially a local phenomenon throughout the decade from its first introduction to the late 1880s. In making such a comparison one has to allow for the much slower overall speed of spread of the railways.

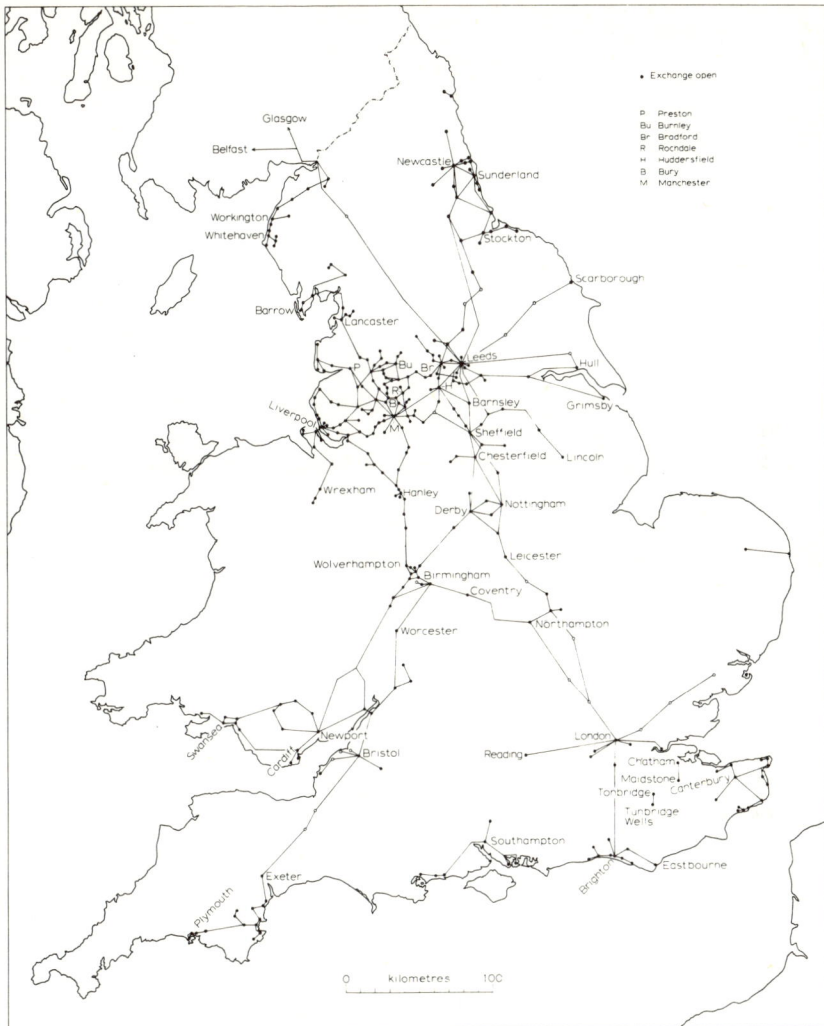

Figure 5.12   The telephone trunk-line network, 1892. *Sources:* National Telephone Company, Trunk lines 1891 (*GPO*. Ref 3/12B); National Telephone Company ... Exchange and Trunkline system 1892 (British Museum. MAPS. 15.a.31)

telephone. Its diffusion must therefore be seen both in terms of an over-riding control being exerted by the size of town, especially in the very early years of development, as well as in terms of a local outward spread — either by imitation or through the effects of the development of a trunk network — to smaller places in the vicinity of the large early adopters.

GASWORKS AND STREET LIGHTING

The development of town gasworks must have been one of the most immediate and striking symbols of the industrial revolution. The very first company – the London Gas-light and Coke Company – was founded in 1812, yet by 1841 a contemporary was able to write that there was 'scarcely a town of any importance' which was not lit with gas (Clegg 1841). For people living in the smaller towns and especially in the non-industrial southern parts of Britain, the spread of gasworks must have been perhaps the one visible sign of the 'progress' of industrialization in the first half of the century. And the visual impact must have been the more marked because the erection of gasworks was almost everywhere associated with the lighting of streets since, in return for the right to break open the street surface to lay pipes, local authorities demanded that gas companies provided street lighting. It was doubtless this fact that gasworks provided so immediate a symbol of the industrial transformation of the age that accounts for the prominence given to them both in contemporary directories and in other general descriptions of towns in the first half of the nineteenth century.

The pattern of the diffusion of gasworks has already been discussed by Falkus (1967) who reached three conclusions which have bearing on the nature of the spread of entrepreneurial innovations: first that, by about the middle of the century, the vast majority of towns with populations greater than 2,500 possessed gas companies; second, that the construction of gasworks took place in surges which corresponded closely with the trade cycle; and third, that throughout the period there was a marked tendency for gasworks to diffuse from larger to progressively smaller towns. As a general indicator of the diffusion of entrepreneurial innovations, the gas industry is in many ways ideal; principally because the towns within Britain were all almost equally feasible as potential adopters. Even though the cost of fuel did differ from one area to another depending on the distance of a town from access to coal supplies, this differential input cost was counterbalanced by the fact that the main by-product, coke, could be sold at higher prices in areas in which coal itself was more expensive (Falkus 1967, p. 500). Further, even though the financial returns were potentially higher in towns with large populations and with a larger number of commercial and manufacturing enterprises, gas companies could be – and, indeed, gradually were – established in relatively small places at quite early dates. The scale economies appear not entirely to have excluded small towns from the ranks of potential adopters of the innovation, and the spread of gasworks extended throughout a wide range of town sizes within two decades after the foundation of the first company. The whole population of towns was therefore equally 'at risk'.

Falkus' conclusion that gasworks diffused regularly down the size hierarchy of British towns during the first half of the century adds considerable substance to the emphasis placed on the size of towns in the study of building societies and telephone exchanges. Is it possible, in studying the data on gasworks, to arrive at some more precise evaluation of the respective importance of hierarchical diffusion and neighbourhood spread for this particular innovation? The details of the earliest dates of establishment of gasworks in towns in England and Wales

Table 5.8   *Hierarchical diffusion of gasworks in English towns, 1812-40*

Rank of towns	Maximum number of towns	Number of towns with gasworks by the end of:			Percentage of places with gasworks by the end of:		
		1820	1829	1840	1820	1829	1840
1- 10	10	8	10	10	80·0	100·0	100·0
11- 30	20	9	20	20	45·0	100·0	100·0
31- 60	30	12	25	25	40·0	83·3	83·3
61-100	40	3	23	32	7·5	57·5	80·0
101-150	50	1	12	32	2·0	24·0	64·0
151-210	60	1	8	36	1·7	13·3	60·0
211-280	70	0	6	39	0·0	8·6	55·7
281-360	80	1	3	35	1·6	3·8	43·7
361-450	90	–	0	24	–	0·0	30·4
'Towns' < 2,500		0	4	33			
Places < 2,500		0	0	26			

Notes
1. Towns are ranked by their populations in 1821, 1831 and 1841 respectively.
2. The two final rows – "'Towns'" < 2,500' and 'Places < 2,500' – are places in which gasworks were built before they reached the threshold of 2,500 population. The first are places which did exceed that threshold at some date before 1911; the second are places which did not exceed the threshold before that date.
3. The figures in the three final columns are calculated as percentages of the number of towns in each category of ranks.
4. Approximations to the population sizes corresponding to town ranks can be taken from fig. 2·3 (p. 30). They will be approximate because of the exclusion of Welsh towns from this table.
Source: Falkus, private communication.

were very kindly made available by M. E. Falkus and it was hoped to be able to suggest answers to this question. Table 5.8 shows the progressive spread of gasworks at three dates for towns within England.[1] The three dates have been selected in the light of the cyclical pattern of the construction of gasworks shown in fig. 5.13: 1820 marks off a period of 'early adopters';[2] 1829 and 1840 include the construction booms in the middle years of the 1820s and 1830s respectively. The most striking feature of the pattern is undoubtedly the close connection between the date of adoption and the size of town. By the end of

[1] Welsh towns have been excluded from consideration since the data appear less reliable in their case.
[2] Indeed by as early as 1822 no fewer than seven gas plants had been established in London (*Parliamentary Papers* 1823, V, 308-41).

1820, all but two of the ten largest English towns, and all but seven of the largest twenty towns had gasworks. Of the exceptions, the great majority had constructed gasworks very soon after 1820: the two towns in the top ten — Plymouth and Portsmouth — by 1823 and 1821 respectively; and of the five towns in the next ten, four had gasworks by 1821 — Norwich, Hull, Leicester and Huddersfield, and the fifth — Sunderland — had a gasworks by 1824. By the end of 1829, all of the thirty largest places had companies and all but five of the top sixty towns had adopted. As Falkus suggests, there was indeed a very close correspondence between size and date of adoption.

The tail of the distribution is, however, fairly distended. At the same time that large places were adopting, gasworks were also being built in very much smaller places. Even before 1820, for example, a town as small as Helston in Cornwall was lit by gas. Other examples of relatively small towns which were

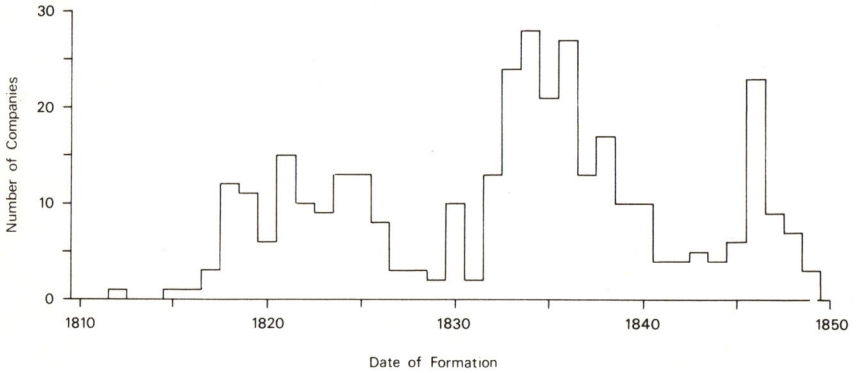

Figure 5.13   Dates of establishment of gas companies in England, 1812-50

'leaders' in the adoption process include Chelmsford in Essex, Newcastle under Lyme in Staffordshire, Chorley in Lancashire, and Gloucester. The spatial patterns of the diffusion are shown in figs. 5.14 and 5.15, and they suggest that, in very qualitative terms, there appears to be some hint of a neighbourhood effect which might go some small way in accounting for this long tail to the distribution of adopters. One marked feature is that gasworks tend to be established early in the county towns of the regions within England, whether or not such places were large. Gloucester was certainly not among the largest of towns; neither were Hereford, Lancaster, Chelmsford, or Reading. All, in fact, fell below the top fifty towns in terms of population size and yet adopted gasworks at relatively early dates. Such 'precocious' adoption might reflect their importance with respect to flows of communication and contact, deriving from their long-standing role as regional centres before the advent of industrialization.

The maps of diffusion also hint at a possible pattern of regional development of gasworks in which towns within a particular area tend to be developed within

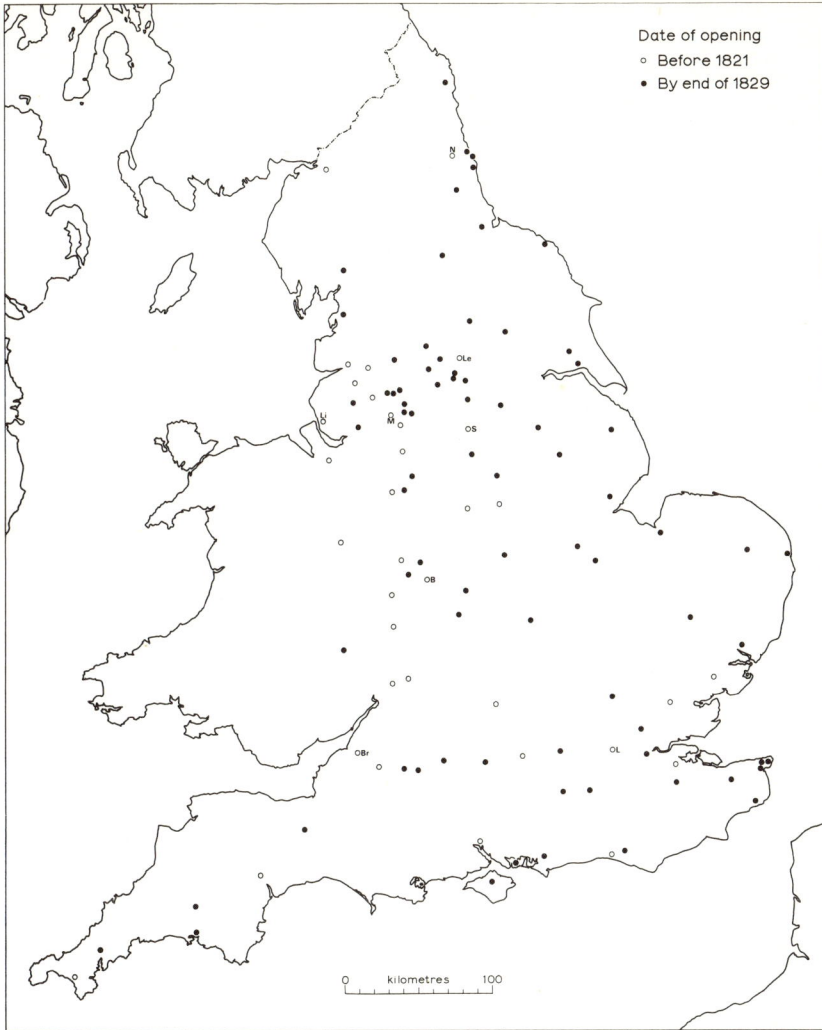

Figure 5.14   Gasworks in England: spatial diffusion 1820-9

a relatively short span of time. Lincolnshire, for example, despite the fact that it contained relatively few large towns, was developed with gasworks relatively early. As in the diffusion of building societies, towns close to London tended to be developed earlier than their size alone might have led one to expect; and this was particularly true amongst the towns in Kent and along the coast of Sussex. The towns of coastal South Devon had gasworks within relatively few years of each other in the decade of the 1830s. The same, again, is true of Dorset towns: Bridport was lit in 1832; Dorchester and Poole were both lit in the following

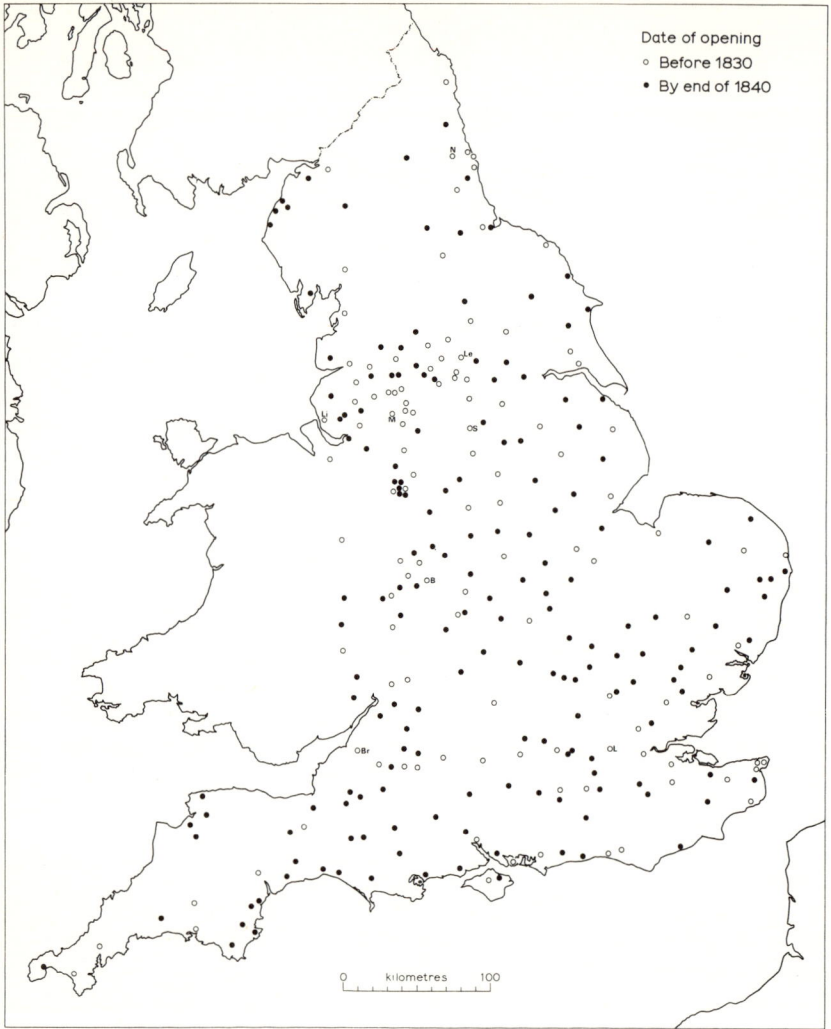

Figure 5.15   Gasworks in England: spatial diffusion 1829–40

year; Lyme Regis in 1835; and Blandford, Shaftesbury and Sherborne all in
1836. Some part of this apparent tendency for neighbourhood diffusion must be
attributed to the contractor system by which many of the gasworks were
constructed; plant being built either on local initiative and under the super-
intendence of a specialist gas engineer called in from outside, or through the
activities of speculators who would build plant and subsequently sell it to a
company of shareholders. Falkus (1967, pp. 505-9) gives instances of the
activities of such promoter-contractors, many of whom appear to have operated

on a regional basis. The Malam brothers, for example, who were responsible for over fifty gasworks before 1846, concentrated their attention primarily within distinct regions of the county: one in Lancashire and the West Riding of Yorkshire; another in Cumberland and the North and East Ridings; and the third in East Anglia.

On the basis of such evidence, it is possible to suggest, in a largely qualitative fashion, that the two principles of hierarchical and neighbourhood diffusion can be seen to have operated in the spread of gasworks in the first half of the century. A more quantitative approach, which might have isolated the respective weightings of the two principles however has been frustrated by the imperfections of the basic data and by the temporal progression of the construction of gasworks. On the first point, it is evident that the dates of first establishment of gasworks are not as reliable as would be required for a more precise analysis. Most of the larger towns were lit by companies which were large enough to justify their incorporation as limited liability companies and the dates of the appropriate Acts provide a good indication of the date of their first operations, but in the smaller places many of the undertakings were not incorporated and, where they were eventually incorporated, the dates of the Acts given in the gas directories usually do not indicate the date at which the original firm began operations. Falkus drew on the records of a firm which supplied castings to the gas companies and, on the basis of a sample drawn from this source, was able to suggest the dates of construction of many gas works in the widely scattered smaller towns throughout the country. The sphere of operations of this firm was, however concentrated in northern and eastern England and there is certainly a number of towns for which the earliest dates which can be established are not those of the first opening of gasworks and the lighting of the town. For example, one of the most obvious anomalies in the data presented here is the town of West Bromwich which was the largest town in 1841 shown as not having been lit by 1840. Indeed, gas directories[1] suggest that a company began operations in West Bromwich as late as 1880. Yet clearly there was a gasworks well before this date. Lewis' *Directory* (S. Lewis 1844, volume 1, p. 389) noted of West Bromwich in 1844 that: 'Very large gas-works have been established by a company of proprietors, from which part of Birmingham, seven miles distant, is lighted, and from which the different towns of Wednesbury, Dudley, Bilston, Darlaston, Tipton, and Great Bridge, are also supplied with gas.' Other such anomalous entries in the data which have been used must doubtless be attributed to similar difficulties in establishing the date of the very first company to start operations in a town — as against the dates of subsequent companies or of extension to existing companies.

The second fact which militated against a more precise analysis of the data on gasworks was the time-curve of construction. The fact that companies were

---

[1] For example, *Gas . . . companies' directory* 1881.

developed in so markedly cyclical a fashion means that equal time increments had very different significance in the cumulative curve of the adoption of gasworks. A difference of five years between dates of openings would be of very different significance during a period of boom in construction than in a period of slump when few plants were built. If a form of regression were to be used in the study of the diffusion of gas lighting, the dependent variable — date of construction — would therefore need to be weighted in some way to take account of this difference and the weighting would be of a complex form, not constant over the entire length of time from 1812 to 1840. The problem is similar to that in Berry's (1972, pp. 343-4) study of the diffusion of television stations in America, where he notes that the two-year freeze on construction during the Korean war had the effect of causing a hiatus in the logistic curve of openings during the years 1950 to 1952.[1] Places which would have been expected to open stations during these years, on the basis of their population size, postponed the openings until the post-war period during which time there consequently was a much wider scatter of sizes of places in which television stations were opened. The same effect must have operated in the case of gasworks because of the correlation of construction with the swings of the general trade cycle.

Despite the absence of a more quantitative analysis of the spread of gasworks, however, the descriptive approach adopted here and in Falkus' analysis, do suggest the importance of town size and, to a lesser extent, of localized spread in the diffusion of gas lighting.

CONCLUSION

The diffusion of gas works at the start of the century, the spread of building societies in the middle years of the century and the development of the telephone in the final quarter of the century each illustrate the operation of the twin processes of hierarchical diffusion down the ranks of the urban size array and the localized 'neighbourhood' spread out from early adopters to smaller towns within their ambit. The relative importance of the hierarchical and neighbourhood effects in each case depends principally on the characteristics of the innovation itself, but, whatever their respective weighting, it would appear that both processes have to be taken into account in any attempt to simulate or to understand the most probable course of the diffusion of entrepreneurial innovations.

The particular innovations which have been looked at in some detail here may in themselves have given rise to relatively little direct employment. The significance of the nature of their spread, however, is that it suggests the validity of using a rather general model of diffusion which incorporates hierarchical and

---

[1] The same tendency was produced by the effects of the Second World War.

neighbourhood principles. Whether or not the particular innovations directly 'caused' population growth in towns, it would certainly seem probable that their more indirect effects were not inconsiderable. The fact that a town adopted gas lighting, or developed telephone exchanges, or that it had flourishing building societies is also in itself some indication of its 'vitality' and 'progressiveness' as a town — qualities held in some esteem in the expansive, quantity-conscious Victorian age. It is not without significance that many contemporaries themselves stressed just these very qualities as ones which attracted immigrants to the towns. H. L. Smith in his well-known discussion of migration in Booth's *Life and labour of the people in London*, considered that the lure of the town was:

> . . . the contagion of numbers, the sense of something going on, the theatres and the music halls, the brightly lighted streets and busy crowds — all, in short, that makes the difference between the Mile End Fair on a Saturday night, and a dark and muddy country lane, with no glimmer of gas and with nothing to do. Who could wonder that men are drawn into such a vortex, even were the penalty heavier than it is?

And if the local 'metropolis' was not only gas-lit, telephone-served and offered the lure of building societies, but also had the hundred-and-one other urban 'improvements' of the age, no doubt the pull of the vortex, both for those within and those without, was stronger still. The nature of the diffusion of entrepreneurial innovations may well serve as a guideline to the manner by which the general growth of nineteenth-century towns took place.

CHAPTER 6

Simulating urban growth

But who Pretender is, or who is King,
God bless us all — that's quite another thing.

JOHN BYROM

The evidence of the three general indicators which have been studied suggests that the diffusion of entrepreneurial innovations through a set of nineteenth-century cities may well be characterized by a simultaneous process of hierarchical space-jumping from larger to smaller cities and of localized spread outwards from regional centres. The particular balance between these two components appears to be determined by the characteristics of the particular innovation being studied — primarily by the importance to it of scale economies and the threshold market size which it requires. Where a large market is called for — because of the need to recoup heavy initial capital outlay, or to minimize the element of risk, or because of marked scale economies — the hierarchical effect may be expected to be commensurately more important in determining the course of the diffusion process. As technical changes alter the costs of installation or operation of a given innovation, it may be that the innovation subsequently filters down to places of much smaller size and that the spread effects become more important in its diffusion — as indeed appears to have been the case with the gas industry. Alternatively, however, it may be that technical improvements may well *increase* the optimal scale of production for an innovation so that, over time, it is less likely to diffuse to smaller places (Pederson 1970, pp. 219-20). Where an innovation is not greatly affected by size constraints — as in the case of building societies — the spread, or neighbourhood, effect may be apparent at the very outset of the diffusion, but it would nevertheless appear that hierarchical diffusion down the ranks of town sizes is rarely, if ever, absent. Even when neighbourhood spread is important, innovations still appear to be diffused to new regions, which are distant from the originating centre, initially through their large towns or regional capitals which act as the organizing poles of economic and social activities within the region.

Underlying the attempts to provide validation of this twin process of diffusion in the nineteenth century has been the assumption that the adoption of innovations is a cause, as well as an indicator, of economic vitality in towns and is therefore closely tied to their population growth. We are now therefore in a position to attempt the development of a model to simulate the growth of towns on the basis of the radically simplified assumption that urban growth is 'caused' by the diffusion of entrepreneurial innovations. Some of these innovations in the real world will, of course, be of a rather specialized technical nature and only those few places which either pursue or which come to pursue the appropriate economic activity will be potential adopters; improvements in mine-ventilation techniques would be of little interest to the inhabitants of Bourne-mouth. Others, however, will be more universal innovations which would have potential benefits to offer to the whole range of places. We can, however, think of the whole set of innovations as averaging out into a 'composite' general innovation which will produce growth in the populations of those places which adopt since the innovation will have both direct effects on the growth of employment as well as more indirect effects by making the towns more efficient or more attractive places both socially and economically. Both in terms of retaining people born within the town and attracting migrants from without, the adoption of the composite innovation will therefore have the effect of increasing the town's population.

Our objective in simulating the diffusion of such a 'composite' innovation will be to see to what extent this urban growth can be produced in a way compatible with the two aspects of the growth of towns suggested by the empirical data; a scatter of growth rates whose variance declines with increasing town size and an average growth rate which can vary between one in which size and growth are positively related to one in which the two are not related. Let us assume that we have a set of towns with given population sizes and given locations and that certain of them have, and others have not, adopted the 'composite' innovation. Those which have adopted will send out messages – or stimuli – about the innovation. For places which have not adopted, these stimuli will represent information about the innovation and, if a non-adopter town receives a sufficient number of such stimuli, it will adopt and in turn will itself begin to emit stimuli. For places which have adopted, the receipt of stimuli will represent agitation in the local economy and will lead to further employment and an increase in the town's population. From our discussion of the nature of innovation diffusion, it can be assumed that the spread of the innovation can be represented by a form of gravity equation, which will combine both hierarchical and neighbourhood effects. For a town, i, with population P_i, the probability of its receiving a stimulus will depend on its population size, its distance from towns which have adopted and which therefore send out stimuli, and the number of stimuli which are emitted by those towns. We therefore have an equation of the following sort which describes the probability of receiving stimuli:

$$\text{Pr}_i = k \left[\sum_{j=1}^{n} (P_i^a . d_{ij}^{-b} . S_j) \right]; \qquad [6.1]$$

where the summation is over all of the set of *j*-places $(j = 1 \ldots n; j \neq i)$ which have already adopted; S_j is the number of stimuli sent out by the *j*th adopter; and *k* is a weight which converts the sum of the expressions for all of the places to 1·0, so that one is dealing with probabilities. For the total set of towns, we therefore have a given number of stimuli being emitted by those places which have adopted the innovation and, for each town, whether or not it has adopted, we have a probability of it receiving a stimulus. The stimuli can thus be allocated amongst the set of towns to cause them either to adopt the innovation if they have not already done so, or to grow in size if they have already adopted. To incorporate into the model the chance elements so characteristic of the real world, this allocation of stimuli can be made on a probabilistic basis. This would involve giving sequential numbers to each of the towns — the range of numbers being dependent upon the town's probability of being 'hit' by a stimulus — and then drawing a random number for each stimulus which is to be allocated. This is a type of Monte-Carlo method which, like Hägerstrand's simulation of spatial diffusion, neatly combines the deterministic and chance elements of the real world: the first in terms of the structure of equation [6.1] which determines the set of probabilities; and the second in terms of the use of random numbers.

To illustrate the procedure with a simple example, let us take a set of five places, only two of which have adopted the innovation and which send out five and three stimuli respectively. The distances and sizes of these towns will be as in table 6.1. If we let the *a* and *b* exponents in equation [6.1] each be 1·0, the calculation of the probability of place 2 being hit would be:

$$\Pr_2 = k \left(\frac{600}{10} \times 3 \right) + \left(\frac{600}{12} \times 5 \right) = k \times 430.$$

The value of k, which converts these sums so that they add to 1·0, will be 1/826 and this produces the column of probabilities given in table 6.1. Since we now wish to distribute the eight stimuli amongst the set of towns, these probabilities are converted to sequential numbers, as in the final column of table 6.1, and eight random numbers are drawn to allocate the stimuli. Supposing that the random numbers were 69, 60, 11, 74, 15, 4, 21 and 97, this would mean that place 1 would receive two stimuli, place 2 would receive three, place 3 would receive two, place 4 would receive one and place five would receive none.[1]

---

[1] It can be seen that equation [6.1], by summing over all towns other than the adopter town itself (i.e. $j \neq i$), sidesteps the question of the number of stimuli a town sends to itself. This broaches the unresolved problem in the literature of social physics of how best one might calculate the 'self-potential' of a town. However the fact that in the development of the simulation model, stimuli are distributed in an aggregate fashion and also that some units of population growth are given to a town once it has adopted, whether or not it receives further stimuli, justify our ignoring the self-potential of adopter towns. The logic of the model is that growth — or agitation to the local economy — will occur principally through the interaction *between* places rather than *within* a place.

Having allocated the stimuli, two things have then to be decided: at what point will adoption occur for a town which has not adopted; and by how much will the population of a town which has adopted grow during the time period represented by this sending-out of stimuli. The first decision would represent the level of resistance which would exist in a town before it decided to adopt and, in the real world, this would depend upon the type of innovation involved, its qualities of perceived risk and its expected costs and returns. Such resistance levels may well differ between towns, with one place being more adventurous or, indeed, more suited to the particular innovation. But in our example we could say that the resistance level was the same for all places and that a place would need to have received three or more stimuli before it would adopt. Place 2 would thus adopt during the time period; place 4 would not adopt, but, having received one stimulus, its resistance would be lowered so that it would require only a further two stimuli in subsequent time periods to cause it to adopt; place 5

Table 6.1   *A simple example of the diffusion model*

Place	Units of population	Units of stimulus emitted	Units of distance to place:					Sum of contacts	Probability of being 'hit'	Sequential numbers allocated
			1	2	3	4	5			
1	400	3	–	10	20	15	5	100	0·12	1– 12
2	600	–	10	–	12	8	8	430	0·52	13– 64
3	1000	5	20	12	–	5	20	150	0·18	65– 82
4	100	–	15	8	5	–	15	120	0·15	83– 97
5	40	–	5	8	20	15	–	26	0·03	98–100

would remain unaffected. Second, for places 1 and 3 which had already adopted, we would need to decide by how much the receipt of their two stimuli would cause their populations to grow. It could be that each stimulus would cause incremental growth of some fixed amount or alternatively of some fixed percentage of the existing town population.

Whatever were the eventual rules which were decided, this outline provides the skeleton of the simulation model to which the details of the operating rules would add flesh. We have a set of towns, some of which have adopted the innovation, and the stimuli sent out from them are allocated amongst the towns, causing certain of those which have not adopted to adopt and producing growth amongst those which have already adopted. This gives one cycle of the model at the end of which there will be a new set of populations, a new set of adopters, and a fresh and larger reservoir of stimuli to be distributed in the next time period. The nature of the model is very simple and, being simple, is far removed from reality. In essence, it is modelling a form of composite innovation which generates factories, employment and general economic vitality. In reality there would be a large variety of innovations, each with different characteristics and

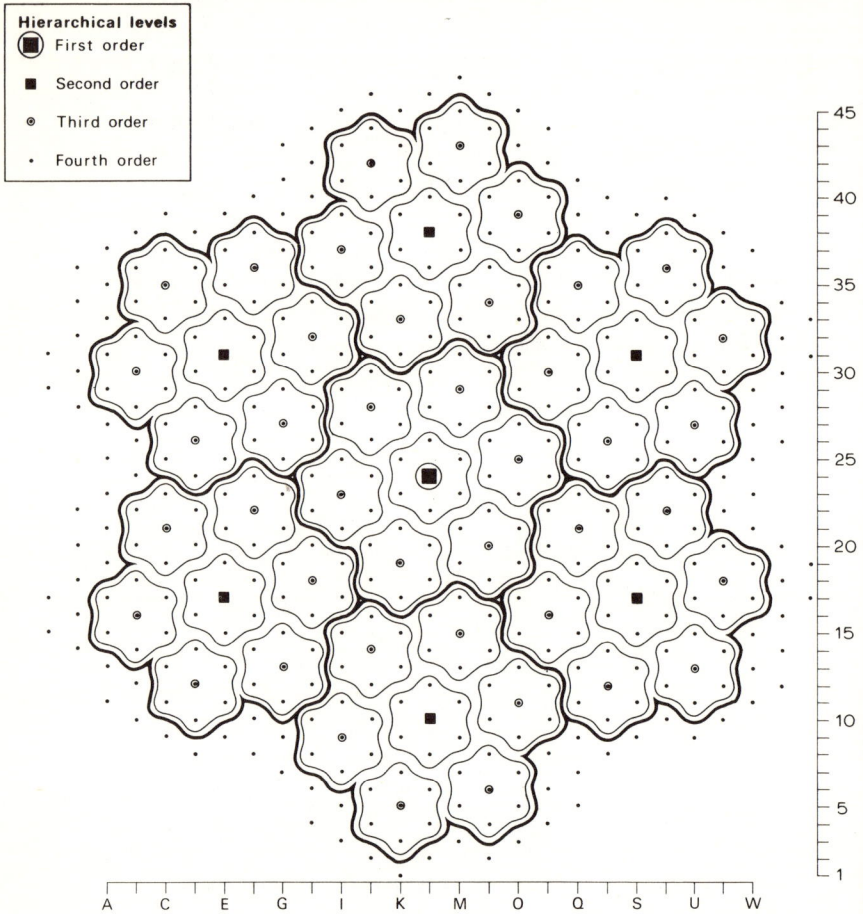

Figure 6.1   An idealized central-place system of towns. An arrangement according to Christaller's K = 7 network

each having effect on the growth of population of either all or some of the towns. For any one of the innovations, the effect on growth would almost certainly decline over time; both in terms of the fact that economic returns may be lower for later adopters and that, within a given town, one innovation would eventually be superseded by others. But, in effect, the simulation model pools together the effects of all of these innovations by assuming a continuing stream of inventiveness and innovation over time. It treats the stream of innovations in an aggregate fashion rather than first diffusing one innovation and, while this first one is still spreading eventually to reach a saturation point, beginning the diffusion of a second, a third, and so forth.

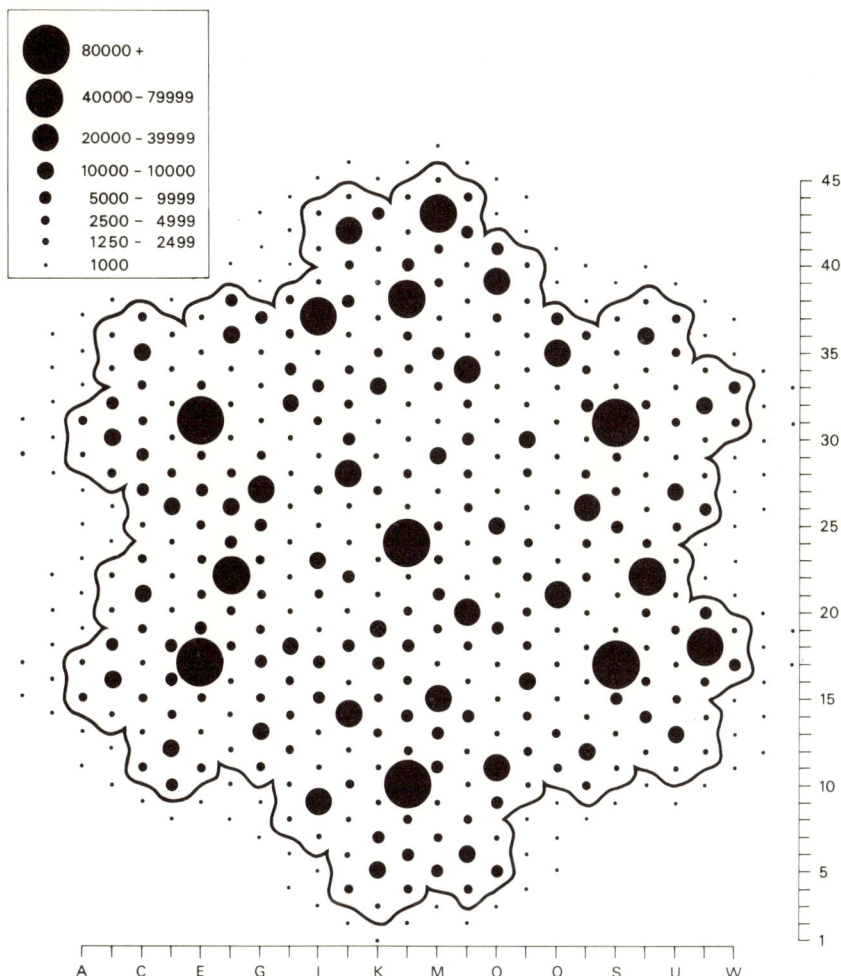

Figure 6.2   Population sizes in the idealized urban system. Populations form a rank-size array and are allocated randomly to cities within each level of the hierarchy shown in fig. 6.1

To examine the nature of the growth processes which this model produces, we shall consider a set of towns distributed in an idealized landscape and arranged according to Christaller's central-place arrangement with $K = 7$.[1] The distribution of towns is shown in fig. 6.1 and it can be seen that there are four

[1] This arrangement was chosen since it is the only one of Christaller's three basic geometrical arrangements in which the boundaries of the market areas of each order of central place coincide. It is therefore possible to draw a 'self-contained' urban system with an overall boundary which includes the market areas of all places.

hierarchical orders of town: one first-order place; six second-order places; forty-two third-order places; and 294 fourth-order places. It is amongst this set of towns that the mythical innovation will be diffused. In addition to the towns within the central-place arrangement, there are also 112 places which have been added around the perimeter of the area. These have been included to add what Hägerstrand calls 'border bounce' into the 'system' and so help to alleviate (but not to solve) the difficulty of dealing with a bounded set of places.[1] Each of the 343 towns was then allocated population sizes in such a way that the overall size distribution conformed to a rank-size curve: the largest place having 500,000 population; the second largest having 500,000/2; the 343rd largest having 500,000/343, or 1,458 population. These populations were randomly allocated within each of the four hierarchical orders of towns, so that the first-order town was given 500,000 population, the six second-order towns were randomly assigned populations of between 250,000 and 71,279, the forty-two third-order towns were randomly assigned populations between 62,350 and 10,204, and the fourth-order towns were randomly assigned populations of from 10,000 to 1,458. The remaining 112 towns which lie outside the boundary of the area were each allocated a population of 1,000. The resulting distribution of towns, shown in groups of town sizes, is given in fig. 6.2. This initial set of towns is obviously only one of an infinite variety of locations and sizes which could have been chosen, but it attempts to approximate the empirical evidence on urban size distributions and also the theoretical notion that the distance between large towns is greater than that between small. Since the form of the basic equation within the model (equation [6.1]) relies both on spacing and town size, however, the results will obviously be influenced by the particular distribution from which one starts, and the pattern of fig. 6.2 needs therefore to be borne in mind in the interpretation of the subsequent results.

We are now in a position to establish the operating rules of the simulation. From the derivation of the model it is evident that there is a variety of parameters and attributes which can be altered. First are the parameters of equation [6.1]; the distance exponent could be raised or lowered so as to give greater or less effect to the neighbourhood process of spread and the weighting of population could equally be altered. Second, there are numerous ways in which one could determine the number of stimuli which would be emitted by an adopter town; the most realistic might be to make the number depend upon the population of the town in some way. Third, there is a variety of ways in which

[1] See Hägerstrand (1967b, p. 18). The boundary problem is a recurring one in spatial studies. Here the difficulty can be seen by comparing the potential set of places from which a central and a peripheral place can receive stimuli: a central place has towns within all quarters of the compass; whereas a place lying close to the southern boundary only has towns lying in the quarter to its north. The 112 border towns are therefore added so that they can 'catch' any stimuli sent outside the 'system' and, if they themselves adopt, can subsequently send stimuli to the border towns within the system. We shall therefore not be interested in the growth rates of the border towns themselves.

population could be increased for each stimulus received by an adopter town; it could be raised by a given number of people or by a fraction of the existing population. Fourth, the levels of resistance which determine the time at which a town adopts could be altered; a higher or lower figure could be chosen or the figure could be made to vary from one town to another in some way. Each of these decisions will have effect upon the operation of the model and each could be interpreted in terms of the changes which it represents in the real world – a topic to which we shall return below.

MODEL 1

The operating rules for the first version of the simulation – Model 1 – were established as follows:

1. At the outset, time t_0, only the largest town has adopted the innovation.

2. Towns adopt once they have received three stimuli from adopter towns. Having adopted, in subsequent time periods their populations grow as specified in rule 5 and they emit a certain number of stimuli as in rule 3.

3. Adopter towns send out S stimuli in each time period subsequent to their adoption:

$$S_j = \sqrt[4]{P_j};$$

where P_j is the population of the jth adopter.

4. The probability of town i being 'hit' by a stimulus is given by the following:

$$k \sum_{j=1}^{n} P_i.d_{ij}^{-1}.S_j \quad (j = 1, \ldots n, j \neq i).$$

5. Once a place has adopted, in subsequent time periods its population grows in the following way:
   (i) every fresh stimulus which it receives generates S additional population ($S_j = \sqrt[4]{P_j}$) in the time period in which the stimulus is received and $\frac{1}{2}S_j$ population in the subsequent period.
   (ii) once it has adopted, a town generates its own further growth by the addition of S_j population in every subsequent period, irrespective of whether or not the place receives stimuli.

For any given period, population growth will therefore be given by the following:

$$N_{j.t}.S_{j.t} + N_{j.t-1}.S_{j.t}/2 + S_{j.t};$$

where $N_{j.t}$ is the number of stimuli received by place j in period t and $N_{j.t-1}$ is the number of stimuli received in the preceding period.

These particular rules for population growth and the generation of stimuli need some brief elaboration. Rule 5(ii) argues that once a town has adopted, it will begin to generate a certain, small, amount of population growth of its own. This is tantamount to adding a 'self-potential' of a place to the gravity-based equation of rule 4[1] which would represent the agitation caused to the urban economy by the fact of its having adopted. This adds a deterministic element to the model since it means that, once having adopted, a place will grow, even if only by a very small amount. The main determinant of growth, however, will still be the stimuli that are received from the 'system' at large and rule 5(ii) argues that a place will grow primarily if, through its contacts with other innovating centres, it continues to take part in the general ferment of the innovative sequence. The effect of each stimulus will have an immediate impact on population growth in the period at which the stimulus was received and also a further, although modified, effect in the next time period. Rule 3 determines that the number of stimuli sent out in each time period is a weighted function of the population size of the town which has adopted; large towns will send a larger absolute number of stimuli, but a smaller proportionate number, than will small towns.

This version of the basic simulation was run over a number of time periods for the set of towns shown in fig. 6.2 and the growth rates of the urban populations were calculated at the end of each period using the compound growth-rate formula given in chapter 3.[2] The pattern of growth rates by the end of the tenth period is shown in fig. 6.3. Only those places which had adopted, and whose population had therefore changed, are shown.[3] The pattern of growth is interesting since, while there is a decreasing scatter of variance at larger sizes of towns, the upward curve of the average growth is far steeper than was ever found in the data of the nineteenth century. The source of this discrepancy is very readily apparent in the nature of the rules of Model 1, since the combination of rules 3 and 5 makes the effect of innovations on urban growth doubly multiplicative; rule 3 making the number of stimuli a function of town size and rule 5 making the increments of additional population also a function of size. If we were considering only a single innovation it would be reasonable to argue that, once a town had adopted, its population would subsequently grow by some fraction of its existing size and thereby simulate the multiplier effect of innovation diffusion, but in our model we are dealing with a whole stream of innovations and the multiplier effect is already incorporated into the model by the increasing numbers of stimuli which a place is likely to receive once it has adopted. It would therefore be more realistic to argue that, given the increasing flow of stimuli in the model, each individual stimulus received by a town would

[1] See above, p. 193.
[2] Equation [3-4], see above, p. 71.
[3] Of the total of 343 places, sixty-nine had not adopted by period 10 and thus had growth rates of zero.

represent a fixed increment of population. This increment would then represent, say, the addition of a factory or of a unit of tertiary employment which would be of the same size irrespective of the size of town to which it was added. The only difference between the likely growth of a large and a small place would then be that the large place would be more likely to attract a greater number of such incremental units by receiving more stimuli through the structure of the equation in rule 4. The multiplier effect would be contained in the tendency for stimuli to increase at something approaching a geometric ratio.

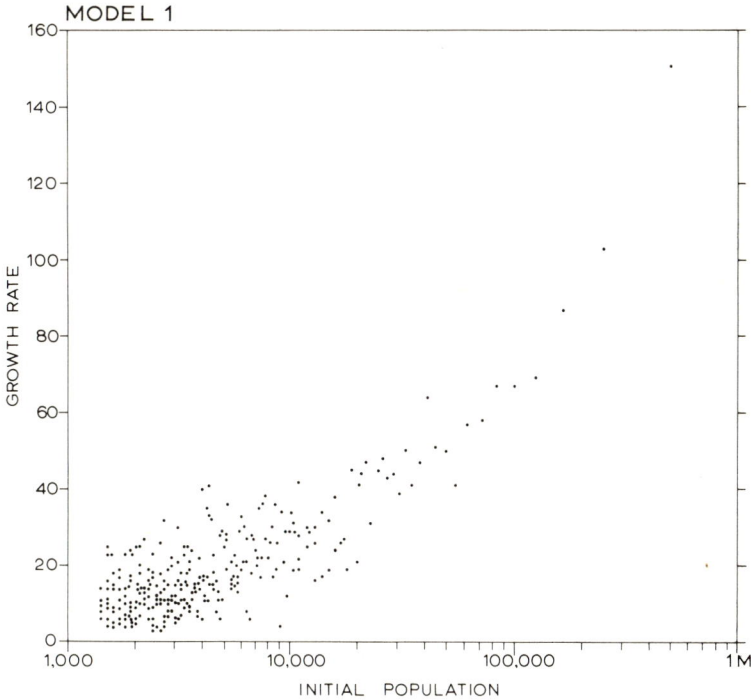

Figure 6.3   Urban growth rates: Model 1 at generation 10

MODEL 2

Model 2 therefore has the following rules:

1-4. As in Model 1.

5. Once a place has adopted, in subsequent time periods its population grows in the following ways:
   (i) every fresh stimulus which it receives generates 100 units of additional population in the time period in which the stimulus is received and 50 units in the subsequent period.

Urban growth

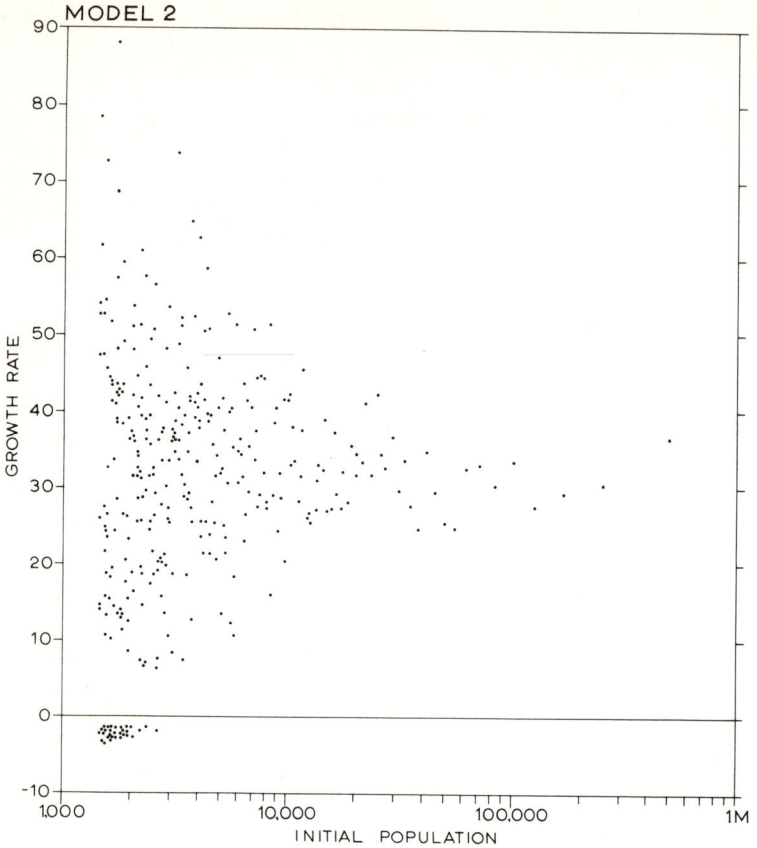

Figure 6.4   Urban growth rates: Model 2 at generation 10

(ii) once it has adopted, a town generates its own further growth by the
    addition of 100 units of population in each subsequent period, irrespective
    of whether or not the place receives stimuli.
For any given period, population growth will therefore be given by the
following:

$$100(N_{j.\,t}) + 50(N_{j.\,t-1}) + 100.$$

Model 2 also differs from Model 1 in that it allows the population of a town
to decline if the town does not receive sufficient stimuli. Since the total number
of stimuli available is small in the first few periods of the simulation this decline
in population only begins to operate after a certain number of cycles of the
model. This additional rule would read:

Table 6.2 *Distribution of dates at which places adopt: Model 2*

Period	1	2	3	4	5	6	7	Total
0	1							1
1	1							1
2	4		1					5
3		4	3	1	1	1		10
4		2	8	3	2	2		17
5			1	15	10	4	5	35
6				6	17	20	4	47
7					15	31	16	62
8					3	23	37	63
9					2	14	28	44
10						4	24	28
11						1	13	14
12							9	9
13							3	3
14							3	3
15							1	1
After 15								0
								343

Note: Size groups are as follows:
1 80,000+
2 40,000–79,999
3 20,000–39,999
4 10,000–19,999
5   5,000– 9,999
6   2,500– 4,999
7   1,250– 2,499

6. If, in the periods after the second cycle of the model, a place fails to receive any stimuli over two consecutive periods, its size will decline by S population $(S_i = \sqrt[4]{P_i})$.

This rule draws some distinction between those places which, irrespective of whether or not they have adopted, continue to receive stimuli and those places which do not. It argues that, whether or not a place has adopted, if it does not take part in the general innovative ferment its population will decline.

Running Model 2 produces a markedly different pattern of growth from that of Model 1. At the end of the tenth period (fig. 6.4), there is only a relatively small number of places which have not adopted. The populations of some of these places have declined by an amount depending on the number of stimuli received since some of the non-adopters may still have received some, but less than three, stimuli which would have had the effect of slowing their rate of decline. The growth rates of the whole set of places shows a scatter which is remarkably, and encouragingly, similar to that of the real world. The largest place, with its initial advantage of having begun the whole growth sequence through having had the innovation from the outset, has a somewhat higher growth rate than expected for its population size, but, overall, the curve of average growth shows a roughly constant average irrespective of size and the most striking feature of the scatter is the way in which the variance decreases with increasing town size. The way in which this declining variance is produced can be seen from the sequence of adoption dates and its relation both to the size and the location of the towns. Table 6.2 shows the date of adoption for groups of towns of different size. The distribution bears a close relationship to the size-related diffusion processes of nineteenth-century entrepreneurial innovations. All of the towns have adopted by the fifteenth period, but the average date of adoption becomes successively later for groups of progressively smaller towns: all of the largest group has adopted by period two; all of the second largest group by period four; all of the fifth largest group by period nine; and so forth. There is, however, an increasing variance in the date of adoption of groups of smaller-sized towns: for example, in the third largest group one town adopts as early as period two, while the latest adopter is in period five; for the very smallest group this range extends from periods five to fifteen. This again was seen to be a feature of the process of diffusion in real-world data; certain small towns adopt precociously early even though the average date gets later for groups of smaller towns.

There are two reasons which account for this variance in the date of adoption (and for the corresponding increase in the variance in growth rates for smaller places).[1] First is the chance or stochastic element in the simulation model which means that, even though the probability of a small place receiving a sufficient number of stimuli for it to adopt may be small, there is still a probability that it will adopt and grow and so will enhance the future likelihood of its receiving stimuli. Second, however, is the influence of the location of the towns which is incorporated into the structure of the model through the neighbourhood effect of distance friction. This second effect can clearly be seen by looking at some specific instances of the adoption sequence which are shown in fig. 6.5. For example, place J.28,[2] with a population in the third-largest group of sizes, adopted as early as the second period, no doubt as a result of its relative proximity to the largest town. This had consequences, subsequently, for the small places in the vicinity of J.28 since they then lay in the vicinity of a place

[1] With so large a number of places, it is easier to examine the results of the model in terms of date of adoption. This is closely related to growth rate in the early generations of the model, but less close at later time periods when the advantage of early adopters tends to be nullified by the rapid growth in the number of stimuli which causes the different variants of the simulation to converge to a similar end-product set of growth rates.

[2] Towns are referred to by the co-ordinates shown in fig. 6.2. The largest, central, town has a co-ordinate reference of L.24.

emitting stimuli from a very early date and thus would have a higher-than-average expectancy of being 'hit' by stimuli. One of them, place J.30, adopted as early as period 4 and had received a total of thirty-nine stimuli by period ten and had a growth rate of 51 per cent — well above the average date of adoption. number of stimuli and growth rate of places of comparable population size. Similarly, the effects of proximity to the central largest town can be seen on the growth of the towns immediately surrounding it. Despite the fact that the random allocation of initial populations to these places happened to give them

Table 6.3 *Diffusion and growth in small towns adjacent to the first-order town: Model 2*

Place	Initial population	Period of adoption	Number of stimuli by period 10	Growth rate by period 10 (%)
L.26	1,736	5	15	88
M.25	3,205	5	23	74
M.23	3,125	8	9	35
L.22	1,565	6	11	73
K.23	1,623	7	7	52
K.25	1,587	9	4	26
M.27	1,930	8	6	39
N.24	1,462	10	3	14
M.21	6,493	4	24	44
K.21	1,511	11	2	−2
J.24	2,415	8	5	25
K.27	4,000	8	12	34

Notes
1. Places are referred to by co-ordinate references as given in fig. 6.2. They are arranged in the table in clockwise order around the central town, L.24. The first six places are closer to L.24 than are the second six places.
2. Dates of adoption should be compared with those of other towns of comparable size given in table 6.2.

very small populations in comparison with the average fourth-order town, their dates of adoption tended to be earlier than the average for their respective sizes. Indeed, if one looks at the fortunes of the twelve fourth-order towns which lie closest to the largest town (table 6.3) the nature of the diffusion process in the simulation model can be seen rather clearly. There is considerable variability amongst the set of towns even though their populations and their locations are not radically dissimilar. This is the consequence of the stochastic element in the model which allocates stimuli to one of the towns which, because of the cumulative and circular process of growth, then tends to be at an advantage with respect to its neighbouring towns as its population begins to rise. Also, however,

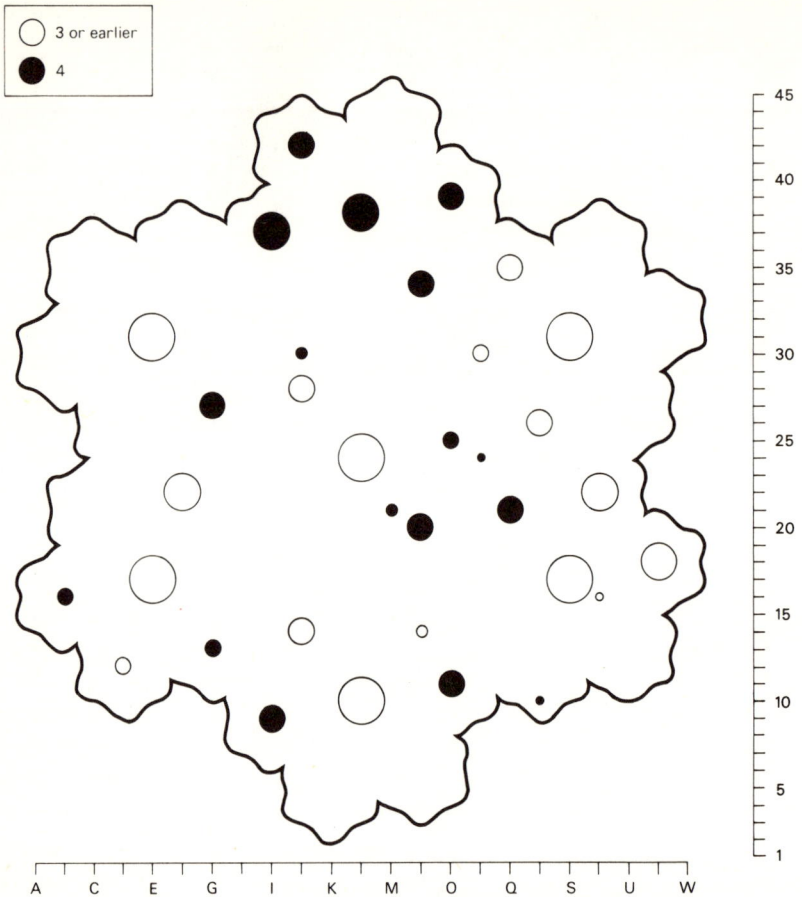

Figure 6.5   The spatial sequence of adoption. Model 2 at generations 3, 4 and 5

one can see that, for all of these places, proximity to the largest town has the effect of increasing the likelihood of earlier adoption and higher growth than in towns of similar size but more remote in the network of the overall set of towns.

Model 2 thus illustrates two points in particular. First, that in dealing with a probabilistic model there is considerable scope for chance happenings to influence the pattern of growth especially in the early time periods of the simulation. Places close to those large centres which happen to adopt early will themselves tend to adopt earlier and grow more rapidly than more distant towns of the same population size, but this is by no means certain. Any particular run of the model will produce a different 'unique' result giving high growth rates to one set of places and lower rates to some other. In all the examples of the application of the simulation model only a single run of each variant of the

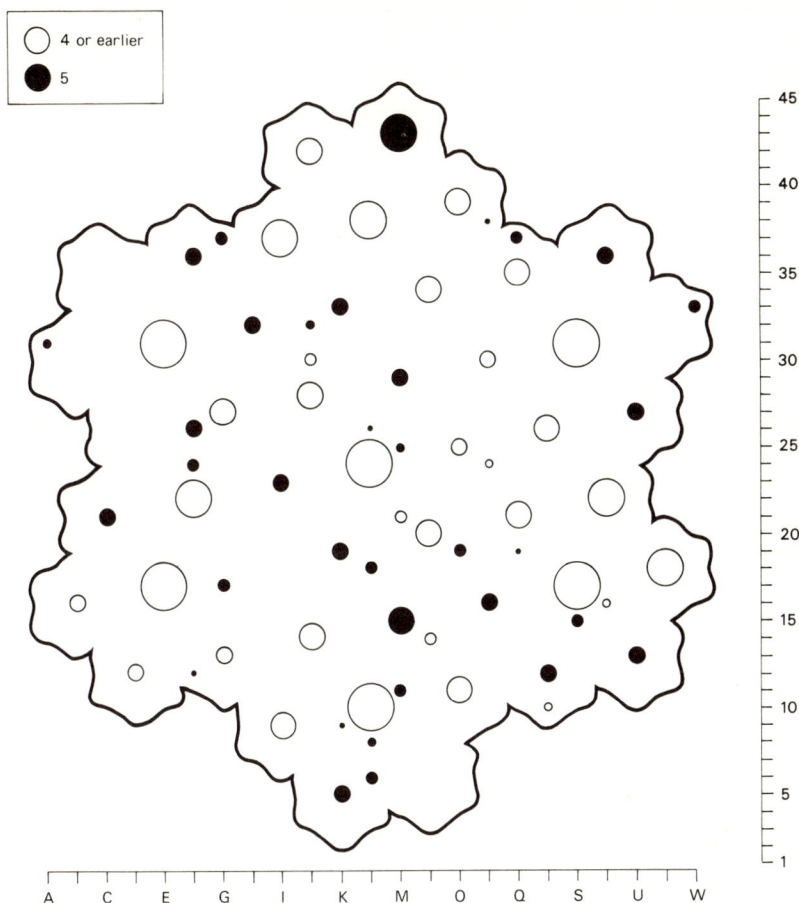

Figure 6.5 (*continued*)   Key to sizes of circles is given in fig. 6.2.

model has been made. The interest lies less in the particular pattern which happens to emerge, than in the general tendencies which are suggested and it has been assumed that a single run of the model over a number of time periods can be taken as representative of a 'mean' of a large number of runs.[1] Second, Model 2 illustrates the effect of the joint operation in the diffusion of the composite innovation of the hierarchical and neighbourhood processes and of their consequences on the aggregate pattern of urban growth rates which are produced by growth-causing innovations. The wide scatter of variance for the growth rates of small towns is the product of the neighbourhood effect operating in a set of towns differently located in space. Suppose, for example, that the structure of the diffusion process had been made to depend purely upon population size. The

[1] See, however, the comments in Brown and Moore (1969, pp. 130-1).

effect would have been a radical reduction in the variance of growth rates; any scatter which did exist would have been due solely to the stochastic nature of the simulation. However, in the model, as in the real world,[1] the variance in the distances between small and large places is greater than the variance between large places, and, when a neighbourhood diffusion principle operates, it is this which produces the increasing scatter of adoption dates of small places. To illustrate the different distance variances between large as against small places, consider the distances involved in our idealized landscape of places (fig. 6.1). If the basic unit of length is the distance between one town and any other town, it can be seen that, with respect to the largest place, all of the second-order towns are equally placed at seven units of distance and their variance in this respect is therefore zero. The third-order places, however, lie at different distances from the first-order place; the closest being less than three units of distance away, while the farthest are over nine units distant. The fourth-order places have an even greater variance since their distances from the first-order place vary from only one unit to over ten units. When only the first-order place is sending out stimuli, therefore, the denominator of equation [6.1], which determines the probability of receiving stimuli, will vary by these increasingly wide margins as one moves from second- to fourth-order places. The nature and operation of the neighbourhood effect can therefore be considered to be an agent of some importance in explaining the increasing scatter of urban growth in smaller size-groups of cities. The correspondence between the pattern of real-world growth rates and those produced by the simulation model suggests the plausibility of the argument that the diffusion of innovations within a set of towns is a contributor to the population growth of those towns. This is not to argue that the adoption of innovations can be thought of as the sole 'cause' of urban growth which obviously is the product of a whole host of events of which innovation adoption is but one. It is, however, of more than trivial interest to find that the patterns of urban growth produced by a diffusion model which combines hierarchical and neighbourhood processes is compatible with that of the real world.

VARIANTS OF THE SIMULATION

Model 2 is, of course, only one variant of a whole family of simulation models which would have different operating rules and parameters even though their structure would be identical. There are three principal ways in which the rules could be changed: the calculation of probabilities of receiving stimuli could be changed by altering the exponents of the distance and population terms in

---

[1] While the vast literature on central-place theory has not established that the uniform spacing and regular hierarchy of that theory are found in the real world, it does suggest the tendency for larger places to be more widely separated than smaller places. See the summary of work in Berry and Pred (1965), and the analysis by E. N. Thomas (1962).

equation [6.1]; the threshold number of stimuli which would be required before adoption occurred could be raised or lowered; and the number of stimuli sent out by towns could be altered. To what extent is it possible to interpret such changes in terms of their meaning in the real world? Altering the distance exponent might be thought of as representing changes in transport in the real world; as movement becomes relatively less expensive or less time-consuming, through technical improvements in transport, so one might imagine that the friction of distance would grow less and the size of the distance exponent would decline.[1] The second change — altering the threshold resistance levels — could be seen in terms of the effects of technical changes upon the optimal scale of production; for any particular innovation, technical improvements might either raise or lower the likelihood of adoption in smaller places either, in the first case, as the risks or the costs of adoption grow less small places can more confidently adopt, or, in the second case, as scale economies increase so will the optimal scale of operation work to the advantage of larger rather than smaller places. The third change — increasing the number of stimuli emitted — could be seen in terms of improvement in general communications. The introduction of electrical means of transmitting messages, the introduction of mass media, improvements in postal services, as well as the improvement of physical transport, all might be expected to increase the total agitation within a national economy and result in an expansion in the overall flow of information and the transmission of ideas (Meier 1962).

It would, however, be difficult to translate into real-world terms any specific change in the operating rules of different varieties of the simulation model since even the three changes noted above are not independent of one another and since the evidence on threshold levels in particular is somewhat ambiguous. On the inter-relatedness of the three examples, improvements in transport, for example, might well have the effect of lowering the distance exponent, but at the same time would doubtless also have the effect of increasing the total flow of information within the system and might too be accompanied by alterations in the threshold levels of adoption. It would, therefore, be difficult to match technical changes during the course of the nineteenth century with specific sets of operating rules so as to develop a version of the model for the early, the middle and the later part of the period 1801-1911, to see whether the changes in the average slope of urban growth rates might be explained by alterations in technology and organization as the period progressed. We might, however, look at two changes in the rules of the simulation to see the direction of their effects and whether these can be made consonant with the empirical changes in urban growth which have been discovered.

Model 3 makes two alterations to the operating rules of Model 2: first by increasing the weighting of the distance term; and second, as a trivial alteration,

[1] See, for example, Olsson 1965, pp. 57-63.

Table 6.4   *Distribution of dates at which places adopt:*
Model 3

Period	\multicolumn{7}{c}{Size group}							Total
	1	2	3	4	5	6	7	
0	1							1
1						1		1
2	1	1				1		3
3	2			1				3
4		1	2			1		4
5	1	4	4	2	2	1		14
6	1		3	8	4	4	2	22
7			4	6	14	10	4	38
8				6	16	22	10	54
9					4	23	26	53
10				2	8	14	19	43
11						12	21	33
12					2	3	15	20
13						3	16	19
14						2	3	5
15							5	5
After 15						3	22	25
								343

Note: Size groups as in table 6.2.

by making the decline in the population of places which do not receive stimuli a decline of a fixed rather than a proportionate amount. The rules of Model 3 therefore read as follows:

1-3. As in Model 1.

4. The probability of town i being 'hit' by a stimulus is given by the following:

$$k \sum_{j=1}^{n} P_i.d_{ij}^{-2}.S_j \quad (j = 1 \ldots n, j \neq i).$$

5. As in Model 2.

6. If, in the periods after the second cycle of the model, a place fails to receive any stimuli over two consecutive periods, its size will decline by 50 units of population.

The growth rates produced at generation 12 by Model 3 are shown in fig. 6.6. The effect of weighting the distance term by an exponent of 2·0 can be seen by comparison with the results of Model 2. Principally, the difference lies in the

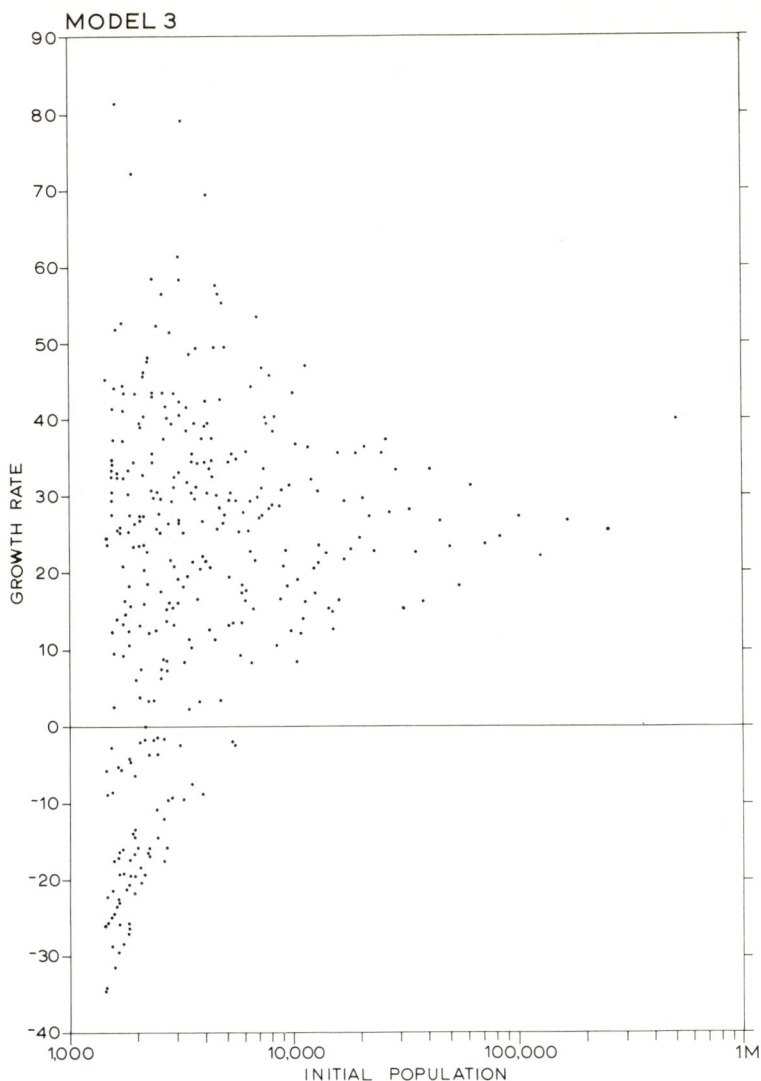

Figure 6.6   Urban growth rates: Model 3 at generation 12

widened scatter of growth rates for each of the size groups in the set of places. Thus, in terms of the date of adoption, table 6.4 shows that there is a much greater spread of dates for the different size groups of towns. This is most noticeable in the group of towns of sizes 2,500-4,999 in which one place adopts as early as period 1 and another as early as period 2. Interestingly, both of these very early adopters are close to the largest place (one is place M.25, the other is

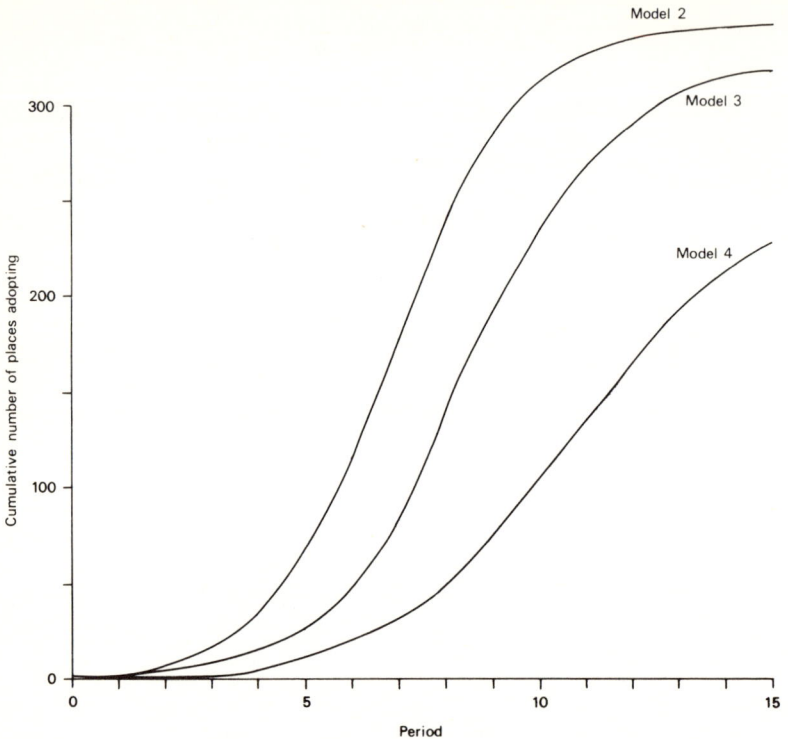

Figure 6.7   Numbers of adopting towns: comparison of Models 2, 3 and 4

place M.23, both of which are small fourth-order towns lying immediately adjacent to the largest town, L.24), thus illustrating the effect of increasing the neighbourhood component of the diffusion process. As was expected, therefore, by giving distance friction a greater weight, certain of the very small places which lie in close proximity to large early adopters benefit more than was the case in Model 2 and the scatter of growth rates in the early periods of the model is consequently somewhat wider. It is apparent too that the greater distance friction also has the effect of slowing up the speed of the whole diffusion process even though the threshold level of adoption is identical for the two models. Figure 6.7 and table 6.5 show the much slower growth curve of adopters in Model 3. The stronger distance constraint has the effect of reducing the probability of stimuli seeping out from the initial adopter town since more of the stimuli are sent to the larger number of small proximate towns each of which takes a longer time than do larger towns to reach the necessary threshold and so adopts later. As the number of adopters is delayed, so the overall growth in the number of stimuli is reduced and a brake is applied to the whole sequence. After

Table 6.5 *Comparison of Models 2, 3 and 4*

Period	Stimuli sent out			No. of places adopting (cumulative total in brackets)		
	Model 2	Model 3	Model 4	Model 2	Model 3	Model 4
0				1 (1)	1 (1)	1 (1)
1	27	26	26	1 (2)	1 (2)	0 (1)
2	46	33	26	5 (7)	3 (5)	0 (1)
3	131	71	26	10 (17)	3 (8)	0 (1)
4	251	124	26	17 (34)	4 (12)	4 (5)
5	447	171	99	35 (69)	14 (26)	7 (12)
6	760	347	203	47 (116)	22 (48)	9 (21)
7	1150	559	301	62 (178)	38 (86)	10 (31)
8	1622	889	394	63 (241)	54 (140)	18 (49)
9	2078	1315	572	44 (285)	53 (193)	29 (78)
10	2437	1689	837	28 (313)	43 (236)	22 (100)
11	2700	2029	1022	14 (327)	33 (269)	31 (131)
12	2933	2280	1269	9 (336)	20 (289)	34 (165)
13	3119	2451	1536	3 (339)	19 (308)	28 (193)
14	3301	2638	1743	3 (342)	5 (313)	22 (215)
15	3467	2740	1919	1 (343)	5 (318)	24 (239)
After 15					25 (343)	104 (343)

a number of generations, however, this initial difference is reduced and the two models rapidly converge to produce very similar patterns of growth rates by the tenth period.

A further alteration can be made to one of the operating rules to produce another version of the simulation. Model 4 raises the level of the threshold of resistance amongst the towns from three to five stimuli, and its rules read as follows:

1. As in Model 1.

2. Towns adopt once they have received five stimuli from adopter towns. Having adopted, in subsequent time periods, their populations grow as specified in rule 5 and they emit a certain number of stimuli as in rule 3.

3. As in Model 1.

4-6. As in Model 3.

The growth rates at generation 15 produced by Model 4 are shown in fig. 6.8. The slowing-down in the rate of diffusion is quite dramatic (fig. 6.7 and table 6.5).[1] Almost one-third of the places have not adopted by generation 15, the

[1] It is because of such differences in the rates of diffusion in Models 2, 3 and 4 that the growth rates produced by the three models are shown for different periods in figs. 6.4, 6.6 and 6.8.

Table 6.6   *Distribution of dates at which places adopt:*
Model 4

| | | | Size group | | | | | |
Period	1	2	3	4	5	6	7	Total
0	1							1
1								0
2								0
3								0
4	3	1						4
5	2	4	1					7
6		1	2	3	2	1		9
7			2	1	4	2	1	10
8			6	4	5	3		18
9			2	8	10	9		29
10				3	7	7	5	22
11				3	7	16	5	31
12				3	7	13	11	34
13					2	14	12	28
14					2	5	15	22
15					1	10	13	24
After 15					3	20	81	104
								343

Note: Size groups as in table 6.2.

period at which cycling of the model was stopped, and, even in the places with populations of from 5,000 to 9,999 three places have not adopted by generation 15. A second difference effected by raising the threshold level, however, is a slight reduction in the scatter of growth rates and adoption dates compared with Model 3 (table 6.6). Again, this is an expected result since it is the consequence of the higher threshold level counteracting the strong distance constraint and thus giving greater weight to population size than in Model 3. With the squared distance term, small places close to a large early adopter are still likely to get some random stimuli because of their proximity and the operation of the neighbourhood effect. However, because there is a large number of such small places, the number of stimuli that any one receives is likely to be relatively few. Thus, with a higher threshold level, these small places are not likely to adopt early and, by later periods, when there is a larger number of stimuli being generated, the more remote small places have had a greater opportunity of catching up the backlog of stimuli so that the proximity advantages of certain of the smaller towns is nullified and they tend to adopt at dates which are not as dissimilar as in Model 3.

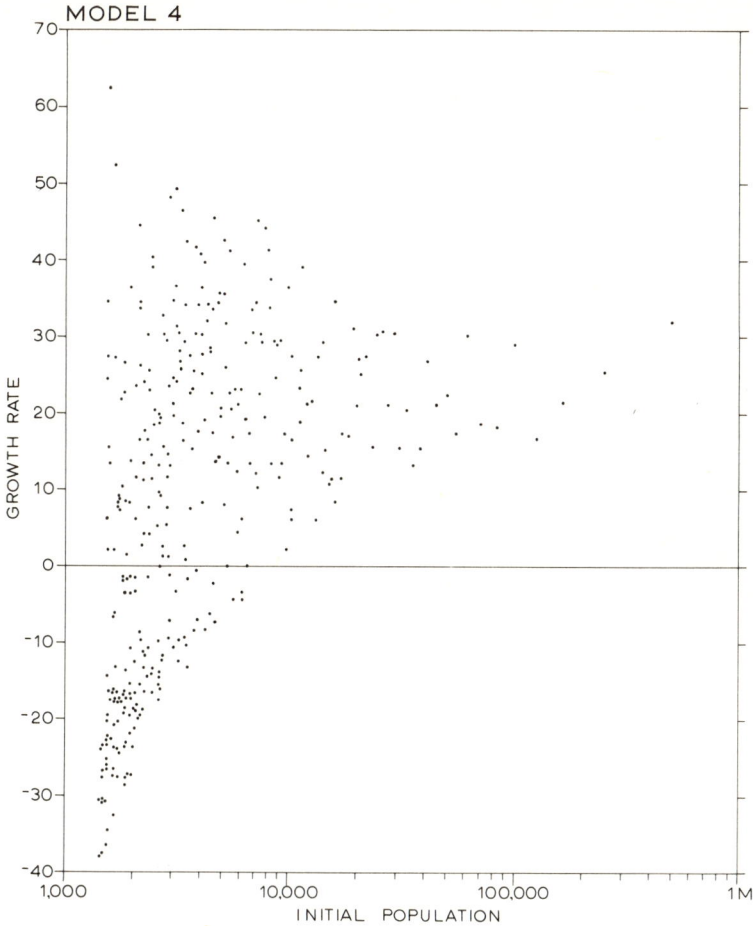

Figure 6.8   Urban growth rates: Model 4 at generation 15

One could continue to play with the permutations and combinations of alternative operating rules for a very considerable time, but the effect is to teach one more about cutting corners in writing computer programmes than about the substantive problem in hand. While a variety of other versions of the basic simulation model were experimented with, sufficient detail has now been introduced for a number of more general conclusions to be drawn.[1]

---

[1] Further alterations included the use of a variable threshold level as well as different weightings of the population and distance terms in equation [6.1]. The analysis of these alternative models by the highly pragmatic means of actually running simulations is both clumsy and time-consuming, but, given the complexity of dealing with the two dimensions of spatial location in a set of towns, no simple analytic approach suggested itself as an alternative to running the simulations.

CONCLUSIONS

The attempt to simulate the diffusion process of a composite innovation was undertaken in an effort to see to what extent the results on the growth of a set of towns appeared to be consistent with the empirical data discussed in chapter 3. It is apparent that one can reconcile the decreasing variance of growth rates in larger towns with our ideas about innovation diffusion. Because the lines of contact and of stimulus are more distended in the case of small towns, but more especially because the lengths of these links are more *variable* for small than for large towns, there will be a tendency for the effects of the diffusion of innovations to be more variable the smaller the town. Certain small places may well join the ranks of adopters, some indeed may well become adopters at very early dates and thus accrue the benefits hypothesized for the early adopter; but other places will not adopt until very late because, being not only small in size, but also being distant from large centres, they have to await the prior adoption by some neighbouring larger centre before they in turn have a high probability of adoption.[1]

This result is of some wide interest. It provides a rather general explanation for the pattern of variance found in the growth of nineteenth-century towns, even though it is only one of a number of explanations. It also implies that the degree of scatter of urban growth rates may be related to the particular spatial distribution of towns in any set of cities being studied. On the basis of our argument about the importance of the variance of the links of contact in influencing the variance of growth rates, one could hypothesize that a uniform distribution of towns — as in the central-place system — would produce a less wide scatter of growth rates than would a more clustered pattern of towns in which only certain regions were densely settled. Both would still show declining variance at larger city sizes, but the overall variance would be larger for the more clustered set of towns since, in this latter arrangement, all of the large and small places in the densely-settled areas might be expected to adopt early, whereas the towns in the more remote areas of more widely-spaced settlement would be expected to adopt considerably later. It might be anticipated that the variance in the growth rates of all sizes of towns might thus be greater.[2] The spatial pattern of towns in Britain is, of course, somewhat closer to the latter pattern rather than to the formal geometry of central-place theory. The nineteenth-century industrial complexes of the North West, the North East, the Potteries, South

[1] This result is not solely the product of the peculiar and regular geometry of the central-place system from which we started since the populations of the towns were made to vary within each of the hierarchical ranks of central places so that the dispersion of probabilities of receiving stimuli was not solely the product of geometry as it would have been if every town in each order had been allotted equal populations.

[2] It would be a similar process which would provide the rationale for patterns of economic inequality — of core and periphery — to persist within national economies.

Wales, West Yorkshire and the West Midlands were each quite widely separated and each, in turn, distant from London, but within each there was a dense cluster of large and small towns. In such a pattern of places, one would therefore expect the variance of growth rates to be higher than in the simulation model. While all of the simulation trials used an identical basic geometry of places, it would therefore be of some interest to see the extent to which alternative geometries had effect upon the rates of diffusion and upon the consequent urban growth rates.

The second aspect of urban growth which was posed as a problem was the change in the slope of the line relating average growth to town size. From the scatter of growth rates produced by the variants of the simulation model it can be seen that, even by relatively early periods, the different operating rules all rapidly converge on a fairly uniform average growth rate as the number of stimuli grows. In the very early generations however, it is apparent that anything which slows down the overall rate of diffusion works to the advantage of the larger towns and gives them a higher average rate of growth. Both a higher threshold level and a stronger distance constraint therefore have the effect of producing higher average growth rates in the larger towns. The latter of these two influences can certainly be interpreted in terms of improving transport; and, in the context of the nineteenth century, the fact that movement became easier and more rapid would thus be consistent with the progressive change from a set of growth rates positively related to size to one in which size and growth were not related.[1]

However, a much stronger reason can be given for the change in the slope of the curve linking growth and size. It is related to the overall rate at which innovations are introduced into an economy as a whole and here the simulation model is less directly helpful. The model treated diffusions in composite terms. Since the number of stimuli continued to grow with the growth of population and the addition of new adopters, the model made the assumption that the stream of new innovations was an unbroken and ever-swelling flow. Now if it is assumed that major innovations occur in swarms or clusters, as did Schumpeter, and if the effects of each individual innovation becomes progressively less over time, an interesting tendency is apparent. The large towns would show the benefits of their early adoption only so long as new innovations were constantly being introduced. Their 'lead' over small places would continue only so long as they were able to draw on new sets of innovations while the effects of earlier innovations were being diffused to places lower in the size hierarchy. Once the stream of new innovations falters or dries up, however, the larger towns have no further sources of growth on which to draw while, for a time, the smaller places would still be benefiting from their adoption of earlier innovations. This can be

[1] This is entirely consistent with Pederson's suggestions in the context of a developing country (Pederson 1970, pp. 224-6).

Table 6.7   *Model 4: distribution of growth rates by generations 10 and 15*

(a) Generation 10 Growth rate (%)	No. of towns in size category						
	7	6	5	4	3	2	1
60– 69							
50– 59							
40– 49	1						
30– 39		2	1				
20– 29		4	4				
10– 19		4	8	6	4	4	3
0– 9	5	12	15	13	9	2	3
–0– –9	6	42	22	6			
–10––19	72	36					
–20––29	50						
–30––39	9						

(b) Generation 15 Growth rate (%)	No. of towns in size category						
	7	6	5	4	3	2	1
60– 69	1						
50– 59	1						
40– 49	2	7	5				
30– 39	7	17	9	4	3	1	1
20– 29	11	19	14	7	6	3	3
10– 19	12	18	13	10	4	2	2
0– 9	16	13	6	4			
–0– –9	13	15	3				
–10––19	42	11					
–20––29	29						
–30––39	9						

Note: Town size categories are as follows
1   80,000+
2   40,000–79,999
3   20,000–39,999
4   10,000–19,999
5   5,000– 9,999
6   2,500– 4,999
7 < 2,500

illustrated by looking at the growth rates produced at successive periods of any one model. Those of Model 4, for example, are shown in table 6.7 for generations 10 and 15. It is apparent that, at the earlier date, the curve relating growth and size slopes upwards since the larger places have higher rates of growth as a consequence of their generally earlier adoption dates.[1] By the later

[1] It is of some interest to note that the one aberrant town with a very early adoption date in the smallest of the size categories is place K.25 – one of the nearest neighbours to the largest town L.24.

date, this difference has almost been eradicated as increasing numbers of smaller places have come to adopt. If the flow of innovations were then t stopped, it would be the larger places whose growth would first suffer while the smaller places would still, for a time, benefit from the effects of earlier innovations which were still diffusing through the lower end of the size hierarchy. The maintenance of an upward-sloping growth-size curve thus depends upon there being a continuing stream of innovations from which larger towns can reap, and maintain, the benefits of their generally earlier adoption dates.

The logic of such an oversimplified picture would be that, if one can think of long waves — or Kondratieff waves — within an economy and if the crests of these waves are periods during which new innovations are being introduced, then

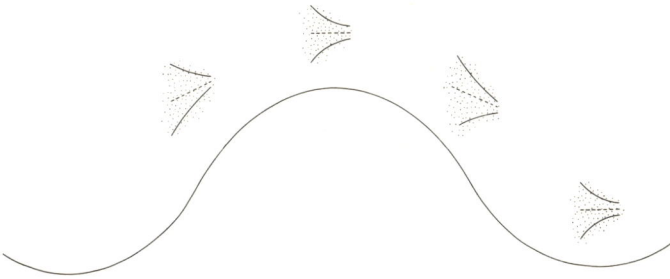

Figure 6.9   The pattern of urban growth and the stream of innovations over time. The solid line suggests an assumed curve of innovations over time in an economy

in these periods of high inventive and innovative activity the large towns would continue to show the benefits of their early adoption of innovations. As the flood of innovations abated so would the advantages of the larger towns begin to decline as the effects of earlier innovations continued in the later-adopting small places while, in the larger towns themselves, no new innovations were available for adoption. The sequence of this idealized relationship might be as portrayed in fig. 6.9 in which the curve of the growth-to-size relationship is shown to alter with the crests and troughs of long waves of innovative activity.

The simulation model of urban growth can therefore suggest reasons both as to why the variance of growth rates grows less in sets of larger cities and why it might be that the relationship of growth and city size may alter over time. Both phenomena can be reconciled with a model suggesting that urban growth is intimately connected with the adoption of innovations which form part of the cumulative and circular process of the growth of an urban economy.

CHAPTER 7

Growth rates and city size: the timing of change

It cannot be said that the country which has produced a Watt, a Stephenson, and an Arkwright is deficient in mechanical inventiveness, but it is impossible to deny that the period of time since 1870 has not been marked by the evolution of distinctly novel electrical inventive ideas proceeding from British minds.

J. A. FLEMING 1901

The diffusion of innovations has been used to explain both of the questions which were posed by the empirical data of nineteenth-century urban growth rates. First, the declining variance of average growth in larger cities has been shown to be compatible with the pattern of growth 'caused' by innovations spreading in a spatial system of towns. Second, the changing relationship between city size and average growth has been suggested as being linked with changes in the flow of innovations; since any cessation in the flow of new innovations in a system of cities could be expected to lead to a relative decline in the average growth rates of larger places, the curve relating size and growth would flatten. The empirical data of the nineteenth century suggest that just such a flattening occurred in the later decades of the period, starting perhaps as early as in the decade 1861-71, but certainly by the decade 1871-81.[1] Since the relationship between size of town and average growth rate changed from being positive to neutral in this period, how reasonable is it to account for the change in terms of a change in the rate of urban innovations?

At first sight, it would appear more profitable to turn to the purely demographic facts of the nineteenth century and seek explanations in them. The rate of population growth certainly fell during the latter part of the nineteenth century, but, for a number of reasons, this does not directly help in any way to explain the change in the relationship between size and growth. First, the fall in the rate of total population growth for England and Wales occurred only in the last two decades of the century and not before 1881 (table 7.1). Secondly, the effect of changes in the overall rate of national population growth would be to change the level of the intercept on the growth-rate axis rather than, by itself, to alter the shape of the curve or the degree of scatter around the average line of

[1] See above, pp. 88–9.

growth. Holding constant the balance of migration, one would therefore expect that, during decades of rapid national population increase, the intercept would be high, and vice versa. Only if the fall in population was differentially concentrated in either large or small cities would the slope of the average growth curve be altered. And the evidence on this question is far from clear. Innes (1938, p. 42) certainly suggests that the fall in the birth rate[1] first occurred in essentially urban occupations, but, on the other hand, it is clear from Welton's (1911, pp. 80-90) calculations of urban population changes, that the fall in fertility in the period 1881-1901 was experienced as early in what he calls 'rural residues' as in the textile and residential towns. Indeed, the fall in the decade

Table 7.1   *Growth of the total population of England and Wales, 1801-1911*

Decade	Decennial increase (%)
1801–11	14·00
1811–21	18·06
1821–31	15·80
1831–41	14·27
1841–51	12·65
1851–61	11·90
1861–71	13·21
1871–81	14·36
1881–91	11·65
1891–1901	12·17
1901–1911	10·89

Source: Mitchell (1962, p. 6).

1881-91 was least in large towns, industrial towns and colliery districts (table 7.2). It would therefore seem unproven that birth rates first fell in larger urban areas.

Changes in the flows of migration could, equally, have effect upon the slope of the growth-size curve, since, if migration was predominantly to large towns, then changes in the streams of migration would have differential effect upon towns of different sizes. Such changes did indeed occur during the late nineteenth century, even though, again, they post-date the period at which the change from a positive to a neutral relationship between growth and size occurred. Welton's figures for 1881-1901, for example, show that the textile towns of the north — and, of course, these included some of the very largest of

---

[1] The report on fertility in the census of 1911 suggested that the fall in fertility may be dated from around 1876 and it found that, by 1911, the lowest effective rates of fertility were in the northern textiles towns which combined low fertility with high child mortality (Census 1923, pp. xxxvii and cxxxv).

the towns — suffered considerable losses especially in the decade 1881-91. The towns which predominantly gained most by migration, in contrast, were the residential and military towns. Cairncross (1953, pp. 68-74) likewise suggests that 1880 marked a watershed in the pattern of migration flows to the northern towns; the migrants, who had constituted a not inconsiderable proportion of the increase in the populations of many northern industrial towns, began, after 1880, to move elsewhere, and particularly abroad, instead of to the large industrial towns within Britain. While London escaped such net losses of population, in the northern industrial towns a pattern of net immigration was changed to one of net emigration, both as people from within the towns moved elsewhere and as the streams of migrants from Ireland and the rural areas were diverted abroad in increasing numbers.

Table 7.2 *Differential fertility*

	Birth rates per 10,000 married women aged below 45		
	1881	*1891*	*1901*
Colliery districts	3244	3156	2880
Industrial places	3196	2988	2683
Rural residues	3117	2838	2473
Old towns	2989	2672	2358
Residential places	2932	2553	2188
Large towns	2898	2657	2407
Miscellaneous places	2884	2623	2202
Military towns	2883	2574	2236
Textile towns	2819	2477	2059

Source: Welton (1911, pp. 84 and 87).

An emphasis upon migration flows, however, points as much to consequences as to causes in the changing relationship between growth and size in the last quarter of the century. Not only do the changes in such flows appear to have occurred after the change in this relationship, but, in any case, it has been argued that migration can be regarded as synoptic of the economic and social attractiveness of cities. We therefore need to look beyond the purely demographic changes to suggest causes of the lower relative growth of large towns. What was it about the larger towns of late nineteenth-century Britain which appears to have made them less economically vital, and therefore relatively less able to retain their own population increases or to attract continuing flows of migrants from elsewhere? Amongst a host of aspects, it would not seem unreasonable to focus on two; the economic opportunities offered in large towns and the internal organization of the towns themselves in terms of such things as housing and the array of services and facilities which they offered.[1] Both aspects, of course, bring us back to the question of the adoption of innovations. The first in that flourishing economic opportunities, particularly in the increasingly competitive climate of the time, would depend on the productivity and vitality of trade and industry which would, in turn, depend much upon the types of technique employed and, hence, upon the adoption of new technologies. The second would equally impinge on the adoption of entrepreneurial innovations since the internal functioning of large towns would be much facilitated by organizational innovations which helped to lubricate the complex business of running large towns — supplying water, heat, food, fuel and power as well as making housing available, all would be improved and made possible by the adoption of new techniques in transport, communication and organizational technologies.

The simulation model of urban growth has already suggested that one can 'explain' the change in the slope of growth and size by postulating a fall in the rate of new innovations, since their absence would first have effect upon the growth of larger towns. We are therefore left with the question of why there might have been a fall in the rate of innovations in the final quarter of the nineteenth century: first in innovations in the general sphere of economic activity; and second in innovations affecting the internal organization and operation of large towns.

TECHNICAL INNOVATIONS

On the economic side, there is a large, and still flourishing debate in the literature of economic history, and the ground has been well covered, even though the debate is by no means yet resolved. That contemporaries in the period considered that the country was falling behind, there is little doubt. Levine (1967, p. 11) suggests that by as early as the 1850s doubts were being expressed about the performance of British industry vis-a-vis that of the United States. By the end of the century, there was a welter of commissions and committees set up to investigate such questions and their conclusions almost invariably bemoaned the laggardly British performance. The Royal Commissions on the Depression of Trade and Industry (1884-6), and on Labour (1892-3), the departmental committees organized by the Board of Trade during the First World War, and the studies of individual industries by the Balfour Committee on

[1] An interesting question is the extent to which the rising social concern expressed in housing, education and welfare in the final quarter of the century, diverted capital resources into fields which did not repay short-term benefits. Ashworth (1966) asks whether the late Victorian educational and sanitary expenditure brought enough economic benefit to avoid slower economic growth: 'It is at least possible that in the nineteenth century it was more economical to keep the labour force up-to-date by letting early death take care of the old-fashioned, and a high birth-rate, plus the spur of insecurity, provide the new recruitment, than it was to make a social investment for the achievement of longevity and adaptability' (p. 30). He stresses, however, that the social services at the time accounted for a very small fraction of the gross national product.

Industry and Trade after the war, were all joined by the more hysterical voices of contemporary writers such as Shadwell (1909) who added to the mounting criticism of, and unease with, the country's economic performance. Current writing in economic history has explored many of the aspects of industrial retardation which gave rise to such concern. Even though different indices suggest different times for the onset of Britain's decline — indices of industrial productivity, for example, suggest the 1870s, whereas figures of gross national product suggest the 1890s (Richardson 1965a) — there is certainly a general concensus that, with respect to the United States and Germany, British industry showed a marked falling-behind in some, if not all, of the final quarter of the century. The reasons suggested in explanation of this decline are many, but might perhaps be summed under four heads: the early start thesis; the relative factor endowment of the country; rigidities in the organization of its firms; and the market opportunities open to British producers.

The thesis that Britain's early start worked eventually to the country's disadvantage is one of long standing since Veblen (1942) was one of its early advocates. It has, however, been carried further by more recent writing (for example, Frankel 1955 and Svennilson 1954). An important plank of the argument is that the country's early industrial start left it with a stock of equipment which acted as disincentive to its replacement by newer machinery and capital goods and thus reduced the likelihood of new innovations being adopted which would have increased productivity and made goods more competitive. Yet, given that other countries equally had stocks of older equipment, it may be that it was less the capital goods themselves, than the rigid attitudes to methods of production and to social and industrial relations which was the more important residue of the early industrial start. Certainly — as an off-shoot of the early-start thesis — the fact of overcommitment to the basic industries on which the country's first industrial success had been based, had subsequent deleterious consequences. Textiles, railways and consumer goods continued to be favoured at the expense of exports of steel to the developed countries of the world (W. A. Lewis 1957; Richardson 1965b). Continuing overcommitment to these activities had the effect of preempting production facilities which might otherwise have been used for newer types of activity; of perpetuating an industrial structure which became less suited to the new industries so that, even where they were introduced, they were often less economic than elsewhere; and of maintaining the industrially-linked development blocks based on coal, steam and iron which which consequently tended to block the development of electricity and of road transport just as the early chemical industry tended to block the progress of petro-chemicals.[1]

---

[1] In a not unrelated argument, there are parallels here with Ajo's (1969) thesis that economic systems develop resistance to innovative stimuli and that acceptance of an early innovation tends to reduce the probability of adoption of later stimuli in related fields. He illustrates his argument with the history of Kylälä's invention of an appliance which, fitted to steam locomotives, effected considerable improvements to their heat economy. Adoption of the device, however, was widespread only within France, Spain and Czechoslovakia.

The second argument, that factor endowments had effect upon the relatively poor British performance, relies on the suggestion that, whereas in the United States, for example, labour was relatively scarce by comparison with other factors of production, in Britain there were equally abundant supplies of all factors (except of land), so that there was little incentive to economize on the use of labour by the introduction of labour-saving innovations or to economize on fuel in the operation of, for example, the steel industry or in shipping or railways (see, for example, Habakkuk 1962a). Likewise, looking at the general absence of economies in the use of capital in the tin-plate industry, Aldcroft (1966, p. 129) argues that British industrialists made 'neutral' investment decisions rather than ones with a factor bias, with the consequence that innovations were less rapid than otherwise they might have been.

The third reason adduced by economic historians is the rigidity of the institutional framework in which investment decisions were made. The persistence of small, family-dominated firms checked industrial progress, so it is argued, because of their insular and parochial attitudes and because of the conservatism which tended to characterize their decisions in the generations following the successes of their first founder. Even though, by the turn of the century, a number of large enterprises had come into being in Britain, their scale was in no way comparable with the size of large firms in the United States which had bigger assets, a larger share of the market and covered a broader range of manufactures. Despite the passing of acts which opened the way for the general development of joint stock and limited liability in the period from the 1840s to the early 1860s, the British reaction was a compromise in the form of *private* limited companies many of which still retained the family heads of the older firms. The benefits of limited liability were thus combined with the minimum loss of independence through the retention of family control. This tendency had implications for the effectiveness of many of the amalgamations, since the boards of directors were often comprised of unwieldy bodies formed of all of the previous directors of the amalgamated companies. Payne (1967, p. 529) quotes the case of the Calico Printers' Association with a board of no fewer than eighty-four members: 'These ruinous weaknesses', he comments, 'resulted directly from the original attempts so to organise the combines that each component part retained a high degree of individuality.' Even where relatively large firms did develop in Britain, they differed from their American counterparts in that the reasons for their emergence were often to be found less in the desire to improve performance than to provide buffers against increasing prices and stiffer competition. Such was the case with the amalgamations arising from the 'Brewers' War' late in the century. By 1905, of the largest fifty firms in Britain, eighteen were in brewing or distilling and ten in textile manufacture; while in the United States, only one such firm represented each of these activities and the bulk of the largest fifty firms was in iron and steel, coal and non-ferrous metals — twenty-three firms in all. Of these top fifty firms, in Britain the numbers of 'producer' and 'consumer' firms were twenty-three and twenty-seven respectively; whereas in the United States, the figures were thirty-seven and thirteen (Payne 1967, pp. 527-9).

Small scales of operation had the effect of reducing the likelihood of standardization of production and this is an important component of the fourth reason suggested for British economic backwardness. The market upon which the British manufacturer increasingly relied was in the under-developed countries of the Empire, which offered safety, but little stimulus to encourage technical innovation. The small size of the home market, added to the fact that it had traditionally been supplied with custom-built rather than standardized products, helped to underline the low probability of the introduction of mass-production techniques. In the motor-car industry, for example, the fact that most firms tried to make as many as possible of the component parts for themselves and that they continued to manufacture for a market which expected highly individual products,[1] meant that the notion of inter-changeable parts caught on very slowly in comparison with the United States and France, despite the fact that the industry was better placed than any other to pursue such a technique. 'In Britain the engineers were obsessed by the technical product rather than by the technique of production' (Saul 1962b, p. 43).

Behind many of these arguments lies the notion of an entrepreneurial failure to adapt to changing competition and changing technical expertise in the latter part of the nineteenth century. The debate about entrepreneurial failure in Britain impinges upon much of the discussion rehearsed above and it invokes a number of further reasons for the poor industrial performance, such as the allegedly poorly developed state of technical education in Britain in comparison with the United States and Germany. But the castigation of the British entrepreneur has been somewhat modified since the early writing of Shadwell (1909) and the more recent work of Landes (1969), Aldcroft (1964) and Burn (1940). The various studies of individual industries have softened much of the sting of this criticism and paint the late nineteenth-century entrepreneur as much less of an inefficient sybarite than the earlier, and more general, studies would have led one to believe.[2]

Such writings and catalogues of explanations, while not as systematic as might be wished, do suggest that Britain did indeed suffer by comparison with American industrial productivity at the end of the nineteenth century and they give grounds for suggesting that the rate of adoption of technical innovations was significantly lower. This is not the place to embark upon historical or economic argument, since it is sufficient that we establish that innovations

---

[1] Such as the habit of manufacturers arranging for customers to fit car bodies of their own design on to a standard chassis.

[2] See, for example, McCloskey and Sandberg (1971) writing, not without irony, in the very journal which gave rise to much of the criticism of entrepreneurial activity. On individual industries, see Saul (1962b, 1967 and 1968) and the contributions in Aldcroft (1968) and McCloskey (1971).

slowed down in late-nineteenth-century Britain and that this could have had differential effect upon the growth rates of the larger towns as against the smaller. Tending to cling to the innovations of the first industrial revolution, British industry did not adopt the wave of newer technologies as rapidly as did certain other countries. The industries which suffered especially in consequence were the steel and chemical industries (for example, Burn 1940; Richardson 1968) and the electrical industries of the 'new' industrial revolution at the end of the century. It was only in the inter-war period that the fuller impact of such newer innovations really took root in Britain so that the impetus of having been the first industrial nation was lost to the United States, Germany and, later, Japan.

ENTREPRENEURIAL INNOVATIONS

While there is some danger in adding endlessly to the list of 'causes' of industrial retardation in the final part of the century, our second emphasis, on entrepreneurial and organizational innovations, does suggest one line of explanation which has not been much followed in the writings of the economic historians. This is the importance of the wider institutional framework in which growth, or lack of growth, occurred. A hostile institutional environment could obviously have marked effects upon the likelihood of innovations being adopted. In particular, stress might be laid upon the importance, in relation to the nature of the innovations at the end of the century, of the size and nature of the control units through which investment, and other decisions affecting innovation adoption, were made. The restrictions which applied to the development of large-scale firms in Britain have already been noted. There is, however, a large number of other fields in which scale of operations was a matter of first importance. The whole question of the servicing of towns at this period depended critically upon the scale of operations. The optimal scale was increasing constantly in terms of a whole variety of servicing activities; from the supply of foodstuffs and retail goods in general, to the supply of gas and other forms of light and power, to the transportation media by which people and information were channelled between and within urban areas. In all of such fields, the nature of late-nineteenth-century innovations laid great stress upon large scale of operation. In the retail trade, this was the period which saw the first developments of departmental stores (Ashworth 1960, pp. 133-7) with the appearance of Marks and Spencer at the turn of the century — with a pattern of diffusion strongly concentrated in the industrial north, the first store opening in Leeds and the first ten including other stores in Warrington, Birkenhead, Castleford, Wigan, Bolton, Manchester and Cardiff — and Woolworths — again with a predominantly northern pattern of diffusion, the first ten stores being in Liverpool, Preston, Manchester, Hull, London, Middlesbrough and Bristol. The development of more extensive supplies of water, gas, electricity, postal services and of internal transport illustrate the importance of scale even more effectively since all required networks encompassing relatively large areas and large numbers of people. The very growth of large towns itself demanded large-scale organization and some increase in the degree of centralization in the control of decision-making.

It might be argued that the functioning of large complexes such as the industrial town might best be achieved in one of two ways: either in terms of a system of *laissez faire* in which few checks were placed on the emergence of a relatively few large-scale private organizations in whose hands many decisions lay; or in terms of a radically-centralized political control by government. At the end of the nineteenth century, Britain was starting to undergo what was to become a major transition towards the latter state, but the lines of battle were only just being drawn in a situation of considerable flux and uncertainty. In the United States, despite the 'trust-busting' exemplified by the Sugar Trust, this was the period of big-business enterprise and one in which the restraints to monopoly had less evident effect. In Germany, by contrast, the state was pre-eminent in a significant number of fields of economic activity. Hartwell (1971, p. 250) suggests that the importance of the differences between English law and continental Roman law may be an important, and certainly an overlooked, element in the timing of the early industrial growth of Britain, but equally it may be argued that it had effect in the later period too since Roman law lent itself much more readily to centralized bureaucratic control and to the large-scale state involvement which characterized many of the continental countries. At the end of the century, when large scale was becoming of growing importance, this might have worked to the benefit of such areas.

Put crudely, therefore, one might argue that, unlike the development of large-scale firms in the United States or the large-scale state involvement in certain European countries, the late nineteenth century in Britain was a period in which no well-crystallized pattern of large-scale control had developed, but one in which the debate about the most optimal units of control was being vigorously, if somewhat damagingly, debated. It was a period of transition in which the old order of mistrust of central authority and a belief in the virtues of free trade, was giving way to the development of a centralized and welfare state. The debate over centralization had, of course, continued throughout the nineteenth century,[1] but it was coming to a head in the late nineteenth century both in the reform of political boundaries and, of more significance, in the advocacy of state involvement in a variety of economic and social matters. There was, too, a notable contribution to this debate in the growing voice of the municipalities which, while formed in the 1830s, had begun to flex both their

---

[1] Earlier reaction to the Poor Law legislation of the 1830s and '40s, to the Factory Acts and to the railway legislation of the 1840s is discussed by Lubenow (1971) who charts the hostility which was expressed towards what were seen by many as instances of an undesirable growth in governmental control in the early Victorian period.

political and economic muscles in the period after 1870. The debate was thus a twin affair; authority versus industry and central versus local authority. The uncertainty of control, and the competition arising from there being a multitude of potential mechanisms of control, undermined much of the social legislation of the late nineteenth century, but it also had profound effects upon the fate of many entrepreneurial innovations at a time when many of the new inventions and innovations required large-scale control and application. The innovations of the electrical age, with their emphasis on size and on wide-ranging networks, coincided in Britain with the emerging, but not yet fully realized, transfer of power and control to central authorities. The clash between the scale of operations demanded by the new wave of innovations and the uncertain scale of control of decision-making may well have been an element of considerable significance in accounting for the lags in the adoption of the new innovations of the 'second industrial revolution' in late-nineteenth-century Britain.

The examples which could be cited by way of illustration are numerous. The lag in the adoption of electricity itself is one. So far as the use of electricity in power and lighting were concerned, the municipal control of gasworks meant that there was considerable opposition from municipal authorities to the adoption of what was rightly seen as a powerful competitor threatening to undermine a source of municipal revenue. And to this was added the restrictive legislation of the Act of 1882 which must itself be seen both as a sign of the temerity of the government as well as its acquiescence to fragmentary municipal control rather than to potentially monopolistic and unitary private control (see, for example, Garke 1907). The effect was that British electrical lighting lagged seriously behind developments in the United States (Hughes 1962) with consequences upon the embryonic electrical industry as a whole (Du Boff 1967) and upon the myriad of industries to which it was potentially linked. The adoption of electricity in Britain would, indeed, have been considerably slower than it was had not American and German firms stepped in at the turn of the century to provide much of the necessary machinery and equipment; the American and German firms of Westinghouse, General Electric, A.E.G., and Siemens contributed greatly to the early installations as did the American firms which were actually established within Britain in the period after 1890.[1]

A second illustration is provided by the lag in internal transport within British cities. The development of tramways was again seriously hampered by the competition between private and municipal desire for control, and supporters of the municipal cause were partly motivated by the uncertain attitudes of the time towards monopoly and large-scale control (Leech 1897-8). The notion that competition was the great economizer and that this could be translated in the

---

[1] An interesting sidelight on the question of scale is provided by the experience of one of these immigrant firms. Ferranti's huge power station which was established at Deptford failed commercially partly through the Board of Trade's policy of establishing very small supply areas (Byatt 1968).

case of private undertakings into the encouragement of developments by more than one company within a single town, made no more sense in the context of internal transportation than it had, much earlier, in the case of the duplication of railway lines. Meyer's (1906) somewhat frenetic denouncements of the evils of municipal control of tramways was in essence an argument for lack of restrictions and for the merits of single- as against multiple-working of such enterprises, and they contain much sound common sense.

These are but some of the many possible illustrations of the retarding effects of the discordance between the necessary scale of operations of certain of the new innovations of the late nineteenth century and the scale at which control and decisions could readily be effected at the time. We might look further at the question by drawing on the history of yet another of the examples – the development of the telephone, whose diffusion was studied in an earlier chapter. This is but one of a multitude of possible examples which illustrate the effect of an inappropriate scale of operations upon the spread of innovations.

SCALE OF OPERATION: THE CASE OF THE TELEPHONE

That the spread of the telephone in Britain lagged behind that in America and other European countries, there is little doubt. Webb (1910, p. 21) calculated that, at the start of 1910, Britain had just over 600,000 telephones and that, had it been as well provided as the United States, it would have had over 2,500,000.[1] *The Electrician* used the theme of the unequal provision of the two countries as a recurring topic of debate, commenting on the disparate sets of statistics with asides of varying acidity: 'Go on America. Tell us the work you are doing and we will follow *afar off*' (*Electrician* 5, 1880, 266). It was claimed that, by the beginning of 1880, America had exchanges in operation in no fewer than eighty-five towns (*Electrician* 4, 1880, 73) and that, by the end of 1881, only one town of those with populations greater than 15,000 and only nine of those with populations greater than 10,000 did not have exchanges (*Electrician* 7, 1881, 178). By the early years of this century, it was claimed that the United States added an annual total of telephones twice the total number in existence in Britain (*National Telephone Journal* 1, 1906, 168).

Two aspects of the development of the telephone in Britain illustrate the types of barrier put in the way of its expansion – barriers which were closely connected with the twin aspects of scale of operation and control of decision-making: first was the role of the state; and second, that of the municipal authorities. The state, given its expensive involvement with the telegraph service which it had taken over from private companies in 1870, had a vested interest in hindering the development of a potential rival in the field of general communications, even though the full extent of that rivalry was not at first

---

[1] Further comparative statistics are given for European cities, for example, by C. E. Webber (1882) and, for America, by Baldwin (1925, pp. 616-17).

realized.[1] State involvement began early with the Post Office challenge that the telephone was but another form of telegraph and so infringed the state monopoly in telegraphs. It was the settlement of the ensuing court decision in favour of the Post Office which gave rise to the compromise by which the companies were made licensees of the Post Office on payment of a 10 per cent royalty on their receipts. This compromise was characteristic of the continuing uncertainty in the government's attitude to the telephone companies. It led to its rather damaging dilatoriness in making an eventual decision to take over the private companies in the early years of this century, more than thirty years after the first introduction of the telephone. The effect, in the meantime, had been that, not only were many companies refused licences to operate, but that the activities of the companies were constantly shackled by the uncertainty which surrounded the long-term future of their investments. Talk of a government take-over had existed from the very early years: even in 1879, consideration of government control of the telephone was being urged (*Electrician* 3, 1879, 258); rumours that the government was seriously considering such a step were being reported in the following year (*Electrician*, 5, 1880, 229); and, again, there were reports in the press that the Postmaster-General had claimed that the government was about to buy-out the companies in 1888 (*Electrician* 20, 1888, 310), reports which were subsequently denied, but which nevertheless added to the uncertainty of the position of the companies. The original telephone licences had been issued so as to expire at the end of thirty-one years after the start of the early licensing system in 1881, but the certainty of take-over and the terms upon which it were to be effected, were not formally agreed until the early part of this century – 1901 in the case of London and 1905 elsewhere. The agreement was for a state assumption of control at the start of 1912 and, since the system was to be bought at replacement cost without allowance being made for goodwill or custom, for the intervening period the National Telephone Company had little incentive to develop its system much farther than that which already existed.

The government's hesitation over assuming control of the telephone was damaging to the development of the service and it can be accounted for not only in terms of its existing vested interests in the telegraph, but also in terms of the prevailing belief in the health of competition and the danger of monopoly. Large companies were suspect, even though the nature of the telephone demanded highly centralized control. The amalgamation of the various private companies into the National Telephone Company by the middle of the 1890s, was greeted with considerable mistrust and, from the early 1880s, the Post Office had both opened exchanges of its own as well as having granted licences to small rival private companies. While the extent and success of the Post Office exchanges were very limited, except perhaps in the North East, the fact that it was seen as

---

[1] See above, pp. 175–6.

desirable to establish rival systems, suggests the belief in the virtues of competition in spite of its evident inappropriateness in the case of a system which was more efficient the greater was its network character and the greater was the extent of that network. By offering alternative telephone systems, the Post Office, or the municipalities, or competing private companies merely duplicated facilities and forced customers to subscribe to more than one network. It was such illogicality which lead inexorably to the gradual emergence of but a single company, but the moral — whose recognition was much delayed by the belief in competition — should have been that, in whatever hands it were to lie — whether state or private company — monopoly or large-scale control was the order of the day where such innovations based on electricity were concerned.

The American experience illustrates a different, and more appropriate, scale of operations. The National Bell Telephone Company had emerged as an amalgamation of two earlier companies by 1879; by 1885, the American Telephone and Telegraph Company had been formed to organize long-distance communications; and, by 1899, this company had merged with Bell to provide a highly centralized administrative system for its associated manufacturing and service companies as well as providing facilities for research.[1] Baldwin concludes that, 'The telephone business in America thus grew to be a huge undertaking long before it became a concern of any magnitude in this country, and it therefore merited an organization and expenditure in research and development which it has been denied here' (Baldwin 1925, p. 615).

The second aspect of the development of the telephone which illustrates the theme of the scale of control units is the involvement of local authorities. Responsible, as they were, for single municipalities their influence was on the whole somewhat parochial and certainly at a scale too small to match the requirements of an evolving network of development. Meyer (1907, p. 266) drew attention to this small-scale parochialism of municipal involvement in urban electrical undertakings in his suggestion that local authorities 'were unable to cooperate for the purpose of serving conjointly a number of districts which the ties of manufacture had united into a commercial and manufacturing unit'. Again, while not painting too crude a dichotomy between the American and British situations, the situation between the two countries was made somewhat different by the less strong position of municipal bodies in the more raw political climate of the United States. In Britain, the provision of way-leaves was one of the recurring and most serious problems hindering the expansion of the telephone and municipal opposition to granting way-leave rights was widespread and consistent. Their refusals to grant extensions to overhead wires were often fully justified since, as well as being unsightly and dangerous, the overhead wires

---

[1] In a wider context, Edison's establishment at Menloe Park in 1871 of a comprehensive research laboratory can be seen as the first development of the concept of centrally-organized technological research.

were increasingly inefficient in the later years of the telephone. But the municipal refusal to grant permission for underground cables can be seen almost as an exercise in flexing their new-found municipal muscle. In the case of both telephones and tramways, the municipalities developed what virtually became a philosophy of the municipal sanctity of the streets in their control – a philosophy which was extended to the air above the streets as well as to the breaking-open of the actual surface. Their attitude was also motivated by the more mundane consideration of the potential income source which telephone development offered. It is not without significance that at the head of many of the deputations demanding lower telephone rates were representatives of the new London County Council, of the Association of Municipal Corporations and of the Scottish municipalities. The Association of British Chambers of Commerce, founded in 1870, also played a part in such movements. It was pressure from such bodies that led to the eventual agreement, by government legislation in 1899, to grant licences to any local authority which applied to operate a municipal telephone exchange. The six municipal exchanges which were actually established as a result of this pressure acted as irritants rather than as serious competitors to the National Telephone Company, since all but the Hull exchange rapidly disappeared, most having been bought by the Company at a loss to the municipalities and never having worked at a profit, being regarded 'by experienced engineers as obsolete even at the time they were installed' (Baldwin 1925, p. 381).

Even though their realization proved so disastrous a failure and even though the government itself regarded the operation with some misgivings, the fact of the pressure for municipal exchanges does illustrate the effects of the contemporary debate on what was the optimal unit of political and economic control in this transition period. Fabian tracts argued for municipal control of a wide variety of undertakings; the heirs of Bentham and of Chadwick argued for greater central control; and the popular spirit lauded the virtues of competition and deplored monopoly in ways at once inconsistent and pragmatic. And in the midst of such uncertainty and of the fluctuating opinions which so characterized the early as well as the later Victorian age, those innovations which increasingly required large-scale control, regardless of whether it was in the hands of private or public agency, languished in the confusion. The nature of so large a proportion of the innovations of the 'second industrial revolution', based as they were on electricity and on networks, demanded a scale of unified control which the current ferment of debate at the end of the century did not provide, even though it heralded the eventual evolution of more centralized and large-scale control.

Most discussion of urban growth has concentrated upon the role of demographic and economic factors, but it is perhaps equally important to study the effect of this factor of control and decision-making, which might be exemplified both in the scale and the intensity of political institutions and in attitudes towards them. In this study, it has been possible to show the importance of the diffusion of innovations upon the patterns of urban growth, just as other studies have shown the impact of innovations upon general economic growth. But in looking at this process, the role of constitutional theory and political power have been highlighted. The tantalizing glimpses of the influence of the struggle between central and local government and between the state and the individual upon the spread of innovations suggest new routes of explanation for the geographer. The scale and nature of power and of the locus of decisions — whether in terms of political power, the activities of manufacturing corporations, or of other sources — have been sadly neglected by geographers, despite their evident impact upon the more tangible aspects of the economic landscape.

In what ways do differences in the real or the perceived structure of power and decision-making vary from place to place and over time, and in what ways do such differences have effect upon the economic vitality and upon the innovativeness of the areas and times concerned? Real differences certainly exist. In terms of the structure of local government at the present, one need only look at the varying stances adopted towards the concept of comprehensive education, at approaches to the management of public housing or at the varying proportions of local finance which are allocated to particular social services, to appreciate the breadth of variation in the interpretation and the exercise of the local government mandate. In what ways do such differences — and in the perception of such differences — affect the buoyancy of local economies? The question takes on added interest at the present, in the context of the current major reform of local government. This reform offers great scope for the analysis of such variation, not only in relation to the efficiency of new local government boundaries and of the appropriateness of the scale of the new units in relation to the various responsibilities which fall within the province of local government, but also on the broader front in relation to the effectiveness of the proposed structure of local government as a mediator between the state and the individual. The major reshuffling of local government in the 1880s, from which the strength of local government derived, can be seen as a compromise solution to the competing claims of *laissez faire* and centralization. Britain today is still left with the legacy of that compromise. To what extent does it better serve the scale requirements of innovations in such varied fields as education, housing, transport, industry and retailing than do other more highly centralized systems on the one hand or more individualistic systems on the other?

The simulation model: urban growth and innovations

In massaging a body of data which covers almost 1,000 towns over a span of eleven decades, a great deal of computer calculation was obviously involved. Throughout the text, the details of statistical techniques and of quantitative methods have been presented in as simple a fashion as possible. For those interested in the details of the simulation model, however, the computer programme which was used is given below. The language used in writing the programme is FORTRAN IV and the programme calls for only one major subroutine — the derivation of uniformly-distributed random numbers.

The data requirements of the programme, for each place, are as follows: a reference number (NAME), an initial population size (XPOP), and locational co-ordinates (XLOC and YLOC). The version given below refers to Model 4 whose operating rules are specified in the text (p. 207). The programme, as written, cycles for fifteen generations and will print out the following: for generations 1 to 4, a list of the number of 'stimuli' received by each town; for generations 5, 10, 11, 12 and 15 the initial population, new population, growth rate, date of adoption, number of stimuli received and probability of being 'hit' for each of the 455 places. Total running time, using an IBM 360/44, is approximately eleven minutes. This can be considerably reduced by calling on a pre-calculated matrix of distances between each of the 455 places used in the simulation, but, for simplicity, the programme shown here includes the calculation of distances as an integral part of the programme (lines 34 to 36).

```
1          SUBROUTINE RANDU (IX, IY, YFL)
2          IY=IY*65539
3          IF(IY)5,6,6
4      5   IY=IY+2147483647+1
5      6   YFL=IY
6          YFL=YFL*0.4656613E-9
7          RETURN
8      END

1          DIMENSION XPOP(455),POP(455), XLOC(455),
       5   YLOC(455),NAME(455),STIM(455),HITS(455),
       5   ITOHIT(455),EXHITS(455),IDATE(455),IPROB(455),
       5   PROB(455),IBLIM(456),GRATE(455)
```

```
2      111  FORMAT('',I5,I8,2F12.0,F16.4,3I10)
3      222  FORMAT('0','STIMULI SENT OUT IN',I3,
          5   'TH GENERATION=',I6)
4      333  FORMAT('0',10X,'CITY',3X,'INITIAL POP',3X,'NEW PO
          5     4X,'GROWTH RATE',4X,'DATE HIT',4X,'NO. HITS',
          5     4X,'PROBS',I6,'TH PERIOD')
5      666  FORMAT(I3,2F3.0,F7.0)
6      777  FORMAT('',I5,I8,2I10)
7      999  FORMAT('0','DIFFUSION OF GROWTH STIMULI-
          5     MODEL 4')
8           DO 3 I=1,455
9           READ(5,666) NAME(I), XLOC(I), YLOC(I),XPOP(I)

C   INITIALIZE ELEMENTS BEFORE STARTING MAJOR
C      GENERATION CYCLES
10          POP(I)=XPOP(I)
11          ITOHIT(I)=0
12          HITS(I)=0.0
13          XLOC(I)=XLOC(I)*8.6605
14          YLOC(I)=YLOC(I)*5.0
15          IDATE(I)=0
16        3 CONTINUE
17          WRITE(6,999)

C START PLACE 1 WITH VALUES APPROPRIATE TO
C    ADOPTION
18          ITOHIT(1)=5
19          STIM (1)=26.5
20          ISTIMT=26

C   ALLOT RANDOMLY-CHOSEN VALUES TO ARGUMENTS
C      IN RANDOM SUB-ROUTINE
21          IYA=24109
22          IXA=567
23          YFLA=0.123

C START MAJOR CYCLES OF GENERATIONS
24          DO 100 JI=1,15
25          PRTOT=0.0
26          DO 10 I=1,455
27          EXHITS(I)=HITS(I)*0.5
28          HITS(I)=0.0
29          IPROB(I)=0
30          PROB(I)=0.0

C   CALCULATE PERIOD AT WHICH EACH PLACE ADOPTS
31          IF(ITOHIT(I).LT.5) IDATE(I)=IDATE(I)+1

C   CALCULATE DISTANCES BETWEEN ADOPTERS AND ALL
C      OTHER PLACES
32          DO 20 K=1,455
```

```
34              DIFFX=XLOC(I)-XLOC(K)
35              DIFFY=YLOC(I)-YLOC(K)
36              DIST=(DIFFX*DIFFX)+(DIFFY*DIFFY)
37              PROB(I)=PROB(I)+(POP(I)*STIM(K)/DIST)
38           20 CONTINUE

  C  CALCULATE TOTAL 'PROBABILITIES' OF ALL PLACES
39              PRTOT=PRTOT+PROB(I)
40           10 CONTINUE
41              IULIM=0

  C  CONVERT PROBABILITIES TO INTEGERS SUMMING TO
  C     1,000,000
42              DO 30 I=1,455
43              IPROB(I)=IFIX((PROB(I)/PRTOT)*1000.0*1000.0)

  C  EXPRESS INTEGER PROBABILITIES AS FIELD OF
  C     CONSECUTIVE NUMBERS
44              IF(IPROB(I)-1) 55,66,66
45           55 IBLIM(I)=0
46              GO TO 30
47           66 IBLIM(I)=IULIM+1
48              IULIM=IULIM+IPROB(I)
49           30 CONTINUE
50              IBLIM(456)=IULIM+1

  C  GENERATE ISTIMT RANDOM NUMBERS BETWEEN 0 AND
  C     1,000,000
51              DO 50 L=1,ISTIMT
52              IXA=IYA
53              CALL RANDU(IXA,IYA,YFLA)
54              IRAND=IFIX(YFLA*1000.0*1000.0)

  C  IF RANDOM NUMBER IS 0, GENERATE AN ALTERNATIVE
  C     NUMBER
55              IF(IRAND-1) 88,99,99
56           88 ISTIMT=ISTIMT+1
57              GO TO 50

  C  ALLOCATE RANDOM NUMBERS TO THE FIELD OF
  C     CONSECUTIVE PROBABILITIES
58           99 DO 50 K=1,455
59              IF(IBLIM(K).EQ.0) GO TO 50
60              IF(IRAND.GE.IBLIM(K).AND.IRAND.LT.IBLIM(K+1))
                5 GO TO 5
61              GO TO 50
62            5 HITS(K)=HITS(K)+1
63              ITOHIT(K)=ITOHIT(K)+1
64           50 CONTINUE
65              WRITE(6,222) JI, ISTIMT
```

```
67              DO 80 M=1,455
  C  POPULATION DECLINES IF, AFTER 2ND GENERATION,
  C    PLACE IS NOT HIT DURING TWO CONSECUTIVE
  C    PERIODS
68              IF(JI-2) 101,101,201
69          201 IF(HITS(M).LT.1.0. AND.EXHITS(M).LT.0.5)
              5    POP(M)=POP(M)-50.0


  C  CALCULATE NEW POPULATIONS AND STIMULI FOR ALL
  C    OTHER PLACES
70          101 IF(ITOHIT(M).LT.5) GO TO 80
71              STIM(M)=SQRT(SQRT(POP(M)))
72              POP(M)=POP(M)+((HITS(M)+1.0+EXHITS(M))*100.0)
73              ISTIMT=ISTIMT+IFIX(STIM(M))
74           80 CONTINUE
75              IF(JI.LT.5) GO TO 12
76              IF(JI.EQ.5.OR.JI.EQ.10.OR.JI.EQ.11.OR.JI.EQ.12.O
              5    JI.EQ.15) GO TO 11
77              GO TO 100
78           12 WRITE(6,777) (I,NAME(I),IPROB(I),ITOHIT(I), I=1,
79              GO TO 100


  C  CALCULATE GROWTH RATES FOR SELECTED GENERATIONS
80           11 WATE=2000.0/FLOAT(JI)
81              DO 22 I=1,455
82              GRATE(I)=((POP(I)-XPOP(I))/(POP(I)+XPOP(I)))*WAT
83           22 CONTINUE
84              WRITE(6,333) JI
85              WRITE(6,111) (I,NAME(I),XPOP(I),POP(I),GRATE(I),
              5    IDATE(I),ITOHIT(I),IPROB(I), I=1,455
86          100 CONTINUE
87              STOP
88              END
```

Appendix A Flowchart of computer programme for the urban simulation model

APPENDIX B
List of towns

(Locations of towns are shown on the reference map, pp. 242–3)

Bedfordshire (BED)

1 Bedford
2 Biggleswade
3 Dunstable
4 Leighton Buzzard
5 Luton
6 Sandy

Berkshire (BER)

1 Abingdon
2 Maidenhead
3 Newbury
4 Reading
5 Wallingford
6 Wantage
7 Windsor & Eton
8 Wokingham

Buckinghamshire (BUK)

1 Aylesbury
2 Bletchley
3 Buckingham
4 Chesham
5 High Wycombe
6 Marlow
7 Newport Pagnell
8 Olney
9 Slough
10 Wolverton

Cambridgeshire (CAM)

1 Cambridge
2 Chatteris
3 Ely
4 March
5 Whittlesey
6 Wisbech

Cheshire (CHE)

1 Alderley Edge
2 Alsager
3 Altrincham
4 Bollington
5 Bredbury
6 Cheadle
7 Chester
8 Congleton
9 Crewe
10 Ellesmere Port
11 Frodsham
12 Hazel Grove
13 Heswall
14 Hollingworth
15 Hoylake & West Kirby
16 Hyde
17 Knutsford
18 Lymm
19 Macclesfield
20 Marple
21 Middlewich
22 Nantwich
23 Neston & Parkgate
24 Northenden
25 Northwich
26 Runcorn
27 Sale
28 Sandbach
29 Staleybridge
30 Stockport
31 Wilmslow
32 Winsford

Cornwall (COR)

1 Bodmin
2 Camborne
3 Falmouth
4 Hayle
5 Helston
6 Launceston
7 Liskeard
8 Looe
9 Newquay
10 Penzance
11 Penryn
12 Redruth
13 Saltash
14 St Austell
15 St Blazey
16 St Ives
17 Stratton & Bude
18 Truro

Cumberland (CUM)

1 Aspatria
2 Carlisle
3 Cleator Moor
4 Cockermouth
5 Egremont
6 Frizington
7 Harrington
8 Keswick
9 Maryport
10 Millom
11 Penrith
12 Whitehaven
13 Wigton
14 Workington

Derbyshire (DER)

1 Alfreton
2 Ashbourne
3 Bakewell
4 Beighton
5 Belper
6 Bolsover
7 Brimington
8 Buxton
9 Chesterfield
10 Church Gresley
11 Clay Cross
12 Clowne
13 Derby
14 Dronfield
15 Elmton

16 Eckington,
   Mosborough &
   Renishaw
17 Glossop
18 Hasland
19 Heage
20 Heanor
21 Ilkeston
22 Killamarsh
23 Long Eaton
24 Matlock
25 Melbourne
26 New Hall
27 New Mills
28 Pilsley
29 Pinxton
30 Ripley
31 Shirebrook
32 South Normanton
33 Spondon
34 Staveley
35 Tibshelf
36 Whitwell
37 Whittington
38 Wirksworth
39 Woodville

Devon (DEV)

1 Barnstaple
2 Bideford
3 Brixham
4 Buckfastleigh
5 Crediton
6 Dartmouth
7 Dawlish
8 Exeter
9 Exmouth
10 Great Torrington
11 Honiton
12 Ilfracombe
13 Kingsbridge
14 Newton Abbot
15 Okehampton
16 Paignton
17 Plymouth
18 Sidmouth
19 Tavistock
20 Teignmouth
21 Tiverton
22 Topsham
23 Torquay
24 Totnes

Dorset (DOR)

1 Blandford Forum
2 Bridport
3 Dorchester
4 Lyme Regis
5 Poole
6 Portland
7 Shaftesbury
8 Sherborne
9 Swanage
10 Weymouth
11 Wimborne Minster

Durham (DUR)

1 Annfield Plain
2 Barnard Castle
3 Birtley
4 Bishop Auckland
5 Blaydon
6 Boldon Colliery
7 Brandon & Byshottles
8 Carrville
9 Chester-le-Street
10 Chilton
11 Consett
12 Cornforth
13 Coundon
14 Coundon Grange
15 Crook
16 Darlington
17 Durham
18 Ferryhill
19 Hartlepools
20 Hebburn
21 Hetton-le-Hole
22 Houghton-le-Spring
23 Hylton
24 Jarrow
25 Langley Park
26 Leadgate
27 Murton
28 Newbottle
29 Pelton
30 Penshaw
31 Ryhope
32 Seaham
33 Seaham Harbour
34 Sherburn
35 Shildon
36 Shotton

37 South Hylton
38 South Shields
39 Spennymoor
40 Stanley
41 Stockton-on-Tees
42 Sunderland
43 Thornley
44 Tow Law
45 Tunstall
46 Usworth
47 Washington
48 West Auckland
49 Whickham
50 Whitburn
51 Willington
52 Wingate
53 Witton Gilbert

Essex (ESS)

1 Braintree
2 Brentwood
3 Buckhurst Hill
4 Brightlingsea
5 Burnham-on-Crouch
6 Chelmsford
7 Chingford
8 Clacton
9 Colchester
10 Coggeshall
11 Epping
12 Grays Thurrock
13 Halstead
14 Harwich
15 Loughton
16 Maldon
17 Romford
18 Saffron Walden
19 Shoeburyness
20 Southend-on-Sea
21 Tilbury
22 West Thurrock
23 Witham

Gloucestershire (GLO)

1 Bristol
2 Cheltenham
3 Coleford
4 Cirencester
5 Dursley
6 Gloucester
7 Nailsworth

8 Stroud
9 Tewkesbury

Hampshire (HAM)

1 Aldershot
2 Alton
3 Andover
4 Basingstoke
5 Bournemouth & Poole
6 Christchurch
7 Cowes
8 Eastleigh
9 Fareham
10 Farnborough
11 Fleet
12 Havant
13 Lymington
14 Newport
15 Petersfield
16 Portsmouth
17 Romsey
18 Ryde
19 Sandown
20 Shanklin
21 St Helens
22 Southampton
23 Totton
24 Warblington & Emsworth
25 Winchester
26 Ventnor

Herefordshire (HFD)

1 Hereford
2 Ledbury
3 Leominster
4 Ross-on-Wye

Hertfordshire (HRT)

1 Barnet
2 Berkhamsted
3 Bishop's Stortford
4 Bushey
5 Cheshunt
6 East Barnet
7 Harpenden
8 Hemel Hempstead
9 Hertford
10 Hitchin
11 Hoddesdon
12 Letchworth
13 Rickmansworth

14 Royston
15 St Albans
16 Stevenage
17 Tring
18 Ware
19 Watford

Huntingdonshire (HUN)

1 Huntingdon
2 Ramsey
3 St Ives
4 St Neots

Kent (KEN)

1 Ashford
2 Bexley
3 Broadstairs
4 Canterbury
5 Chislehurst
6 Crayford
7 Dartford
8 Deal
9 Dover
10 Erith
11 Farnborough
12 Faversham
13 Folkestone
14 Gravesend
15 Herne Bay
16 Hythe
17 Maidstone
18 Margate
19 Medway Towns
20 Orpington
21 Queenborough
22 Ramsgate
23 Royal Tunbridge Wells
24 Sandwich
25 Sevenoaks
26 Sheerness
27 Sidcup
28 Sittingbourne
29 Southborough
30 Stone
31 Swanscombe
32 Tonbridge
33 Whitstable

Lancashire (LAN)

1 Abram
2 Accrington

3 Adlington
4 Aspull
5 Ashton-in-Makerfield
6 Ashton-under-Lyne
7 Atherton
8 Bacup
9 Barrowford
10 Barrow-in-Furness
11 Blackburn
12 Blackpool
13 Blackrod
14 Bolton
15 Brierfield
16 Burnley
17 Bury
18 Carnforth
19 Chorley
20 Clayton-le-Moors
21 Clitheroe
22 Colne
23 Crompton
24 Darwen
25 Dalton-in-Furness
26 Denton
27 Eccles
28 Farnworth
29 Fleetwood
30 Formby
31 Golborne
32 Great Harwood
33 Haslingden
34 Haydock
35 Heywood
36 Hindley
37 Horwich
38 Huyton-with-Roby
39 Irlam
40 Kirkham
41 Lancaster
42 Leigh
43 Leyland
44 Littleborough
45 Little Hulton
46 Little Lever
47 Liverpool & Birkenhea
48 Longridge
49 Lytham
50 Manchester & Salford
51 Middleton
52 Milnrow
53 Morecambe
54 Mossley

55 Nelson
56 Newton
57 Oldham
58 Orrell
59 Ormskirk
60 Padiham
61 Pendlebury
62 Prescot
63 Preston
64 Radcliffe
65 Rainford
66 Ramsbottom
67 Rawtenstall
68 Rishton
69 Rochdale
70 Royton
71 St Annes on Sea
72 St Helens
73 Skelmersdale
74 Southport
75 Standish
76 Thornton
77 Tottington
78 Tyldesley
79 Upholland
80 Ulverston
81 Urmston
82 Walton-le-Dale
83 Wardle
84 Warrington
85 West Houghton
86 Whiston
87 Whitefield
88 Whitworth
89 Widnes
90 Wigan

Leicestershire (LEC)

1 Ashby de la Zouch
2 Barwell
3 Coalville
4 Earl Shilton
5 Enderby
6 Hinckley
7 Hugglescote
8 Ibstock
9 Leicester
10 Loughborough
11 Market Harborough
12 Melton Mowbray
13 Oadby

14 Shepshed
15 Sileby
16 Syston
17 Whittick
18 Wigston Magna

Lincolnshire (LIN)

1 Alford
2 Barton-on-Humber
3 Boston
4 Brigg
5 Gainsborough
6 Grantham
7 Grimsby
8 Horncastle
9 Lincoln
10 Louth
11 Market Rasen
12 Scunthorpe
13 Sleaford
14 Spalding
15 Stamford
16 Skegness

London

Middlesex (MDX)

1 Ashford
2 Enfield
3 Feltham
4 Friern Barnet
5 Hampton
6 Harrow
7 Hayes
8 Hounslow
9 Pinner
10 Southall
11 Staines
12 Sunbury-on-Thames
13 Teddington
14 Twickenham
15 Uxbridge
16 Wembley
17 Yiewsley &
     West Drayton

Norfolk (NFK)

1 Cromer
2 Diss
3 Downham Market
4 East Dereham

5 Fakenham
6 Great Yarmouth
7 Hunstanton
8 King's Lynn
9 North Walsham
10 Norwich
11 Thetford
12 Sheringham
13 Wells-next-the-Sea

Northamptonshire (NTS)

1 Burton Latimer
2 Daventry
3 Desborough
4 Earls Barton
5 Finedon
6 Higham Ferrers
7 Irthlingborough
8 Kettering
9 Northampton
10 Oundle
11 Peterborough
12 Raunds
13 Rothwell
14 Rushden
15 Wellingborough

Northumberland (NLD)

1 Alnwick
2 Amble
3 Ashington
4 Bedlington
5 Berwick
6 Blyth
7 Cramlington
8 East Chevington
9 Haltwhistle
10 Hexham
11 Morpeth
12 Newbiggin-by-Sea
13 Newburn
14 Newcastle &
     Gateshead
15 Pegswood
16 Prudhoe
17 Tynemouth
18 Wallsend
19 Whitley Bay

Nottinghamshire (NOT)

1 Arnold
2 Beeston

3 Carlton
4 East Retford
5 Eastwood
6 Hucknall
8 Kimberly
9 Kirkby in Ashfield
10 Mansfield
11 Mansfield Woodhouse
12 Newark
13 Nottingham
14 Radcliffe on Trent
15 Skegby
16 Southwell
17 Stapleford
18 Sutton in Ashfield
19 Warsop
20 Worksop

Oxfordshire (OXO)

1 Banbury
2 Bicester
3 Chipping Norton
4 Henley-on-Thames
5 Oxford
6 Thame
7 Witney

Rutland (RUT)

1 Oakham
2 Uppingham

Shropshire (SAL)

1 Bridgnorth
2 Broseley
3 Dawley
4 Ludlow
5 Market Drayton
6 Newport
7 Oakengates
8 Oswestry
9 Shrewsbury
10 Wellington
11 Whitchurch

Somerset (SOM)

1 Bath
2 Bridgwater
3 Burnham-on-Sea
4 Chard
5 Clevedon

6 Crewkerne
7 Frome
8 Glastonbury
9 Midsomer Norton
10 Minehead
11 Portishead
12 Radstock
13 Shepton Mallet
14 Street
15 Taunton
16 Wellington
17 Wells
18 Weston-super-Mare
19 Yeovil

Staffordshire (STF)

1 Amblecote
2 Biddulph
3 Bilston
4 Brierley Hill
5 Brownhills
6 Burslem
7 Burton-on-Trent
8 Cannock
9 Coseley
10 Darlaston
11 Fenton
12 Hanley
13 Kidsgrove
14 Leek
15 Lichfield
16 Longton
17 Newcastle under Lyme
18 Quarry Bank
19 Rowley Regis
20 Rugeley
21 Sedgley
22 Short Heath
23 Stafford
24 Stoke-on-Trent
25 Stone
26 Tamworth
27 Tipton
28 Tunstall
29 Uttoxeter
30 Walsall
31 Wednesbury
32 Wednesfield
33 West Bromwich
34 Willenhall
35 Wolverhampton

Suffolk (SFK)

1 Beccles
2 Bungay
3 Bury St Edmunds
4 Felixstowe
5 Hadleigh
6 Halesworth
7 Haverhill
8 Ipswich
9 Leiston-cum-Sizewell
10 Lowestoft
11 Newmarket
12 Southwold
13 Stowmarket
14 Sudbury
15 Woodbridge

Surrey (SRY)

1 Ashtead
2 Byfleet
3 Camberley
4 Caterham
5 Cheam
6 Chertsey
7 Dorking
8 Egham
9 Epsom
10 Esher
11 Ewell
12 Farnham
13 Godalming
14 Guildford
15 Haslemere
16 Kingston upon Thames
17 Leatherhead
18 Malden
19 East & West Molesey
20 Purley
21 Reigate
22 Sutton
23 Wallington
24 Walton-on-Thames
25 Warlingham
26 Weybridge
27 Woking

Sussex (SSX)

1 Arundel
2 Bexhill
3 Bognor

4 Brighton & Hove
5 Burgess Hill
6 Chichester
7 Eastbourne
8 East Grinstead
9 Hastings
10 Haywards Heath
11 Horsham
12 Lewes
13 Littlehampton
14 Newhaven
15 Rye
16 Seaford
17 Shoreham
18 Uckfield
19 Worthing

Warwickshire (WAR)
1 Atherstone
2 Bedworth
3 Birmingham &
  Smethwick
4 Coventry
5 Kenilworth
6 Nuneaton
7 Royal Leamington
  Spa
8 Rugby
9 Stratford-on-Avon
10 Sutton Coldfield
11 Warwick

Westmorland (WLD)
1 Ambleside
2 Bowness
3 Kendal

Wiltshire (WIL)
1 Bradford-on-Avon
2 Calne
3 Chippenham
4 Devizes
5 Malmesbury
6 Marlborough
7 Melksham
8 Salisbury
9 Swindon
10 Trowbridge
11 Warminster
12 Westbury

Worcestershire (WOR)
1 Bewdley
2 Bromsgrove
3 Cradley
4 Droitwich
5 Dudley
6 Evesham
7 Halesowen
8 Kidderminster
9 Lye
10 Malvern
11 Oldbury
12 Redditch
13 Stourbridge
14 Stourport
15 Worcester

*Yorkshire – East
Riding* (YER)
1 Beverley
2 Bridlington
3 Filey
4 Gt Driffield
5 Hessle
6 Kingston upon Hull
7 Pocklington

*Yorkshire – North
Riding* (YNR)
1 Brotton
2 Eston
3 Guiseborough
4 Loftus
5 Malton
6 Middlesbrough
7 Northallerton
8 Redcar
9 Richmond
10 Saltburn
11 Scarborough
12 Skelton
13 Thirsk
14 Whitby
15 York

*Yorkshire – West
Riding* (YWR)
1 Adwick le Street
2 Altofts
3 Ardsley

4 Aston cum Aughton
5 Baildon
6 Barnoldswick
7 Barnsley
8 Batley
9 Bentley with Arksey
10 Bingley
11 Birkenshaw
12 Birstall
13 Bolton upon Dearne
14 Bradford
15 Brighouse
16 Burley in Wharfedale
17 Calverley
18 Castleford
19 Cleckheaton
20 Clayton
21 Conisbrough
22 Cudworth
23 Dalton
24 Darfield
25 Darton
26 Denholme
27 Dewsbury
28 Dinnington
29 Dodworth
30 Doncaster
31 Drighlington
32 Earby
33 Elland
34 Ferry Fryston
35 Featherstone
36 Farsley
37 Garforth
38 Gildersome
39 Glass Houghton
40 Glusburn
41 Goole
42 Greasbrough
43 Greetland
44 Guiseley
45 Halifax
46 Harrogate
47 Hebden Bridge
48 Heckmondwike
49 Hemsworth
50 Hipperholme
51 Honley
52 Horbury
53 Horsforth
55 Hoyland Nether
56 Huddersfield

57 Ilkley
58 Keighley
59 Kippax
60 Kirkburton
61 Kirkheaton
62 Knaresborough
63 Knottingley
64 Leeds
65 Lepton
66 Linthwaite
67 Meltham
68 Menston
69 Methley
70 Mexborough
71 Mirfield
72 Monks Bretton
73 Morley
74 Mytholmroyd
75 Normanton
76 Ossett
77 Otley
78 Penistone
79 Pontefract
80 Pudsey
81 Queensbury
82 Rawdon
83 Rawmarsh
84 Ripon
85 Rotherham
86 Rothwell
87 Royston
88 Saddleworth
89 Selby
90 Sheffield
91 Shelf
92 Shipley
93 Silsden
94 Skelmanthorpe
95 Skipton
96 Slaithwaite
97 South Elmsall
98 Southowram
99 Sowerby
100 Sowerby Bridge
102 Stainland
103 Stanley
104 Stocksbridge

105 Swinton
106 Tadcaster
108 Todmorden
109 Wakefield
110 Wales
111 West Melton
112 Wombwell
113 Woodlesford
114 Worsborough
115 Wath upon Dearne
116 Yeadon

Monmouthshire (MON)

1 Abercarn
2 Abergavenny
3 Abersychan
4 Abertillery
5 Bedwellty
6 Blaenavon
7 Chepstow
8 Ebbw Vale
9 Llanfrecha Upper
10 Monmouth
11 Mynyddislwyn
12 Nantyglo & Blaina
13 Newport
14 Panteg
15 Pontypool
16 Rhymney
17 Risca
18 Tredegar

North Wales (NWA)

1 Holyhead
2 Aberystwyth
3 Cardigan
4 Bangor
5 Bethesda
6 Caernarvon
7 Conway
8 Llandudno
9 Penmaenmawr
10 Portmadoc
11 Pwllheli
12 Colwyn Bay
13 Denbigh
14 Llangollen

15 Llanrwst
16 Ruthin
17 Wrexham
18 Buckley
19 Connah's Quay
20 Rhyl
21 Flint
22 Holywell
23 Mold
24 Llanidloes
25 Newtown
26 Llandrindod Wells

South Wales (SWA)

1 Brecon
2 Brynmawr
3 Ammanford
4 Burry Port
5 Carmarthen
6 Cwm Amman
7 Kidwelly
8 Llanelli
9 Aberdare
10 Barry
11 Bridgend
12 Briton Ferry
13 Cardiff
14 Caerphilly
15 Gelligaer
16 Maesteg
17 Merthyr Tydfil
18 Mountain Ash
19 Neath
20 Ogmore
21 Penarth
22 Pontypridd
23 Porthcawl
24 Port Talbot
25 Rhondda
26 Swansea
27 Fishguard
28 Haverfordwest
29 Milford Haven
30 Neyland
31 Pembroke
32 Tenby

Appendix B Reference map overleaf

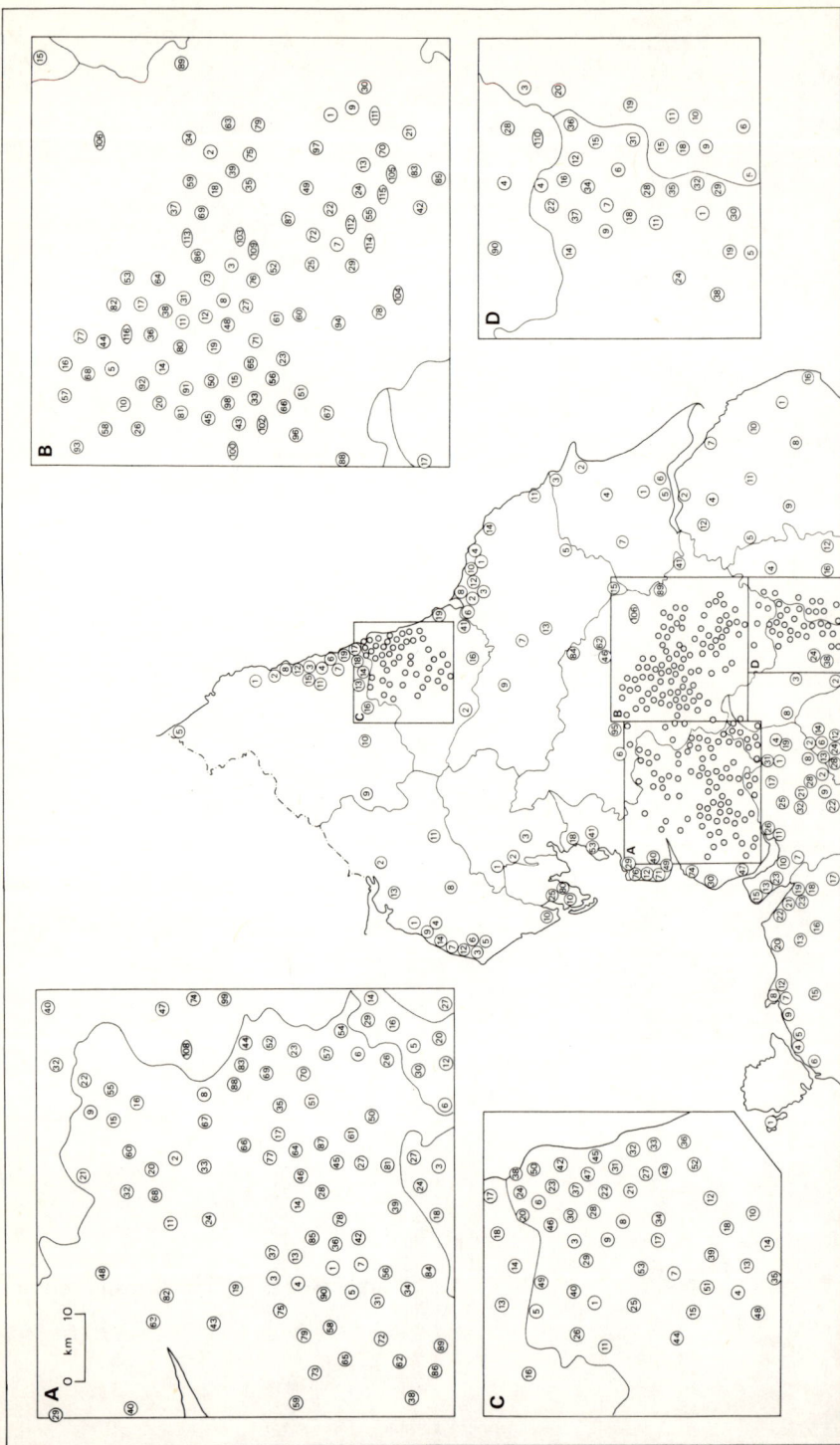

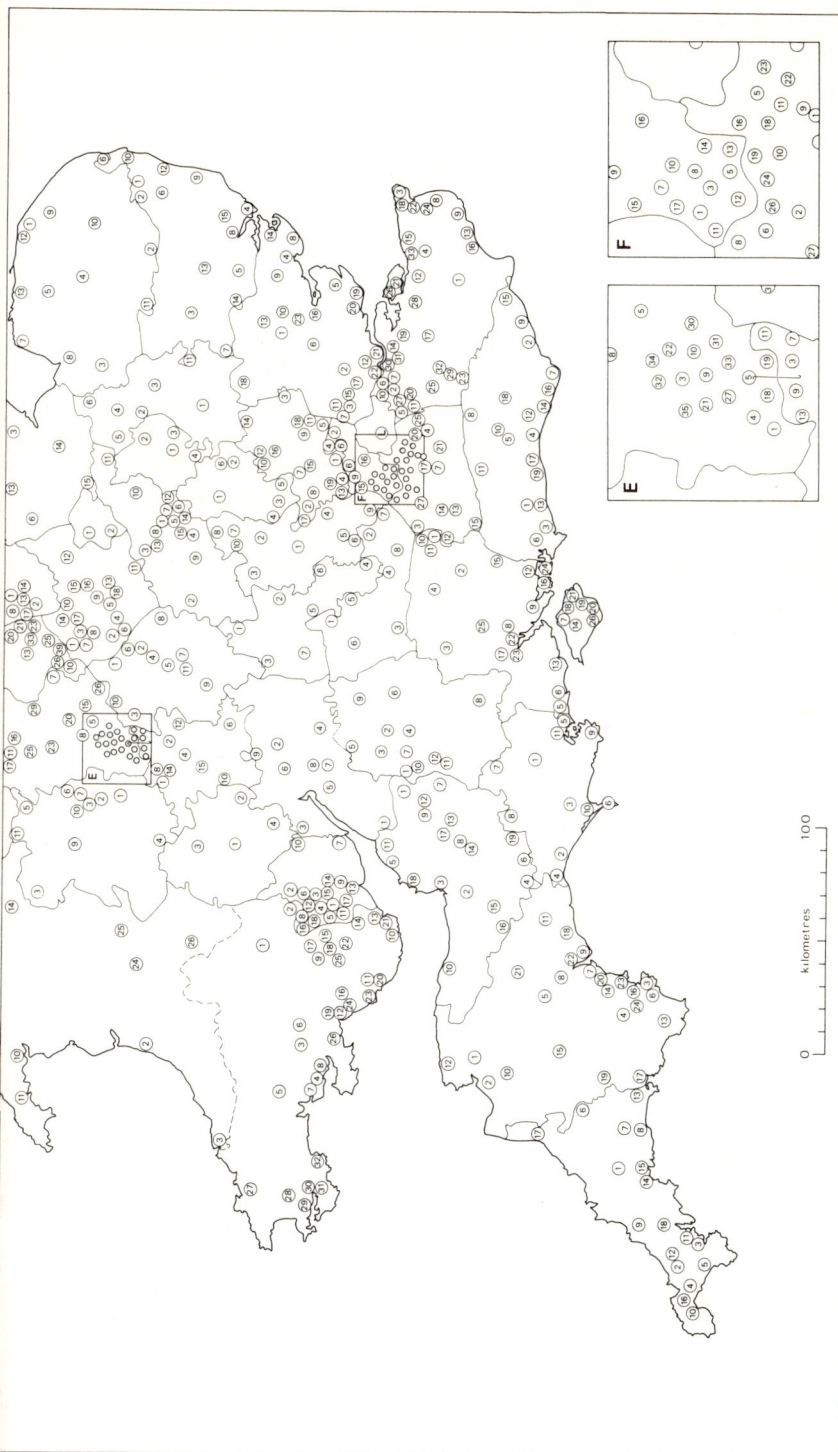

Appendix B Reference map: towns used in the analysis

Sources

The following is a list of sources rather than a bibliography, since, in covering a topic which straddles so many fields, a comprehensive bibliography would be impossible. Many primary sources were consulted, especially in connection with the material on urban innovations. The assistance given by numerous librarians and keepers of archives — especially those of the Post Office archives — was of great value and I should like to record my appreciation of their help.

Of the primary sources consulted — in addition to the *Reports* of the Census for England and Wales — the following were most extensively relied upon:

(i) PARLIAMENTARY PAPERS

For the regulation of Benefit Building Societies, 1836.I.

Return relating to the condition of Benefit Societies, etc. 1859.XXIII.

Return(s) of Societies Incorporated under the Building Society Acts, etc: 1876.LXVIII; 1877.LXXVI; 1878.LXVIII; 1878-9.LXV; 1880.LXVII; 1881.LXXXIII, 1882.LXIV; 1883.LXIV; 1884.LXXII; 1884-5.LXXII; 1886.LXII; 1887.LXXVIII, 1888.XCIII; 1889.LXXII; 1890-1.LXXIX.

Return of Building Societies . . . which have terminated, etc. 1892.LXXIII.

Tables showing Number of Building Societies . . . Registered . . . in each year 1874-91, etc. 1893-4.LXXXIV.

Reports to Government respecting Gas-Light Establishments. 1823.V.

Statement from every Gas Company established by Act of Parliament etc. 1874.XLIV

Abstract of Return of Gas Companies, etc. 1850.XLIX.

Return from every Gas Company, etc: 1865.L; 1866.LXVI.

(ii) DIRECTORIES

The Building and Freehold Land Societies' Directory and Almanack for 1853, etc. Rouse & Co. (London) 1853.

The Building Societies' Directory and Almanack for 1854; idem, 1855, Edited by Henry Brooks (London) 1854, 1855.

Directory and Handbook of Building and Freehold Land Societies etc. Building Societies' Gazette (London) 1874.

The Directory of Building Societies, etc. Compiled by H. Kent and V. M. Braund (London) 1884, etc.

Gas and Water (and electric lighting) Companies' Directory (London) 1877-94.

Gas and electric lighting companies' (works) directory and statistics (London) 1895-9.

Gas works directory and statistics (London) 1900-30.

Electrician's Directory (London) 1883-5.

The Electrician: electrical trades' directory and handbook (London) 1894-1918.

Manual of electrical undertakings etc. Compiled under the direction of E. Garcke (London) 1896-1947.

(iii) TELEPHONE HISTORY

Material on the dates of opening of exchanges was drawn largely from the periodical *The Electrician*, from early telephone directories (see above, p. 169*n*) and from local newspapers. In addition, the records of the Post Office archives, Post 30, proved invaluable for the wider history of early telephone development.

References

Ackerman, E. A. (1963) Where is a research frontier?, *Ann. Ass. Am. Geogr.* 53, 429–40.

Adelman, I. G. (1958) A stochastic model of the size distribution of firms, *J. Am. Statist. Ass.* 53, 893-904.

Ajo, R. (1969) Response of geographical systems to repeated psychological shock, *Geogr. Annlr, Ser. B.* 51, 8–14.

Aldcroft, D. H. (1964) The entrepreneur and the British economy, 1870–1913, *Econ. Hist. Rev.* 2nd Ser. 17, 113–34.

Aldcroft, D. H. (1966) Technical progress and British enterprise, 1875–1914, *Busin. Hist.* 8, 122–39.

Aldcroft, D. H. (ed.) (1968) *The development of British industry and foreign competition, 1875–1914: case studies of ten industries* (London).

Allen, G. R. (1954) The 'courbes des populations': a further analysis, *Bull. Oxf. Univ. Inst. Statist.* 16, 179–89.

Angyal, A. (1941) *Foundations for a science of personality* (Cambridge, Mass.).

Anthony, J. and Baxter, R. (1971) The first stage in disaggregating the residential sub-model, *Working Pap.* No. 58, Land Use and Built Form Studies, Univ. of Cambridge.

Armstrong, W. (1972) The use of information about occupation, in Wrigley, E. A. (ed.), *Nineteenth-century society: essays in the use of quantitative methods* (Cambridge), pp. 191–310.

Ashworth, W. (1960) *An economic history of England, 1870–1939* (London).

Ashworth, W. (1966) The late Victorian economy, *Economica* 33, 17–33.

Aspin, A. C. and Welch, B. L. (1949) Tables for use in comparisons whose accuracy involves two variances, separately estimated, *Biometrika* 36, 290–6.

Association of American Geographers (1968) A systems analytic approach to economic geography, *Publication*, No. 8, Commission on College Geography Publications, Ass. Am. Geogr.

Auerbach, F. (1913) Das Gesetz der Bevölkerungskonzentration, *Petermanns Mitt.* 59, No. 1, 74–6.

Bailey, N. T. J. (1957) *The mathematical theory of epidemics* (New York).

Baldwin, F. G. C. (1925) *History of the telephone in the United Kingdom* (London).

Banks, J. A. (1968) Population change and the Victorian city, *Victorian Stud.* 11, 277–89.

Bassett, K. A and Haggett, P. (1971) Towards short-term forecasting for cyclic behaviour in a regional system of cities, in Chisholm, M. *et al.* (eds), *Regional forecasting* (London), pp. 389-413.

Beckmann, M. J. (1958) City hierarchies and the distribution of city size, *Econ. Dev. cult. Change* 6, 243-8.

Beckmann, M. J. and McPherson, J. C. (1970) City size distribution in a central place hierarchy: an alternative approach, *J. reg. Sci.* 10, 25-33.

Bell, G. (1962) Change in city size distribution in Israel, *Ekistics*, 13, No. 75, 103.

Bellamy, J. (1952) Occupations in Kingston upon Hull, 1841-1948, *Yorks. Bull. econ. soc. Res.* 4, 33-50.

Beresford, M. W. (1971) The back-to-back house in Leeds, 1787-1937, in Chapman, S. D. (ed.) (1971), pp. 93-132.

Berry, B. J. L. (1961) City size distribution and economic development, *Econ. Dev. cult. Change* 9, 573-87.

Berry, B. J. L. (1964) Cities as systems within systems of cities, *Pap. Reg. Sci. Ass.* 13, 147-63.

Berry, B. J. L. (1967) *Geography of market centres and retail distribution* (Englewood Cliffs, N J).

Berry, B. J. L. (1968) Metropolitan Area redefinition: a re-evaluation of concept and statistical practice, *Working Pap.* No. 28, US Bureau of the Census, Washington DC.

Berry, B. J. L. (1969) City size and economic development: conceptual synthesis and policy problems, with special reference to South and South-East Asia, *Unpublished ms.* Dept. of Geogr., Univ. of Chicago.

Berry, B. J. L. (1970) The geography of the United States in the year 2000, *Trans. Inst. Br. Geogr.* 51, 21-53.

Berry, B. J. L. (1972) Hierarchical diffusion: the basis of development filtering and spread in a system of growth centres, in English, P. W. and Mayfield, R. C. (eds), *Man, space and environment: concepts in contemporary human geography* (London), pp. 340-59.

Berry, B. J. L. and Garrison, W. L. (1958) Alternate explanations of urban rank-size relationships, *Ann. Ass. Am. Geogr.* 48, 83-91.

Berry, B. J. L. and Horton, F. E. (1970) *Geographic perspectives on urban systems* (Englewood Cliffs, N J).

Berry, B. J. L. and Pred, A. R. (1965) Central place studies: a bibliography of theory and applications including supplement through 1964, *Biblphy Ser.* No. 1, Reg. Sci. Res. Inst., Philadelphia.

Beshers, J. M. and Laumann, E. O. (1967) Social distance: a network approach, *Am. sociol. Rev.* 32, 225-36.

Best, G. (1971) *Mid-Victorian Britain, 1851-75* (London).

Boal, F. W. (1968) Technology and urban form, *J. Geogr.* 67, 229-36.

Bogue, D. J. (1950) *The structure of the metropolitan community* (Ann Arbor, Mich.).

Boon, F. (1967) A simple model for the diffusion of an innovation in an urban system, *Reg. Econ. Dev. Stud.* No. 1, Center for Urban Studies, Univ. of Chicago.

Booth, C. (1886) Occupations of the people of the United Kingdom, 1801–81, *Jl R. Statist. Soc.* 49, 314-435.

Booth, C. (1902–3) *Life and labour of the people in London, etc.* (London), 17 vols.

Borchert, J. H. (1967) American metropolitan evolution, *Geogrl Rev.* 57, 301-31.

Boulding, K. E. (1956) General System Theory: the skeleton of science, *Mgmt Sci.* 2, 197–208.

Bowers, R. V. (1937) The direction of intra-societal diffusion, *Am. sociol. Rev.* 2, 826–36.

Bowkett, T. E. (1844) *Alchemy, or, the art of converting the baser metals into gold . . . a highly valuable receipt for the manufacture of an accumulating fund, investment, provident, building, equitable association* (London).

Bowkett, T. E. (1850) *The bane and the antidote, etc.* (London).

Briggs, A. (1963) *Victorian cities* (London).

Briggs, A. (1968) The Victorian city: quantity and quality, *Victorian Stud.* 11, 711–30.

Brooks, E. (1967) Public housing and labour mobility in Britain, *Unpublished Pap.* Study Group in Urban Geogr., Inst. Br. Geogr.

Brown, L. A. (1968) Diffusion processes and location: a conceptual framework and bibliography, *Biblphy Ser.* No. 4, Reg. Sci. Res. Inst., Philadelphia.

Brown, L. A. and Moore, E. G. (1969) Diffusion research in geography: a perspective, in Board, C. *et al.* (eds), *Progress in Geography*, Vol. 1 (London), pp. 119-57.

Browning, H. L. and Gibbs, J. P. (1961) Some measures of demographic and spatial relationships among cities, in Gibbs, J. P. (ed.) (1961), pp. 436–59.

Burn, D. L. (1940) *The economic history of steelmaking, 1867-1939* (Cambridge).

Butlin, N. G. (1964) *Investment in Australian economic development, 1861–1900* (Cambridge).

Byatt, I. C. R. (1968) Electrical products, in Aldcroft, D. H. (ed.) (1968), pp. 238–73.

Cairncross, A. K. (1949) Internal migration in Victorian England, *Manchr Sch.* 17, 67–87.

Cairncross, A. K. (1953) *Home and foreign investment, 1870–1913: studies in capital accumulation* (Cambridge).

Carr-Saunders, A. M. and Jones, D. C. (1927) *A survey of the social structure of England and Wales as illustrated by statistics* (Oxford).

Carter, H. (1955) Urban grades and spheres of influence in south-west Wales: an historical consideration, *Scott. Geogr. Mag.* 71, 43–58.

Carter, H. (1969) The growth of the Welsh city system, *Inaugural lecture*, University College of Wales, Aberystwyth (Cardiff).

Carter, H. (1972) *The study of urban geography* (London).

Casetti, E. (1967) Urban population density patterns: an alternate explanation, *Can. Geogr.* 11, 96–100.

Casetti, E. and Semple, R. K. (1968) A method for the stepwise separation of spacial trends, *Mich. Int-Com. Math. Geogr.* No. 11.

Casetti, E. and Semple, R. K. (1969) Concerning the testing of spatial diffusion hypotheses, *Geogrl Analysis* 1, 254–9.

Census (1923) *Census of England and Wales, 1911. Fertility of marriage*, Part 2 (London).

Champernowne, D. G. (1937) The distribution of income between persons, *Unpublished Fellowship Dissertation*, Vol. 2, King's College, Cambridge.

Chapman, G. P. (1970) The application of information theory to the analysis of population distribution in space, *Econ. Geogr.* 46, 317–31.

Chapman, G. P. (1971) The object of geographical analysis, *Unpublished Pap.* Comn Quant. Meth., Int. Geogrl Un., Budapest conference.

Chapman, S. D. (ed) (1971) *The history of working-class housing: a symposium* (Newton Abbot).

Childe, V. G. (1936) *Man makes himself* (London).

Chisholm, G. G. (1897) On the distribution of towns and villages in England, Part 2: Historical aspects, *Geogrl J.* 10, 511–30.

Chisholm, M. (1967) General Systems Theory and geography, *Trans. Inst. Br. Geogr.* 42, 45–52.

Chorley, R. J. and Haggett, P. (1965) Trend-surface mapping in geographical research, *Trans. Inst. Br. Geogr.* 37, 47–67.

Chorley, R. J. and Kennedy, B. A. (1971) *Physical geography: a systems approach* (London).

Christaller, W. (1933) *Central places in southern Germany* (original publication, 1933: English translation by C. W. Baskin, 1966) (Englewood Cliffs, NJ).

Church, R. A. (1966) *Economic and social change in a Midland town: Victorian Nottingham, 1815–1900* (London).

Clark, C. (1951) Urban population densities, *Jl R. Statist. Soc., Ser. A.* 114, 490–6.

Clark, C. (1967) *Population growth and land use* (London).

Clark, G. Kitson (1962) *The making of Victorian England* (London).

Cleary, E. J. (1965) *The building society movement* (London).

Clegg, S. (1841) *A practical treatise on the manufacture and distribution of coal-gas* (London).

Cliff, A. D. (1968) The neighbourhood effect in the diffusion of innovations, *Trans. Inst. Br. Geogr.* 44, 75–84.

Cliff, A. D. and Ord, K. (1970) Spatial autocorrelation: a review of existing and new measures with applications, *Econ. Geogr.* 46, 269–92.

Crain, R. L. (1966) Fluoridation: the diffusion of an innovation among cities, *Social Forces* 44, 467–76.

Cripps, E. L. and Foot, D. H. S. (1969) The empirical development of a residential location model for use in sub-regional planning, *Envirmt Plann.* 1, 81–90.

Crowther, D. and Echenique, M. (1972) Development of a model of spatial structure, in Martin, L. and March, L. (eds), *Urban space and structures* (Cambridge), pp. 175–218.

Curry, L. (1964) The random spatial economy: an exploration in settlement theory, *Ann. Ass. Am. Geogr.* 54, 138–46.

Curry, L. (1967) Central places in the random spatial economy, *J. reg. Sci.* 7, No. 2, 217–38.

Dacey, M. F. (1966) Population of places in a central place hierarchy, *J. reg. Sci.* 6, No. 2, 27–33.

Dacey, M. F. (1968) An empirical study of the areal distribution of houses in Puerto Rico, *Trans. Inst. Br. Geogr.* 45, 51–69.

D'Arcy Thompson, W. (1917) *On growth and form* (Cambridge) (abridged ed., edited by J. T. Bonner, 1961).

Davies, A. (1926) Critical analysis of the census returns of the Merthyr Tydfil area, *Geogrl Teacher* 13, 473–9.

Deane, P. and Cole, W. A. (1962) *British economic growth, 1688–1959: trends and structure* (Cambridge).

Dickinson, R. E. (1947) *City, region and regionalism: a geographical contribution to human ecology* (London).

Donnison, D. V. (1967) *The government of housing* (London).

Drake, M. (1972) The Census, 1801–1891, in Wrigley, E. A. (ed.), *Nineteenth-century society: essays in the use of quantitative methods* (Cambridge), pp. 7–46.

Du Boff, R. B. (1967) The introduction of electric power in American manufacturing, *Econ. Hist. Rev.* 2nd Ser. 20, 509–18.

Duncan, O. D. and Reiss, A. J. (1956) *Social characteristics of urban and rural communities, 1950* (New York).

Duncan, O. D. *et al.* (1960) *Metropolis and region* (Baltimore).

Dyos, H. J. (1953) Workman's fares in south London, 1860–1914, *J. Transp. Hist.* 1, 3–19.

Dyos, H. J. (1955) Railways and housing in Victorian London, *J. Transp. Hist.* 2, 11–21, 90–100.

Evans, A. W. (1972) The pure theory of city size in an industrial economy, *Urban Stud.* 9, 49–77.

Falkus, M. E. (1967) The British gas industry before 1850, *Econ. Hist. Rev.* 2nd Ser. 20, 494–508.

Feller, I. (1966) The draper loom in New England textiles, 1894–1914: a study of diffusion of an innovation, *J. econ. Hist.* 26, 320–47.

Feller, I. (1971) The urban location of U.S. invention, 1860–1910, *Explor. entrepreneurial Hist.* 8, 285–304.

Ferguson, R. I. (1969) The rank-size rule. Parts 1 and 2, *Geogrl Artic.* No. 12, 36–42 and No. 13, 25–44, Dept. of Geogr., Univ. of Cambridge.

Fiebleman, J. K. (1954) Theory of integrative levels, *Br. J. Philos. Sci.* 5, 59–90.

Fisher, F. J. (1935) The development of the London food market, 1540–1640, *Econ. Hist. Rev.* 5, 46–64.

Frankel, M. (1955) Obsolescence and technological change in a maturing economy, *Am. econ. Rev.* 45, 296–319.

Friedlander, D. (1970) The spread of urbanization in England and Wales, 1851–1951, *Popul. Stud.* 24, 423–43.

Friedlander, D. and Roshier, R. J. (1966) A study of internal migration in England and Wales, Part 1: geographical patterns of internal migration, *Popul. Stud.* 19, 239–78.

Friedmann, J. (1966a) *Regional development policy: a case study in Venezuela* (Cambridge, Mass.).

Friedmann, J. (1966b) Two concepts of urbanization: a comment, *Urban Affairs* 1, No. 4, 79–84.

Friedmann, J. and Miller, J. (1965) The urban field, *J. Am. Inst. Planners* 31, 312–20.

Fuguitt, G. W. (1965) The growth and decline of small towns as a probability process, *Am. sociol. Rev.* 30, 403–11.

Garke, E. (1907) *The progress of electrical enterprise* (London).

Geddes, P. E. (1949) *Cities in evolution* (London, revised ed.).

Gibbs, J. P. (ed) (1961) *Urban research methods* (New Jersey).

Gibrat, R. (1931) *Les inégalités économiques* (Paris).

Goheen, P. G. (1970) Victorian Toronto, 1850–1900: pattern and process of growth, *Res. Pap.* No. 127, Dept. of Geogr., Univ. of Chicago.

Goodrich, E. P. (1926) The statistical relationship between population and the city plan, in Burgess, E. W. (ed.), *The urban community* (Chicago), pp. 144–50.

Gottmann, J. (1961) *Megalopolis: the urbanized northeastern seabord of the United States* (New York).

Granger, C. W. J. (1964) *Spectral analysis of economic time series* (Princeton, N J).

Gras, N. S. B. (1922) *An introduction to economic history* (New York).

Gunston, W. H. (1907–8) The development of the telephone in the English counties since 1892 geographically considered, *Natn. Teleph. J.* 2, 134-5, 158-9, 183-5, 228-30.

Gunston, W. H. (1910) The National Telephone Company in country districts, *Natn. Teleph. J.* 6, 73–4.

Habakkuk, H. J. (1962a) *American and British technology in the nineteenth century: the search for labour-saving inventions* (Cambridge).

Habakkuk, H. J. (1962b) Fluctuations in house-building in Britain and the United States in the nineteenth century, *J. econ. Hist.* 22, 198–230.

Hägerstrand, T. (1966) Aspects of the spatial structure of social communications and the diffusion of innovations, *Pap. Reg. Sci. Ass.* 16, 27–42.

Hägerstrand, T. (1967a) *Innovation diffusion as a spatial process* (Chicago, English translation by A. R. Pred) (original Swedish edition, 1953).

Hägerstrand, T. (1967b) On Monte Carlo simulation of diffusion, in Garrison, W. L. and Marble, D. F. (eds), Quantitative geography, Part 1: economic and cultural topics, *NWest. Univ. Stud. Geogr.* No. 13, 1–32.

Hall, A. D. and Fagen, R. E. (1956) Definition of system, *Gen. Syst.* 1, 18–28.

Hall, P. G. (1962) *The industries of London since 1861* (London).

Hall, P. G. (1966) *The world cities* (London).

Harris, C. D. (1970) *Cities of the Soviet Union: studies in their functions, size, density and growth* (Chicago).

Hartwell, R. M. (1971) *The industrial revolution and economic growth* (London).

Harvey, D. (1966) Geographical processes and point patterns: testing models of diffusion by quadrat methods, *Trans. Inst. Br. Geogr.* 40, 81–95.

Harvey, D. (1968) Some methodological problems in the use of Neyman Type A and negative binomial probability distributions in the analysis of spatial series, *Trans. Inst. Br. Geogr.* 44, 85–95.

Harvey, D. (1969) *Explanation in geography* (London).

Higgs, R. (1969) The growth of cities in a midwestern region, 1870–1900, *J. reg. Sci.* 9, 369–75.

Hirschman, A. O. (1958) *The strategy of economic development* (New Haven, Conn.).

Hobsbawm, E. J. (1964) The nineteenth century London labour market, in Centre for Urban Studies, *London: aspects of change* (London), pp. 3–28.

Hudson, J. C. (1969) Diffusion in a central place system, *Geogrl Analysis* 1, 45–58.

Hughes, T. P. (1962) British electrical industry lag, 1882–1888, *Technology Cult.* 3, 27–44.

Ijiri, H. and Simon, H. A. (1964) Business firm growth and size, *Am. econ. Rev.* 54, 77–89.

Innes, J. W. (1938) *Class fertility trends in England and Wales, 1876–1934* (Cambridge).

Interdepartmental Committee on Social and Economic Research (1951) Census reports of Great Britain, 1801–1931, *Guides to Official Sources*, No. 2 (London).

International Urban Research (1959) *The world's metropolitan areas* (Berkeley, Calif.).

Jefferson, M. (1939) The law of the primate city, *Geogrl Rev.* 29, 226–32.

Jones, G. S. (1971) *Outcast London: a study in the relationship between classes in Victorian society* (Oxford).

Kalecki, M. (1945) On the Gibrat distribution, *Econometrica* 13, 161–70.

Keeble, D. E. (1967) Models of economic development, in Chorley, R. J. and Haggett, P. (eds), *Models in geography* (London), pp. 243–302.

Kellett, J. R. (1969) *The impact of railways on Victorian cities* (London).

Kemeney, J. G. and Snell, J. L. (1960) *Finite Markov chains* (Princeton, NJ).

Kendall, M. G. (1961) Natural law in the social sciences, *Jl R. Statist. Soc., Ser. A.* 124, 2–16.

King, L. J. E., Casetti, E. and Jeffrey, D. (1969) Economic impulses in a regional system of cities, *Reg. Stud.* 3, 213–18.

Kingsbury, J. E. (1915) *The telegraph and telephone exchanges: their invention and development* (London).

Krause, J. T. (1958) Changes in English fertility and mortality, 1781–1850, *Econ. Hist. Rev.* 2nd Ser. 11, 52–70.

Krim, A. J. (1967) The innovation and diffusion of the street railway in North America, *Unpublished MA Dissertation*, Univ. of Chicago.

Lampard, E. E. (1968) The evolving system of cities in the United States: urbanization and economic development, in Perloff, H. S. and Wingo, L. (eds), *Issues in urban economics* (Baltimore), pp. 81–139.

Landes, D. S. (1969) *The unbound Prometheus: technological change and industrial development in Western Europe from 1750 to the present* (Cambridge).

Langton, J. (1972) Potentialities and problems of adopting a systems approach to the study of change in human geography, in Board, C. *et al.* (eds), *Progress in Geography*, Vol. 4 (London), pp. 125–79.

Law, C. M. (1967) The growth of urban population in England and Wales, 1801–1911, *Trans. Inst. Br. Geogr.* 41, 125–43.

Lawton, R. (1968a) The journey-to-work in Britain: some trends and problems, *Reg. Stud.* 2, 27–40.

Lawton, R. (1968b) Population changes in England and Wales in the later nineteenth century: an analysis of trends by Registration Districts, *Trans. Inst. Br. Geogr.* 44, 55–74.

Leech, B. T. (1897–8) Tramways and their municipalisation, *Trans. Manchr Statist. Soc.* 129–52.

Lever, W. F. (1972) A Markov approach to the optimal size of cities in England and Wales, *Unpublished Pap.* Quant. Meth. Stud. Group, Inst. Br. Geogr., Sheffield conference.

Levine, A. L. (1967) *Industrial retardation in Britain, 1880–1914* (New York).

Lewis, J. Parry (1965) *Building cycles and Britain's growth* (London).

Lewis, S. (1944) *A topographical dictionary of England, etc.* (London 4 vols. 5th ed.).

Lewis, W. A. (1957) International competition in manufactures, *Am. econ. Rev.* 47, No. 2, 578–87.

Liepmann, K. K. (1944) *The journey to work: its significance for industrial and community life* (London).

Loewenstein, L. K. (1965) *The location of residences and work places in urban areas* (New York).

Lopes, A. S. (1972) The economic functions of small towns and rural centres, *Unpublished PhD Dissertation*, Univ. of Oxford.

Lord, J. (1923) *Capital and steam-power, 1750–1800* (London).

Lotka, A. J. (1924) *Elements of physical biology* (Baltimore) (new ed., New York, 1965, entitled *Elements of mathematical biology*).

Lotka, A. J. (1926) The frequency distribution of scientific productivity, *J. Wash. Acad. Sci.* 16, 317–23.

Lubenow, W. C. (1971) *The politics of government growth: early Victorian attitudes towards state intervention* (Newton Abbot).

Luckermann, F. (1966) Empirical expressions of nodality and hierarchy in a circulation manifold, *E. Lakes Geogr.* 2, 17–44.

McCloskey, D. N. (ed.) (1971) *Essays on a mature economy: Britain after 1840* (London).

McCloskey, D. N. and Sandberg, L. G. (1971) From damnation to redemption: judgements on the Late Victorian entrepreneur, *Explor. entrepreneurial Hist.* 9, 89–108.

McElrath, D. C. (1968) Societal scale and social differentiation: Accra, Ghana, in Greer, S. *et al.* (eds), *The new urbanization* (New York), pp. 33–52.

McKenzie, R. D. (1933) *The metropolitan community* (New York).

Mackinder, H. J. (1902) *Britain and the British seas* (London).

McVoy, E. C. (1940) Patterns of diffusion in the United States, *Am. sociol. Rev.* 5, 219–27.

Madden, C. H. (1956a) On some indicators of stability in the growth of cities in the United States, *Econ. Dev. cult. Change* 4, 236–52.

Madden, C. H. (1956b) Some spatial aspects of urban growth in the United States, *Econ. Dev. cult. Change* 4, 371–87.

Madden, C. H. (1958) Some temporal aspects of the growth of cities in the United States, *Econ. Dev. cult. Change* 6, 143–69.

Maine, H. J. S. (1861) *Ancient Law* (London).

Maitland, F. W. (1898) *Township and borough: together with an appendix of notes relating . . . to Cambridge* (Cambridge).

Mandelbrot, B. (1953) An informational theory of the statistical structure of language, in Jackson, W. (ed.), *Communication theory* (London), pp. 486–502.

Mansfield, E. (1969) *The economics of technological change* (London) (first published, New York, 1968).

Mantoux, P. (1928) *The industrial revolution in the eighteenth century: an outline of the beginnings of the modern factory system* (English translation by Marjorie Vernon) (London).

Marsh, D. C. (1958) *The changing social structure in England and Wales, 1871–1951* (London).

Marshall, J. D. (1968) Colonisation as a factor in the planting of towns in north-west England, in Dyos, H. J. (ed), *The study of urban history* (London), pp. 215–30.

Meier, R. L. (1962) *A communication theory of urban growth* (Cambridge, Mass.).

Mesarovic, M. D. (ed.) (1964) *Views on general systems theory: proceedings of the second systems symposium at Case Institute of Technology* (New York).

Meyer, H. R. (1906) *Municipal ownership in Great Britain* (New York).

Meyer, H. R. (1907) *Public ownership and the telephone in Great Britain* (New York).

Minchinton, W. E. (1956) The diffusion of tinplate manufacture, *Econ. Hist. Rev.* 9, 349–58.

Mitchell, B. R. (1962) *Abstract of British historical statistics* (Cambridge).

Moses, L. and Williamson, H. F. (1967) The location of economic activity in cities, *Am. econ. Rev.* 57, 211–22.

Mumford, L. (1938) *The culture of cities* (London).

Mumford, L. (1961) *The city in history: its origins, its transformations, and its prospects* (London).

Myrdal, G. M. (1957) *Economic theory and under-developed regions* (London).

National Academy of Sciences (1965) The science of geography, *Report*, Natn. Res. Coun.-*ad hoc* Comm. on Geogr. (Washington).

Neft, D. S. (1966) Statistical analysis for areal distributions, *Monogr. Ser.* No. 2, Reg. Sci. Res. Inst., Philadelphia.

Newling, B. E. (1966) Urban growth and spatial structure: mathematical models and empirical evidence, *Geogrl Rev.* 56, 213–25.

Newling, B. E. (1969) The spatial variation of urban population densities, *Geogrl Rev.* 59, 242–52.

Newton, M. P. and Jeffery, J. R. (1951) *Internal migration: some aspects of population movements within England and Wales* (London).

Nordbeck, S. (1965) The law of allometric growth, *Mich. Int-Com. Math. Geogr.* No. 7.

Nordbeck, S. (1971) Urban allometric growth, *Geogr. Annlr, Ser. B.* 53, 54–67.

Olsson, G. (1965) Distance and human interaction: a review and bibliography, *Biblphy Ser.* No. 2, Reg. Sci. Res. Inst., Philadelphia.

Olsson, G. (1967) Central place systems, spatial interaction, and stochastic processes, *Pap. Reg. Sci. Ass.* 18, 13–45.

Osborne, R. H. (1964) Changes in the regional distribution of population in Great Britain, *Geography* 49, 266–73.

Parr, J. B. (1969) City hierarchies and the distribution of city sizes: a reassessment of Beckmann's contribution, *J. reg. Sci.* 9, 239–54.

Parr, J. B. (1970) Models of city size in an urban system, *Pap. Reg. Sci. Ass.* 25, 221–53.

Payne, P. L. (1967) The emergence of the large-scale company in Great Britain, 1870–1914, *Econ. Hist. Rev.* 2nd Ser. 20, 519–42.

Pearson, E. S. and Hartley, H. O. (1966) *Biometrika tables for statisticians*, vol 1 (Cambridge, 3rd ed.).

Pederson, P. O. (1970) Innovation diffusion within and between national urban systems, *Geogrl Analysis* 2, 203–54.

Perloff, H. S. *et al.* (1960) *Regions, resources and economic growth* (Baltimore).

Pirenne, H. (1925) *Medieval cities: their origins and the revival of trade* (Princeton).

Pollins, H. (1964) Transport lines and social divisions, in Centre for Urban Studies, *London: aspects of change* (London), pp. 29–61.

Popenhoe, D. (1965) On the meaning of 'urban' in urban studies, *Urban Affairs* 1, No. 1, 17–33.

Prais, S. J. (1955) Measuring social mobility, *Jl R. Statist. Soc., Ser. A.* 118, 56–66.

Prais, S. J. and Hart, P. E. (1956) The analysis of business concentration: a statistical approach, *Jl R. Statist. Soc., Ser. A.* 119, 150–75.

Pred, A. R. (1966) *The spatial dynamics of U.S. urban-industrial growth, 1800–1914: interpretive and theoretical essays* (Cambridge, Mass.).

Preece, W. H. (1882) Recent progress in telephony, *J. Soc. Arts* 30, 965–9.

Price, S. J. (1958) *Building societies: their origin and history* (London).

Price-Williams, R. (1880) On the increase of population in England and Wales, *Jl R. Statist. Soc.* 43, 462–96.

Pritchard, R. M. (1972) Intra-urban migration in Leicester, 1860–1965. *Unpublished Ph.D. Dissertation*, Univ. of Cambridge.

Quandt, R. E. (1964) Statistical discrimination among alternative hypotheses and some economic regularities, *J. reg. Sci.* 5, No. 2, 1–23.

Read, D. (1964) *The English provinces: a study in influence* (London).

Richardson, H. W. (1965a) Retardation in Britain's industrial growth, 1870–1913, *Scott. J. political Econ.* 12, 125–49.

Richardson, H. W. (1965b) Overcommitment in Britain before 1930, *Oxf. econ. Pap.* New Ser. 17, 237–59.

Richardson, H. W. (1968) Chemicals, in Aldcroft, D. H. (ed.) (1968), pp. 274–306.

Rodda, J. C. (1970) A trend-surface analysis for the planation surfaces of North Wales, *Trans. Inst. Br. Geogr.* 50, 107–14.

Rogers, E. M. (1962) *Diffusion of innovations* (New York).

Rogers, E. M. and Shoemaker, F. F. (1971) *Communication of innovations: a cross-cultural approach* (New York).

Rosing, K. E. (1966) A rejection of the Zipf model (rank size rule) in relation to city size, *Prof. Geogr.* 18, 75–82.

Ryan, B. and Gross, N. C. (1943) The diffusion of hybrid seed corn in two Iowa communities, *Rur. Sociol.* 8, 15–24.

Saul, S. B. (1962a) House building in England, 1890–1914, *Econ. Hist. Rev.* 2nd Ser. 15, 119–37.

Saul, S. B. (1962b) The motor industry in Britain to 1914, *Busin. Hist.* 5, 22–44.

Saul, S. B. (1967) The market and the development of the mechanical engineering industries in Britain, 1860–1914, *Econ. Hist. Rev.* 2nd Ser. 20, 111–30.

Saul, S. B. (1968) The machine tool industry in Britain to 1914, *Busin. Hist.* 10, 22–43.

Saville, J. (1963) Internal migration in England and Wales during the past hundred years, in Sutter, J. (ed.), *Human displacements: measurement, methodological aspects* (Paris), pp. 1–21.

Schumpeter, J. A. (1939) *Business cycles: a theoretical, historical and statistical account of the capitalist process* (New York, 2 vols.).

Scratchley, A. (1867) *A treatise on benefit building societies* (London, First ed., 1849).

Shadwell, A. (1909) *Industrial efficiency: a comparative study of industrial life in England, Germany and America* (London, First ed., 2 vols, 1906).

Shannon, H. A. (1935) Migration and the growth of London, 1841-91: a statistical note, *Econ. Hist. Rev.* 5, 79–86.

Shannon, H. A. and Grebenik, E. (1943) The population of Bristol, *Occasional Pap.* No. 2, Natn. Inst. Econ. Soc. Res., London.

Shevky, E. and Bell, W. (1955) *Social area analysis: illustrative application and computational procedure* (Stanford, Calif.).

Simon, H. A. (1955) On a class of skew distribution functions, *Biometrika* 42, 425–40.

Simon, H. A. and Bonini, C. P. (1958) The size distribution of business firms, *Am. econ. Rev.* 48, 607–17.

Singer, H. W. (1936) Courbes des populations: a parallel to Pareto's law, *Econ. J.* 46, 254–63.

Singh, A. and Whittington, G. (1968) Growth, profitability and valuation, *Occasional Pap.* No. 7, Dept. of Applied Econ., Univ. of Cambridge.

Sjoberg, G. (1960) *The preindustrial city: past and present* (New York).

Sjoberg, G. (1965) Cities in developing and in industrial societies, a cross-cultural analysis, in Hauser, P. M. and Schnore, L. F. (eds), *The study of urbanization* (New York), pp. 213–63.

Smailes, A. E. (1947) The analysis and delimitation of urban fields, *Geography* 32, 151–61.

Smith, C. T. (1951) The movement of population in England and Wales in 1851 and 1861, *Geogrl J.* 117, 200–10.

Smith, W. (1953) *An economic geography of Great Britain* (London, 2nd ed.).

Starr, R. B. (1878) *Starr-Bowkett Societies as they are* (London).

Steindl, J. (1965) *Random processes and the growth of the firm* (London).

Stewart, J. Q. (1947) Empirical mathematical rules concerning the distribution and equilibrium of population, *Geogrl Rev.* 37, 461–76.

Stewart, J. Q. (1958) The size and spacing of cities, *Geogrl Rev.* 48, 222–45.

Stewart, J. Q. and Warntz, W. (1958) Physics of population distribution, *J. reg. Sci.* 1, 99–123.

Svennilson, I. (1954) *Growth and stagnation in the European economy* (Geneva).

Tanner, J. C. (1961) Factors affecting the amount of travel, *Road Res. Tech. Pap.* No. 51, Dept. Sci. Ind. Res., London.

Taylor, A. J. (1951) The taking of the Census, 1801–1951, *Br. Med. J.* Vol. 1, 715–20.

Temin, P. (1966) Steam and waterpower in the early nineteenth century, *J. econ. Hist.* 26, 187–205.

Thoman, R. S. (1965) Some comments on 'The science of geography', *Prof. Geogr.* 17, 8–10.

Thomas, B. (1930) The migration of labour into the Glamorganshire coalfield, 1861–1911, *Economica* 10, 275–94.

Thomas, B. (1954) *Migration and economic growth: a study of Great Britain and the Atlantic economy* (Cambridge).

Thomas, B. (1972) *Migration and urban development: a reappraisal of British and American long cycles* (London).

Thomas, E. N. (1962) The stability of distance-population-size relationships for Iowa towns from 1900–1950, in Norborg, K. (ed.), 'I.G.U. symposium in urban geography', *Lund Stud. Geogr., Ser. B.* No. 24, 13–29.

Thomas, E. N. (1967) Additional comments on population size relationships for sets of cities, in Garrison, W. L. and Marble, D. F. (eds), 'Quantitative geography, Part I: economic and cultural topics', *NWest. Univ. Stud. Geogr.* No. 13, 167–90.

Thompson, W. R. (1965a) *A preface to urban economics* (Baltimore).

Thompson, W. R. (1965b) The future of the Detroit Metropolitan Area, in Haber, W. (ed.), *Michigan in the 1970s: an economic forecast* (Ann Arbor, Mich.).

Tisdale, H. (1942) The process of urbanization, *Social Forces* 20, 311–16.

Tobler, W. R. (1963) Geographic area and map projections, *Geogrl Rev.* 53, 59–78.

Tompkins, H. (1845) *Building societies: their formation and management* (London).

Udry, J. R. (1964) Increasing scale and spatial differentiation: new test of two theories from Shevky and Bell, *Social Forces* 42, 403–13.

Ullman, E. L. (1941) A theory of location for cities, *Am. J. Sociol.* 46, 853–64.

U.S. Bureau of the Budget (1967) *Standard Metropolitan Statistical Areas* (Washington, DC).

Usher, A. P. (1921) *An introduction to the industrial history of England* (London).

Vance, J. E. (1967) Housing the worker: determinative and contingent ties in nineteenth century Birmingham, *Econ. Geogr.* 43, 95–127.

Vance, J. E. (1971) Land assignment in the precapitalist, capitalist and post-capitalist city, *Econ. Geogr.* 47, 101–20.

Veblen, T. (1942) *Imperial Germany and the industrial revolution* (New York).

Vince, S. W. E. (1955) The rural population of England and Wales, 1801–1951, *Unpublished Ph.D Dissertation*, Univ. of London.

Von Bertalanffy, L. (1950) An outline of general system theory, *Br. J. Phil. Sci.* 1, 134–65.

Von Tunzelmann, N. (1970) Technological diffusion during the industrial revolution: the case of the Cornish pumping engine, in Hartwell, R. M. (ed.), *The industrial revolution* (Oxford) pp. 77–98.

Walsh, W. D. (1966) The diffusion of technological change in the Pennsylvania pig iron industry, 1850–1870: a summary, *J. econ. Hist.* 26, 591–4.

Ward, B. (1963) City structure and interdependence, *Pap. Reg. Sci. Ass.* 10, 207–21.

Wärneryd, O. (1968) *Interdependence in urban systems* (Göteburg).

Warnes, A. M. (1970) Early separation of homes from work-places and the urban structure of Chorley, 1780–1850, *Trans. Hist. Soc. Lancs. Chesh.* 122, 105–35.

Warntz, W. (1967) Global science and the tyranny of space, *Pap. Reg. Sci. Ass.* 19, 7–19.

Webb, H. L. (1910) *The development of the telephone in Europe* (London).

Webber, C. E. (1882) Telephonic communication, *J. Soc. Arts* 30, 607–19.

Webber, M. M. (1963) Order in diversity: community without propinquity, in Wingo, L. (ed.), *Cities and space: the future use of urban land* (Baltimore), pp. 23–54.

Webber, M. M. (1964) The urban place and the nonplace urban realm, in Webber, M. M. *et al.* (eds), *Explorations into urban structure* (Philadelphia), pp. 79–153.

Webber, M. M. (1968) The post city age, *Daedalus*, 1091–1110.

Weber, A. F. (1899) *The growth of cities in the nineteenth century: a study in statistics* (New York) (republished, Ithaca, NY, 1967).

Weber, M. (1958) *The city* (English translation by D. Martindale and G. Neuwirth) (New York).

Wells, H. G. (1902) *Anticipations* (London, 3rd ed.).

Welton, T. A. (1868–9) On population statistics, *Trans. Hist. Soc. Lancs. Chesh.* New Ser. 9, 55–92, 93–164.

Welton, T. A. (1869) On the classification of people by occupations; and on other subjects connected with population statistics of England, *Jl R. Statist. Soc.* 32, 271–87.

Welton, T. A. (1897–8) On forty years' industrial change in England and Wales, *Trans. Manchr Statist. Soc.* 153–243.

Welton, T. A. (1900) The growth of population in England and Wales and its progress in the period of ninety years from 1801–91, *Jl R. Statist. Soc.* 63, 527–89.

Welton, T. A. (1911) *England's recent progress: an investigation of the statistics of migrations, mortality, etc. in the twenty years from 1881 to 1901* (London).

Wetham, E. H. (1964) The London milk trade, 1860–1900, *Econ. Hist. Rev.* 17, 369–80.

Wilbanks, T. J. and Symanski, R. (1968) What is systems analysis? *Prof. Geogr.* 20, No. 2, 81–5.

Willatts, E. C. and Newson, M. G. C. (1953) The geographical pattern of population changes in England and Wales, 1921–51, *Geogrl J.* 119, 431–50.

Williams, T. (1969) Social gradients in the city: a trend-surface analysis of enumeration district data for inner London, *Discussion Pap.* No. 32, Dept. of Geogr., London Sch. Econ.

Williamson, J. G. (1965a) Regional inequality and the process of national development: a description of the patterns, *Econ. Dev. cult. Change* 13, 3–45.

Williamson, J. G. (1965b) Antebellum urbanization in the American northeast, *J. econ. Hist.* 25, 592–608.

Williamson, J. G. and Swanson, J. A. (1966) The growth of cities in the American north east, 1820–1870, *Explor. entrepreneurial Hist.* 4, 44–67.

Wilson, A. G. (1970) *Entropy in urban and regional modelling* (London).

Woldenberg, M. J. (1967) Concepts and applications: spatial order, *Harvard Pap. Theoretical Geogr.* No. 1, part 2.

Wrigley, E. A. (1965) Geography and population, in Chorley, R J. and Haggett, P. (eds), *Frontiers in geographical teaching* (London), pp. 62–80.

Wrigley, E. A. (1967) A simple model of London's importance in changing English society and economy, 1650–1750, *Past and Present* 37, 44–70.

Yeates, M. H. (1965) Some factors affecting the spatial distribution of Chicago land values, 1910–60, *Econ. Geogr.* 41, 57–70.

Zipf, G. K. (1941) *National unity and disunity* (Bloomington, Indiana).

Zipf, G. K. (1949) *Human behavior and the principle of least effort* (Cambridge, Mass.).

Author index

General index